Fall of Light

Fall of Light

Nina Kiriki Hoffman

ACE BOOKS, NEW YORK

THE BERKLEY PUBLISHING GROUP
Published by the Penguin Group
Penguin Group (USA) Inc.
375 Hudson Street, New York, New York 10014, USA
Penguin Group (Canada), 90 Eglinton Avenue East, Suite 700, Toronto, Ontario M4P 2Y3, Canada
(a division of Pearson Penguin Canada Inc.)
Penguin Books Ltd., 80 Strand, London WC2R 0RL, England
Penguin Group Ireland, 25 St. Stephen's Green, Dublin 2, Ireland (a division of Penguin Books Ltd.)
Penguin Group (Australia), 250 Camberwell Road, Camberwell, Victoria 3124, Australia
(a division of Pearson Australia Group Pty. Ltd.)
Penguin Books India Pvt. Ltd., 11 Community Centre, Panchsheel Park, New Delhi—110 017, India
Penguin Group (NZ), 67 Apollo Drive, Rosedale, North Shore 0632, New Zealand
(a division of Pearson New Zealand Ltd.)
Penguin Books (South Africa) (Pty.) Ltd., 24 Sturdee Avenue, Rosebank, Johannesburg 2196,
South Africa

Penguin Books Ltd., Registered Offices: 80 Strand, London WC2R 0RL, England

This is an original publication of The Berkley Publishing Group.

This is a work of fiction. Names, characters, places, and incidents either are the product of the author's imagination or are used fictitiously, and any resemblance to actual persons, living or dead, business establishments, events, or locales is entirely coincidental. The publisher does not have any control over and does not assume any responsibility for author or third-party websites or their content.

Copyright © 2009 by Nina Kiriki Hoffman.
Text design by Laura Corless.

FIRST EDITION: May 2009

Library of Congress Cataloging-in-Publication Data

Hoffman, Nina Kiriki.
    Fall of light / Nina Kiriki Hoffman.—1st ed.
        p. cm.
    ISBN 978-0-441-01468-2
    1. Makeup artists—Fiction.   2. Magic—Fiction.   I. Title.

    PS3558.O34624F35 2009
    813'.54—dc22

                                    2009001833

PRINTED IN THE UNITED STATES OF AMERICA

10   9   8   7   6   5   4   3   2   1

To my sister. Thanks.

Acknowledgments

I am eternally grateful to E. Larry Day, special effects makeup artist of Chimera Studios (www.chimerastudios.com), who let me ghost him for a day on a movie set and was nice in every other way. My thanks to his crew as well, especially Molly, who answered many questions and showed me makeup tools and continuity Polaroids of actors being very silly.

I also owe a huge debt of gratitude to my sister, Valley Via Reseigne, production manager (among other things), and her husband, Richard Reseigne, construction coordinator (among other things), for help with the technical details of life on a movie set.

To Valley I am also grateful for introducing me to E. Larry and letting me tell movie people I am related to her. After that, people told me how great she is to work with and answered my questions.

What I got right, I got right because of these people. The wrong stuff is all mine.

1

When Opal LaZelle arrived at the Makeup trailer on the set of *Forest of the Night*, she found her personal employer, Corvus Weather, asleep at her station. The chair had been specially designed to hold his seven-foot two-inch length and generous, muscular frame. It had to be comfortable for hours at a time, the period it took her to transform him from a strangely stretchy-faced, gentle man into the monster of whatever movie they were working on.

She and Corvus had one end of the trailer to themselves. Four other makeup chairs stood in a line between the brightly lit mirrored walls and the many-drawered desk cupboards below them where the makeup artists stored their supplies. Doors opened into the trailer at either end. Both doors were propped open; a cool breeze spiced with pine eased through the trailer, accompanied by the hum of generators.

Opal could have transformed Corvus in minutes using her special skills, but she and Corvus had only worked together on one film so far, and, though she was afraid she loved

Corvus, she didn't trust him yet. Applying the latex prosthetics to turn Corvus into the Dark God of *Forest of the Night* would take four hours; they were heading into a night shoot, so she had to start now. This was the first day of shooting for her and Corvus; most of the rest of the cast and crew had been on location in backwoods Oregon for a week.

Girl One and Girl Two were in other chairs in the trailer. Rodrigo Esposito, a dark, shaggy-haired man and the key makeup artist on the shoot, was working on Girl Two, the fair one, and supervising his first assistant, Magenta, as she worked on Girl One, the dark one. Opal knew Rodrigo from *Twisted* and *Deviant*, where he had been her boss, and she one of a small pool of makeup artists. He hadn't worked on *Dead Loss*, the film where Opal had met and been hired exclusively for Corvus. Corvus had been the ghost of two merged serial killers, an interesting challenge for Opal's skills as special effects makeup artist and Corvus's skills as actor. Unfortunately, though they both did worthy work, the writers' skills hadn't been up to creating a memorable movie. DVD afterlife was the only thing that saved the movie from being a dead loss itself.

"Opal," Rodrigo murmured as she set out her equipment. "Come meet the girls."

She glanced at Corvus. He sprawled in his chair, a dark blue fleece blanket over him, with black-jean-clad legs and giant black boots sticking out the bottom. He smiled in his sleep. His breathing was so quiet. It surprised her; most of the big men she'd known snored.

She slipped down the trailer to where Magenta, a short, stocky woman with short black hair that had broad pink streaks, stood by Girl Two. Opal knew Magenta from *Deviant* and *Twisted*.

"This is Lauren Marcos, our Serena," Rodrigo said. Lauren had large, dark eyes and a generous mouth, not yet colored; its natural color was dusky pink. She was a character actor with a string of successful comic sidekick roles behind her.

In *Forest of the Night*, she was tackling a different role, a serious, even depressing character, one of the two leads. Her dark, curly hair was pulled back from her face by a stretchy foam band so Magenta could lay the foundation.

"Hi, Lauren," Opal said.

"Hey, doll," said Lauren in a warm, low voice. "You got the big job, huh?" Her eyebrows twitched, and she glanced toward Corvus, her mouth edging into a small smile.

"Opal's a genius," Rodrigo said. "She has magic hands. She could turn you into a warty old witch your mother wouldn't recognize and the witch's mother would."

"That so?" The edges of Lauren's eyes crinkled. "Could we maybe do that sometime, Hon? Like, when my mother's actually visiting the set?"

Opal laughed.

"This is Blaise Penny, our Caitlyn." Rodrigo nodded toward Girl One in the other chair. "Blaise, Opal LaZelle."

"Hi, Opal," said Blaise. She was a gorgeous green-eyed woman with high cheekbones and a mass of crinkled silver blond hair. Blaise and Lauren played sisters in the film, but no effort had been made to cast for family resemblance. Lauren looked Hispanic; Blaise, Caucasian. They were different body types, too—Lauren solid without being fat, Blaise ethereal, the sort of person you expected to see tripping through the woods in a filmy gown and fairy wings. In *Forest*, Blaise was playing against type as the evil sister, which Opal thought promising.

Blaise had just come off two hit films. Opal wondered why she'd chosen a monster movie for her next project; she could have easily been cast in another big budget movie.

"Why aren't you in one of these chairs yourself?" Blaise asked.

Opal glanced at the nearest mirror, wondering if she'd made herself too pretty today. Sometimes she did that inadvertently, since she'd done it on purpose every morning for several years while she was a teenager. But no, she looked like her birth self, clean-faced, violet-eyed, her hair brown with gold highlights, cut even with her jaw so as not to get in her way. She had the same distinctive good looks that made her mother a successful newscaster, but mostly she didn't inhabit her face the way a star would.

Blaise was probably just being polite. "I could never do what you do," Opal said, and smiled.

Blaise tilted her head. Something edged the air between them, a recognition, or perhaps just an electric prickle. "I don't quite believe you," Blaise murmured. "I guess we all tell ourselves the lies we need to believe. Nice to meet you, Opal."

Disconcerted, Opal nodded. She glanced toward Corvus. "I better get to work. Excuse me."

"Later," said Lauren.

Opal returned to her workstation. She got out the full-sized head of Corvus she had made when she built his Dark God; it held all the pieces of his facial prosthetics. She had made stacks of each piece, enough for him to have a new mask every day he was shooting, and a few extra in case things went wrong. "Hey, big guy," she murmured, and Corvus opened his deep brown eyes.

He smiled. "You smell like apples."

"Shampoo. How long have you been awake?"

"Since the others got here," he murmured. His voice was deep and velvety, one of the things she loved about him. He had a career in audiobooks most of his coworkers didn't know about; he was especially popular as a reader of children's books, since he could do so many different voices. His voice had been wasted in *Dead Loss*, which had been about the menace of appearance, not about lines. Corvus's character had a lot to say in *Forest of the Night*. The Dark God had the ability to seduce, a welcome challenge for Corvus after years of playing unspeakable and unspeaking menaces. "Didn't feel like talking."

She smiled at him, folded back the blanket to expose his neck and bare shoulders, and got out her razor and shaving cream. She shaved him, even though he had shaved himself earlier. She talked to his hair follicles while she did it, asked them to lie dormant for a while. She cleaned his face and neck carefully, then applied a long-lasting moisturizer that would keep his skin safe under the adhesives she was about to use.

"Hang on," said a shadow against the afternoon sun in the doorway at their end of the trailer.

Opal's back stiffened. Erika Dennis.

The film's publicist swept in in a cloud of musky perfume and lifted one of her cameras from the interlaced straps of them around her neck. "First transformation," she said. "Gotta document it for the DVD."

"No," said Corvus. His voice held so much menace Opal would have run if it were directed at her.

Erika was oblivious, or maybe just strong-willed. "Yes." She aimed the video camera at Corvus's face and pressed the record button. "It's in your contract."

"No."

"Erika, get out," Opal said. She hadn't started making Corvus into the Dark God yet. They had done all the prep work during preproduction—studied the script, the story-boards, the costumer's concept of the character. They'd talked to the art director, exchanged sketches. She and Corvus had discussed what Corvus wanted to bring to the role, and what he hoped Opal would do to augment it. They had made Corvus's life-mask, the armature on which Opal built her monster. He had built the character inside himself. She felt it rising in him now as she prepared for his transformation.

She didn't think Corvus had magical abilities—he'd never exhibited anything overt—but something about the chemistry of interaction in the trailer charged the air. Opal felt a surge under her skin, her own power readying for a fight. It frightened her. She never had this kind of fight away from her gifted family. People said there were others with powers out in the world, but Opal hadn't yet met many.

Rodrigo took Erika by the shoulders and pushed her out of the trailer. "Not this time," he said. "Film it some other day and say it's the first time. This time they need to focus. Get out of our workspace, Ere. You're upsetting the talent." He closed the door in her face.

The scent and feel of threat faded.

Rodrigo said, "It probably *is* in your contract, Corvus. She'll have to film it sometime."

"It's not in my contract." Corvus had his eyes closed. "I specifically struck that clause. I always do. I'm going to play monsters all my life. I decided early in my career that I wanted to do it mysteriously. Nobody outside of cast and crew gets to see me transform."

"Yikes. That raises the stakes for *National Enquirer* opportunists."

Corvus sighed. "I know. Could you help me, Rodrigo? No cameras in the Makeup trailer."

"That's already the rule, except for my continuity cameras."

"Finished work is okay. It's the process I want to guard."

"You got it. I can't police the area all the time, though. If someone's determined to plant a camera in here and has the tech, I don't know that I can stop them. Cameras can be so small now. You can get spytech at Sharper Image, for God's sake, and this is not a secure shoot; lots of holes."

"Noted."

"I'll guard the workspace," Opal said. She could add a level of awareness every time she entered the trailer, check for hidden things. She was hypersensitive to anything that watched; it would be simple. She opened one of her extra senses and glanced around. "Who put that there?" She moved to the mirror and plucked a suction-cup-backed rubber eye from it. It had been staring down at Corvus.

The back of her neck prickled. No one else should touch her things or invade her space. She had proprietary processes. She realized she needed to set traps.

Rodrigo's eyes widened. "I vaguely remember somebody coming in and sticking that up. They said it was a joke."

Opal closed her hand into a fist. The eye looked like rubber, but things inside it crunched. She opened her hand again, revealed a crushed mess of machinery. "Man or woman?"

"Male," said Rodrigo. "Not somebody I know yet, but someone whose presence here didn't surprise me. One of the electricians, I think." He closed his eyes. "Seal brown hair, olive tan skin, shadowed eyes. Rangy frame. White T-shirt, jeans. Toolbelt with the requisite rolls of tape. I don't think I noticed him before or since, but I don't pay a lot of attention to them."

"May I see that?" Corvus asked. He held out a hand and Opal dropped the mashed electronics into it. His hand could have closed around both of hers and hidden them completely.

"God. I hate this. I guess we'll need to set watch here, or lock up when we're not in. I better check for others," said Rodrigo. He went down the trailer, looking everywhere. Opal expanded her awareness the length of the trailer. No sense of any more invading eyes.

Opal shrugged and went to work on Corvus. They sank into collaboration then, all her focus on his face as she applied the adhesive and then attached the different prosthetics that would alter him but leave him with the ability to govern his expressions. His deep, shadowed eyes watched her face most of the time. It was unnerving. Other actors she'd worked with fell asleep while she was applying their prosthetics and makeup, or listened to music with their eyes closed. It made them much easier to deal with.

She didn't notice when others entered or left the trailer, though she was half-conscious of surrounding murmurs, and then, finally, silence.

Corvus sighed.

Opal wanted his head to belong to her, to be the armature for her artwork. She wasn't ready to let him be a person yet. *You are mine,* she thought as she narrowed her eyes and stared into his. *You are calm and receptive. You wait without complaint.* He became very still then, but his gaze never left hers. She worked with adhesive and latex, and after she had applied all the pieces (some of her magic slipped out her fingertips, she couldn't stop herself; but only she would take off the mask, so she should be able to undo it), she painted on the colors. Last of all, she put in his monster contact lenses, glittery metallic green with no whites or pupils except for clear spots in the centers so he could see through them.

At last she stood straight and stretched, her shoulders creaking from her working stoop. She glanced at the clock. Their call time was for 6 P.M., and it was 5:30 now. Not much time to dress him! But he looked perfect, and the costume for his role was simple, an enveloping black robe. In the scene scheduled to film tomorrow, she'd need to put on the upper body and hand appliances, and that would take more time.

She flexed her fingers, stepped back, and studied the overall effect; she had been too lost in the details to notice the whole before.

She was looking at someone new.

Working off images of the Green Man and legends of the Bogeyman, she had crafted someone leafy and scary, overhanging brow, jutting chin, details of oak leaves and maple leaves starting at his nose and raying out across his cheeks, forehead, and chin; his skin was light brown, layered in leaf veins with green highlights and scatterings of powdered gold, intermittent gleams that would catch the firelight of the night filming. The strange eyes almost frightened her as they stared into hers. He looked like something from a dream.

The mouth moved. She jumped.

"Opal," Corvus murmured.

"Yes?"

"Did you paralyze me? I can't move."

"Oh. Oops. Sorry, Corr." She touched her palm to his newly leafy forehead and released him. She didn't remember spelling him still. She could tell she had done it, though; her signature was on the magic. Maybe a thread of something else.

He shook his shoulders, turned his head. "How did you do that?"

"Hypnosis." One of her stock answers. She usually didn't do things like involuntarily paralyze other people anymore, unless the circumstances were dire. Why had she done it to Corvus?

It had certainly made the work easier.

"I don't like hearing that," he murmured. "I'm not supposed to be an easy subject. You didn't do this to me on the last picture."

"No."

"I guess I must trust you." He blinked. His eyelids were brown, now, blended with the rest of his face. When had she colored his lids? All she remembered from their session was his unblinking stare.

And the magic that had seeped from her fingertips into his skin . . . She must have done it then, tinted his face the color she wanted.

With his eyes closed, Corvus looked almost like forest floor. Opal shot some Polaroids for continuity, asked him to open his eyes and shot a couple more.

Corvus turned and stared at his reflection in the wall of mirrors beside his seat. "Oh. My." A hand rose to his mouth, hovered but did not touch. He noticed the hand was normal, held it out, and frowned at it. The facial prosthetics worked well; she could read his expression without trouble.

"You're not going to need the hands in tonight's scene," she said.

His eyes closed, opened. "You're right. Do you have the mock-up gloves, though? I'd like to put something on. It'll help with the character."

She opened the drawer that held the hand work and got out the prototype gloves she had made. The real prosthetics were pieces again, finger sheaths, backs and palms of hands, a several-layer process to apply, but she had made the gloves to get the overall look, a template she could cut apart. She held the gloves open and he slid his large hands inside. She had worked from casts of his hands; the gloves fit absolutely.

She had used the leaf pattern and earth colors to craft the gloves, too. The fingernails were long, horny, and dark.

"Lovely," he murmured, his voice dark, rich, velvety. He gave her a Dark God smile. She swayed, wanting to fall forward into his lap.

"Are you all right?" He pushed up out of the chair, braced her shoulders in his gloved hands, and steadied her.

Opal blinked up into his face, pulled herself together. "I've got to get Wardrobe in here," she said. Had she laid an Attract Spell on him and not noticed? What was wrong with her? Usually she leashed her powers completely in situations like this.

She sniffed. No smell of an Attract Spell, but there was something at work here, something strange. It must be her, in love with her own creation and how Corvus embodied it. She'd had this problem before, especially at the start of a shoot, before she got tired of all the time it took to create her creatures over and over again. He was just so—perfectly monstrous.

Better ditch this attitude fast.

She picked up the "Ear," the communications headset that linked her to the rest of the crew, slipped it on, and hooked the battery/control box to her belt. She hated the headset. Its electric energy field messed up her thinking. She wore it as little as possible, but right now she needed it to drop back into the web of everything going on with the film.

She called the head of the teamsters and put in a request for Corvus's driver to be ready soon. Then she switched channels. No local traffic on the Makeup channel. She switched to Wardrobe, clicked the transmit button. "Betty?"

"Who is this?"

"Opal, makeup for Dark God."

"I'm still at the B&B set. You need something?" The key wardrobe artist sounded gruff and irritated.

"Costume for Dark God. Call time in half an hour."

"You're one of those last-minute emergency people, huh? Great," said Betty.

Turf wars, thought Opal. *Wonderful.*

"I'm still needed here," said Betty, still grumpy. "Pick up Kelsi, my assistant, at the trailer. She'll get you geared up."

"Is she on this channel?"

"She probably doesn't have her Ear in. She hates it."

"That makes two of us."

"Great. More idiots out of the loop. Go to the trailer and tell her I said she should help you. She can confirm if she wants."

Opal sighed and switched off. "Don't go anywhere," she told Corvus. "I brought you some water." She handed him a sports bottle with a straw, something he could sip from without upsetting the prosthetics. "I'll be right back with Wardrobe." She dashed out of the trailer, locked the door behind her.

In the Wardrobe trailer, Opal introduced herself to Kelsi Martini. Kelsi, her short bobbed hair lime green, her skin pale, her lips painted black, helped Opal track down Corvus's costume. "I'll suit him up," Kelsi said as she draped the long black robe twice over her arm.

"All right."

Opal's Ear crackled. Rodrigo's voice said, "What's your status? Ready to head out?"

She pressed the transmit button. "Not dressed yet."

"We're wrapping with Unit One, but there's been some traffic on another channel about the forest shoot. You should hurry."

"On it," she said.

"Can't wait to see what you've done to the big guy," Kelsi said as they left the trailer. "Sure looked spooky in the story-boards."

"Yeah, well . . ." Opal unlocked the Makeup trailer.

"What's with the extra security?" Kelsi asked as she entered the trailer.

"We found a hidden camera. Somebody's going tabloid on our asses."

Kelsi gasped, and Opal turned from locking the door to stare.

The Dark God loomed at the far end of the trailer. He was a large, ominous shadow against the light—all the other makeup stations had been shut down; only Opal's was still lit. His naked upper body looked bull-like, dense with muscles, and the silhouetted shape of his head was odd and wrong, different from her vision of him. Fear thrilled in feathering ripples up Opal's spine.

A sucking sound came from the Dark God's direction. "Got any more water?" Corvus said, his voice higher than usual.

"*Gaah,*" said Kelsi. "You scared me, dude!"

"Good." He had dropped the register into deep and rich again. Opal wondered if he'd spoken high to break the tension. She wouldn't put it past him. He was always sensitive to emotional atmospheres. "That's my job."

Kelsi headed toward him. Opal followed. As Corvus turned toward the light, she saw that he was just as she had left him, a demon–wood god mix, his mane of black hair raying out around the prosthetics that covered his face and neck. She had carried the dark brown/gleaming gold skin color of the Dark God a short way down his black-furred chest; below that, he was light tan, normal. She hadn't seen him out from under the blanket yet today; she didn't remember him being this buff during their last movie.

Kelsi walked all the way around Corvus. "Wow, Opal! Wow! That's amazing! I'd heard you were good, but I never—"

Corvus posed while Kelsi examined him.

"Fantastic," Kelsi whispered.

Opal crossed her arms. "Thanks. It helps to have good base material."

Corvus grinned, his Dark God expression more sinister than reassuring, but she could read beneath the layers she had applied to his face, and knew he was teasing her. She was glad they'd forged a good connection. Some of the actors she had worked with in the past had been horrors in several senses of the word.

Kelsi held up the black robe. "Well, so, want to slip into this, Mr. Weather?"

He put down the sports bottle, and Opal grabbed it. There were crates of water bottles on the Craft Services truck. She should stock some by her station.

Corvus stretched his arms behind him so Kelsi could slip on the sleeves. She slid the black robe up over his shoulders. "Any of this stuff bleed?" she asked Opal. "Do you have solvents to get it out of cloth?"

"It shouldn't stain; it's set until I use the removal goop."

"No stains, huh?" Kelsi fastened the robe at Corvus's neck with a silver brooch shaped like a five-pointed star, center point down. She straightened the hood. The back of her hand brushed the colored part of Corvus's neck. She studied her hand, flashed it at Opal: no makeup adhered. "Neat."

"Ticktock," Corvus said.

Startled, Kelsi glanced at Opal's Batman clock. It was almost six; they were due at the forest clearing location. "Sorry." She used hidden snaps to fasten the rest of the robe down the front, then reached way up to lift the hood and settle it, veiling most of his head. The hood left his face in shadow; only the extended chin, with its leaf beard, jutted out far enough to catch much light. "Okay. I'll ride over with you guys, if that's all right."

"Sure," said Opal. Then she glanced at Corvus: it was really his decision. He was the star, the one who could have tantrums and snits if he liked, so long as they stayed on schedule. He was so laid back she had forgotten he was talent and she was second- or third-class citizen. On some shoots, nobody ever let you forget your status; other shoots were more relaxed. Opal hadn't spent enough time on this shoot to get a sense of how it worked.

"Glad to have you," Corvus said to Kelsi.

"I'll get my kit. Meet you at the car."

Opal packed solvents and brushes and touch-up equipment in her makeup kit, along with duplicates of the pieces of latex she had applied to Corvus's face, in case of wardrobe malfunctions. "I have to stop at Craft Services and pick up more water—"

"Could you get me something to drink with calories in it? I don't want to eat with this on," Corvus said.

"Yeah. Patty stocked protein shakes for you. I'll walk you to the car and get you settled, then run for it."

"Good. I can see, but my vision is limited, and I don't want to bump my hands."

"Rest your hands on my shoulders." She stood in front of the door and waited until Corvus was right behind her, his large, warm, rubber-gloved hands heavy on her shoulders.

They had done this before, too: she had acted as guide dog on *Dead Loss*. The doubled head he had worn for that role was much more of a challenge for him visually.

Opal opened the door at her end of the trailer and flicked off the lights. "Three steps down," she said, "and the last one is—yikes!"

Erika's camera flashed, blinding her. She would have stumbled without Corvus's steadying grip on her shoulders.

"Stop it!" she yelled at Erika.

"No way. I've waited all afternoon for this." Erika shot a stream of pictures, alternating between two cameras on straps around her neck.

"If we're late because of your interference," Corvus said, his voice a low rumble, "we'll redirect the wrath to you."

"I'm done for now," Erika said. She smirked. "Thanks so much. Catch you later. Nice job, Opal." She strolled away, taking her musky scent cloud with her.

Opal shivered with suppressed rage. The wrappings on her powers unwound; she felt red rivers rise. Energy pooled in her palms. She hadn't been this angry since she was sixteen, newly powerful, and her younger brother and sister had teased her beyond bearing. She could hold up her hands and let the power jab out of her into Erika's back. Erika would melt into a puddle of steaming flesh, her cameras slag.

Opal clenched her fists to restrain the eager power.

Corvus's hands on her shoulders steadied her. He leaned down and whispered in her ear, "Not yet," in a Dark God voice, and that gave her the strength to chill her power and send it back to sleep. In the shocky aftermath, she swayed, and Corvus held her steady.

How could she even contemplate such a devastating thing? She was Opal, low-powered Opal who only used her gifts to change how things looked. Who inside her rose up in a killing rage?

Corvus's rubber-taloned fingers massaged her shoulders

a little. His regular voice said, "You okay, Opal, hon? I guess we should have expected that. She's a pit bull."

She hugged herself, settled down. "Sure. Sorry, Corr. Let's go. Three steps down, and the last one is steeper."

"I'll find it by feel."

They descended the steps. Once they touched down on the parking lot between the bed-and-breakfast, where the first unit had been filming all day, and the abandoned grocery store the production company had taken over as a housing for sound stages, Corvus moved up to walk beside her, one hand still on her shoulder. They walked to the black Lincoln the production manager had rented for Corvus's use.

A short dark man leaned against the car, reading a magazine. He wore pointy boots, jeans, and a brown leather jacket. "Hitch," Corvus said. "This is Opal, my makeup artist. She comes with me every time. Opal, Hitch, my driver."

"Pleased," said Hitch, holding out a hand. Opal shook it and smiled.

Kelsi joined them. "I'm geared up! Let's rock and roll."

"Boss?" Hitch said.

"Kelsi. Wardrobe. She's with us, too."

Hitch shrugged and held the door for Corvus.

"I've got to get food and water," Opal muttered.

"There's another Craft Services van at the site," said Kelsi. "Dinner break's at nine. Somebody'll bring a load of sandwiches."

"Oh, good."

Kelsi jumped into the backseat. Opal joined her. Hitch piloted them away from the trailer village.

From the supermarket parking lot, people could walk anywhere in town; it was that small. Corvus, the director, and an actor Opal hadn't met yet were staying upstairs in the B&B. Most of the crew and any day players they needed stayed at a budget motel ten miles out of town, in the larger city of Redford off the highway. The production manager had rented a house across the square from the B&B in Lapis where she set up the office, reception, accounting, and a small room where the director, the director of photography, and anyone else who needed to could watch the dailies on DVD. The director of photography and the producer lived upstairs in the house. Other principal actors were living with various families around town.

Lapis had been small but busy before the Interstate was finished in 1966 and business and traffic moved a few miles west. One main road ran from north to south through town; two smaller roads ran east–west past the outskirts. Hitch took Sixth Street to Lost River Road. A mile east out of town, they came to a post with a paper plate stapled to it. One of the crew had written FOREST and an arrow pointing away from the road on the plate. There was a rutted track where the equipment trucks had churned up late spring mud on their way to the clearing where demonic rituals involving the Dark God were going to be filmed.

Mud spat up into the undercarriage of the Lincoln as they took the squishy road into the forest. The terrain was slippery. Opal wondered why the location manager had picked this place—until they broke out of the trees into a perfect clearing, firm ground, clear of trees, with a small brook running through one corner, and a stone altar and lichen-starred standing stones at the far end.

It was Magic Hour. Twilight still lightened the sky; the trees were visible but dark against the lingering light. Someone had brought in small bronze censers on tripods, suitably smoking, and an open fire danced in a ring of stones in front of the altar. A group of extras in long white robes were bunched up at the far end of the meadow. Light racks, camera tracks, and sound equipment stood ready near the altar. Chairs, the Craft Services truck, and equipment vans were arrayed at the near end of the meadow, hidden behind a photographed forest backdrop.

One of the young men directed Hitch off the road into a makeshift parking lot where someone had cleared a few trees. He pulled in and turned off the engine, which didn't silence the night. Portable generators roared near the equipment.

Hitch rounded the car and opened the door, helped Corvus out. Opal and Kelsi emerged. "The ground's pretty good here, but you better let me lead you anyway," Opal said, turning so Corvus could rest his hands on her shoulders again.

"Anytime, hon," said Corvus. He sounded distracted.

"Come on, come on," yelled Neil Aldridge, the director, "we're eating energy here." He wore black slacks and a black shirt. He was tall and muscular, with a shock of dark hair, heavy brow ridges, and a dissatisfied, thin-lipped mouth. He stood with his arms crossed, looking irritated. He appeared about forty-five. She hadn't seen any of his earlier movies. She and Corvus had wanted to consult with him about the Dark God in preproduction, but he had fobbed them off on the production designer, Dathan Riley, who was excited about the concept and worked with them to define and fine-tune it. Aldridge's voice was mellifluous, and carried well. He sounded kind. That was not his reputation.

The script supervisor, a sturdy woman with a clipboard, stood one step behind him. "The call was for six," Neil said.

"Sorry," said Opal. She checked her watch. They were a minute late. "Erika."

"Damn," muttered Neil. "Well, get out here and let me see what we've got."

Opal led Corvus past Neil into the full glare of the lights near the altar. Something itched her feet, some dazzle or discomfort she didn't recognize.

"Ladies, gentlemen, and others, our monster," said Neil. Like a ringmaster, he swept an arm toward Opal and Corvus.

All sound aside from the generators stopped.

Corvus gripped Opal's shoulders once, then gently pushed her aside. He stood with his arms crossed and looked over the assembled cast and crew. He moved his head and the hood fell away, revealing a stranger.

The horns weren't part of her prosthetics. They looked right, though, two short forward-thrusting spikes growing from Corvus's leafy temples, gleaming gold in their grooves. Opal opened her senses wide. Stranger magic tickled the bottoms of her feet, met her own force without meshing with it.

It climbed Corvus, enveloped him, resided most strongly in the places where she had changed him. Her alterations had left toeholds for it.

"Corvus," she whispered.

The face turned toward her. The eyes were dark now, not so green, and the soul looking out was not the man she knew.

He smiled. His teeth were pointed, serrated like a shark's.

Applause burst out around the circle.

Corvus lifted both arms, basking, circled with his hands, then took a very theatrical bow, one leaf-skinned hand lifting a segment of his robe behind him.

"He's going to steal the picture," Neil muttered. Then, louder, "All right, everybody, find your marks for a run-through. Can you see all right, Weather?"

"Perfectly," said Corvus.

"I want you looming on the far side of the fire, behind the altar, looking hungry while your minions dance for you. Menace and lust."

Corvus nodded. Opal raised her eyebrows, her gaze on his face. Did he want her to help him across the clearing to his mark? He nodded, gesturing from her toward the location. She stepped closer, and he settled his hands on her shoulders. They walked in tandem toward the fire and the altar. "Corr, are you all right?" she murmured.

He laughed. "Better than ever." He didn't sound like himself.

A tall man in a black robe backed away as they approached, Corvus's stand-in. He had the height, and his face was the same color greeny brown as Corvus's mask, but nothing else about him looked like Corvus. "Evening," he said.

"Hi, Fred," Opal said. Fred had been Corvus's stand-in on *Dead Loss*, too.

"Whoa, Nellie," said Fred when he saw Corvus. He hurried off to where the other stand-ins stood, behind the camouflage backdrop and out of sight of the cameras, smoking and whispering.

"Can you see your mark?" Opal asked. There was a piece of black electrician's tape on the ground beyond the altar.

"I know my place. Thanks, honey." He let her go, and she edged away from him, turned to look back. She stared at the pointy-toothed smile, the too-dark eyes, as a flicker of firelight ran over his face.

She hoped he was okay.

"Stand by for rehearsal. All nonactors off the set," Neil yelled.

Opal fled. She ran back to the car and pulled out her traveling kit, then joined Wardrobe, Makeup, and Hair at the cluster of canvas-backed chairs on the edge of the clearing, behind the backdrop.

"Cue music," called Neil. Someone punched a tape player. Eerie music full of whining wind instruments from unnamed countries and the thud of deep drums started up. "Action!" The frozen people in white, the looming figure in black all responded to the music. their motions small and restrained at first, growing wilder and looser.

"Okay, great," said Neil. "Let's do it from the top with the cameras."

"Last looks!" called the first assistant director, George Corvassian.

Opal grabbed her kit and joined a rush of Makeup, Hair, and Wardrobe people to the actors. Corvus started the scene with the hood up; midway through, when the minions had loosened up and didn't look like bad 1980s dance party victims, he would drop the hood.

He lowered the hood when she approached him and bent so that his face neared hers. She studied his face and could find nothing to correct.

"This is so strange," he murmured, in almost his own voice, and then, the Dark God spoke: "I like you. I like this. I wasn't sure at first, but now I'm glad you're all here."

She backed away again, her heart beating too fast. The hair on her arms stood; her skin prickled everywhere.

"Starting marks," yelled Neil. "Here we go, people. Start the music again."

A bell rang. George cried, "We're on bell. Roll sound, please."

"Rolling."

"Roll camera."

"Rolling."

"Action," Neil said.

Opal settled into Corvus's giant custom canvas-backed chair, opened her senses, and reached for what disturbed her here.

The ground was alive with more than scuffed grass. She had a sense of profound sleep, with an edge of waking, of old wounds, covered but not healed, and of something unhuman, a mind that didn't work like anything she had ever encountered.

She had had a brief career as a tree talker when she was sixteen—the family invited a tree to live in their house over the Christmas season every year, and the youngest with gifts was the one who issued the invitation. She had only done it once before her younger brother Jasper came into his power and took over the job. Communicating wasn't one of her stronger gifts; she had had to listen hard to find a tree that volunteered to travel. Even then she wasn't sure if she'd chosen the right one, not until her mother spoke to the tree and confirmed it. Since then—twelve years ago—she hadn't tried to talk to anyone but humans, and that using her mouth.

"What are you?" she whispered.

The ancient sleeper surged beneath her, alive with an energy she could sense but not see. It didn't answer.

It was this that was seeping up into Corvus's skin, shifting him in ways Opal hadn't. She wondered what it wanted, whether it would hurt him.

Magenta, in a chair next to hers, cradled a tiny portable TV that showed a black-and-white version of what the hot camera on the set was filming. At the moment, the camera was focused on Corvus's face. Magenta whispered, "What you did with him? That's amazing. How did you do it? Can I watch you next time? I want to learn."

"If it's all right with Corvus," Opal whispered.

"Cut! Let's run it again," Neil called.

Usually everyone had magazines to flip through while they waited, but tonight, Wardrobe, Makeup, Hair, and drivers all watched whatever monitors they had, even three takes in. Opal couldn't stop staring at Corvus. Whatever was in him worked on her, inviting her to fall in love with him even more than she already had.

During one of the touch-up moments between takes when everyone rushed to fix whatever had gone awry during the last take, Opal said, "Corr, are you okay in there?"

He just smiled. She lifted a gilt-dipped brush, lowered it. He needed no help from her.

"Starving," he whispered then, and she went to the mobile Craft Services van and got him a protein shake. He sipped while they reset the cameras, but he didn't speak to her again.

They closed down at midnight, just before the rain started. Hitch drove Corvus and Opal back through sweeping rain as other crew broke down sets and sheltered equipment under tarps. Someone rushed the exposed film off to be developed.

In the Makeup trailer, Corvus sprawled in his chair. Opal got out the Polaroid camera and shot more pictures of him, compared them to her earlier shots. She wrote time and date across the bottoms of the new Polaroids in Sharpie permanent ink.

The horns on his forehead were the most obvious change, and they still looked good. The rest of her forehead pieces didn't have them, though. She'd have to spend the rest of the night making new appliances.

Or maybe she could cheat. As long as she had the photos for continuity, she should be able to manage. She wasn't sure how to manage the wild magic out in the clearing, though.

"Ready for removal?" she asked Corvus when she had satisfactory shots from several angles.

"Please," he said. He held out his hands. She pulled the latex mitts off gently. They came off all in a piece. She handed Corvus a towel, and he wiped sweat and moisturizer off his hands. She set the gloves up on spikes to dry; she would powder, maybe blow-dry them tomorrow, as necessary.

She got out her special solvent and prepared to take the first section of his facial prosthesis off. It clung to his face. She eased a brush loaded with solvent along the edges. As the outside edge of her finger brushed over the prosthetic, she felt not latex but flesh, warm, with pores and tiny hairs.

She set the brush down across the solvent tin. Her hand shook. She stroked Corvus's leafy cheek, pointed chin, horns. The eyes, a solid dark green color, watched her, and the mouth quirked in a small smile.

"Let him go," Opal whispered. Warm power gathered in

her fingertips. She touched them lightly to his face, and the foreign power that had been riding him since they had arrived at the clearing seeped away. Her fingernail flicked up the edge of a cheek piece.

She reached for her brush and worked carefully, pulled the pieces off, and tossed them in the trash. The horns came off as though they were part of the forehead pieces. She set them on the counter near his life-mask so she could match tomorrow's mask to them. She worked with haste, hoping the new energy wouldn't return and force Corvus back into character.

She took care with his skin, finishing with another round of moisturizer.

"Feels good," he said as she massaged lotion into his face. He still wore the dark contacts and watched her face more than her hands.

"Good," she echoed, distracted. "How are you, otherwise? Did you notice anything different?" She finished and capped her bottles.

Corvus popped out the contacts, set them into the solution-filled container she held out. He studied the more recent Polaroids. "I don't know. It doesn't look like the prototype, or even what I looked like when we left the trailer. Looks much better, actually. When did you change it?"

"Um—last looks, right before the first shot."

"I don't remember. Guess I was distracted. Did you watch the monitors while we shot?" asked Corvus.

"Sure."

"How'd I come across?"

"Amazing."

He smiled, seemed entirely himself again. "Good. I wonder if the D.P. will let me see the dailies. Do you know when they're supposed to arrive?"

"Three sets tomorrow night, but I'm pretty sure Aldridge

doesn't want any of the actors looking at them. News at supper was he's an overcontrolling asshole." There had been a half-hour meal break in the midst of the night's filming; Corvus had been restricted to protein shakes, but Opal had wolfed a sandwich and listened to other crew members talking.

It wasn't the first time she and Corvus had heard these rumors about the director. They had done research on cast and crew while Corvus contemplated the project, mostly quizzing other people who had worked with the principals before. The part was too good to turn down, even though it wasn't a great script.

"Frustrating," Corvus said. He moved his shoulders, still clothed in the black robe. "A good night's work."

"Time for your beauty sleep," Opal said. She checked the call sheet the assistant director had handed out just before they stopped filming for the night. "Call's for four P.M. tomorrow—we'll have to start makeup around noon."

He sighed and pulled himself to his feet. "Thanks for taking care of me." He gave her a hug, then ambled out of the trailer.

She policed her area, straightening, cleaning, restocking supplies. She got out the new set of latex appliances she'd use on Corvus tomorrow, draped them over the life-mask, checked to make sure there was no one nearby, and then, studying the Polaroids and the previous pieces of altered mask, she let her power seep into the forehead pieces to form the horns. A tiny touch of alien power still lingered in the horns from that day's mask; when she touched their tips, the power jumped into her fingers. She touched the new horns and the power flowed into them.

Disturbing. Yet it helped, added some quality that made the horns match absolutely with the earlier set.

When she had finished, she curled up in the residual warmth Corvus's body had left in his oversized chair. She studied pictures of the face she had built, with its later additions. Who had shifted her work? She'd never encountered outside magic on a set before, even though she had done most of her work in weird supernatural movies.

The face, with its blank white eye sockets, stared back at her. A corner of its mouth quirked up into a smile.

2

The following day, Corvus had a scene on the soundstage with Lauren Marcos, who played the older sister, Serena, in the film. Opal was thrilled. He almost never got close-ups— she'd spent hours watching his old movies on DVD after she met him on *Dead Loss*, and he was mostly a shambling monster in the distance, obscured by fog and darkness and attended by scary musical cues. Even when his face appeared full screen in the scary psycho shots, he was always projecting rage or madness. This was going to be different.

Corvus and Lauren had run lines during a late breakfast just before Corvus's makeup call time, off in a corner, hunched (at least, Corvus hunched; Lauren, two feet shorter, had cricked her neck to keep his face in view) together. Opal, eating a breakfast burrito with Makeup and Wardrobe, had felt a familiar flare of jealousy, and had, with a practiced mental motion, tamped it down. Corvus wasn't her creation at breakfast; he was entirely his own self, and he could be interested in Lauren if he liked. Or just work with her.

Opal fell in love with everyone she worked on. She had to love them. Otherwise what she did to them wouldn't look convincing. She loved them, and she had to convince herself to leave them alone. She throttled her urge to claim Corvus and ate the rest of her burrito, then went to the Makeup trailer and rechecked her preparations.

Corvus was quiet when he came in, silent as he stretched out, shirtless, in his chair and lay back so she could work. Today, because of the close-ups, Opal was applying neck and chest prosthetics as well as face and hands. Lauren, in the next chair being tended by Rodrigo, was quiet, too. Opal cleansed, shaved, moisturized Corvus's face, letting the magic seep from her fingertips into his skin only a little. The pieces of the false face slid on smoothly. When she pulled up out of her creative trance and glanced at the clock, she saw she had finished an hour early.

Lauren was still sitting in the nearest makeup chair, flipping through a fashion magazine. Rodrigo was gone.

"That was intense," she said. "You always get so wrapped up in your work?"

"Yep." Opal shook her head to wake herself, checked Corvus. He looked great. She studied the Polaroids she'd taken the night before and compared them with Corvus now, was satisfied with the match. She took more shots and dated them.

"Opal," whispered Corvus. "You did it to me again."

"Oh, God," she said, and pressed her palm to his enhanced forehead, released him from paralysis. "Sorry. Are you all right?"

"Feeling strangely fine." He stretched and rose to his feet, all the visible skin on his front altered into Dark God, though Opal had done less work on his upper arms and lower abdomen. "It's not something I enjoyed, that sense of utter helplessness, but it didn't leave me stiff the way I expected. I almost trust you enough to relax, and it does make it easier for me to stay still. Nothing even itched. Posthypnotic suggestion?" He paused, arrested by his own image in the mirror. "Oh, I *am* someone else now," he murmured low.

Lauren set aside her magazine without looking and studied him. Her eyes widened.

Corvus smiled at her, his look strangely tender. The energy in the air feathered against Opal's skin, unspoken messages involving warmth and desire, persuasion and invitation. She fell under the spell herself, and wondered if Lauren had any defenses against it, or wanted any.

She couldn't let Corvus and Lauren make out now; it might mess up the makeup. "Wait until after your scene," Opal said, her voice cross.

"What?" Corvus's voice was deep and Dark Godly, but startled.

"Oy," said Lauren, and shook herself. "Yeah. Focus, Laur," she muttered.

"I need to put one last piece on the back of your neck," Opal said to Corvus.

"Right." He dropped to his knees on the floor and leaned forward, braced his arms on the seat of his chair. She applied the last piece of the prosthesis, almost certain not to be seen, but still necessary.

When she had finished, Opal thumbed a button on her walkie and switched to Wardrobe frequency. "Betty? This is Opal. The Dark God is ready for wardrobe."

Corvus stood, his back still tan and human-colored below the darker brown, green, and gold of his neck and the black of his hair.

"Okay, Opal, good. You're early. Kelsi's in the trailer. I'll tell her to come to you. They're still filming scene nine on the stage, but what the heck."

"How close are they to done?" Scene nine was supposed to

wrap by four, when Corvus and Lauren were due on the set. Opal checked her watch. They were still an hour early.

"Aldridge is throwing a hissy fit about rounded vowels," Betty whispered. "Millie has the wrong accent."

"Great."

"He might finish this scene on time, though. Better be here."

"We will." Opal signed off. "Kelsi's bringing the robe here."

Lauren stood. She was already dressed in her costume for this scene, flat black kung fu shoes, jeans with wear-whitened knees, and a chocolate brown blouse that buttoned all the way to her throat. Her street makeup was minimal, subdued, almost not there. In her first confrontation with the Dark God as an adult, she was restrained, self-protective, making no attempt to look good. Her childhood encounter with the Dark God had driven her character underground, hiding from herself and the world. She would shift over the course of the film, and so would her costume, hair, and makeup.

Kelsi knocked. Opal let her in. "Hey, big guy," Kelsi said. Corvus stooped, and Kelsi settled the robe around his shoulders, adjusted its folds, mated the hidden snaps to each other, and fastened the upside-down star at his throat. Covus lifted the hood. His horns tented the material.

Opal grabbed her set makeup kit and went to the door. "Wait," she said. She closed her eyes and tuned in to the air. She had already checked for spies in the trailer, and now she pushed her senses farther out. Was Erika lying in ambush again? It occurred to Opal that the pictures the publicist had taken the day before were now inaccurate, but maybe Erika didn't know that yet. It would be better if no one knew, but she wasn't sure how to manage that.

No one waited outside, so Opal opened the door and led Corvus down the steps. His hand on her shoulder was warm again, but he squeezed her and let go at the base of the stairs.

"I don't know what it is," he said, "but I can see better today. Thanks for your help."

The construction crew had built a mock-up of the forest altar on the soundstage inside the old supermarket, so they didn't have far to go.

This shoot had a bigger budget than most of the other movies Opal had worked on. She felt a brief pang for previous pictures, when, as chief makeup assistant, she had had more to do, helping out with makeup for everybody from the stars to the extras. Even though she loved Corvus, it was a pain being attached to one person; everybody else got variety in their work.

The crew had been out in the forest all day shooting a flashback to Serena's earlier life, when she had participated in the demonic rituals of her mother's coven in the forest, summoning the Dark God. Splices of Corvus's image from the previous day's filming would be cut in later. Gemma Goodwin, a fourteen-year-old child actor, was playing ten-year-old Serena.

People were already complaining about Aldridge in corners during meal breaks, though Opal thought he had been businesslike on the set yesterday. People said he was a stickler for getting done on time, whether it was quality work or not, and he had a reputation for reducing people to tears by yelling at them. It was part of his theory about getting the best performance out of an actor: break them down completely until he could build them back in the form he desired. Corvus wasn't his first choice for monster. Aldridge had a protégé he had wanted to use, but the studio executives had overruled him.

They crossed the parking lot toward the abandoned supermarket. Under a canopy tent that made the old parking lot look like a garden party, the stand-ins smoked or drowsed or played computer games at a picnic table. The red light over the door to the building was off; no filming was happening at the moment. They passed a security guard on their way into the chilly building, then headed over to the clutter that wasn't one of the sets, a hanging clothing rack, stacks of flats full of bottled water, masses of Medusa wires coiling across the floor and dangling from the ceiling, and all the canvas chairs with actors', producers', and directors' names on them. The director's, assistant director's, and producer's chairs huddled on a platform a short distance from the cast's chairs.

Opal and Corvus went to Corvus's specially constructed chair. She helped him settle into it and got him the novel he was reading, complete with its own book light; the waiting area was indifferently lighted. A few of the other actors were there, sipping water; Rod and Magenta perched in chairs with absent actors' names on them.

Opal went back outside to the Craft Services trailer to fetch a couple of the butterscotch protein shakes for Corvus, then returned and wandered over to the Props department monitor, a small black-and-white TV that showed the view through whichever camera was hot on the set. The camera was focused on a table topped with a doily, with a lamp sitting on it. The light was made from an old brass carriage lamp. Opal hugged herself. She had forgotten how cold they kept it on the soundstage to offset the melting heat of the lights.

"Fascinating, isn't it?" said a stocky older man, his hair solid, grease-tamed gray, his face set in a wide smile like a frog's.

"What's going on?"

"Wait for it, wait for it," he said. Someone put a small, carved wooden box beside the lamp, angled it sideways, held a Polaroid next to it and moved it again. "Excitement unlimited!"

"That's the magic box?" Opal asked. The script mentioned a magic box, left by the dead mother at the bed-and-breakfast, discovered by the two daughters when they returned after an absence of years. The box held the key to unlocking the daughters' magical natures. It was made of some varnished wood, and the figures carved into it were geometric rather than representational. Inlaid diamonds of mother-of-pearl gleamed under the light.

"That's the magic box. You like? Say, who are you, anyway?"

She held out her hand, and he shook it. "Opal LaZelle. Special effects makeup." She hitched a shoulder toward Corvus.

"Joe Lazarus, prop master."

"Pleased to meet you."

A bell rang. "Roll sound," called someone. "Rolling," called someone else. "Roll camera." "Rolling." A clapperboard showing production, scene, take, roll, date, sound, director, and cameraman came into view on their screen. Someone bumped it. It pulled out of frame. "Action!"

Opal stood beside Joe and watched as a slender hand moved into the shot, rested on the box a moment, then slipped it out of frame. Blaise Penny, as Caitlyn Lost, the younger sister, was stealing the box.

"Cut," cried a voice. Two bells rang.

"Sixth time he's done that one," Joe muttered. "Is it over yet?"

"And print! Break, everybody. Ready set two for scene nineteen!" one voice called, and a second voice echoed it. Activity surged around another part of the soundstage, and the sound of hammering and an electric saw.

"Better scoot," said Joe. He headed into the storm of activity around the forest altar set.

Opal went back to the gathering of canvas-backed chairs. Corvus's oversized chair had accompanied him from *Dead Loss*. While he was on the set, Opal curled up in his chair, but now she settled into the chair assigned to Blaise. Blaise wasn't going to be in the scene with Corvus and Lauren, so she would probably quit for the day. If not, Opal would move. This might be a good time to take a set temperature, see how Blaise treated the help. Lauren was friendly, which was good to know.

"Stand-ins," yelled someone. Corvus's stand-in, Fred, and Lauren's stand-in headed for the set, a tall man in a black robe and a compact woman in brown blouse and jeans.

"How you doing?" Opal asked Corvus, who sprawled in his chair, his hood low over his face, his altered hands sticking out the ends of his black sleeves, the leafy fingers curled under into loose fists. The novel she had brought him earlier lay closed on his lap.

"Strangely," Corvus murmured. "Did you give me post-hypnotic suggestions to help me find the character? I don't know that I signed on for that."

"No," said Opal. "Honestly, Corr. I didn't even know I was hypnotizing you. I didn't tell you to do anything."

"I'll vouch," said Lauren, lazily. "I was watching the whole time she did you. She didn't tell you anything."

"I'm not exactly myself, here," he said.

"Who are you?" asked Opal.

One of the great hands clamped over her wrist. "I think you know," said a low voice from under Corvus's hood. His mouth, the only visible part of his original face, smiled slowly. "You are my handmaiden, are you not? The facilitator who brought me this more-than-perfect vessel? You will be rewarded." The voice had dropped to a whisper.

Opal twisted her arm, tried to free it from the vise of his fingers. He gripped her more tightly.

"Hey, big guy. Save your energy for the shooting," Lauren said.

"Corvus," Opal whispered.

He released her, then ran his clawed fingertips gently

down her arm, ended with them resting on her knuckles. "I don't wish to frighten you," he said. "Yet."

"Could you *be* any more creepy?" Lauren asked. "Leave the handmaiden alone, will you?"

"What?" Corvus asked in his normal voice.

"You're getting eerie, Corvus. Stop it. At least until we're acting."

"I'm eerie?" He sounded surprised.

"Opal, come sit by me," Lauren said. "Could you check my eyelashes?"

Opal left the chair beside Corvus and moved to the one on the far side of Lauren. It was Dirk Baptiste's chair—he played the mysteriously ambiguous sheriff in the film, and Opal hadn't met him yet. His only scene with Corvus happened during the climax, which wasn't scheduled to be filmed for a week.

Opal leaned to look at Lauren's eyelashes.

Lauren winked.

"Thanks," Opal whispered.

"I've got some questions for you later," murmured Lauren. "For now, could you take a quick look at my makeup?"

"No, she cannot," said Rodrigo, beside them suddenly. "That is not her job. It is mine."

"Sorry," said Lauren. "*You* check my eyelashes, then."

Rod put a Set2Go kit labeled "Caitlyn" in his black duffel and took out one labeled "Serena." He leaned close and peered at Lauren's face. "Close your eyes," he murmured. She did, and he blew across her eyelids. A loose lash lifted, drifted. "As for the rest, let's wait until they call for last looks. Everything looks pretty good for the moment."

"Scene nineteen. Ten-minute warning," called one of the assistant directors over by the forest altar set.

Opal got to her feet and grabbed her own kit, a small wheeled suitcase. Special effects makeup called for a lot more equipment than street makeup. She returned to Corvus, wondering who would meet her there. She fished one of the protein shakes out of her bag. "You hungry?" she asked.

"Not really, but I'll drink. It might be a while before I get another chance." He sounded normal again, no more creepy whispering.

Opal popped the top of the can and slid a straw in, held it up where Corvus could easily sip. He steadied her hand with his own, but didn't close his hand on her again; he drank from the straw. She watched his mouth to see if the makeup survived its encounter with the straw. His mouth looked different, and real. The straw didn't disrupt it at all.

"Here we go, people," called the A.D. "Stand by for blocking rehearsal."

Corvus pushed Opal's hand away gently. He and Lauren rose and headed for the set. Opal set the half-finished drink on a nearby table, grabbed her kit, and followed, with Rod.

The stand-ins moved off the set. The boom operator adjusted a microphone to give Corvus more headroom.

SCENE 19

EXT. ALTAR STONE. TWILIGHT.

The DARK GOD stands at the head of the altar stone, which is stained with dark splatters. SERENA, clutching a big sack of a purse, stands beside the stone, not too near the Dark God.

DARK GOD
You've come here for a reason.

SERENA
That's right, to find out what happened to my mother in this forest. Something killed her . . .

Neither Cait nor I believe she committed suicide.
Who are you? Some Halloween nutcase who goes
around dressed like that all year? You get a kick
out of scaring people?

DARK GOD
We have known each other before. Don't you remember?

He reaches out, tips her chin up. Eye contact. They transfix each
other. Serena breaks contact, shakes her head.

SERENA
(agonized whisper)
No.

DARK GOD
(low, hypnotic)
You were dedicated to me at your birth. I tasted
your blood when you were thirteen, and you
pledged to serve me then. Don't you remember?

SCENE 19b

EXT. ALTAR STONE. NIGHT.

Flashback sequence. YOUNG SERENA at the altar stone where a
small fire burns in a circle of black stones, with bowl, goblet, gold disk
with mystic writing on it, three red roses. SERENA'S arm is held steady
by a FIGURE in a hooded green robe, her mother, her arm stretched
above the altar, a gleaming bronze knife flickering in firelight above the
child's wrist. Other ROBED FIGURES dance in the background, eerie
FLUTE AND DRUM MUSIC, flickering light indicating firelight,
torches. CLOSE-UP on child's eyes, with wildly dilated pupils.

                    MOTHER
(portentous voice)
Do you give yourself to the God for the greater
good of us all?

                  YOUNG SERENA
I do!

The knife descends, slashes a shallow cut on the child's wrist, and
blood splashes into the fire. Horrid cries of ghoulish delight from all
the robed figures; music picks up a notch, and dancing grows more
frenzied. Dark figure looms behind them, head nodding to the music. It is the DARK GOD. For a moment his face is visible, smiling,
the eyes glowing green with satisfaction.

BACK to present.

                    SERENA
No, that never happened! It was just an awful
dream!

                   DARK GOD
You cannot deny it. You bear the mark of that
day.

He traces the scar on her wrist with his index talon.

                   DARK GOD
It is written here, and also on your heart. My
name. Speak it.

                    SERENA
(whisper)
Is . . . bry . . . Isbrytaren.

DARK GOD

Yessssss.

He raises her hand to his face, presses his lips to the scar on the inside of her wrist, then to the back of her hand.

DARK GOD

Now you remember. You know. You can deny your destiny no longer. You are mine.

SERENA

No! No!

DARK GOD frames her face with his hands as her mouth goes wide to scream. He stares into her eyes and she stills like a hypnotized rabbit facing a snake.

DARK GOD

Do not imagine serving me will be terrible. I treasure your fear, but I will also give you gifts. Gifts that can help you in your quest. We will work together.

DARK GOD strokes SERENA'S cheek gently. Her face shifts through a range of responses from horror to acceptance, then finally to anticipation. He tilts her chin again and leans down to kiss her. His hood falls forward so that the kiss is implied rather than overexplicit.

"All right, everybody, stand by for rehearsal." "Rehearsal's up!" "Here we go . . . and . . . rehearsing!" "Rehearsing!" "And . . . action."

Opal had retreated with Rod and the other Hair, Makeup, and Wardrobe people to the tangle of cast and crew chairs behind the walls that simulated night forest. They could hear but not see as Corvus and Lauren ran their lines. Rod got a small portable TV set from his duffel and tuned in to UHF channel sixteen, which, in the vicinity of the soundstage, carried the signal from the hot camera, visual without sound. All of them bent their heads to watch the rehearsal from the view of the master shot camera.

"Dark God looks so real," Magenta muttered.

"You're a genius, Opal," Rod said.

"Thanks," murmured Opal. She felt both proud and disquieted; she knew she was good at her job, no matter how she did it, but this time she couldn't take total credit. Something had worked through and with her to turn Corvus into who he was now.

"But the lines," Betty muttered. "This is so cheesy. I hope they can pull it off."

The rehearsal ended.

"All right, kids," said the director, "Last looks."

Opal got Corvus's Set2Go bag out of her suitcase. It held sponges, gilding powder, adhesive, and other things she could use to tweak Corvus's prostheses and bring them back to their original look. She and the other Hair, Makeup, and Wardrobe people took their kits and continuity Polaroids and went on the set to make any necessary last-minute touch-ups.

Opal made the transition from the shadows around the edges to the set, where everything was subject to observation. The lights were bright and hot. Two different worlds existed side by side, the visible world that created the film's fictional reality, and the invisible world where the illusionists lurked. Opal didn't like being on the set; she kept most of herself submerged while she was working, and even though she knew she was skilled enough to maintain her mask of normal, being onstage made her nervous. Nobody would be interested in her; she was part of the scenery that moved, and yet, a camera might turn her way, capriciously, and show a part of her she hadn't hidden well enough. She glanced at the cameras. None had a red light lit. Not a guaranteee.

Coming on set to make sure everything was right was an important part of her job, so she did it. Corvus dropped his hood and leaned forward so Opal could inspect the prostheses on his head. She couldn't find anything she needed to fix. He held out his hands, turned them up and down. Again, they looked perfect. "Any problems?" she asked.

"No." He stood to his full height and pulled the hood up.

"Ready? All nonactors, clear the set," said Aldridge.

Hair, Makeup, and Wardrobe retreated. Opening bell rang; sound and camera rolled, slate bumped, action called. Rod got out his TV again. Everybody watched the first three takes of the master shot, but then interest dwindled. People settled back in the canvas-backed chairs, pulled out books or magazines. Rod worked on a crossword puzzle. Craig Orlando, key hair, had a book of sudoku puzzles.

Opal opened her letter case, got out a pen and a piece of stationery with red maple leaves across the top.

"Dear Mom," Opal wrote. Maybe she was nuts to write an actual physical letter. Magenta thought so. E-mail was easier and faster. Opal's mother liked something she could hold in her hand, and ever since Opal's younger sister's accident with one of the household computers, Mom had been suspicious of them. Maybe even before the computer went wild and caused plants to overgrow the guesthouse. Mom had never been fond of technology, though, as a TV news personality, she tangled with it every day. When she got really mad, studio equipment around her broke down.

"Lapis is tiny and dusty. The sets look good, though, and so does my Monster. You met Corvus Weather at the premiere of *Dead Loss* last fall, remember? This costume is much better. He doesn't have to kill anybody in this movie, either, just corrupt them, so less mess to mop up."

Maybe she better not mention the human sacrifices. Her mother hated film representations of witchy religions, especially the bloody ones that made witches look bad. Her dad laughed about all the things the movies got wrong, but sometimes Mom had no sense of humor.

Not that her family were technically witches, or used magic as a religion; magic was something they were born with, though it didn't manifest until they reached their teens. Their family had many traditions associated with magic use. They had met witches—a variety of them, some professing Wiccans or Pagans with power and without, and some, well, just witches. The word *witch* didn't explain the LaZelles, but Mom could get upset about almost anything.

The Dark God didn't commit any of the film's murders—that was all human stuff. Opal had read the script a number of times and she wasn't sure if the humans were supposed to be acting under the influence of the Dark God, or on their own, thinking they could tell what the God wanted without asking him. She was pretty sure the film had, as part of its agenda, a veiled indictment of organized religion. Which was pretty silly for a horror film no one important would ever see. Then again, the director had pretensions to art. Always a problem, in Opal's experience. People who thought they were doing art were much harder to work for.

Second bell rang twice, signalling the end of the take. "All right," called the A.D., "we're switching to Dark God's POV of Serena. Last looks."

Opal set her letter aside and grabbed her bag. Corvus wouldn't be in this shot, but she might as well check on him anyway.

He smiled at her, and his green eyes glittered. Unnerved, she ducked away from him and left the set. The rest of the day was like that: nothing ever went wrong with the makeup, and each time she faced Corvus, she felt a chill—this was a stranger, and she wasn't sure if he was friendly.

3

Shooting finished at eleven, and afterward, it took Opal an hour to photograph and then remove Corvus's face and hands. The pieces came off easily. The good thing was Corvus slept through most of it. By the end, he looked like his normal self. She astringed the last of the glue from his face, moisturized his skin, and prodded his shoulder gently. He woke with a start.

Except for them, the Makeup trailer was empty. A production assistant had been by earlier to leave off call sheets and script pages for tomorrow's scene. Lauren had an early call the following morning, and had left as soon as she was clean. Rod and Magenta had cleared all the counters and locked all the drawers and cupboards, then left. Hitch had left the Lincoln's keys with Opal before he clocked out; he was done for the day and Corvus wasn't working any longer, so Corvus had control of the car.

"Are you hungry?" Corvus asked as he levered himself out of his chair. He went to the clothes valet and pulled on a shirt.

"I suppose," said Opal. "Are you? I have a couple more of those liquid diet things." She checked the tiny fridge that was part of her counter. A few diet drinks, some protein shakes, and some makeup items that needed refrigeration.

Lapis had a coffee shop and a family restaurant, but neither stayed open late at night. There was no place nearby to get food. "I'm hungry, but not for another shake," Corvus said. "Want to go out for dinner?"

Opal checked the call sheet for the following day. Corvus had a scene where he incited the sisters to fight with each other. They wouldn't need to get to makeup until ten A.M. "Sure," she said, feeling a little strange. She had spent hours and hours with him, but mostly in the context of playing with his face, or waiting to play with his face. They had lunch together, catered meals—along with all kinds of other people at the same table. Most dinnertimes, each of them took their per diem and went separate ways, but that was when they were on a more normal schedule.

The nearest open restaurant Opal knew about was on the highway, ten miles from Lapis, near the characterless hotel where most of the crew and the lesser cast had rooms. Opal drove the Lincoln there with Corvus relaxing in the passenger seat. The restaurant was an IHOP truck stop, and none of the strangers sipping coffee inside had ever seen someone Corvus's height before, from the reaction they got when they walked in. Everybody gawked. Corvus was used to it.

"You movie people?" the waitress asked. She was young and blond and looked wilted but game.

"Yep," said Corvus. "How could you tell?"

She grinned and avoided the obvious answer. "Don't get many black Lincolns in the parking lot, not till you folks started dropping by. You want to sit with the others?"

"Where?" asked Corvus.

She gestured with a pink-feather-poof-topped pen toward the corner booth. Travis Roy and Bethany Telfair, the *Forest of the Night* scriptwriters, were holed up there with pots of coffee, laptops, and color-coded pages of script. Opal had met with Bethany in preproduction to discuss her concept for the Dark God. In those meetings, the young scriptwriter had been energetic and confusing, full of contradictory details. Opal had gotten a clearer picture from the production designer, who would dictate the look of the whole picture anyway.

Now Bethany looked frazzled. Her hair, ginger, thick, and shoulder length, stood up in tufts, as though she had been tugging at it.

Travis, Bethany's husband and mentor, blinked blearily at his screen. He was older than Bethany. His hair was a thick shock of gray, and he had deep character brackets around his mouth. He wasn't smiling now.

"They look busy," Corvus told the waitress. Then Bethany glanced up, brightened, and beckoned them over.

Opal wondered what Corvus really wanted to do. He was good-natured enough to head for the table.

"Want something to eat?" asked the waitress, following them.

"Yes, please," said Opal.

"You one of the stars, hon?" asked the waitress.

Opal smiled and shook her head. "I do makeup. Mr. Weather is the star."

Corvus slid into the booth beside Bethany, then shook his head. "The makeup is the real star, Jenny," he said.

Opal checked the waitress's nametag, saw that Corvus had her name correct. She sat next to Travis, who scooted over to make room. He stacked some of the pages and pulled them closer to his laptop.

"You been in anything I might have seen?" the waitress asked Corvus.

"Depends on whether you like horror films," Corvus said. "I play a lot of monsters."

She shook her head, handed them menus. "Naw. I got

enough scares in my daily life. Rather see romances. Your voice sounds familiar, though."

"I don't usually have speaking parts. Could I get some coffee, please?"

She started. "Oh, sure. You want some, too, hon?"

"Please," Opal answered.

The waitress went to a neighboring table and grabbed mugs and silverware wrapped in white paper napkins, set them on the table in front of Opal and Corvus, and headed for the kitchen and the coffeepot.

"What are you guys doing?" Opal asked the writers.

"Rewriting scenes twenty-five, twenty-six, and twenty-seven," said Bethany.

"Adding in scene twenty-five A. Aldridge wants more monster, Corr," said Travis. "After he saw yesterday's dailies, he decided to beef up your part. You got an extra week?"

"If they have the budget for me, sure. What am I supposed to be doing now?"

"He wants you to do an extra scene with child Caitlyn, really mess her up."

"It makes dramatic sense," said Bethany. "I always wondered about her motivations, anyway, Trav. She has everything going for her, looks, talent, youth, and she's just so *bad*."

"Caitlyn and Serena both have father issues," said Travis. "Their mom killed their father, remember? Years before she killed herself."

"What? That's not in the script," Corvus said.

"It was part of the brainstorming we did early on. Serena was out there at one of the rituals. She was five or six. Mom was high on something. Dad was, too. In the grip of the drug, Mom sacrificed Dad. Lots of blood. Dark God shows up. Serena saw what happened, but she suppresses it. Caitlyn never found out. To Caitlyn, Dad went away one night and never came back. She's been searching for him or a reasonable facsimile ever since."

"*Eww.* Serena thinks Dad's blood was spilled to summon Dark God? So maybe she thinks of Dark God as her replacement father?" Bethany tugged at her hair, then attacked her laptop's keyboard.

"Which is pretty disgusting, since *he* thinks she's his *bride*," said Travis.

Bethany shrugged. "Hey, they're creepy witches. What more do you need?"

"Where do you guys get your ideas about witches?" Opal asked, with a touch of acid. She regretted the question the moment after it came out. It wasn't her job to critique scripts or supply magical reality.

Travis and Bethany grinned. "Watching other peoples' movies," said Travis.

Bethany lost her smile. "Yeah, but Trav, this particular project—"

"Oh, right. We actually did some original work on this project. Bethany got the idea while she was staying at the Lapis B&B," Travis said.

"You visited Lapis before you wrote the script?" asked Corvus. "Why on earth?"

Bethany said, "My folks live in Lapis. I grew up around here. A couple years ago, we were having a big family party, and not everybody could stay at my folks' house, so I spent my first night ever in the scary B&B. When I was a kid"— Bethany's gaze softened—"I thought the B&B was run by ghosts. Mr. and Mrs. Gates—well, they're still there. I thought they were old when I was a kid, but now they're positively ancient. You can see the cobwebs on 'em. They manage to keep the place clean, though.

"Anyway, I had such a dream in that house. More like a nightmare. Most of the plot for the movie, in fact. The next morning I got my cousin to drive me out to that clearing, which was a place we never went when we were kids. It was supposed to be haunted, too. I mean, when I'd sleep over at my girlfriends', all the kids knew some story about something horrible that happened there. And it was creepy out there. That altar, those stains. The story kind of—well, I talked it over with Trav, and we figured we could make something out of it. It's one of those gift things. Kind of drops into your lap."

The waitress finally brought them coffee and took their sandwich orders.

"You thought that clearing was haunted when you were a kid?" Opal repeated after the waitress left.

"Yeah. My brother wanted to sneak over there one Halloween, but I was petrified and wouldn't do it. Everybody said kids had died there in some horrible way—bled out on the altar rock, or something worse. There were lots of rumors of Bad People in the woods. Nobody said the *W* word, though. They were more like bogeymen and bogeywomen."

She went on, "Now that I think about it, there are lots of places around here that felt off when I was a kid. We had a few places it was safe to go, like the lake and the library, and the rest of the world was filled with scary places."

"You have any trouble getting permits for the locations?" Opal asked. She knew some sites where people practiced magic; the sites had their own powers, and made it hard for nonmagical people to find them or stay on them. Was Lapis trying to protect itself from her or from others?

"I don't know. Not my department. The locations were perfect, though, which I guess they would be, since this is the place I was describing in the script."

"I wonder if they scouted anywhere else," Opal muttered.

"Is there something wrong with here? I thought everything was going great," said Travis.

"This place feels weird to me," Opal said. "Which doesn't

make a bit of difference to anybody who matters. I just—I think there's something going on under the surface."

"You *trying* to creep me out?" Bethany asked.

"No. No, sorry. Corr—"

"Maybe I know what you're talking about," he said. "The non-posthypnotic suggestions?"

"Right. Really, I'm *not* trying to force you anywhere near your role."

"You guys are speaking code now," said Travis.

Opal bit her lip, tried to figure out whether to share her concern with anyone. What the heck. Travis and Bethany were writers. They were close to being wallpaper, too . . . depending on whether the director and his team included them. "Corvus falls further into character than he needs to, even when he's not on the set," she said. "And that Dark God guy—not really a fun person."

"I thought he was fun," said Travis. "I love writing for him. Stuff almost writes itself. Deliciously creepy."

Opal frowned and checked Corvus's reaction to this. He looked puzzled.

The waitress brought their sandwiches, and they ate.

"So," said Bethany when Opal had finished half her sandwich, "what's not to like about Dark God? Personally, I think he's not creepy enough. Trav made him all seductive instead of terrifying."

"It's a trend," Travis said. "Horrifying heroes. Vampires and werewolves are really hot in romance right now. Why not gods?"

"We're writing a romance?" asked Bethany.

"Of course. Twisted, but that resonates with people at the moment."

"Oh. I wish I'd known. Well, anyway, Opal—"

"He called me a handmaiden and thanked me for selecting such a perfect vessel for him."

"I what?" said Corvus. "Are you saying I said that?"

"You did. Ask Lauren. Also, his face is alive," Opal said. The minute it was out of her mouth, she thought, *This is a mistake. I shouldn't be talking to outside people about this stuff. Never break the wall of silence that surrounds our magic.*

But this is not our *magic. I don't have to keep it secret.*

"My face is alive?" Corvus asked, more confused than ever.

"The face I put on you is alive."

"Can I use this stuff in the script?" Travis asked.

"How are you going to use something about a mask being alive?" said Bethany. "It's been done, and it's not our movie."

"Not the mask," Travis said. "The handmaiden and vessel stuff."

Opal sighed, and decided that on the whole, it was probably a good thing they weren't taking her seriously.

"I called you a handmaiden?" Corvus said, and pressed the knuckle of his index finger against his lips, then dropped his hand. "I wonder what I meant."

"I *am* a handmaiden," said Opal. "I wait on you and serve you."

He studied her, his brows lowered. Finally a smile flared, as though he knew she was kidding. His gaze was warm, and she felt again the queer tight twist in her chest, the love she couldn't stop. She wanted to help and protect him, give him all the tools he needed to be great.

She had felt like this about Gayle Graceland, the first star she had been personally attached to on a project, in *Weather Witch*, even when Gayle was a raving bitch, throwing things that broke and couldn't easily be replaced, and occasionally hitting crew with them. Adoration had engulfed Opal. She had put up with all kinds of lunatic behavior from Gayle; the love pressed her into servitude, pulled her best skills out of her, forced her to make sure Gayle was perfect in every take, even when others whispered commiseration to Opal behind the scenes.

After Gayle's part wrapped, Gayle had invited Opal on a spa vacation. The grip on Opal's heart had vanished. She envisioned the trip: Gayle behaving badly, abusing Opal, Opal picking up after her and trying to calm everyone hurt by her. Opal had refused the invitation. Later, she read all about Gayle's supposed spa antics in the tabloids—slapping a masseuse, starting a mud fight—and she felt nothing but relief that she hadn't gone. The picture came out; Gayle's performance got great notices, while her personal life was chewed up and spit out by the media.

Opal got a better job, and fell in love again. Her next film hadn't been a monster film and she'd been one of a core of makeup artists under the supervision of a key artist. She'd fallen for Gerry that time, even though she didn't always make him up. He looked good enough not to need much help. They'd gone out after the film wrapped. The relationship had died a natural if public death.

Corvus was the only person she'd worked with so far who kept a grip on her heart, all unknowing, even after they finished a picture. She had gone on thinking about him, wishing she were with him, even after *Dead Loss* was made and out.

He had never given her a reason to think he reciprocated her feelings.

Now they were working on a second job together. She hadn't had to let go of the love.

In the break between pictures, Opal had gone home and talked to her mother, a newscaster and social commentator, who knew about being famous and loved for how she looked and behaved on camera.

"Crushes are strange," her mother said. "I have fans who send me all kinds of things. Photographs. Poetry. Pastry. Underwear, some of it used. Impassioned letters begging me for fingernails or locks of hair or a lipstick kiss on the return envelope. I use my talents to turn on the charm, but I always try not to turn it too high. People watch me. They feel they know me. They want to own me. Sometimes it's disturbing, and other times it's my dream come true, the height of my desire. If it gets sick and twisted, I can deal with it: I have the skills to shut the fans down before they hurt me or themselves.

"So, my dearest daughter, have you asked yourself what you get from this love, why you let yourself fall into it?"

"No," Opal said, after consideration. "I wondered whether I should try to cure myself of it."

"You could shut it off with a thought," said her mother. "It's a choice you've made. It must pay off somehow."

Opal thought about Gayle. Everyone else on the *Weather Witch* shoot had hated the star, but she looked so good on film they had to work with her. Not hating her had helped Opal get her job done, no matter what Gayle did. If Opal had stood her ground against unreasonable behavior or demands, or even asked for the respect she deserved, everything would have taken twice as long. Her love for Gayle had been useful; it kept the film close to budget and gave Opal the power to do her job even after it would have become unbearable for anyone in her right mind. She had cruised through work in an altered state of fatuous adoration and done fine.

Later she had bumped into the key makeup artist from *Weather Witch* at a party, and been confused by the contempt the man showed her. It took her a while to remember what she had been like under the influence of Gayle.

Corvus was a different story. Gentle, likable, helpful, talented, and willing to work with her. Somebody she wasn't embarrassed to be in love with.

"You do an amazing job no one else could do," Corvus said to her now. "Somehow I don't think 'handmaiden' covers it."

"Thanks," she said. She stared down at her plate, then raised her eyes to meet his gaze. The smile he gave her was her favorite, the one that promised laughter. "I'm not so worried about the handmaiden part. It's the part where he said he was using you for a vessel that really bothers me. It was like you were possessed."

His laugher came, deep and infectious. "I was pulling your leg," he said.

4

Opal slid up her sleeve below the table, checked the bruises on her wrist where the Dark God had gripped her. Pretty strong pressure for a joke. Didn't jibe with anything she knew about Corvus: he had never hurt anybody that she'd heard of, and she'd spent months in his orbit.

More was going on here than an actor acting like someone he wasn't. She knew the feeling of power settling on someone, knew it had come from outside of him.

She tilted her head to look at him again, and found him leaning forward, the smile gone, his heavy brows pinched together in worry. "I didn't mean to upset you."

She sucked on her lower lip. "Big guy, I'm the one who knows who you are under the mask. You shouldn't even *think* about messing with me."

"Define *messing*."

"Yeah, Opal, define *messing*," said Travis.

Opal flushed. Stupid writers, always looking for hidden

meanings. "Pulling my leg. Corvus, you wouldn't play a mean joke on me for no reason. Why pretend you would?"

"I'm not comfortable with the direction the conversation's going."

"Oh." She thought about that, smiled. "Let's change the subject, then." She needed to collect more information before she decided what to do about it.

"All right."

"Let's finish eating and I'll take you back to your room," Opal told Corvus.

"I'm done." Corvus rose, loomed over the table.

Opal unfolded her paper napkin and wrapped the second half of her sandwich in it. She stood, too, and tucked it into her coat pocket to eat after she had dropped Corvus off in Lapis. "Good night," she said to Bethany and Travis. "Hope you can finish and get some sleep."

"We never sleep," said Travis. "Thanks for the ideas."

Corvus got the check from the waitress and paid before they headed out into the night. Opal drove with him sprawled in the passenger seat beside her. By the time they reached the bed-and-breakfast, he was asleep. She debated the merits of waking him versus using a persuasion on his sleeping self, and, after a scan of the area to make sure no one else was around, decided on the second option. She went around the car, opened his door, and spoke to his body, bypassing his mind. "Gently, gently, and all in concert," she whispered, "rise from where you are, walk in beauty, stealth, and grace; carry yourself to where you can rest."

Corvus got out of the car, his eyes closed. Opal took his hand. "Come," she whispered. He didn't take much persuading; somehow he was tuned to her already, receptive to suggestion, and that worried her. Maybe it explained the paralysis she had put on him without meaning to earlier.

Early in her dating career, Opal had learned to be wary of where her unconscious talents took her: she had tranced boys without even trying, had not realized that their perfect behavior toward her was the product of her own desires rather than their characters. Her younger brother Jasper was the one who alerted her to what she was doing. He'd asked her if she really needed to spell a guy to get a date. "Jeez, Opal, you can look like their dream girl; how come you need to put them under to get them to go out with you?"

The front door to the bed-and-breakfast was locked. Opal and Corvus stood under the orange porch light while she pondered this.

The house distracted her. The door felt almost as though it were warded. The house, too, put out some nonvisual darkness. With Corvus swaying slightly beside her, Opal studied the face of the house. The front windows were lace-curtained. Dim orange lights glowed behind the two windows to either side of the front door. Opal felt as though the house were watching her.

The script described this house as possessed by a spirit of evil. Maybe Bethany was sensitive. Opal wasn't sure the house was evil, but she thought it was possessed. One of her cousins had a gift of sensing the histories of places. Some houses made him sick; he could tell that people had been murdered in them, or hurt in other ways. Opal had never thought she had that kind of sense.

She flattened her palm on the front door and felt an uneasy shift under her hand. Huh.

Still, she needed to get Corvus to his room.

Corvus had the key on him somewhere, but asking him to find and use it might wake him up. He looked so peaceful. She murmured to the lock. It opened for her. Again she sensed a shift in the house, not like the lurch of an earthquake, more like something stirring under the surface of a street. When she touched the door handle, she felt a slight squirm, as though the metal were the skin of some smooth reptile. Then a low-level rumble, like purring.

Uneasy, she crossed the threshold with Corvus in tow.

In the front hall they had to maneuver between movie equipment; parts of the B&B's downstairs were being used as a set. Corvus moved just as she had told him to, gracefully and stealthily. "Go to your room," she said. He led her up the stairs, his hand still in hers, and down the hall to one of six doors. She talked to the lock on his room and opened the door, and then the door to the next room down the hall opened. Neil Aldridge leaned out.

"What the hell is going on out here?" he said.

"We just got back from supper. I'm putting him to bed," Opal answered.

Aldridge glared at her. "No games," he said. "I need him fresh tomorrow." He glanced at his watch, shook his head, and retreated into the master bedroom. As he shut the door, Opal heard him say, "The monster is bedding the makeup girl," and a murmur from someone else, a woman.

Opal sighed and drew Corvus into his room. It looked nice, spacious, brown-walled and ruffly, everything gingham or patterned with tiny flowers and edged with fussy lace. The bed was huge, a good thing; Corvus could fit on it if he lay diagonally from one corner to the other. The weird household spirit, ominous yet welcoming, was present under the surface here, as well. It didn't really feel as though something was ready to pounce or menace. Just as though something was watching. Maybe licking its lips. Opal shuddered and closed the door behind her.

"All right," she said to Corvus. "Do everything you need to, to put yourself to bed comfortably."

He went into the bathroom and only partially closed the door. Water ran, and toothbrushing sounds drifted out to her. The sound of a long and abundant piss. The toilet flushed, the water ran again. Good. Even in his sleep, he washed his hands after using the john.

Now was a good time for her to leave. She glanced around

the room, wondering if she should do anything else for him before she headed back to her own hotel. Tell him he could wake up when he'd rested or when the alarm went off, she supposed. She went to the bedside table to check the alarm clock. They had to be in Makeup at ten. She had no idea how long it took Corvus to wake up, shower, eat. Should she set the alarm for eight thirty? Nine? Maybe it was time to wake him up and let him run his own life. Then again, that might just confuse him. She set the alarm for eight thirty.

He emerged from the bathroom, naked, eyes closed. He gathered her up and pulled her onto the bed with him. There was a folded quilt at the bottom of the bed, and he tugged it up over them, then settled on his side, his arm tightly around her, snugging her back against his front. He was so large she felt as though she had a warm, breathing mountain behind her. His arm was muscular and heavy. She had seen his upper body before, but now she thought about what else she had just seen when he came out of the bathroom: respectable, but not intimidating. Oddly attractive, like the rest of him. Not at all erect, however.

He sighed into her hair and dropped more deeply into sleep.

She lay in his embrace, her heart bumping, and wondered what to do next. Wake him? Escape by persuading his arm to let go? Stay where she was? The director already thought they were sleeping together, and hadn't told them they couldn't.

This was a bad idea, though. Corvus didn't know what he was doing. Besides, she was still fully clothed, including her shoes, and she was lying on half a squashy sandwich in the pocket of her coat. She hadn't brushed her teeth or gone to the bathroom.

"Let me go," she murmured to his arm. At first it tightened. "Please let me go," she whispered, with persuaders, and he sighed again and lifted his arm. She scooted out. "Rest well," she told him, "and wake when you need to." She slipped out of the room, got it to relock itself, and then left the house, locking it behind her.

———————

At the hotel ten miles away where the lesser cast and crew were staying, Lauren was waiting in the utilitarian, sterile lobby with her feet up on a coffee table, reading a novel. She put it down as soon as Opal entered. "Did it really take that long to take off his makeup?" she asked.

"What are you doing here?" said Opal. As a lead actor, Lauren had her own private room in someone's house in La-pis. All the principal cast and crew had been quartered close to the locations and soundstage.

"Waiting for you," Lauren answered.

"Did you get supper? We went to the restaurant and ate."

"My host family left me a meal. I stopped at the restaurant to look for you, though, on my way here, and you weren't there. Where've you been?"

Opal checked her watch. Two A.M. She needed to get up in about six hours. "Is there something I can do for you?"

"Can I come up to your room? I'd rather not discuss this in public."

There was no one behind the front desk, and no one else in the lobby. Opal supposed someone might come in at any moment. She looked across the parking lot to the restaurant where she and Corvus had had dinner, which was open twenty-four hours and had lots of glass. Travis and Bethany were still ensconced in the corner booth, arguing about something.

"All right," Opal said at last, and headed for the elevator. Lauren followed.

Opal switched on the light in her room and glanced around. She spent so little time here she had made no effort to soften it away from its budget motel one-size-almost-fits-people-with-no-expectations. The maid had made the bed.

There was a chair at a rudimentary desk, and a television bolted to a wall shelf. She had to pay extra if she wanted the cable turned on. Her per diem would cover it, but she didn't need TV after a day working on the film.

Opal gestured toward the chair. "Please have a seat. I'm sorry. I don't have anything to offer you. There's a pop machine down the hall. . . ."

"I don't need anything," Lauren said. She took the chair, though.

Opal dropped onto the bed and fished the squashed half sandwich out of her pocket. "What's on your mind?"

"I was wondering if I could hire you for a side job."

"I think I'd get in trouble with the union if I did that."

Lauren considered. The corners of her generous mouth stretched into a small frown. "Cash under the table? It's not complicated. Just a simple disguise. Here's what's happening. I got involved with one of my costars on my last film. His name's Norman Davis. What I didn't know going in was he's a nutcase, kind of an obsessive stalker type, and right now he's unemployed. Somebody said they saw him at the supermarket down the road. I'm kind of afraid of him. I wondered if there was something simple I could do to hide myself from his regard. What if he's been savaging things for fun ever since I broke up with him? I don't want to be one of them."

"Oh," said Opal.

"Security's tight enough on the shoot to keep him out. I'll talk to the chief about this. But I'd also like to be able to go out and wander around, shop, whatever, without being paranoid all the time. Can you help me?"

"I'm sure Rod—"

Lauren leaned toward Opal, her large dark eyes intent. "I watched you work," she said.

Opal waited.

"My grandmother's a witch," said Lauren, "and my sister has a little talent. Not like you."

Opal straightened. Calm flowed into her. It was a first for her, being discovered by someone she didn't want to know about her talent. Since she had started in the business, she had revealed herself to a few people, but never by mistake. She could take care of an unintended revelation. The family had techniques to deal with outsiders. Opal had mastered persuaders. She hadn't used them much until tonight, with Corvus and the locks, but she knew her own strengths.

"I'll never, ever tell," said Lauren.

"Even if I don't help you?"

Lauren shook her head. "Your choice. I'll ask Rod for disguise advice if I have to, and Craig. I know a blond wig would change me, and I can walk and act differently. I just thought—"

"How much would you pay me?"

"How much would you want?"

Opal sucked on her bottom lip, rose, and wandered to the dresser. She opened the top drawer and looked at her underwear, shook her head. She opened another drawer. More clothes. What was she expecting? "Money's not much of a motivating factor for me," she said. She got good pay doing special effects makeup, and she didn't spend much. Her bank balance was almost big enough to buy real estate in California.

"Is there something you'd prefer? I don't have a lot of pull with the Makeup people. It's not like I could get you a promotion."

"I don't want a promotion. I have the job I want." Opal wandered into the bathroom and looked at her toiletries. She picked up her hairbrush, then her comb. She set them down again. She had no cosmetics of her own, just soap and shampoo and moisturizer. "Oh," she said, "I know." Out in the room again, she went to the closet and opened her suitcase, pulled out a bag of new makeup brushes, her spares. She selected a broad brush, the kind one used to whisk powder onto a face.

"What can I do in return?" Lauren asked.

"You were there when the other person talked to me," said Opal. She sat on the bed with the brush cupped in her hands. She strengthened its psychic shape so it would be able to hold power, and then she sent power into it.

"The one who talked through Corvus?" Lauren said.

"You understand that there was someone else?"

"I don't know what to think, except that was a lot different from the way he usually talks. But he's such a good actor, he could do a voice and persona like that without any trouble. Was it a joke?"

"He said it was, but I don't believe it. Something worked through him and through me, something I don't know. I'm afraid of it. What you can do for me . . ." She finished imbuing the brush with power and set it on her thigh. "Listen to my fears. I don't have anyone else I can talk to about this right now."

"I can listen. Of course I can listen," said Lauren. "Does this mean you trust me?"

"I don't know yet. I'd like to trust you. But how can I?"

"I don't know," Lauren said. "My *abuela* said she could tell when a person was being straight with her, but my sister, not such a good lie detector. Lots of boys fooled her into thinking they meant everything they said when they were trying to get into her pants. You do any truth detecting?"

"My talents lie in the opposite direction," Opal said. "Come in the bathroom and let me show you how to use this."

"What?"

"C'mon." Opal rose, and Lauren followed her into the bathroom, where the mirror was just wide enough for both of them to see themselves at once. "Sometimes I use tools in my work," Opal said. "I've just made this one different. I hold it, and think about the effect I want to achieve, and then I apply it." She thought about pale, crystal green eyes. When she had the image clear, she closed her right eye and brushed the brush over the lid. She opened her eye and stared at herself:

one violet eye, one pale green one. The effect was spookier than she expected. The green eye looked wicked, somehow, as though it saw too much. Her color sense was a little off, too. She closed her violet eye and looked at the world with the green one; suddenly the utilitarian, beige-colored bathroom had secret sparkling diamonds hidden in its corners, and strange patterns in its wallpaper. "Whoa."

"My god!" said Lauren. "That's amazing. Amazing!"

"It's peculiar," Opal said. She held out the brush. "This thing is charged right now. What you should do is think of something simple. The more complicated and extreme you make it, the faster the charge gets used up, and if you run out of charge, you can get stuck that way."

"This'll work for *me*?" Lauren took the brush gingerly.

Opal nodded. "Once I put the power in the tool and tell the tool how to work, anybody can use it, if they know what they're doing. Think about the change you want, then brush it into being."

Lauren held the brush up as though it were a magic wand or a conductor's baton. She closed her eyes, took a deep breath, and opened them. She brushed her cheeks. The shape of her face changed, became thinner. Her jawline softened. She brushed her lips. They also thinned.

She was unrecognizable.

"Oh, God," she whispered. "Unreal." She set the brush down and placed her hands on her cheeks, pressed her fingertips to her mouth. "Oh, God," she repeated. "It feels like it looks. Oh, God!"

Her eyes were still large and dark, wide in their astonishment. "How—"

Opal stood back, her arms crossed over her chest.

Lauren swallowed. "How long does it last?"

Opal touched Lauren's cheek and thought about it. "I guess about two hours. It's hard to tell. You can change back with the brush, too. You don't want to try this too often. I can't put too much into the brush—I need to save power for my own work."

"Is this what made Corvus strange?"

"I don't think so. I only change the outer layer, what the light falls on. It shouldn't go any deeper. Do you feel like someone else?"

Lauren stared at her new self. "I think I'm myself inside, but if I went on looking like this for a while, I'd feel different. Wearing this face, I'm not so sure of myself or what signals I'm sending. This is *so* strange."

Opal checked her watch again. Nearly three. "I've got to get some sleep or I might mess up tomorrow."

"Oh. Oh, yes, sorry. Thanks, Opal. This is unbelievable."

"You might want to practice undoing it before you leave, so I can help if anything goes wrong."

Lauren nodded. She picked up the brush, held it, thought, then stroked the brush gently over her cheeks and mouth. Her face filled out, generous, sensuous, arresting, and Opal felt a twist in her chest again. Though she hadn't made any choices about Lauren's changes, her power had worked them, and now she was engaged, like it or not. A warm affection welled up in her, a longing to protect Lauren and help her, spend time with her in any capacity Lauren allowed.

She felt stupid. Why hadn't she foreseen this outcome?

Maybe it was for the best.

"I look like myself again, right?" Lauren asked. She patted her cheek. "I did all right?"

"You did great."

"Do you need this for your eye?" Lauren held out the brush to her.

"No," said Opal. "I wonder." She closed both her eyes and thought her other eye green. She studied herself with the new eyes. "It's weird, isn't it, how such a small thing can make someone look completely different?"

"You look lethal, somehow."

"Hmm." What would the Dark God make of that? "Hey, wrap the brush in a handkerchief, if you have one. Because it's a touch power, it might affect random things it comes in contact with, like stuff in your purse."

"You're giving me this?"

"Sure. You can pay me back for the cost of the brush if you like. That's one of the expensive ones. Be careful with it."

"I will." Lauren went back to the bedroom and rummaged in her purse, found a small silk Japanese pouch with coins in it, dumped the coins out and put the brush gently in. "Thank you," she said, and hugged Opal awkwardly. "See you in the morning." She let herself out.

"Good night," Opal said. She just remembered to set her own alarm before she fell exhausted into bed with all her clothes on.

"You sleep all right?" Opal asked Corvus when he arrived at the Makeup trailer at ten. She had gotten there about twenty minutes earlier and had almost finished prepping for him.

"Great. Suspiciously great, when I don't even remember how I got to bed last night. What happened?"

"You fell asleep in the car. You took direction, though, even asleep. Did you know you sleepwalk excellently?"

"No one has ever told me that before. Opal?" He reached for her hand, tugged her away from setting out her brushes. "Things seem much stranger on this shoot. What's going on?" He stared into her face, started. "Good lord, what happened to your eyes?"

She had forgotten the change. She glanced at the mirror and saw pale, crystal green eyes staring back. They looked like someone else's eyes, mysterious and unsettling. "I'm trying out a new effect. You like?"

He frowned. "It's interesting, anyway."

"What's he talking about?" Rodrigo asked from the second chair. He and Magenta were taking a break before Blaise and Lauren arrived. Their call for makeup was much later. Opal had more to do for Corvus.

Opal opened her eyes wide and stared at Rod. "Whoa!" he cried. "Where'd you get the contacts? They're great! You look so different!"

"It's not a commercial company. I'm a beta tester. Guess I better take them out before I spook anyone else."

"Thumbs up for looks," said Rod, and Magenta nodded.

Opal gave them a big smile. She knelt over her counter and pretended to pop contacts out and put them into an illusory case, letting her eyes go back to their natural violet. She locked the intangible case into one of her drawers and turned to look at Corvus. "You ready?" Opal asked.

He leaned back and stared at the ceiling. Finally he clasped his hands over his stomach and nodded to her. "Apprehensive, but ready, I guess."

"I'm sorry I've broken your trust," she said gently to him as she shook a can of shaving cream. "I never meant to."

"Things are happening I don't understand."

"Me, too."

"I never sleep well on a shoot. Too much to obsess about."

"Do you consider that time well spent?" she asked.

"In fact, I do; it's those after-midnight skull-sweat sessions that lead me to character breakthroughs—when I get a chance to act a character. They don't stop me from doing a good job, not when you can't see my real face."

She sighed. "I chose not to wake you when it turned out you could walk while asleep, and get ready for bed, too. It's my fault. Seemed like you were tired enough to need whatever rest you could get. I apologize."

"You're going to take responsibility for my sleeping so deeply?"

She hesitated, then said, "I made a suggestion to you while you were under."

He caught her hand before she could apply the shaving cream. "What was it?" he asked, his voice grating.

" 'Rest well,' " she said. "Just 'rest well.' "

His face went more still than she had ever seen it. He stared at her, motionless, her hand caught in his. She felt the hot track of a tear streak down her cheek and blinked to stop any others from falling. He might hate her now, but that wouldn't change how she felt about him, which meant she was in for misery.

He opened his hand and released her, then lay back in his chair and closed his eyes. She shaved him and prepped his skin and laid the prosthetics on gently and silently. This time, she noticed when Blaise and Lauren came in, was remotely aware of their being prepped by Rodrigo and Magenta. She did nothing to Corvus but attach necessary things to his face, arms, hands, and upper body; she made sure she didn't paralyze him this time, but he didn't move; he barely breathed. She ornamented him the way she would have painted a statue.

Lauren, ready for her scene, sat in the next chair and watched, silent.

"Time for the contacts," Opal said at last, her voice choked.

"Can I put them in myself?" he asked.

"Not with the hands you've got now."

"Oh." He stared down at his hands. This time she had done his whole chest and arms, and the hand prostheses. Today there would be close-ups. He blinked twice. "Go."

She couldn't help saying a small spell to herself, that she would slip the contacts in perfectly, not harm him, that he would be comfortable with them as long as it took. She lifted his leaf brown eyelids and slid the contacts in, which gave him the stare of a stranger.

"Good job," he said. He pulled the lever that straightened his chair so he could stand up easily. He shook his shoulders, and said, as if to himself, "Good."

"I'll call Kelsi."

Corvus studied himself in the mirror while Opal called Kelsi on her walkie to come over with the Dark God's robe.

"I need jewels," said Corvus, his voice low and thrilling. "Why would I not adorn myself? It is too simple. Have you people no sense of pageantry? Handmaiden." He turned to Opal.

Opal glanced at Lauren, who had straightened, her eyes wide.

"I want something that sparkles. A diamond star for my forehead."

"I can't do that, sir. It would ruin the continuity."

"You *can* do it," he whispered. "You *will* do it." He gripped her wrist again, bent forward, and brought her hand up to touch his forehead. "Give me a small fraction of your power. A tiny taste, a promise of what we will share later."

"I don't want to share with you. I don't even know you."

"You know my vessel," he whispered. "You love it."

"You're not that person."

"I can give you that person."

"I only want him if he gives himself."

"Foolish denier of dreams."

"Yep, that's me," Opal said. "Give up this dream of jewels, will you? You're here to play a part, that's all."

He grinned, suddenly, just as Kelsi's knock sounded on the door. Lauren jumped up and opened it.

"How little you know," the Dark God said to Opal. "It's delicious."

Lauren closed and locked the door after Kelsi came in, the Dark God's robe over her arm.

"I am surrounded by beauty," said Corvus, smiling at all three of them. "It's a fine time to be awake."

"Mr. Weather, could you hold out your arms behind you so I can slide this on, please?" Kelsi asked.

Corvus posed. She slid the robe onto him. After she had

snapped it shut and fastened it with the silver star, he took her hand and pressed his lips to the back of it.

"Won't you screw up your—" she began, but then her eyes met his, and she blinked and swayed, leaned into him. His arms folded around her; her face pressed against his sculptured abdomen. He closed his eyes and drew in a long breath, his smile widening.

Kelsi sagged in his arms. He lifted her and set her gently on his abandoned chair, where she curled up, snoring softly.

"What did you do to her?" Opal demanded.

"You wouldn't give me what I needed, so I had to go elsewhere." He stretched as best he could in the cramped quarters of the Makeup trailer. "I feel stronger now."

"She going to wake up okay?" Lauren asked.

"Of course. She will just—*rest well.*" He turned his luminous eyes to Opal, who had flinched at his words. "You could both rest well, if you liked."

"Get out of here. We have a job to do. Do you have your lines memorized?" Lauren said.

"My lines?" He cocked his head. "My lines. Oh, yes, they're in here."

"Well, I hope you can act," said Lauren. She unlocked the door, flung it open, and stomped down the stairs.

Opal packed her makeup suitcase for the walk across the parking lot to the soundstage. She was conscious of Corvus's body hovering above her, of the absence of his spirit and the presence of someone else's. She wasn't sure how to handle that. She wanted to rescue Corvus, bring him back to himself, but—what if she confronted the new guy and lost? She had never been the most powerful person in her family. She had no idea how to kick a spirit out of a body where it didn't belong. No way could she act like an exorcist. No religious training. She used her power to alter appearances, not to change the cores of things.

Her options were to try something desperate that might

not work or wait him out. See if the new guy could act. Maybe the new guy was the character, and wouldn't need to act.

The new guy had been present before, and Corvus had returned to the body without any damage but lost time. Maybe the new guy had a time limit on how long he could stick around. Although the fact that he had sucked something out of Kelsi and left her asleep didn't bode well. Powering up, stealing energy, it looked like. If he could do that to Kelsi, he could probably do that to other people. Opal wondered how hungry he was, and how far he'd go.

Kelsi was still breathing. That was good.

Opal had done her best to leave the magic out of changing Corvus into the Dark God this time, but she had let a little trickle in at the last moment, and the new guy had brought his own. Looking at the Green Man face on him, she didn't think it was latex any longer.

Corvus didn't trust her. This wasn't going to help.

She needed to figure out how to deal with the new guy. Though she had known some roughhousing techniques when she was younger—she had needed them to deal with aggressive siblings and unkind cousins—she was out of practice.

She had a cell phone in her pocket. As soon as she got a minute—and there were lots of hurry-up-and-wait minutes on the set—she'd call home, see if her relatives had any ideas on how to deal with this.

She turned toward the door, and the thing in Corvus's body said, "Just one taste," pulled her to him, pressed his lips to hers.

His mouth had a flavor like a ripe, juicy peach, something she had never tasted in a kiss before. She struggled with several impulses: slap him and maybe mess up four hours' work, cost the picture who knew how much time and money to repair the face. Relax into it: she'd dreamed Corvus would fall for her, in the way of hopeless fantasies. Her sensible streak said it would never happen naturally (it could be made to happen without much effort, she knew), and she wouldn't force it. This wasn't Corvus, though; it wasn't even someone she liked. This was the opposite of her fantasy, an unpleasant reality she didn't want. While she debated, she felt him drawing power from her. Not good. She needed to cut him off. She could change herself into something without a mouth and break the connection. Shock him away from her. Slide sideways—

Light flashed, a camera's shutter clicked, and then more flashes and clicks. "Work it, work it," said Erika from the door.

Opal gripped the Dark God's shoulders and pushed him away. She wiped her mouth with the back of her hand. "Stop."

"This is terrific stuff," Erika said, staring at the screen on her digital camera. "Couldn't have asked for anything better—bye, now!" She raced away as Opal advanced on her, and just then, Opal's Ear crackled. "Where are you?" asked one of the A.D.s.

Opal glared at the new guy. "You're coming," she said, grabbed her suitcase, and headed down the stairs.

Laughing, he followed her.

5

The new guy in Corvus's body went to the altar set for blocking rehearsal with Blaise and Lauren, and Opal slumped into a chair next to Magenta, who watched a monitor as the cast ran the scene.

"You probably don't need to hear this again," said Magenta, "but he looks absolutely awesome."

"Thanks."

"You getting ideas about him?"

"What?"

"I am. I thought he was weird-looking at first, but man, he's hot, in or out of makeup. I usually skip the stars—can't deal with those messed-up egos, and most of them don't respect us—but him, there's something about him—"

"I know."

"There's a rumor you were in his room last night."

"I was."

"Business or pleasure?"

"Business. I put him to bed. But just now, Erika shot us kissing." Her hands closed hard on the chair arms. "It's not just us in an awkward moment," she muttered, "it's the makeup. Nobody's supposed to see that until the trailers. If she leaks any of those—"

"Uh-oh," said Magenta. "What were you doing, messing around when you were due on the set? How could you do that when he's already in makeup?"

"It wasn't my idea. He just grabbed me."

"Whoa. He doesn't seem like the type."

"He's kind of schizo. I like the other one, not this one."

"He musta grown up weird, had to deal with all kinds of body image shit from other people. No wonder he split himself in two."

"Hmm," said Opal. She pulled out her cell phone, but just then, someone called out, "Last looks!" She grabbed her suitcase, and she and Magenta went to the set.

"Can he act?" Opal muttered to Lauren as she passed her.

"Enough," Lauren answered, then tilted her head to catch light so Magenta could look her over and see if she needed powdering or lipstick repair. Rod hovered near Blaise, who looked amazing, an angel, though her expression was marred by some form of distaste. Rod said something to her and her face cleared. She closed her eyes as he whisked powder across her nose and cheeks.

Opal faced the new guy. "Come on down, big guy," she said. "Let me check your looks."

Obligingly, he bent over. She studied her Polaroids from the night before against his face. He looked better today, though nothing substantial had changed—continuity should be all right. She touched one of his horns, and it felt solid and rooted into his forehead. The point of his chin, the built-up brow ridges had the heat and solidity of living skin. There was no rubbery give to them.

He pressed his hand over hers as she felt his face. His palm was warm, the gesture gentle. Had her problem solved itself? Unlikely, with her latex acting alive.

"Corvus?" she said, hoping anyway.

He smiled, but didn't answer.

"Clear the set. Let's go, people. Starting marks. Starting marks." Opal and the others fled back to the chairs in the outer darkness.

"Blaise is a bitch," Magenta whispered to Opal as they settled. "I'm lucky she wants Rod to do her. 'Nothing but the best,'" she mimicked.

"Do you like Lauren?" Opal whispered back.

"She's not fussy. She looks good, too—not much to correct for."

"Quiet," yelled one of the assistant directors. "We're on bell. Roll sound, roll camera, please." The starting bell for filming rang. Casual conversation died. The voices of the actors spoke their lines from behind the walls of the altar set.

Opal wished she could go outside and phone her family, but now was when she had to be present and silent, in case anything went wrong. She slid a notebook out of her suitcase, opened it to a blank page, and wrote down everything she knew about the person who was not Corvus but wore his body.

It wasn't much of a list.

What if Magenta was right, and this was a case of multiple personality, some other facet of Corvus taking charge? She didn't have to like him, she just had to work with him. It would explain Corvus Prime's lost time, but not the new guy's use of magic. He could be a natural, she guessed. But Corvus had never behaved anything like this on *Dead Loss.*

Option two: local phenomenon. Bethany's story about how

she wrote the screenplay added weight to this option. They were messing with sites that might hold old history, old tragedy, old power. Opal had heard stories about places of power. She knew how to send power into objects. Maybe someone had sent power into the ground at the altar location, and Corvus had accessed it somehow. She hadn't seen that happen before, but it seemed plausible.

Option three: some inimical and possibly noncorporeal person was stalking someone on the movie, and picked this weird way to get at them. She, Opal, seemed like the most likely candidate for a haunting, since Corvus had spent the bulk of his haunting time with her. She couldn't remember anything she had done recently that would have upset anyone magical. Since magical people tended to hide their talents, she could have offended someone with power and never noticed. She never set out to offend people, though.

Maybe the power was haunting Corvus. Maybe Corvus had a curse on him, and this was how it manifested. Maybe he'd angered someone who could do this sort of thing. Hard to imagine. His reputation was solid: a professional in every way, easy to work with, someone who would put up with a lot and give you a good performance even in adverse conditions. She'd never heard a negative story about him.

"Cut!" yelled Aldridge. "Dark God, could you play this a bit more sinister?"

"Of course," said the new guy.

Opal closed her notebook and went to the Prop Department monitor. They were shooting a master shot, an overview of the scene, with everyone in frame; the viewpoint was from the foot of the altar stone. Dark God stood at the head of the altar stone, with Serena (Lauren) to his left and Caitlyn (Blaise) to his right. Magenta joined Opal and Joe.

The slate moved into frame: Roll 32 Scene 23A Take 2, FOREST OF THE NIGHT Dir. Neil Aldridge Cameraman: T. Yamanaka.

CAITLYN

She doesn't deserve you. She abandoned you years ago. I'm the one who's been faithful! I'm the one who's honored you since I was a child! Give me the power!

DARK GOD

She is my promised bride. We have a blood connection. It is her destiny.

CAITLYN

But she doesn't even want it! Pick me instead.

SERENA

I do want it.

CAITLYN

That's not what you said yesterday!

SERENA holds her wrist above the altar stone, turns it so the underside is up. She pulls a knife from a sheath at her waist. It gleams. She touches the tip to her skin.

SERENA

Isbrytaren, I am ready to pledge myself to you again.

DARK GOD

I accept your pledge.

He takes her hand.

The Dark God took the knife from Serena. "Wait a sec," Magenta whispered. "That's not in the script." She glanced at

Opal and Joe, but they shook their heads. Opal had read the script, but not recently. She supposed she ought to read the scenes listed on the call sheets, but her job didn't change; the Dark God had pretty much one look all the way through the film; she just had to make sure it was consistent. The only question from day to day was whether he'd be in close-up or distance shots, which governed how much of the other prostheses and body makeup she applied and how long the call sheet budgeted for application.

"Are you ready?" the Dark God asked, with peculiar intensity.

"That's in the script," Magenta whispered.

On the set, Caitlyn said, "Wait. This isn't right. She's supposed to cut herself."

"Not in the script," muttered Magenta.

The Dark God said, "Do you presume to tell me my business?"

"Not script."

Caitlyn: "But the book says—"

"Not script."

"Serena," said the Dark God.

"I'm ready," Serena replied.

"Script," whispered Magenta.

The Dark God drew the tip of the blade from Serena's palm a little way up her arm, and blood welled in its wake. He leaned forward and licked the blood, his eyes half-closed in ecstasy. Serena swayed, held upright only by his grip on her arm. Her eyes closed. Her face showed something that could be pain or absolute joy.

"Ick," whispered Magenta. "*So* not script."

Opal jumped to her feet, galvanized by a fear come to life. How could they trust someone else inside Corvus's body? There was no indication he cared about the same things everyone else cared about. Why should he?

If he wasn't following the script (and she didn't

remember—but Magenta did), he must have his own agenda. He was a power person, and she didn't trust him. Her great-uncle Tobias, her family's magic teacher, said blood carried power and could be used in both good and bad ways to transfer energy and other influences. She strode toward the set, marshaling her resources.

George Corvassian, the first assistant director, grabbed her arm and pulled her away. He dragged her all the way to the second set, then put his mouth right next to her ear. "We know it's not in the script," he whispered to her, "but Neil wants to let it play out and see what happens. It's looking great."

"It's a real wound," she whispered, furious.

"Special effects knife," George whispered. "Ask Props."

"I don't think so. What if he really hurt her?" She decided to speak in a language he could understand. "She could sue the company!"

"Anyway, it happened, and we might as well see if we can use it."

"But he—"

"It was superficial," George said.

"You don't understand," said Opal. She pulled loose, but he grabbed her again.

"Wait," he whispered in her ear. "If there's something seriously wrong, Neil will stop and take care of it."

Opal didn't trust Neil to do any such thing. "The Dark God'll get Lauren. He'll own her."

"It's only a movie," muttered George. "There are worse tragedies at sea."

Opal opened her mouth to scream and interrupt the filming, but just then two bells rang, signaling the end of the take, and George let her go. Opal raced to the other set. The set doctor was treating Lauren's arm. The actress stared at it blankly.

Opal touched Lauren's shoulder, sent as much spirit protection as she could. She remembered doing this for her sisters and brothers when they were little; sometimes she had had to protect them against each other, and sometimes she gave them a layer of safety against their mother. It had been a long time since she had done it.

Lauren blinked and woke, gasped and jerked her arm. The doctor held it firm: he was applying antiseptic. "What?" Lauren said. "How'd that happen?"

"Dark God did it. During a take."

"Damn it!" Lauren jerked free of the doctor's grip, marched over to the Dark God, and shook her arm at him. "You did this to me?"

"You said yes," he said, speaking in Corvus's voice, gentle. He smiled, almost benevolently, despite the monster face he wore.

"Looked great on film," said Neil. "Print that." The script supervisor made a mark on her script. "We'll do the other shots with fake blood, naturally," he said. "Did you get down the new dialogue?" he asked the script supervisor, and she nodded.

"All right, actors take ten or fifteen while we set up for the next shot and get some typing done," an assistant director called. "Stand-ins to the set. Lighting crew. D.P. and camera crew. Next shot POV Caitlyn on Serena and the D.G."

Magenta approached Lauren. "We have to cover the scratch with something for the next take."

"In a minute." Lauren turned to the Dark God. "How'd you make me stand still for this?"

"You have many desires, all competing. This was one of them; I only teased it closer to the surface."

"Don't do it again."

"I make no promises."

She glared up at him, then turned and took a few steps, lost. Her hand rose to touch the new wound, now dabbed with ointment. Lauren glanced around until her gaze encountered Opal, and then she went to her, pulled her away from the others. "Help," Lauren whispered.

Opal touched her shoulder, tried to sense what had happened the way she used to. When she was younger and most of the childcare in the family devolved onto her, she had come up with shortcuts for finding out who hit whom, and later, when some of them got their powers and one of them didn't, she'd learned to trace power use even more.

"It's bad," she said. "There's a reason why the devil gets you to sign a contract in blood. It carries a blueprint of your identity with it. Now he has that, and he got you to give it to him."

"I feel like I was drugged."

"Yeah, I think you were. Maybe not drugs, but some kind of altered state. Hypnosis."

"He doesn't play fair."

"I know."

"What's he going to do with me now that he's got me?"

"I don't know. I think him kissing me was the same kind of deal. Saliva has all that genetic information, too. Not as popular in mystic circles, but still potent, and he stole some of mine."

"He kissed you?"

"Right after you left. While he was doing it, Erika caught us. Photo op city."

"Great," said Lauren sarcastically.

Opal shook her head. "I don't know what she's going to do with those pictures, but maybe I better tell somebody about them. Someone with actual veto power might be able to block her using them."

"Talk to the production manager. Fran. You know? She's in charge of all the stuff that happens on location, and she might be able to control Erika. I don't know. Erika's a really good photographer, Opal. She gave me some great head shots."

"Thanks for the tip. I'll see what I can do. I might be able to take care of the pictures another way. They involve the fall of light." She thought about that. She could affect film, and probably digital media, too. She'd have to get specific, though; just fog the ones of her and the new guy, and see if Erika had backed up her photos anywhere.

"What can we do about D.G.?" Lauren asked.

"I'm going to ask my mom for advice."

"I'll call my *abuela*."

"Tell me if you find out anything."

"Will do. You tell me, too, okay? Not that I'll be able to do anything about it. You think he plans any more conquests?"

They both looked at Blaise, pouting by the fake altar stone.

"Has he shown any interest in her?" Opal wondered.

"Nothing obvious. I think that pisses her off. Before he turned into D.G., she was trying to get his attention, but he's, you know, all reserved and quiet. You can't tell where he's looking, or if." They watched Blaise, who seemed to feel their regard. She glared back at them. "She really gets into that character," Lauren muttered, "and sometimes she doesn't come out. It's disturbing. Her character hates and despises me. Or maybe my character. It's not always clear."

"We have to find out what he wants," Opal muttered.

The Dark God put arms around both their shoulders, and came to stand between them, startling them. Opal had thought he was still by the altar stone with Blaise, but that was Corvus's stand-in, Fred, with his hood up, a respectable distance from Blaise.

Should have known it was Fred from the way she's not paying attention to him, Opal thought.

"What who wants?" the new guy asked. "Do my hand-maidens conspire?"

"Stop it, for God's sake. That's creepy," Lauren said. "My

mom didn't spend years cleaning other people's houses to turn me into some handmaiden."

"What *do* you want with us?" said Opal.

"Do you know the child who wrote this play?" he asked.

"Sure, Bethany. We talked to her last night in the restaurant." Opal shook her head. She and Corvus had talked to Bethany, anyway. The new guy hadn't been around for that discussion. She thought.

"You know she grew up here?"

"You're not going to make us live the script, are you?" Lauren asked. "If that's your plan, I'm quitting right now. I don't care what it costs."

He laughed. Then he patted her head. "You can't leave," he said, still smiling.

"Just watch me, buster. No way am I going to turn into some sexy vamp girl and go around killing people to serve your need for blood."

"I won't ask you to," he said. "It's not really blood I need." He stroked her hair. She stood rigid, but then she relaxed into it, shoulders lowering, her head tilting toward him so that his hand had easier access. She blinked, and closed her eyes, a contented smile on her face.

Trance technique, thought Opal. *Hair involved.* The new guy's arm still rested on her shoulders, but he wasn't stroking *her* hair. She glanced up at his face, the lace of leaves across his skin, the horns, the jutting brow and chin, the lakes of shadow, the internal glow of the eyes, the quiet smile. He did not look malevolent or dangerous, despite the monster outer layer. She and Corvus and the art director had wanted him to be strange rather than terrifying. How informed had they been about his real nature? He was local; he had almost said so, talking about Bethany and the script. Opal had built the pieces of his face in Los Angeles, nine hundred miles away. Maybe his true face was completely different, and now he was just a squatter behind her creation. The horns, though—those weren't hers.

Magenta stalked over to them. "Stop that," she said to the new guy. "You want to mess everything up for the next take? Serena's on camera for it. I still need to fix her arm, and now I have to call Craig and get him to redo her hair. What is *wrong* with you?"

The Dark God stared at Magenta, his face expressionless. Her breath caught, and then she held a hand to a reddening cheek. "What are you doing to me?" she cried. "Why does it burn?"

"You mustn't speak to me that way." He continued to stroke Lauren's hair.

"This is crazy," Magenta said. She looked at Opal. "Am I crazy?"

Opal shifted, uncomfortable with the new guy's arm over her shoulder. Strange overlays webbed them: the power structure of the film, where the stars ruled, sometimes on a level with the director, sometimes above or below, but all the service people, she and Magenta, were lower-class citizens, not supposed to speak sternly to those above. Plus, whoever the presence behind Corvus's mask was, he seemed at home as an aristocrat. He took without asking, and considered everyone else his playthings. Handmaidens. Like one of the worst stars, although he hadn't been mean or really petty yet, just bossy and demanding.

Lauren, waiting for Opal at her hotel the night before, well, that had been odd. The structure had tilted. Lauren knew Opal was a magic user, and that changed their status in the eyes of each other. Right now, since Lauren had spoken to her on a topic other than makeup or special effects, in full view of the other cast and crew, people would be making up stories about that, if they had the attention to spare.

Opal had hooked up with stars before, in a variety of ways. She'd almost thought she was marrying one. A mistake. Location shoots often threw people together in odd combinations. The intensity and isolation drove them into each other's arms and beds, and sometimes exhaustion made them mistake physical release for something more important. As soon as their reasons for living in each other's shadows evaporated, so did the connections.

Her connection to Corvus hadn't behaved like that. After this, though, who could tell? The new guy was messing everything up, in more than one way.

"I don't think you're crazy," Opal told Magenta. "I think he's hypnotic. D.G., please don't hurt Magenta. She's just doing her job."

"I don't care for her tone."

"She gets that. She won't talk to you like that again." Opal nodded to Magenta. Magenta didn't respond.

One of the assistant directors called, "Ten minute warning, everyone."

"We have to fix Lauren's hair and that great gaping slash you made on her arm right now," Magenta said, "your majesty."

The new guy stopped stroking Lauren's hair, gripped her shoulder, gave her a gentle push. "Go and be repaired," he said. She only half awoke. She glanced back at him, her dark eyes sleepy, before she wandered off in Magenta's wake to one of the canvas-backed chairs behind the scenes, where Craig, the key hairstylist, waited with a Polaroid and a set of combs.

"Are you going to do the work, or screw up the production?" Opal asked.

"I am going to do many things," he said in a low voice. "Right now, it amuses me to put my face and my voice inside these machines. This is a new way to work. It may aid me greatly. It's a wonderful time to be awake."

"Are you ever going to let Corvus come home?"

He smiled, stroked her hair, offered no answer.

6

As soon as the stars were safely trapped acting in front of the cameras, Magenta grabbed Opal's hand and dragged her as far from the altar set as they could get inside the building. They huddled inside the bathroom, soundproofed enough that they could talk in low voices, with walls thin enough they'd be able to hear the two bells that signaled the end of the current take. "What the hell is going on?" Magenta asked. One of her cheeks still blazed.

"Have you ever worked on a picture that was cursed?"

"Cursed? I've been on one where everything went wrong. We were filming in Mexico, and bandits stole the equipment trucks while they were driving to the location, and one of the stars died, killed by a freak accident with a dollycam, and the weather kept screwing us up. Nobody got any sleep, and everybody got mean. Cost overruns, sniping tempers, infighting—we all hated what we were doing by the end. Then, you know, they couldn't save it in post. The thing was a huge flop. Worst shoot of my life. Is that what you mean?"

"Sort of." Opal frowned. "In a more supernatural way, though."

"What, that old you're-doing-something-commercial-on-top-of-an-Indian-graveyard riff?" asked Magenta. "Who believes *that* shit?"

Opal touched Magenta's reddened cheek.

"Ow!"

"He burned you by looking at you," said Opal.

"I've seen that happen in hypnotist acts. Okay, not the burned part, but I've read about that. Freaky powers of the human mind, turned against itself. You said it was hypnosis."

"It might have been, I guess, but I'm exploring other options. You asked what the hell's going on. I think Corvus is possessed."

"Oh, please!"

"That's my explanation. I can't make you believe it, but there it is. Bethany wrote the script here, where she grew up, surrounded by things she was scared of. Whatever's creepy here got inside her head and helped her write it."

"What about Travis? He cowrote."

"Bethany did the first draft while she was staying at the B&B. Travis doctored it. They find a producer and put together a package, and hey! Creepy evil guy gets people right where he wants them so he can use them to further his creepy agenda. I build the mask. Corvus steps into the role. Creepy guy crawls into Corvus, and here we are."

"That is so lame."

"I would love," Opal said, "to be wrong about this."

Magenta mini-paced. Two steps one way, two steps the other. The sink and the toilet precluded her having room to really pace. "Okay," she said, "your explanation covers his bad behavior, my cheek. What the *hell* is happening with Lauren?"

"The not-script part. He drank her blood, and now he can control her."

"Melodrama!"

Opal snorted. "All right. Melodrama. And yet. Can you picture Lauren standing there like an idiot while someone strokes her hair and ruins her look, in the time it takes to set up a different camera angle? She strikes me as much more professional than that."

"She's his love slave."

"Since when? She wasn't dopey like that yesterday."

"Nope."

"Would she have looked at him twice yesterday?"

"Yes, of course she would, and did. Now, maybe you didn't notice this, because you get so wrapped up in your work, but the whole time you're slapping bits of rubber on Gigantor, Lauren's perched in the next chair, watching, even after the rest of us have left the trailer. You don't call that a crush? Admittedly, you can work magic—"

Magenta halted, turned, stared at Opal with narrowed eyes. "Damn! All that time Rod spied on you, then tried to repeat what you were doing later? He could *never* get it to work, even though he got hold of every ingredient you ever used. He snooped your trash! You mean nobody can replicate your processes because you're *cheating*?"

"What cheating? The whole point is to do something nobody else can do."

Magenta growled, then paced away and back.

Finally, she said, "Well, the crucial question is, are we going over budget?"

"Creepy evil guy says no. He likes being in the movies."

"Well, okay," said Magenta, and two bells rang. "The show must go on." They left the bathroom and rushed to their equipment.

Blaise, Dark God, and Lauren came off the set and settled into their chairs. Rod was ready with bottles of water for everybody. Opal fished one of the protein shakes out of her suitcase. She presented it on her open palm to the Dark God.

"What is it?" he asked.

"Nourishment." She shook it vigorously, then popped the top. "I think you could probably use this about now."

He took it, studied it, sipped from it, and frowned. "Tastes vile." He sipped again. "But I take your meaning. It satisfies a certain hunger." He drank the rest and handed her the empty can. As soon as she set it down, he took her wrist and tugged her toward him. "I have another hunger," he said, staring at her lips.

"Please," she said, conscious of Rod and Blaise and Lauren and Magenta, conscious that she had no interest in another kiss from him. "No."

He lifted her hand to his lips and pressed them to the back of it. Her shadow self, the one who held her magic, startled and tried to retreat, but he had forged a connection with her earlier, and she didn't know how to break it. He drew a long draft of her magical energy, leaving her wilted and confused. She swayed and sat down beside him.

"Thank you," he said, his eyes glowing even brighter.

She pressed her hand to the cell phone, a lump in her pocket. She had to call home.

This time, when the actors were called back to the set, Magenta came to her. "What happened? What did he just do?"

"Kind of a vampire thing." Opal pressed her palm to her forehead. "I don't know if I'll ever get Corvus back." She dug through her bag for another protein shake, opened and drank it. She checked her watch. They should break for lunch in twenty minutes. She felt better after the shake, but she could tell she was still depleted.

They did a quick last looks after the rehearsal. Opal didn't even touch the Dark God. The A.D. called for silence, and the bell rang.

Rodrigo and Magenta joined Joe at the Props monitor again to watch the filming. Opal stayed where she was. She needed time to think.

He got the drop on me. I've let him have his way too much. I have to fight. I have to fight! For Corvus, for Lauren, for herself, against whatever plans the Invader had, she had to pull herself together and remember who she was and where she came from.

When she was younger and first came into her power, tired of being the good child, the oldest, the caretaker, the one who put up with shit from her mother and all the younger kids, she had flirted with turning really, really bad. She had explored dark powers her great-uncle had frowned at and warned her against. Maybe that made her more susceptible to the Invader's powers. Maybe it gave her tools. Her magical self had been living so far underground since she left her family's house that she'd practically trained herself to be normal. Time to loosen up and find her secret self again.

First, she needed distance, a shield, so the Invader couldn't just walk up to her and suck her dry.

He's taken my identity inside him, but he gave me his, too. Their morning kiss had been hours ago, and she'd eaten and drunk since then, but at some point she had swapped spit with the Invader—or Corvus's body—and that should give her some kind of hold over him. She tasted the interior of her mouth, a little sour with the aftertaste of energy drink, and could find no trace of him. She needed to seek with a different sense. She closed her eyes.

Who has entered into my house of self without an invitation? She saw a room, comfortable, with a desk she could work at, a swivel chair more like a throne than office furniture, shelves along the wall holding all sorts of materials she could use to shape masks, craft colors, make salves, ointments, creams that could dull skin or shine it, draw attention to or divert it from any feature of the human face, pencils and putty, spirit gum and mustache hair, terror and beauty.

Life-masks of previous clients stood on pedestals on a second desk, with bright but diffuse light shining on them, a place where she could create. Books of reference photos stood in staggering stacks along another wall. In a corner was a second chair, broad and adjustable and comfortable, with a red velvet pillow on it for her to hug while she sat and thought. Nearby was a fireplace, clean now, with a ball of green witchfire burning coolly in it.

Above the desk, a wide window that looked out into a sunlit garden.

Her interior office, her safe place where she met her muse for tea.

In the back corner across from her thinking chair stood a tall featureless shadow, a stain on the air. It had a scent of metal and machine oil that didn't belong in her place. She rose from her office chair and turned toward the shadow, but it flickered, only visible from the corners of her eyes; she couldn't look directly at it. It faded from direct gazes.

She needed to know more about him if she were going to defeat him. So a shadow of him had invaded her private place? At least she knew one place to find him.

"Opal." Rod joggled her shoulder. "You okay?"

"Not really. I'm worried and tired."

"Oh."

"Not what you were asking." She straightened. "What's up?"

"Lunchtime. Betty went on ahead, and reported back on the walkie that it's that rosemary chicken thing again, with the greasy potatoes."

"Oh, boy!"

"She's not sure if it's leftovers from yesterday, or the only thing they know how to cook. You ready?"

She rose, locked her case. "Cast already went?"

"Yeah."

"I didn't take my continuity Polaroids."

"Magenta did it for you. You missed some last looks, too,

but he looked fantastic. Didn't need any touch-ups. Magenta checked. Not that she wanted to. She's scared of Corvus now."

Opal wondered if Magenta had shared Opal's theory of Corvus's possession with Rodrigo. She decided to wait before she broached the subject with him. After they finished shooting for the day, maybe they could meet for dinner and talk about what was going on, and whether there was anything they could do about it. She said, "Well, I owe her, and I know it. I've got to make a call, and then I'll be right there. Thanks for waking me."

"You're welcome. Say . . ."

She waited for it.

"I thought you got the easy job, but now I see it isn't so. Is your guy on the rag or something?"

"I don't know."

"Sympathies, anyway. Still looks good, even when he acts nuts."

She smiled and headed outside. Around back of the building, she got out her cell phone and dialed the number of a house she hadn't lived in for seven years.

"Hey," said Flint, one of her younger brothers.

"Hey yourself. Mama home?"

"Um, no. She left for the TV station about ten minutes ago."

Opal checked her watch. "Damn! Uncle Tobias there?"

"Hang on. I'll find out." There was a clunk as he set the handset down—probably on the kitchen table, Opal thought—and then his footsteps receded. She waited, checked her watch, waited. She should eat. They only had half an hour for lunch. Then again, she'd had that protein shake . . . Presently footsteps approached, and she heard heavy breathing. "Hey," Flint said, "astonishing as it is, Uncle Tobias is not in his tower. I don't know where he went."

"Damn! I really need to talk to someone!"

"I'm someone," said Flint plaintively.

"About dealing with magical possession."

"Oh. Okay. Not one of my things. Are you possessed?"

"No, my friend is, and the possessor guy is a—well, I need help."

"Do you want me?"

She smiled and stared into the forest behind the old supermarket. Her younger brother was a screwup. He had trouble getting his powers under control. They were good powers, but nobody understood them—they were different from anyone else's. She loved him dearly, but even she, in her role as second mother, hadn't been able to help him figure out how to make his powers work reliably. "I might. Not just yet, but thanks for the offer."

"You want someone else? Jasper? Gyp? Beryl?"

"Are they home?"

"No."

"If I get desperate, I'll call you back," she said. "Thanks, little brother."

"Must be serious. You never asked for help before," he said.

"Never?"

"Not in living memory. Hang on."

"Flint, I have to go to lunch."

"Hang on," he said again. "I'm going to try something."

"Flint—no, don't—"

He grunted.

Something punched Opal in the stomach so hard she fell down. She dropped the cell phone, and it skittered away. She lay on the damp, packed earth and tried to catch her breath. She could barely hear Flint's voice: "Hey? Did that work? Something happened. Are you okay? Opal? Opal?"

She wondered if she was okay. Why would her little brother send her a body blow? Her stomach felt—hurt, and warm. Warmth spread through her like a liquor afterglow. She closed her eyes and went to her inner office. In the middle of the room, an exercise-ball-sized fireball hovered, glowing orange and red in streaks, sending out arcs of random heat. She held a hand out to it, and a prominence flared up, scorched her fingertips. She tried to pull her hand back, but the light locked onto her. The burn spread up her arm into her shoulder and then— cooled, effervesced, moved through her like water flowing up the stem of a dehydrated plant. More than half the ball burned its way into her and cooled down, refreshing and reinvigorating her in an unfamiliar way. Even after she felt restored, the fireball floated in her office, diminished but lively.

Presently she sat up and reached for the phone, which hadn't stopped squawking.

"Don't do that again," she said in her big sister voice.

"Oh, God, are you okay?"

"I think so. It hurt me, but then it helped. Thanks for the thought, anyway, little brother. The delivery method needs work. We operate from different places. Your energy needs to be converted before it can turn into my energy."

"You'll be okay?"

"Yes. After the initial shock, I recognized what it was, and you know, I *do* need energy right now, so this is a help. You need to ask before you do things like that, though, bud. Okay?"

"Okay." He sounded so forlorn she wished she could hug him.

"Tell Mama I'll try calling later tonight. I'm not sure how late. We don't get many breaks here. You might tell Tobias, too. Okay?"

"Sure." He still sounded subdued.

"Got to run," she said. "Love you."

"Love you."

By the time she reached the out-of-business café the caterers had taken over while they were in town, the buffet was almost empty of food and she had five minutes to grab something, eat, and head back to the Makeup trailer. She wolfed a banana and grabbed a chicken leg to eat while she walked.

The Dark God wasn't there when she arrived, nor was Kelsi still curled up asleep in his chair. Opal opened the door and glanced across at the trailer next door, a three-banger Star Waggon with private rooms for Lauren, Blaise, and Corvus to use when they weren't required on the set. Corvus had the room at the end nearest his special station in the Makeup trailer. All three rooms were veiled with curtains, and no lights were on in any of them.

Magenta and Rod came in and set out their tools. Magenta dropped off a set of Polaroids with date and time written across the bottom in Sharpie.

"Thanks," Opal said to Magenta. "Thanks for picking up all my slack. God. Sorry I was so out of it."

"Vampires," said Magenta, with a shrug. "What can you do? You feeling better yet?"

"Yeah. Who knows how long that'll last. You didn't touch him, did you?"

Magenta shook her head. "For one thing, his makeup was fine. If it hadn't been, I would have woken you. Union rules. I'm not allowed to touch him."

"I know."

"And, after seeing what he did to you and Lauren, my hots for him went right out the window."

Opal nodded.

"Good luck. If you know how I can help you if he sucks on you again, tell me now."

"Keep your distance. No sense both of us going down."

Magenta bumped fists with her and went back to her station to finish laying out her brushes.

Opal set up her station. She didn't expect to have much to do, unless Invader had lost hold of Corvus since she last saw him. He had just stolen energy from her; he could probably hold out for a while.

She had to prevent him from stealing more energy from her. Flint's fireball—how could that boy transfer energy along a phone line? Maybe she shouldn't ask. He often couldn't repeat his feats. Trying just made him mess up in more spectacular ways.

Flint's fireball still warmed her insides, still felt like a transplanted organ from someone whose blood type she didn't share. Maybe she could use its foreignness to protect herself from predation. She dropped into Corvus's chair, went inside herself, and sat cross-legged in her mental study. A fireball half the size of the original one still burned there. She looked around for the shadow the Invader had left in her study earlier, but didn't see even a flicker in the corner of her eye.

She focused on the fireball. *Please give me an outer skin of unfriendly fire,* she thought, and the fireball brightened, almost smiled at her, and sent out a sheet of fire that formed a thin glowing layer around her.

Thanks, she thought. *You are beautiful. You are good. You are my friend.*

The fire laughed at her in Flint's voice.

He will come with a kiss and a siphon, Opal thought. *Do not enter him. Keep him back. Burn him.*

I hear, the fire sang, cheerful flames dancing.

She felt someone looming over her and looked up into the green glow of the Invader's eyes. She rose from the chair and gestured toward it. "Have a seat?"

Lauren and Blaise were in the other chairs. Rod and Magenta went to work repairing the damage lunch had caused without conversation. Magenta watched Opal and the Invader covertly.

The Invader settled into the chair and looked up at her, a faint smile on his leafy face. She got the Polaroids Magenta had taken before lunch and studied them, holding them near his face. Perfect match—nothing had come loose. She wondered if he had eaten greasy potatoes and rosemary chicken with the rest of the cast and crew. Corvus couldn't eat solid food with appliances on his face, but if it was the Invader's real face, he could eat anything he liked, she supposed.

Would the prostheses ever come loose again? She opened a drawer and took out the Polaroids she'd shot the first day and studied them against his face. He had still been Corvus—though already troubled by the intrusion of the Invader. He had changed since—the color of his skin was a trace greener now, the horns more pointed, the eyes larger and the brows more peaked. Subtle changes. She wasn't sure she should tell anyone. Possibly it could pass as normal character change. They were shooting the scenes out of sequence, but a lot of them were dim light, so it probably wouldn't make much difference.

The finished film was shipped to L.A., where the editor cut it together into rough scenes, transferred them to DVDs, and overnighted them back. Only three copies were made; they went to the director, the director of photography, and the producer, to share with subordinates as necessary.

Opal remembered earlier days in moviemaking, when everybody who was interested gathered to watch the processed dailies from the day before. The system had changed; too many actors, seeing their earlier work, wanted to do it over. Big names like Schwarzenegger and Cruise could do that, but none of the actors on this picture had that kind of clout.

She decided to wait until someone mentioned the difference in the Dark God's looks from shot to shot, if anybody did. They couldn't be as alert to his face as she was.

"Well?" he asked.

"You look perfect," she said.

"Of course."

"Have you always looked like this?"

He turned and studied himself in the wall of mirrors above her built-in makeup cabinet. "Never have I looked like this until now. I admire the design. This is a good face for me, I think; it startles those who see it for the first time, but does not send them away screaming. I want them to sit still for my approach. You are an excellent mask maker."

"Thanks," she said.

"So you don't need to touch me now?"

"Not unless there's something wrong with the facade."

"You'd touch me if I lost something vital?" He reached up with his transformed hand and wiggled one of his horns. It was too solid to come loose. He glanced toward Magenta, who suddenly focused intently on painting Lauren's lips. "Your friend also doesn't wish to touch me."

"We're not running away screaming, but we've learned to fear you."

"I am not doing my work correctly, then. I don't wish you to fear me, my handmaiden."

"I'm afraid of people who steal vital energy without asking, or put people into trances with a touch, or cut people without permission, or burn someone with a look because she said something disrespectful. How am I not supposed to be afraid of that?"

"I should give you something in exchange for your energy. I would, if you would let me." His voice was caressing, low and warm. "I would give you pleasure," he murmured. "I would give you almost anything in my power, my glorious wellspring of delight."

"Right now, your cooperation is really sexy," Opal said. "Do a good job on the picture, and I'll try to relax about the fact that you've displaced someone I love."

"Do you love me, Opal?" he asked in Corvus's voice.

"Corr! Are you in there?" She gripped his shoulders and leaned to look in his eyes. The green glow had dimmed, but he was still hidden behind the mask she had put on him that morning.

"Do you mean it?" he asked.

"Yes, I love you." Now was not the time to explain what kind of love it was, or that it wasn't exclusive. "Are you okay?"

"I don't know," he said. "I don't seem to be tracking very well."

"But you're not suffering?"

"Suffering? I've been asleep, I think. Did I mess up my scenes? I don't remember doing them. Was I sleepwalking?"

"I don't think so. Do you realize you're not alone in your body?"

"What? I don't understand."

"You're possessed by some god-thing. Maybe it's the Dark God of the script. He's been acting the part, anyway, maybe as well as you can, with more motivation."

"I don't understand," he said again, and then his eyes changed, and it was the Other staring out at her. "He doesn't have to understand, if you are good to me," whispered the Invader. "If you resist, I can help him understand in many unpleasant ways. Shall I let him sleep, or wake him up and make him suffer? The choice is yours."

Why had she brought up suffering to Corvus? Had she given the Invader ideas? Damn it. "What do you want?"

"Touch me."

She touched the horn he had wiggled, found that it was still seated well on his forehead and wouldn't move without—without, perhaps, a bone saw. He reached up and took her hand, brought the palm to his mouth and pressed his lips to it—

Then cried and thrust her hand away, tapped his lips gently with his fingertips. "What did you *do*?"

"I got some help," she said.

"Well, dispense with it, unless you want me to do something to your beloved."

She clenched her fists. She wanted to pound him. How

would that serve Corvus? It probably wouldn't help him. If she had her sister Gypsum's power to curse things—

"Where the hell are you guys?" yelled one of the assistant directors from the door. "You were due on the set fifteen minutes ago!"

"Give me something," whispered the Invader as Blaise and Lauren—both fully made up and ready—stood.

Fire, leave me a finger free, Opal thought, and her fire skin retreated from her right index finger. She touched the Invader's lips with it, and he took it into his mouth, sucked on the first knuckle, and released her. She felt only a little faint this time. He surged to his feet and swept out of the trailer, followed by Opal, Blaise, Lauren, Magenta, and Rodrigo.

Lauren gripped her arm. "Did Corvus really come back?"

"You heard that?"

"We were all listening as hard as we could."

"I don't know if it was Corvus or a trick. I don't trust the new guy at all."

"None of us do," said Lauren. Blaise, beside her, shook her head. Rod and Magenta had gone on ahead.

"Blaise?" Opal said.

The fair-haired woman stared after Corvus's tall, black-clad form. "He has a good professional reputation. That's not the behavior I'm observing. I don't want him to sabotage the picture. If you can come up with a way to handle this, deal me in."

"Thanks," said Opal. She felt a weight settle on her shoulders. They were all worried, and they thought she was the one to deal with the problem. Well, maybe she *had* given the Invader an opening to Corvus by using the techniques she had used to create his face, so she *should* fix the problem. She had more magical resources to fight the Invader with than anybody else on set, as far as she knew.

At least everybody was on the same side, or said they were.

Filming resumed with different angles on the same scene. The Invader behaved very well, saying his lines over and over again; he didn't forget the dialog he had improvised. They had a stunt knife for the part where he sliced open Serena's arm, and some stage blood for him to lick when they did the new takes, and he seemed okay with that, too. Opal went on the set to do last looks any time they paused long enough to need it, and she never had to work on the Invader's face. After a while, her tension evaporated.

It was only after filming had finished for the day, around eleven P.M., and the Invader was sitting in his chair in the makeup trailer, that she went back on high alert.

He had taken off the robe and given it to someone from Wardrobe, and he sat there in his black jeans and leafy skin and horny hands, smiling. "What are you going to do with me?" he asked.

"You tell me. Are you going to stay in there all night?"

"Would you like me to?"

"No," she said, unsure whether a statement of her desire would help or hinder. She wanted Corvus back so much she was going to ask her mother for help, something she couldn't remember doing since she had reached the age of eight. She didn't have the tools to force the Invader out by herself. She needed her mother or Tobias. Would either of them be up this late?

"If I come out, you must promise me you will restore me tomorrow," he said.

If you come out, how can you make me let you back in? she wondered. They had two more weeks of work on location, though, maybe longer, depending on the rewrites Travis and Bethany were doing. Every time she put the face on Corvus, it was another invitation to the Invader.

"Make me a promise or I won't leave," he said.

She clenched her fists and looked away, down the trailer

toward the chairs where Blaise and Lauren sat, Magenta and Rod standing beside them, no one else moving.

She could lie. Make a promise and not keep it.

That went against everything she believed about herself. It had always been vital to her to keep her word when she gave it. She tried not to ever give it if she didn't mean it, even though she saw people around her break promises all the time.

Still, she could do it. Maybe.

"All right," she whispered. "I promise."

7

The Invader heaved a deep sigh and relaxed in the chair, his shoulders slumping and his eyes falling shut. She hadn't known he was so tense. It was a clue. Possessing another was exhausting. She might be able to use that, or at least take note of it to report to her mother.

She got out her solvents and makeup removers and went to work on Corvus.

He slept through the removal. A production assistant brought in the call sheet and new script pages for the following day early in the process. Opal paused long enough to glance at their start time for the next day. The weather forecast was for rain, so they were filming on the soundstage again. Corvus was supposed to be in the Makeup trailer by ten A.M.

She stuffed the call sheet and the script in her messenger bag and moisturized Corvus's hands, arms, upper body, and his face, which was empty of the Invader but also of consciousness.

Lauren and Magenta hovered as Opal finished.

"Corr?" Opal whispered, gripping his shoulder.

It took him a long time and some serious shaking to wake up. "What?" he said at last, opening eyes still hidden behind the Dark God's contact lenses. "What happened? How'd I get back in the trailer?" He glanced toward the clock on the mirror. "Is that A.M. or P.M.?"

"It's midnight," said Lauren. "What do you remember about today? Anything?"

He groaned, and said, "This morning. Opal and I were— you said you told me to rest well, and I was a little upset. I don't like to sleep soundly. It makes me nervous. Have I slept through the whole day?" He gripped Opal's arm. "Did you hypnotize me into it?"

"No, I didn't!"

"I'm sorry." He let her go.

"Corvus, you spent most of the day being someone else," said Lauren. "Someone incredibly creepy, a lot like the role you play, a manipulator who gets off on other people's pain."

"What?"

"The good thing is, he can act," she continued. "He's doing you proud. But we'd much rather have *you* around."

He looked at his watch, pressed a button to get the date. "It's November, not April First," he said. "I don't like this joke, Lauren."

"Are you hungry?" Opal asked.

Distracted, he glanced toward his stomach and frowned. "Ravenous. Opal—"

"Come on, big guy. Let's go get some supper."

He let her pull him to his feet. He accepted the shirt she handed him. Magenta and Lauren were watching him so intently he turned his back to them and whispered, "What do they want?"

"They want to make sure you're okay."

"It's not just my shoulders or my ass, eh?" He flexed his biceps and glanced back.

"Those, too," Opal whispered, and smiled.

He put on the shirt and buttoned it to the top button. He set the back of his hand on his forehead. "I'm so tired," he said.

"Let's get you to the car. You can nap on the way to the restaurant." Hitch had left Opal the keys again once Corvus was off the clock. "You've got to eat, though, Corvus. I don't know if you had anything all day aside from a protein shake I forced on you."

"You were really talking and interacting with me all day?"

"Not you. Someone else in your body." She snagged the last set of Polaroids she'd taken before she removed his makeup, rubber-banded them together, and stuck them in her messenger bag. The Invader had posed for the Polaroids, showing his teeth, his horns, and the unlikely gleam in his eyes. She would show them to Corvus at the restaurant; maybe that would help bring this home to him.

"This feels like a bad extended jape," he said. He shook his head. "It's hard for me to take seriously."

"It's outside your experience. Of course it'll take you a while to get used to it," Opal said. She remembered the steps she and her family had to take every time they introduced outsiders to who they really were. "You don't have to believe us, Corr. You *do* have to decide what to do next."

He followed her down the trailer stairs, Magenta and Lauren in their wake. Opal pressed the keychain button to unlock the Lincoln, and Magenta and Lauren climbed into the backseat. Corvus stared at them. "You're coming?"

"We've been waiting all day to talk to you," said Lauren, "and we're not letting you out of our sight."

He shrugged massively. "I'm not up to much conversation, I'm afraid," he said.

"That's okay. Whatever you've got."

"All right, then."

Opal held the door so Corvus could climb into the passenger seat, then went around the car and got behind the wheel. She started the car and drove.

"Did you dream?" Lauren asked from the backseat.

"What?" Corvus said.

"While you slept through the day, did you have any dreams? Say, one where you woke up for a second and talked to Opal?"

"Was that not a dream?" he asked. Opal, watching the view out the front window of light blades on a dark road, with tree shadows crowding close, was conscious of Corvus's regard. His gaze prickled against the skin of her right cheek like sunlight.

"What do you remember?" she asked, without looking toward him.

"Did you tell me you loved me?"

She closed her eyes, then opened them so she could watch the road. "That was really you I was talking to? I wasn't sure."

"It wasn't a dream?"

"No, I really said that."

"Did you mean it?" He shifted in his seat, turned to peer toward the backseat. "Or should we have this conversation later?"

"They heard everything I said before," she said. "I meant it, sure. How could I not love you? I don't like the one who's been using you, though, and he has me over a barrel now."

"What do you mean?"

"He only let you out tonight after I promised to help him back inside you tomorrow."

"*You're* the one who put him in me?"

"Not exactly. I put the Dark God's face on over yours, and he used that, somehow. I don't know what to do. Do you want to quit the film?"

"No," he said. "I still have dreams that this'll be a break-out role for me. I want to act this part."

"But when I put the face on you, you're gone—I think."

"Lauren?" Corvus said.

"You and I and Blaise did scene twenty-three all day to-day, Corvus. Do you remember any of it?"

"No," he said.

"Well, you were great, whoever you were, creepy as hell," said Lauren. "I have to tell you, if you quit now, the whole production will fall apart, and it won't be doing your career any favors, either. But if it's a matter of survival, well, you should do whatever you have to."

"I'm not doing my own acting," he muttered, "but I'm do-ing all right. That troubles me. I want to do the work . . . I feel okay now. As soon as you put the face on me, I return to being this other guy?"

"That's the impression I get," Opal said. "Magenta and Lauren and I have been speculating about how it works. We have ideas, but no certainties."

Corvus shook his head. "This is crazy."

"Yeah," said Opal. "Just deal with as much of it as you can. Ignore the rest."

"How's that going to help us get rid of the Dark God?" Magenta asked.

"We can't force Corvus to believe something he's not ready for," Opal said, "no matter how urgent it is."

"How urgent is it?" Corvus asked.

"It's hard to say. Is he hurting you? You don't seem to have suffered today, but he says he might hurt you tomorrow un-less I do what he says."

"What he makes her do is let him suck on her like a vam-pire," Lauren told Corvus. "Except it's not blood he takes, but her life force. He did that to me, too, or something like it. I'm not sure what he did to me, but it was horrible."

"Shit, Lauren, he drank your blood," said Magenta.

"Didn't drink it, more like licked it, and then he put a spell on me that turned me into a drooling idiot, worshipping him just like Serena. All the rest of today's filming! I didn't come out of it till you stripped off my makeup, Madge. I remember it all, though. I was awake and watching. I just couldn't come to the surface."

"You all believe this happened today," said Corvus.

"We were there, and you weren't," said Magenta.

"But I—" He pressed his face into his palms. "I can't think about this now."

"Don't worry, Corr," said Opal. "We're almost at the restaurant. Guys, give it a rest. Let him eat."

"We need a plan," said Magenta.

Opal said, "The call sheet said we're filming scene twelve C tomorrow, and I got a stack of new script pages for Corvus. Are you in that scene, Lauren?"

"No. That's afternoon, Corvus with Gemma and Bettina. It's a new one about how messed up the sisters get as kids. In the morning, Blaise and I are filming in the B&B. One of our fabulous bitch-fight scenes."

"What's your call time tomorrow?" Opal asked.

"I need to be in Makeup by seven thirty," said Lauren. "We're supposed to be on the set by eight. What's yours?"

"Corvus goes into Makeup at ten so we can film at two. They give me four hours to put together Dark God. With the Invader's help, it takes less time. If there's any time after you finish and before we start filming, maybe we can talk, if Corvus is too out of it tonight." She pulled into the restaurant parking lot and turned off the engine.

Magenta and Lauren got out of the car. Opal reached for her door handle, but Corvus grasped her wrist. "Wait," he murmured.

Opal opened her window. "You guys get a table, will you? We'll be in soon."

Magenta saluted and headed into the restaurant with Lauren.

"I'm fuzzy on a lot of details," Corvus said in the relative darkness of the car, "but I remember you said you loved me."

"So what?"

"What does it—where do we—I'm not sure—"

"It's not a trap or an obligation, Corvus. It's just part of the way I work. To change someone so completely, I must love them in both their personas, before makeup and after. It usually wears off when the picture's over."

"This happens to you a lot."

"Only when I'm at the top of my game."

"Do you ever follow up on the feeling?"

"Oh, come on. Who needs the tsuris?"

He stared out the windshield, his large hand still loosely circling her wrist. "Did you feel like this during *Dead Loss?*"

"Immediately," she said. "You're not hard to love."

He sat silent, his fingers warm around her wrist, his palm a warm, dry pressure against the back of her hand. "Did it wear off afterward?"

"No."

"Why didn't you—"

She blew out a breath. "You try to maintain a low profile, but those people at *Entertainment Tonight* and *Access Hollywood* just love pictures of you with starlets, you know?"

"I think that's why those girls call me. Guaranteed exposure. The Beauty and the Beast captions write themselves. It means nothing."

She laughed. "Oh, *they* call *you*, eh?"

"Most of the time, I'd rather stay home and read a book," he said. She heard an undertone of laughter. "Opal," he said, the laughter gone.

She waited. She had gotten involved with one of her other special projects, a popular leading actor who could have picked anyone. He professed to be tired of high-maintenance relationships—not the most promising opening, but she had loved him deeply, or the character he was playing, anyway, a tortured soul with interesting facial scars she applied as necessary. He had been sweet, tender even; on idle days, they had spent time in the wilderness, where he could be someone he wasn't: unrecognized. But she always knew who he was.

He took her to a couple of premieres, too; he wasn't ashamed to be seen with someone who gave him no extra clout. He never treated her as a lesser being, the way some stars treated all the people whose names came at the end of the movie rather than the beginning, but she never cut her self-imposed tethers while she was with him and showed him she could fly.

Later, the news stories weren't kind to her: another in the chain of broken hearts he'd left behind, but this time, they said, given her profession, at least she knew how to conceal the tracks of her tears. Dreadful stuff.

Corvus tugged gently on her wrist. She unbuckled her seat belt and waited. He looped an arm around her, and lifted her (with some help from her) over the center console to settle in his lap. She relaxed against his chest; she had dreamed of being there, curled in his arms, his heart beating in her ear, and now she could hear it. She nestled against the huge warm mountain of him. His arms circled her, and his breath stirred her hair. He smelled like the sandalwood-scented moisturizer she'd rubbed on him, and underneath it, his own scent, that of a large, powerful, clean male animal.

A voice whispered: *Don't be stupid; we've been down this road before. Nothing good can last. You don't know him. You don't know anything about him. How can you trust him?*

Who needs trust? some other part of her asked. *I just want to fool around.*

He tipped her chin up and lowered his face, touched his lips to hers. His kiss was gentle and tasted sour. She gripped his face and explored his mouth, then pushed away. "I can taste how hungry you are," she whispered. "You should eat. We can do this later."

He groaned and hugged her almost too tight, then unlatched the door and helped her out of the car.

The same waitress was working again.

"Hey," she said. "I read your name off your credit card and rented one of your movies when I got off shift this morning. I watched it over lunch."

Corvus smiled. "I wouldn't eat while watching any of them. Did you like it?"

"You were really scary!" she said.

"Thank you."

"But I'm not scared of you now. I think that's strange. Oh, don't mean to hold you up. You guys want a table to yourself tonight, or are you joining someone?"

Corvus pointed toward the corner booth, where Magenta and Lauren sat, eating French fries and drinking soda.

"Her I've heard of," said the waitress, nodding toward Lauren. "She was great as Bitsy in *Fooled Me Twice*. Is she really as nice as she was in the movie?"

"She is," said Opal.

"Oh, good. We had a couple other stars in here around dinnertime, and they were—well, you don't need to hear. Please, seat yourselves. Here's some menus. I'll be right over to take your orders."

"Thanks, Jenny," said Corvus. He and Opal headed for Magenta and Lauren's booth. "Opal, you said something about new pages?"

"Yes. Sorry." She fished a sheaf of marigold-colored paper out of her messenger bag and handed it to him. Opal slid in beside Magenta, and Corvus beside Lauren.

He took reading glasses out of his shirt pocket and skimmed through the pages. There were six. "I've never seen this before."

"They were writing it last night, remember? In this same booth."

"Any good?" Lauren asked.

He flipped back to the start and frowned. "I—"

Jenny came up, pencil poised over her order pad. "Steak?" Corvus asked, peering at her over his glasses.

"Sure. T-bone or top sirloin?"

"T-bone."

"How you want that?"

"Medium rare. And a big salad if you have one."

"Sorta," she said. "Anything to drink?"

"A pitcher of coffee." He flipped through the marigold pages. "Gotta stay awake awhile longer. Got some memorizing to do."

"How about you, hon?" Jenny asked, turning to Opal.

For the first time Opal remembered her own hunger. It had been a long time since lunch, which she had barely had. She ordered a turkey sandwich, salad, and a glass of milk.

"Be right back," said Jenny, and bustled off.

"So what did you figure out in the car after we left?" Lauren asked.

"Not much," said Opal.

"Took you pretty long," said Magenta.

Lauren kicked Magenta under the table. "Meanwhile, we're still trying to figure out what to do about the D.G.," she said. "I don't want him to get to me again the way he did today. Tomorrow I'm safe, because we're not working together, but I think day after tomorrow, we're scheduled to do another forest shoot, if the weather cooperates. What I want to know is, are you *completely* unconscious the whole time he's here?"

"I don't remember anything about today, aside from sitting down to get made up, our fight, the dream about Opal," he said, "and then waking up after the day was over."

"I wonder if there's some part of you that remembers," said Lauren.

"What's your point?" asked Opal.

"If they're two separate people, we have to figure out how to manipulate the D.G. without Corvus's help—if he's stuck down in the basement and can't affect the D.G. while he's in charge, that's no good. If there's some kind of connection, we might be able to get Corvus to work on the guy from inside. Assuming Corvus is on our side, and doesn't want the D.G. torturing us all day while he's gone. But if there's a connection, that might mean the D.G. could figure out everything we plan, so I don't know whether to talk about this anymore in front of him."

"This film has been an eye-opener, and I've been here less than a week," Corvus said.

"What do you mean, big guy?" asked Magenta. She sipped soda from the bottom of the glass through her straw.

Jenny came and put food down in front of Corvus and Opal.

Corvus salted his steak, sat with his fork poised, frowned at his food. "Why did I say that?" he asked himself. "I'll tell you why. My flight lands in Portland, and I'm in charge of my life, about to start work on a new project. Good step on my career path, a role with meat to it. I know I can do a good job. I've memorized the most current version of the script. I've got a good room right in town, with a bed that's big enough for me for once, and my trailer's decent. First weird thing I learn on this shoot: Opal can hypnotize me."

"Oh?" Lauren glanced at Opal, eyebrows up.

Opal shrugged. "Not on purpose. Just so he could lie still comfortably while I was changing him into Dark God."

"I'm helpless in her hands," Corvus said. He straightened to his full height, which was impressive, sitting or standing. He shook his head slowly. "Long time since I've been helpless for anybody. I hate that."

"How come you can hypnotize him?" Magenta asked. "Is that part of your general witchiness?"

"I guess," Opal said.

"Wait," said Corvus. "You're a witch?"

"Close enough."

Corvus glanced at Lauren and Magenta. "Not news to them," he said to himself. "Okay. Maybe I knew it, too. So anyway, that's the first step to my discovery that I don't rule my own life. Now this other person is running around wearing my—wearing me, and alienating my coworkers and friends."

"You could leave," Opal said. "While you're still you. I'll drive you to Portland if you want."

"Breach my contract? Mess up this multimillion-dollar production and screw over everybody working on it?"

"Yep," said Opal.

"I don't think so. Talk about a career-killing move."

Opal had the impulse to stick it out, too. The shoot had to end sometime. They might be able to figure out how to deal with the Invader, keep him tame enough to work with. He was her best creation to date, though she couldn't take full credit for him.

"Is this movie going to be any good?" she asked the others.

"It'll be okay if they don't completely screw it up in post," said Magenta. "Nothing everybody hasn't seen before, but that's good, if it's something everybody wants to see again."

"Like everything I've done so far," Corvus said. "Anyway, in terms of career, I'm working my way toward where I want to be. Maybe next picture, I get to wear my own face, who knows? I know that's not likely; not many roles written for seven-foot leading men, but it could happen, right?"

"If anybody can do it, it's you," Lauren said. "You've got a great face. I wonder if Travis and Beth would write you a picture."

"To get to that point," he said, "I should probably get through this picture first. Agreed?"

The women looked at each other and nodded.

"All right, then. I vote we wait and see what happens tomorrow. Though I'm not looking forward to it." He sighed and settled into eating.

Opal had finished her sandwich. She checked her watch—after midnight—then opened her messenger bag to search for her cell phone, even though she was sure her mother had already gone to bed.

Lauren leaned across Magenta and touched Opal's arm. "Sorry to change the subject," she said. "But there he is."

"Who?" Opal asked.

"The ex." She nodded toward the front of the restaurant. "I wonder how long he's been here."

They all looked. A dark-haired man was sitting at the counter with a mug of coffee in front of him. He held something in his hand, stared down at it. It winked.

"Is that a mirror?" Magenta asked.

"Subtle, isn't he?" said Lauren.

"Who is he?"

"The guy who's stalking me, Norman Davis."

"You have a stalker?" Magenta said.

"Yep. Not just trendy, but nerve-racking."

"Do you know what he wants? An autograph?" asked Corvus.

"Not hardly," said Lauren, while Magenta said, "He's a movie star, big guy, not an autograph hound."

"Oh?" Corvus looked at the back of Norman's head again. He frowned.

"He was the male lead's sidekick in *Fooled Me Twice*," said Magenta. "Mr. Comic Relief. The B-story romance with Lauren's character."

"Oh. That was a charming subplot," Corvus said.

"You've actually seen the movie?" Lauren said.

"Of course. I like to know who I'm going to be working with. You were great. He was good," Corvus said.

"Thanks. Yeah. Snowed me enough I said yes when he wanted to take the relationship outside the script."

Jenny leaned forward at the counter, smiled at Norman while she refilled his coffee mug, laughed at something he said. She gestured past his shoulder toward their table and asked a question. Norman shook his head without turning around.

Still staring at Norman, Lauren said, "Will you guys leave with me?"

"Sure. Anyway, we have to, don't we? I've got the car," said Opal.

"Oh. Yeah," said Lauren. She smiled.

"Corvus will pretend he's your boyfriend," Opal said.

"I will?" said Corvus. "Of course I will, if that's what you want."

"Not sure that's a good idea," Lauren said. "I know Norm is whacked. I don't know exactly how. He might get weird and destructive toward you, as well as me, if he thinks we're together. Anyway, tabloids will be announcing you two as a couple any day now, right?" She smiled at Corvus and Opal.

"Are there actual press leaks on this shoot?" asked Magenta. "Erika is irritating, but she doesn't seem to have sent out a story yet. We had some security scares in the Makeup trailer, but I haven't seen anything in the tabloids about this shoot yet, and yeah, I'm checking out the *World Weekly News* and the *Enquirer* every time I'm at a cash register in the supermarket."

"I could start some stories," said Lauren.

"Please don't," Opal said. "Been down that road. Hated it."

"Really?" Lauren asked.

"That was with Gerry?" Corvus said.

"Gerry who?" asked Magenta.

"Gerard Shelley." Opal hunched her shoulders. Her relationship with Gerry hadn't ended badly. They were still friends, but he had moved on. Really, so had she; she'd been working with Corvus by the time she and Gerry wished each other well. The tabloids had invented their own sour ending. "Why do you know about that, Corr?"

"I told you, I research the people I work with."

"You hooked up with Gerry?" Lauren said. "I worked with him once. One tiny scene. I was a funny library lady and he had a question. He's awesome. Or—does it turn out he's not?"

"No. He's a good guy," Opal said.

Jenny came by with a coffeepot and a pitcher of cola, offered refills. She glanced over her shoulder toward the counter, then looked at Lauren.

"Sweetie, we're not together any longer, and I'm totally uninterested in him," Lauren told her. "So please don't tell him what I'm doing or who with, okay?"

Jenny flushed. "He said he wanted to surprise you."

"Yes, but not in a good way."

"Oh," said the waitress. "I'm sorry."

"No way you could know that. He's an actor. It's his job to convince people he's nice. Underneath—well, my advice would be don't go there, but it's up to you."

Jenny's eyes widened. "No." She gave her head one shake. "I wasn't even thinking that. I thought you were a couple."

"Nope. So don't tell him any more about me than you have to, okay?"

"All right. Boy, having you guys around sure makes life interesting."

"We live for that," said Lauren with a grin. Jenny topped off everybody's drinks and went away again.

"Well, I've got pages," Corvus said. "Or does the other guy need to memorize them?" He shuddered.

"He knows what you know," Lauren said. "We found that out today. If you get your lines in your head, he can get to them. Hmm. That may answer my earlier question. You guys are connected somehow. Any plans we make with you, he can figure out, maybe. That's not good."

Opal dropped her hands to her thighs and fisted them under the table. She needed to talk to her mother. The previous Christmas, her sister had done a strange spell that revealed how people connected to each other in her family, and Opal had seen strings leading from her mother to everyone else. If she could connect to Corvus that way, maybe she could talk to him, even while he was submerged under the Invader. She dug out her cell phone. "Excuse me," she said. "Gotta make a call."

"Don't go too far," Lauren said. "Please."

"Right out front," said Opal. "I'll keep an eye on you through the glass."

They all watched her leave, and she realized everyone was depending on her. It felt like she was back at home, herding her younger siblings around, being their mother because Mama wasn't really good at that, listening to every complaint, fixing things that went wrong. Familiar, and in a way almost sweet, and also annoying.

She stood just to the side of the door. She could see the back booth from there, and she also saw Norman's profile. He was handsome, and looked grumpy.

She called home.

"Opal, is that you? I've been waiting to hear from you," said her mother after one ring.

"Oh, good. I'm sorry to call so late. Glad you're up."

"I'm not, really. Your father and I are reading in bed. What's the problem? Flint wasn't very coherent."

"Mama, I put a face on my friend to turn him into a monster, and a monster came with it. What do I do?"

"Can you give me some real information, honey? It's hard to diagnose from this distance."

Opal explained as much as she understood about the Invader, how the location had influenced the writing of the script, the script had dictated the nature of the monster, and the monster she had assembled had taken on a life of its own. She also talked about the Invader's blackmail scheme. "How did you make those strings that hooked us all together, Mama?" she asked.

"What are you talking about?"

"Remember Gyp's Reveal Spell, how it showed strings between us? She broke the string you had to her, and—"

"What are you talking about, Opal?" Mama asked again. "I don't remember any Reveal Spell."

"It was at that special meeting we had before last Christmas, just before Gyp got her curses under control. Actually, it was the meeting where she figured out how to control them, and she—" Opal thought about the meeting, remembered her own astonishment when her sister and her sister's new lover had showed the family many things, most of them unpleasant.

So many things had happened during the meeting that Opal didn't remember it very clearly, but she remembered the image of her whole family draped in webs of many colors, and how her mother had spun most of the webs to snare the rest of them. Looking at the webs had told Opal so much: why her younger brothers and sisters never moved out, and how scared her mother must have been, to hang on to them so tightly.

Opal had carried the web image to the extended family party in Los Angeles after Christmas, had wished she could see the webwork among her cousins and grandparents, aunts and uncles. Mama had four sisters and two brothers, and she didn't get along with any of them. Opal had lost her special vision by then, though, and she had to guess rather than know. She had studied her grandparents afresh, noticed how Grandmère pitted her children against each other. "Well, Anise," Grandmère had said to Opal's mother, "I hear your oldest boy is learning to use his talents in music. Sage, what's wrong with your daughter? She was studying flute last year. Why did she give it up?"

Aunt Sage had been upset. "How did you know?"

"I know everything," Grandmère had said. And then, to another aunt: "Well, Lily, I understand your youngest daughter transitioned at last. At fifteen! I hear she has cooking talents. So sad, Anise, about your girl Gyp, having to do it all without talent—"

But that was where the party got interesting. "As to that," Mama said, "Gyp brought her usual array of cookies and brownies to the party. We had more to share this year than usual, but I notice there are almost none left. I wouldn't say she's not talented."

"Not talented with a capital *T*," said Grandmère, with a tiny shark smile.

"I suppose," Mama said brightly, "it depends on how you define talent. Gyp finally transitioned, although her talent is like Aunt Meta's."

"What?" Grandmère spoke so loudly everyone turned to look and listen.

"Gyp has the power of curses," said Mama, almost proudly.

Opal was surprised the whole family didn't already know. She remembered how distracted Mama had been before Christmas, and realized part of her distraction must have been due to planning how to introduce the family to this new development. Play it up? Play it down? Mama had picked the first alternative.

Opal checked for Gyp. It should have been her information to share. Gyp was talking to two of the cousins, admiring a brag book one held, maybe photographs or artwork. Like everyone else nearby, the cousins heard Mama's declaration. They stepped away from Gyp.

Opal had headed toward her. So had Flint and Jasper and Beryl. Opal slowed when she saw other cousins gathering around Gyp, asking questions, touching her arms and shoulders, one or two embracing her. Gyp was smiling.

Mama continued, "She even uses her power in cooking, though she has to have help, or what she makes comes out cursed. Don't worry. We made sure our contribution to the potluck was curse-free."

"Curses? Curses?" Grandmère muttered.

Mama took top news honors with that information, no matter what this cousin or that cousin had managed to do with their powers last year. In fact, Grandmère was so surprised she lost control of the party for at least half an hour.

"Strings," Mama said on the phone, bringing Opal back to the present. "I don't remember any strings."

"Oh. Well, do you have any other good ideas?"

"I just have bad ideas, like flying up there to help you, and bringing the kids with me. Do you want any or all of us with you?"

"How would that work with your job?"

"It wouldn't be convenient, but I can escape if I have to. Do you want me to send Tobias?"

Opal's great-uncle Tobias was the family teacher. He knew more magework than any of the rest of them, and had been practicing longer than the rest of them had been alive. He was a stick in the mud, though; didn't even leave the house to accompany the family on vacations. Hell, he claimed he liked having the time alone, and he probably meant it.

"I don't know," Opal said. "If he could come, that would be great. I don't know if we're in enough danger to warrant emergency measures, though."

"I'll check with him in the morning," said her mother. "Call if you need help sooner than that. Here's your father."

"Opal? What can I do to help?" asked her father, and suddenly she felt like crying. Dad was great. But he had no more than normal human powers.

"Same deal as always, Dad. Be yourself. Listen and think. If you come up with any ideas, let me know."

"All right," he said. "Love you, Opal."

"Love you," she whispered, closed the phone, and wiped her eyes.

8

Opal peered into the restaurant—she had forgotten to watch what was happening between Norman and her friends—but everything looked the same. She opened the door and went back to the corner booth.

"Thanks for the offer, Lauren," Corvus was saying when Opal settled next to Magenta again. "I'll ask Opal to run lines with me." He turned to Opal. "You'll spend the night, won't you?"

"What?"

"You'll stay with me tonight."

Immediately she felt like saying no. Did he think a declaration of love made her stupid or weak? Did he think it gave him permission to order her around?

"Please," he said.

"Sure," she said, shaking her head.

"And on that note, maybe we better get back to town," he said, "so I can practice and get some sleep."

"I'll want my toothbrush and a change of clothes," said Opal.

"Of course."

Corvus paid for everybody, and linked arms with Lauren on the way out. They swept past a frowning Norman. Lauren never even looked at him.

Across the parking lot at the budget motel, Magenta bid them goodnight and went to her room. Lauren and Corvus followed Opal into her room. Having Corvus there made Opal conscious of how low the ceilings were, how small the room really was. She liked his room better, despite the brown gingham and chintz, and the sense of the house watching.

"How much should I pack?" she asked. If Corvus had an agenda, she wanted to know what it was.

"Doesn't that kind of depend on who he is after shooting tomorrow?" asked Lauren. "You don't want to move in with D.G., do you?"

"Good point." Opal packed essential toiletries, the oversized T-shirt she wore as a nightgown, and one change of clothes. It all fit into her messenger bag.

She drove them both back to Lapis. A car followed them—Lauren pointed it out.

"Don't worry," Opal said. "I can take care of this."

As soon as they reached town, Opal parked and conjured an image of their car, while hiding the real car in unreal shadows. The imaged car drove on past them.

"What was that?" Lauren asked as she watched the image of a car drive away from them, with Norman's car following. She leaned forward in the backseat, gripping Opal's seat.

"An illusion," said Opal.

"But how—Oh. You can do that?"

"It's light. I can work with light. That's my gift."

"If you can do that—you could make your own movies. Without the benefit of actors or sets."

"Not interested," said Opal. "At least, not at the moment. Where are you staying, again?"

Lauren was quiet as Opal drove her to her host family's home, speaking only to give directions. She gripped and released Opal's shoulder before she climbed out of the car. "Later." Opal watched as Lauren went up the front walk and into the house. One light burned beyond the front door; the rest of the house was dark.

No other cars drove down this street. Opal pulled out and drove slowly back to the bed-and-breakfast, watching for Norman's car, but her illusion car had apparently led him far from downtown Lapis. All to the good.

At the B&B, Corvus took her bag out of the backseat and carried it up. The house didn't feel menacing tonight, more curious. Again, when they reached the upstairs hall, the director glanced out of his room as their footsteps sounded. He frowned and shook his head, disappeared back into his room without a word.

"Who's he shacking up with?" Opal asked as a woman murmured beyond the wall Corvus's room shared with Aldridge's.

"They're very discreet," said Corvus. "I've never seen her, only heard that voice. Can you tell from listening?"

Opal leaned her ear against the wall, but couldn't make out the words, only the tone. She glanced at Corvus.

"I think it's Blaise," he said. "Trav and Beth just rewrote a key scene and gave her five more lines. They cut Lauren's part by three lines. Lauren was looking over her new pages while you were on the phone. She's mad."

"She should be. Serena's the main character," Opal said.

"That could change."

It was true. Lots of things could change during production, and even more drastic changes sometimes took place in postproduction.

"That sucks," said Opal.

"We'll see what happens," Corvus said. "From everything going on, nobody knows how this will play out. Too many wild cards. Will you read lines with me?"

"Yeah, I guess," she said. "I have to brush my teeth."

"Go on. I'll change."

She changed into the T-shirt nightgown she usually didn't wear—when she was alone, she slept naked—and wrapped herself in a man's triple-X corduroy work shirt, the closest thing she had to a bathrobe. She washed up.

When she came out of the bathroom, Corvus was lounging on an overstuffed brown and white gingham couch; it was big enough to support him without parts of him hanging over the edge. He wore blue pajamas and his reading glasses, and he was studying the script. Love swept through her, startling and inconvenient. He glanced up at her over the tops of his glasses, and her throat tightened. He could immobilize her with a look; better not let him know. She forced herself to walk forward and sat on the bed across from him.

"It's only six lines," he said. "I think I've got it. Would you help me?"

"Sure." She took the script from him and read the parts of Young Serena and Young Caitlyn. The Dark God was already sharpening up the rivalry between them, pretending he favored one, then the other.

Opal was intrigued by the young girls' parts. They had seen this monster accept the sacrifice of both their parents. Well, according to Beth and Travis, Serena had seen her mother sacrifice her father to him, and both of them had witnessed their mother's suicide on the Dark God's altar. Why were they even talking to him? Neither of them seemed scared of him. Young Serena even clung to his hand. By the end of the scene, he had stooped and gathered her to him. Young Caitlyn stood outside of the embrace, her face cold.

Did this make psychological sense? Opal wasn't sure it

did, but then, maybe it didn't need to. Most horror movies she'd worked on weren't that long on sense. People always wandered off alone in time to get killed, when any sensible person would cling to the others and head for someplace with lots of light.

"Both of you may be my handmaidens and help me," said Corvus, "but I will always love one above the other." He was almost whispering by the time he finished.

"Love me," said Young Caitlyn. "I'm strong and beautiful."

"Love me," said Young Serena. "I'll do whatever you want."

Corvus laughed a villain's laugh. It went on too long. Opal dropped the pages and stared at him. His eyes glowed green.

"Go away," she said. "You said you wouldn't come back until tomorrow!"

"What?" Corvus blinked, and the extra light in his eyes faded.

"Let's go to bed," Opal said. "Which side do you prefer?"

"The left side," he said. "Now *I've* got to brush my teeth. Did you want to—? Because I'm not sure I have the energy."

"I'd rather just get some sleep," she said. While he was in the bathroom, she curled up under the covers on the right side of the bed.

Water ran. She needed to collect more power. She might need enough to offer some to the Invader and keep some for herself, or she might need enough to fight him. Either way, she needed to engage in power collection.

She thought about the person she had been in her teens, her brief period of rage and revenge, when she had attacked her irritating brother, Jasper, in ways creative, devious, and mean. It had been so foreign to her character she hadn't maintained it for long. Also, Jasper had gone through transition soon after she had, and once he had his own powers, he was too formidable for her to fight. She had read some of the

Forbidden Texts during her brief flirtation with the dark side, though, and learned a few handy things.

She reached into her shadow and summoned the Sifter Chant, the one that threw out a net to snare any stray power in the environment and store it in her power reservoir. There was nothing inherently evil about this chant. It could work in the background once she set it going; she would only need to check on it now and then to make sure what she was collecting wouldn't make her sick. The world was full of different-flavored powers in various stages of existence, and some of them weren't good for anyone.

She scribed three symbols on her palm with her index finger and spoke the Sifter Chant three times, felt the opening out of her nets and the first tiny tugs as she collected. The power flowed into her reservoir and stored itself, quiescent. *Good,* she thought, drowsy now, warmed by the very act of summoning.

The next time she opened her eyes, it was because she smelled coffee. Corvus stood beside the bed holding a mug near her face. "I don't even know if you drink coffee in the morning," he said as she sat up. "I do. Copious amounts, usually, unless I'm about to put on a costume it takes an hour to get out of. Thank God this picture isn't like that."

She took the mug from him and drank from it. It had lots of cream and sugar in it; usually she didn't use either, but she liked it this time. The coffee tasted like hot ice cream.

"Thanks," she said.

He was already dressed, black jeans and a blue shirt, and his hair was wet from a shower. Opal lifted her wrist to check the time. Six thirty. She groaned and glanced at the pillow, imagined flopping down to sleep another couple hours.

"We gather for breakfast between six and nine. The hostess is kind of strict about that," Corvus said.

"You go ahead," said Opal. "I'll go back to sleep and drive out to the IHOP later."

"Come on. You can eat here. Bess always makes too much of everything."

She downed the rest of the coffee. "Okay, if you want to be public about this, us being a couple, if that's what we are. I'll be down after I shower. You sure?"

"How secretive have we been so far? If you think Magenta and Lauren aren't going to tell anyone, think again."

"And anyway, it's only half a couple. You never said anything," she muttered. "I feel like your all-access stalker."

He sat on the bed beside her and pulled her into his arms, kissed her with his eyes shut; she knew, because she kept hers open, and saw the trouble in his face, the lowered brows, tightened cheeks. She flattened her hand against his chest and pushed him back until he lifted his face away from hers. "Please. Don't torture yourself. I said a stupid thing, all right? I meant it before, about this not demanding any specific response from you."

"Am I that bad a kisser?"

"Go on down to breakfast. I'll shower and sneak out. I can get something to eat at Craft Services."

"No. We need to straighten this out before I turn into that other guy you don't like." He shook his head. "Still not sure I believe that, but I'm afraid of it anyway. What's wrong?"

She blew out a breath, got up, and paced. "It's much easier to love you when you don't know about it. I don't want everything to shift around because this information is in the way. I can love you from a distance, from the other hotel. I can love you whatever you do, including if you get involved with someone else. I can have this as my own background feeling and do my job just fine. This foreground stuff isn't working for me. I don't want to think about whether you care about me. If you do care, I don't want you worrying about how to treat me, or whether I'll explode if you make the wrong move, or whatever's going through your head that makes you feel like you have to prove something to me.

If you want to prove something to me, this isn't the way. Okay?"

"What do you think I'm trying to prove?" he asked.

"God, I don't know. You don't have to act like you want me, Corr. That's not what I need."

"But I—I *do*—" He dropped his forehead to his palm. "What do you need?"

"Go back to normal. Think about the role, worry about your lines, be here because you're doing a job. You do yours; I'll do mine. We'll be fine."

"Except for the other guy who walks around inside me."

"Well, there is that."

"Give me a kiss before you leave," he said. "We might not have another chance."

She huffed, exasperated, then went to him. He embraced her and kissed her, and this one went better; with him sitting and her standing, they were well matched in height. This time she tasted desire and desperation, two things she felt, too. Eventually, he eased away from her and smiled. She smiled, too.

"Okay. I'll see you in the trailer at ten." She grabbed her bag and went into the bathroom to shower.

On her way down the back stairs ten minutes later, she ran into Blaise. They slipped out of the house in silence. Blaise walked away down the street in the early morning light, then glanced over her shoulder. "Come on," she said.

Opal followed her to a small but ornately gingerbreaded house in the next block. Blaise gestured her up the front porch steps. "Neil initially set me up with a room at the B&B, but I didn't want it," she said. "Didn't want to be housed with the movie people. Said it'd be too noisy. More fool I."

"So this is your lodging?"

"Right, a nice lady in her seventies with cats. A fan. Sickening, really, in a way, but handy, too. She always gets up and makes me breakfast if I'm here, no matter what time the

call's for. She made me a four A.M. breakfast one morning.
She stocks my favorite foods. I bet she'd be thrilled if I
brought another movie person to breakfast."

Opal raised her eyebrows.

"Yes, you're enough of a movie person to impress her.
Come on in." Blaise tapped on the door and opened it.
"Myrna?" Blaise called softly as she and Opal entered the
foyer. The walls were dark maroon with sparkles in the paint,
and a strange, complicated coatrack stood against the right
wall, with dangling garments hanging on it that looked a
little like the cult robes in the film. A large, fluffy, tabby-
striped cat stropped Opal's legs, purring. "You up?" Blaise
called.

"In the kitchen, dear," called a pleasant alto voice from the
back of the house.

"I've brought a friend. Is that all right?"

"Oh, who? Who?" A door flapped open in front of them.
A stout woman with short curls of bright, copper-washed
hair stood there in a gray silk dressing gown covered with
blue butterflies.

"This is Opal LaZelle, who does the creature makeup for
Forest," Blaise said. "Opal, Myrna Partridge, my excellent landlady. Myrna, is it too late for breakfast?"

"Too late? Of course not. I was hoping you'd make it
home in time." Myrna held the door open and they walked
past her into the kitchen, all white counters and yellow, flower-
sprigged wallpaper and sunny floor tile. A black cat clock
with wagging tail and shifting eyes ticked loudly on the wall
by the fridge. Everything looked unnaturally clean, considering there were six cat dishes on the floor near the back door,
each with a little kibble remaining, and three large water
dishes on the floor near the sink. "What's your pleasure this
morning, Blaise? My goodness, Ignatious certainly has taken
a liking to your friend."

The big tabby had followed them into the kitchen, where

he settled on Opal's feet. The cat's purrs were audible from the floor. He stared up at Opal with wide green eyes.

"Is there any more of that strawberry Special K?" Blaise asked.

"I bought a new box just yesterday," said Myrna, "and more skim milk for you."

"Thank you, Myrna. You're much too good to me," Blaise said.

Opal knelt and stared into the cat's eyes. Their green glow looked familiar. The cat licked her nose.

"Oh, please," she said.

He did it again, the rasp of a wet tongue against her nose. She sighed and stood up.

"What would you like for breakfast, dear?" Myrna asked.

"Cereal sounds good," said Opal. "Thanks so much, ma'am."

"You're so welcome." The landlady got down two large pottery bowls and poured cereal in one, eyebrows quirked as if to ask *how much?* Blaise held up her hand after only a little cereal had gone into her bowl. She took the bowl to the fridge and poured milk into it, then grabbed a couple of spoons from a drawer and returned to the kitchen table.

Opal waited until the bowl was half-full before cutting off the flow of cereal. "Okay if I get my own milk?" she asked.

"Surely. Help yourself." Myrna sat down at the table with a large mug of coffee. "If you want coffee, there's a full pot in the coffeemaker, and mugs in the cupboard above it. So you're making the Lapis monster?"

"Well, the monster for the movie, anyway."

"That creature is a local celebrity."

"Oh? Did the writers base him on an actual local legend? They didn't tell me. Are there any descriptions of him?"

"Tall and dark, they say, and he stalks the young girls. I remember when I was fifteen, all the girls talked about him, and none of us were allowed out alone at night. We had some shivery sleepovers, I can tell you."

"Did he have a name?" Opal asked. She poured milk onto the cereal and set the bowl on the table next to Blaise's place. Blaise handed her a spoon.

"There was something romantic we called him. Let me think." She sipped coffee, narrowed her eyes, and stared into the past. "So sad, it was. The Last of the Lost."

"Last of the Lost," Opal repeated.

"There was a girl I knew then—what was her name? Linda, I think—who felt sorry for the Last."

Opal got some coffee and sat beside Blaise. "What happened?"

"She had some idea that he was a sad and lonely creature someone had abandoned. This was the early fifties, and there were lots of things we didn't talk about. Linda never had us over to her house after school, and she came to school with bruises she never explained. She had a terrible time at home; I think that's why her heart went out to him. Anyway, at one of our sleepovers—now that I think about it, I remember she didn't make it to many of those; her mother didn't let her out of the house—she wanted us to sneak out the basement window and go to the forest with food for the Last. None of us would do it. We were all terrified. She snuck out after the rest of us went to sleep, and we never saw her again."

"Whoa," said Blaise.

"Was there a search?" Opal asked.

"Oh, yes. Everybody and their dogs were out in the forest looking for her. Somebody found her hair ribbon on a bush. Someone found a few bloodstains on those strange rocks out there in the clearing where you all are filming, but they looked old. I think some of the boys went out there and played weird games. Nobody who had a cat let it out of the house at night, I recall." Myrna drank more coffee, sleepwalked to the coffeemaker for a refill. "They said it wasn't the first time something like that happened. People went missing—that was why our parents were always telling us not to go out at night."

She settled in her chair. "Sometimes I envied Linda. I thought she went off somewhere and found another life, and it had to be better than here. Maybe she found someone to care about. Maybe someone did her in. I did think about that, too. Might have been better for her, either way.

"Even these days, I don't much sit on my porch after sunset. I'm still afraid of the night. I remember my husband and I went to Mexico on a trip one time, and there were all kinds of people out after dark, and music and drinking and dancing. It was like visiting another planet."

Opal ate cereal and drank coffee and thought about the Invader. "Why did you stay here?" she asked. "Why not move away?"

"Oh, well. I inherited this beautiful house, and it was all I ever knew, really. My husband and I both grew up here. He went away to college, but something scared him and he dropped out his junior year and came home. He worked in the gravel pit here ever since. Died last year." She shrugged. "I asked him what happened out there in the world, but he never did tell me. Boys do all right here, but we had no children, and not for lack of trying. If we'd had girls to look after, we might have made different choices."

"Can I ask you more about the Last of the Lost?" Opal said. "Did anybody ever know where he came from or why he was here?"

Myrna closed her eyes and thought. "Collected girls," she muttered. "Nobody ever said what he did with them, but it was probably about sex, which we never talked about, or murder, which we did talk about, but only from what we saw in the movies. Nobody ever found bodies or bits of them. We said the missing girls were runaways in the police reports. Why was he here? Well, because he'd always been here, forever and ever. Before there was a town, he was here. He was here because of the people who were here before." She opened her eyes, stared into Opal's eyes. "Isn't that odd? I don't think there *were* any people here before. Maybe Kalapuya Indians, but I don't think so."

"Opal, I've got to get to my seven thirty makeup call. I'm going to head over now," said Blaise.

Opal checked her watch. "Shoot. I better go, too. Mrs. Partridge, thanks so much for everything. Is there anybody else around who might be able to tell me more about this Last guy?"

"Old Bessie Gates at the Early Bird Bed-and-Breakfast, where you folks are filming. She's even older than I am, and she's lived here all her life. Haven't spoken to her in a long time, myself. Don't get along with her. But if anybody knows local history, she's the one."

"Thanks. Should I wash this?" Opal held up her bowl.

"No, no, don't worry about it. You kids just go. A pleasure, Opal."

"Likewise," said Opal. She grabbed her messenger bag and followed Blaise out.

"So that was quite the fishing expedition," Blaise said.

"You know there's something going on with Corvus," said Opal. "This is all background."

"You think the thing she was talking about is the thing that's taken him over and molded him into a better actor?"

"He could always act!" Opal said. "You are such a snot!"

Blaise laughed. "You're easy to tweak," she said.

"Why would you want to?" asked Opal.

"I need to find out who you are," said Blaise. "If we're arming for some kind of war, I like to know who I'm fighting with."

"Okay, maybe you're right. Who are *you*?" Opal asked.

"It's not that easy," said Blaise. "It's not my habit to get along with anyone, and I have my reasons for that."

"You're sleeping with the director, and suddenly you have more lines."

Blaise laughed again. "Sure. I want to shine in this picture. It has potential. People aren't expecting much, but some of the writing is sharp, and I must say, your work with Corvus, however it's happening, is quite astonishing. I wouldn't be surprised if you were nominated for an Oscar— or, I guess Dathan would get nominated for art direction, and take all the credit. Of course I'm angling to get more and better lines. Lauren's not good at guarding her territory. Right now, the picture has two leads, and I don't like that. I'd like to emerge the winner, the one people remember. The writing isn't quite aimed that way yet. But I can work it around."

"So you really are a bitch."

"Yep." She smiled. "We all would be, if we weren't so busy being nice. Let that be a lesson to you. You could use a little bitching up, too."

9

They arrived at the Makeup trailer. "Be right back," said Blaise. "Gotta make a pit stop." She headed toward the B&B.

Opal unlocked the trailer door. She figured she could nap in Corvus's chair until he arrived—that would be easier than sneaking back into the B&B or driving her little economy car back to the motel in Redford.

Lauren, Rod, Corvus, and Magenta were already in the trailer. Corvus sprawled in his chair, his reading glasses perched on his nose, a novel in his hands and one of her lights angled so it shone on the pages. He straightened.

Opal wondered why he hadn't gone either to his room or to his private dressing room in the trailer next door. Maybe he was feeling social. She said good morning to everyone and hopped up on the makeup counter to think about Blaise. She had seen principal actors behave in ways that led to increased roles for them, decreased roles for others, but she'd never had an actor be so up front about it. You were supposed to maintain an attractive surface.

Well, in public. Lots of stories made the rounds about stars whacking their personal assistants with phones or other handy objects. Opal had observed some bad behavior, experienced some herself, and heard many stories about much worse.

Corvus watched her. "Where'd you go?" he asked.

"I had breakfast with Blaise," she said.

He quirked both eyebrows.

Lauren was already in her clothes for the shoot. The fight Serena was having with Caitlyn today was apparently early in the picture, when Serena was still dressed in dowdy, repressed clothes—a khaki skirt, a bulky oatmeal-colored shirt with long sleeves—before her relationship with the Dark God opened her up to her dark side, and she went wild and vampy. She was in her chair, waiting for makeup. Magenta was still setting out her tools.

"How'd that happen?" asked Lauren.

"We were leaving the B&B at the same time," said Opal.

Magenta and Lauren looked at each other, then at Opal with varying degrees of dismay.

"Well, okay, I heard something like that was going on," said Lauren, "but I didn't want to believe it."

"Believe it," said Opal. "Corr said you mentioned rewriting last night, losing some of your lines, Blaise getting extra."

"Yeah. It makes sense now."

"She's angling for even more, Lauren. I hope you figure out how to handle this."

"I'll come up with something."

"Meanwhile, at breakfast, Blaise's landlady told us about a local monster that stalked women here in the fifties."

"What?"

"We need to ask the woman at the B&B about this. Blaise's landlady said she would know about the monster if anybody did."

"You could ask me," said Corvus, "sometime in the near

future." His voice was deeper than usual. He stared at the new face of the Dark God, on its life-mask head on Opal's counter where she had set it out the night before. She had already altered the rest of the stack of latex to add the horns and the other slight changes the Dark God had made, matching the rest of her mask supplies to the Polaroids, using magic without qualm because there was no other way around the continuity problems.

"I'll do that," said Opal. "You ready for this, Corr?"

He closed his eyes, sighed, and nodded. "Let's go. Wait. A kiss for luck first?"

She held his head between her hands and touched lips to his. He ringed her with his arm and drew her closer. She thought about what she had learned about him overnight, and some of it was funny and sad. She still loved him. Plus, he tasted wonderful, even flavored with coffee. At last he loosened his hold around her, and she pushed up and away.

She pressed the back of her hand against her mouth, as though to print his kiss on memory, and said, "Try to hang on while I'm doing this, okay?"

"I will."

She shaved him and moisturized him, and he watched her, smiling. "How can I not love somebody who treats me this way?" he asked as she mixed the adhesive.

"How many of your barbers have you fallen in love with?" she asked.

"All of them."

She lifted the brow piece and applied fresh adhesive to the back of it, then laid it carefully across his temple. She checked the Polaroid she had taken the night before and nudged it a little sideways, then lifted the second piece of leafy latex skin. By the time she turned around, his eyes had changed, and it was the Invader looking at her with most of Corvus's face. The effect was eerie. She hadn't seen him using Corvus's real features before. He looked almost natural there.

"Thanks," he said. "I respect your honor."

"Well," she said, and laid the next piece of his face on over Corvus's. "Are you an ancient entity?"

"I don't care to discuss that."

"Did you steal girls fifty years ago from this town?"

"Let's get to know each other better before I tell you my personal history," he said. "Where's my kiss?"

She wondered if she still had Flint's energy to shield her from him. It hadn't stopped her from kissing Corvus, or even sleeping with him. She held out her hand, trying to ignore the shudder in her flesh. He took it in hands she had just been embraced by and brought it close to his mouth. The burn of Flint's blessing heated her hand as the Invader drew her hand toward his mouth. "Clear a little space," she said to herself, reassured and again charmed by Flint's gift. She gave him the back of her hand to kiss, but then brought back the shield before she lost much energy to him.

"Strict," he said.

"We have work to do," she said. "If you're hungry, I'll get you food. Right now, let me finish putting on the mask, okay?"

He stared up at her, and leaves pushed up out of his skin, tracing themselves in the same paths as those on the mask she had made, changing his face from within.

"Don't!"

"It's more comfortable this way," he murmured.

She saw Lauren watching her and Corvus. Magenta watched in the mirror. She looked pale.

"Turn him back and let me do it my way," she said. "You have to be honorable, too, or I'll leave right now."

"You won't," he whispered. "You can't."

She set down her tools and walked toward the door.

The whisper followed her. "You'd leave him to me?"

She gripped the doorknob, turned it, and opened the door. He asked a good question, but she had to stay strong, or she might lose Corvus altogether. She stepped out of the trailer onto the landing. The door almost closed behind her before she heard the voice of the Invader.

"All right," he said. "Come back."

She stood on the landing under the overcast sky, savoring a brief moment of the other choice. Walk away from all of this. Never do this job again. Her mother still kept her room for her at home. It would drive Opal insane to live at home for any length of time, but she could rest there and figure out a different way to use her gifts, begin a whole new career. It wasn't too late.

Or, less dramatically, just get a job on a movie filming on another location.

Lose Corvus, with whom she was still hopelessly in love. There was a chance he would be back. Maybe she could increase the likelihood of that if she stuck around.

She turned and went back into the trailer.

Corvus looked like himself again except for the two pieces of prosthesis she had attached. His eyes had extra light in them, so she knew the one she loved wasn't present.

"I *will* walk," she said.

"I understand," said the Invader.

"All right, then." She went back to work, and he left the face in its natural state, letting her do the crafting to make it unnatural. She did not let even a little magic help her.

By the time she had almost finished fitting the Invader into his face and looked up again, Lauren was gone; Blaise had come and gone without her noticing; and the two girls who were playing Serena and Caitlyn as adolescents were in the chairs. Magenta was working on them; Rod was undoubtedly on the set with Blaise and Lauren.

"Have you met the girls yet?" Magenta asked Opal, her tone flattened.

"Not yet," said Opal. She dipped a brush in gilt, another in adhesive. She painted a thin outline around one of the leaves on Corvus's cheek and scattered gold over it. The Invader watched her, smiling. She checked his face against last night's Polaroid and decided he would do.

Opal called Kelsi, who said she'd bring Corvus's robe right over. There was something to be said for the convenience of a simple costume without changes. She wandered over to where Magenta was working.

"Hey, guys," Magenta said. "This is Opal. She's the creature wrangler. Opal, this is Gemma Goodwin and Bettina Lysander."

"Nice to meet you," Opal said.

"Hey," said the darker girl, slightly plump, who looked pretty much like a younger version of Lauren. She looked about twelve. Her voice was deep. "I'm Serena the younger, aka Gemma."

The other girl, who looked even younger, was a match for Blaise in cherubic beauty and silver-gilt crinkled hair. Maybe she also matched Blaise in temperament; she scowled at Opal, turned back to Magenta. "Yeah, so? Finish up, will you?"

"You're done," said Magenta.

Bettina slitted her eyes and glared at Magenta. "You spent ten more minutes on Gemma than on me. I'm telling."

"Please do."

Projecting anger with every motion, Bettina pushed herself up from the chair and stalked out of the trailer.

"Well, that was dramatic," said Gemma.

"It *is* nice to meet you," Opal said.

Gemma laughed. "Thanks."

Kelsi came in and stood beside Corvus's chair, not too close. Corvus rose and put on the robe. Kelsi hesitated, then fastened the star at his throat. He didn't reach to touch her, which relieved Opal's mind. Kelsi had reason to be skittish. He lowered his chin and smiled at Gemma.

"Whoa!" said Gemma, staring.

Opal said, "This is—what *is* your name?" Kelsi slipped out of the trailer.

"Isn't it Corvus Weather?" Gemma said in a slightly choked voice. "I've seen some of your work. I was going to say it was awesome, but I get the feeling this project's going to be different, and even more intense."

"I want a name to call him when he's in this state, because he doesn't act like Corvus," Opal said. "Is your name Last of the Lost?"

He smiled at her, his eyes glowing green and hot. She had not put the contacts on. That much costuming, she figured, she could leave to him. It gave her a quick way to know who was behind his eyes.

"That's a trifle cumbersome. I'll give you a name which isn't mine, but to which I'll answer. Phrixos."

"Phrixos," Opal repeated.

"Prick," said Magenta.

He glared at her. Her cheeks reddened. She gasped and turned away, her hand rising to hover near one cheek.

Opal gripped his arm. "Stop it."

"God!" said Gemma. "What was that?"

"Overreacting," said Opal. "Stop it, Phrixos. Magenta—"

"Damn, I keep forgetting," Magenta muttered. "All right. Phrixos. What the hell kind of name is that?"

"One I like," said the Invader. "Child, I am pleased to meet you." He held out a hand to Gemma.

"I'm scared to meet you," she said, and slowly placed her hand in his. He lowered his head, lifted her hand, kissed the back, a linger of lips, and she suddenly relaxed and smiled at him.

Before she could worry about Phrixos brainwashing a child, Opal's Ear crackled from its resting place around her neck. Magenta tapped her Ear. Opal put the Ear on. "Where are you people?" asked the assistant director.

Magenta checked her watch. "Shit."

Opal pressed the transmit button. "On our way," she said, and then, to the others, "Let's go." She grabbed her messenger bag and makeup suitcase and followed Gemma, Magenta, and Phrixos out of the trailer, and locked it behind them.

Magenta fell back to walk with her. "Figures the little princess would actually get to the set on time," she muttered. "Brownie points for her and demerits for the rest of us. Are my cheeks red?"

"Wait a sec." Opal had a spell she had used often on her younger siblings, a healing for scrapes, cuts, and bruises. She held her hands palms out near Magenta's face and murmured. The red faded.

"Wow. Lots better. Thanks, Opal."

"You're welcome. I think your nickname for him is right, but we can't use it when he can hear us," she muttered.

"Yeah. I get that. I'm a slow learner, but I learn."

The red light over the door to the soundstage was out. A security guard held the door open for them. They went to the backstage grouping of chairs near the clearing set. Bettina was already in her own chair, hunched tight and frowning, so that she looked more like an unpleasant old lady than a young girl. An older, baggier version of her sat in a nearby chair reading a fashion magazine.

"Gemma?" said a slender, dark-haired woman in another chair. "What was the delay?"

"Sorry, Mom," said Gemma, settling beside the woman. "This is Magenta, my makeup lady, and Opal, who does the Dark God makeup, and that's, uh—Phrixos? Everybody, this is my mom, Doreen Goodwin."

Phrixos came forward and held out his hand. "Corvus Weather," he said. "Pleased to meet the mother of such a talented child."

Gemma's mother did not look as pleased as Phrixos

sounded, but she was polite. "Nice to meet you. Please call me Doreen." She extended a hand to Phrixos, gave a slight shudder when he accepted it. He didn't try to kiss the back of her hand, which Opal thought was interesting.

"My pleasure." He glanced toward the woman who was apparently Bettina's mother. She didn't look up from her magazine. Phrixos smiled and sat in Corvus's chair.

"Hey," said Neil. "Lighting's up. Cast to the set for blocking rehearsal."

Gemma, Bettina, and Phrixos headed for the set. Opal slumped in Corvus's chair, hugging her messenger bag, and Magenta took the chair next to her, which had the name DIRK BAPTISTE on it. Dirk played the suspicious and *Twin Peaks*-ish sheriff in the film. Opal had never met him; Corvus had only one scene with him, tentatively scheduled to be filmed next week.

Craig Orlando sat in one of the other chairs. He smiled at Opal and Magenta.

Doreen sat in Gemma's chair and stared at Magenta.

"What is it, Mrs. Goodwin?" Magenta asked.

"Why do you choose to look so strange when your job is to make people beautiful?" she asked.

"Because I don't have to be in front of the camera. I can look any way I want," said Magenta, smoothing back her heavy black and pink hair. "I did a fine job with your daughter, didn't I?"

"Yes," said Doreen. "I was just wondering. If your job is—"

"Yes, but I already got the job, ma'am. I don't have to keep interviewing for it. This is the me I feel like being now." She ran her fingers through her hair and smiled.

"Ah." Doreen subsided.

Magenta got a pad of paper out of her duffel and wrote, *Was that weird, or is it just me?* She slid the pad into Opal's lap.

It was weird, Opal wrote back. She rose and set her messenger bag in Corvus's chair. "I'm going to check the camera," she said.

"Me, too," said Magenta. They went over to the Props area and joined Joe at his monitor. The camera was set for the master shot, showing everything. Bettina and Gemma sat on the altar stone, side by side, Bettina looking fierce, Gemma hesitant. Phrixos stood at the head of the stone, face-to-face with them. They spoke, but the monitor had no sound. Opal mouthed the lines, having memorized them from practice with Corvus the night before.

"Louder," said Magenta, and Opal whispered them a little louder, lip-synching as well as she could.

"This scene's new, huh?" Joe said after the first run-through.

"Yep."

"Creepy as hell. The more they write on this, the worse it gets. Only good thing about this scene, no props to manage, and I still get paid."

"Hey," said Opal. It was true. All she saw in the camera's view were the actors and the standing stones. The stones were set decoration. The actors didn't pick up or move anything in this scene. Although they did interact with the stones—touch them, sit on them. No knives or cups or censers or braziers. Daylight in the forest—a whole different animal from the night rituals.

Opal left the Props area and edged around the backdrop of photographed forest to watch Phrixos as he ran through the scene with the girls. No doubt about it, he looked the part, and he gave her the creeps. In the script, he didn't actually seduce the underage girls, but he was asking them for a commitment to belong to him in later life. "Handmaiden," whatever the hell that was supposed to be. Damn it, Travis had used it after all. Phrixos was infecting her brain, and she was infecting the writers.

He had been infecting the writers all along.

"A little more hunger, Caitlyn. A little more revulsion, Serena," said Neil.

"But I don't—" Gemma said.

Phrixos placed his palm on her forehead. She blinked in confusion. "What?"

"You're supposed to be more afraid of me," he said, his voice low and thrilling.

"But I—"

"You fear me," he murmured, "you resist me, you are fascinated by me."

Her face changed as he spoke. Fear dawned, and she couldn't look away from him. She did not blink.

"Thanks for the direction, Corvus," the director said dryly. Phrixos smiled at Neil as though taking his remark at face value. "All right, we're almost ready to shoot. Last looks!" he said.

Opal got her bag, and she, Craig, and Magenta went to the set.

Phrixos knelt and stared into her eyes. As always, his makeup looked perfect, if that was what it was. "I'm hungry," he whispered.

"You pick now to tell me?" she whispered back. She dug an energy drink out of her bag. "It's not very cold."

"You know that's not what I want," he said.

She studied her hand. She could almost see the flaming shield Flint had given her, still strong after a day—self-sustaining, or was she feeding it? Either way, she was grateful for this warm invisible cocoon. She stroked her smallest finger until it emerged from its shelter. It felt strangely bare. She curled the other fingers toward her palm.

He leaned forward and took her finger in his mouth. The touch of his tongue, his lips, was strangely erotic. She felt the draw on her magical energy, and that was erotic, too, the mother's power to feed another from her body.

"What are you doing?" whispered Bettina. She sounded appalled.

Opal felt a little faint. She touched Phrixos's face as though redrawing one of his cheek leaves and slid her finger from his mouth. His eyes glowed brighter than they had, and he smiled.

"Thank you, my handmaiden."

"Hey. She's not your handmaiden. I am," said Bettina.

"Save it for the take," said Neil. "Come on, people, let's get to work! Clear the set. Starting marks. Okay. We're on bell . . ."

Opal joined Magenta and Joe at the Props monitor and watched the scene come alive. Now that the actors were projecting, they could hear the lines. Gemma went through a series of emotions. Opal found her so fascinating she couldn't look at Bettina or Phrixos.

"Wow," muttered Magenta. "She's really good."

"She's in a trance."

"Prick can hypnotize other people into acting, too?"

"Apparently."

"Cut. Good work," said Neil after the second bell had rung. "Got it in one, people. Print that. Take a break while we light for close-ups."

The actors came off the set. Someone went outside and summoned the stand-ins.

Phrixos claimed Corvus's chair. Gemma's mother tugged Gemma toward a chair beside hers. The woman who might be Bettina's mother took her a little way off and lectured her. She didn't go far enough that everyone couldn't hear every word she said. "I saw the whole thing on the Casio," she said, "and that girl stole the scene. What's the matter with you?"

"She has better lines," Bettina said.

"You're making excuses."

"What do you expect me to do? She has the interesting part."

"There are no small parts, only small—"

"Minds," said Phrixos.

The woman glared at him. "This is a private conversation," she said.

"Perhaps you should take it farther away," he said. Then his voice silkened. "Perhaps you should leave the child alone. She gave an adequate performance."

"Adequate is not good enough," said the woman.

"Cast back to the set," called one of the A.D.s. "Last looks."

They all went to the altar, except for the mother and the maybe mother. As she touched up the powder on Gemma's nose, Magenta muttered, "Who is that woman, and why is she tormenting Bettina?"

"That's her on-set guardian," Gemma said. "I forget her name. She's always mean, and she torments our tutor, too."

"Shut up," said Bettina, beside Gemma. "You don't know anything."

"What, you *like* the way she treats you?"

"She wants what's best for me."

"Clear the set," called Neil. "Let's go, camera two."

Back in the chairs, Magenta got out an *InStyle* magazine and flipped quietly through it. Opal thought about watching the Props monitor again, but ended up curled up in Corvus's chair instead. Doreen came and sat beside her. The woman took a small pad of paper out of her purse and wrote a note on it, then shoved it in Opal's face.

What is that man doing to my daughter?

Opal took the pad and pen. She wasn't sure what to write. Finally she settled on *Coaching her.*

I don't like the way it looks. Is he a Svengali?

Opal tapped the pen on the pad. She couldn't remember how the movie had turned out. *I don't know. Maybe. ???* she wrote.

Don't you leave him alone with my daughter.

Opal stared at the note, then snatched the pen and wrote, *I can't control him.*

I see how he treats you. He's more interested in you than anyone else. Keep him on a leash.

Opal shook her head. *He's the one pulling strings.*

Doreen clutched the pen and pad in her hands, stared at the backdrop separating them from the set. Her hands tightened until the pad bowed. Finally, she wrote, slowly, *Do what you can? Please. Help my daughter.*

If I can, I will.

"Cut," yelled the director. Two bells rang. "Print. Good work, people! Caitlyn, you're a little stiff; let's do another one. Relax. Don't be the actor playing the girl. Be the girl."

"Yes sir."

Phrixos's voice murmured something, and Bettina murmured something in response. A moment's silence.

"Last looks," called someone, and Magenta, Craig, and Opal headed for the set.

Phrixos was kissing the back of Bettina's hand this time. She stared into his eyes.

The director grabbed Opal's arm as Opal passed her. "Is the monster schizo?" he whispered.

"Not exactly. More like multiple personality," Opal whispered.

"Damn it. This upsets me. But it's working on film. Damn it! Nobody told me!"

"It's a recent development."

Neil blew air out through his nostrils, a subvocal snort. "Rein him in."

"How? Why does everybody think *I* can control him?" Opal's whisper came on a gush of breath.

"You're sleeping with him."

"In a master-servant way," Opal muttered.

"Oh? Damn. That's no help. Anyway, do what you can, will you?"

"I already am, and it's not a whole lot."

Neil released Opal and pushed her toward the set.

Opal went to Phrixos. He leaned forward. "Trouble?" he muttered, and for a second she felt comforted by his concern, as though she had a coconspirator.

Then she remembered what everybody was complaining about. "You're creeping everybody out, and they want you to stop it."

He smiled, and his eyes glowed brighter. "Don't worry," he said, but not in a way that convinced her. "Things will fall into place."

"And then what?"

"You'll see."

10

He dropped a brief kiss on her cheek—no draw, only a touch—then turned her by her shoulders and aimed her off the set with a push on her rear. She stumbled two steps, then whirled and walked backward as she studied him. She hadn't touched him up again. If it were Corvus, that kiss on the cheek would have mandated some kind of makeup repair, and so might the swat on the butt, but Phrixos was fine.

In the next take, Bettina and Gemma gave fantastic performances, and Phrixos was superb.

"Cut and print," Neil said. "Now we need some hand shots. Off the set, everybody! We need to reset the cameras."

———————

They wrapped early, around eight in the evening. They had shot every shot listed on that day's schedule, and, partly because of Phrixos's influence on the young actresses, they had shot fewer takes. Everything seemed aligned to give the best results. Neil had consulted with the production manager about whether they should try something that wasn't scheduled, but each scene took hours to set up. A production assistant came by with call sheets and script revisions for tomorrow as the actors headed toward the Makeup trailer or the Wardrobe trailer to escape the people they had been playing all day.

Opal hadn't found a minute to call her family. She only thought of doing it when a scene was shooting or when she was summoned to the set. She had spaced it during lunch, worn out by wondering what could go wrong next. Plus, Phrixos had drained her with another kiss, despite the new power collecting she had been doing. She needed to collect even more energy, but she hadn't found time and space to do the necessary meditations. Tonight, she promised herself.

Phrixos followed Opal into the Makeup trailer. She wondered if he would leave Corvus's body tonight, or if she had another fight on her hands. She didn't want to spend any more time with him than she had to.

He had taken the call sheet before she could look at it, and was studying it as she nudged him toward the chair. She had been fighting him all day and was tired of the constant energy it required. She'd look at the call sheet later.

Lauren waited in one of Rod's chairs, looking rumpled, unmade up, and worried. Bettina and Gemma came in and sat down, Bettina glaring at the older actress, but there were enough chairs for everybody. Rod and Magenta went to work taking off the girls' makeup.

Lauren didn't seem to notice Bettina's irritation. She didn't even pay attention to Phrixos; her look was all for Opal.

Opal settled Phrixos in his chair. "Go on," he said. "Check with her." He leaned back and closed his eyes, call sheet and script pages—pale blue this time—in a loose pile on his lap.

"Thanks." She felt again the momentary and confusing sense of collaborating with the enemy. Why did she trust him even to this extent? She needed to, she guessed. She went to Lauren and took her hands. "What's wrong?" she murmured.

"Norman's here, and I can't get the brush to work. I forgot what you told me about it."

"How'd he get on set?"

"He's not, really, but he's found a place to stay in town, and he's lurking outside every time I walk across to the B&B."

"Has he approached you yet?"

"I've been shadowing Blaise, and she's shadowing Aldridge, so we're always surrounded by people. Traveling in a pack is more tiring than you'd think. Plus some of the pack keep breaking away and I can't figure out who to follow. So the answer is no, but now we're done for the day and I need to go home and rest, which makes me feel vulnerable. Also I'm starving. Did you try that pasta at lunch? Could anything taste more like glue and Styrofoam?"

"It was bad," Opal said. "Okay, you relax here and I'll see what I can do with the big guy."

"Thanks." Lauren sighed and dug through a hobo-style purse, produced a battered paperback romance.

Opal returned to Phrixos. She tugged the papers out of his grasp and set them on the counter.

"Lauren is in danger?" he asked.

"Do you remember about that?" asked Opal. "You learn what Corvus knows, right? He heard about her stalker last night at dinner."

The green glow in his eyes dimmed a fraction as he looked inward. Then he returned and stared up at her. "I remember now." He gripped the arm of his chair as though to rise.

"What?" said Opal.

"The man is a gnat. I can dispose of him."

"No disposing, all right? Not that I know exactly what you mean by that. If you could send him off to mind his own business, that would be good. No murdering, all right?"

"You prefer he leaves here alive?" said Phrixos.

"I insist on it," she said. A chill shivered in her shoulders. She had been frightened of Phrixos before, but hadn't let herself think about whether he was truly dangerous.

He smiled at her, the leaves shifting on the planes of his face until he looked truly demonic.

"Stop that," she said.

He raised his eyebrows, but he still looked scary. She grabbed the Polaroid and took some continuity pictures, dated and time-stamped them with a Sharpie. In the process, Phrixos's face relaxed back into the role of supernatural monster, losing its disturbingly human cunning.

Good. Phrixos responded to routine.

Opal got out the solvents that would loosen the adhesive on his face.

"I could approach him as I am now," he said before she started removing the top layer of appliances.

"You think he's going to be scared of a costume? He's a professional. Relax. Nothing's going to happen right away, except I'm going to take off your mask, okay? Then we're going to dinner."

"Whom do you want to escort you?" he asked.

Was this an opening? Could she just ask for Corvus and get him back? How useful would Corvus be in dealing with Norman? Corvus had physical presence; he worked out. Opal had never heard of him getting into fights with anyone.

On the other hand, maybe Phrixos really could solve their problem in a nonlethal way. He had certainly hypnotized people into doing his bidding on the set today and yesterday. Possibly he could give Norman a mental twist that would keep him away from Lauren forever.

"You," Opal said. She tried not to be disturbed by the smile he kept all through his unmasking and subsequent cleansing and moisturizing.

By the time she restored him to Corvus-normal, everyone

had left the trailer except for her, Phrixos, and Lauren. As Phrixos buttoned himself into Corvus's shirt, Opal packed her messenger bag, stuffing call sheet and script pages in, in addition to everything else she imagined she might need. Their call for tomorrow was five A.M. The weather was supposed to clear so that they could film in the forest. This was an early scene, the coven in the forest summoning the Dark God, and involved Gemma and some actors Opal hadn't met yet, including Ariadne Orullian, the woman who played Caitlyn and Serena's mother; this was her bloody death scene.

Five A.M.. They had left the set on time and a half, since the shoot plus makeup application and removal had taken eleven hours. First three hours of tomorrow would be time and a half until they reached turnaround. Well, a person had to take advantage of the weather when the opportunity arose. They'd been waiting to shoot on the forest set for too long already. It was possible they would shoot a piece of the scene with Dark God and Lauren on the altar rock if the light held out, her "come to the dark side" scene.

Lauren was curled up in the chair, the book in her lap, her eyes shut and her mouth slightly open, soft snores coming out. Opal shook her shoulder gently and she gasped and sat up. "Huh?"

"Let's go to supper," said Opal.

Lauren looked up at Phrixos, narrowed her eyes. "Who are you?"

"Phrixos."

"Have you been that before?"

"That's his Scary Dark God name. It's not his real name," Opal said, "but it comes in handy."

"Oh. Okay. So anyway, not Corvus. How come you're not Corvus?"

"Opal asked me to stay," he said, and smiled his demon grin. "I understand you have a problem with someone. I can help you deal with it in ways he can't."

"Why would you?"

"I protect my own."

"I'm not yours," she said.

"Do you wish to test that assertion?"

"Stop arguing," said Opal, "and let's go take care of this guy."

"Wait a sec," said Lauren. "How do we plan to do that? Norman creeps me out, but I'm not ready for full-scale violence."

"It would solve your problem," said Phrixos.

"Not going to work for me," Lauren said.

"Opal says the same thing. It's a timid generation you are. Very well. I will settle for a less permanent solution, and merely persuade him away."

"Okay. Thanks."

"First I want a kiss."

"What?" She shrank back. "No."

"Payment in advance. What's wrong with that?"

"You gonna knock me out the way you did Kelsi?"

"I won't," he said.

"I'll be able to walk and talk and think afterward?"

Phrixos sighed. "Very well."

"I don't like you," she said. He smiled gently, cupped the back of her head in his hand, and leaned forward to press his lips to hers, gently, gently, working slowly up to more pressure. Lauren stood passive at first, her eyes closed. Her hands crept up to grip his shirt. Their mouths engaged more fully, and Lauren's posture softened.

Opal struck Phrixos on the back of the head with the flat of her hand. "Stop that!"

He pulled away from Lauren, licked his lips, grinned sideways at Opal. "Jealous?"

"Oh, please," said Opal.

Lauren moaned, opened her eyes. She looked dazed. She

blinked, shook her head. "You are so—" she said, her voice rising with each word.

"Tasty? Helpful? Pleasurable?"

"Infuriating."

Phrixos laughed. "You, on the other hand, are another source of pure pleasure. Let's go." He threaded her arm through his and went to the door, helped Lauren down the steps. They left the trailer-laden parking lot with its saggy insta-fence and a guard sheltering under an overhang on one of the Star Waggons from the constant misty drizzle. As they crossed the street toward where Hitch had parked the car, a form detached itself from one of the droopy-branched evergreens in the town square and came toward them.

"Norman," said Lauren. She gripped Phrixos's arm more firmly. Opal came up on his other side, and he crooked an elbow so she could hang on him, too. What the hell. This was why she endured his presence without protest. She hooked her arm through his.

The man walked into the light of the nearby streetlamp, staring at Lauren's face. He had an engaging best-friend type of face, not leading man; slightly disheveled and good-humored, friendly blue eyes and a wide smile. His bangs flopped half over his eyes. "Evening," he said.

"Norman," said Lauren.

"Lauren."

"What are you doing here?"

"Well, waiting for you, I guess."

"I told you to stop that," she said. "It's over, Norman. Find someone new."

"It's not that easy." He came closer. "There's no one else." He bent to peer at her. "No one else is you."

"Well, okay, I'll live with that hypothesis. I'm the only me. And I'm telling you to leave me alone, Norman. Seriously. Get over it and move on."

He smiled as though that would change things. Opal, an educated observer, had to admit that he had an excellent and inviting smile.

"I'm not ready," he said. "I can't stop thinking about you, Lauren. You won't leave my mind. I need you."

"I don't need you, and I don't want you," said Lauren. "Do you hear me?"

He shook his head. "I hear you, but I don't believe you."

"Phrixos," Lauren said.

"Come here, little man," Phrixos said, his voice gentle and rich.

Norman backed up a step. "I'm not getting in range of those fists of yours. I'm besotted, not insane."

"I won't hit you. I just want to shake the hand of the man who recognizes treasure when he sees it."

"I'm not touching you," said Norman.

"Very well. I'll touch you, then." Phrixos eased out from between the women. In one stride, he stepped into Norman's breathing space, crowding him. He cupped his hands around Norman's head, tilted it back until Norman was staring up at his face. Norman shoved at Phrixos's chest, but the taller man didn't budge, even when Norman pounded on him. "Quiet," Phrixos said, his voice gentle and thrilling. Norman slowed and stopped, hung limply in Phrixos's grasp.

"Good," said Phrixos. "Listen to me. Hear me. Your memory and desire for this woman fade. They seep away. She is not in your blood. She is not in your brain. You do not need or want her. She is just another woman you worked with once. A pleasant acquaintance, nothing more. You have somewhere else to go, something else to do. She leaves your mind and you find another star to fix on. Say it."

"She is not in my blood. She is not in my brain," Norman whispered.

"You release her from your thoughts and let her go her own way."

"I release her," he muttered, almost too low to hear.

"You are content."

"I am content."

Phrixos lowered his hands from Norman's head to his shoulders, stabilized him. "Are you all right?" he asked.

Norman shuddered, shook his head as though he could cast off thoughts like water, and said, "Okay."

"Can you stand?"

"Okay."

Phrixos lowered his hands. Norman swayed a moment, then found his feet. "What am I doing here?" he asked.

"We don't know. You were following us," said Phrixos.

"I was? Where are we?" He glanced around at the nearby forest, the mist, the night. He looked closer to home. "Hi, Lauren. Who are you?" he asked Phrixos, ignoring Opal. "You were in a horror movie, right?"

"Several. We're in Oregon, shooting a movie, but you're not in it. You just showed up here. Where's your home?"

"Los Angeles." Norman frowned and got out his wallet, checked the currency compartment, pulled out some receipts. "Looks like I ate at an IHOP this morning, but I don't remember it at all. Here's a keycard for a hotel, the Bugle Arms. Wonder which room I have. What time is it?" He looked at his watch. "That late?" He glanced around. "I don't know what's the matter with me. Maybe I'm having a psychotic break. What's the date?"

Lauren said, "November seventh."

Norman looked confused, unfocused. "I've lost a week. Last thing I remember was calling the airline to book a flight. Guess I was coming here, but I don't know why."

"Maybe there are clues in your hotel room," Lauren said. "What are you driving?"

Opal tried to remember what kind of car had followed her last night when they left the restaurant, but it had been dark.

Norman reached into his pocket, came up with a key attached to a plastic tag with writing on a slip of paper inside: Enterprise Rent-A-Car, and SILVER CAPRICE LIC. # KKO 951.

"Huh," said Norman.

Lauren glanced around at nearby cars. She pointed. The Caprice was parked down the block from the B&B. They strolled over and checked the license plate. The numbers matched. Norman unlocked the passenger-side door and looked in. A litter of fast-food wrappers and white paper bags with a doughnut shop logo emblazoned on their sides lurked in wadded disarray in the footwell, and on the seat were a pair of binoculars, three bottled waters, a half-eaten sandwich falling out of its paper wrapper, a notebook with crabbed blue ballpoint handwriting in it, and a handheld digital recorder.

"Jeez," said Norman. "What the hell have I been doing?"

Opal reached in and snatched the notebook and recorder.

"Hey!" Norman said.

"I'm pretty sure you don't need these anymore," she said.

"How would you know? Have we even met? If that stuff belongs to me, I want it back."

"No, you don't," Phrixos said, a hand on Norman's shoulder.

"I sure do. Are you people robbing me?"

Phrixos rested a hand on Norman's head again, only this time Norman sidestepped. "Quit touching me! What are you, a pervert?"

"That and much more," said Phrixos, gripping Norman's shoulder in one hand and his head in another. He aimed Norman's eyes toward his own again, and stared down with that peculiar intensity. "Let go of any records you have of Lauren. She's just someone you know, not someone you obsess about. You don't need anything you wrote down or spoke about her. Let it go. Repeat that."

"Let it go," Norman whispered.

"You feel all right, and you don't suspect us of any ill intentions toward you. You feel we are your friends."

"You're my friends."

Opal slipped the notebook and recorder into her messenger bag.

"You remember what number your room is in the hotel, and where it is. You remember a creative reason why you came up here that has nothing to do with Lauren. Maybe you're researching something for your career. Understand?"

"Yeah," said Norman.

"Good," said Phrixos. He stroked Norman's hair, then released him again.

Norman shuddered and said, "Where were we?"

"Hard to tell," said Phrixos. "You ready to go back to your hotel now?"

"Yeah. I feel tired. Can't remember what I've been doing, but I'm worn out."

"We'll see you later," Phrixos said, and gave Norman's shoulder a little shove.

"All right. Good night." Norman slammed the passenger door shut and rounded the car to climb in behind the steering wheel.

Opal stood beside Phrixos in the cold evening air and watched Norman drive away. When the car turned a corner and the taillights were no longer visible, Lauren let out a sigh.

"I don't know that that is permanent," said Phrixos, one arm dropping to lie across Lauren's shoulders, the other resting on Opal's. "I didn't want him to forget forever, because there might be something in his memory we need later. Also, I'm low on energy right now. I could do a better job if you would feed me more."

"Quit whining," said Opal. "You drew from him, didn't you?"

He laughed and squeezed her shoulder. "A little. He can't

supply the quality of energy I get from either of you. So, Lauren, a kiss as thanks?"

"Must I? I'm tired, too."

"I see I have not sufficiently impressed you with my awesome majesty," Phrixos said, but it was hard to tell whether he was joking. "In any case, my internal self grows restless, so I'll say good night. Opal." He bent and pressed his lips to hers, and she let him, because no matter how tired she was, she was glad he had solved Lauren's problem, even if only temporarily. When his lips touched hers, though, he jerked back, and she realized Flint's shield of fire was still working, bless the boy for giving her weird energy that didn't get used up. She thought her lips free of the shield and reached for Phrixos, pulled him down and kissed him, sending him some of the extra power she had collected during the day.

He moaned with delight and drew more, but just when she was going to struggle and stop him, the draw halted; his taste changed, and so did his posture. She was kissing Corvus, who held her closer, then finally raised his head and looked around. "What a nice way to wake up," he said. The green glow in his eyes had dimmed but not extinguished. "What are we doing now?"

"Solving Lauren's stalker problem, at least for the moment."

"Oh?"

"Let's get food," she said, and they headed back to the lot by the supermarket/soundstage where Hitch had left the Lincoln. On the drive to the IHOP, Opal brought Corvus up to speed on the Dark God's new name, Phrixos's behavior on the set with the girls, and his confrontation with Norman.

"He wanted to kill him?" Corvus asked as Opal parked on the edge of the IHOP lot.

"He didn't exactly say that," said Opal.

"But he implied it," Lauren said.

"Do you think he could?" Corvus asked. He held the restaurant door for them as they went in.

Tonight a different waitress seated them, a small, young brunette with black-framed glasses, a narrow smile, and a mouthful of chewing gum. "Hi, Erin. Jenny off tonight?" Corvus asked.

"Yeah." The girl glanced down at her nametag, as though confirming her name was Erin. "You guys in the movie?"

"Sure," said Corvus.

"Cool. This table all right?" She showed them to a table for four, not the corner booth they'd been in the last two nights.

"Sure."

Opal hesitated to look around, wondering whether she would see someone she knew and get drawn into someone else's drama. She had plenty of her own. She hadn't seen any of the cast or crew's rental cars in the lot, but that didn't necessarily mean no one was here. It was a short walk from the crew hotel to the IHOP.

She saw only strangers. She sat facing the door, and Corvus seated himself beside her, Lauren on his other side. After the waitress asked them about beverages and went to get them, Corvus leaned forward, inspiring the women to lean forward, too. "Do you think he could kill someone?" he repeated.

"We don't know enough about him," said Lauren.

"This morning one of the town old-timers told me a story about a monster who used to haunt Lapis during the fifties," Opal said, then remembered she had mentioned this to both of them that morning. "He was called the Last of the Lost, and he stole young girls. Nobody ever found any bodies though. Plus, it's one of those stories you tell tourists to make your town more interesting. But what if there's some truth to it?"

"Did you ask him?"

"Yeah. He only answers questions when he feels like it."

"We need you to be more active," Lauren said. "Be our spy. Pay attention to what he's thinking. Were you awake at all today?"

"I was asleep again the whole day," he said. "I kissed Opal in the morning, and then I woke up kissing her in the evening. Nice, but odd."

"Your eyes are still glowing," Opal said, "so I think Phrixos is still awake. Can you tell?"

"What?" He sat back, stared beyond her, then looked up at the ceiling. He put his hands on his cheeks, touched his lips. He held his palm in front of his eyes and stared, as though looking for a reflection of the glow. Frowning, he lowered his hand.

Opal dug a mirror compact out of her bag and presented it to him. "Take a look."

He stared into the little mirror, blinked at his own green-enhanced eyes. "You left the contacts in."

"Didn't use them today."

"That's eerie," said Lauren. "I never noticed."

"I think you're blending now, Corr, and you should stop pretending you're not. Phrixos, are you present?"

Corvus frowned. He looked so like himself and so unlike Phrixos she felt like backing down, but she changed her mind. They needed to know who they were talking with.

"I don't feel like he's here," said Corvus at last. "Still, there's the evidence of my eyes. Maybe we should talk about something else. Lauren, how did your day go?"

The waitress came and took their order, and then Lauren talked about the fight scene she had shot with Blaise that day. "Neil yelled at both of us equally. The writers were there, and he made them rewrite a piece of the scene so Blaise lost a couple of lines. They both seemed kind of irritable."

"I wonder what's going on," said Opal. "Tonight, I'll try a

glass against the wall to see if I can hear them better. Trouble in paradise?"

"They have my corruption scene scheduled for tomorrow afternoon if you guys can finish up with the kids on time," Lauren said, "which, considering how things are going so far, seems likely. Did you look at the pages?"

"I did," said Corvus.

"It's mostly the same as it was before, but we have one set of rewritten lines," Lauren said. "I asked Travis to do it, because there was a jawbreaker line in there. I think your line's the same, though."

"Yes. 'What do you *really* want?'" he quoted, in Phrixos's voice, thrilling, deep, and compelling.

"I want to be discovered by you movie people, get a role in the film, and then run away with you to Hollywood," said Erin the waitress as she set salads down in front of them. "Oh, God. Did I say that out loud?" She flushed and darted away.

"Interesting," said Corvus, looking after her. "I have the power to cloud women's minds. *Moo hoo hahahah!*"

Opal thumped his arm with her fist. "Don't laugh about it, big guy. What if it's true?"

He smiled the big goofy smile she considered pure Corvus, light dancing in his eyes, then sobered when she didn't smile back. "I pledge to use my powers for good."

"That's nice," said Lauren, "but I don't think it stops the other guy from using them for whatever he wants. What do you think *he* really wants?"

Corvus stared at his salad, his brow furrowed. He stroked a spiral pattern on his forehead with the first two fingers of his right hand. Finally he shook his head. When he looked up, his eyes had no extra light in them. "There's something there, but I can't get hold of it. It's red, though."

11

Before she drove them back to Lapis for the night, Opal stepped outside with her phone and called the family again. Her mother answered, peevish at the late hour. "There wasn't a single other time you could try us?" she demanded.

"I'm sorry, Mom."

"Yes, well, all right. Tobias considered your case and threw some auguries and said it's serious, but he can't leave until tomorrow. He'll fly to Portland and find some way to get where you are. He got Gypsum to MapQuest it for him. Expect him tomorrow night. You'll have to leave word with security."

"Did he get a cell phone yet?"

"He refuses to carry something on his person that concentrates signals from the ether," said her mother. "You'll just have to let him find you."

"If you see him before he leaves, please tell him thank you for me."

"I will." Her voice softened. "Opal, call anytime if the need is great. Call if you need reinforcements. We'll find some way to work it out."

"Thanks, Mom." She had to hang up before she started crying. For years she'd been handling her own problems. She felt silly going to the family for help when she wasn't even sure it was real trouble. It surely felt good to know someone else was concerned, though.

In the restaurant, Corvus was paying the bill again, smiling at Erin, who blushed while waiting for credit card approval.

"We ran through our scenes for tomorrow while you were outside," said Lauren. "Any satisfaction from your phone?"

"My uncle's coming tomorrow night."

"*Brujo?*"

"*Sí.*"

"*Bueno.*"

"Your *abuela?*" Opal asked.

Lauren shook her head. "She's sending me some charms to protect me, but she doesn't feel well enough to travel."

Opal drove them back to Lapis and let Lauren off at the house where she was staying, then parked the Lincoln in the guarded lot by the soundstage and walked Corvus back to the B&B. She lingered on the sidewalk in front of the building, and he stood beside her. Together they stared up at the front of the Victorian building with its tooled gingerbread eaves and strange bits sticking out where modern houses were smooth. The house was pale in the streetlight, with darker trim. No lights shone inside; lace curtains draped the lower floor's windows like an arrested fall of flour, hiding the interior.

"You coming up?" Corvus asked in a low rumble. He stood near her but didn't touch her.

Tonight the house didn't purr, but she still had the sense that something coiled inside it, and that the front door was a mouth that would swallow her and Corvus. She gripped his hand, and his fingers closed gently around hers. When she looked up, she saw green glow in his eyes. "Once we go in, we can get out again, right?" she said.

"You're safe with me," he said, using his Dark God voice.

"I don't believe that at all." Yet somehow she felt reassured.

He laughed and released her hand. "Stay the night or don't, my dear; it's your choice."

She had left her toiletries bag in his room after her shower that morning, unsure of anything, though it wasn't exactly a lifelong commitment. The hotel where most of her things were gave her fresh shampoo, soap, and conditioner every day in tiny plastic bottles, and she could always get a toothbrush and toothpaste from a nearby 7-Eleven, or even the front desk.

She glanced up at his face, saw the rueful smile that always captivated her, the faint tilt to the eyebrows indicating a person waiting for an answer. The glow was gone again.

"I'd like to," she said.

His hand rested on her shoulder, then, the heat of it welcoming and welcome, and they walked up the flagstone path together. He let her into the house. This time they got all the way to his room without rousing the director or anyone else.

"Wait here," he whispered at the threshold, then crossed the dark room and turned on the bedside light. He nodded and she came in and eased the door shut, locked it. The atmosphere was different in the room tonight; the light lower, and no sense of tiredness or settling for comfort.

Corvus picked up the alarm clock and set it, placed it on the bedside table again, then only looked at her, most of him in silhouette with the lamp almost behind him. She stepped away from the door without speaking. Her breath quickened as she kicked off her shoes, dropped her messenger bag on the couch, and went to him. His huge hands were gentle and deft, the knuckles brushing her breasts as he unbuttoned her shirt. She worked his belt free of its buckle. Only their breaths sounded in the room, ragged and harsh, along with the small thuds of discarded garments dropping to the floor.

Everything that followed had its own logic and rhythm. She ended up drowsing across him afterward, riding the rise and fall of his chest, one of his hands resting on the small of her back. He pulled the covers up over them and was gone into sleep like a candle snuffed out.

The alarm woke them far too early, while the sky was still dark. Corvus groaned, a sound and a vibration against her cheek. She lay soaking in his warmth, comfort, and scent, until he finally rumbled, "Opal? I think we better get going," and she remembered where and who she was.

They shared the shower and brushed teeth beside each other, dressed out in the open space of his room. She was on her third day with this set of clothes; they stank. She glanced at Corvus to make sure his back was turned, then ran her clothes through a Refreshing Spell, and stroked pale green into the shirt.

"We don't have time to go anywhere but here for breakfast," Corvus said, and she checked her watch. Almost four fifteen A.M., and they had to be in the Makeup trailer at the location by five. "Bessie sets out coffee and toast and cereal and juice. Sometimes more, if she's feeling perky. Neil or George will have told her we're getting up early today."

"Okay."

Neil and Blaise were in the dining room when they arrived. None of them spoke. Neil had a plateful of scrambled eggs and sausages, things Corvus hadn't mentioned in his menu report, and Blaise had a big mug of coffee and a piece of dry toast.

Opal got coffee and a buttered English muffin from an array of food on the sideboard. She sat at the table to slather the muffin with blackberry jam. Corvus got a huge bowl of oatmeal into which he dumped raisins, milk, and syrup. "Sleep well?" he asked Neil.

"Well enough," said Neil. "You?"

"Yeah. Blaise, you're on hold today, right?"

Blaise shrugged. "Yes, but I'm going to the location with you anyway. I want to watch you seduce my sister."

Opal glanced at Neil to see if he had any objections, but he was absorbed in his breakfast.

An old woman with silver hair, a softly wrinkled face, and a cushiony, comfortable-looking shape clothed in a red plaid dress and a white apron came through the swinging door from the back of the house, bearing a plate of crisp bacon, which she set down in the center of the table. "My, my," she said, looking from Blaise to Opal with a smile. "More company. You ladies care for anything you don't see here?"

"No," said Blaise.

"The bacon looks great," Opal said. This must be Bessie Gates, the woman Mrs. Partridge said she didn't get along with. Opal wondered if now was a good time to ask about ancient history, but before she could frame her question, the woman turned to Corvus.

"Master?" Bessie said.

He paused, a spoon loaded with oatmeal on its way to his mouth, and cocked his head at Bessie. "Ma'am?"

"What may I feed you?" There was silk in her voice, Opal thought, spider silk or something else, something worshipful and seductive and a little sticky.

The house was watching and listening to them.

"I'm happy with oatmeal and bacon," said Corvus, his voice at its most gentle.

The woman smiled, bobbed her head, tucked her hands into her apron pockets, and headed toward the door back to the kitchen.

Neil looked grumpy. No one had called him *master* or asked what he wanted.

"Ma'am?" Opal said.

Bessie paused with her shoulder against the swinging door. She turned reluctantly. "Miss?"

"I was wondering if you could tell us about the Last of the Lost?"

Bessie laughed. "Where'd you hear that old wives' tale? From an old wife, I'll wager! Who was it? That tattletale busybody, Myrna Partridge?"

"She did say some girls disappeared in the fifties and were never seen again."

"It makes a good story, doesn't it?"

"Do you know what happened to them?"

"Well, now." Bessie came back into the room and stood beside the table, looming over Opal, her hands still hidden in her pockets. She seemed taller than she had before. Her eyes were hungry. "Sometimes a woman has to get away from a place," she said. "There was just no help for her there. I think it's likely those girls hiked over to the highway and hitched a ride up to Portland. I know it seems like we're at the back of beyond here, but even back then, the big city wasn't so far away. Who knew what happened to any of them once they left?"

"You don't think they went to the forest to join the Last of the Lost?"

Bessie laughed again. "There is no Last of the Lost." She strode toward the door. "He's not lost, and he's not last anymore," she muttered, with a glance at Corvus before she disappeared.

Opal looked at Corvus, too. He was shoveling oatmeal into his mouth; it took him a couple of seconds to notice her regard. When he did, he raised an eyebrow.

"Maybe she'd answer if you asked the questions," Opal said.

"What *are* the questions?" asked Corvus.

"There are no more bloody questions," said Neil, "Only

timing, and you need to shove off if you're going to make your call."

————————

Hitch drove Blaise, Opal, and Corvus to the location. Blaise didn't say anything snide on the way.

The Makeup trailer, Cast trailer, Craft Services trailer, generator, camera truck, all the equipment had been moved to the location during the night. The morning was misty but not drizzling, a relief to everyone. Gemma and Bettina weren't in Makeup yet; their call was for eight A.M. Transportation had started the Makeup trailer's generator and turned on the heat already, but Rod and Magenta hadn't come to open up the trailer, since they didn't have to arrive until Gemma and Bettina did. Opal turned on the lights as Corvus and Blaise settled into chairs. She unlocked the cupboard where she stored the prosthetics and set up for work. Blaise lounged in one of the chairs, opened a copy of *Harper's* and effectively vanished, but Opal, conscious of her presence, didn't talk with Corvus. There was nothing she wanted to say to him where anybody else could hear.

She wondered if she wanted to do a postmortem on their first actual night together anyway. Maybe she should just let it lie.

She was ready for Corvus's transition into Phrixos, she thought, but this time it happened while she was shaving him, before she had applied any of his face. The glow grew in his eyes, and his smile widened. She hesitated, then finished the stroke she had started. Blaise glanced up, but she was behind Corvus's head and couldn't see his eyes.

Phrixos closed his eyes and relaxed under her hands. Only once did he break her concentration, when she had leafed over his nose and let one hand rest on his leafy cheek while she thought about her next step. He pulled her hand toward his mouth. She sighed and drew the shield away from her smallest finger, let him feed from her. The Sifter Chant had been running in the background; her reservoir felt pleasantly full. She narrowed the channel, though, so he could not draw too quickly or too much. She shut down the feed before he released her, testing the limits of their boundaries.

"Unfair," he muttered.

"Live with it." She wiped her hand on her jeans and finished matching his face with yesterday's Polaroids. "Arms, please."

Gemma, Bettina, their guardians, Magenta, and Rod all arrived at the trailer at the same time, as Opal was finishing Phrixos's chest leaves. Another actress Opal hadn't met yet arrived as well, a dark-haired woman who displaced Blaise. Blaise hopped up on a counter near Corvus's chair, still clutching her magazine. Magenta went to work on Gemma, while Rod started with the strange woman.

When Opal finished turning Phrixos into the Dark God, Rod called her over. "This is Ariadne, the mom who gets to die in today's scene. Day player—she's only got the two scenes, this one and one with the kids we're shooting on a different set tomorrow. Today we have a call in for all the other coveners, but they'll be wearing hooded robes, so not much makeup on them. Ariadne, Opal LaZelle, special effects makeup."

"Hi," said Ariadne. "You doing my blood?"

"If I am, nobody told me," said Opal.

"She's special to the Dark God. Fake blood is not her department," Rod said.

"Oh. Well, hi," said Ariadne.

"Hi." Opal smiled and went back to Phrixos, who was drowsing.

The mist had lightened by the time they came out of Makeup and headed for the stones. The clearing was silent, the air cold. Opal felt again the undertone of hum, an anticipatory sensation. Something waited.

She walked with Phrixos over to the altar stones as the stand-ins came off the set. Then, suddenly, he lifted her and set her on the altar. She felt a vibration all through her. "What are you doing?" she asked.

"Lie down," he whispered. He gripped her shoulders and pushed down on them. "Just for a second."

"What? No!" She tried to wrench free, but he didn't let go.

Lightning flashed. Or, no, it was a camera flash. Erika stood just outside the circle of stones, taking pictures one after another.

"Hey," said George, the first assistant director and Neil's shadow. "What's going on here? No horseplay, Corvus! You're going to knock something out of alignment if you're not careful."

"Lie still," Phrixos said, his voice soft and fierce.

She couldn't break his grip. Furious, she lay on the stone and glared up at him.

He spoke a phrase in a language she didn't recognize. Something burned and buzzed against her back. She felt the flare of Flint's shield along her skin as something tried to enter her and failed.

"Corvus!" said Neil.

"Let go!" she said. Finally he released her and she sat up, shoved off the altar stone, and ran from the set to the cast corral behind the backdrop. Shuddering, she curled up in Corvus's chair.

Erika ambled over, camera still in hand. Opal hid her face in her hands and Erika strode past.

"What was *that*?" Magenta asked.

"Things getting worse," Opal whispered. "He stopped playing nice."

"Oh, God." Magenta touched her shoulder, glanced toward the set. They were behind the backdrop and couldn't actually see what was happening at the altar directly. "Did he hurt you?"

"He tried to get something to—possess me. I mean, I'm not sure about that, but he—" Opal shuddered again, pulled arms and legs tight to her center, hugged her knees to her.

She remembered one of her high school boyfriends. Once she had come into her powers, she had experimented with boys, changing her appearance in little ways to see which features attracted which boys, then trying some of the nastier spells in her repertoire, the ones Great-Uncle Tobias had scolded her for studying, to see how much she could bend people to her will. She had had no idea back then what kind of boyfriend she really wanted.

Somebody sweet like her father, the only one in the house who could actually make her mother slow down and think before she acted? Opal could force boys to be sweet, but she couldn't make them sweet and strong enough to stop her from doing anything she wanted to them. She didn't know what Dad's secret was.

Somebody who could resist her? No, she got enough of that with her younger brother Jasper and the rest of the kids. Even when she was just trying to help them, they fought back. It wasn't fair. She wasn't really their mom, just the one who took care of them. Mom was gone most of the time, and even when she was home, she was absorbed in her own affairs. The kids had minded Opal when they were little, and she loved them so much it hurt. Now they were teenagers and didn't mind much anymore.

And then she met Keith. At first he behaved like the other boys she'd experimented on, falling under her spell, responding to her smaller manipulations. Her friends thought he was so agreeable. Her most recent ex-boyfriend, still obsessing about her, wilted and faded away: Keith was stronger, better-looking, smarter. Plus, Opal suspected, but never confirmed, that Keith had beat up the previous boyfriend at one point. That sort of thing could drum even enchanting girlfriends out of people's brains, and a good thing, too, because Opal hadn't yet learned other, cleaner ways of dumping boys.

Keith behaved like all her previous boyfriends . . . up to a point. They'd been on the beach at night when she realized he wasn't like the others. They were alone on a blanket, the repeating hush of waves not far from them, faint fog rising to mask the stars. He had given her the kind of sexual experience that was all she knew, a gentle, prolonged session she had orchestrated with subtle precision, culminating in a small orgasm for her and a release and collapse for him. They lay silent. She stared sleepily up at stars. He sat up and said, "This is your idea of a good time? Let me show you something, babe."

None of her spells affected him. Nothing she did even slowed him down. He took her hard. He hurt her. The things he whispered to her hurt, too, almost worse than the physical experience.

Afterward, when she curled up and cried, he sat beside her and said, "You have no right to complain, babe. That's what you've been doing to all those boys. They were okay before they met you. Think about it."

She couldn't get herself to go back to school for a week, though she knew she was setting a bad example for the other kids in the family. When she did go back, she practiced a new way of altering her appearance: she made herself invisible. She watched the boys she had messed with and saw that some of them hadn't recovered particularly well. Keith would meet her gaze if he caught her looking at him, but he never smiled at her. Every time she felt herself drawn to someone new, though, she'd glance around and realize Keith was watching her.

She finally went to Uncle Tobias and forced herself to tell him everything. He set her new studies, strict lessons about how to unspell people and free them. She worked hard.

Her final assignment was to find as many of her old boyfriends as she could and take whatever spell threads she had left on them off. Tobias helped supervise. Afterward, most of them were mad at her, if they had memories at all. Tobias gave her permission to protect herself with illusion when necessary.

But it was uncomfortable living in a place where so many people had the wrong kind of history with her. She reengineered herself: moved to Los Angeles, ninety miles from home, got a real job—in the movies, like many in her family, but not with any of her cousins or aunts or uncles. Not with anybody she'd ever met before. She started at the bottom, assisting a makeup artist on a low-budget horror movie, and kept her talents under wraps while she learned how normal people worked. Anonymity and distance gave her the strength to examine everything she'd done so far, think about it, make different decisions.

Now *she* was like one of those ineffectual boyfriends she'd mistreated in her teens, at the mercy of a power greater than her own. She hadn't even tried to resist yet. She needed to resurrect Evil Opal.

"He tried to get something to possess you?" Magenta whispered, her grip on Opal's shoulder tightening.

"Keep away from him if you can," Opal said. She took a deep breath. Evil Opal. Her shadow self. Somewhere in her memory house, probably behind a closed door in the basement or the attic, Opal had locked her away. Time to dig her out.

"You bloody fool, you don't go messing with anyone in public," Neil said to Phrixos, behind her. "Especially you don't manhandle any talent necessary to the successful completion of the picture, not unless it's something she wants, and then you do it in private. I won't have this kind of upset on my set."

"Just a joke," Phrixos said.

"Nobody's laughing. Now straighten up and find your character. Time for blocking rehearsal. Ariadne? Where's my mini Caitlyn and Serena?"

Magenta loosened her grip on Opal's shoulder as the other

stars went onto the set. Doreen, Gemma's mother, stared at Opal. Perhaps she hadn't seen or heard what had just happened. Maybe she had. Nothing to do about it now.

The actors walked through blocking rehearsal. Neil yelled at them a lot.

"The big boss is grumpier than usual," Magenta muttered. "Wonder how things went with him last night."

Neil didn't have a light touch with the actors; instead of getting them to work with him, he made them resentful and defensive. The rehearsal repeated several times.

Blaise drifted over from the trailer that held her dressing room, along with Lauren's and Corvus's. "Trouble in paradise?" she asked.

"Did you kick the boss out of bed last night?" Magenta asked. "What chemistry there is is all bad."

Blaise raised her eyebrows, but didn't answer.

"Might as well shoot the fucking scene and hope for a miracle," Neil yelled. "Last looks! Somebody make these people look better than they can act!"

Opal collected her kit, but she waited until Magenta, carrying a different Set2Go bag for each of the teen actors, joined her before she headed for the set.

Opal mentally stroked Flint's shield, made sure it surrounded her completely. She checked her reservoir for power: plenty. She flexed her fingers, remembered ribbons of invisible smoke she had sent out to do her bidding when she was controlling people. A tiny puff of smoke from her index finger reassured her.

As usual, Phrixos didn't need touch-ups. He stood silent, looming above her, his expression unreadable, observing, as she focused on the separate details that made up his character's whole. He touched her face without making any attempt to draw from her. His eyelids flickered. She wondered if Corvus was trying to surface. At least he didn't grab her and lay her on the altar again.

One of the special effects crew was on the set to orches-
trate the blood spatter from the mother's horrifying death.
He had practiced with a Styrofoam mock-up of the set inside
the soundstage building, and thought he knew where all the
spray and spatter would go, but when they actually started
filming, things kept going wrong with the direction of the
blood. Some of the blood spattered across the camera lenses,
which entailed an extended cleanup. The altar stone got lib-
erally spattered and needed scrubbing every time, though
they couldn't get all the stain off—some of it was original,
and old. They decided to leave it, but the continuity shots
looked different every time.

The onsite showers in the trailers didn't have strong enough
water pressure. The stars were miserable after every take—
and wardrobe was running out of copies of the clothes, even
though they were pretty generic, white robes for the coveners,
including Ariadne, the girls' mother, the black robe for the
Dark God, and special ritual dresses for the two girls in honor
of their induction into the Dark God coven. The girls weren't
supposed to be in range of the blood spatter, though Neil had
reserved the right to drench them if he thought it made dramatic sense. Bettina and Gemma had changed out of gory
dresses twice already, and there had been big gaps in the filming while their hair was restored. Special Effects was using
peppermint-flavored stage blood, so at least everybody would
have clean-tasting mouths if they ate any by mistake.

"Break for fucking lunch," the director finally said. "I
don't know if we can salvage anything out of this fucking
mess. Come back ready to work." He wandered off, mutter-
ing curses, while people mopped up behind him. Everybody
went to the folding tables set up behind the drapes that hid
the trucks, trailers, and cast corral from the cameras. Cater-
ing had dropped off a big box of mixed sandwiches wrapped
in plastic an hour earlier, and a tub full of varied canned
beverages buried in ice.

The hum under Opal's feet had grown more insistent during all the mishaps of the afternoon. As everyone else left the ritual rocks, she wandered toward them, hands stretched before her, palms aimed downward. Something under the ground was awake. She'd never felt anything quite like it before. Her family home was full of spirit-haunted things, some of them active, because people with power had been using them for years; but none of them purred like this. The energy didn't get through her shield, yet still she sensed it, a warmth, a summons, almost a song.

The altar stone, still damp from being cleaned of special effects blood, vibrated with enticing energy. A sweet taste thrummed on Opal's tongue. She reached, for what she didn't know; she only knew something invited her, promising things.

"Open to me," it whispered. "I will be your strength. I will be your spine. I will be your friend and protector. I will be your wings."

She flattened her hands against the altar stone, felt the surge of a warm sea of power under her palms. Only Flint's shield kept it separate from the sea inside her. She could make the shield retreat, bare her skin, wrap herself in that warmth, finally find something that would take care of her instead of her taking care of everyone else—

"What are you doing?" asked someone behind her.

She blinked, glanced back. Phrixos stood silent a foot behind her, his hood up, his face shadowed in the black robe of his character. She was startled. She hadn't known he was there.

He was not the one who had spoken. Beyond him stood Erika, frowning, no cameras raised, curiosity marking her face.

"What?"

"Something special about the rock?" Erika asked.

"I'm sorry?" Opal said.

Erika came forward, stared at the altar stone. She sucked in her lower lip, then touched the stone. "Ow!" Her hand jerked, a drop of blood spilling free of her finger to splash on the rock. "What? How'd that happen?"

The music streaming from the rock rose from a single voice to an orchestra, full of ominous chords, woodwinds, and triumph, strings singing, deep notes of percussion.

Erika froze. Then her hand lowered, drops of blood welling from her fingertip and dripping on the stone, where they wet the surface and vanished. She set both hands against the stone, leaned on them, her shoulders hunching.

Manipulating her arms as though she were a rag doll, Phrixos gently stripped the cameras and her shoulder bag from her, then lifted her and laid her on her back on the stone. She stared up at him, only her eyes moving. "What," she said, her voice a thread now as the music of power lapped at her, loudest where her blood fed the rock. "Don't," she said. Her hand jerked, though, pressed the bleeding finger to the rock, pressed the palm, and then the wrist. "Stop it," she whispered.

12

Opal stood, battered by wild waves of energy coming from the rock, from the ground below. Even the grass was dancing. Phrixos stood beside her, an absence of light and sound. Before her on the altar stone, Erika closed her eyes, her face drawn into a grimace. As her blood dripped into the stone, something flowed from the stone into her finger, a trickle of blue green energy Opal could not quite see but could sense. It sparked up Erika's arm, seeped through her torso, climbed her spine, and burst into her brain. Erika jerked again, and Opal woke out of the trance the music had put her in.

She stepped forward, lifted Erika's wounded hand from the stone, and broke the connection. Erika's body stiffened, all muscles tight, then relaxed. The music faded, still present but not so overpowering.

"Hey!" yelled someone from behind them. "What are you doing?"

"Are you okay?" Opal asked Erika.

"No," Erika said. Her voice was strained, as though her

throat had closed around the word and didn't want to let it escape. Her hand encircled Opal's forearm, the grip hard enough to hurt. "Yes. No! Help me!"

Opal helped Erika sit up, supported her as she slid off the altar stone. Phrixos stood silent, while Neil stumped across the clearing toward them. "You people know better than to mess with the set between shots! Have you gone mad?"

Opal lifted Erika's arm over her shoulder and snaked an arm around her waist to help her walk. Phrixos still held Erika's camera bags and shoulder bag. He followed.

"What the fuck is this?" Neil cried. "Someone better answer me, or there'll be hell to pay."

Phrixos halted beside him and stared into his face from under that dark hood.

"Don't you play a part with me, you great lurching golem. I admire what the camera does with your image, but I was against hiring you from the start, and I haven't changed my mind yet—what's that look? What? Stop that! Stop . . ."

Opal left them both behind. Erika's muscles had been stiff when she came off the altar, but they loosened as she walked, and her breathing eased, opened. "What happened?" she asked.

"You tell me," said Opal.

"I don't know. I feel like I walked into an electric fence. Everything in my head is still going *kabong*." She lifted the hand she had bled from, stared at her finger. "Can a rock be a vampire? What's wrong with this shoot, Opal?"

"You're the professional observer," Opal said. She was relieved Erika was talking like a person with sense after whatever had happened to her on the rock. It didn't make her feel like sharing anything with a woman who had been nothing but an irritation in her life so far.

"Yes, but you're the one with all the secrets."

"Let me know when you decide to respect my privacy," Opal said. "Until then, I'm not telling you a thing."

"But I—but—" Erika gripped her forehead with her free hand. "My head hurts."

The crew had finished devouring all the sandwiches, and most were on their feet again, leaving behind wads of plastic wrap, dented aluminum cans, crumpled paper napkins, and crumbs on the folding tables the caterers had set up for lunch.

Magenta rose from the table. "I saved you a cheese sandwich. Something happen?"

Opal glanced behind her. Phrixos had his palm on Neil's forehead now, and the director wasn't fighting him anymore; his eyes were closed.

"I think it's bad," she muttered.

Magenta looked where Opal was looking. "Uh-oh. What's D.G. doing to our director? What's with Flashbulb here?"

"She bled on the altar stone. Then Dark God put her on it."

"That does sound bad," Magenta said.

"Whyever would you say that?" Erika asked. "Because that shambling monster as good as assaulted me? Or because the rock bit me, then Tasered me, and Miss Too-Big-for-Her-Britches let it happen?"

"What?" Magenta asked Opal. "This was going on and you just stood there?"

"I was sort of—in a trance myself."

"The rock Tasered Erika?"

"I touched it and it paralyzed me! It drank my blood! Then that giant goon laid me out on it like a sacrifice, and"—she put her hand to her forehead, gripped it as though she could squeeze a memory out—"and I'm not sure what happened next, except it hurt, and I feel really weird. Kind of—not alone."

"Opal," said Magenta.

The first assistant director called, "All right, people. We're burning daylight. Let's get back to it. Stand-ins, we need to check the lighting again. Cast, go to Makeup for repairs. Crew, assume the position!"

The pull of work tugged them back to their stations. Erika, her cameras once again draped around her, trailed Magenta and Opal back to the trailer, but Rod turned her back at the door. Her screeches of rage in response were only halfhearted, trailing off with one last nonspecific, "I'll get you, bitch!" before Rod shut the door in her face.

Phrixos sat in his chair with his hood down, his eyes burning, looking like some wild thing captured against its will and ready to attack. Bettina and Gemma waited in their chairs, both pale and unhappy. Doreen hovered near Gemma, though technically she wasn't supposed to be in the trailer during makeup unless there was trouble. Rod had already gone to work on Ariadne. No one spoke, the sign of a truly troubled shoot.

Opal stood at her workstation facing the mirrored wall, her back to the trailer. She could see the others reflected as they went to work. She placed her palms flat on the counter. The tools of her trade were around her, and she pulled together the identity she had built for herself since she left home: skilled, respected, solid and reliable, invisible, accomplished, creative, resourceful, inspired.

Not enough, she thought, and remembered the new people she had become on this particular project: witch friend to Lauren and Magenta, Corvus's girlfriend, Phrixos's walking nourishment supply, information collector.

Not enough, she thought again. She closed her eyes and found her inner study. Some of Flint's energy still floated there, a bumbling fireball. *Come,* she whispered to it. *Help me open to my shadow self.*

Obedient, the fire seeped through her, sent bright warmth into all her dark corners, found the door she had shut on the self who knew how to manipulate and hurt other people, the part of her that most resembled Phrixos. Fire formed the key to pick the lock for her, but she had to turn the doorknob herself. She reached out and did it, pulled the door open and stepped through.

A skin of darkness settled over her, snugged against her in every expanse, crease, recess, every fine hair and blemish. It seeped under her surface. She twitched, settling it, then scratched an elbow. The new self itched! *Hey, hey,* it said, *what have I missed? Whoa, lots of life! Wow, what's going on here? How neat is that?*

She lifted her eyelids and stared at herself in the mirror, saw darkness staring back. She closed her eyes and asked herself what the hell she had just done. *What I needed to,* she decided, and shuddered. She studied herself again, smiled, and saw the extra intensity darkness gave her, the beckoning that said, *Come closer. I have such interesting things to tell you.*

Hey, said her second self, *show me the guy.*

She turned. Phrixos stared at her, his face unreadable beneath its overcoat of leaves and glitter. He sat up straighter. "What have you done?" he asked.

She felt wings at her back, flames at her fingertips, a blaze behind her eyes. All defenses, because her second self could tell how dangerous Phrixos was. She smiled at him, too, because second self felt the pull of attraction between them. It wasn't Corvus her second self wanted.

"Ready?" asked one of the production assistants from the trailer door.

"She never even touched him," Bettina said, pointing to Opal and Phrixos.

"He doesn't need any help," said Opal. "He's perfect."

"You didn't even look at the photos," said Bettina. "You're a total slacker."

Opal raised her brows and looked at Bettina with the glare of an older sister who can do things to you while you're asleep if you piss her off. Bettina lost color. She leapt to her feet and fled the trailer.

"How'd you do that?" Gemma asked, rising from her chair as Magenta tried to pat her cheek with a powder puff.

"I'll demonstrate, if you bother me," Opal said. Her voice had deepened just a little.

Everyone in the trailer turned to look at her. In the resulting silence, the P.A. said, "We needed you ten minutes ago, people! Come on!"

Phrixos rose, tipped Opal's chin up, and kissed her. Instead of letting him draw from her, she drew from him, sucked off a draught of his energy. He tasted sweet and sour, smoky and sharp, scary. He tried to move into her as his essence crossed her tongue, but Evil Opal knew how to drag all of him out of Corvus's body. Something in her spun darkness to wrap him tighter and deeper in a cocoon of night, though she couldn't paralyze him; she felt him struggling, and countered with more until at last he lay silent.

Corvus staggered when he let her go. She stared up at him and saw that Phrixos's green glow had faded from his eyes. "What?" he said in Corvus's voice.

She smiled. "Well, that's a handy trick. You're wanted on the set, Corr."

"I am?"

She turned him and aimed him toward the door. "I'm right behind you." She felt drunk and a little staggery herself. The taste of the banished god was still on her tongue, intoxicating to her second self. She grabbed her bag and followed Corvus down the steps in the wake of Ariadne, the two girls, their Makeup and Wardrobe people, the mother, and the guardian.

"Which scene are we doing?" Corvus asked Opal as they rounded the backdrop and headed for the altar.

"Mom's death scene. You studied it last night with Lauren at the restaurant, remember?"

"Vaguely," he said.

"So far it hasn't been working out very well. Everybody's

in a mood, especially Neil. We spent six hours getting it wrong, and then we broke for lunch."

"How did I get to be me in the middle of the day? I'd pretty much given up on that."

"I forced it," said Opal.

"You did?" He studied her as they walked. "How?"

"I used a trick that probably won't work twice," she said. "Now you're going to have to act happy while you're sprayed with special effects blood. Oh, and just before lunch, Phrixos actually woke the rock by spilling Erika's blood on it." The grass was still vibrant with energy, and the rocks glowed with it. The music was there, too, half a melody that played, cut off, started again. Beneath it all was a slow pulse, the heartbeat of something huge, old, and resting. Resting, but awake now.

The hairs on Opal's arms and legs bristled. The muscles in the back of her neck twitched. Whatever lay under the ground recognized her presence, and wanted her.

"Over here," bellowed Neil. "Quit lagging!"

They reached the altar, where the coveners in their recently dried robes, Ariadne in period clothes as the mother doomed to die, and Gemma and Bettina in their white lace dresses as witnesses and innocents waited. Corvus took his mark at the head of the altar, straightened, and turned into a close approximation of Phrixos; it was hard to distinguish them by sight when they were in full makeup, but Opal could sense the spiritual difference.

Phrixos was inside her, and not lying quiet, either, though she had tried to lock his essence away. Her second self was intrigued by him; she let small bits of him out to play, enjoying his dark impulses, though not giving them any weight or power. Opal felt things going on in the back of her mind while she was focused on what was in front of her: Neil harangued his cast about their previous inadequacies and demanded better of them.

"Does that kind of screeching ever work?" Magenta muttered, from beside Opal.

"Sure," Opal said. "Fear works. You should know that by now."

Magenta stared into her eyes, then stepped back.

Opal considered this. She had opened to her dark half, and anybody smart *should* be scared of her, if that change was visible. Maybe she should mask it better. She closed her eyes and thought *disguise*, one of her best and most practiced skills. She felt the spin of energies as her looks reformed into something nonthreatening, knew each change; she had done this a lot when she was a teenager, to convince her parents she was innocent. Her great-uncle Tobias hadn't been fooled; he could see under surfaces. She looked toward Magenta again.

"What did you just do? I hate it that you can do makeup without tools."

"Is it working? Are you reassured?"

"Yeah, and I don't like that either. Jerk me around! Who were you a minute ago? Almost as scary as the prick."

"Takes one to deal with one," said Opal.

Magenta half smiled and glanced toward Opal's crotch. Opal laughed, and said, "Not quite that way, but yeah, I decided to be my own mean self. Somebody I haven't been in a long time."

"Well, that's weird. Makes me wonder who you normally are. Did it make a difference?"

"Yeah. I did a job on him, locked him up. Right now, he's Corvus, not Phrixos. Not sure that was smart, and I don't know that it'll last, but I managed it."

"Cool," said Magenta. "You gonna get nasty, too?"

"I hope not. Can't rule it out, though."

"Can you give me some protection?"

Protection. Why hadn't she thought of that before? She could make talismans for everybody—except Lauren, who had already been tapped by Phrixos, and Erika, who had been attacked by the altar. Maybe she could come up with something that would help even those who had been compromised.

She didn't have much experience with it, though. Her brother Jasper had worked on it more. Maybe when Uncle Tobias came, which should be any time now, he could help her.

"I—" Opal began, but then Neil yelled, "Is my goddamned blood ready to go?"

"Ready," said the pale-faced special effects man.

"And it'll go the right direction this time? It'll land where I say it's supposed to land?"

"Yes," squeaked the man.

"All right, then. One final blocking rehearsal without the blood, and then you lot have no excuses left!"

Opal kept her attention on Corvus, listened to make sure he remembered his lines and knew where he was supposed to go. The girls were flat in their delivery, having said everything twenty times already, but Corvus brought a new spirit to his gloating over the death of one of his character's most devoted followers.

"Good," Neil said at last. "Last looks, and let's make this the actual last, shall we?"

Opal checked Corvus over carefully, referencing Polaroids from the morning shoot. He looked a little less realistic now, but nothing needed work.

"All right, clear the set," said Neil. His call was repeated, louder, by the first assistant director. Opal fled with all the others to the cast corral. Rod got out his little TV, and they watched as the take went perfectly for the first time that day.

Everyone involved relaxed as soon as Neil called cut. He and the A.D. and the D.P. gathered around a monitor and watched a playback, with the script supervisor right behind them to take notes. Everyone else waited for the verdict.

"All right," George, the first assistant director, called out, "looks like we got the master shot, finally! Two angles on it. Thank God. Clear the set. We'll go to close-ups on the principals next. Coveners, you're done for the day. The rest of you, take five while we set up."

The actors went to the Wardrobe trailer, where they changed out of fake-blood-soaked robes into lounging wear. They came to the cast corral and settled into chairs, most leaning back as though exhausted. The makeup artists cleaned fake blood off everyone who had been spattered for the umpteenth time, and restored their pre-suicide makeup. Doreen, Gemma's mother, went to the Craft Services truck and came back with several bottles of water. She offered them to Gemma, Bettina, Ariadne, and Corvus, who all accepted.

"Do you want something to eat?" Opal asked Corvus.

He caught her hand and lifted it to his lips. She wondered if Phrixos had found his way back inside—she hadn't had time to tend to what she had pulled from Corvus earlier. The little dark flurries and explorations some part of her had entertained while the rest of her was being Opal LaZelle, special effects makeup queen, had slowed.

Something moved inside her, something that was not either of her selves. She closed her eyes and tried to wrap it in darkness again, but she felt the taint of it, itchy and exciting, glowing along her mental entrails and trails.

There was no sense from Corvus of threat or invasion, even as his lips pressed against the back of her hand, only a warmth that wakened memories of last night.

The ground was alive with excited anticipation, and it kept trying to send exploratory feelers up through her feet. Something inside her reached down toward the invading energy, but explorations from both directions stubbed against Flint's shield. She needed time and space to figure out what had happened.

"Actually," Corvus said, in his own voice, letting her hand

slip from his, "I'm starving. I don't know what he had for lunch, but I don't think it was enough. Could you get me one of those energy drinks? I don't have his power over the makeup, to eat with it on and not mess it up."

"Sure." Opal went to the Craft Services wagon and got some cold protein drinks and a couple of straws. She brought them back and then stood behind Corvus as he drank, contemplating her inner universe.

Magenta tapped her shoulder, startling her, and she looked up without thinking about who she was. Magenta sucked in breath and took a step back, and Shadow Opal smiled wide, the smile of seduction that said, *you're the most interesting person I've ever seen. Come closer.* Magenta wavered, not fleeing, not approaching.

Opal straightened, tried to find her usual face. "Sorry. Identity crisis."

"Are you a good witch or a bad witch?" Magenta asked after a pause.

"Hard to tell at this point."

"If you have a choice, could you veer toward the good witch end of the spectrum? We really don't need more bad blood on the set."

"That's my usual inclination, when I act like a witch at all," said Opal.

Magenta glared at her, then said, "Well, anyway, about protection."

"Protection?" said Corvus.

"Not that kind," Magenta said. "If this is the good witch I'm talking to, can you say a spell that will protect me from you and the prick?"

"Let me think." One thing that had worked for her was Flint's shield, but she didn't want to give any of that away; she needed it herself. She held up her hand, studied it, turned it over and back, and tried to see how Flint's shield surrounded her like a clear second skin. What were the components of this energy? It came from Flint, which made it something other people usually couldn't make or use. She wanted to make more of it. She stroked fingers across it, trying to taste its ingredients. Her younger sister Gypsum was a cook who could analyze components of baked goods by savoring a bite. Opal wondered if she could sample spells the same way, though her darker power might taint them somehow. Opal had never paid much attention to food, and she hadn't done much magical investigating since she was a teenager, hungry for skills and knowledge that would help her outfight her younger and more powerful siblings.

She lifted her hand to her mouth and pressed her lips to the back of it, touched the tip of her tongue to it. She could barely tell the fireskin was there; it wasn't trying to protect her from herself. She sucked on it, and then a taste flared in her mouth, a jalapeño scorch across her lips and tongue. *Analyze,* she thought to herself and to Evil Opal. *Replicate.*

Offer it energy, and ask it to change the new energy into itself, responded one of her.

Is it a living thing with its own mind?

Don't know. Can't break it down, but maybe we can get it to work with us.

She lowered her hand and closed her eyes, shutting out the sight of Corvus staring up at her from the chair, Magenta focused intensely on her, Rod down the trailer tending to Bettina, Gemma in one of the closer chairs with Doreen hovering over her.

In her mental study, Opal talked to the small ball of Flintfire that remained after it had built her shield. "Can you make more of yourself to share with my friends?" she asked it.

Let's try, it thought.

She opened her power reservoir and trickled power toward the fireball. It ate the power and grew. When it was the size of a small weather balloon and she had almost exhausted her reserves, she opened her eyes. Magenta waited.

"I think I can give you a shield," she said. "My little brother gave me a kind of bodyshield that protects me from Phrixos's power, unless I take it off. I was rolling it back from just one finger, or my lips, when he made me feed him. I don't know about using this power on someone who isn't—isn't a witch herself—so this might not work. It might fail spectacularly. Do you want to try anyway?"

"How wrong could it go?" Magenta asked.

"I don't know. I've never done anything like this before."

"What if it cripples me, or makes it so I can't work?"

"Yeah," said Opal, "what if?"

Magenta frowned ferociously at her, then lifted a leg and propped her running-shoe-clad foot on the back of Corvus's makeup chair. "Maybe you could put it around my foot and see if it works."

"Take off your shoe and sock," Opal said.

Magenta glared at her, then did it. Opal cleared a section of counter. "Sit here." Magenta hopped up, and Opal took her foot—toenails neatly trimmed and coated in sparkling black polish, the long slender muscles and bones an elegance of form—between her hands. Opal went into overawareness, her body's eyes focused on her hands and Magenta's foot, her mind's self engaged with Flint's fireball in her study, consulting and interacting with it. "We want to protect someone who is not like we are," she told it, and it sent out a thin, questing thread that eased along the lace of her veins, arteries, muscles, and nerves to her fingers and palms, to lie like a simmering sea of fire just under her skin.

"Okay," she said, her voice tight, her attention split, "I'm going to start now. Tell me if it hurts and I'll try to reverse it. Ready?"

"I guess," said Magenta. She scrunched up her face.

Opal stroked two fingers along the arch of Magenta's foot, spreading the smallest flush of fire along the skin. She glanced toward Magenta's face, looking for signs of pain.

"Oh," Magenta said. "That's warm."

"Does it burn?"

"No. Feels nice."

"Okay, I'm going to be a little bolder." She tapped into the stream of Flintfire lying under her skin and spread it over Magenta's foot in a sweep of her whole hand.

"Yikes!" said Magenta.

Opal looked at her, but she looked more surprised than pained. Opal waited for a more telling reaction.

"It's okay," said Magenta.

Opal gloved her whole foot in shield, then let go. Magenta stared down at her foot, kicked it, flexed her toes. "It's a little warm, but other than that, I can't even tell anything's there. So now my foot's safe?"

"Safe as I can make it," Opal said, "with what I know right now."

"Do the rest of me?"

Opal sucked on her lower lip, then held out her hands. "Give me your foot again."

Magenta held out her foot, and Opal grasped it, spoke to the fireball. "Send energy from me to her, slide along all her skin, and protect her from outside sorcery."

"Including yours?" asked the fireball. As she spoke to it, it had acquired personality. She had a sense that she was talking to a separate self. One of hers? More like Flint's, though she didn't think he was inside her. The fireball was itself and could make decisions. So she had her usual self, her evil self, a semicorralled Phrixos, and the self-aware fireball colonizing her. It was almost like being back home.

"Probably best if you do," she told the fireball.

"This won't be me anymore once we sever the connection,"

said the fireball, "so there's no guarantee you'll be able to talk to the shield."

"Okay, maybe we'd better leave it vulnerable to me a little, in case something goes wrong." She wished she trusted herself more. Dark Opal might decide to make mischief; she already felt the urge percolating. "Ready?"

A sound outside her internal conversation penetrated her concentration; she woke to herself in the outside world, Magenta's warm foot in her hands, Corvus, his chair turned so he could see what she was doing. "We need Dark God on the set," repeated her Ear.

"Oh, God," she said. "I forgot." She looked Corvus over; he still looked flawless. "We've got to get out there."

Magenta gripped her shoulder. "Do me first."

"But—all right." Opal closed her eyes and focused on the fireball, big with all she had given it. "A shield for all of her," she whispered, and the fire flowed through her. It streamed up from Opal's hands along Magenta's skin under her clothes. There wasn't time for finesse; they would be in big trouble with the director if they were late to the set. She waited until she got a sense from the shield that it had enveloped Magenta completely, then cut it off and felt it flex and tighten around the other woman, settle against skin.

Opal grabbed her on-set kit and Corvus's leafy hand and pulled him toward the door. Magenta, dazed, sat behind them, breathing loudly. Opal chanced a glance behind her, unsure if Magenta was all right, but then they were out of the trailer and crossing the lively ground toward the altar again, and something dark and fiery battered inside her, trying to free itself. The attack was so sudden and surprising she couldn't counter it. In that way, Phrixos pulled back the shield protecting her hand, and flowed from Opal into Corvus. They both stumbled and caught themselves as their insides reorganized. Then Phrixos stared down at her with Corvus's eyes and his own unsettling half smile, and Opal had time to wonder what he had learned while she had held him inside herself.

"That's better," he said, and laughed. "You are so full of lovely things. I'm glad you're the first handmaid I found."

"Bite me," said Opal.

13

She flexed her fireskin, made sure it was complete.

He lifted her hand toward his mouth, but then they stepped into a hailstorm of the director's disapproval. Phrixos pulled away from Opal and took his mark; Opal returned to the others who spent most of their time waiting; the cameras rolled, the scene unfolded again, smaller now, the cameras focusing on faces, hands, angles that menaced.

The Dark God maintained character this time, and gave the two girls looks that straightened them out—or reduced them to authentic fear and longing, appropriate to the scene. They did lines until the director was satisfied, and held the blood until the very end. Opal watched Phrixos lick blood from his leafy lips, saw the glow blossom in his eyes on camera, though this was stage blood—how could he get joy from that? Acting? Or maybe symbols spoke as loudly as the real thing to him, in which case, they were in even more trouble than she thought.

Magenta tugged on Opal's arm as Opal watched a scene unfold on Rod's Casio, and she looked up. "What?"

"I feel—strange," Magenta whispered.

"Good strange or bad strange?"

"I don't know. I'm warm—"

"But not burning up?"

"No, it's more, sort of, comfortable." Magenta shifted shoulders up and down, first one, then the other. She scratched the back of her neck. "But a little itchy. Could you—"

"What?"

"Could you cast a spell on me so I can see if it works?"

Opal glanced around. Rod was standing within hearing distance. He didn't look surprised. Maybe Magenta had told him about their experiment while Opal was busy working over Phrixos. She wasn't sure she liked Rod being in the loop.

Don't worry about it, said one of her. *The more people who know, the more we can do to them without having to break through disbelief. Less worry about repercussions. If everyone's expecting me to be a witch, what's the downside to witchy behavior?*

Being burned at the stake?

That's not going to happen to us, one of her thought. *One of us is of the fire. If they try to burn us, we can swallow the fire.* Flint's fireball stroked flame across her face. All she felt was warmth and comfort. *Good.*

Opal straightened and looked at Magenta, considered. A hair-color-changing spell would do, simple, not very energetic, nonthreatening. Turn Magenta's black, pink-streaked bob purple and green. Opal closed her fist, opened it, sent a small moth of spell toward Magenta. It stuttered out against the shield, a tiny purple spark.

Magenta gasped. Rod jerked as though pushed by an invisible hand against his shoulder.

"Did you see it?" Opal asked. She was never sure whether others could perceive magic working. Sometimes it hid itself, sometimes not.

"Fireworks in my face," said Magenta.

"The shield works well enough to block a spell like that, anyway," said Opal.

"What did you try to do?"

"Change your hair color."

"You can do that? Of course you can. I—"

All their Ears crackled, summoning them to the set for another round of fixing marred makeup. By the time they returned to the chairs, they had lost the thread of the conversation.

Opal curled up in Corvus's chair and closed her eyes. "Okay," she whispered. She had shielded Magenta. Should she extend that shield to others? She checked her power reservoir. Still low from supplying Magenta's shield, so she stepped her Sifter Chants up to more actively seek local power. She felt them hum as they teased strands of power from the lively ground. She sent some of the new power toward Flint's fireball to replenish it. It was the best thing she had going for her.

She wasn't sure the shield worked the way it was supposed to. Magenta had agreed to be a guinea pig; let her. Maybe after a day's trial to make sure there were no negative side effects, Opal would protect Kelsi, Lauren, Blaise, Rod, the girls.

Maybe.

Maybe she would only help people who were nice to her.

Maybe she should harm people whom she didn't like. She contemplated the universe of people she knew on the set. Bettina was the person she was most irritated with currently. Bettina's on-set guardian was worse than the kid. Erika was an irritant, too, though maybe she was already messed up enough by her contact with the rock, the mixing of her blood with whatever lay below the ground here.

Phrixos. Talk about troubling. She had locked him up inside herself, but he had freed himself. What had he done to her before she noticed his escape?

She went back to her study. Flint's fireball had settled on

the hearth and was now acting like an overactive but almost respectable fire. "Did you see where I put the Dark God while he was here?" she asked it.

"Some other room," it said, and sent a finger of flame to point toward the main door into her study. She went out, found herself lost in the castle of self. A tatter of black on the floor: she moved toward it, recognized a shred from the co-coon her dark half had used to bind Phrixos. She picked it up and ventured down the stone-floored hallway. Veins and striations of some other material striped the dark rock walls. Jewels glinted here and there, and other things gleamed in the matrix, shapes that whispered and promised.

Doors opened here and there in the living rock, different shapes, sizes, and compositions, most of them ajar. She had never been into any of these rooms. She peeked into one and saw a baby, apparently about two years old, asleep. It could have been any of her siblings; it was her favorite state for them, quiet, comfortable, completely trusting, beautiful in their innocence. So easy to care for; a hug could nourish them. She stepped into the room and contemplated the baby. Finally she realized it wasn't breathing.

She darted forward, arms out, ready to give it mouth-to-mouth. One of her selves stopped her. "It's not dead," said some other Opal. "Just frozen. They're easier to take care of that way."

"What?" she asked.

"If you could have, wouldn't you have frozen them once in a while? When they had colic, when they were screaming, when they turned into brats? If only you had had your powers while you were small. Our mother made you take care of them all by the time you were ten. Couldn't you have used a nice freeze ray on them then?"

"No. That would make me just like Mom!" she cried.

"Mom has her good points," said the other.

"Neglect and misuse of power aren't good points."

"Kinda depends."

Opal turned and found a Goth version of herself, dark brows, pale skin, golden eyes, and her naturally light hair darkened to black with one white streak above her left eye. She wore a gray body stocking. Had she ever been this self? Opal couldn't remember a time. Maybe for Halloween? *No.*

"Am I the shadow self or are you?" said Goth Opal. She smiled. Pointy teeth.

"Cliché and obvious," Opal said.

Other Opal shrugged. "I can be whatever I like. Right now, this is working for me. I'll change if you want me to; I don't care about the form."

"No, it's all right. I like that you're different from me."

"Just a surface. The fall of light."

Opal looked back into the crib at the frozen baby. "Why do you know about this?"

"You gave me this baby a long time ago. Sometimes I wake her up and play with her."

"Who is it?"

Dark Opal stepped past her and lifted the baby in her arms, cradled it. The baby breathed. Her brow wrinkled, her eyes opened. Violet eyes. She looked preternaturally aware.

Opal half reached for the child, and Other Opal handed it to her.

A strange frightening tenderness swamped Opal as she held her baby self in her arms. She wanted to wrap the baby in love and safety. The baby's own feelings of fear and abandonment swept through her. When Opal was this little, there hadn't been anyone to do for her what she managed to do for the others: guard them, hug them, whisper them past their nightmares, warm them when they were cold, feed them when they were hungry. Opal was the oldest. Daddy had gone to work every day, leaving Opal home alone with Mom, who liked being pregnant but didn't like taking care of babies once they were external to herself.

At some point an aunt and uncle had moved into the guest-house, and Mom often dumped baby Opal on them while she was out building her career as a television personality. The relatives were better about tending to Opal when she needed things than Mom had ever been. For a little while, Opal had felt cared for and beloved. But then the aunt and uncle had twins of their own, and their attention was split.

Opal learned not to need things. She grew up a little ahead of the twins. She learned how to take care of babies from watching her aunt and uncle.

The baby was quiet and still in her arms, eyes wide and watching.

Opal hugged her, filled with wordless longing for many things that had never happened.

The baby opened her mouth and screamed and cried, wracking sobs alternating with shrieks.

Opal rocked the baby and murmured to her, but nothing halted the shuddering, piercing cries. She held her out so she could see her. "What's wrong?"

"She's the first version of me," screamed the Other Opal above the noise. "Sometimes she wants to do all the things we never did, and that's one of them. You can't shut her up once she gets started, no matter what you do. That's why I always end up freezing her."

Opal held her smaller self as she sobbed. Each sob and cry grated against her heart. How long could this go on?

"Hours," said her other self, even though she hadn't spoken aloud. "I've timed it. I've never ridden it out. We stored up a lot of trouble, sister. You're more patient than I am."

Opal kissed the baby's cheek and set her in the crib, tucked the blanket around her small thrashing form. The baby paused in midscream and stared up at her with glistening violet eyes. Her cheeks were wet with tears, ruddy with crying.

"Love you," Opal whispered.

Baby opened her mouth, and Other Opal touched her forehead gently. She froze, stiller than death. Other Opal touched her eyes closed, tapped the chin to close the mouth.

"She'll be all right," she said. "She always is."

Opal backed away from the baby, fighting all the compulsions that said the baby was her responsibility and she had no right to leave it. What the baby needed was love and affection. She could give that. How could she walk away?

Roaring fire swept through her, a rage so big she couldn't keep it inside. Flames rose from her skin, formed a hot, flaring cocoon around her. The stone under her feet scorched, but she didn't feel the heat. She stared at the baby. Why should she be the one who took care of the baby? Where was the baby's mother? How could she leave such a tiny creature alone, surrounded by cold, uncaring stone?

"This is the safest place she could be," said Other Opal, and then, "no place is safe."

Opal stood on the threshold to the hallway, flames flickering the air around her, glanced once more at the baby, then crossed into the hall. Her rage died down. The door closed most of the way behind her. Other Opal stood beside her.

"What were we doing before we went in there?" Opal asked Other Opal.

"Seeing what Phrixos did while he was here."

"Where was he?" She liked Other Opal having a form she could question.

Other Opal pointed down the hallway toward a three-way branching. A fragment of black cocoon lay on the floor, and beyond it, down the left-hand branch, another. They moved that way. Down the hallway, soft gold light spilled from an open door, and another black tatter lay in the fallen gold. A shadow flickered past the edge of Opal's eye, and she almost turned, but Other Opal took her hand, tugged her onward. They hastened toward the open door—

Someone shook Opal's shoulder. She gasped and pulled free of the inner world. "God, Opal, where were you?" Magenta demanded. "I've been shaking you forever!"

"Sorry. What's up?"

"Last looks again!"

Opal jumped up, staggered; her legs were shaky from sitting. She grabbed her kit and followed Magenta at a run to the set.

The energy state of everything has changed, Opal thought—the ground more alive and awake than it had been, people in sharper outline and color to her eyes. Night was coming, and the lighting crew had put up banks of lights to replicate the amount of daylight they'd started shooting in. She felt as though she was moving through a liquid, something denser than atmosphere. Every move anyone made, every word they spoke, even their thoughts and feelings, reached out through the rippling air, responding to every other thing going on, all of them trapped together, working on each other at a distance. She turned to Magenta, wondering if she felt it, too, but Magenta only frowned fiercely at her and ran ahead.

Opal sped to the set. Phrixos caught her before she crashed into him. "Whoa," he said. "Something wrong?"

She looked up at him, checking for smug. Had he left traps in her head? She still didn't know. "I'm late," she said. "Sorry."

"Need a little blood cleaning," he said. "Splatter misfired again."

He had blood spots across the leaves of his face, and a big splotch on his chest. She muttered under her breath and opened her kit to do repairs. If things were normal, she would have had to take him back to the Makeup trailer, undo half of what she had done that morning, and redo it—hours of work. But because Phrixos was alive inside of Corvus and had chosen to manifest as something that looked just like the monster she had created, all it took was a little water sponged across his face and chest.

He pressed his hand over hers as she wiped a droplet of false blood from his cheek. The leaves of his face crinkled under her hand, not dry as fallen leaves, more like living leather. He pushed his face against her palm.

Scarves of red, yellow, and orange energy shimmered up around her, hovered around both of them.

"What the hell are you doing?" Neil demanded, his naturally loud voice even louder than usual.

The ground was alive with the exhalations of something that breathed out color and light. The air vibrated with anxious anticipation. Phrixos snaked his arm around Opal's waist and pulled her close. Light danced around them.

"Stop that! You're screwing up everything! What's with all this light? I didn't authorize that shit! Stop—oh, damn it, roll cameras."

Phrixos turned his face and kissed her palm. His tongue left a hot wet firekiss in the center. Slowly, he drew her hand from his face, pulled her up against him, lifted her from her feet. Her fireskin tightened all around her as colors sheeted up in plumes and sprays, fountains of light, the ground alive under her feet and pulsing hypnotically. Sparkles and streamers of light curled around them, sent questing fingers to stroke her, only to stub against her shield. Then the fireskin flexed and melted, fled into the air to dance with all the other colors of fire.

Other Opal opened golden eyes inside her and smiled, grew from an idea into an inhabiter, stretched out to fill Opal's skin, tingling in the fingertips and toes, a stitchery of silvery mesh under the surface. She pushed into Phrixos's embrace, sought his mouth against hers, and the energy from underground, the fire in Phrixos that had burned others, rose up to wrap them in heat, cinnamon and ginger, saffron and bittersweet, peach and henna, heedless of everything around them. He tasted of milk flavored with Indian spices, cardamom, nutmeg.

"This is what he left in us," Other Opal whispered to Opal. "A door." She wrapped their arms around Phrixos, embracing everything he was and wasn't. For the first time, she opened herself wide to him, and he came in, unrestrained now, flooding through her like shadowed water, drawing her to mingle with him. He laughed aloud, startled by who she had become since he escaped her. Other Opal shoved at him, and he encompassed the push, still laughing.

"I like this you better," he said.

She shoved him again, but ended up laughing, too, then pulled him back into a kiss, let herself disappear into the heat.

14

When Opal opened her eyes to the outside world again, she was lying on the altar. Night sky was above, beyond the reach of the banks of lights that shone full on her and on Phrixos, who lay across her, his arms around her, his leathery, leafy face against her cheek. Glow still surrounded them, hazy, golden and green.

The eyes of the cameras watched them.

She took a breath.

The one under the ground had sent Phrixos out as scout and envoy, point man and first negotiator in this latest of its ventures into the world above. All these people had moved willingly into its orbit, with only the most tenuous of invitations. They had danced on its head and let it taste them. They had come bringing treasures. Nourishment, playthings, converts.

Opal blinked, glanced around. Everyone she could see looked stunned and strange. She heard the muffled machinery of filming. People were scattered amongst the lights, cameras, tracks, boom mikes, all the hidden structures associated with capturing a momentary fall of light. Those who manned the machines seemed to still be on the job, though they looked blank, not present. None of them looked like themselves.

She pushed Phrixos back so she could sit up. He was limp, spent, still smiling, asleep or comatose, dead weight across her legs, a huge lump of flesh. She was naked. She touched his chest, made sure he was still breathing. She leaned forward, smelled the cinnamon on his breath, felt warmth under her palm when she laid it against his cheek.

She wasn't sure she wanted him to wake, so she eased out from under him and slipped off the rock. She leaned against the altar stone and tried to get her bearings.

She had been out of her mind, drowned in fire and water, lost to thought. Had they fucked? In front of the cameras? Apparently they had. Her coverall lay draped across the top of the altar, and her underwear had disappeared. She straightened, retrieved her coverall and stepped into it, carefully zipped up so she wouldn't snag her skin or anything else. She felt awash and sticky with the secretions of someone else, invaded, unalone, colonized. There was a salt taste in her mouth, a wet heat still between her legs, an uncomfortable itch and burn. She had a sense of incomplete separation; he was still inside her, though not physically; or he had left his flag planted, or some other sign of occupation: threads of him woven into her fabric, things he could call to that would open a door in her and invite him back.

"Rod? Magenta?" she said. She glanced at the nearest cameraman. "Ben?" He didn't even blink. "Neil?" She looked for the director. People stood all around the altar, with vacant faces and staring eyes, many in states of undress. Those who still wore clothes didn't seem at home in them; shirts were untucked, zippers not zipped, buttons in various states of joining with buttonholes, or not. Many went barefoot. Some were frozen in the act of coupling. Everywhere she looked, people were paused, trapped, as though she had arrived between one moment and the next.

Neil was nowhere nearby.

Magenta edged out from behind the backdrop, held onto the edge of the fake-forest-photographed cloth as though ready to flee. "Is it over?"

"What happened?" Opal asked.

"I don't know. It was hard to see through all that crazy special effects stuff. Light and magic. I thought they put that in afterwards now, but man! It was intense!"

"The light?" Opal asked.

"Yeah, it was everywhere, like fog. It kind of—people sucked it in their mouths, you know? Even little Gemma, she tried to run from it, but it followed her and got in her face until she had to breathe it. It came at me, too, but—I don't know. Maybe that shield you gave me? I didn't breathe any of it in."

"Oh. Oh. Good," said Opal. "So everybody else got caught in the light? Then what?"

"It was like they had a script. They were acting it out, like the coveners in the film, except the people running the lights, camera, and sound—they stayed on the job. The rest of them, all of them got into some kind of chanting and dancing, and you guys up there, too, kind of, dancing, and getting naked, and—did you know he was allover leaves? I sure didn't see you do that to him in the Makeup trailer."

"I got naked?" Of course she had. No use trying to deny it. Where had her mind gone?

"Uh-huh. I, uh, well. Didn't think I should watch that part, but I couldn't look away. Anyway, you two weren't the only ones. There was a lot of that going around, only nobody was home in their heads." She looked toward the forest. "I tried to stop Rod. I called his name, I pulled on his shirt. He acted like I was invisible! Off he went in the crowd."

"The girls?" Opal whispered.

Magenta licked her lips. "They, uh." She pointed toward the forest. "The girls ran off, but they had those blank eyes, too. There was so much going on I couldn't keep track of everybody. That Evil Guardian Witch of Bettina's, she was in the thick of the crew cluster, but Gemma's mom kind of panicked. She hid in one of the trailers. And then just now all those lights faded and everybody stopped. Then you're awake, but nobody else is. Huh?"

"What happened?" Opal muttered to herself. She reached out with hands and mind to feel where the energy lay. What had possessed her? Who was she now? She sketched a mirror in the air and stared into her own eyes, reassured by their violet color, then flicked it away and took in a breath, tasting for information.

"What did you just do?" Magenta asked. Focused elsewhere, Opal glanced toward her, and Magenta said, "Never mind."

The ground was quiet, the people absent inside themselves, maybe, except Magenta, whom Opal could now see was outlined in Flint's familiar flame.

"I need to think," Opal told Magenta.

"What am I supposed to do? If I try to wake people up, will it hurt them? I don't want to be here all alone."

"You're safe here," Opal said. "You have a magic shield, and it works."

"But—" Magenta looked around at a world on pause. "Nobody's themselves. What if they—You don't know. It was so crazy before. Where did it all go? They ought to be tired after what they did. Why aren't they sleeping?"

"I can't answer you until I figure out what just happened. I need to think."

"But—Oh, dammit, go ahead, then," said Magenta. She sagged in one of the chairs.

Opal sat in Corvus's chair, hugged herself, closed her eyes, went inside to see what she could learn.

Golden-eyed Shadow Opal sat on a couch in the mental study with a big cup of hot chocolate. She smiled and stretched out a hand toward the fire, which reached from the fireplace and wound through her fingers. "Have fun, honey?" she asked.

"I don't know. Did I?"

"Oh, yes, you did, in ways you never have before."

"Why did we do that? What happened?"

"Part of it was just letting go of all those wrappings you keep around your talents and your heart. Do you *ever* remember having fun, Opal?"

"Lots of times."

"Like?"

"Taking the kids to the county fair."

"Hands to hold, noses to wipe, vomit to clean up, children to keep track of, everybody asking for money, none of them happy for very long."

"Taking the kids to the beach."

"Sunburn, sand in their swimsuits, salt water in their eyes, always watching to make sure they're not drowning themselves or each other. Who carried the cooler? Who made all the sandwiches? Who shook the sand out of the towels at the end of the day? Who took the blame when we got home late because Flint ran off and got lost?"

"Bathing the kids. Tucking them in at night. Some of that was really—"

Shadow Opal waited for her to finish, and Opal inexplicably found herself in tears.

"You had tender moments," said Shadow Opal after Opal had rubbed her eyes without managing to stop the tears. "That's not the same as fun."

"When I was working on *Dead Loss*—when Corvus and I first met—"

"You focused on the job. Did you ever notice he asked you out for drinks after work? You always said no."

"He asked me out?"

"Six times. You filter out anything that might be fun. I'm tired of that."

"So you—so *we*—find ourselves on *Girls Gone Wild*? Scratch that—put ourselves there on purpose?"

Golden-eyed Opal looked past her. "Wilder than that," she muttered, "and oh, it was delicious. Delightful. Astonishing. He has powers he hasn't shown you yet, and he's part of a larger community here, with its own agenda. You weren't there, though. You still didn't have fun. You abdicated while I made you these memories."

"You made memories?"

"They're here." Shadow Opal glanced toward the study door. "Want to see?"

Opal shuddered, then shook herself like a dog shaking off water and headed for the door. Shadow Opal opened it for her and led the way into the hall beyond. They traveled down a hall that got darker and narrower as they went. At its very end was a thick steel door barricaded with bolts, bars, and locks.

"You're good at this sort of thing," said Shadow Opal.

Opal put her hand on a padlock the size of a pumpkin, with a cartoonishly large keyhole. "I did this?"

"You've got a lot of doors like this scattered around. Lots of things you don't want out roaming, I guess. I don't know how I got out."

"How do I open it?"

"Give me a key."

"A key?" Opal looked down at what she was wearing. The same olive green denim coverall she had just shrugged into back in the real world, with lots of pockets, and black boots. She pushed her hands into the pockets, pulled things out. Tape, scissors, lip gloss, a tin of Altoid peppermints, a Swiss Army knife, six quarters and two shiny pennies, a packet of airline pretzels, a wad of Kleenex. A pad of paper, a telescoping pen, two paper clips.

"Close enough," said Other Opal. She took a paper clip, held it in her closed hand, produced a skeleton key. "Are you ready?"

"No," said Opal, "but go ahead."

Other Opal touched the key to the locks—she didn't even have to turn it. They snapped open one by one. Finally the door was no longer locked. Other Opal stood back. She gestured toward the doorknob. "Your turn."

Opal gripped the doorknob, turned it, opened the door, and looked in at the altar in the forest.

Everything about the scene was different from the way it had been when she'd awakened. Here, the forest was a wilderness of strange, exotic trees, with leaves the shapes of violins, harps, hearts, arrowheads. The greens shone in many vibrant shades, and the tree bark was rich colors as well, red brown, cream yellow, slivers of peeling, textured silver. The altar glowed with gray light. A version of Opal stood on it, embraced by a version of Corvus in his Dark God shell. Phrixos's energy wasn't there. Opal stood rigid on the stone, though wrapped in his embrace. No one else was present.

"Relax," said the Dark God, in Corvus's beloved voice, the voice she had listened to many nights as she fell asleep, audiobooks that murmured to her in different hotel rooms, the voices of different characters, all, somehow, contained inside Corvus and let out to play. "Let go, Opal. Let go."

She watched her other self melt. The starch leached out of Opal on the altar, and she leaned against Corvus's chest. His arms supported her. His head dipped so he could speak near her ear. His voice softened; still, she heard every word.

"You don't have to be in charge. You don't have to take care of everyone but yourself. Let me take care of you," he whispered, and she melted more. Her eyes closed. Her mouth smiled.

He eased her down onto the rock, cupping the back of her head so that it didn't bump. He held himself above her, stared down at her face. "Let me hold you. Let me be in you. Let me be part of you."

Opal on the altar let him do all those things, moaning with delight. Her fingers unclenched, her shoulders eased, her body lay boneless, as though she no longer had to hold up the world. Her face relaxed into bliss. It lost the rigid look of someone who knows who she is.

Opal turned away, headed toward the door back into the hallway, but Shadow Opal gripped her shoulders and turned her to face the altar again. "Stop running away," she said. "Stop standing aside. Be there." Shadow Opal pressed on her shoulders, and Opal found herself compressing, deflating, narrowing into something not herself until she was something her other self could hold between her hands. Shadow Opal pressed her palms together, and Opal felt a disorienting upending of the world, a shriek of colors, a breeze brushing tastes against her, a swirl of scents, and then she blinked eyes open and looked up into Corvus's face, the monster she had made and grown to fear and love. His eyes glowed with green light around pupils slit up and down like a cat's. He closed them and pressed close, and then his lips touched hers and she gave herself up to that sense, his heat and pressure and tenderness, gentle in everything he did; he had buried himself in her, but he held himself up enough to not crush her; he had to tilt to reach her mouth, but he managed, despite his length. Something of the god worked in him to make it possible, and everything about him embraced her, made her feel safe in a way she could never remember feeling before.

She wanted to laugh, and she wanted to cry. How strange it felt, being here, at the mercy of someone else, having let loose of all the things she usually kept track of, her lists of things she needed, things she planned to do, things she would check to make sure everyone else around her had what they needed and knew what they were going to do next.

Most of her work was preparing. She spent hours setting

up the makeup and tools she used for her job, even though she could have worked faster and better without them. She planned ahead, usually, so she would be where she needed to be in plenty of time. Cars she drove never ran out of gas, and if she had to change a tire she always had a well-inflated spare. When she cooked, which she only did if she were expecting company, she had all the ingredients and instructions ahead of time and never missed a step.

She had spun webs of control around everything she touched.

A vision from Christmas vacation came to her.

Mother might not remember the strings she had threaded through everything and everyone around her, but the image of it was clear in Opal's memory, a horrifying truth revealed by her sister's magic during a family meeting: their mother had bound her children, husband, relatives up in magic threads that trapped them in the family home; only Opal had escaped. She had moved out into the world and spun threads of her own.

Opal opened her hands and let go of all those controls.

She opened her heart, let it lie revealed, unprotected. Corvus's whispers as he embraced her nudged her heart, as he drove into her, nested inside her. The edge of pain and yearning that rode him bumped into her heart, touched her own longing for something she had never yet found, wove into it. She found herself up against his heart as well, a large mass of all the colors of amber spiderwebbed in silver and gold, pulsing, with many chambers, slivers of secrets and wonders, memories and wounds, slender syllables of bliss and tiny grains of pain.

She slipped her hand inside his heart, let things flow across her palms and along her fingers. She tasted loneliness, longing, tenderness, fear. Solitude: long stretches of solitude.

"What are you doing?" he whispered. He had stilled above her and within her. His forehead rested on her cheek.

"I don't know," she said. Why had she thought it was his heart she touched? It wasn't shaped like any heart she had ever seen in an anatomy chart, or even in horror movies where people ripped the hearts out of each other's chests. She turned her inward vision toward what she had been thinking of as her own heart, and saw a landscape of walls. She went toward the first wall, looking for a door, but she couldn't find one, so she climbed up the wall—it had things sticking out of it, sharp things, but she found a way up them without cutting her feet.

Why did she have feet, she wondered, when she was shifting across impossible landscapes? There was no reason she should be one form or another. She paused, standing on a wall in her own heart, and thought, usually I work with surfaces; but I have practiced greater shifts. I have turned my siblings into objects of convenience on occasion, though not often, and not after they got their own powers. I have changed myself in all kinds of ways, sometimes so much that I had trouble remembering what my previous form was. Now I want to be something that can fly above walls and see beyond them.

She stared down at hands that looked like the hands she wore in waking life, then glanced down at her breasts, her front, her legs beyond the slope of her stomach. She was naked now, three steps away from the coverall-dressed self she had been and still another step from the physical body she wore in the waking world. How many layers down was she? She had left Corvus in midquestion, but it was Corvus in memory, not in real life; she could pause a memory without upsetting anybody, surely.

Shift, she thought, and she turned into winged mist, a thin and less connected-to-itself creature. *Eyes,* she thought after a moment's blind confusion, and she grew several eyes. She looked up, down, forward, backward, inward at the same time. It took a while to integrate all the visions into a coherent picture. The color of the sky had changed from standard blue to scarves of varied colors, blue, green, shades and nuances. Seeing many directions at once, vision was a three-dimensional experience. She was enveloped in sight the way she would be embraced by warm water in a hot spring.

She hovered above the courtyard protected by the first wall and saw a pale statue of a child in the center. The child had blind white eyes and short curls. It gazed toward the ground, its mouth in a faint frown, brows drawn together above its nose. The cloud that Opal was drifted closer to the child, saw her own features on the statue. Another younger, frozen self. She rose again and headed inward across the landscape toward another walled fortress. This one had a roof over it, but when she flew closer, she found that there were chinks in its armor; she flowed in through one of them and found herself in a chamber. Light shone in through the stained-glass walls, a mosaic of many different colors of red and dark orange, ruby, crimson, rust, coral, salmon, sunset colors. In the center of the chamber, on mounded velvet cloth, nestled a red jewel—or if it were a paler color, she couldn't tell, because the colored light coming through the walls and striking gleams off its faceted surface stained everything it touched.

She drifted down to the jewel. How vulnerable it was to anything in mist form. She had built all these walls, but did they really protect her? In this landscape, people could be so many other ways than merely human-shaped. She had protected herself so far, though—or had she? She and her shadow had still not found out where Phrixos had gone or what he had done while she held him inside, and now she was layers deep into herself and didn't know how to navigate.

She touched the red jewel. Passion flared through her, washed her up out of the walled landscape, back into Corvus's arms.

"Stop slipping away," he whispered. He braced her and

pumped into her, and it sent her spasming over the edge into complete loss of control.

He smiled when she came back to herself. "How was that?"

"Terrifying."

He kissed her, his lips soft. "Was anything about it good?"

"Are you fishing for compliments?" she asked, strangely detached from what had happened, but not outside of it anymore.

"No. I'm trying to learn you. Maybe next time I'll do better."

"Corr. This isn't even real. I don't think you're real. I don't know where we are, but look at these trees . . ." She lifted her head and looked, then gasped. She was back out in the real world, on the altar, with people and cameras all around them, and some of the people were waking up.

"I don't claim to be an authority on reality," he murmured, "but—"

15

"What the *hell* has happened to my production?" screamed the director, rising from a tangle of bodies in various states of clothed and unclothed just beyond the trees that ringed the clearing on the far side of the altar. "You! Put your pants on! Oh my gawd. Where are *my* pants? Oh my gawd. Where's the damned publicist? Someone lock her up before any of this gets out! What—"

"Say, boss," said George. "Is this a classic case of dope in the water or what?"

No one spoke. Neil found his clothes and hurried into them, as did anybody else who could locate what they or someone else had been wearing before the big meltdown. "All right," Neil said at last. "Dope in the water supply. That could work. Might even be true. Sabotage! Damage control . . . Loaders, I'm confiscating all the film we shot since—Juanita, when did you stop taking notes?" he asked the script supervisor, who was struggling to tie her hair back into a knot at the nape of her neck. It turned out she had a wealth of sleek dark hair, long enough to reach her hips. Opal had never seen her disarrayed before; she was in charge of keeping track of everything about the script—what was written before they filmed, what lines and angles changed in the course of filming, what time everything happened, and which take it happened on. She always wore her hair wadded at the back of her neck, with a baseball cap on top of her head.

Juanita buttoned her pants, tracked down her clipboard and a couple of pens from a scatter of things in the grass, then checked her watch. "Um," she said. "We had just finished take nine, scene twelve C, reaction shots to Mom's death. Another splatter misfire. One forty-five point thirty seconds. Three hours ago, boss. God."

"Everyone? Everyone, listen to me absolutely. You are gagged about this. Talk about it and risk being blacklisted. We have to figure out what happened. We have to . . . we have to examine the film for clues. No one who wasn't here is to know what happened. Understand?"

"But boss—"

"What *did* happen?"

"Who's going to pay for it?"

"Some of us are working overtime now," said one of the teamsters with satisfaction.

"If you call what just happened work!" Neil cried.

"Are you gonna?" asked someone else.

Neil growled, and then said, "That's enough for tonight! To your scattered domiciles go, you wretches! Where's my call sheet? Where's my A.D.s? We're going to have to redo the schedule for tomorrow, and you've got to let everyone know once we finalize it. The rest of you, clean up and clear out. Get off the damned clock!"

Continuity came by the set and shot pictures of everything there. Opal closed her eyes; Corvus lay quietly over her, shielding her from sight while keeping himself up on his elbows enough not to crush her. Her hand had settled just above his hip, and she left it there. The skin of leaves over him covered him everywhere. As Magenta had said, that wasn't something Opal had ever put on him. Phrixos must have arranged it. Where was *he*?

People moved, shutting down equipment, turning off lights, wrapping set pieces in waterproof protection for the night. Still, Opal and Corvus lay entwined, the center of the scene as lights shut off, generators powered down, and people moved around them, eyes lowered. People still surreptitiously searched for lost articles of clothing and equipment.

"Hey," said someone nearby. Opal opened her eyes and found Kelsi standing beside the altar. "Brought you some wardrobe." She held up a big black robe, one of Dark God's standard outfits, and a white covener's robe.

"Thanks, hon," said Corvus. "Could you drape the black thing over me? Maybe I can get up and wrap it around both of us. Not the first time I've been glad I have such loose robes for this role."

Opal tried to remember what she had been wearing before the forest took over. Before she let it take over.

One of her green denim coveralls with lots of pockets, and those black boots. She could not remember getting out of her clothes again, but she'd been walking between several worlds. She wondered who she had left in charge of the body. She rolled her head and looked around as much as she could. No sign of her clothes.

Corvus rose, draped in black, pulled her up with him, edged awkwardly around until they were both sitting on the altar with scarves of black lapped around them from behind. Opal glanced down at her body and saw stone scrapes, bruising, bite marks she didn't remember from the sex she had just had, awake, with Corvus, where everything had been a kind of gentle she wasn't used to in sexual encounters. The marks must have happened during the earlier sex, when Other

Opal was running things, and maybe Phrixos was around. If they got all that on tape—

She rubbed her face, reached inside for the healing she used to apply to scrapes and bruises on her siblings until they came into their own powers, and later, something she had practiced on the sly on various movie shoots. Usually on other people, not so much on herself. She didn't take these kinds of risks.

Kelsi stretched up and handed her the white robe, and she shrugged out of Corvus's embrace and slid it on, even as her skin repaired itself and bruised flesh healed. Power came easily. What had just happened hadn't drained her. She wanted to go back to her study and check how much Flintfire she had left, how much power her Sifter Chants had stored for her, but then she decided maybe she better come into the world for now and see what needed doing.

She wanted to figure out what had happened in the clearing, not just to her, but to everyone. What had the thing under the ground accomplished, and why? Had they fulfilled its desire, or was this just the beginning? It must have wanted all that energy for some reason, all that procreative power. She didn't know much about major ritual workings—that was not magic as her family practiced magic—but she had heard stories.

"Thanks, Kelsi," Opal said as she belted the white robe. "What happened to you?"

Kelsi's gaze dropped. Her head drooped. "I, uh," she said, and red flushed across her forehead and cheeks.

"Sorry," said Opal. "Shouldn't have asked. I guess everybody knows what happened to me and Corr, huh?"

"Not all of us were paying attention."

"Oh. Right." Opal looked up at Corvus's face, but he was staring past her toward the trucks. People were striking everything strikable. The security guards had arrived for the night so that they didn't have to move all the equipment back to the parking lot by the old supermarket. The guards looked confused.

"Better get to the Makeup trailer and take this off," Corvus said, stroking a cheek leaf.

"Right," said Opal. She led the way across the battered grass to the trailer, part of her mind wondering if the girls, Gemma and Bettina, had made it back from wherever they had gone when the wave of orgy energy hit. Maybe they had done things that would scar them for life under the influence of it. Opal hadn't done much memory mending, but she knew there were charms for it.

Uncle Tobias was supposed to arrive tonight. He could help. In fact—she checked her watch, then remembered she didn't know what time to expect him.

In the Makeup trailer, Rod and Magenta had closed up their stations and were gone. The trailer was dark except for a nightlight by Opal's station. Corvus settled into the big chair and Opal turned on more lights, snapped Polaroids of his head and shoulders and dropped them haphazard on the counter. "Does it even come off anymore?" she muttered to herself as she approached Corvus with her solvents. She wondered again what had become of Phrixos.

Corvus pulled his arms out of the robe and studied his chest and arms, leaved all over. These leaves weren't the ones she had applied to him at the start of the workday. They hadn't come off during the day, despite strenuous contact with other surfaces, including the altar stone and her. A memory of the leaves against her skin, rough, strange, smelling of autumn, abrading her like the scales of a dragon, chased through her mind and vanished.

She loaded a makeup sponge with solvent and lifted it, ready to press it against Corvus's chest. "Shed, skin," she whispered. She tugged gently at the edge of a leaf, and the leaf skin split and slid beneath her fingers, baring Corvus's chest, its halves sliding off him like silk to pool around the chair in heaps. Detached, the leaves looked like net fabric painted with color, dull and dark on the inside. It was like nothing she had ever worked with.

"Wow," she said. She touched his face. "Shed, skin," she whispered again, and the mask split down along the middle of his forehead, the spine of his nose, the philtrum beneath, the middle of his mouth, the cleft in his chin. It fell apart in two soft halves and pooled above his shoulders against the back of the chair. She gathered the halves and placed them on her plaster cast of his head, where they welded together and formed the face he had just worn.

She looked back at Corvus, restored to his nonmonster face, his smile steady, his hair rumpled, a few leaves still caught in it. He looked like her Corvus, except for the resident green glow in his eyes.

"Phrixos," she whispered.

He smiled at her with Corvus's tenderness, then rose and stretched, settled his robe on his shoulders again. "It's been an interesting day," he said, in Corvus's voice. "A pleasurable day, a profitable day in so many ways."

"What did you do to us?"

"What did I do? People did what they wanted. I just gave them an atmosphere of permission, maybe a few nudges in the right direction."

She shook her head. "No, I can't believe everybody wanted to do that."

"Why not?"

She flipped through memories, not all of them clear, of people in positions she'd never seen people in in real life, faces taut with pain or pleasure, the chant some of them chanted— nonsense words, or maybe not; words she didn't understand. Maybe they had all done what they wanted. But if that was the truth, why had they fled, shamefaced, afterward?

"Why did you do it?" she asked.

He looked at her then, and she saw that he was completely Phrixos, though he had all of Corvus in his gaze and look, the parts of Corvus he hadn't been able to successfully mimic before, tenderness and wry humor, sweetness, a self-effacing air despite his size.

A shadow self hovered above him, huge, glittering, and beautiful. It radiated power and satisfaction.

The ground? She had thought the ground was quiet, but now she realized it was warm, almost hot, with a long, slow pulse.

"We were starving, sleeping, hibernating with no spring promised," Phrixos said. "We lay here like husks a long long time, dreaming of waking. The girl came, the one who makes stories, with her promises of bringing others. She let us into her dreams. She listened to our story and took it out into the world. She told others and enlisted them into the service of the story." He glanced around the trailer, nodded toward the location beyond the walls. He spread his hands, as though to indicate everything about the production. "Many people work to make the story take form. Now we are awake again."

Opal pulled the covener's robe tighter around herself and stared at the man in front of her. "You gave Bethany the first draft of the script?" she said.

"She used her own skills to shape it, but we gave her dreams to draw from."

"The script is full of blood and terror and death."

Phrixos shrugged. "She seemed to think it needed it."

"So—no one has to die on the altar to satsify you in real life?"

"You and I have already done the necessary ritual there. Several times."

"But you used Lauren's blood, and Erika's—"

"Blood has its own power. I do seek and treasure it. There are some doors it is a key to unlock."

"What did you do to the inside of my head?" Other Opal had told her one thing about that—that he had left his own door into her there. Was that all? Maybe it was plenty.

He smiled and climbed to his feet, pulled the black robe up to cover his shoulders. "There are other hungers," he said, pressing a hand to his stomach. "Let's get something to eat."

"What did you do to Corvus?" she asked.

"Did anyone ever tell you you worry too much?"

"Worrying is an integral part of my character," she said, "so yeah, people tell me that all the time, but it doesn't change what I do. What did you do to Corvus?"

"I ate him."

"What?" she cried.

"Get your things and let's go." He nudged her shoulder.

She glanced around, frantic, wondering which spells to invoke to make Phrixos tell her the truth. If he had actually eaten Corvus, was there any way she could save him? Make Phrixos regurgitate him, the way Chronos had been tricked into coughing up his Greek god children after he had swallowed them? Was Corvus even still alive? Phrixos was full of power from what had happened in the clearing. Opal wasn't sure she could force him into anything.

"Kidding," said Phrixos. "Come on, let's get out of here."

Opal swallowed her terror and chose to believe him so she could focus on practical matters. She locked up her supplies, including the strange new leaf skin Phrixos had shed, grabbed her messenger bag, and followed him out of the trailer, turning off lights as she went.

She locked the door and glanced around. Most of the crew had driven away; a few were still packing up equipment. "The girls," she said. Worry flared, the same kind of worry she used to spend on all her younger siblings. "Magenta? Doreen?" Magenta had said Doreen, Gemma's mother, was hiding in one of the trailers.

Magenta had said that to Opal the first time Opal woke

up. She had had her clothes then. Gone inside herself, and awakened again in the real world, back on the altar. A time jog had happened, or something else. "How many times did we—were you always out here?" she asked Phrixos.

"No," he said. "Sometimes I was in two places at once. You took me with you."

"There's a clear piece of time in the middle of it all when Magenta and I were awake and everyone else was still under the influence."

"Yes," he said.

"When I woke up again—"

"It was fun, wasn't it?"

"You're gloating. I hate gloaters."

He smiled, stroked his hand down her hair. She jerked out from under his caress and strode toward the crew corral. It was deserted. The canvas-backed chairs with the names on them had been packed. Opal found Doreen's yarn bag in the half-crushed grass, with its crochet projects inside. Knitting needles might have made noise during takes, so Doreen had been teaching herself this new skill.

"I used to have clothes," Opal muttered, abandoning the bag. "What happened to my damned clothes?"

More important than clothes, what had happened to the young actresses? Into her mind rushed a spell she had often used as a teenage mother surrogate, a Locate-Lost-Objects Cantrip, because the kids were always losing things, and they got in deep trouble if the things were important and stayed lost. She visualized Gemma and whispered the spell. A thin thread of silver faded into view in the air before her, leading toward the forest. She raced off along the line, stumbling as she left the lighted clearing and headed into the trees.

No sound followed her, but she felt his presence behind her, Phrixos, a large displacement of space, a traveling nexus of energies. The thread led her past bushes and under branches, over roots and rocks. Some small animal startled out of her path, the sudden rustle of it scaring her so she stumbled, but he reached from behind and steadied her. She stilled, her elbow cupped in his hand, and paused to listen to the night, the diminishing racket of the animal crashing away, an owl calling from farther, and the sound of the stream. The night was damp and smelled of fallen leaves. In the still, she suddenly realized her feet were bare and battered, that she'd stubbed her toe against a rock. Pain signals flared, all the feelings she had blocked in her sudden panicked desire to find the children. Her calves were scratched and bleeding.

She muttered, set healing in motion, stood with the warmth of his fingers braceleting her elbow.

The crickets started up again, a song she had interrupted by running.

"They're all right," he said.

She was angry all over again that he could use Corvus's voice so well she couldn't tell the difference. "Whose definition of all right are you using?"

"Good point."

She pulled her arm out of his grasp and started forward again, slower this time. She flicked a small greenish globe of witchlight from her fingers so she could see where to put her feet down.

The silver seek-thread shimmered in the darkness ahead of her. It led her, eventually, to a nest of dried ferns and damp earth, where the two girls, still in their special ritual dresses, all tatters now, were curled up in each other's arms, their faces and arms smudged, their hair full of twigs, their breathing slow and steady.

Phrixos stood beside her as she stared down at the sleeping girls.

"They weren't part of it?" she asked.

"Not really."

"What does that mean?"

"The energy affected them, but I sent them away from it."
Now he spoke in a distant voice, the voice of someone else,
not Corvus nor Phrixos, someone she hadn't met. The glittering shadow she had seen hovering above him when she first
woke up.

"Why?"

"I knew you wouldn't like it," said the stranger.

"You care what I think?"

"You're a key element," it said. "I wish to keep you happy."

Good news and bad. She didn't necessarily want to be a
key, but if it wanted to keep her happy, maybe she had leverage. "Who are you?"

"I was asleep and now I'm wide awake, thanks to everything you've done for me." He stroked a hand along her
shoulder, down her back, trailing warmth and pleasure.

Creepy. She knelt and touched Gemma's shoulder. Gemma's
face contracted into a frown. She rubbed her cheek against
Bettina's shoulder, frowned again, and opened her eyes.
"What?" she asked, as though puzzled by everything. She
rubbed her eyes with dirty fists, then stared at Bettina's an-
gelic sleeping face so close to her own. She glanced around,
found and fixed on Opal's face. "What's going on?" This time,
her voice had sharpened into confusion and dismay.

"Lots," said Opal. "Strange things happened to everyone.
You and Bettina went off in the woods. Can you get up?"
Opal touched Bettina's shoulder. "Bettina?"

Bettina burrowed deeper into the hollow where she lay,
hunched her shoulders and hid her face.

"Bettina," Opal repeated. "It's dark and cold. I should get
you back to your hotel, or wherever you're staying. Wouldn't
you like a hot bath?"

Bettina slowly turned toward them. Her face showed traces
of muddy tears. She opened her eyes. A new tear ran down into
her hair. "I would like that above all things," she whispered.

Gemma sat up. She worked her legs free of Bettina's skirts, rested her hand on Bettina's shoulder. "Let's get out of here."

Bettina nodded, mashing her crinkled hair against the damp earth. She let Gemma pull her upright. She and Gemma worked together to scramble out of the hole they were in. Phrixos reached down and helped haul them to their feet. "You will never," Bettina said in a low voice to Gemma, "tell a soul what we did. Ever."

"What did we do?" Gemma asked. "I fell asleep and had really weird dreams. God, where are we?" She turned her head, glancing at the darkening forest around them.

"We're a ways into the forest." Opal touched the witchfire ball with a finger, fed it more energy so that it brightened enough to light the ground for a few feet in all directions. She lifted it so it hung in the air just above their heads, though not so high as Phrixos's head. "Let's go back."

"What's that thing?" Gemma asked in a flattened voice.

"Special effects," said Opal.

Phrixos strode in front of them, the light at his back, coating his robe with soft greenish yellow color. The two girls held hands as they walked just ahead of Opal. She didn't think they even knew.

As they forged toward the clearing, she said her cantrip again, this time focusing on Doreen. A slender thread of rose pink led toward Doreen; Opal broke away from Phrixos and the girls and followed her thread. It led to one of the crew Porta-Johns. The door was locked. Opal knocked several times and got no answer, so at last she unlocked the door with a tiny push, another skill she'd honed while caring for her siblings, though she'd only seriously used it a few times. Usually, she figured that if they were hiding, they needed to hide, not be found. Once in a while, necessity had pushed her.

"Doreen," she murmured. She opened the door half a foot. "Doreen?"

The door pulled out of her hand, opening wider. Doreen sat on the floor, a miserable ball, her eyes puffy, her face stained with salt tear tracks, her hair greasy as though sweaty hands had stroked through it too many times. She groaned and climbed to her feet.

"Whore," she said.

Opal flinched, straightened. She thought about what had happened that afternoon and wondered who and what she really was. Had she had any control over events? Had she given control away? She had definitely had sex in public, which was pretty skanky, but . . . "It had nothing to do with money," she said at last.

"Not you," said Doreen. "Well, you, but . . ." She ran her fingers through her hair again, pulled herself together. "God, I need a bath. A shower. Another bath."

"Mom?" Gemma said, tentative.

"Gemma! Oh my god! Are you all right?" Doreen came out of the Porta-John and reached for her daughter, who flinched and backed away, pulling Bettina with her. The girls still held hands; it was as if they didn't know how to disconnect.

"I'm fine," Gemma said, and held up her free hand in a "stop" gesture.

"Did you—where were you when—are you going to need therapy?" Doreen asked.

"Oh, who doesn't," said Bettina, her voice acid.

"Whatever it was, I kind of slept through it," Gemma said. She looked around. The clearing and the waiting area were trashed in some strange ways, but empty of people. Most of the equipment had been put away for the night. "What happened?"

"Thank God for small mercies," said Doreen.

"You really don't remember any of it?" asked Bettina.

"Why? What do you remember?"

Bettina's gaze went to their linked hands. She bit her lower lip. Her brow furrowed, and she said, "Well, I shan't tell you now. I wonder what it means in the long run. Perhaps nothing, if it wasn't as real for you as it was for me."

"But, on a more immediate note . . ." Opal glanced around. "It looks like everybody left. Or maybe they're hiding. I have a car. Doreen, did you drive yourself, or do the three of you want a ride somewhere? Phrixos and I were going to supper."

"After everything that's happened, you're going to eat?" Doreen asked, outraged. Her stomach rumbled and she glanced toward it. Her eyebrows rose. "Oh."

"Has anyone seen Rica?" asked Bettina. "I can't remember the last time I saw her."

Opal said, "Do you want me to find her now? I'll need something of hers. I don't know her well enough to track her."

"What are you, psychic or something?" Bettina said.

"Something," said Opal, as Gemma said, "She found Mom, didn't she?"

"Good grief, that's right." Bettina bit her bottom lip, swung Gemma's hand. "Well, I suppose I don't really want to find Rica. I suppose I hope she's all right. If what happened to her is the same as what happened to everyone else, I wish I'd had a camera. Pictures would be worth a lot in our future relationship."

"Eww," said Gemma.

"If you can drive us to our B&B, that would be good," Doreen told Opal. "I did drive myself and Gemma to the location this morning, but now it looks like my car is gone."

Bettina said, "May I stay with you two? I don't want to go back to my room alone."

"Okay," said Gemma, then glanced at her mother.

Doreen nodded, her face pale. "I don't want you to be alone, either."

Opal led the way to the Lincoln. Everyone piled in. She

didn't think she should let the girls and Doreen go without making sure they were all right, but she didn't know what to do for them. She was still appalled and confused about what to do for herself.

Doreen, her voice tired, directed Opal to another early-twentieth-century house in town, where the girls and the woman got out and slammed the car doors without saying good-bye.

"What do you think?" she asked Phrixos after they had sat in silence, parked outside the B&B. "Where do we go next?"

He smiled down at her. "Back to the nexus?"

"Is that the altar?"

"Yes. We could go back and add to the work we've started. We are close to completing all the necessary steps."

She didn't want to know about steps, or where they led. "I don't want to go back. I'm dirty and tired and hungry. The choices are your place or mine." She thought about running into Neil at the bed-and-breakfast. He'd been pretty mad when the confusion wore off. It was possible he would blame her for everything. He wasn't pleasant at the best of times. "Scratch that. We're going to my hotel."

"Do you have clothes for me there?"

"Nope, but I've got clothes for me. I can make clothes for you. I have an industrial-strength shower, too."

"You've made up your mind."

"I have." She started the car and they drove back to the hotel in silence.

The front desk clerk in the lobby opened his mouth to speak when he saw them, but they pushed past to the elevators without giving him time to say anything. Opal pressed the up button, then leaned on the wall, tiredness weighing her down. She knew how to deal with that, didn't she? She could draw energy from her reservoir and pull herself together. Just now, she felt too tired to do it.

Before the elevator arrived, she heard a voice greeting the desk clerk in jovial tones. "I'm looking for my niece," said Great-Uncle Tobias. "Opal LaZelle."

The clerk said, "I think she's registered here—"

Opal opened her eyes and straightened. "Uncle."

16

Tobias crossed the lobby. He looked thin and tired and older than usual, though his thick white hair crowned his head like an energetic bush. He carried a small duffel bag and a jacket. "Oh, no," he said, studying Opal and Phrixos, his face stretched with dismay.

The elevator dinged and the doors opened. "Come up," she said, and she, Phrixos, and Tobias got into the car.

Opal's room had a deserted air, a little stuffy, the bed made up and everything hidden away. The air tasted sterile. Opal opened the curtains and then the window, which stopped after a two-inch gap. Damp, fresh, chilly air came in.

"There's a lot to tell you," Opal said to Tobias, "but I need a shower first."

"I'll wait." Tobias settled in one of the chairs by the little round table, with his bag beside his feet.

Phrixos followed Opal into the bathroom, out of his robe, and on into the shower as soon as she got it going. His head brushed the ceiling even when he hunched over, and he took up so much space she could barely turn around, but she decided she didn't care; she was closer to the showerhead and the delicious stream of hot water than he was, and that was all she focused on, until he helped her soap up and scrub. At which point she leaned back against him, both of them steamy, soapy, slippery, comforting, with warm water pounding on them. She said, "Let me think."

He closed his arms around her and stilled.

At last she had time to count her blessings. Hot water. The girls were safe. Tobias was here. She had enough power—

She closed her eyes and went inside herself, to the study. The fire—Flint's fire, augmented by some of her sifted power—burned in the fireplace. Her second self wasn't there.

She grabbed a poker and stooped before the fire. "Hey, you traitor," she whispered to it, stirring it with the poker. "You deserted me and left me open to him."

Open to a kind of mad transcendence she had never experienced before, a memory she wanted to consider and strengthen, even though it frightened her. "Let go," Corvus or Phrixos or both of them had said, and for once in her life she had. He had not let her fall.

The fire sent apologetic flames to stroke her hand, then flooded through the air to wrap around her, but she said, "Wait," and sent it back into the fireplace. It burned bright and comforting, the promise of protection.

Something outside her shifted, and she left her study. Phrixos's arm reached past her to turn off the water. She gasped and shivered as the warmth stopped, though they were both wrapped in steam, and he was warm against her back still, and her lower legs were also warm.

"Was that long enough?" he murmured. Water had gathered around their feet and calves, rising to the level of her knees, almost spilling over the edge of the tub; she had dropped a washcloth on the drain where he couldn't reach it, and it had acted like a plug.

She bent and pulled it loose. The water rushed away. "Is my hair clean?" She worked her fingers through it. She couldn't remember using shampoo.

"Clean enough," he said. He pushed aside the curtain and grabbed towels from a shelf of metal bars above the toilet, shook one open and draped it over her, then scrubbed at his head with another.

She stepped out onto the linoleum and dried off. She hadn't brought any clothes into the bathroom except the white robe. It was tattered and stained from her passage through the forest. She wrapped a towel around her and went through the steam to the bedroom.

Tobias had the overhead light on and was studying various drafts of the script, which she had left lying on the table. Opal sighed and pulled a brown coverall out of the closet, grabbed some underwear, and went back into the bathroom to change.

Phrixos stood there, flushed from the heat, a towel wrapped around his waist. "I'm guessing you don't own anything in my size." He had used her deodorant and smelled like hot male mixed with baby powder. He reached for the black robe he had hung on the hook on the back of the door.

"I can at least clean it for you." She held the robe and sent a Cleaning Spell through it that left it soft, clean, and scented like lemons and wind-washed sunlight. He smiled at her and pulled on the robe.

They went out and sat on the bed, facing Tobias.

Tobias set aside the script. "I believe the nature of your trouble has changed?"

"Yes," said Opal.

"When I threw the auguries last night, there was urgency implied, and a suggestion to prevent something from happening. My sense now is that I came too late to stop it."

"What did they say? Was it a dire reading?"

"The reading was muddled and confusing. It wasn't dire

enough to make me hurry. I was worried about you—there was a death threat—but here you are, alive, thank goodness."

"A death threat!" Opal glared at Phrixos, who smiled and shrugged. She made a fist and tapped his bicep with it. "There was a death threat?"

"It depends on your definition of death," he said.

"What does *that* mean?"

"There was a death, I think—"

"Who? What else happened while I was out of it? Someone died?"

"You," he said.

She punched him again. "What? I'm a walking corpse?"

"For a time you were alive with your walls down. A state you thought of as death, and so, for you, a little death."

"Uncle?" she asked, turning to Tobias.

"Niece, you haven't introduced us yet," said Tobias.

"What?" She looked at Phrixos. Tobias had met Corvus on the *Dead Loss* set. But now he was speaking to a deeper reality. "My apologies, Uncle. This is—I am not sure, exactly. Some parts of him seem to be Corvus. A portion is an entity I call Phrixos, an agent for the local power that possessed Corvus. There's another part, I think, that is the actual local power speaking for itself through him. Phrixos is capable of deceit, so I don't know whether to believe him when he pretends to be Corvus. All of you inside the body of my boyfriend, this is my great-uncle Tobias, who has come to help me solve the problem you present."

"To whom am I speaking?" Tobias said. Opal heard the undertone in his voice; he was asking a question with more than words.

Phrixos straightened, his gaze sharper, more alert, and then a level of character faded from his face, leaving him still sitting up, but different. Opal flattened her hand over his on his thigh. He flashed her a brief glance, then turned to Tobias. "Corvus Weather," he said.

"Were you really here when Phrixos sounded like he was you?" Opal asked.

"Some of the time. It got complicated. He decided to bribe me instead of continually putting me to sleep."

"Were you you while we—" She stopped, conscious of Tobias's regard.

"Bribe you with what?" Tobias asked.

"Presence."

"Explain," said Tobias.

"Phrixos tells me I invited him in, but I don't remember that. I was sleeping through my days while he walked around in my body and did my job. I woke up and time had passed. While I was asleep, he hurt my friends and colleagues, and used me to do it. I don't understand much about this, except that most of what I've believed all my life isn't true, and I have even less control over myself than I thought I did. Anyway, this visitor in my head figured out that Opal responds better to me than to him, so he lets me wake up for key parts of the day now. Sometimes he even tells me what he wants to do next, and gives me the chance to ask people for their cooperation, instead of him trying to force his plans on people."

"Do you know what he wants and why?" Tobias asked.

"Sometimes I know a minute before he asks. I don't have the big picture."

Opal squeezed his hand. "Not even a little part of the big picture?"

"Some of the outlines. But he's already told you some of that. They were asleep and they want to be awake, and now they have a bunch of people they can use to help them wake up."

"Who are they?" Tobias asked. "The auguries—"

Corvus shook his head. "I don't know enough. He guards himself from me. Also, he's so different, even when I see some of his thoughts, I don't understand them. They're in a different language, or they happen at a different speed, or there's an extra dimension I don't grasp."

"You get nothing at all?" asked Tobias.

Corvus bent his head. His hand turned upward under Opal's, and his fingers closed over hers. "There's a shine to it. It's too bright for me to look at."

"Is it something that hurts people?" Opal asked.

"I don't know. I don't think so. It's—it might change people, but I'm not sure it's supposed to hurt them. I would hope I could stop them from jerking me around if I thought it was going to hurt people, but since it's unclear to me, I can't—stand against it."

"Some part of you understands it on a deeper level," Opal said.

He shook his head while saying, "Maybe."

"You're not frightened of it."

"I am, a little. But Opal—cliché, I know, but this gives me power beyond my wildest dreams. I had no idea any of this was possible. What you can do, and what they can do. I've been playing monsters for fifteen years, and I never believed in any of them except when I was being them. God."

"What do you want power for?"

He hesitated, staring toward a wall. "I hit my growth spurt when I was around thirteen," he said. "It didn't all happen at once, but it came before any of the other kids my age got that tall. By the time I was sixteen, I was seven two, and no one else was my size. Nothing fit—clothes, furniture, doorways, social situations. People didn't know how to respond to me, and I didn't know how to get my body to work. I tried basketball, because that was the best typecast I could think of, but back then, I had no coordination. I retreated into quiet, studying too much, exercising on the sly at three A.M., when I could count on being alone. Most of the teasing wasn't meant to be mean. The only girls interested in me, though, were looking for a freak, and that wasn't what I wanted to be."

He frowned. "One of my friends from the nature club decided he wanted to be a moviemaker, and he asked me to be the monster. At first I was really mad at him, but then I thought, why not? I loved being a monster, because I could take off the costume and turn back into myself afterward, pretend I was normal. When I made the jump into real movies, things got much better. Everyone involved in this business is weird one way or another, so they can accept me the way I am, pretty much. There's still no way for me to step out into the regular world and not be noticed, and I—I can't help wondering what that would be like. Phrixos says—" His voice trailed off and he stared down at his feet.

"That's the bribe he offered you? He can make you shorter? I can make you look shorter, if that's what you want," Opal said.

"Can you?"

"Illusion is my business," she said. "I can make you look like whatever you want."

"But you never would have told me that."

"True. Probably. I don't know. If we got involved, I might have told you."

"He offered first."

Tobias opened his bag and pulled out a smaller bag, unzipped it to reveal compartments filled with different ingredients. "Maybe the auguries will tell me more, now that I'm in the presence of what's been warping them."

Opal stood. "Can we do that after supper? We haven't eaten in hours."

Tobias frowned. He opened one compartment, pulled out a pinch of yellow fragments, rubbed them between fingers and thumb, and tossed them into the air with a muttered phrase. An image formed and faded. "I guess it can wait," he said.

"If you can make me look like anything," said Corvus, "make me look like a normal guy now. Let me try having a meal as someone besides me or a monster."

Opal closed her eyes, so deeply tired she wasn't sure she could handle anything demanding. She went to her study and checked her power reservoir. It held an assortment of shades of power. She held out a hand toward a streamer of blue that looked friendly and uncomplicated, and it rose from the array, touched her palm, slid into her. The blue power revived her, like three sips of water on a hot day—a temporary but convincing state.

She envisioned a Corvus shorter than the one she knew, shrank his features and his stature until he looked—strangely normal, almost nondescript. She decided to dress him in a brown sports jacket, pale blue shirt, dark slacks, and brown shoes. When she had the vision complete, she flicked it over the tall black-robed man in front of her and opened her eyes.

Corvus reduced: she wouldn't have looked twice, except he smiled, and his eyes lit up, and then he was present in a way she knew and loved, from the inside. "Done?" he asked.

"Done. I haven't changed your size, just how you look. You'll need to be careful moving around; you take up more room than it appears. Or did you want the complete transformation? I'm not sure I have enough energy for that right now."

"You can do that?"

She smiled, shrugged with shoulders and eyebrows.

"Let me see." He rose, stared into the mirror over the dresser. His eyes widened. "Heavens. Do you see what I see?" He turned to Tobias, eyebrows up.

"Opal is very good at what she does. You look like someone I would pass on the street without a second thought."

His eyes danced. "Let's go out. I want to walk this one around. Possibly the most peculiar part I've ever played."

In the elevator down, Opal tried to make sense of her impressions of Corvus. She was aware of the space he took up. He hovered over her, even though she looked at him and saw someone only an inch taller than she was, smiling at her. She refined the illusion to damp the space-taking vibes he was giving off. By the time the door opened on the lobby, she had made the transformed Corvus so convincing she believed his apparent size herself.

Tobias bumped into Corvus's elbow as they got off; he had tried to occupy space Corvus was already using.

"Sorry," they both said simultaneously. Corvus made his first frown in his new face. "I see what you mean," he said to Opal.

"This might not be the best idea I ever had," she said. "I should do the whole thing. I'm too tired, and it might hurt you, though. I was never big on total transformations, so I'm out of practice. My brother could do a better job."

"Your whole family has skills?" Corvus asked as they exited the hotel.

"Opal," said Tobias.

"Sorry, Uncle. Corr, we don't talk about that."

"I met a bunch of siblings," he said thoughtfully as they crossed the parking lot. "I—" His eyes glowed green for a second. She would have missed it, but she was still studying the effect of her magic, still trying to reconcile what she knew and what she saw. "Oh, yes. There were three more of you, and two parents, yes?" he said. Though his voice hadn't changed much, she knew Phrixos was the one asking.

She smiled and didn't answer. She had four siblings; one hadn't made the meeting. No need to correct Phrixos's impressions. The less he knew, the better.

Corvus strode ahead to open the door to the IHOP for them. She brushed his arm without intending to. He shifted so there was no more contact.

It took a while for the waitress to notice them. Corvus smiled the whole time. The waitress was Jenny again, and she looked very frazzled. "You movie people?" she asked.

"Not right now," said Corvus.

"Booth or table?"

"Booth," said Opal. Less chance of someone bumping into the invisible parts of Corvus if he was in a booth.

Jenny waved toward a booth. It was next to the corner booth where Travis and Bethany were sitting, again, their laptops out, scripts scattered around. They both had headphones on and gave off an aura of not knowing the other existed. They frowned ferociously at their screens, unconsciously mimicking each other.

Opal wondered if they had been on location that evening. Maybe her party should sit farther away from people they knew. The waitress hadn't recognized Opal from earlier—what casual acquaintance would notice Opal when Corvus was with her?—but surely Bethany and Travis would know her . . .

Corvus took her arm gently and steered her toward the booth beside Bethany and Travis's. Tobias followed. Corvus moved in first, pushing the table out with what appeared to be air in front of his stomach. Tobias and Opal slid in on either side of him.

Bethany took off her headphones and tapped Opal's shoulder. Opal turned to look at her over the back of the booth. "Hey, hon," said Bethany, "whatcha doing here?"

"Need food," said Opal.

"Were you on location tonight?"

Opal relaxed. "Yeah. You miss the whole thing?"

"Yep. We were right here, reworking some of the kid scenes. What the hell happened? No one answers their phones! But Neil came along and dropped a bunch of changes on us. He wouldn't say anything, either, except the whole script is scrapped, practically!"

"Let me eat, and then I'll try to explain it," Opal said.

"Okay," Bethany said, but she looked frustrated, and so did Travis, who hadn't taken off his headphones, but was listening to their conversation. Bethany looked past Opal. "Oh. You've got company. I'm sorry. I'm being rude. But it's like—he's throwing out everything we did! He wants the movie to be romantic! Maybe with a brand-new female lead, but can he give us any background on the new lead? No! I can't believe he's throwing out everything we've done. What about all those days of filming? He didn't seem to care whether he can use any of the stuff he already shot. He can't have talked to the producers. When do they *ever* scrap everything? God, Opal, the whole thing's going to hell!"

Jenny returned. "Have you decided?" she asked, poof-topped pen poised over her order pad.

Corvus ordered a club sandwich. Opal hadn't thought to disguise his voice; the rich words came from his mouth, making the sandwich sound like luxury.

"Hey!" said Bethany.

He glanced over at her and smiled.

"No way!" Bethany said. "Corvus? How can that be you? What the hell?"

17

Travis tore his headphones off and stared.

"I'm not Corvus," said Corvus. "I'm his shorter brother."

"You sound just like him. It's eerie!" Travis said.

"No, seriously," said Beth, "how the hell are you doing that?"

Corvus drank coffee and smiled.

"This is my uncle, Tobias." Opal pointed to Uncle Tobias. "Uncle Tobias, this is Bethany and Travis. They wrote the script for the movie. Dreams came into Beth's head while she was visiting here, and she wrote from them. She grew up here."

"Ah," said Tobias.

Opal turned to Jenny, who was still waiting for their order, though her gaze had settled on Corvus. "Can I get one of those sandwiches, too? Tobias?"

"Just coffee," he said. "I ate on the way."

Jenny smiled, nodded, and headed for the kitchen.

"Stop jerking us around," Travis said, "and tell us what you did to Corr."

"I didn't do anything to him," Opal said. She had only altered the air around him; he remained internally intact.

"Corvus, how is that—what happened?" Bethany asked.

"Nonmovie magic," Corvus said.

"What?" Bethany asked, her voice almost a whisper.

"It's just an illusion, Beth. I wanted to see what it was like to look normal for once. So far, it's very interesting. I'm not used to being ignored. I rather like it. In the short term, anyway."

"How could you possibly get that to work?" Bethany asked.

"Opal managed it. You do miss out on a lot, not being on the set," Corvus said.

Jenny put a coffeepot and plates full of sandwiches on the table, and Corvus said to Bethany and Travis, "Excuse us, please. It's been too long since we ate, and we really used up a lot of energy today—"

Opal socked the air near where his arm appeared to be, and hit an elbow. He flinched and smiled, so strange with his smaller face, nearer to hers. It made her wonder how the illusion worked; he could still use his face as an actor did, even though it was far from the face he actually lived in. She had worked with light to create his false self, but hadn't noticed how intimately entwined this atmosphere she had created was with his actual person. She knew what she had done, and still she found him completely convincing.

Bethany and Travis stared at him. Then Bethany waved a hand, and she and Travis put their headphones back on.

"We can't plan strategy here," Tobias said.

"We'll go back to the room afterward." Opal ate. The first bite was bliss, the second even better. She had eaten half the sandwich before she knew it, and Corvus scarfed his even faster. She watched him eat. It really looked like the sand-wich went into his illusion self's mouth. How on earth was that working? She was a better craftswoman than she knew.

"Why are you staring?" asked Corvus.

"What does it look like from inside?" she asked.

"You're staring at my chest," he murmured. "Maybe this is what it's like for well-endowed women. I'm imagining you're looking into my eyes, and responding accordingly. Are we making eye contact?"

"Yes. I can't figure out how the food gets into your mouth."

"How strange," he said, and stared at his empty plate. "I guess I've had enough."

"You haven't," she said. "You've got a lot of self to main-tain." She handed him the other half of her sandwich.

"Thanks. I'll eat it in the room." He wrapped it in a nap-kin and made it disappear somehow. She couldn't remember if his robe had pockets.

She ate her fries. He had already eaten his. "Okay. You finished?" she asked Tobias.

Tobias drank the last of his coffee and didn't pour more. Even the parsley had vanished from Corvus's plate. Opal rose. She grabbed her messenger bag. This time, she would pay; Corvus didn't match his ID.

"Hey," Bethany said. "Not so fast! You promised us an explanation after you ate."

"We're not going to tell you here," said Opal.

Bethany packed her computer, headphones, and script pages and was on her feet before Corvus even finished get-ting out of the booth. Travis, slower on the uptake, stared after her with confusion on his face. "You pay, hon. I'll be back once I find out what's going on. Opal, you're in a little bitty single room, right? Trav and I have a suite. We needed work room, even though we spend most of our writing time over here. You can meet in our room."

Opal glanced at Tobias, then up where she suspected Corvus's real face was. Both of the men shrugged. "Lead the way," Opal said.

————

On the elevator, Opal said, "Are you ready to be yourself again?" to Corvus.

He glanced into the mirrored back wall of the elevator, smiled at his smaller self, turned to Opal with a faint smile still in place. "Okay. Which one?"

She poked his chest and let the illusion dissolve, and then, there he was, taking up a fourth of the available space, dressed in the black robe of his monstrous self. Bethany and Tobias gasped and stepped back against the wall.

"How the *hell* did you do that?" Bethany demanded.

"I forgot how large you are," said Tobias.

Corvus beamed. "It was educational, wasn't it?"

"Come on," Bethany said, "that works in movies and on-stage, but—how the hell?"

The doors opened and Opal marched out onto Bethany's floor, ignoring the rumble of Corvus's voice behind her. The other three caught up with her when she paused in the hall. She realized she didn't know Bethany's room number. Bethany gave her three eyebrow waggles and walked past to open double doors into a suite with the legend "Senator" over the doorway.

As soon as Bethany dumped her backpack on the coffee table and they all sat on the two couches in the suite's sterile-looking living room, Bethany said, "All right, tell me what happened on location today."

"What have you heard?" Opal asked.

"Zip! Zero! Zilch! Nada! We're in our usual booth, arguing about how bad to make the kids' trauma, when in walks Neil, his shirt and pants stained in interesting places, his hair sizzling around his head, and his eyes shooting lasers.

Bam! He hits the table so hard the coffeepot wobbles. 'This changes everything,' he says. Travis and I go, 'What? What?' like dummies, and he says, 'The film's going in a different direction. We'll know more after we look at the dailies. You people are going to have to be ready for a lot of rewriting. Just so you know.' Like that's any help at all!"

Bethany went to the sideboard and grabbed a bottle of whiskey, whipped off the cap and drank. "This job is already so stressy," she muttered. "Do something you think works, you're proud of it, it's great, he says it's great, then an hour later somebody else complains about something and then he hates what you've done, and you have to do it all over again, and there's no guarantee any of it's going to work, and it's not because of anything you can control. I mean, I've worked like this before, don't get me wrong, but Neil is the worst slave driver I've ever worked with. All directors piss on your work to prove it's theirs, but he's just a big gushing fountain of urine." She recapped the bottle and set it on a tray again. "Yesterday, though, it felt like everything was going to work out all right. We were sliding right along toward getting out of here. What the hell happened today?"

"The whole cast and crew were possessed," Opal said.

Bethany strolled over and dropped onto the couch beside Tobias. "Possessed? That makes no sense. You know that, right? Possessed. Huh. By what?"

"The spirit of the place. Same thing that stole women in the fifties, and made your childhood scary, and crawled into your dreams at the B&B while you were writing the script."

"But that's—but you—but that's crazy."

"Get over it. There's something underground here that's been sleeping a long time, and it's awake now. It's been messing with the production all along, one way or another, and today it went crazy and we all had a great big lovefest out there in the woods, with the cameras rolling. So maybe this turns out to be porn."

"Porn? Porn? Goddamn it. Not again."

"I was kind of out of it while it was happening, so I don't know if anybody got decent tape. But—" Opal felt her cheeks heat. Maybe she should just say it now. Tobias, watching alertly, needed to know this, too, no matter how embarrassing it was. "Corr and I were the stars out there on the altar. Not that we were the only ones. Just—we were the ones with the good lighting and camera angles. But pretty much everybody went nuts simultaneously."

"Whoa," said Bethany.

"So that's what happened." Opal slumped back on the couch. Corvus eased an arm around her shoulders. She wasn't sure that was what she wanted, given how little she knew about who he actually was, but it felt good. She relaxed into the embrace and closed her eyes.

Other Opal was waiting for her on the inside of her eyelids. "Do you remember what happened this afternoon yet?"

"Go away."

"Come on, this is part of our journey now. You stop running away from who you are and what you've done. Remember what you know about this guy's body, and what else we touched while we were with him. Decide from an informed place whether you want his arm around you right now."

"Is there a reason why I might not want that?"

"I'm not going to tell you. You need to decide for yourself."

Opal let her memory open on the afternoon. She had been in two or three places at once: on the altar; on a version of the altar in a dream; inside her own mind, flying around and looking at her fortifications, which guarded against some things and not others. An edge of the memory flapped at her like a flag in wind. What was that? She leaned over and gripped the loose corner, lifted it, opened a door into a fourth reality.

Lying under a bumpy transparent surface like a frozen sea

lay a rivery network of lights and darks, a lacework in three dimensions through which green and blue colors pulsed and flowed, although they were running slowly, and many parts of the network were dim. There was such depth to the vision she could not see the bottom, only that the roots of the rivers twisted down into darkness and faded from view. From the surface of the sea rose many tall columnar shapes with nets of faint light threading through them, but they were hard to see in this dark expanse.

In one place the lines of light converged, braided amongst themselves and rose upward into one of the surface bumps, upwelling, reaching tendrils up toward—

Two forms in the rough shape of humans lay on top of one of the shorter bumps; it was squat, like a table. The larger one, whose body was interwoven with the same sorts of light rivers as the ground, and another, smaller, beneath the first, who was laced through with interlocking snowflakes of red and orange fire.

Opal focused and found herself drawing closer to the two. She stared at the transparent hands of the lower figure, which were bright with internal mehndi lacework, the fingertips alight with whorls and flowers of pulsing red light. The hands, the arms, reached up from the lower figure to embrace the other on top of her, and where their bodies intersected, his cooler colors of light exploded into her, and her own fires dived under his transparent skin to mix with his, to feed his, until the dimmer lines of light inside him grew brighter, their colors shifted toward the red end of the spectrum. This was where she had surrendered, let her shield drop, and she and whatever it was that laced all through the ground under Lapis, whatever it was that had invaded Corvus, had connected. The ground brightened and stirred with the influx of light. Though she fed her energy into the other's net, she did not become depleted. The rivers of green energy had flowed into her as she had flowed into them.

So he, the presence under the ground, Phrixos, whoever it was, had drawn from her even as he put himself into her—and where was Corvus in this equation? She hadn't had a moment alone with him to find out how much of Corvus was left.

A rosy flush ran all through the networks, then faded, leaving the whole of the webwork brighter than it had been before. All around the two figures were other faint networks she had ignored while she had watched herself. Where these networks touched the surface, water from the underground rivers flowed up into them. The whole of the film crew and cast, doing whatever they had done while she and Corvus's body had been engaged with each other. Lines of green force ran through everything, faintly, then faded again, leaving the people more transparent, still alive in faint lingers of light, but not as influenced from the underground as before.

This was when they woke.

Opal opened her eyes. Tobias and Bethany were staring at her. "What?" she said.

"Waiting for an answer," said Tobias.

"Was there a question?" She glanced toward Corvus.

"Where were you?" he asked.

"I was thinking back to what happened in the clearing." She watched as his face rippled in search of an expression. Two or three people inside him seemed to be trying to decide who would control the surface. She felt a brief prickle of grief at the thought that she was losing Corvus before they'd had time to explore each other.

He settled for looking worried.

"So was there a question? I'm sorry I missed it. Could you fill me in now?"

"Your uncle wants to know what you want him to do," said Bethany.

"Yes," said Opal. "That's a good question. Corr, you stay here, all right?" He shifted his arm, tightened it around her.

She straightened, and he relaxed his grip so she could rise. "Tobias, will you come with me?"

"Assuredly," he said. He followed her out of Bethany's room and down two floors to Opal's.

They sat facing each other across the table. She stretched out her hands, and he laid his own on them, staring into her eyes. "What on earth has been happening?" Tobias asked.

"Oh, Uncle," she said, and lifted her hands to press them to her eyes.

He was beside her then, his hand on her arm, the weight of a fallen leaf, a chance gift. She lowered her hands and took one of his, careful not to squeeze. When she was younger, she had thought Uncle Tobias would go on forever, like the tides and the moon, but ever since Christmas Eve, when her sister's spell had given her a glimpse of the hidden ways of things, she had known her uncle was ancient and more fragile than he appeared. His skills and wisdom still burned with clear flames, some of them clearer and stronger as his physical powers faded. He had lost his role as the all-powerful elder, though, whether he recognized it or not. His hand was warm, but felt breakable.

He sat silent while she explained the changes Corvus had undergone since they started filming, the surges of power she had felt underground, her own confusion and participation, culminating in the orgy that afternoon. "Nobody's blamed me for that, as far as I know," she muttered, "but I'm no longer hidden in my talents. Four or five people know I'm not just another normal human being."

"Given the circumstances—forces acting on them, and the peculiar atmosphere that gives people permission to believe the unlikely," Tobias said, "this is not terribly surprising."

"I think it's the first time since high school that I might need to clean up after I've made a mess, though."

"Or maybe not," he said.

"Not? After yesterday?"

"Let's wait and see how all this plays out. It sounds like it's already self-correcting. One of my questions now is, are you in personal danger? Should we work some wards for you?"

"Flint sent me some nonstandard energy that works as a shield."

"What? Explain that."

She told him about Flint's attack over the phone, and he said, "I keep forgetting to watch that boy! This is fascinating! Can you manifest some of this power for me?"

She closed her eyes and went into her mental study. The fire was faint in the fireplace. She stooped before it and held out her hand. "What's the matter?" she asked.

"You don't need us anymore," it said, flames reaching out to brush her skin with heat.

"I do, though. Don't go away. You're some of the best stuff I've got."

"Are you sure?" The flames grew.

"I'm sure. Thanks. Please stay lively." She fed the fire sticks of dried, seasoned wood. She didn't remember putting wood into this room, but it was handy that there was some close at hand. Then she wondered if someone had meddled with the wood, but by that time the fire had eaten three big sticks and burped.

Opal sat on the floor and laid her hand over the remaining wood, sought through it for an explanation.

"I put it there," Other Opal said from behind her.

"Did Phrixos mess with it?"

"No. It came from our own forest. Flame, eat more. We need you. I didn't mean to dismiss you altogether; I just needed you to lie low for a while." Other Opal fed the fire with Opal, and the flames reached up to lap at her hands as she added wood.

"We have a forest?"

"There are a lot of rooms here you haven't seen. We have all kinds of things." Other Opal held a hand near the fire, and a flame jumped to hover above her palm. She turned and held it out to Opal, who accepted it. It melted down over her hand like hot butter, a golden haze of light. "Open your eyes," Other Opal whispered, and Opal opened her eyes to stare into Tobias's face as he leaned over her.

She lifted her hand, and it wore the flame like a translucent glove, a beautiful color of yellow orange like sunset light. Tobias sucked in breath, untucked something from a pocket and held it out to the flame. The flame wicked toward it, a twist of pale string, made the jump, sizzled at the end of the twine for a moment, then faded. The string turned ocher. Tobias held it close to his face and sniffed it.

Opal rubbed her hands across each other. The flame seeped under her skin, a transient warmth, a continuing comforting presence.

"Strange and elegant," said Tobias. "And, of course, unprecedented. Is it entirely Flint's?"

"I had to transmute it so I could use it, but I think it's the Flint part that makes it work."

"His gift may lie in mixing his magic with others'," Tobias muttered. "But that's something to explore another time. This worked as a shield?"

Opal spoke to the Flintfire, asked it to shield her the way it had before, and it rose up and enveloped her, not visibly, but in an embrace she could feel. She held out her hands palms facing her uncle, and he closed his eyes and sent questing fingers of power toward her. They stubbed against her shield. He opened his eyes. Their normal pale blue flared brighter, and he sent a spear of power at her that made her gasp. If she had seen it coming toward her in a regular argument with someone in her family, she would think she had really hurt someone's feelings and they wanted to kill her.

It splashed against her shield and parted, went around her and sizzled against the chair she was sitting in. "Uncle!" she cried, leaping up. Parts of the chair were history; some of them were still smoking.

"As I thought. An amazingly effective tool."

"You could have killed me!"

"True," he said, "but I didn't think you would let me, and I was right. I'm glad you've got this kind of armor, Opal. The situation calls for it."

"What do you see as the situation?"

"You already know it. An uppity dormant god power has grasped opportunity and seeks to rise again. It's a smart one, and it sees you as its chief vehicle. This is a role you've been preparing for much of your life. You know, when I was teaching you as a teenager, you took some of the lessons wrong. I never meant for you to suppress your powers; I just wanted you to learn to use them responsibly. Don't let this thing take you over and use you, Opal. Make your choices. Lay it to rest. If it gets out, who knows what it will do?"

Opal felt strange, listening to Tobias. He said aloud things she had been worrying about, and suddenly she felt contrary and didn't want to believe them. Or she wanted to reframe them.

"The question is: Do you need my help?" he said. "You have your armor, and you have your powers; there's some shifting going on inside you that I'd like to explore; it feels weighty. I think you have the power to stop this yourself, but I'll help if you want me to."

"Would you turn around and go home now if I asked you to?"

"Yes," he said.

"Even though you never leave home, and now you have? Seems like a long time since you went out in the world. I appreciate your coming. Would you be mad at me because you made this trip for nothing?"

"It was not for nothing. You're right, it's been a long time since I was out in the world, and I know now I should do it more often. Santa Tekla is not the world. I feel invigorated, in fact, by having brushed up against so many different kinds of powers and people and communities on my journey. Will you dismiss me, Opal?"

"What would be wrong with your staying, at least over-night?"

"Is that what you want?" He was staring at her as though her answer was important.

She sat back and closed her eyes, and inside, she found herself in a forest, facing her other self. "What is he up to?" she asked Other Opal. Had she seen this forest before? While they were making love to Corvus, these were the trees that surrounded them. And yes, some were dead and could serve as firewood. Twilight made the trees into silhouettes. Other Opal glowed with a pale radiance of her own. One of her hands was still gloved in the warm orange of Flint's fire.

"You can ask him," Other Opal said, "but I don't think he'll answer."

"What's important about this choice?"

Other Opal looked off toward the trees. An owl flapped out of the forest, crossed the clearing where they stood, and was gone. "We left home, and none of the rest of them has," she said slowly.

"Yes," said Opal.

"Since we left, have we ever asked for help before?"

"No. Well, just with Flint."

"If we accept his help now," said Other Opal, "we're bind-ing ourselves back to the family."

"I never left all the way," Opal said.

"From their perspective, it looks as though you've left."

"I come back every year."

"You're the only one Mama doesn't have bound to her with all those strings she laid on the other kids. We really got away from her."

"Do you remember if Tobias was bound up in that web?"

Other Opal looked at her and they both thought. No, Tobias had not been tied to Mama with the network of threads she'd laced into the siblings.

"There are other ways of being bound," said Other Opal. "That vision only showed one surface. Gyp was checking for what she needed to know. She wasn't looking at the whole constellation. She most needed to know how Mama was controlling them all. Look now."

Opal opened her eyes and studied Tobias, but he just looked like himself, waiting, maybe a bit exasperated, or maybe that was just his normal expression. His white hair still bushed up in an untidy bunch, and his face, though weary, was almost more familiar to her than her own, after all the hours of lessons and training he had put her and the other kids through. She had relied on him in many ways to be her compass while she navigated the world of her powers. She had used her skills and strength to care for her siblings when their mother hadn't had the attention to pay them, and Tobias had been one of the powers who supported her in that. A surge of love and gratitude warmed her as she studied her great-uncle. She smiled, and he smiled back.

"Look again," whispered Other Opal inside her. "Widen your eyes. Here. I'll help you."

Other Opal settled into Opal like a dream self coming home, blinked her eyes, and then Opal saw the world draped in webs and colors. Tobias was wrapped in ragged threads of silver and gold, the way he had looked under Gyp's reveal spell, but beneath that lay a soft cashmere-looking layer of blue green, with strings that led away, including one that led from Tobias's chest to Opal's.

"Family ties," Other Opal murmured, using Opal's voice. Tobias, dimly seen through his wrappings, frowned and leaned toward her.

Other Opal pulled back from Opal's edges and retreated to the forest, where they could talk without being overheard.

"So the question is, do you want to lean on your family now, or stand on your own feet? You've been standing on your own feet for years. Do you want to slide back?"

"It's not a final decision, is it? If I ask for help once, I don't become dependent again. Or do I?" Opal had structured her life so she didn't have to depend on anyone. She didn't remember when that had become her goal. But even before she had seen an enmeshed vision of her family, she had felt that their mother was strangling them. She had burned herself out making sure that her younger brothers and sisters were okay, and then they had grown into their powers and gotten snotty. They didn't want or need her help.

So fine, she had left and found other communities where she was necessary and appreciated. They were temporary communities, lasting the length of a shoot, but once one was gone, she could always find another. She had more job offers than she could accept.

Other Opal answered her: "I don't know if it's a final decision, but Tobias is making it seem extra important. You could tell him to go fuck himself."

"Great way to ask for help," said Opal.

"Look at the question he really asked. Do you need help, Opal?"

Opal thought about everything that had happened. The gradual shift toward what Phrixos and the thing under the ground wanted, and then the not-so-gradual shift. Everyone blinking and waking up after the orgy—a change that they had yet to process. Could she grasp the various forces at play and turn them back? Could she send the underground thing, the no-longer-dormant god power, to sleep, and make the world safe for moviekind?

She hadn't bested Phrixos in most of their encounters. Had she truly tried? Did she have the power to control him, make him let go of the other people he'd laid claim to, Lauren, the girls, Erika, Magenta, others she might not know about?

"Do you like it when Tobias says you've spent your life preparing to be a handmaiden?"

"Not a lot," said Opal.

"Who do you really want to be?"

All her life, she had built skills that made her a consummate helper, except those times in her teen years when she experimented with being a user, like many people in her extended family. Helper had felt better, and the fallout was pleasure rather than regrets and pain. She took care of people. She stepped in when a job needed doing and did it. She made people look better, or worse, or whatever way they wanted to look, and in Hollywood, that was a significant power.

"Who else *could* I be?" she asked.

"Mother. Builder. Witch. Fortune-teller. Wife. Sanitation worker. Wizard, baker, actress, seamstress, director, writer, musician, retail worker, teacher, nurse, president, cook, accountant, whore. Soldier. Folklore collector. What do you want? You could spend the rest of your life being lazy, or you could be a drudge, or you could turn into an animal and ditch all human responsibilities."

"Huh."

"It's taking you a long time to make a simple choice," said Tobias in her ear.

"There's nothing simple about this choice, is there?"

"Do you want my help?" he asked. "Yes or no?"

"I don't know if I can handle this on my own," she said slowly. "What if I need your help, whether I want it or not? Is there something wrong with wanting to be safe and sure?"

"Set those questions aside and answer: do you *want* my help?"

"No," she said.

He smiled. He leaned forward and kissed her forehead. "All right," he said. "Now that I'm away from home, I think I'll do some exploring. I've taken a room in a hotel in Salem. Give me a piece of paper and I'll write down the phone number. I won't be in the room during the day, but I will check for messages. I may not be able to respond right away, but I'll try to come if you need me."

She dug a scrap of paper out of her messenger bag. Tobias wrote the name and number of a chain hotel on it. "Good luck," he said, picked up his duffel, and left.

18

She sat alone in her hotel room for the first time in a long time. "What am I going to do?" she asked.

She went into the bathroom. The damp towels from her and Corvus's impromptu shower were still neatly folded and stacked on the floor under the sink, and she didn't have any fresh ones left for the next morning, but the steam had cleared off the mirror. She looked at herself, really looked at herself: violet eyes just like her mother's, the gleam of gold in the soft brown of her hair, her clear features: her birth self, not altered in any of the ways she could have altered herself.

Her reflection doubled. Other Opal stood shoulder to shoulder with her, the nose, cheekbones, mouth the same, hair black with a white streak above her left temple, her eyes golden and softly glowing, lit from within.

"What's our next move?" Opal asked her second self.

"What do you really want?" Other Opal said.

"I don't know! I don't know! You must know if I don't, right? You're all the me I don't let out."

"Not all of you. There are more of us; we have different jobs. Baby you is one, and—"

"Do I need to know this now?" Opal asked.

"Maybe not." Other Opal smiled, a little sadly. "I asked you what we really want, and that's a complicated question, because we want a bunch of different things. You're the one who lives out there in the visible world, though, the one who has the riskiest job. What *you* really want is to go to sleep."

"That's what I want?" Suddenly Opal sagged, feeling the exhaustion of the day catch up to her. The shadows under her eyes darkened.

"Yes, but we can't do that, can we? There are too many things left hanging. So I'll help you." Other Opal laid hands on Opal's shoulders. Opal felt fire shift through her, burn away fatigue, energize her.

She hunched her shoulders, stared at herself, paused long enough to get a glass of water from the tap and drink it, then straightened again. "All right. Ready for our next move."

"Do we want to do the job Tobias outlined? Put the god-let back to sleep?"

Get the movie back on track, make everything go back to normal? Wash out whatever memories people had of strange events? Turn back into Opal, shadow-person, attached at the hip to Corvus, with no current role outside of making him look like a forest god?

Sink into that comfort, that invisible existence. That would be okay.

Lose the friendships she had started with Magenta and Lauren.

Force Corvus back into his unmonsterlike self.

Warp a lot of images taken earlier in the day, make the orgy unhappen, quiet the exciting energy under the ground, relieve Bethany's mind of all the dreams her home place had laid on her to make her write the script. Take the magic out of the movie.

If it had magic. She hadn't seen any dailies. She wasn't sure what the end product was going to be. She usually didn't concern herself much with what the movie looked like when it was finished. She just made sure her work was done well.

This project would have been different if everything had gone according to plan. Corvus was her focus, and he had so much to do in this one. She wanted to see him on the screen in a role that would take him to a level where his talents wouldn't be wasted anymore.

There was little chance in a movie like this there'd be any award-level recognition—most horror movies never got noticed by the Academy—but producers would see her work and think of her when they needed excellent makeup in films. They would see Corvus act.

Now, who knew.

Other Opal shook her shoulder. "Quit thinking about long-term career goals and get back to the present," she said.

Someone pounded on her hotel door. Opal sighed and snapped back together, with Other Opal inside again.

She went to the door, wondering if it was Bethany or Corvus knocking. She opened it to find Neil.

"You're the goddamned special effects makeup artist," he yelled.

"That would be me, yes."

"You're not the producer or the D.P. or the A.D. You're not anybody important. How come you're now central to this godforsaken movie we're stitching together?"

Opal crossed her arms over her chest. The fingers of her left hand tapped her right upper arm. "What do you want?"

He pushed past her into the room, slamming the door behind him. "Violating every order I gave when we started on this shit-spewing project, one of our cameramen took a digital movie of events this afternoon, and he gave it up when I threatened to fire him if he didn't. Of course there hasn't been time to process what was in the real cameras, but we took a look at his movie. George and Basil and I have been reviewing every shit-spattered thing that happened today," he said, still at pretty high volume. Opal glanced at her watch. After three A.M. She wondered if anybody in a neighboring room was going to call the front desk to complain about noise, but then she realized most of her neighbors were probably crew, and would either recognize Neil's voice or be out cold with exhaustion after the day they'd all had. "And even though we can't quite figure out how, you have somehow become central to this bleeding project. My first impulse was to kick you off the film, because I don't like having people around who can screw up my work. I've thought twice, because what started out as a nice little money-maker has the potential to turn into something wilder, something that could take off if we figure out how to frame it. So we've decided the thing to do is pick your brain."

Opal sighed and sat on the bed. Neil dropped into a chair facing her and leaned forward, his hands gripping his thighs, his face thrust toward hers as though he were about to bite off her nose. "What the hell have you done to my film?" he yelled.

Opal took a breath and felt her Flintfire spark up. Suddenly her shield was back, a second and invisible skin. She laughed, because she hadn't thought of the fire in terms of shielding her from a normal human assault, but she still felt better than she had without it.

"What are you laughing at?" Neil yelled, even louder.

"What the hell *could* I do to your film?" she asked.

"Rumor has it you're some kind of witch," said Neil, in a more conversational tone of voice. "After what I saw in that flaming handheld playback and what I know about where I've spent our special effects budget, I believe it. Of course, I absolutely do not believe in anything supernatural. I know how people get effects. I can debunk anything—one of the reasons I relish making monster films. Gives me a chance to see what fools these mortals really can be. But this afternoon, you—and he—and good Lord, the rest of us—Fran can say anything she likes about spiked water or hallucinogenic mold spores or some kind of hypnotism, but that doesn't explain what I saw on the handheld."

"I like the mold spores theory," Opal said.

"I don't give a damn what you like. Tell me what happened today, and whether you can make it happen again."

Tobias had talked about the atmosphere of people believing what they usually wouldn't. Atmosphere. Hmm. "I'm not making strange things happen. There's a local power that's doing it," she said.

"What does that mean, *a local power?*" Neil jumped to his feet and paced the narrow aisle between the end of the bed and the dresser. "Politics? I've met the mayor in Lapis. Fran told me I had to make nice. Guy couldn't sell shelter in a blizzard."

"Do you have a religion?" Opal asked.

"Religion is for idiots. Will you quit stalling and get to the point?"

"All right. A local god wants to use your movie to get famous."

"What?"

"He gave the writers the idea for the script. He influenced the choice of locations. That altar stone and all that, what did you think when you saw it? Those were naturally occurring rocks?"

"I thought the locals were very odd. I assumed some local lunatic built it for some weird thing they do at a harvest festival or something. Then again, the rocks are very solid, and—right, it was there already, wasn't it? Even getting permissions from the owner of the site—Fran said it was dead easy."

"There's a god in the ground there, and people used to

worship him, and he wants them to start up again. If the movie gets distribution, and people see it and feel even the slightest hint of belief, maybe he gets—"

"He *wants* the movie to succeed. He's not trying to sabotage it," Neil said. "Well, what the bloody hell was this afternoon about, then? That footage isn't going to edit well with everything else we've done. What was the point? Was he trying to communicate with us? Are we reduced to hand signals and semaphores? Can't we just ask him what he wants, and give it to him?"

"Well, we kind of can," she said, "because he's been possessing Corvus."

"The god wants to fuck you! What's it like being fucked by a god?"

"Do you want to try it?"

"Hell, yes, or the possession—no, cancel that, I don't know what it means. It could be like a really bad drug and leave me a wreck. I don't take chances like that anymore. But if he could possess Blaise—"

"Don't even think it," Opal said, her voice freezing.

"Why not?"

"Possession is a serious business for everybody concerned."

"If it makes your boyfriend more convincing in the part, then it's a good thing . . . Hmm. The script is about an evil god who makes his followers suffer." He dropped into the chair again and peered at her. "Are you suffering?"

"I think Bethany came up with the suffering part," Opal said. "I don't know for sure what this god wants his followers to do. The jury's still out on whether he's evil, though I've seen him do some things I thought were questionable."

"If the god didn't hurt people, would you support him? I'm pretty sure we can't use most of what we shot this afternoon without going to a completely other market, but maybe there's some other way we can salvage this. I mean, even though I resent him like hell, I have to confess Weather is a genius in the part. He could *make* this film, if we can finish it. I need a success. My last film tanked."

"I don't know what the god wants," Opal said, "or if I'll ever get Corvus back. Did you see what he did to Erika?"

"Erika? Who's that? Oh, that p.r. bitch? What happened to her?"

"He laid her on the altar and drank her blood. Hell, you were there. You almost interrupted. But then Phrixos—" Phrixos had pressed Neil's forehead. Neil had changed from a yelling tyrant to someone calm.

"Phrixos?"

"That's what I call the entity possessing Corvus."

"Phrixos. All right. What did Phrixos do? I don't remember anything about this."

"I guess he messed with your memory," said Opal.

Neil looked thoughtful. "That doesn't sound good. How was the woman afterward?"

"I don't know. Right afterward, she was mad about it, but then we went back to work. I had other things on my mind, and I haven't seen her since. When's the last time you saw her?"

"Can't remember. Didn't care enough to pay attention." Neil shifted in the chair, frowned mightily. "That's neither here nor there. What I want to know is whether we can get back to work tomorrow." He heaved himself to his feet, gripped handfuls of hair. "Gawd," he said. "I can't believe I'm discussing this with the makeup girl!"

Opal dug through her messenger bag, sorting through various pieces of multicolored script pages, looking for the call sheet for the next day. All she dug up was a couple of crumpled call sheets from earlier in the shoot. "What are we shooting tomorrow?"

Neil went to the door, stooped, lifted an envelope lying on the floor. "George didn't get them made up until after we finished our meeting. He was supposed to wake everybody up when he passed them out, make sure everyone knows what the plan is for tomorrow. Guess he figured I'd clue you in." Neil slipped a finger under the envelope's flap and pulled out a call sheet. "First we'll shoot the girls on the soundstage, and then the seduction scene between the devil and Serena on location. What I really need to know is whether *I'm* going to be the director, or if everything will go to hell again."

"I don't know," Opal said.

He glared at her with intense dislike. His eyes narrowed, and he said. "Very well, then. One more day like today, though, and—" He snarled and paced away from her, then glanced down at the sheet of paper in his hand, which he had crumpled in his fist. He straightened it, then handed Opal the sheet. "You're supposed to prep Weather at ten A.M. We shoot at noon. George said you budget four hours for prep time, but it doesn't take that long, does it?"

Opal stared down at the call sheet.

"Rod said you whiz through it," said Neil.

"It's true," she said in a low voice. "It's been going much faster than I expected. The possession helps speed it up." Rod was ratting on her now? She'd have to find out what that was about.

"I don't care how you do it. I don't want you padding my budget and charging for extra hours you don't need, understand?"

"Yes," she said.

"Get some sleep and be ready for anything, all right? Did you put my star to bed yet?"

"No."

"Is he here? I could take him back to the B&B." Neil shuddered, then firmed his chin. "If you come with us."

"I think we'll stay here tonight," she said.

"Where is he?"

"In Bethany's room."

Neil glanced toward the ceiling, shook himself, and headed for the door. "Get him to the location on time and in costume," he said over his shoulder.

19

When she went upstairs, Opal found that Travis had come back from the restaurant, and he and Bethany were knee-deep in arguments, which continued even as Travis answered the door and let her in. Corvus sat on the couch, arms along the couch's back, eyes closed, head back, apparently asleep. *Death takes a holiday,* she thought, appreciating the contrast between his large, black-robed presence and the standard beige furniture and vanilla floral prints and landscapes on the walls.

There was an energy in his presence that hinted he was awake on several levels.

Opal sat down beside him, touched his hand. His arm slid around her shoulders, though he didn't open his eyes. "Who's awake in there?" she whispered to him.

He opened his eyes and smiled at her. The green glow showed in a subdued rim around his irises, so she guessed he was both Corvus and Phrixos. Maybe that was who he would be from now on. "Where's your uncle?" he asked.

Travis and Bethany paused to look toward her, interested in her answer.

"Gone," said Opal.

Corvus leaned closer, studying her face, his own concerned. "Why?"

"I wasn't sure what to do with him," she said.

His fingers tightened on her shoulder, then relaxed.

"Let's go to bed," said Opal. "We've got a ten o'clock call tomorrow."

"Shooting what?" asked Bethany.

"Did you get a call sheet?" Opal said. She looked at the floor by the door and saw another envelope, production stationery. "I guess George dropped it off. But he didn't knock and give it to you. Do you guys ever get called?" She tried to remember. During the shoot Opal had never seen the writers on the set except on their own time, and then, if Neil noticed them, he chased them off.

"Just on the phone," said Travis, "or when he comes in here to scream at us. That's one of the reasons we write in the restaurant. Even Neil doesn't want to make a scene there. Fran really gets on his case when he alienates locals, especially in places where cast and crew need service. When Neil needs something, though, we better be ready to write it, print it, leap in the car, and drive it to wherever the hell he is, and he needs it yesterday." He went over, picked up the envelope, opened it, and shook out the call sheet.

To save him time, Opal said, "We're shooting the seduction of Serena tomorrow."

"Which draft are we on with that?" Travis asked Bethany.

"I think it's the marigold pages," Bethany said, searching down through her stack of many-colored papers, some sheafs of them fastened together with brass brads.

Opal had left her messenger bag in her room. She couldn't remember if she had any marigold pages. "Do you have an extra copy? I didn't get the call sheet until about ten minutes ago because everything was so chaotic on the set today. Neil just stopped by my room—"

"Why?" said Bethany, her expression a mixture of fascination and distaste.

"To pick my brain, ask me if I could make whatever happened today not happen again."

"He thinks you're the agent of strange?" asked Bethany.

Opal smiled. "He did. I told him it was really the local god. He doesn't believe in any of this, but he kind of believes in that."

"Oh?" said Corvus.

She looked at him directly. "As long as you support the film instead of trying to sabotage it, he's happy. When we go back to the forest location, are we all going crazy again?"

He smiled. "Wait and see."

She held a fist up to his chin, tapped it. "Don't tease me. I've had a long, weird day."

"The answer is, I don't know."

Bethany pulled some pages out of her stack, leafed through them, brought them to Corvus and Opal. "This hasn't changed a whole lot. This *is* the most recent version we've written, though with Neil, who knows, maybe he wants the pink pages or something. It's my only copy, though, so don't you dare lose it. I want it back when you're done."

Corvus took the pages and read through them. "Pretty close to what I've already memorized," he said. "Let me just make sure." He went back through the pages and reread them.

"Travis, we're going on location tomorrow," Bethany said.

"But the retool on the big finale?"

"I don't think we should do any more work until Neil gets his head out of his ass and figures out where the film is going. Which probably depends on what happens on location tomorrow. Can we ride with you, Opal? Maybe he won't notice us if we come in one of those black cars instead of that powder blue Nissan we got."

"Corvus?" Opal said.

"Fine with me."

"Okay." Opal slipped from the claim of Corvus's arm and rose. "Breakfast at 8:30, and we're out of here by 9:30." She took his hand and tugged him toward his feet. It helped when he got the message and cooperated with her. "See you tomorrow."

"Night," said Travis.

Downstairs, Corvus sat on the bed and Opal on a chair and she ran his lines with him. The energy she had given herself from her internal stash was wearing thin; she read the lines without paying attention. Corvus tried several different readings on some of his lines, but he noticed her sagging at last, took the pages out of her hands, lifted her onto the bed, and pulled off her shoes. She was asleep before he stripped and crawled in beside her.

———

The next morning, Opal didn't recognize the waitress at the IHOP, a teenager with pink hair, black lipstick, and an eyebrow piercing, but the girl seemed to know them. She nodded to Bethany and Travis and put them all in the big corner booth. "Will you have enough room?" she asked.

"We're actually eating today and then leaving," Bethany said with a smile. "We don't need to spread out."

"Oh, so you're down to two pots of coffee instead of six?"

"Probably," said Travis. "Thanks, Tera."

"You guys have the menu memorized already, right? What would you like this lovely morning?"

They ordered, ate, paid, and left. Opal called Hitch at about 9:15. He had the car waiting out front by the time they got to the parking lot.

On the drive to the location, Opal glanced at Corvus. He looked back at her, his gaze quiet. *Where do we go from here?* she wondered.

The closer they got to the location, the stronger and wilder grew the buzzing under Opal's skin. The ground was wide awake today. She put up her shield as Hitch drove, thickened it as more and more energy radiated against it. She wasn't ready to collapse into Other Opal this time.

By the time they parked, Corvus's face had already changed partway. Leaf outlines lay just under his skin.

"How'd you do that?" asked Bethany as they climbed out of the car.

He gazed at her. She swallowed, backed up, and grabbed Travis's arm. Corvus raised the hood of his robe to cover his head.

"Do you sense anything different about this place?" Opal asked Bethany. On this project, Bethany had been the first one influenced by the god under the ground. Was she still being affected by it? To Opal, the trees shimmered with energy, and there was a glow surrounding the altar stone she wasn't seeing with her eyes.

"I'm totally spooked by Corvus," Bethany said, "so yeah, I'm feeling kind of fucked up."

"Anything else?"

"I've got this crawly feeling under my skin," said Travis. "More static than anything else. I feel jumpy."

"Want to leave?"

"No way," said Bethany, as Travis said, "Are you kidding? We've got to see what happens next." He grabbed Bethany's hand and pulled her toward the altar.

Opal shrugged and headed to the Makeup trailer, trailing Corvus.

Kelsi intercepted them, gripped a fingerful of Corvus's robe. "So that's where that got to," she said. She frowned. "Did you clean it?"

"I did," said Opal.

Kelsi narrowed her eyes, leaned closer, peered at the material, sniffed it. "Looks like you didn't destroy it, so okay. Next time, ask before you take something off the set."

"We didn't have anything to change into yesterday."

"Sure," said Kelsi, "that's what everybody says. And yeah, I was there, so I guess I know it's true, though I'm kind of fuzzy on what happened. You should see what the kids did with their clothes, damn it. Yesterday was a nightmare with those kids' clothes! First the blood, and then the dirt! There wasn't one intact dress for either of them, so Betty and I were up all night making new ones . . . Glad you took good care of this robe. The other two we have are still spattered with that damn peppermint blood. It's supposed to be washable, but I soaked them all night, and they're still not right." She released Corvus's robe and headed for the Wardrobe trailer.

Inside the Makeup trailer, Lauren was sitting in one of the normal-sized chairs, with Magenta working on her. Rod lounged in another chair, flipping through a magazine. Blaise sat cross-legged in the chair next to Rod's. She wore a gauzy purple and gold Indian-print hippie dress her character wouldn't have worn, and she gripped her bare feet with her hands. She gazed at Opal and Corvus as they passed the other chairs to get to Corvus's custom chair.

"Blaise?" Opal paused next to the actress. "You're not on the call sheet."

"Right, I'm not working today, but I decided to come watch. Neil was interesting and mysterious and way too secretive when he got back last night."

"We heard we missed the party of the year yesterday," Lauren said.

"Don't talk." Magenta was outlining Lauren's lips.

"Sorry," Lauren said, without meaning it. "Would someone please fill us in? Blaise said Neil wouldn't tell her much. Everybody in town seems to know something except us; my hostess at the B&B was all, 'You wouldn't believe what happened at the altar yesterday,' and then she wouldn't give me any details."

"The townies know?" Rod said. "Oh, God. Can the media be far behind?"

"Neil was trying to keep it under wraps," said Magenta. "I wonder how they found out."

Rod said, "Everybody and his sister was out here working yesterday. It's hard to keep every mouth shut. I didn't think the crew knew the townsfolk, though, since we're all staying by the highway."

"Some of the hotel staff live in Lapis," said Blaise. "One of the grips is sleeping with the desk clerk, and the desk clerk's parents are second-generation Lapislanders. That could be one avenue of information."

"How do you *know* these things?" Lauren asked.

"Please," said Magenta. "Keep still."

"It pays to be informed," Blaise said. "Stop being evasive and tell us what happened. Opal?"

"Drugs in the water, or mysterious spores, that's what I've heard," said Opal.

Blaise glared at her. "Right, those are the fake stories Neil's telling. Cough up a few actual details, witch."

Opal grinned. "Calling me names, great way to get me to talk to you. I've got something else on my mind." She turned to Rod and lost any impulse to smile. "Why'd you tell Neil it doesn't take me long to put Corvus in his makeup?" Corvus moved past her and settled into his chair, his head still hidden in his hood.

Rod glanced at her, then back down at his magazine. Without looking at her, he said, "All these years, Opal, working side by side, I thought we were friends."

"I did, too."

"But I don't even know you," he said to his magazine. "Blaise is right, you're a witch. You never told me."

"I never tell anybody. That's your excuse to snark about me behind my back?" She leaned forward, tilted Rod's chin up so he was looking at her.

"A small, petty revenge, but mine own," he said.

"You were friends with the person I used to be," she said. "Due to circumstances beyond my control, I don't think I'm that person anymore. You might think about whether you want to be friends with who I am now. I imagine I'm a better friend than an enemy."

"Do you really care about your hours, Opal?" asked Rod, staring unflinchingly into her eyes. "Does any of that matter to you, given what you can do? The minute I said that to Neil, I regretted it, but I couldn't take it back. Now that you're acting like Threaten-Me Barbie, I'm not sure what I want. Would you quit being such a badass?"

"Um," she said. She released his chin and straightened, felt the starch drain from her shoulders. "Okay. Sorry about that. I'm pretty confused."

"And scary," muttered Magenta.

Opal glanced at Magenta before she headed for Corvus and her tools. Magenta was focused on her work and didn't meet Opal's gaze. Another thing to worry about?

Not right now.

Opal opened her locked cupboard and pulled out Corvus's head mold, with its mask of leaves. It looked alive, the blank eyes forbidding. She knelt and searched the cupboard for the leaf skin she had taken off him yesterday, but there was no sign of it. Well, that was going to be trouble—today's scene had chest nudity in it, and the leaf skin had made that simple. She might need more time after all.

"You guys, sorry to interrupt a personality conflict, but nobody's answering my questions. We're not the public," Lauren said. "And we're not just asking for fun. We *need* to know what happened yesterday, and if we're expecting more of the same today. I didn't volunteer for total insanity."

"Stop talking!" Magenta said. "You made me smear!"

"Opal, please. Please tell me *some*thing," Lauren said, even though Magenta looked mad enough to spit fire.

"Yesterday we were all possessed by a spirit of sex, and some of it got on tape," Opal said. "We fucked like rabbits. No one was in their right mind except Magenta, who was protected. Something's going to happen today, but I'm not sure it'll be the same. That's what I know. Okay?"

"Um," said Lauren. "No."

"If you would let me do my job," Magenta said, "maybe we could film everything and get out of here before another sexquake happens. Will you *please* shut up now?"

Lauren subsided.

"Why were you protected?" Blaise asked Magenta.

"Opal fixed me up way before it happened."

"Like with a charm or something?"

"I don't know. Don't say it," she said to Lauren. She finished filling in the lip color, having repaired earlier mishaps, and Lauren sat still for it.

"Opal," said Blaise.

"Give me a break. I have work to do." She tapped the mask, whispered, "Shed, skin." It split neatly down the center of the face. It was warm in her hands as she fitted it over Corvus's head. It molded to his skin immediately, and a gilded flush ran over it. Buried leaves rose from the skin of his neck, raced down under his robe. She undid the brooch at the throat and bared his chest, which was now as leafy as his head. "Good," she said, and got out yesterday's Polaroids for comparison. He looked exactly the same, down to the green glow in his eyes.

She put the Polaroids in a drawer and came back to take more pictures and another look at him, just to make sure everything worked together.

He pulled her into his lap and kissed her.

At first she resisted. This was where she worked, not where she kissed. She was working with materials she didn't understand and wasn't sure she could fix if they got messed up.

But her work was done, by someone other than herself, and

even though she didn't like or trust Phrixos, his kiss felt wonderful, promising that she could relax into the self who didn't have to be in charge. He tasted of forest and sleep and comfort. Her Flintfire kept her from sinking into him completely, but she let herself respond to the promises as though she believed them.

Someone tapped her shoulder. She opened her eyes, broke contact with Phrixos's mouth, and looked up. Magenta stood above her, frowning.

Opal pushed away from Phrixos. He let her go, his fingers lingering and sliding along her hips as she pulled away.

"It pisses me off to no end that he doesn't smear," Magenta said. "Anyway, it's time to get to the set."

"But I thought—" How long had the kiss lasted? Lauren and Blaise were no longer in the trailer. Opal checked her watch. All the time budgeted for applying makeup had melted away. Weird that a kiss could relax her instead of exciting her, and weird that whatever it was had happened in spite of her shield. Things had changed while she'd been lost; a kind of nervous energy flooded her now, something ambient that almost sounded like a song. "Come on, big guy." She tugged Phrixos to his feet.

Everything felt electrified. Phrixos's hand in hers was hot and buzzing, as though she touched bees. "What is it?" Opal asked. The mirrors on the trailer walls reflected back scenes brighter than the one they were standing in.

Magenta looked around, too. Rod glanced up from his magazine. "Here we go again," he said. "I think I'll lock myself in the restroom this time. I didn't like who I ended up with last time."

"Is that what's happening?" Magenta asked.

"Don't you feel it?" asked Rod. "That urge to merge—but maybe different from yesterday. I don't—I'm not sure what I want, but—"

Magenta cocked her head. "There's some kind of weird

sound, like one of the generators is running too fast or something, but I don't feel anything."

"You are shielded," Phrixos said. "Do you want to open to this?"

"Nope, no thanks," said Magenta. "Rather sit it out, like I did yesterday."

"As you like." Phrixos tugged Opal with him toward the door to the trailer. She grabbed her messenger bag on the way. Rod headed toward one of the trailer's restrooms. Magenta took her duffel and followed Opal and Phrixos out, locked the door as she left the trailer.

Everyone they passed on their way to the altar looked alert and itchy, most glancing this way and that in search of something nobody seemed to find. Suspicious glances followed Phrixos.

"This is where I get off," Opal said as they came abreast of the cast corral. Phrixos's grip on her hand tightened, then released.

"Don't go anywhere," he said. "I need you."

"Sure," she said, uncomfortable. Did he really need her, or did he just want to own and control her? "Something's going to happen today."

"If everything works out," he said.

"It's not going to be the same as yesterday, is it?" she asked.

"No," he whispered, and walked on, toward where Lauren, in her character's dumpy-phase clothes, stood. Lauren looked lost and sad. Corvus's stand-in, Fred, walked into the circle of light and stood facing her. They murmured to each other. Everyone glanced around uneasily.

Blaise stood in the trees, out of sight of where the cameras aimed at the moment, a pale forest dryad spying on invaders.

Magenta set her duffel on the ground and sat in Lauren's chair, her hands gripping each other in her lap.

Opal settled in Corvus's chair and closed her eyes. "What's going on?" she asked Other Opal.

Other Opal took shape in the air beside her, glanced around. "Interesting," she said. "Gearing up."

"For what?"

"Can't tell, but it feels like everything around us is awake." Other Opal looked toward the ground. "We're standing on another kind of person. He lies there and smiles at us. He's glad we're here. He wants us."

Opal stroked her shield. Part of it had opened for Phrixos's kiss, but now it gloved her. She could resist what was about to happen. As long as that door Phrixos had made in the shield stayed shut. *Damn.*

"You gonna keep that shield up the rest of your life?" asked Other Opal.

"Maybe," said Opal. She had lowered it during the kiss, though, and whatever Phrixos had done to her still resonated inside. She sighed and opened her eyes to the outside world.

Neil yelled by the altar. "Am I surrounded by dolts and donkeys? Would you all stop shaking the equipment? News flash: we're not sitting on a volcano!"

Opal went to the Props department to get a camera-eye view.

"Blocking rehearsal's over," Joe said. "Looked good. Neil's like a cat on a hot griddle today."

"Who isn't?" asked Opal.

"Good point." They watched Lauren and Phrixos. The scene took place after Caitlyn had practically kidnapped Serena and forced her back to the forest, where Serena had sworn she would never go again. Caitlyn told Serena she had to help Caitlyn figure out how their mother had died. At this point, the flashback of the mother's death would show, as Serena regained her lost memory. And then the Dark God would talk her into accepting his proposal. There was a lot of verbal persuasion involved; it was one of Corvus's best scenes in the movie, all talking instead of anything that smacked of scare tactics. Opal had drowsed through the scene the night before, even as she mouthed Serena's lines, but this time she leaned in close as Phrixos and Lauren spoke the lines. Joe's TV didn't pick up sound, but as Opal watched the actors' lips, she remembered.

> DARK GOD
>
> All your life you have denied your power and hidden from yourself. It is time for you to become who you really are.

> SERENA
>
> Wouldn't my sister be better? She's already given heart and soul to you.

> DARK GOD
>
> *You* are the one with the gifts I want. Accept your destiny. How long will you hide in the shadows? Show the world your true self. Open to your power.

"Last looks," the A.D. called.

Opal and Magenta went to check their respective charges. Phrixos's leaves had darkened, turned more realistic. Opal wasn't sure how to reverse that. "Can you step it down a notch? This is bad for continuity," she said to him.

"I can't," he said. "It's not in my control. It never really has been." The green in his eyes was only half-lit, and he spoke to her in Corvus's voice. She stepped back and stared up at him. The nervous energy in the air vibrated against her shield.

"I can't wait until you get all trampy and rampagy," Magenta was saying to Lauren. "That's going to be the fun makeup."

"Looking forward to it." Lauren's voice sounded tight.

From just behind Opal's shoulder, Neil said, "What's the

problem here?" He touched a leaf on Corvus's cheek and grunted. "The color palette changed, eh? Why's that?"

"Um," said Opal, "it wanted to, I guess. I don't know how to change it back, unless I cover it with something lighter, which would take a while."

"Oh fuck oh dear." He stepped back. "Well, maybe we can fix it in post. Prognostications for today?"

Opal shook her head.

"Damn and thunderation. All this itchy energy, too. Please. Just let us shoot the scene as written at least once, all right?"

Opal wasn't sure who he was talking to. She knew she couldn't say yes to that; like Corvus's makeup, the whole situation was beyond her control.

"Maybe if we do it quickly," Corvus said.

"I despise *quickly*," said Neil, "no matter how many people tell me it's important. Today, though—let's do this thing right now."

"Clear the set," George yelled.

Opal and Magenta hid behind the backdrop. Someone yelled for quiet on the set. The bell rang, sound rolled, the camera assistant called scene and take number, the slate was bumped, Neil yelled, "Action," and the lines ran.

How long will you hide in the shadows?

20

Corvus spoke with a clarity that brought the lines to her even this far from the set. Was she hiding in the shadows still? No, people were looking at her in the light, more than she was comfortable with. She wanted to fade into the background again.

Which was hard when everyone was aware of her now. She glanced at Magenta, Blaise, random other not-working-at-the-moment crew. Everyone was silent while the scene played out, but none of them were reading, puzzle solving, distracting themselves today. They all stood listening, and many of their gazes rested on her.

Were they remembering her as half of the center of yesterday's tossed human salad? Or was everyone remembering she was a witch equivalent?

Oh, come on, thought Dark Opal, *it's not always about you.*

It's almost never about me, thought Opal. *That's the way I like it.*

Keep telling yourself that. I'll hang onto the other thoughts for us.

Are you saying I want *to be the center of attention?*

Every little once in a while, thought Dark Opal.

Opal straightened, pushed her shoulders back, and took a deep breath. *Okay. Yesterday was enough of that for now. Agreed?*

Dark Opal laughed. *You got it, sister.*

Maybe everyone was tense because of the ubiquitous hair-raising, nerve-tingling energy, its pitch rising, that tightened the air until it was hard to breathe.

Barefoot, an almost unrecognizable Erika came to stand beside Opal. This Erika's hair was loose around her shoulders, and she wore not a single camera around her neck. She had on some kind of springy, flower-laden dress and wore an unfamiliar nongloating smile.

Brainwashed, Opal decided. "You okay?" she whispered.

"I'm so happy," Erika murmured. "I've found my true happiness."

"Cut. Print," called Neil and two bells rang.

"Weren't you happy before?" Opal asked Erika. "Taking pictures and torturing people?"

A shadow of Erika's triumph smile flashed across her face. "Yes," she said. Then she looked confused. "This is different."

Handmaiden, thought Dark Opal. *She's a total handmaiden. Don't go there. I'm sick of being a handmaiden.*

I'm with you there.

The cast and the director came off the set. Phrixos took his own chair. Lauren retreated to the cast trailer.

Neil grabbed a cold frappuccino from the Craft Services cooler and came over to Opal. He said, his gaze directed between Opal and Phrixos, "The master shot is in the can. Three takes, at least one of which is good enough, if we revert and follow the original script, and ignore everything that happened yesterday, which, at this point, I'm inclining toward."

She wasn't sure why he was telling her this, or how to respond. She tried a smile.

He scowled and strolled off to where Blaise was lurking, then wandered back to watch people position equipment. Lauren returned from the trailer and sat in her chair.

The undertone of frenzy intensified.

"What is it?" Opal asked Phrixos. "What's going to happen?"

"It takes the right trigger," Phrixos said.

"And then what?"

"I'll ask you a question. I'll ask everyone a question."

"What's the question?" Magenta said from beside Lauren's chair. Lauren looked anxious and sweaty. She was drinking orange juice.

"You have to wait for it."

"Waiting is driving us all crazy," said Lauren.

"Only a little longer, and all the steps will be complete," said Phrixos. He closed his eyes and leaned back, cutting off the conversation.

The next shot was of the Dark God, speaking seductively to Serena, or, more realistically, directly into the camera. Lauren wasn't in the shot, but she stood nearby to speak her lines off camera. Opal hovered behind one of the cameras filming the shot.

The energy erupted while the Dark God spoke.

DARK GOD

Will you spend the rest of your life hiding from your true nature? Now is the time to surrender all the things that keep you locked up inside yourself. Come to me. Worship me. Give me strength, and I will set loose the power you already have.

His voice, Corvus's best voice, reasonable, enticing, seductive, was everywhere. Opal heard it in her ear, felt it sliding through the clearing and even into the trees. Her heart raced. Heat flooded her face. She yearned toward him, almost stepped past the camera, then recalled herself, glanced at the cameraman and the focus puller, and saw that they were leaning forward, too.

> DARK GOD
> All you have to do is say yes. Will you say yes to me?

He held out his hands, palms up. His voice was irresistible. The green rose from the ground, coruscating around his hands and face. He smiled, turned to look straight at Opal, then swept the crew with his gaze.

"Yes," said Lauren, her line, but "yes," cried everyone else, everyone, boom mike operator, electricians, grips, director, cameramen, set dressers, wardrobe, props, supervisors, writers, everyone.

Opal opened her mouth, a "yes" shaping her lips. Dark Opal invaded her muscles and changed her response to "No!" spoken in a whisper. *No! You don't need him to make you whole. You have me! You have all of us. Frozen baby, marble child, your internal forest, all those rooms you haven't looked in, all the yous you've locked up, and even Flintfire that's you and not you. I can help you out of the shadows.*

Can you help me let go of everything holding me back and locking me up?

Oh, yes, thought Dark Opal. *You know I can.*

After the chorus of "Yes!" swept the clearing, the Dark God laughed and held out his hands. Green rushed from him, enveloped each one of them and sank under their skin. It tried to enter Opal. She could feel its promises and whispers: warmth, love, safety, the death of worry, the comfort of being cared for. She held out a hand, but it shone faintly orange—shielded—against the invading green.

"You are mine now," said Phrixos. He turned and stared at each of them in turn. *Not in the script.* "I thank you and welcome you. We will do great things together."

He smiled, a benediction. Even shielded, Opal felt its glow.

"Is that it?" said Magenta, and everyone turned on her.

"Cut," cried Neil. "Damn you! How dare you interrupt my take?"

Everyone did their jobs; stopped taping, finished the shot. Second bell rang shrilly through the clearing.

Everyone again turned on Magenta.

"What? It's a special effect? Everybody gets a green dot? What?" she asked.

"A green dot?" Neil said. People glanced at each other and saw that she was right, everyone else had a small, glowing green dot just above their noses.

Nice redirect, thought Dark Opal.

Opal touched her forehead, glanced at Magenta, caught her attention, and lowered her finger. Magenta's eyes widened.

Corvus stepped out from under the lights, touched his own forehead, and frowned. Opal walked to him, stared up into his leafy face. There was green among the leaves; she couldn't tell whether he had a dot. His eyes were his own color, no trace of Phrixos in them. "What just happened?" she asked.

"I don't know."

"Um," said Magenta. She pointed past them, and they turned.

A giant green figure faded into view on the altar, spinning out of air, sunlight, and diffused klieg lights. People gasped.

"Cameras," Neil yelled, and dazed camera people started film rolling.

The green mist took vaguely humaniform shape as a seated person. It pushed stumpy arms toward the sky, opened a hole the shape of an orange slice in the lump that was its head, and sighed with pleasure. "So long," it said, its voice warm and musical, "since I've had the strength to manifest. Thank you, my new children."

"What are you talking about?" Magenta asked, striding toward it.

"My poor orphan," said the creature. Something Opal could barely see was rising from all the people in the clearing, including those who had come from behind the backdrop and out of the trailers while Phrixos was talking. A faint mist lifted from each of them and flowed toward the green thing. The form got solider and better defined. It looked cheerful, benevolent, and enormous; it stopped being lumpy and turned nearer to human, as muscular, sculpted, and sexless as an Oscar. It smiled at all of them and rose to its full height, perhaps nine feet tall.

"Do you want to join the rest of your people, or are you determined to be alone?" It leaned toward Magenta, its face blank but somehow attentive.

"Join my people in what?" She thrust her jaw out. "Did you turn them all into your handmaidens? What kind of verbal contract did they just agree to, huh?"

"Nothing that will kill them," it said gently.

"That covers a lot of ground, some of it pretty bumpy. I say no thanks."

The god brushed Magenta's cheek with a fingertip—she flinched from his touch, and he smiled gently—and walked past her to Opal. He towered above her. He bent, his face kind, his eyes irisless almonds.

"You," he said. "My most ardent supporter."

"Me," Opal said.

"We have made homes in each other. Why do you cast me out now?"

A whir of replies whizzed through her head—I don't like your use of force/I'm not sure who you are or what you want/I don't trust you, and for good reason/You hurt me, and you hurt my friends. Ultimately, she said, "I got a better offer."

He looked sad. "I want you back."

She studied everyone else. They stood quiet, almost like the trance state they had been in yesterday, waiting. Opal shook her head. "No."

He gazed at her, his attention concentrated, a force that almost made her take a step back. Then he rose. "I will never stop wanting you. For now, I don't need you. I'll ask you again later." He straightened to his full height. "Now," he said to all of them, "where shall we start?"

Everyone woke. "We start with making this a damn good film," roared Neil, "and that's going to take the lot of you working like demons, hear me?"

"We hear you," said someone, and the rest of them laughed.

"So what else is new?" muttered Magenta. She grabbed Opal's hand and stomped back to the Makeup trailer while the crew, supervised by the tall green man, set up for the next shot, which would be Lauren saying her lines on camera, with Corvus interpolating his lines out of sight. The god helped the electricians and grips move equipment. No one said anything about him being nonunion.

Corvus and Lauren followed Opal and Magenta.

"What just happened out there?" Magenta asked after she had slammed and locked the door with the four of them inside. "Did you become happy little cult members? Who *is* that guy, anyway?" She stomped up to Corvus and stared up into his eyes.

"Isbrytaren, I guess. Who knows who that is."

"I Googled it," Magenta said. "It's not a god's name. It means *icebreaker* in Swedish."

"Icebreaker?" Corvus repeated. He started laughing, and fell into his chair clutching his stomach.

"Yeah, it's these ships that go out and break ice to let shipping operate in the winter in the northern ports—what's so funny about that?"

He leaned his leafy head over the back of the chair, trying to catch his breath, his belly rippling the black robe as he laughed. Opal and Lauren exchanged a glance. For Opal, it was almost a reflex; she had become used to exchanging glances with her friend. Who had Lauren become since she had said yes to the god?

Lauren shrugged. She smiled the same smile she had used before her conversion. So maybe you didn't have to go all the way into goofiness, the way Erika seemed to have, under the influence of the god.

When Corvus conquered his laughter, he said, "*Icebreaker.* I was thinking more in terms of conversation starters at parties. Weird function for a god."

"Does this mean he's some kind of Norse god? How'd he get here?" Magenta asked.

"I don't know," said Corvus. "Why don't you ask him?"

"Maybe I will. But you never did answer my other question. What are you now that you said 'yes' to him? Slaves? Clones? Handmaidens? Religion pushers?"

"Lauren?" Opal asked.

"I don't know. I don't think the terms were outlined anywhere. I feel really weird, like I just agreed to be the evil girl in the movie, and now I'm going to have to curse all my friends, sacrifice small animals, and run around in slut makeup. But when he asked me, it wasn't like that, it was sort of like he was saying, 'I'll love you the way no one else ever has, accept you as you are, help you do what you most want, no matter what it is.'"

"Corr? You were saying all the lines. You didn't say yes. Are you included in this agreement?" Magenta asked.

Corvus straightened, stroked a forehead leaf. "Uh—

another good question. I'm not sure. I've already been invaded and possessed. I don't really understand whether the person who's been walking around in my skin, the one Opal calls Phrixos, is the same as the green thing we saw outside. But I didn't answer Phrixos's question with a yes, and I didn't feel quite what Lauren felt. I just felt like I loved everybody. A lot."

"If that thing walks in here right now and orders you to lick its feet, what do you think will happen?" Magenta asked.

Lauren made a face. Then she made a different face. The first conveyed disgust, and the second dismay. "Shit."

Someone tapped at the door. Magenta huffed a sigh and went to peek out.

George stood there. "We need Lauren and Corvus on the set."

They all went back outside.

The god walked behind Neil as the director strode around the set, peering through the camera, speaking with the crew at a much lower volume than he usually employed. Neil stopped to consult with the script supervisor and the director of photography, and finally got mad. "Would you cease *looming*? Why must you be so green?" he yelled up at the god.

"Oh, God," muttered Lauren. She lifted her skirt and hurried past her lighting stand-in to take her mark.

"Am I bothering you?" the god asked, his tone jolly.

"The green. The glowing. It's fucking with my light balance."

"I don't want to interfere with your work. I'll go out of sight," said the god, but instead of backing off, he leaned closer, lowering his face to Neil's as though seeking a kiss from a reluctant partner.

"You great gob, that's worse—" Neil cried, and the god turned to mist and flooded into his mouth. Neil shrieked. His belly pushed out against his clothes like the surface of boiling water, bumps rising and collapsing. He stopped screaming and pressed both hands against his stomach, which continued to bubble under its taut layer of shirt, skin, muscle, and fat. Finally he let out a belch and wiped his forehead. "That's better," he said.

"Is it?" Magenta muttered.

Neil turned toward Opal and Magenta, his eyes alight with green glow, and said, "Yes. It is. Now let's get this done. Serena?"

Lauren, standing on her mark beside the altar, had her hand over her mouth. Her eyes were wide.

"Don't worry, love. We'll smooth it out. Ready? Last looks."

Magenta edged past him and checked Lauren's makeup, then ducked away. She gripped Opal's arm and pulled her toward the backdrop.

"Dark God. You set?"

"I am," said Corvus.

"Right, then. Sound the bell."

The bell rang.

"Quiet on the set," George yelled.

Behind the backdrop, Opal and Magenta collapsed into the actors' chairs, muffling the crack of canvas an instant too late. They both froze, waiting for a scream from the set, but the only sound was Lauren and Corvus, continuing their lines, with the same energy and passion they'd used all day, barring Corvus's brief foray into ad-libbing with the whole crew.

Magenta tugged her duffel out from under Lauren's chair, pulled out a pad and a pen. *Do you think he'll keep being creepy?* she wrote.

Opal took pad and pen and wrote, *I'm not an expert.*

You slept with him.

Still doesn't make me an expert. I'm not even sure it's the same guy.

Great.

They both sighed and sat back. The Props table and Joe's monitor were near. He stared at the screen, transfixed. Finally Opal rose and went to look. It was only Lauren, or Serena, really, looking alternately horrified, fascinated, and excited. Her face was so expressive. Her hesitation, her final surrender, the naked ecstasy of the moment—

Lauren opened her eyes and stared as though she were looking at Christmas morning.

"Cut. Print. Next setup," Neil's voice called.

"He swallowed a god and he's just going to go on directing?" Magenta muttered.

"Looks like it," said Opal.

By suppertime they had finished all the filming for the day and shut down the set.

This time, Opal had to use solvents to remove Corvus's makeup, and he scratched frantically at his chest. "I forgot how irritating this can be," he said as she collected scraps and damp cotton balls into a trash sack.

"Me, too."

"Could you cheat?"

She cleaned leaves off his face and moisturized his skin. "Maybe. It might invite Phrixos back, though. Is that what you want?"

He sighed. She finished wiping leaves off his neck and gently detached the points elongating his ears.

One of the A.D.s came by with a call sheet for the next day, and Opal paused to study it. Dark God invaded the bed-and-breakfast where Serena was staying—dream or haunting? After lunch, a scene with Caitlyn, her betrayal, eclipsed in all ways by her renegade sister. Lauren would finally get to be evil.

Magenta set her call sheet on the counter. "That's it?" she asked. "We just keep going?"

Opal, too, felt the sense of waiting for something to fall, a boulder, an avalanche, an earthquake, tornado, or tsunami. She glanced toward the door, saw that Neil, eyes still glowing, stood there.

"Is that it?" she asked.

He smiled and nodded. "We'll finish the project. I'll follow it south into postproduction, and give it all the extra help I can, weaving the right kinds of influences into it, and then—"

"Then what?" Magenta asked.

He smiled wide, like someone with a bellyful of good food, and said, "Distribution! People see it. They meet me." He nodded a head toward Corvus. "Or one part of me. They think about me, and send me energy, and I stay awake."

"Unless it totally tanks," said Magenta.

"In which case—in any case—we move on, and make another one. I know I have the support of the crew."

"What about everybody who wasn't here today?" Magenta asked.

"There's time. We're all working on the same project already. I'll speak to them."

"In your own special way," Magenta said, with a sneer in her voice.

"Yes. Will you join us?"

"Not yet," said Magenta.

"Your choice," said whoever was inside of Neil. He looked kind.

Opal thought of Other Opal, dressed in knee-high black boots and tight black clothes, like a thief who might need to slip through slender openings. Her black hair was tied back, the white streak swooping along the side of her head and diving into the clubbed ponytail at her nape. She stood, arms crossed, ass toward the fire as she leaned against the mantel. Her amber eyes glowed golden.

No way we're going to join him, not if I have my way, said Other Opal. *Gonna miss the wild sex, though.*

Corvus rose, took her hand. "Let's go home," he said.

Or maybe not, one of them thought. Perhaps both of them.

American Public Policy
Promise and Performance
FIFTH EDITION

B. Guy Peters
Maurice Falk Professor of American Government
University of Pittsburgh

CHATHAM HOUSE PUBLISHERS

SEVEN BRIDGES PRESS, LLC

NEW YORK • LONDON

American Public Policy: Promise and Performance
Fifth Edition

SEVEN BRIDGES PRESS, LLC
135 Fifth Avenue, 9th Floor
New York, NY 10010-7101

Publisher: Robert J. Gormley
Cover design: Lawrence Ratzkin
Managing Editor: Katharine Miller
Production Supervisor: Melissa A. Martin
Composition: Bang, Motley, Olufsen
Printing and Binding: Phoenix Color Corp.

Library of Congress Cataloging-in-Publication Data

Peters, B. Guy.
    American public policy : promise and performance / B. Guy Peters.
—5th ed.
        p.   cm.
    Includes bibliographical references and index.
    ISBN 1-56643-067-4
    1. United States—Politics and government.   2. Political planning—United States.   3. Policy sciences.   I. Title.
JK271 .P43   1999
320'.6'0973—dc21

98-40204
CIP

Manufactured in the United States of America
10   9   8   7   6   5   4

Contents

Part Three: Substantive Policy Issues

Part Four: Policy Analysis

Tables and Figures

Figures

Preface to the Fifth Edition

Here we go again. The government of the United States continues to churn out policies and in the process reveals much about itself and about American society. The prefaces to the earlier editions commented that there had been a great deal of policy change in the years prior to each new edition. That is both true and untrue for this fifth edition. On the one hand, there have been a number of major innovations in public policy—implementing welfare reform and balancing the budget in particular—and the climate of public policy apparently has changed after several years of Republican domination of Congress, reflecting in part a more conservative set of assumptions about what constitutes good policy. Moreover, the climate in Washington is also now more partisan and conflictual than in the past, and any sense of a bipartisan consensus over policy has long since disappeared in a flurry of ideological claims and counterclaims.

On the other hand, while there have been some real changes in policy and politics, there are also a number of continuities. Many issues that have been on the agenda since our first edition in 1982 remain unresolved at this writing. There is still no form of comprehensive health insurance, leaving millions of Americans with little access to care, and even more Americans live in poverty than at the first writing. The public remains discontented with many aspects of the educational system, despite some apparent improvements in this policy area. Many Americans are also unhappy about their taxes, and they want to find some way of reforming the system of revenue collection. There have been some successes in addressing the problems of economy and society, but many more remain.

Bringing this edition to completion involved a great deal of hard work, and patience, on the part of Bob Gormley and the rest of the Chatham House team; in particular, Katharine Miller ensured that the manuscript was complete and accurate, tracking me down in the far corners of the earth. I am indebted to them all for their assistance.

Completing a manuscript is always a good feeling, but finishing this edition also brings more than a little sadness. I began planning this edition with Ed Artinian, who has since passed away. Ed was a superb editor and publisher, a good friend, and a singular individual. This edition is dedicated to his memory.

PART ONE

The Nature of Public Policy

1. What Is Public Policy?

Government in the United States has grown from a small, simple "night watchman state" providing defense, police protection, tax collection, and some education into an immense network of organizations and institutions affecting the daily lives of all citizens in countless ways. The United States is not a welfare state in the sense of most European countries, but there is now an extensive array of social and health programs that serve much of the population. The size and complexity of modern government make it necessary to understand what public policies are, how those policies are made and changed, and how to evaluate the effectiveness and morality of policies.

Government in the United States is large. Today its revenues account for one dollar in three of total national production. This money is rarely wasted; most of the money returns to citizens through a variety of cash-benefit programs or in the form of public services. Likewise, one working person in six is employed by government. But the range of activities of modern government in the United States is not confined to such simple measures as spending money or hiring workers. Governments also influence the economy and society in many less obvious ways, such as regulation, insurance, and loan guarantees.

Government in the United States today also is complex and is becoming more complex every day. The institutions of government are becoming more complicated and numerous. More public business is now conducted through public corporations and quasi-autonomous public bodies, and over 86,700 separate governments now exist in the United States.[1] There are also a number of increasingly complex relationships between the public and private sectors for the delivery of services. In addition, the subject matter of government policy is more complex and technical than it was even a few years ago. Governments must make decisions about the risks of nuclear weapons, the reliability of technologically sophisticated weapons systems, and the management of a huge economic system. Attempting to influence socioeconomic problems—poverty, homelessness, education—may be even more difficult than addressing problems arising in the physical and scientific world, given the absence of a proven method of solving social problems.[2] Even when the subject matter of policy is less complex, increasing requirements for participation and accountability make managing a public program a difficult undertaking—often more difficult than managing in the private sector.

This book is intended to help the reader understand the fundamental processes and content of public policy that underlie the size and complexity of government. It is meant to increase knowledge about how public policies are made, what the policies of the United States are in certain areas, and what standards of evaluation should be applied to those policies. I begin with a discussion of the policy process in the United States—concentrating at the federal level—and the impact that the structures and procedures of that government have on the content of policies. I then discuss the means that professionals and citizens alike can use to evaluate the effects of public policies, and the methods that will enable them to decide what they want and can expect to receive from government.

Defining Public Policy

Mark Twain once commented that patriotism was the last refuge of fools and scoundrels. To some degree, "public policy" has become just such a refuge for some academic disciplines. As public policy studies are now popular, everything government does is labeled "policy." I adopt a somewhat more restrictive definition of public policy.

Stated most simply, public policy is the sum of government activities, whether pursued directly or through agents, as those activities have an influence on the lives of citizens. Operating within that definition, we can distinguish three separate levels of policy, defined by the degree to which they make real differences in the lives of citizens. At the first level, we have policy *choices*—decisions made by politicians, civil servants, or others granted authority and directed toward using public power to affect the lives of citizens. Congressmen, presidents, governors, administrators, and pressure groups, among others, make such policy choices. What emerges from all those choices is a policy that can be put into action.

At the second level, we can speak of policy *outputs*—policy choices being put into action. Here the government is doing things: spending money, hiring people, or promulgating regulations that are designed to affect the economy and society. Outputs may be virtually synonymous with the term "program" commonly used in government circles.[3]

Finally, at the third level, we have policy *impacts*—the effects that policy choices and policy outputs have on citizens. These impacts may be influenced in part by other factors in the society—wealth, education, and the like—but they also reflect to some degree the success or failure of public policy. Also, these policy outputs may reflect the interaction of a number of different programs. Successful alleviation of poverty, for example, may depend on a number of social programs, economic programs, and the tax system.

Several aspects of public policy require some explanation. First, although we are focusing on the central government in Washington, we must always remember that the United States is a federal system of government in which a large number of subnational governments also make decisions. Even when they attempt to cooperate, those levels of government often experience conflicts over policy. For example, attempts by the Clinton administration to enforce national standards for education have encountered opposition from the states, and from Congress, each with their own ideas about what those standards should be.[4] Even within the federal government, the actions of one agency may conflict with those of another. The Department of Agriculture, for example, subsidizes the growing of tobacco, while the Office of the Surgeon General encourages citizens not to smoke.

Second, not all government policies are implemented by government employees. Many are actually implemented by private organizations or by individual citizens. We must understand this if we are to avoid an excessively narrow definition of public policy as concerning only those programs directly administered by a public agency. A number of agricultural, social, and health policies involve the use of private agencies operating with the sanction of, and in the name of, government. Even the cabin attendant on an airplane making an announcement to buckle seat belts and not to smoke is implementing a public policy. As government has begun to utilize an increasing number of alternative mechanisms, such as contracts, for implementation, these private-sector providers are becoming increasingly important actors in public policy.

Even if a government is to implement a program using public employees, it may not necessarily make use of its own employees. The federal government in particular depends on state and local governments to implement a large number of its programs, including major social programs such as Medicaid and the recent "workfare" reforms to the welfare system. The degree of control that the federal government can exercise in these instances may be as little as, or even less than, when the program is delivered through private-sector actors. The private-sector actors often depend upon government for contracts and loans and therefore may be very compliant with the demands from Washington.

Third, and most important, we are concentrating on the effects of government choices on the lives of individuals within the society. The word *policy* is commonly used in a number of ways. In one usage it denotes a stated intent of government, as expressed in a piece of legislation or a presidential speech. Unfortunately, any number of steps are required to turn a piece of legislation into an operating program, and all too frequently significant changes in the intended effects of the program result from difficulties in translating ideas and intentions into actions. In this analysis we evaluate policies on the basis of their effects rather than on their intentions. We must also have some degree of concern for the legislative process, which produces the good intentions that may or may not come to fruition.

Our definition recognizes the complexity and the interorganizational nature of public policy. Few policy choices are decided and executed by a single organization or even a single level of government. Instead, policies, in terms of their effects on the public, emerge from a large number of programs, legislative intentions, and organizational interactions to affect the daily lives of citizens. This conception of policy also points to the frequent failure of governments to coordinate programs, with the consequence that programs cancel out one another, or create costly duplication of effort.[5] The question about government posed many years ago by Harold Lasswell, "Who gets what?" is still central in understanding public policy.

The Instruments of Public Policy

Governments have a number of instruments through which they can influence society and the economy and can produce changes in the lives of citizens. The choice of which instrument to employ in any particular instance may depend on the probable effectiveness of the instrument, its political palatability, the experiences of the policy designers, and national or organizational tradition. Further, some policy instruments may be effective in some circumstances but not in others. Unfortunately, governments do not yet have sufficient knowledge about the effects of their "tools," or the relationship of particular tools to particular policy instruments, to be able to make effective matches.[6] It appears that most choices are now made out of habit and familiarity, not out of certain knowledge of effectiveness.

Law

Law is a unique resource of government. It is not available to private actors who have access to the other instruments of policy discussed here.[7] Governments have the right to make authoritative decrees and to back up those decrees with the legitimate power of the state. In most instances, simply issuing a law is sufficient to produce compliance, but monitoring and enforcement are still crucial to the effectiveness of the instrument. Citizens may obey speeding laws most of the time, but the prospect of a policeman hiding with a radar set makes compliance even more probable. Citizens daily obey many laws without thinking about them, but police, tax collectors, and agencies that monitor environmental damage, occupational safety, and product

President Clinton and Vice-President Gore pose with park service and environmental group representatives to promote new initiatives in conservation of public
lands. (Reuters/Luc Novovitch/Archive Photos)

safety (to name only a few) are also busy trying to ensure enforcement and
compliance.

We should make several other points about the use of law as an instrument of public policy. First, laws are used as the means of producing the
most important outputs of government: rights. Such laws are usually of a
fundamental or constitutional nature and are central in defining the position
of citizens in society. In the United States the fundamental rights of citizens
are defined in the Constitution and its amendments, but rights also have
been extended in a variety of other legislation. This extension has been most
significant for the rights of nonwhites and women, as reflected in the passage
of the Voting Rights Act of 1965, the Equal Employment Opportunity Act of
1972, and the Civil Rights Act of 1991. The Americans with Disabilities Act
(1990) extended a variety of rights to people with various forms of disability
and handicap, with the courts tending to expand the applicability of that
law to groups, such as AIDS sufferers,[8] for whom it was perhaps not intended by the framers of the legislation.

7

Second, the United States uses laws to regulate economic and social conditions to a greater extent than most countries do. The United States is frequently cited as having a small public sector in comparison with other industrialized countries because of lower levels of taxing and spending. If, however, the effects of regulations are included, government in the United States approaches the pervasiveness of European governments.[9] The costs of government's interventions in the United States tend to appear in the price of products, however, as much as in citizens' tax bills.[10]

Third, law can be used to create burdens as well as benefits. This is certainly true for tax laws and is also true for legislation that mandates the recycling of metal or glass. Often a law that creates benefits for one group of citizens is perceived by others to be creating a burden; environmental laws answer the concerns of conservationists but often impose costs on businesses. Any action of government requires some legal peg on which to hang, but the ability of a simple piece of paper to create both rights and obligations is one of the essential features of American public policy.

Services

Governments also provide a number of services directly to citizens, ranging from defense to education to recreation. In terms of employment, education is by far the largest directly provided public service, employing almost 8.5 million people. Defense employs just under 3 million, both military and civilian. Government tends to provide services when there is a need to ensure that the service is provided in a certain way (education) or where the authority of the state (policing) is involved.

The direct provision of public services raises several questions, especially as there are continuing pressures for government to control expenditures and to "privatize."[11] An obvious question is whether the direct provision of services is the most efficient means of ensuring that a service is delivered to citizens. Could it be contracted out instead? A number of public services have been contracted out to private corporations, including traditional government services such as firefighting, tax collection, and prisons.[12] Contracting out removes the problem of personnel management from government, a problem made greater by the tenure rights and pension costs of public employees under merit systems. Also, government tends to build a capacity to meet maximum demands for services such as fire protection and emergency medical care, resulting in an underutilization of expensive personnel and equipment. This capacity problem can be corrected in part by contracting out.

Another interesting development in the direct provision of services is the use of quasi-governmental organizations to provide services.[13] There are some services that government does not want to undertake entirely but that require public involvement for financial or other reasons. The best example here is AMTRAK, a means of providing passenger train service with public subsidies in the face of declining rail service in the United States. Government may also choose quasi-government organizations for programs that require a great deal of coordination with private-sector providers of the same service, or when the service is in essence a marketable service.

Money

Governments also provide citizens, organizations, and other governments with money. Approximately 51 percent of all money collected in taxes by the federal government is returned to the economy as transfer payments to citizens. Transfers to citizens range from Social Security and unemployment benefits to payments to farmers to support commodity prices. Interest on the public debt is also a form of transfer payment. Another 12 percent of tax receipts is transferred to other levels of government to support their activities.

The use of money transfers to attempt to promote certain behaviors is in many ways an inefficient means for reaching policy goals. The money paid out in Social Security benefits, for example, is intended to provide the basics of life for the recipients, but nothing prevents them from buying food for their pets rather than food for themselves. The claims about how Aid to Families with Dependent Children payments were used and abused are legion, if often inaccurate. Thus, while the direct provision of services is costly and requires hiring personnel and erecting buildings, many less expensive transfer programs are much less certain of reaching the individuals and achieving the goals for which they were intended.

Money dispersed to other levels of government can be restricted or unrestricted. Of the $110 billion given in 1996 to state and local governments, most was distributed as categorical grants, with an increasing proportion being given as block grants. Categorical grants channel resources more directly to the problems identified by the federal government as needing attention, but they also tend to centralize decision making about public policy in Washington.[14] Categorical grants also tend to encourage state and local spending through matching provisions and to create clienteles that governments may not be able to eliminate after the federal support has been exhausted. Although this pattern of funding is largely associated with social and economic programs, the Clinton administration's program for funding the hiring of local policemen may create expectations among citizens that local governments will have to fulfill in the future.

The federal government has less control over the impact of block grants than over the effects of categorical grants.[15] Block grants allow greater latitude for state and local governments to determine their own priorities, but most still have some strings attached. Also, giving block grants to the states tends to concentrate power in state governments, rather than allowing local (especially city) governments to bargain with Washington directly. Given that state governments are, on average, more conservative than local governments—especially large city governments that need federal grant money the most—block grants have been a useful tool for Republican administrations, as well as for the Republican Congress.[16]

Taxes

The government giveth and the government taketh away. But the way in which it chooses to take away may be important in changing the distribution of burdens and benefits in society. In the United States we are familiar with tax "loopholes," or, more properly, "tax expenditures."[17] The latter term is derived from the theory that granting tax relief for an activity is the same as subsidizing that activity directly through an expenditure program.[18] For example, in 1996 the federal government did not collect $47.5 billion in income tax payments because of mortgage interest payments, and another $16 billion because state and local property taxes were deductible. This is in many ways exactly the same as government subsidizing private housing in the same amounts, a sum far greater than the amount spent on public housing by all levels of government. The use of the tax system as a policy instrument as well as for revenue collection is perhaps even less certain in its effects than transfer payments, for the system is essentially providing incentives instead of mandating activities. Citizens have a strong incentive to buy houses, but there is no program to build houses directly. These instruments are, however, very cheap to administer, given that citizens make all the decisions and then file their own tax returns.

Taxes may also be used more directly to implement policy decisions. For example, there are proposals to substitute taxes on pollution for direct prohibitions and regulation of emissions. The logic is that such action would establish a "market" in pollution: those firms willing to pay the price of polluting would be able to do so, while those less willing (or, more important, less able because of inefficient production means) to pay would have to alter their modes of production or go out of business. The use of market mechanisms is assumed to direct resources toward their most productive use; regulations at times may inhibit production and economic growth. Critics argue that what is being created is a "market in death," while the only real solution to the problem would involve the prohibition or severe restriction of pollution.

Tax incentives are a subset of all incentives available to government to encourage or discourage activities. The argument for their use, as well expressed by Charles Schultze, is that private interests (e.g., avarice) can be used for public purposes.[19] If a system of incentives can be structured effectively, then demands on the public sector can be satisfied in a more efficient and inexpensive manner than through direct regulation. Clearly, this form of policy instrument is applicable to a rather narrow range of policies, mostly those now handled through regulation, but even in that limited range the savings in costs of government and in the costs imposed on society may be significant. The use of such incentives also conforms to traditional American ideas about limited government and the supremacy of individual choice.

Other Economic Instruments

Government has a number of other economic weapons at its disposal.[20] Governments supply credit for activities such as a farmer's purchase of land and supplies.[21] When it does not directly lend money, government may guarantee loans, thus making credit available (e.g., for student loans or FHA mortgages) where it might otherwise be denied. Governments can also insure certain activities and property. For example, federal flood insurance made possible the development of some lands along the coasts of the United States, thereby creating both wealth and environmental degradation. Almost all money in banks and thrift institutions is now insured by one of several insurance corporations within the federal government.

Although these instruments of government may be important to their beneficiaries and may influence the spending of large sums of money, they do not appear as large expenditures in most government accounting schemes. Thus, as with regulations and their costs, the true size of government in the United States may be understated by looking simply at expenditure and employment figures. In addition, the ability of these programs to operate "off budget" makes them not only less visible to voters but also more difficult for political leaders and citizens to control. Only when there are major problems, as in the savings-and-loan industry in the early 1990s, do government insurance or guarantee schemes make the news.

Suasion

When all other instruments of policy fail, governments can use moral suasion to attempt to influence society. Government as a whole or particular political officials are often in good positions to use such suasion. They have the ability to speak in the name of the public interest and to make those who oppose them appear unpatriotic and selfish. As Theodore Roosevelt said, the presidency is a "bully pulpit." Suasion, however, is often the velvet glove disguising the mailed fist, for governments have formal and informal means of ensuring that their wishes are fulfilled. So when Lyndon Johnson "jawboned" steel industry officials to roll back a price increase, the patriotism of the steel officials was equaled by their fear of lost government contracts and

Internal Revenue Service investigations of their corporate and personal accounts.

Suasion is an effective instrument as long as the people regard the government as a legitimate expression of their interests. There is evidence that the faith and trust of American citizens in government is declining (see table 1.1) in response to the excesses of Vietnam, Watergate, the savings-and-loan crisis, Iran-*contra,* Whitewater and the Lewinsky scandal, budget deficits, and so forth. This decline may also have been exacerbated by the economic problems of the 1980s and early 1990s, especially decreasing wages and relatively high unemployment, although the economic well-being of the late 1990s does not appear to have restored much confidence. As governments lose some of their legitimacy, their ability to use suasion naturally declines. One exception may be in times of war, as President Bush showed during the Persian Gulf crisis. In the event of declining ability to use suasion, government may have to resort to more direct tools of intervention, which may

TABLE 1.1

PUBLIC PERCEPTION OF HONESTY AND ETHICS
OF VARIOUS PROFESSIONS
(PERCENTAGE "VERY HIGH" AND "HIGH" COMBINED)

	1976	1981	1985	1988	1990	1992	1995
Pharmacists	n.a.	59	65	66	62	66	66
Clergy	n.a.	63	67	60	57	54	56
Medical doctors	56	51	50	53	52	52	54
College teachers	49	45	53	54	51	50	52
Engineers	49	48	53	48	50	48	53
Policemen	n.a.	44	47	47	49	42	41
Journalists	33	32	31	23	30	27	23
Bankers	n.a.	39	38	32	32	27	27
Lawyers	25	25	27	22	22	18	16
Business executives	20	19	23	16	25	18	16
Local officeholders	n.a.	14	18	14	21	15	21
Real estate agents	n.a.	14	15	13	16	14	15
Labor union leaders	12	14	13	14	15	14	14
U.S. senators	19	20	23	19	24	13	12
State officeholders	n.a.	12	15	11	17	11	15
Congressmen	14	15	20	16	20	11	10
Car salesmen	n.a.	6	5	6	6	5	5

SOURCE: *Gallup Poll Monthly,* November 1995, 31.

lead to increasing government employment and taxation and perhaps to an accelerated downward spiral of government authority.

The Effects of Tools

Governments have a number of instruments with which they attempt to influence the economy and society. Using these various instruments, governments distribute what burdens and benefits they have at their disposal. The most fundamental benefits governments have to confer are rights. These are largely legal and participatory, but with the growth of large entitlement programs that distribute cash benefits to citizens, rights may now be said to include those programs as well.

Governments also distribute goods and services. They do this directly by giving money to people who fall into certain categories (e.g., unemployed) or by directly providing public services such as education. They also do this less directly by structuring incentives for individuals to behave in certain ways and to make one economic decision rather than another. Governments also distribute goods and services through private organizations and through other governments in an attempt to reach their policy goals. A huge amount of money flows through the public sector, where it is shuffled around and given to different people.[22] The net effect is not as great as might be expected, given the number of large expenditure and revenue programs in operation in the United States, but that effect is to make the distribution of income and wealth somewhat more equal than that produced through the market.[23]

Finally, governments distribute burdens as well as benefits. They do this through taxation and through programs such as conscription for military service.[24] Like expenditures, taxes are distributed broadly across the population, with state and local taxes tending to be collected from an especially broad spectrum of the population. Even the poorest citizens have to pay sales taxes on many things they purchase, and they must pay Social Security taxes as soon as they begin to work. In other words, everyone in society benefits from the activities of government, but everyone also pays the price.

The Environment of Public Policy

Several characteristics of the political and socioeconomic environment in the United States influence the nature of policies adopted and the effects of those policies on citizens. Policy is not constructed in a vacuum; it is the result of the interaction of all these background factors with the desires and decisions of those who make policies. Neither individual decision makers nor the nature of "the system" appears capable alone of explaining policy outcomes.

Instead, policy emerges from the interaction of a large number of forces, many of which are beyond the control of decision makers.

Conservatism

American politics is relatively conservative in policy terms. The social and economic services usually associated with the mixed-economy welfare state are generally less developed in the United States than those in Europe, and to some extent they have declined in the 1990s. This is especially true of government involvement in the management and ownership of economic enterprises such as public utilities and basic industries such as coal and steel. In general this is the result of the continuing American belief in limited government. As Anthony King has said: "The State plays a more limited role in America than elsewhere because Americans, more than other people, want it to play a limited role."[25]

Several points should be brought out in opposition to the description of American government as a welfare state laggard. First, the government of the United States regulates and controls the economy in ways not common in Europe, and in some areas, such as consumer product safety, it appears to be ahead of European governments. If the effects of regulation are tabulated along with more direct public interventions into the economy, the government of the United States appears more similar to that of other industrialized countries. We also have a tendency to forget about the activities of state and local governments, which frequently provide gas, electricity, water, and even banking services to their citizens.

Also, it is easy to underestimate the extent of the changes in public expenditures and the public role in the economy that followed World War II. Let us take 1948 as the starting point. Even in that relatively peaceful year, defense expenditures were 29 percent of total public expenditures and 36 percent of federal expenditures. At the height of the Cold War in 1957, defense expenditures were 62 percent of federal expenditures and 37 percent of total public expenditures. In contrast, 1996 defense expenditures were 17 percent of federal expenditures and 10 percent of total expenditures. Spending on social services—including education, health, social welfare, and housing—increased from 21 percent of total spending in 1948 to over 70 percent in 1996. Even for the federal government, social spending now accounts for 48 percent of total expenditures. American government and its policies may be conservative, but they are less so than commonly believed, and less so in the 1990s than in the 1950s.

It is also easy to overestimate the conservatism of the American public because Americans are often very ambivalent about government.[26] Lloyd A. Free and Hadley Cantril referred to Americans as "ideological conservatives" and "operational liberals."[27] Americans tend to respond negatively to the idea of a large and active government, but they also respond positively to individual public programs (e.g., Social Security). For example, a majority of voters leaving the polls in California after voting in favor of Proposition 13 to cut taxes severely in that state were in favor of reducing public expenditures for only one program—social welfare. For most programs mentioned by the researchers, larger percentages of respondents wanted to increase expenditures than wanted to reduce them.[28]

The huge federal deficit is to some degree a function of this set of mismatched ideas about government; politicians can win votes both by advocating reducing taxes and by advocating spending for almost any program. For example, surveys show that the majority of Americans believe that they pay too much tax and that the federal government wastes almost half of all the tax money it collects.[29] On the other hand, there are generally majorities in favor of a variety of social programs, especially those for the "deserving poor"—the elderly, unemployed workers whose companies have closed, divorced and widowed mothers, and the like.

Participation

Another attitudinal characteristic that influences public policy in the United States is the citizen's desire to participate in government. A natural part of democratic politics, public participation has a long history in American politics. The cry of "No taxation without representation!" was essentially a demand to participate. In a large and decentralized political system that deals with complex issues, effective participation may be difficult to achieve. The low rates of participation in most elections appear to indicate that citizens do not consider the voting process a particularly efficacious means of affecting government. Further, many experts believe that citizens are not sufficiently informed to make decisions about such complex technical issues as nuclear power. Citizens, however, argue that they should and must have a role in those decisions.

Government has increasingly fostered participation. The laws authorizing community action in 1964 were the first to mandate "maximum feasible participation" of the affected communities in renewal decisions. Similar language was then written into a number of other social and urban programs. Also, the regulatory process has requirements for notification and participation that, in addition to their positive effects, have slowed the process considerably. Government also has been allowing more direct participation in making rules, with the affected interests allowed to negotiate among themselves the rules that will govern a policy area.[30]

The desire for effective participation has to some degree colored popular impressions of government. Citizens tend to demand local control of policy and to fear the "federal bulldozer." Although objective evidence may be to the contrary, citizens tend to regard the federal government as less benevolent and less efficient than local governments. The desire to participate and to exercise local control then produces a tendency toward decentralized decision making and a consequent absence of national integration. In many policy areas, such decentralization is benign or actually beneficial. In others, it may produce inequities and inefficiencies. But the ideological and cultural desires for local control may override practical arguments.

Ideas about participation in the United States also have at times had a strong strand of populism, meaning the belief that large institutions—whether in government, business, or even labor—are inimical to the interests of the people. Further, there is a belief that those institutions are structured to prevent effective participation. Those institutions have, however, themselves begun to respond to the demands for effective participation, and "empowerment" has become one of the more commonly used words in government circles.[31] Balancing popular demands for greater direct democracy with the demands of governing an immense land mass with over 250 million citizens will continue to be a challenge for American democracy.

Pragmatism

The reference to ideological desires seemingly contradicts another cultural characteristic of American policymaking that is usually, and quite rightly, recognized. This characteristic is pragmatism, the belief that one should do whatever works rather than follow a basic ideological or philosophical system. American political parties have tended to be centrist and nonideological; perhaps the surest way to lose an election in the United States is to discuss philosophies of government. Ronald Reagan to some degree questioned that characteristic of American politics and interjected an ideology of government that was to some extent continued by George Bush. Bill Clinton's self-description as a "New Democrat" represented a return to greater pragmatism. This pragmatism tends to make American politics a clash of platitudes and narrow programmatic issues rather than of ideas such as Marxism or fascism—probably mercifully.

One standard definition of what will work in government is "that which is already working," and so policies tend to change slowly and incrementally.[32] The basic centrist pattern of political parties tends to result in agreement on most basic policies, and each successive president tends to jiggle and poke policy but not to produce significant change. A crisis such as the Great Depression or a natural political leader such as Reagan may produce some significant changes, but stability and gradual evolution are the most acceptable patterns of policymaking. Indeed, American government is different after Reagan, but not as different as he had hoped or intended.[33]

The pragmatism of American politics appears to have been declining.

Several issues over which there appears to be little room for compromise have split the American public. The obvious example is the abortion issue. Abortion intruded into the debate over national health-care reform, with some members of Congress refusing to support any bill that paid for abortions, and another group refusing to support any bill that did not fund abortions.[34] Other issues of a moral or religious or ethnic basis also have taken more prominent places in the political debate, with fewer possibilities for compromise or pragmatic resolution of disputes. The religious right has become especially important in the internal politics of the Republican Party, with groups such as the Christian Coalition and the Family Research Council taking over the party at local and even state levels and attempting to shape national party policy.[35]

Wealth

Another feature of the environment of American public policy is the great wealth of the country. Although it is no longer the richest country in the world in per capita terms, the United States remains the largest single economy in the world by a large margin. This wealth still permits great latitude for action by American government, so even the massive deficits of recent years have not required government to alter its folkways. The federal government can continue funding a huge variety of programs and policy initiatives (see chapter 5), despite its own efforts to control the size of the budget.

This great wealth is threatened by two factors. First, the U.S. economy is increasingly dependent on the rest of the world. This is true in financial and monetary policy as the United States becomes the world's largest debtor, but it is true especially in terms of dependence on raw materials from abroad. We are familiar with this nation's dependence on foreign oil, but the economy is also heavily dependent on other countries for a range of commodities necessary to maintain our high standard of living. The American economy historically has been relatively self-sufficient, but the increasing globalization of the 1980s and 1990s has emphasized its relationship to the world economy.[36]

Wealth in the United States is also threatened by the relatively slow rate of productivity growth and capital investment. The average American worker is still productive but has lost some ground to workers in many other countries. Also, many U.S. factories are outmoded, so competition on the world market is difficult. These factors, combined with relatively high wages, mean that many manufacturing jobs have gone overseas, and more are likely to do so. The U.S. government has had to borrow abroad to fund its deficits, and we also have chronic balance-of-payments problems because of a relative inability to export. These international trade problems are not often direct domestic concerns of American politicians, other than a few such as Congressman Richard Gephardt (D-Mo.), but they do affect the ability of the nation to spend money for the programs that many politicians and citizens want.

Diversity

The American society and economy are also diverse. This at once provides a great deal of richness and strength to the country and presents real policy problems. One of the most fundamental diversities is the uneven distribution of income and wealth in the society. Even with the significant social expenditures mentioned earlier, approximately 38 million people in the United States live below the poverty line (see pp. 313–16). The persistence of poverty in the midst of plenty remains perhaps the most fundamental policy problem for the United States, if for no other reason than that it affects so many other policy areas, including as health, housing, education, crime, and race relations.

Diversity of racial and linguistic backgrounds is also a significant factor affecting policy in the United States. The underlying problems of social inequality and racism persist despite many attempts to correct them. The concentration of minority-group members in urban areas, the continuing influx of immigrants, and the continuing economic problems of some cities all combine to exacerbate these underlying problems. Again, this diversity affects a variety of policy areas, especially education. Race in particular pervades policymaking and politics in the United States, and this fundamental fact conditions our understanding of education, poverty, and human rights.[37]

The social and economic characteristics of the country taken as a whole are also diverse. The United States is both urban and rural, both industrial and agricultural, both young and old. It is a highly educated society with several million illiterates; it is a rich country with millions of people living in poverty. American policymakers cannot concentrate on a single economic class or social group but must provide something for everyone if the interests of the society as a whole are to be served. But, in serving that whole range of social interests, policymakers must expend for other purposes the resources that would be required to rectify the worst inequalities of income and opportunity.

World Leadership

Finally, the United States is an economic, political, and military world leader. With the collapse of the Soviet Union, it is the only remaining superpower. If America sneezes, the world still catches cold because the sheer volume of the American economy is so important in influencing world economic conditions. Also, despite the upheaval in global political alignments, the world still expects military leadership for the West to come from the

United States. The initial failure of the world to make a systematic response to the war in former Yugoslavia was due in large part to American diffidence on the subject; the subsequent American involvement produced an effective response. The United States also has become a leader in international bargaining and negotiation, as first Camp David and more recently the Middle East peace accords have demonstrated.

The position as world leader imposes burdens on American policymakers. This continues to be true of defense policy even after the end of the Cold War; the role of peacekeeper requires a good deal of military might. This also is true for the need to provide diplomatic and political leadership. The U.S. dollar, despite some battering and significant competition, is still a major reserve currency in the world economy, and this status imposes additional economic demands on the country. The role of world leader is an exhilarating one, but it is also one filled with considerable responsibility and economic costs for the United States. Indeed, the globalization of the economic system is making many Americans rethink the desirability of playing such a major international role.

The policies that emerge from all these influences are filtered through a large and extremely complex political system. The characteristics of that government and the effects of those institutional characteristics on policies are the subject of the next chapter. Policy choices must be made, and thousands are made each day in government; the sum of those choices, rather than any single choice, will decide who gets what as a result of public policies. In the United States more than in most countries, there are a number of independent decision makers whose choices must be factored into the final determination of policy.

Conclusion

American public policy is the result of complex interactions among a number of equally complex institutions. It involves a wide range of ideas and values about what the goals of policy should be, and what are the best means of reaching desired goals. In addition to the interactions that occur within the public sector, there are a number of interactions with an equally complex society and economy. Indeed, society is playing an increasingly important role in policymaking and implementation, with reforms in the public sector placing increasing emphasis on the capacity of the private sector to implement, if not make, public policy.

Making policy requires obtaining some form of social and political consensus among all these forces. There does not have to be full agreement on all the values and all the points of policy, but enough common ground must be found to pass and implement legislation. Building those coalitions can extend beyond reaching ideological agreement to include bargaining and "horse-trading" that in turn assigns a central role to individual policy entrepreneurs and brokers. There is so much potential for blockage and delay in the American political system that some driving force may be needed to make the system function.

2. The Structure of Policymaking

The structures through which public policy is formulated, legitimated, and implemented in the United States are extremely complex. It could be argued that American government has a number of structures but no real organization, for the fundamental characteristic of these structures is the absence of effective coordination and control. This absence of central control is largely intentional. The framers of the Constitution were concerned about the potential for tyranny of a powerful central executive within the federal government; they also feared the control of the central government over the constituent states. The system of government the framers designed divides power among the three branches of the central government, and further between the central government and state and local governments. As the system of government has evolved, it has become divided even further, with individual policy domains able to gain substantial autonomy from central coordination. To understand American policymaking, therefore, we must recognize the extent of fragmentation and the few mechanisms devised to control that fragmentation and enhance coordination.

The fragmentation of American government does present some advantages. First, having a number of decision makers involved in every decision should reduce errors, as all must agree before a proposal can become law or be implemented as an operating program, and there will be full deliberation. Also, the existence of multiple decision makers should permit greater innovation in both the federal government and state and local governments. And, as the framers intended, policymaking power is diffused, reducing the capacity of one central government to run roughshod over the rights of citizens or the interests of socioeconomic groups. For citizens, the numerous points of access to policymaking permit losers at one level of government, or in one institution, to become winners at another.

Americans also pay a price for this lack of policy coordination. It is sometimes difficult to accomplish *anything,* and elected politicians with policy ideas find themselves thwarted by the large number of decision points in the policymaking system. The policymaking situation in the United States in the 1980s and 1990s has been described as "gridlock," in which the different institutions block each other from developing and enforcing policies.[1] Likewise, programs may cancel out each other, as progressive (if decreasingly so) federal taxes and regressive state and local taxes combine to produce a tax system in which most people pay about the same proportion of their income as tax, or as the surgeon general's anti-smoking policies and the Department of Agriculture's tobacco subsidies attempt to please both pro- and antitobacco advocates.[2] The apparent inability or unwillingness of policymakers to choose among options means that policies will be incoherent and the process seemingly without any closure and that decisions may cancel each other out. It also means that because potential conflicts are resolved by every interest in society receiving some support from the public sector, taxes and expenditures are higher than they might otherwise be.

I have already mentioned the divisions that exist in American government. I now look at the more important dimensions of those divisions and the ways in which they act and interact to affect policy decisions and real policy outcomes for citizens. "Divided government" and "gridlock" have become standard descriptions of American government, and the impact of these divisions, as well as that of federalism, must be considered in analyzing the way in which policy emerges from this political system. Further, we need to be careful to determine the extent to which gridlock really exists, as more than simply a convenient description of institutional conflict.

Federalism

The most fundamental division in American government traditionally has been federalism, or the constitutional allocation of governmental powers between the federal and the state governments. This formal allocation at once reserves all powers not specially granted to the federal government to the states (Ninth and Tenth Amendments) and establishes the supremacy of federal law when there are conflicts with state and local law (Article 6). Innumerable court cases and, at least in part, one civil war have resulted from this somewhat ambiguous division of powers among levels of government.

By the 1990s American federalism had changed significantly from the federalism described in the Constitution. The original constitutional division of power assumed that certain functions of government would be performed entirely by the central government and that other functions would be carried out by state or local governments. In this "layer cake" federalism, or "separated powers model," the majority of public activities were to be performed by subnational governments, while a limited number of functions, such as national defense and minting money, were to be the responsibility of the federal government.[3]

As the activities of government at all levels expanded, the watertight separation of functions broke down, and federal, state, and local governments became involved in many of the same activities. The layer cake then was transformed into a "marble cake," with the several layers of government still distinct, although no longer vertically separated from one another. This form of federalism, however, still involved intergovernmental contacts through central political officials. The principal actors were still governors and mayors, and intergovernmental relations remained on the level of high politics, with the representatives of subnational governments acting almost as ambassadors from sovereign governments and as supplicants for federal aid. Further, in this form of federalism, the state government retained its role as intermediary between the federal government and local governments.

Federalism evolved further from a horizontal division of activities into a set of vertical divisions. Whereas functions were once neatly compartmentalized by level of government, the major feature of "picket fence" federalism is the development of policy subsystems defined by policy rather than level of government.[4] Thus, major decisions about health policy are made by specialized networks involving actors from all levels of government and from the private sector. Those networks, however, may be relatively isolated from other subsystems making decisions about highways, education, or whatever. The principal actors in these subsystems frequently are not political leaders but administrators and substantive policy experts. Local health departments work with state health departments and with the Department of Health and Human Services (HHS) in Washington in making health policy, and these experts are not dependent on the intervention of political leaders to make the process function. This form of federalism is as much administrative as it is political, and it is driven by expertise as much as by political power.

In many ways, it makes little sense to discuss federalism in its original meaning; it has been argued that contemporary federalism is as much facade as picket fence. A term such as *intergovernmental relations* more accurately describes the complex crazy quilt of overlapping authority and interdependence among levels of government than does a more formal, constitutional term such as federalism.[5] In addition to being oriented more toward administrative issues than high politics, contemporary intergovernmental relations is more functionally specific and lacks the coordination that might result if higher political officials were obliged to make the principal decisions. Thus, like much of the rest of American politics, intergovernmental relations often now lacks the mechanisms that could generate effective policy control and coordination.

Despite the complexity, overlap, and incoherence that exist in intergovernmental relations, one can still argue that centralization of control in the federal system has increased.[6] State and local governments are increasingly dependent on central government financing of their services, given the more buoyant character of federal revenues and the ability of the federal government to borrow more readily. With financing has come increased federal control over local government activities. In some cases that control is absolute, as when the federal government mandates equal access to education for the handicapped or sets water-quality standards for sewage treatment facilities. In other instances the controls on state and local governments are more conditional, based on the acceptance of a grant; if a government accepts the money, it must accept the controls accompanying that money.

In general, the number and importance of mandates on state and local governments, and the number of conditions attached to those grants, have been increasing. For example, the Department of Health and Human Services has threatened to cut off funding for immunization and other public health programs in states that do not implement restrictions on procedures performed by doctors and dentists with AIDS. Even the existence of many federal grant programs may be indicative of control from the center, inasmuch as they direct the attention and money of local governments in directions those governments might not otherwise have chosen.

In addition to controls exercised through the grant process, the federal government has increased its many controls over subnational governments through intergovernmental regulation and mandating. These regulations require the subnational government to perform a function, such as wastewater treatment, whether or not there is federal money available to subsidize the activity. These regulations are certainly intrusive and can be expensive for state and local governments. Even when the mandates are not expensive and are probably effective, such as the requirement that states raise the minimum drinking age to twenty-one or lose 5 percent of their federal highway money, they can still be perceived as "federal blackmail" of the states.[7] Even the Reagan and Bush administrations, dedicated to restoring the balance in favor of the states in federalism, found mandates an almost irresistible means for implementing their policy goals.

One part of the Contract with America promoted by the incoming Republican majority in Congress in 1994 was to end unfunded federal mandates, and this assault on mandates was the first section of the "contract" enacted into law. In particular, the 1995 legislation[8] requires the Congressional Budget Office to estimate the mandated costs in legislation reported out of committee in Congress. This by no means outlaws mandates, but it does require that members of Congress at least know what they are doing to the states and localities if they pass the legislation. Also, this legislation did not in any way affect existing mandates, nor will the federal government have to pay the bill. In practice, conservatives believe that the legislation has been largely toothless,[9] while liberals believe that environmental and consumer standards are in danger of being undermined. The shift from mandates to suggestions to control drunk driving in the 1998 highways bill may indicate something of the change in attitudes about mandates.

One complicating factor for intergovernmental relations in the United States has been the proliferation of local governments. As fiscal restrictions on local governments have caused problems for mayors and county commissioners, a number of new local governments have been created to circumvent those restrictions. States frequently restrict the level of taxation or bonded indebtedness of local governments. When a local government reaches its legal limit, it may create a special authority to undertake some functions formerly performed by the general-purpose local authority. For example, as Cleveland faced severe fiscal problems in 1979 and 1980, it engaged in a "city garage sale" in which it sold its sewer system and transportation system to special-purpose local authorities. The fiscal crisis in New York in the early 1990s prompted the city and even the state to sell off facilities such as roads and prisons to special-purpose authorities.[10]

During the 1980s and 1990s, an average of almost 500 local governments have been created every year, primarily special districts to provide services such as transportation, water, sewerage, fire protection, and other traditional local government services.[11] These new special-purpose governments present that many more problems of coordination and may pose a problem for citizens who want to control the level of taxation but find that every time they limit the power of one government, a new one is created with more fiscal powers. The new forms of local governments also present problems of democratic accountability. The leaders of special-purpose governments often are not elected, and the public can influence their actions only indirectly through the general-purpose local governments (cities and counties) that appoint the boards of the special-purpose ones.[12]

The Reagan and Bush administrations attempted to reverse some of the historic course of centralization in federalism. One approach was to reduce the amounts spent for intergovernmental grants, especially general-purpose subsidies for subnational governments. Their strategies also involved eliminating a number of categorical (program) grants and providing more federal grants to subnational governments in the form of large block grants to the states. Block grants provide for all programs in a broad policy area, such as maternal and child health care or community development. These grants at once give state governments power over local (especially city) governments and provide those governments with more capacity to make decisions about how the money will be spent.

The economic circumstances of the late 1980s and 1990s—the mounting federal deficit and the then-healthy state treasuries—tended to push power back toward the states.[13] The recession of the early 1990s ended public surpluses in almost all states and turned eyes in state capitols back toward Washington. Those eyes became even more hopeful and searching with a Democratic administration in Washington. The Clinton administration, however, proved to be as decentralizing as most previous Republican administrations, and perhaps even more so. For example, the welfare reform passed in 1996 was a major decentralization of power to the states, and the general pattern of policy change has been to increase the powers of states and localities vis-à-vis Washington. President Clinton's experience as a governor and his natural inclinations, in conjunction with those of the Republican Congress, have pushed power to the states.

Despite recent changes, the American federal system still centralizes power more than was planned when the federal system was formed. The grant system has been purchasing a more centralized form of government. The shift in power appears to have resulted less from power-hungry federal bureaucrats and politicians than from the need to standardize many basic public services and the need to promote greater equality for minorities. Further, even if programs are intended to be managed with "no strings attached," there is a natural tendency, especially in Congress, to demand the right to monitor expenditure of public funds and to ensure that those funds are used to obtain desired goals. In an era in which the accountability of government is an increasingly important issue, monitoring is likely to increase in intensity, even with a Republican Congress stressing the need to limit federal power.

Separation of Powers

The second division of American government exists within the federal government itself and incidentally within most state and local governments as well. The Constitution distributes the powers of the federal government among three branches, each capable of applying checks and balances to the other two. In addition to providing employment for constitutional lawyers, this division of power has a substantial impact on public policies. In particular, the number of "veto points" in the federal government alone makes initiating any policy difficult and makes preventing change relatively easy.[14] It also means, as I mentioned when discussing the incoherence of American public policy, that the major task in making public policy is forming a coalition across a number of different institutions and levels of government. Without "legislating together" in such a coalition, either nothing will happen or the intentions of a policymaker will be modified substantially.[15] The United States is not a tightly administered political system in which one actor makes a decision and all other actors must fall neatly into line. This country has an intensely political and highly complex policymaking system

Secretary of State Madeleine Albright is greeted by Senators Joseph Biden and Jesse Helms as she arrives to testify before the Senate Foreign Relations Committee. (Agence France Presse/Corbis-Bettmann)

in which initiatives must be shepherded through the process step by step if anything positive is to occur.

The president, Congress, and the courts are constitutionally designated institutions that must agree to a policy before it can be fully legitimated. The bureaucracy, however, although it is only alluded to in the Constitution, is now certainly a force with which elected politicians must contend in the policy process. Despite its conservative and obstructionist image, the bureaucracy is frequently the institution most active in promoting policy change, given government workers' close connections with the individuals and interests to which they provide services.[16]

The bureaucracy, or more properly the individual agencies of which it is composed, has interests that can be served through legislation. The desired legislation may only expand the budget of the agency, but it usually has a broader public policy purpose as well. Administrative agencies can, if they wish, also impede policy change or perhaps even block it entirely. Almost every elective or appointed politician has experienced delaying tactics of nominal subordinates who disagree with a policy choice and want to wait until the next election or cabinet change to see if someone with more compatible policy priorities will come into office. The permanence of the "bureaucrats," and their command of technical details and of the procedural machinery, provide bureaucratic agencies much more power over public policies than one would assume from reading formal descriptions of government institutions.

The institutional separation in American government has led to a number of critiques based upon the concept of "divided government."[17] The argument is that American government is incapable of being the decisive governance system required in the late twentieth century, and that some means must be found of generating coherent decisions. This was especially true when the two major institutions were controlled by different political parties, as they were during the Reagan and Bush presidencies. The early days of the Clinton presidency, however, indicate that even when the same party controls both branches, there are still enough differences within parties, and enough institutional rivalry, to make cooperation difficult.[18] In contrast, David Mayhew, Charles O. Jones, and other scholars have argued that the system is capable of decision making and even of rapid policy innovation, and that it can govern effectively.[19]

Whether the system is efficient or not, one principal result of the necessity to form coalitions across a number of institutions is the tendency to produce small, incremental changes rather than a major revamping of policies.[20] This might be best described as policymaking by the lowest common denominator. The need to involve and placate all four institutions within the federal government—including the many component groups of individuals within each—and perhaps state and local governments as well means that only rarely can more than minor changes be made in the established commitments to clients and producer groups if the policy change is to be successful.[21] The resulting pattern of incremental change has been both praised and damned. It has been praised as providing stability and limiting the errors that might result from more significant shifts in policy. If only small policy changes are made, and these changes do not stray far from previously established paths, it is unlikely that major mistakes will be made.

The jiggling and poking of policies characteristic of incremental change is perfectly acceptable if the basic patterns of policy are also acceptable, but in some areas of policy, such as health-care and mass transportation, a majority of Americans have said (at least in polls) that they would like some significant changes from the status quo.[22] The existing system of policymaking appears to have great difficulty in producing the major changes desired. In addition, the reversibility of small policy changes, assumed to be an advantage of incrementalism, is often overstated.[23] Once a program is implemented, a return to the conditions that existed before the policy choice is often difficult. Clients, employees, and organizations are created by any policy choice, and they usually will exert powerful pressures for the continuation of the program.

The division of American government by the constitutional separation-of-powers doctrine represents a major institutional confrontation in the center of the federal government. Conflicts between the president and Congress over such matters as war powers, executive privilege, and the budget represent differences over those manifest issues as well as a testing and redefinition of the relative powers of institutions. Is the modern presidency inherently imperial, or is it subject to control by Congress and the courts? Does too much checking by each institution over the others generate gridlock and indecision? Likewise, can the unelected Supreme Court have as legitimate a role as a rule-making body in the political system as does the elected Congress? Further, do the regulations made by the public bureaucracy really have the same standing as law as the legislation passed by Congress or decrees from the court system? These are the kinds of questions posed by the separation-of-powers doctrine. These questions influence substantive policy as well as relationships among the institutions.

Subgovernments

A third division within American government cuts across institutional lines within the federal government and links the federal government directly to the "picket fence" of federalism. The results of this division have been described variously as "iron triangles," "cozy little triangles," "whirlpools," and "subgovernments."[24] The underlying phenomenon described by these terms is that the federal government rarely acts as a unified institution making policy choices, but tends instead to endorse the decisions made by portions of the government. Each functional policy area tends to be governed as if it existed in splendid isolation from the remainder of government, and frequently the powers and legitimacy of government are used for the advancement of individual or group interests in society, rather than for a broader public interest.[25]

Three principal actors are involved in the iron triangles so important for explaining policymaking in the United States. The first is the interest group. The interest group wants something from government, usually a favorable policy decision, and it must attempt to influence the institutions that can act in its favor. Fortunately for the interest group, it usually need not influence all of Congress or the entire executive branch, but only the relatively small portion concerned with a particular policy area. For example, tobacco growers who want continued or increased crop supports need not influence the entire Department of Agriculture but only those within the Agricultural Stabilization and Commodity Service who are directly concerned with their crop. Likewise, in Congress (although the heightened politicization of the smoking issue requires a somewhat different strategy), they need only influence the Tobacco Subcommittee of the House of Representatives Agriculture Committee; the Senate Subcommittee on Agricultural Production and Stabilization of Prices; and the Rural Development, Agriculture, and Related Agencies Subcommittees of the Appropriations Committees in the Senate and House. In addition to the usual tools of information and campaign funds, interest groups have an important weapon at their disposal: votes. They represent organizations of interested individuals and can influence, if not deliver, votes for the congressman. Interest groups also have research staffs, technical information, and other support services that, although their outputs must be regarded with some skepticism, may be valuable resources for congressmen or administrative agencies seeking to influence the policy process.

The second component of these triangular relationships is the congressional committee or subcommittee. These bodies are designated to review suggestions for legislation in a policy area and to make recommendations to the whole Senate or House of Representatives. An appropriations subcommittee's task is to review expenditure recommendations from the president, then to make its own recommendations on the appropriate level of expenditures to the entire committee and to the whole house of Congress. Several factors combine to give these subcommittees substantial power over legislation. First, subcommittee members develop expertise over time and are regarded as more competent to make decisions concerning a policy than is the whole committee or the whole house.[26] Norms have also been developed that support subcommittee decisions for less rational, and more political, reasons.[27] If the entire committee or the entire house were to scrutinize any one subcommittee's decisions, it would have to scrutinize all such decisions, and then each subcommittee would lose its powers. These powers are important to individual congressmen, and each congressman wants to develop his or her own power base. Finally, the time limitations imposed by the huge volume of policy decisions being made by Congress each year mean that accepting a subcommittee decision may be a rational means of reducing the total workload of each individual legislator.

Congressional subcommittees are not unbiased; they tend to favor the very interests they are intended to oversee and control. This is largely because the congressmen on a subcommittee tend to represent constituencies whose interests are affected by the policy in question. As one analyst argued, "a concerted effort is made to insure that the membership of the subcommittee is supportive of the goals of the subgovernment."[28] For example, in 1996 the Energy and Mineral Resources Subcommittee of the House Resources Committee included representatives from the energy-producing states of Texas (2), California (2), Louisiana, West Virginia, Tennessee, Wyoming, and Ohio and from the mining states of Arizona, New Mexico, Idaho, and Colorado; there was also one representative from Hawaii. This pattern is not confined to natural resources. The Housing and Community Development Subcommittee of the House Banking, Finance, and Urban Affairs Committee has representatives from all the major urban areas of the United States. These patterns of committee and subcommittee membership are hardly random; they increase the ability of congressmen to deliver certain kinds of benefits to constituents as well as their familiarity with the substantive issues of concern to constituents.

Subcommittee members also develop patterns of interaction with the administrative agencies over which they exercise oversight. The individual members of Congress and agency officials may meet informally and discuss policy with one another. As both parties in these interactions tend to remain in Washington for long periods of time, the same congressmen and officials may interact for twenty years or more. The trust, respect, or simple familiarity this interaction produces further cements the relationships between committee members and agency personnel.

Obviously, the third component of the iron triangle is the administrative agency. The agency, like the pressure group, wants to promote its interests through the policymaking process. The principal interests of an agency are its survival and its budget. The agency need not be, as is often assumed, determined to expand its budget. Agencies frequently do not wish to expand their budget share, but only to retain their "fair share" of the budget pie as it expands or contracts.[29] Agencies also have policy ideas that they wish to see translated into operating programs, and they need the action of the congressional committee or subcommittee for that to happen. They also need the support of organized interests.

Each actor in an iron triangle needs the other two in order to reach its goal, and the style that develops is symbiotic. The pressure group needs the agency to deliver services to its members and to provide a friendly point of access to government, while the agency needs the pressure group to mobilize political support for its programs among the affected clientele. Constituents must be mobilized to write letters to influential congressmen arguing that the agency is doing a good job and could do an even better job if given more money or a certain policy change. The pressure group needs the congressional committee both as a point of access and as an internal spokesperson in Congress. And the committee needs the pressure group to mobilize votes for its congressmen and to explain to group members how and why they are doing a good job in Congress. The pressure group can also be a valuable source of policy ideas and research for busy politicians. Finally, the committee members need the agency as an instrument for producing services to their constituents and for developing new policy initiatives. The agency has the research and policy analysis capacity that congressmen often lack, so the committee can profit from its association with the agency. And the agency obviously needs the committee to legitimate its policy initiatives and provide it with funds.

All the actors involved in a triangle have similar interests. In many ways they all represent the same individuals, variously playing the role of voter, client, and organization member. Much of the domestic policy of the United States can be explained by the existence of functionally specific policy subsystems and by the absence of effective central coordination. This system of policymaking has been likened to feudalism, with the policies being determined not by any central authority but by aggressive subordinates—the bureaucratic agencies and their associated groups and committees.[30] Both the norms concerning policymaking and the time constraints of political leaders tend to make central coordination and policy choice difficult. The president and his staff (especially the Office of Management and Budget, or OMB) are in the best organizational position to exercise this control, but the president must serve political interests, just as Congress must, and he faces an even more extreme time constraint. Thus, decisions are rarely reversed once they have been made within the iron triangles.

One effect of this subdivision of government into a number of functionally specific subgovernments is the incoherence of public policy already mentioned. All societal interests are served through their own agencies, and there is little attempt to make overall policy choices for the nation. Further, these functional subgovernments at the federal level are linked with functional subsystems through the intergovernmental relations described earlier. The result is that local governments and citizens alike may frequently receive contradictory directives from government and may become confused and cynical about the apparent inability of their government to make up its mind.

A second effect of the division of American government into a number of subgovernments is the involvement of a large number of official actors in any one policy area. This is in part a recognition of the numerous interactions within the public sector, and between the public and private sectors, in the formulation and implementation of a public policy. For an issue area such as health care, the range of organizations involved cannot be confined to those labeled "health" but must inevitably expand to include consideration of the social welfare, nutrition, housing, education, and environmental policies that may have important implications for citizens' health.[31] But the involvement of an increasing number of agencies in each issue area also reflects the lack of central coordination so that agencies can gain approval from friendly congressional committees for expansion of their range of programs and activities.

From time to time, a president attempts to streamline and rationalize the delivery of services in the executive branch and in the process frequently encounters massive resistance from agencies and their associated interest groups. For example, in creating the cabinet-level Department of Education, President Jimmy Carter sought to move the educational programs of the (then) Veterans Administration into the new department.[32] In this attempt he locked horns with one of the best organized and most powerful iron triangles in Washington—the Veterans Administration, veterans' organizations, and their associated congressional committees. The president lost. Subsequently the veterans' lobby was sufficiently powerful to have the VA made into a cabinet-level department.

As easy as it is to become enamored of the idea of iron triangles in American government—they do help explain many of the apparent inconsistencies in policy when viewed broadly—there is some evidence that the iron in the triangles is becoming rusty.[33] More groups are now involved in making decisions, and it is more difficult to exclude interested parties from decisions; Charles O. Jones describes the current pattern as "big sloppy hexagons," rather than "cozy little triangles."[34] For example, the health-care debate in 1994 included not just representatives of the medical professions, hospitals, and health insurers, but a range of other interests such as small businessmen, organized religion, and trade unions. A simple search of the internet on a policy issue will reveal a wide range of groups expressing their opinions and attempting to influence public—and congressional—opinion.[35]

The concepts of *issue networks* and *policy communities,* involving large numbers of interested parties, each with substantial expertise in the policy area, now appear more descriptive of policymaking in the United States, as well as in other industrialized democracies.[36] These structures of interest groups surrounding an issue are less unified about policy than were "iron triangles," and they may contain competing ideas and types of interests to be served through public policy—the tobacco subsystem may even be invaded by health-care advocates. As important as the network idea is to explain changes in federal policymaking, it does not detract from the basic idea that policymaking is very much an activity that occurs within subsystems.

American government, although originally conceptualized as divided vertically by level of government, is now better understood as divided horizontally into a number of expert and functional policy subsystems. These feudal subsystems divide the authority of government and attempt to appropriate the name of the public interest for their own more private interests. Few if any of the actors making policy, however, have any interest in altering

33

these stable and effective means of governing. The system of policymaking is effective politically because it results in the satisfaction of most interests in society. It also links particular politicians and agencies with the satisfaction of those interests, thereby ensuring their continued political success.

The basic patterns of decision making in American politics are *logrolling* and *pork-barrel* spending, through which, instead of clashing over the allocation of resources, actors minimize conflict by giving each other what they want. For example, instead of contending over which river and harbor improvements will be authorized in any year, Congress tends to approve virtually all so that all congressmen can claim to have produced something for the folks back home. Or congressmen from farming areas may trade positive votes on urban development legislation for support of farm legislation by inner-city congressmen.

Although such logrolling does tend to spread benefits widely, direct involvement in the subsystem making decisions tends to produce even more benefits for congressmen and their constituents. This could be seen easily in the distribution of funds from the 1998 highways bill, one of the largest public works bills ever passed by Congress. Although the bill tended to dispense highway funding widely, it still rewarded House Transportation committee members disproportionately. As shown in table 2.1, states that had one or more representatives on this committee received substantially more per capita than did states without such a representative. It could be that the states with representatives needed more highway repair and construction, but the pattern does appear suspiciously political.

TABLE 2.1

PER CAPITA APPROPRIATIONS IN HIGHWAYS BILL OF 1998

No representatives	One representative	Multiple representatives
$29.70	$40.40	$43.20

SOURCE: *Almanac of American Politics, 1998;* and "A Close Look at the Highway Bill," *New York Times,* 28 May 1998.

This pattern of policymaking is effective as long as there is sufficient wealth and economic growth to pay for the subsidization of large numbers of public programs.[37] Nevertheless, this pattern of policymaking was one (but by no means the only) reason for the federal government's massive deficits in the 1980s and early 1990s, and it appears that the pattern can no longer be sustained comfortably. Various budget reforms (see pp. 149–60) have attempted to make pork-barrel politics more difficult to pursue. In particular, the institutionalization of the PAYGO system in Washington, by requiring consideration of the alternative uses of the money or an alternative source of revenue, has made it more difficult to spend (see pp. 156–58). Given the divisions within American government, however, it is difficult for the policymaking system as a whole to make the choices among competing goals and competing segments of society that would be necessary to stop the flow of red ink from Washington.

Public and Private

The final qualitative dimension of American government that is important in understanding the manner in which contemporary policy is made is the increasing confusion of public and private interests and organizations. These two sets of actors and actions have now become so intermingled that it is difficult to ascertain where the boundary line between the two sectors lies. The leakage across the boundary between the public and private sectors, as artificial as that boundary may be, has been occurring in both directions. Activities that once were almost entirely private now have a greater public-sector involvement, although frequently through quasi-public organizations that mask the real involvement of government. Also, functions that are nominally public have significantly increased private-sector involvement. The growth of institutions for formal representation and for implementation by interest groups has given those groups perhaps an even more powerful position in policymaking than that described in the discussion of iron triangles. Instead of vying for access, interest groups are accorded access formally, and they have a claim to their position in government.

The other major component of change in the relationship between public and private has been the push toward privatization of public activities.[38] This trend began to some degree in the 1970s with Presidents Ford and Carter, but it became more pronounced during the 1980s under President Reagan. The United States traditionally has had an antigovernment ethos; that set of values was articulated strongly, and the positive role of the federal government minimized, during the 1980s.[39] For example, a large amount of federal land was sold by the Department of the Interior, and a number of public services were contracted out to the private sector. At one extreme, security checks for the Department of the Navy were being contracted out to a private security firm. It was not only at the federal level that privatization and contracting was popular. At the state and local levels, a large number of functions—hospitals, garbage collection, janitorial services, and even prisons—were contracted out or sold off as a means of reducing the costs of government.[40]

The blending of public and private is to some degree reflected in employment.[41] Table 2.2 (p. 36) demonstrates public and private employment

35

TABLE 2.2

PERCENTAGES IN PUBLIC EMPLOYMENT,
SELECTED POLICY AREAS, 1970–90

Policy area	1970	1980	1985	1990
Education	87	85	84	83
Post office[a]	92	73	74	70
Highways[b]	74	68	68	62
Tax administration[c]	90[d]	57	57	55
Police[e]	85	60	58	56
Defense[f]	63	59	60	62
Social services[g]	26	35	34	32
Transportation	33	31	32	34
Health	26	30	33	37
Gas/electricity/water	25	27	26	24
Banking	1	1	1	1
Telecommunications	<.5	1	1	1

SOURCES: Bureau of the Census, *Census of Governments,* quinquennial; Department of Defense, *Defense Manpower Statistics,* annual; Employment and Training Administration, *Annual Report.*

   a. Private-sector counterparts are employees of private services, couriers, etc.

   b. Private-sector counterparts are employed by highway construction contracting firms.

   c. Private-sector counterparts are tax accountants and staffs, H&R Block employees, etc., some only seasonally.

   d. Rough estimate.

   e. Private-sector counterparts are security guards, private policemen, etc.

   f. Private-sector counterparts are employed by military suppliers.

   g. Private-sector counterparts are employed in social work and philanthropy, many only part-time.

in twelve policy areas, as well as changes that occurred from 1970 to 1990. By 1980, for example, only education retained more than 80 percent public employees, and that percentage was dropping. Even two presumed public monopolies—defense and police protection—had significant levels of private employment. These two policy areas differ, however, in the form of private employment. Defense employment in the private sector is in the production of goods and services used by the armed forces, whereas in police protection a number of private policemen actually provide the service.

The development of mechanisms for direct involvement of interest groups in public decision making is frequently referred to as *corporatism* or *neocorporatism*.[42] These terms refer to the representation in politics of members of the political community not as residents of a geographical area but as members of functionally defined interests in the society—labor, management, farmers, students, the elderly, and so forth. Associated with this concept of representation is the extensive use of interest groups both as instruments of input to the policy process and as a means of implementing public policies. The United States is a less corporatist political system than most industrialized democracies, but there are still corporatist elements. Most urban programs mandate the participation of community residents and other interested parties in decision making for the program. Crop-allotment programs of the Department of Agriculture have used local farmers' organizations to monitor and implement the programs for some time. County medical societies have been used as professional service review organizations for Medicare and Medicaid as means of checking on quality and costs of services, and medical and legal associations license practitioners on behalf of government. In addition, as of the mid-1990s there were approximately 6,000 advisory bodies in the federal government, many containing substantial interest-group representation.[43]

In addition to the utilization of interest groups to perform public functions, a number of other organizations in the society implement public policy. For example, when cabin attendants in an airplane require passengers to fasten their seat belts, they are implementing Federal Aviation Administration policies. Also, universities are required to help implement federal drug policies (statements of nonuse by new employees) and federal immigration policies (certification of citizenship or immigration status of new employees). Manufacturers of numerous products must implement federal safety and environmental standards (e.g., seat belts and pollution-control devices in automobiles), or they cannot sell their products legally.

The increasing use of quasi-public organizations, changes in the direction of a limited corporatist approach to governance in the United States, and privatization (largely through contracting) raise several questions concerning responsibility and accountability in government. These changes involve the use of public money and, more important, the name "public" by groups and for groups that may not be entirely public. In an era in which citizens appear to be attempting to exercise greater control over their governments, the development of these forms of policymaking "at the margins of the state" may be understandable in terms of financial hardships but may only exacerbate the underlying problems of public loss of trust and confidence in government.

The Size and Shape of the Public Sector

We have looked at some qualitative aspects of the contemporary public sector in the United States. What we have yet to do is to examine the size of that public sector and the distribution of funds and personnel among the various purposes of government. As was pointed out, drawing any clear distinctions between public and private sectors in the mixed-economy welfare state is difficult, and it is growing more difficult, but we will concentrate on the expenditures and personnel that are clearly governmental. As these figures are only those that are clearly public, they inevitably understate the size and importance of government in the United States.

Table 2.3 contains information about the varying size of the public sector in the United States during the post–World War II era and the changing

TABLE 2.3

GROWTH OF PUBLIC EMPLOYMENT AND EXPENDITURES, 1950–94

	Public employment, civilian (in thousands)			Public expenditures (in thousands)		
Year	Federal	State and local	Total	Federal[a]	State and local	Total
1950	2,117	4,285	6,402	$44,800	$25,534	$70,334
1960	2,421	6,387	8,808	97,280	54,008	151,288
1970	2,881	10,147	13,028	208,190	124,795	332,985
1975	2,890	12,083	14,973	341,517	218,612	560,129
1980	2,876	13,315	16,191	576,700	432,328	1,009,028
1990	3,105	14,976	18,081	1,243,125	976,311	2,219,436
1994	2,952	16,468	19,420	885,324	1,264,348	2,149,672

	As percentage of total employment			As percentage of GNP		
1950	3.6	7.3	10.9	15.7	8.9	24.6
1960	3.7	9.7	13.4	19.2	10.7	29.9
1970	3.7	12.9	16.6	21.2	12.7	33.9
1975	3.4	14.2	17.6	22.5	14.4	36.9
1980	2.9	13.1	16.0	20.0	16.4	36.4
1990	2.6	12.5	15.1	23.2	18.2	41.4
1994	2.0	12.5	14.5	19.5	21.4	40.9

SOURCE: *Statistical Abstract*, 1997.

a. Does not include federal monies passed through grant programs to states and localities for final expenditure at state and local levels.

distribution of the total levels of expenditures and employment. Most obvious in this table is that the public sector has indeed grown, with expenditures increasing from less than one-quarter to more than one-third of gross national product. Likewise, public employment increased from 11 percent of total employment in 1950 to over 17 percent in 1975. The relative size of the public sector, however, has since decreased, especially in terms of percentage of employment. Although the number of public employees increased by more than 3 million from 1980 to 1994, government's share of total employment dropped slightly. Government in the United States is large, but it does not appear to be the ever-increasing leviathan that its critics portray it to be.[44]

It is also evident that growth levels of public expenditures are more than twice as large, relative to the rest of the economy, as public employment figures. Also, public expenditures as a share of gross national product have continued to increase slightly. The differences relative to the private sector and the differences in the patterns of change are largely the results of transfer programs, such as Social Security, which involve the expenditure of large amounts of money but require relatively few administrators. In addition, purchases of goods and services from the private sector (e.g., the Department of Defense's purchases of weapons from private firms) involve the expenditure of large amounts of money (over $110 billion in 1994) with little or no employment generated in the public sector. In 1988, however, those purchases did create approximately 2.1 million jobs in the private sector, a figure similar to the number of people then in the armed forces.[45] From these data it appears that some portions of "big government" in the United States are more controllable than others, even during the eight-year term of a popular president determined to reduce the size of the public sector.

The distribution of expenditures and employment among levels of government also has been changing. In 1950 the federal government spent 64 percent of all public money and employed 33 percent of all public employees. By 1994, the federal government spent approximately 60 percent of all public money but employed only 14 percent of all civilian public employees.[46] The remarkable shift in employment relative to expenditures is again in part a function of the large federal transfer programs, such as Social Security. It also reflects the expansion of federal grants to state and local governments and the ability of the federal government to borrow money to meet expenditure needs, as contrasted to the necessity for state and local governments to balance their current expenditure budgets.

In addition, the programs provided by state and local governments —education, social services, police and fire protection—are labor intensive.

The major federal program that is labor intensive, defense, had declining civilian and uniformed employment even before the apparent end of the Cold War in the late 1980s. These data appear to conflict somewhat with the characterization of the federal government as increasingly important in American economic and social life. While certainly it is a large institution, employing over 4 million people when the armed forces are included, it actually has been declining in some respects, with the major growth of government occurring at state and local levels.

Another factor involved in the declining share of employment in the federal government is the shift from defense programs toward social programs. In 1952, national defense accounted for 46 percent of all public expenditures and for 49 percent of all public employment. By 1995, defense expenditures had been reduced to 13 percent of all expenditures and 5 percent of public employment. By contrast, a panoply of welfare state services (health, education, and social services) accounted for 20 percent of public expenditures in 1952, and 24 percent of public employment. By 1995 these services accounted for 52 percent of expenditures and 53 percent of all public employment. Within the welfare state services, education was the biggest gainer in employment, with over 6 million more employees in 1996 than in 1952. And Social Security programs alone increased their spending by well over $300 billion during that time period. The United States is often described as a "welfare state laggard," but the evidence is that although it is still behind most European nations in the range of social services, a marked increase has been occurring in the social component of American public expenditures.

It was argued that the landslide victories of the Republican Party in the presidential elections from 1980 to 1988 were a repudiation of this pattern of change, and that they should have produced little increase, or actual decreases, in the level of public expenditures for social programs. There was a slight relative decrease in social spending from 1980 until 1992—in part a function of increasing expenditures for other purposes, such as interest on the public debt—but sustained decreases will be difficult to obtain. Most social programs are entitlement programs, and once a citizen has been made a recipient of benefits or has made the insurance "contributions" for Social Security, future governments will find it difficult to remove those benefits. This is especially true of programs for the retired elderly, as they cannot be expected to return to active employment to make up losses in benefits. Unfortunately for budget cutters, public expenditures are increasingly directed toward the elderly. For example, in the late 1990s, over 50 percent of the federal budget went to programs (Social Security, Medicare, housing programs, and so forth) for the elderly. As the American population continues to grow older, expenditures for this social group can only be expected to increase. What is true in particular for the elderly is true in general for all entitlement programs, and reducing the size of the government's social budget will be difficult indeed.

The 1990s have been something of a surprise in other ways. The election of a moderate Democrat as president might have been expected to produce a rise in public expenditures, especially for social purposes. The election of an extremely conservative Republican Congress in 1994 and the fiscal conservatism of the Clinton administration, however, actually generated a relatively smaller increase in social spending than might have been expected. The issue of controlling the budgetary deficit, so central to the politics of the 1990s, has mandated slow growth in social spending and, indeed, in public spending more generally.

We have been concentrating attention on public employment and public expenditures as measures of the "size" of government, but we should remember that government influences the economy and society through a number of other mechanisms as well. For example, the federal government sponsors a much larger housing program through the tax system (deductibility of mortgage interest and property taxes) than it does through the Department of Housing and Urban Development (see table 9.2, p. 221). Likewise, through subsidized student loans, the government provides a major education program that shows up only indirectly in public expenditures.

In the United States, regulation has been the major form of government intervention in the economy, rather than the more direct mechanisms used in other countries, because of the generally antistatist views of many American citizens. The regulatory impact of government on the economy can be counted in the billions of dollars—one estimate was $542 billion in 1992.[47] Reliance on these indirect methods of influence has been heightened by the conservative administrations of the 1980s and early 1990s, and the conservative Congress since 1994. The conservatives in Congress have, however, been successful in creating requirements for government to report on the estimated size of the regulatory impact.[48] Therefore, we must be very careful in making an assessment about the size, shape, and impact of government in the United States based solely upon figures about public expenditures and public employment.

American government at the end of the century is large, complex, and to some degree unorganized. Each individual section of government, be it a local government or an agency of the federal government, tends to know clearly what it wants, but the system as a whole lacks overall coordination and control. Priority setting is not one of the strongest features of American government. An elected official coming to office and attempting to give direction to the system of government will be disappointed by his or her inability to produce desired results, by the barriers to policy success, and by

41

the relatively few ways in which the probability of success can be increased. These difficulties of control, however, may be compensated for by the flexibility and multiple opportunities for citizen inputs characteristic of American government.

Despite the problems of coordination and control, and the tradition of popular distrust of government, contemporary American government is active. It spends huge amounts of money and employs millions of people to perform a bewildering variety of tasks. These activities are not confined to a single level of government; instead, all three levels of government are involved in making policy, taxing, spending, and delivering services. This activity is why the study of public policy is so important. It is a means of understanding what goes on in the United States, and why government does the things it does. The emphasis in the next portion of the book is on the processes through which policy is made. All governments must do much the same things when they make policy: identify issues, formulate policy responses to problems, evaluate results, and change programs when they are not producing desired results. American governments do all these things, but they do them in distinctive ways and produce distinctive results.

PART TWO

The Making of
Public Policy

3. Agenda Setting and Policy Formulation

This chapter discusses two aspects of the policymaking process that occur rather early in the sequence of decisions leading to the actual delivery of services to citizens but are nonetheless crucial to the success of the entire process. These two stages of policymaking—agenda setting and policy formulation—are important because they establish the parameters for any additional consideration of the policies. Agenda setting is crucial, for if an issue cannot be placed on the agenda, it cannot be considered and nothing will happen. Similarly, policy formulation begins to narrow and structure the consideration of the issue placed on the agenda, and to prepare a plan of action intended to rectify the problem identified. These two stages are also linked because it is often necessary to have a solution before an issue can be accepted on the agenda. In addition, the manner in which an issue is defined as it is brought to the agenda determines the kinds of solutions that will be developed to solve the problem.

Agenda Setting

Before a policy choice can be made by government, a problem in the society must have been accepted as a part of the agenda for the policymaking system—that is, as one member of the set of problems deemed amenable to public action and worthy of the attention of policymakers. Many real problems are not given any consideration by government, largely because the relevant political actors are not convinced that government has any role in attempting to solve those problems. Although problems once accepted as a part of the agenda tend to remain there for long periods of time, problems do come on and go off the active policy agenda.

One of the best examples of a problem being accepted as part of the agenda after a long period of exclusion is the problem of poverty in the United States. Throughout most of this nation's history, poverty was perceived not as a public problem but as merely the result of the (proper) operation of the free market. The publication of Michael Harrington's *The Other*

America in 1963 and the growing mobilization of poor people brought the problem of poverty to the agenda and indirectly resulted in the launching of a "war" dedicated to its eradication.[1] Once placed on the agenda, poverty has remained an important public issue, although different administrations definitely have given different amounts of attention to the problem.

Another obvious case of external events contributing to setting the policy agenda is that the perceived poor quality of American elementary and secondary education, especially in science and technology, did not become an issue at the federal level until the Soviet Union launched *Sputnik I* in 1957. Although now redefined in terms of economic competitiveness rather than the Cold War, educational quality has remained on the agenda and has gained renewed importance as an issue in the 1990s (see chapter 12). The celebrated murder trial of O.J. Simpson may yet place issues of domestic violence in a more prominent position on the agenda of American governments. In each of these examples some dramatic public event awakened the populace to an existing social problem that needed to be addressed.[2]

The best example of an issue being removed from the policy agenda is the repeal of Prohibition, when the federal government said that preventing the production and distribution of alcoholic beverages was no longer its concern. Despite the end of Prohibition, all levels of government have retained some regulatory and taxing authority over the production and consumption of alcohol. The movement to privatize some public services (mainly at the local level) also has removed some issues from direct concern by the public sector, although again a regulatory role usually continues.

What can cause an issue to be placed on the policy agenda? The most basic cause is a perception that something is wrong and that the problem can be ameliorated through public action. This answer produces a second question: what causes the change in perceptions of problems and issues? Why, for example, did Harrington's book have such far-reaching influence when earlier books about social deprivation, such as James Agee's *Let Us Now Praise Famous Men,* had relatively little impact?[3] Did the timing of the "discovery" of poverty in the United States result from the election of a young, seemingly liberal president (Kennedy) who was succeeded by an activist president (Johnson) with considerable sway over Congress? When do problems cease to be invisible and become perceived as real problems for public consideration?

Issues also appear to pass through an "issue attention cycle," in which they are the objects of great public concern for a short period and generate some response from government.[4] The initial enthusiasm for the issue is generally followed by more sober realism about the costs of policy options and the difficulties of making effective policy. This realism is in turn followed by a period of declining public interest as the public seizes on a new issue. The histories of environmental policy, drug enforcement, and to some degree the women's movement illustrate this cycle very well. More recently, the "discovery" of sexual harassment as a policy issue during the confirmation hearings of Clarence Thomas for the Supreme Court was followed relatively quickly by doubts about the possibility of effective enforcement of the laws and even the exact definition of the offense. Attention to the issue, and its possible ambiguity, was reinforced by allegations against Senator Robert Packwood and later by the several claims against President Clinton.

Just as individual issues go through an issue-attention cycle, the entire political system may experience cycles of differential activity. One set of scholars has described this pattern as "routine punctuated by orgies."[5] A less colorful description developed by Frank Baumgartner and Bryan D. Jones is "punctuated equilibria."[6] Some time periods—because of energetic political leaders, large-scale mobilization of the public, or a host of other possible causes—are characterized by greater policy activism than are others. Those periods of activism are followed by periods in which the programs adopted during the activist period are rationalized, consolidated, or perhaps terminated.[7]

This chapter discusses how to understand, and how to manipulate, the public agenda. How can a problem be converted into an issue and brought to a public institution for formal consideration? In the role of policy analyst, one must understand not only the theoretical issues concerning agenda setting but also the points of leverage within the political system. Much of what happens in the policymaking system is difficult or impossible to control: the ages and health of the participants, their friendships, constitutional structures of institutions and their interactions and external events, to name but a few of the variables. Some scholars have argued that agendas do not change unless there is an almost random confluence of events favoring the new policy initiative.[8] Such random factors may be important in explaining overall policy outcomes, but they are not the only pertinent factors to consider when one confronts the task of bringing about desired policy changes. Despite all the imponderables in a policymaking system, there is still room for initiative and for altering the political behavior of important actors in the system.

It is also important to remember that social problems do not come to government fully conceptualized with labels already attached. Policy problems need to have names attached to them if government is to deal with them, and that is in itself a political process.[9] For example, how do we conceptualize the problem of illegal drugs in the United States? Is it a problem of law enforcement, as it is commonly treated, or is it a public health problem, or a problem of education, or a reflection of poverty and despair? Perhaps drug use indicates something more about the society in which it occurs than it does about the individual consumers usually branded as criminals.

There are a number of possible answers to the definitional questions raised above, but the fundamental point is that the manner in which the problem is conceptualized and defined determines the remedies to be proposed, the organizations that will be given responsibility for the problem, and the final outcomes of the public intervention into the problem.

Kinds of Agendas

Until now we have been discussing "the agenda" in the singular and with the definite article. There are, however, different agendas for the various institutions of government, as well as a more general agenda for the political system as a whole. The existence of these agendas also is to some degree an abstraction. The agendas do not exist in any concrete form; they exist only in a collective judgment of the nature of public problems or as fragments of written evidence such as legislation introduced, the State of the Union message of the president, or notice of intent to issue regulations appearing in the *Federal Register.*

Roger Cobb and Charles Elder, who have produced some of the principal writing on agendas in American government, distinguish between the systemic and institutional agendas of government. The systemic agenda consists of "all issues that are commonly perceived by members of the political community as meriting public attention and as involving matters within the legitimate jurisdiction of existing governmental authority."[10] This is the broadest agenda of government, including all issues that might be subject to action or that are already being acted on by government. This definition implies a consensus on the systemic agenda—a consensus that may not exist. Some individuals may consider a problem—such as abortion (whether to outlaw it or to provide public funding for it)—as part of the agenda of the political system, while others regard the issue as entirely one of personal choice. The southern states' reluctance for years to include civil rights as part of their agendas indicated a disagreement over what fell within the "jurisdiction of existing governmental authority." Setting the systemic agenda is usually not consensual, as it is a crucial political and policy decision. If a problem can be excluded from consideration, then those who benefit from the status quo are assured of victory.[11] Only when a problem is placed on the agenda and made available for discussion do the forces of change have some opportunity for success.

The second type of agenda that Cobb and Elder discuss is the institutional agenda: "that set of items explicitly up for active and serious consideration of authoritative decision-makers."[12] An institutional agenda is then composed of the issues that those in power within a particular institution actually are considering acting on. These issues may constitute a subset of all problems they will discuss, as the complete set will include "pseudo issues" discussed to placate clientele groups but introduced without any serious intention to make policy.[13] Actors within institutions do run a risk, however, when they permit discussion of pseudo issues; once they appear on the docket, something may actually happen about the problem.

A number of institutional agendas exist—as many as there are institutions—and there is little reason to expect any agreement among institutions as to which problems are the most appropriate for consideration. As with the discussion of conflicts over placing issues on the systemic agenda, inter-institutional conflicts will arise about moving problems from one institutional agenda to another. The agendas of bureaucratic agencies are the narrowest, and a great deal of the political activity of those agencies is directed at placing their issues onto the agendas of other institutions. As an institution broadens in scope, the range of agenda concerns also broadens, and supporters of any particular issue will have to fight to have it placed on a legislative or executive agenda. This is especially true of *new problems* seeking to be converted into active issues. Some older and more familiar issues will generally find a ready place on institutional agendas. Some older issues are *cyclical issues:* a new budget must be adopted each year, for example, and changes in the debt ceiling must be adopted as frequently (or more frequently in recent years). Other older agenda items may be *recurrent issues,* indicating primarily the failure of previous policy choices to produce the intended or desired impact on society. Even recurrent issues may not be returned easily to institutional agendas, when existing programs are perceived to be "good enough" or when no new solutions are readily available.

Jack Walker classes problems coming on the agenda in four groups.[14] He discusses issues that are dealt with time and time again as either periodically recurring or sporadically recurring issues (similar to our cyclical and recurrent issues). He also discusses the role of crises in the placement of issues on the agenda, as well as the difficulties of selecting new, or "chosen," problems for inclusion on agendas. Within each institution, the supporters of an issue must use their political power and skills to gain access to the agenda. The failure to be included on any one institutional agenda may be the end of an issue, at least for the time being.

Who Sets Agendas?

Establishing an agenda for society, or even for one institution, is a manifestly political activity, and control of the agenda gives substantial control over the ultimate policy choices. Therefore, to understand how agendas are determined requires some understanding of the manner in which political power is exercised in the United States. As might be imagined, there are a number of different conceptualizations of the manner in which power is exercised. To enable us to understand the dynamics of agenda setting better, we should discuss three important theoretical approaches to the exercise of political power: pluralist, elitist, and state-centric.

Pluralist Approaches

The dominant, though far from undisputed, approach to policymaking in the United States is pluralistic.[15] Stated briefly, this approach assumes that policymaking in government is divided into a number of separate arenas and that those who have power in one arena do not necessarily have power in others. The American Medical Association, for example, may have a great deal of influence over health-care legislation but little influence over education or defense policy. Furthermore, interests that are victorious at one time or in one arena will not necessarily win at another time or place. The pluralist approach to policymaking assumes that there is something of a marketplace in policies, with a number of interests competing for power and influence, even within a single arena. These competitors are perceived as interest groups competing for access to institutions for decision making and for the attention of central actors in the hope of producing their desired outcomes. These groups are assumed, much as in the market model of the economy, to be relatively equal in power, so on any one issue any interest may be victorious. Finally, the actors involved generally agree on the rules of the game, especially the rule that elections are the principal means of determining policy. The principal functions of government are to serve as an umpire in this struggle among competing group interests and to enforce the victories through law.

The pluralist approach to agenda setting would lead the observer to expect a relatively open marketplace of ideas for new policies. Any or all interested groups, as a whole or within a particular public institution, should have the opportunity to influence the agenda. These interest groups may not win every time, but neither will they systematically be excluded from decisions, and the agendas will be open to new items as sufficient political mobilization is developed. This style of agenda setting may be particularly appropriate for the United States, given the multiple institutions and multiple points of access inherent in the structure of the system.[16] Even if an issue has been blocked politically, the courts may enable otherwise disadvantaged groups to bring it into the policy process, as has happened with civil rights and with some aspects of sexual harassment.

Elitist Approaches

The elitist approach to American policymaking seeks to contradict the dominant pluralist approach. It assumes the existence of a "power elite" who dominate public decision making and whose interests are served in the policymaking process. In the elitist analysis, the same interests in society consistently win, and these interests are primarily those of business, the upper and middle classes, and whites.[17] Analysts from an elitist perspective have pointed out that to produce the kind of equality assumed in the pluralist model would require relatively equal levels of organization by all interests in society. They then point out that relatively few interests of working- and lower-class individuals are effectively organized. While all individuals in a democracy certainly have the right to organize, elitist theorists point to the relative lack of resources (e.g., time, money, organizational ability, and communication skills) among members of the working and lower economic classes. Thus, political organization for many poorer people, if it exists at all, may involve only token participation, and their voices will be drowned in the sea of middle-class voices E.E. Schattschneider describes.[18]

The implications of the elitist approach are rather obvious. If agenda formulation is crucial to the process of policymaking, then the ability of elites to keep certain issues off the agenda is crucial to their power. Adherents of this approach believe that the agenda in most democratic countries does not represent the competitive struggle of relatively equal groups, as argued in the pluralist model, but the systematic use of elite power to decide which issues the political system will or will not consider. Jürgen Habermas, for example, argues that the elite uses its power systematically to exclude issues that would be a threat to its interests and that these "suppressed issues" represent a major threat to democracy.[19] If too many significant issues are kept off the agenda, the legitimacy of the political system can be threatened, along with its survival in the most extreme cases.

Peter Bachrach and Morton Baratz's concept of "nondecisions" is important here. They define a nondecision as a decision that results in suppression or thwarting of a latent or manifest challenge to the values or interests of the decision maker.[20] To be more explicit, nondecision making is a means by which demands for change in the existing allocation of benefits and privileges in the community can be suffocated before they are even voiced; or kept covert; or killed off before they gain access to the relevant decision-making arena; or, finally, maimed or destroyed in the decision-implementing stage of the policy process.[21] A decision not to alter the status quo is a decision, whether it is made overtly through the policymaking process or whether it is the result of the application of power to prevent the issue from ever being discussed.

State-Centric Approaches

Both the pluralist and elitist approaches to policymaking and agenda setting assume that the major source of policy ideas is the environment of the policymakers—primarily interest groups or other powerful interests in the society. It is, however, quite possible that the political system itself is responsible for its own agenda.[22] The environment, in a state-centric analysis, is not filled with pressure groups but with "pressured groups," activated by government. As governments become more interested in managing the media and in influencing public opinion, the state-centric view may be more viable.[23]

The state-centric concept of agenda setting conforms quite well to the iron-triangle conception of American government but would place the bureaucratic agency or the congressional committee, not the pressure group, in the center of the process.[24] This approach does emphasize the role of specialized elites within government but, unlike elitist theorists, does not assume that these elites are pursuing policies for their own personal gain. Certainly their organizations may obtain a larger budget and greater prestige from the addition of a new program, but the individual administrator has little or no opportunity to appropriate any of that increased budget.

In addition, the state-centric approach places the major locus of competition over agenda setting within government itself, rather than in the constellation of interests in society. Agencies must compete for legislative time and for budgets; committees must compete for attention to their particular legislative concerns; and individual congressmen must compete for consideration of their own bills and their own constituency concerns. These actors within government are more relevant in pushing agenda items than are interests in society.

One interesting question arises about agenda setting in the state-centric approach: what are the relative powers of bureaucratic and legislative actors in setting the agenda? An early study by the Advisory Commission on Intergovernmental Relations argued that the source of the continued expansion of the federal government at that time was within Congress.[25] The authors of this study claimed that congressmen, acting out of a desire to be reelected or from a sincere interest in solving certain policy problems, have been the major source of new items on the federal agenda. Other analyses have placed the source of most new policy ideas within the bureaucracy as much or more than in Congress.[26] Also, the nature of American government requires that president and Congress work together to set agendas and make policy.[27] Given the complexity of the chains of events leading to new policies, it may be difficult to determine exactly where ideas originated, but there is (at least in this model) no shortage of policy advocates.[28]

The agenda resulting from a state-centric process might be more conservative than one resulting from a pluralist process but less conservative than one from the elitist model. Government actors may be constrained in the amount of change they can advocate on their own initiative; they may instead have to wait for a time when their ideas will be more acceptable to the general public. Congressmen can adopt a crusading stance, but this is a choice usually denied to the typical bureaucratic agency. Except in rare instances—the surgeon general and the Food and Drug Administration concerning the regulation of cigarette smoking perhaps—a government-sponsored agency may be ahead of public opinion, but only slightly so.

Which approach to policymaking and agenda formation is most descriptive of the process in the United States? The answer is probably all of them, for the proponents of each can muster a great deal of evidence for their position. More important, policymaking for certain kinds of problems and issues can best be described by one approach rather than another. For example, we would expect policies that are very much the concern of government itself (e.g., civil service laws or perhaps even foreign affairs) to be more heavily influenced by state-centric policymaking than would other kinds of issues. Likewise, certain kinds of problems that directly affect powerful economic interests would be best understood through elite analysis. Energy policy and its relationship to the major oil companies might well fit into that category. Finally, policy areas characterized by a great deal of interest-group activity and relatively high levels of group involvement, both by clients and producers—education is a good example—might be best understood through the pluralist approach. Unfortunately, these categorizations are largely speculative, for political scientists have only begun to produce the kind of detailed analysis required to track issues as they move on and off agendas.[29]

From Problem to Issue:
How to Get Problems on the Agenda

Problems do not move themselves on and off agendas. Nevertheless, a number of characteristics can have an influence in their acceptance as part of active systemic and institutional agendas. We should remember, however, that most problems do not come with such characteristics clearly visible to most citizens, or even to most political actors. Agendas must be constructed and issues defined by a social and political process in a manner that will make them most amenable to political action.[30] Further, an active policy entrepreneur is usually needed to provide the political packaging that can make an issue appear on an agenda.[31]

The Effects of the Problem

The first aspect of a problem that can influence its placement on an agenda is whom it affects and how much. We can think about the extremity, concentration, range, and visibility of problems as influencing their placement on agendas. First, the more extreme the effects of a problem, the more likely it is to be placed on an agenda. An outbreak of a disease causing mild discomfort, for example, is unlikely to produce public action, but the spread of a life-threatening disease, such as the AIDS epidemic, usually provokes some kind of public action.

Even if the problem is not life threatening, a concentration of victims in one area may produce public action. The sudden unemployment of 50,000 workers, while certainly deplorable, might not cause major public intervention if the workers are scattered around the country, but it may well do so if the workers are concentrated in one geographical area. Most industries in the United States are concentrated geographically—automobiles in Michigan, aerospace in California, oil in Texas and Louisiana—and that makes it easier for advocates of assistance to any troubled industry to get the help they want from government. Even conservatives who tend to oppose government intervention in the economy appear happy to assist failing industries when it is clear that there will be major regional effects.

The range of persons affected by a problem may also influence the placement of the issue on an agenda. In general, the more people affected or potentially affected by a problem, the greater the probability that the issue will be placed on the agenda. There are limits, however; a problem may be so general that no single individual believes that he or she has anything to gain by organizing political action to address it. An issue that has broad but only minor effects therefore may have less chance of being placed on the agenda than a problem that affects fewer people but affects them more severely.

The intensity of effects, and therefore of policy preferences of citizens, is a major problem for those who take the pluralist approach to agenda setting.[32] Many real or potential interests in society are not effectively organized because few individuals believe that they have enough to gain from establishing or joining an organization. For example, although every citizen is a consumer, few effective consumer organizations have been established, whereas producer groups are numerous and effective politically. The specificity and intensity of producer interests, as contrasted to the diffuseness of consumer interests, creates a serious imbalance in the pattern of interest-group organization that favors producers. An analogous situation would be the relative ineffectiveness of taxpayers' organizations compared to clientele groups, such as defense industries and farmers, which are interested in greater federal spending. The organizational imbalance against consumers and taxpayers was mitigated somewhat during the 1980s, but it still exists.[33]

Finally, the visibility of a problem may affect its placement on an agenda as an active issue. This might be called the "mountain climber problem." Society appears willing to spend almost any amount of money to rescue a single stranded mountain climber but will not spend the same amount of money to save many more lives by, for example, controlling automobile accidents or vaccinating children. Statistical lives are not nearly so visible and comprehensible as an identifiable individual stuck on the side of a mountain. Similarly, the issue of the risks of nuclear power plants have been highly dramatized in the media, while less visibly an average of 150 men die each year in mining accidents and many others die from black-lung disease contracted in coal mines. Likewise, the existing environmental effects of burning coal, although certainly recognized and important, appear to pale in the public mind when compared to the possible effects of a nuclear accident.

Analogous and Spillover Agenda Setting

Another important aspect of a problem that can affect its chances for placement on an agenda is the possibility of analogy to other public programs. The more a new issue can be made to look like an old issue, the more likely it is to be placed on the agenda. This is especially true in the United States because of the traditional reluctance of American government to expand the public sector, at least by conscious choice. For example, the federal government's intervention into medical-care financing for individuals with Medicare and Medicaid was dangerously close to the (then) feared "socialized medicine."[34] It was made more palatable, at least in the case of Medicare, by making the program appear similar to Social Security, which was already regarded as legitimate. More recently, the Clinton administration attempted to make its plan for health-care reform appear as much as possible like the health maintenance organizations (HMOs) that earlier had been sponsored by federal policy.[35] If a new agenda item can be made to seem only an incremental departure from existing policies rather than an entirely new venture, its chances of being accepted are much improved.

Also, the existence of one government program may produce the need for additional programs. This spillover effect is important in bringing new programs onto the agenda and in explaining the expansion of the public sector. Even the best policy analysts in the world cannot anticipate the consequences of all the policy choices made by government. Thus, the adoption of one program may soon lead to the adoption of other programs directed at "solving" the problems created by the first program.[36] For example, the federal government's interstate highway program was designed to improve transportation; it was also justified as a means of improving transportation for defense purposes. One effect of building superhighways, however, has been to make it easier for people to live in the suburbs and work in the city. Consequently, these roads assisted in the flight to the suburbs of those who could afford to move, which, in turn, contributed to the decline of central cities. In consequence, the federal government had to pour billions of dollars into urban renewal, Urban Development Action Grants, and a host of other programs for the cities. The inner cities, of course, probably would have de-

Children from a local Head Start program join parents and educators to rally in support of day-care legislation at the Illinois State Capitol. (AP/Wide World Photos)

clined somewhat without the federal highway program, but the program certainly accelerated the process.

Policies in modern societies are now tightly interconnected and have so many secondary and tertiary effects on other programs that any new policy intervention is likely to have results that seem to spread like ripples in a clear lake. To some degree the analyst should anticipate those effects and design programs to avoid negative interaction effects, but he or she can never be perfectly successful in so doing. Tax policies in particular tend to spawn unanticipated responses, as individuals and corporations attempt to find creative ways of legally avoiding paying tax and the Internal Revenue Service tries to find ways to close unanticipated loopholes.[37] As a consequence, "policy is its own cause," and one policy choice may beget others.[38]

Relationship to Symbols

The more closely a particular problem can be linked to certain important national symbols, the greater is its probability of being placed on the agenda. Seemingly mundane programs can become involved in rhetoric about freedom, justice, and traditional American values. Conversely, a problem will not be placed on the agenda if it is associated primarily with negative values. There are, of course, some exceptions, and although the gay community is not a positive symbol for many Americans, the AIDS issue was placed on the agenda with relative alacrity even before the possibilities of other sectors of the population becoming infected with the disease became widely known.[39]

There are several interesting examples of the use of positive symbols to market programs and issues that might not otherwise have been accepted on the agenda. The federal government traditionally eschewed most direct involvement with education, but the success of the Soviet Union in launching *Sputnik I* highlighted the weaknesses of American elementary and secondary education. This led to the National *Defense* Education Act, which associated the perceived problem of education with the positive symbol of defense, a long-term federal government concern. More recently, increased federal involvement in education has been associated at least in part with problems of global economic competitiveness.[40] In addition, although the American government has generally been rather slow to adopt social programs, those associated with children and their families have been more favorably regarded. So, if one wants to initiate a social welfare program, it is well to associate it with children, or possibly with the elderly. It is perhaps no accident that the basic welfare program in the United States was for decades known as Aid to Families with Dependent *Children*. Similarly, the 1994 crime bill contained a variety of social programs (i.e., the famous "midnight basketball" provisions) that might not have even made it to a vote if they had not been attached to the symbolic issue of crime control.

Symbol manipulation is an extremely important skill for policy analysts. In addition to being rational calculators of the costs and benefits of their programs, analysts must be capable of relating their programs and program goals to other programs and of justifying the importance of the program to actors who may be less committed to it and its goals. Placing a problem on the agenda of government means convincing powerful individuals that they should take the time and trouble, and should make the effort necessary to rectify the problem. The use of symbols may facilitate this process when the problem itself is not likely to gain wide public attention.

The Absence of Private Means

In general, governments avoid accepting new responsibilities, especially in the United States with its laissez-faire tradition and especially in a climate of budgetary scarcity (even after a balanced budget has been attained). The market, rather than collective action, has become the standard against which to compare good policy.[41] There are, however, problems in society that cannot be solved by private market activities alone. Two classic examples are social problems that involve either public goods or externalities.

Public goods are goods or services that, once produced, are consumed by a relatively large number of individuals, and whose consumption is difficult or impossible to control—they are not "excludable." This means that it is difficult or impossible for any individual or firm to produce public goods, for they cannot be effectively priced and sold.[42] If national defense were provided by paid mercenaries rather than by government, individual citizens would have little or no incentive to pay that group of fighters; citizens would be protected whether they paid or not. Indeed, citizens would have every incentive to be "free riders" and to enjoy the benefits of the service without paying the cost. In such a situation, government has a remedy for the problem: it can force citizens to pay for the service through its power of taxation.

Externalities are said to exist when the activities of one economic unit affect the well-being of another and no compensation is paid for benefits or costs created externally.[43] Pollution is a classic case of an externality. It is a by-product of the production process, but its social costs are excluded from the selling price of the products made by the manufacturer. Thus, social costs and production costs diverge, and government may have to impose regulations to prevent the private firm from imposing the costs of pollution—such as damage to health, property, and amenities—on the public. Alternatively, government may develop some means of pricing the effects of pollution and then imposing those costs on the polluter.

All externalities need not be negative, however, and some activities create public benefits that are not included in the revenues of those producing them. When a dam is built to generate hydroelectric power, the recreational, flood-control, and economic development benefits cannot be reckoned as part of the revenues of a private utility, although government can include those benefits in its calculations when considering undertaking such a project with public money (see chapter 15). Thus, some projects that appear infeasible for the private sector may be feasible for government, even on strict economic criteria.

Public goods and externalities are two useful categories for consideration, but they do not exhaust the kinds of social and economic problems that have a peculiarly public nature.[44] Of course, the consideration of issues of rights and the application of law is considered peculiarly public. In addition, programs that involve a great deal of risk may require the socialization of that risk through the public sector. For example, lending to college students who have little credit record is backed by government, as a means of making banks more willing to take the risk. These loans are only one example of the general principle that the inability of other institutions in society to produce effective and equitable solutions may be sufficient to place an issue on the public agenda.

The Availability of Technology

Finally, problems generally will not be placed on the public agenda unless there is some technology believed capable of solving the problem. For most of the history of the industrialized nations, it was assumed that economic fluctuations were, like the weather, acts of God. Then the Keynesian revolution in economics produced what seemed to be the answer to these fluctuations, and governments soon placed economic management in a central position on their agendas. In the United States this new technology was reflected in the Employment Act of 1946, pledging the U.S. government to maintain full employment. The promise of "fine tuning" the economy through Keynesian means, which appeared possible in the 1960s, has now become extremely elusive, but the issue of economic management remains on the public agenda.[45] Subsequent governments have provided new technologies (e.g., "supply-side economics" during the Reagan years), but they have not been able to evade responsibility for the economy.

Another way of regarding the role of technology in agenda setting is the "garbage-can model" of decision making, in which solutions find problems, rather than vice versa.[46] Problems may be excluded from the agenda simply because of the lack of an instrument to do the job, and the example of economic management points to the danger of the lack of an available instrument. If government announces that it is undertaking to solve a problem and then fails miserably, public confidence in the effectiveness of government will be shaken. Government must then take the blame for failures along with the credit for successes. The garbage-can model also illustrates the relationship between agenda setting and policy formulation because issues are not accepted as a part of the agenda unless it is known that a policy has been formulated, or is already on the shelf, to solve the problem. Solutions may beg for new problems, like a child with a hammer finding things that need hammering.[47]

As with all portions of the policymaking process, agenda setting is an intensely political activity. It may well be the most political aspect of policymaking, because it involves bringing into the public consciousness an acceptance of a vague social problem as something government can, and should, attempt to solve. It may be quite easy for powerful actors who wish to do so to exclude unfamiliar issues from the agenda, making active political mobilization of the less powerful a requirement for success. Rational policy analysis may play only a small role in setting the agenda for discussion; such analysis will be useful primarily after it is agreed that there is a problem and that the problem is public in nature. In agenda setting, the policy analyst is less a technician and more a politician, understanding the policymaking process and seeking to influence that process toward a desired end. This involves the manipulation of symbols and the definition of often vague social problems. Nevertheless, agenda setting should not be dismissed as simply political maneuvering: it is the crucial first step on the road to resolving any identified problem.

Policy Formulation

After the political system has accepted a problem as part of the agenda for policymaking, the logical question is what should be done about it. We call this stage of the policymaking process *policy formulation,* meaning the development of the mechanisms for solving the public problem. At this stage in the process, a policy analyst can begin to apply analytic techniques to attempt to justify one policy choice as superior to others. Economics and decision theory are both useful in assessing the risks of certain outcomes or in predicting likely social costs and benefits of various alternatives. Rational choice, however, need not be dominant; the habits, traditions, and standard operating procedures of government may prevail over rational activity in making the policy choice. But even such seemingly irrational sets of choice factors may be, in their way, quite rational. This is simply because the actors involved have experience with the "formula" to be used, are comfortable with it, and consequently can begin to make it work much more readily that they could a newer instrument in which they might have no confidence, even if that instrument were technically superior.

The Clinton administration's formulation of its health-care reform proposal demonstrates some of the potential pitfalls of rationalistic and expert policy formulation. Technically this proposal may have been excellent, but it simply did not correspond to the familiar political and administrative patterns of the United States. The plan was excessively complex and could easily be labeled "bureaucratic," whereas more successful social programs have been simpler insurance-based systems. Further, the formulation was carried out largely behind closed doors, rather than permitting affected groups to help shape the proposals and perhaps save the administration from some of the more egregious errors.

The federal government has followed several basic formulas in attempting to solve public problems. In economic affairs, for example, the United States has relied on regulation more than on ownership of business, which has been more common in Europe. In social policy, the standard formulas have been social insurance and cash transfer programs rather than direct delivery of services. The major exception to this pattern has been the reliance on education as a means of rectifying social and economic inequality. And finally there has been a formula involving the private sector as much as possible in public-sector activity through grants, contracts, and use of federal money as "leverage" for private money and money from state and local governments.

We should not, however, be too quick to criticize the federal government for its lack of innovation in dealing with public problems. Most governments do not use all the "tools" available to them.[48] In addition, there is little theory to guide government policymakers trying to decide what tools they should use.[49] In particular, there is very little theory, or practical advice, that links the nature of public problems with the most appropriate ways of solving them. As a consequence, a great deal of policy formulation relies on inertia, analogy, or intuition.

Who Formulates Policy?

Policy formulation is a difficult game to play because any number of people can and do play, and there are few rules. At one time or another, almost every kind of policy actor is involved in formulating policy proposals. Several kinds of actors, however, are especially important in formulating policies. Policy formulation is also very much a political activity, but not always a partisan activity. Political parties and candidates, in fact, are not as good at promulgating solutions to problems as they are at identifying problems and presenting lofty ambitions for society to solve the problems. Expertise begins to play a large role here, given that the success or failure of a policy instrument will depend to some degree on its technical characteristics, as well as its political acceptability.

THE PUBLIC BUREAUCRACY

The public bureaucracy is the institution most involved in taking the lofty aspirations of political leaders and translating them into more concrete proposals. Whether one accepts the state-centric model of agenda setting or not, one must realize that government bureaucracies are central to policy formulation. Even if programs are formally introduced by congressmen or the president, it is quite possible that their original formulation and justification came from a friendly bureau.

Bureaucracies presumably are the masters of routine and procedure. This is at once their strength and their weakness. They know how to use procedures and how to develop programs and procedures to reach desired goals. Yet an agency that knows how to do these things too well may develop an excessively narrow vision of how to formulate answers for a particular set of problems. As noted earlier, certain formulas have been developed at the governmental level for responding to problems, and much the same is true of individual organizations that have standard operating procedures and thick rulebooks. Many of the administrative reforms of the 1990s have sought to jog bureaucracies from these established routines, but old habits are difficult to break.

Certainly familiarity with an established mechanism can explain some of the conservatism of organizations in the choice of instruments to achieve ends, and faith in the efficacy of the instrument also helps explain reliance on a limited range of policy tools. One important component of the restrictiveness of choice, however, appears to be self-protection. That is, neither administrators nor their agencies can go very wrong by selecting a solution that is only an incremental departure from an existing program. This is true for two reasons: (1) such a choice will not have as high a probability of going wrong as a more innovative program; and (2) such an incremental choice will almost certainly keep the program in the hands of the existing agency. Hence, reliance on bureaucracy to formulate solutions may be a guarantee of stability, but it is unlikely to produce many successful policy innovations.

Also, agencies will usually choose to do *something* when given the opportunity, or the challenge. Making policy choices is their business, and it is certainly in their organizational self-interest to make a response to a problem. The agency personnel know that if they do not respond, some other agency soon will, and their agency will lose an opportunity to increase its budget, personnel, and clout. Agencies do not always act in the self-aggrandizing manner ascribed to them,[50] but when confronted directly with a problem already declared to need solving, they will usually respond with a solution—one that involves their own participation.

There is one final consideration about bureaucratic responses to policy problems: agencies often represent a concentration of a certain type of expertise. Increasingly this expertise is professional, and an increasing proportion of the employees of the federal government have professional qualifications.[51] In addition to assisting an agency to formulate better solutions to policy problems, expertise narrows the vision of the agency and the range of solutions that may be considered. Professional training tends to be narrowing rather than broadening, and it tends to teach that the profession possesses *the* solution to a range of problems. Consequently, an agency having a concentration of professionals of a certain type will tend to produce only incremental departures from existing policies. For example, although both the Federal Trade Commission and the Antitrust Division of the Department of Justice are concerned with eliminating monopolistic practices in the economy, the concentration of economists in the former and of lawyers in the latter may generate different priorities.[52]

The occupation of public manager itself is becoming more professionalized, so the major reference group for public managers will be other public managers, a factor that may further narrow the range of bureaucratic responses to policy problems. Much of the drive of the New Public Management,[53] however, is to empower public managers to make more of their own decisions and to be more significant forces in public policy. Thus, senior bureaucrats may be expected to employ their professional expertise, and that of their colleagues, to develop new programs and strategies.

THINK TANKS AND SHADOW CABINETS

Other sources of policy formulation are the "think tanks" that encircle Washington and the state capitals around the country. These are organizations of professional analysts and policy formulators who usually work on contract for a client in government—often an agency in the bureaucracy. We would expect much greater creativity and innovation from these organizations than from the public bureaucracy, but other problems arise in the types of policy options they may propose. First, an agency may be able virtually to guarantee the kind of answer it will receive by choosing a certain think tank. Some organizations are more conservative and will usually formulate solutions relying more on incentives and the private sector, while other consultants may recommend more direct government intervention. These reports are likely to have substantial impact, not only because they have been labeled as expert, but also because they have been paid for and therefore should be used.

Another problem that arises is more of a problem for the consultants in think tanks than for the agencies, but it certainly affects the quality of the policies recommended. If the think tank is to get additional business from an agency, the consultants believe—perhaps rightly—that they have to tell the agency what it wants to hear. In other words, a consulting firm that says that the favorite approach of an agency is entirely wrong and needs to be completely revamped may be at once technically correct and politically bankrupt. Hence, a problem of ethical judgment arises for the consulting firm, as it might for individual analysts working for an organization: what are the boundaries of loyalty to truth and loyalty to the organization?

Three particular think tanks have been of special importance in U.S. policy formulation. Traditionally, the two dominant organizations were the Brookings Institution and the American Enterprise Institute. During the Nixon, Ford, and Reagan administrations, the Brookings Institution was described as "the Democratic Party in exile." The Carter and Clinton administrations did indeed tap a number of Brookings staff members for appointments. On the other side of the fence, the American Enterprise Institute (AEI) housed a number of Nixon and Ford administration personnel, although relatively few of its staff members were tapped by the more conservative Reagan administration. Both of these think tanks support wide-reaching publication programs to attempt to influence elite public opinion, in addition to their direct involvement in government.

The third major think tank is the Heritage Foundation, which came to prominence during the 1980s as an advocate of a number of neoconservative policy positions, especially privatization and deregulation.[54] It was less prominent in the Bush administration than during the Reagan administration, when its proposals were central to policy formulation in some fields.[55] Since that time there has been an increase in the number of think tanks on the political right, funded largely by contributions from industry and wealthy individuals. Prominent among these are the Cato Institute, Citizens for Tax Justice, and the National Center for Policy Analysis.

Universities also serve as think tanks for government. This is true especially for the growing number of public policy schools and programs across the country. As well as training future practitioners of the art of government, these programs provide a place where scholars and former practitioners can formulate new solutions to problems. For instance, Robert Reich, while at the Kennedy School of Government at Harvard, formulated some of the ideas he would later attempt to implement as Secretary of Labor.[56] In addition to the policy programs, specialized institutes such as the Institute for Research on Poverty at the University of Wisconsin and the Joint Center on Urban Studies at Harvard and MIT develop policy ideas concerning their specific policy areas.

It is sometimes difficult to determine where think tanks end and interest groups and lobbying organizations begin. The term "think tank" has a more positive connotation than does "interest group," so the lobbying groups have gone to some lengths to appear as if they were providing objective public policy research. Again, if we go to the internet and begin to look at the range of opinions that appear on any issue, we can see a number of "institutes," "centers," and "foundations" that are attempting to influence opinion. A somewhat more careful analysis will reveal that these are really subsidiaries of interest groups.[57]

INTEREST GROUPS

Interest groups are also important sources of policy formulation. In addition to identifying problems and applying pressure to have them placed on the agenda, successful interest groups have to supply possible remedies for those problems. Those cures will almost certainly be directed at serving the interests of their group members, but that is only to be expected. It is then the task of the authoritative decision makers to take those ideas about policy choices with as many grains of salt as necessary to develop workable plans for solving the problems. Given the existence of iron-triangle relationships, a close connection is likely to exist between the policy formulation ideas of an agency and those of the pressure group. The policy choices advocated by established pressure groups will again be rather conservative and incremental, rarely producing sweeping changes from the status quo in which they and their associated agency have a decided interest.

Some interest groups contradict the traditional model of policy formulation by interest groups. These are the public-interest groups, such as Common Cause, the Center for the Public Interest, and a variety of consumer and taxpayer organizations. Perhaps the major task of these groups is to break the stranglehold that the iron triangles have on policy and to attempt to broaden the range of interests represented in the policymaking process. These groups are oriented toward reform of policy and policymaking. Some of the issues they have taken up are substantive, such as the reform of safety requirements for a variety of products sold in the marketplace. Other issues are procedural, such as campaign reform and opening the regulatory process to greater public input. In general, however, no matter what issue these groups decide to interest themselves in, they will advocate sweeping reforms as opposed to incremental changes, and these groups are important in providing balance to the policy process and in providing a strong voice for reform and change.

CONGRESSMEN

Finally, individual congressmen are a source of policy formulation. We have previously tended to denigrate the role of politicians in formulating policy, but a number of congressmen do involve themselves in serious formulation activities instead of simply accepting advice from friendly sources in the bureaucracy. Like the public-interest groups, these congressmen are generally interested in reform, for if they were primarily interested only in incremental change, there would be little need for their involvement. Some congressmen are also interested in using formulation and advocacy as means of furthering their careers, adopting roles as national policymakers as opposed to the more common pattern of emphasizing constituency service.

Congress in the 1990s is better equipped to formulate policy than it has ever been, even given the nature of the policy challenges it faces. There has been a continuing growth in the size of congressional staffs, both personal staffs of congressmen and the staffs of committees and subcommittees.[58] For example, in 1965 Congress employed just over 9,000 people; by 1990 the number of employees had increased to over 21,000. These employees are on the public payroll at least in part to assist Congress in doing the research and drafting necessary for more active policy formulation, and they are quite important in rectifying what some consider a serious imbalance between the power of Congress and that of the executive branch. For example, the Congressional Budget Office now shadows the Office of Management and Budget and provides an independent source of advice on budgeting and a range of other issues. The Republicans in control of Congress after 1994 reduced their staffing as a good example to the rest of government, but after the large initial reductions, staffing has tended to creep back upwards toward the 21,000 mark.

How to Formulate Policy

The task of formulating policy involves substantial sensitivity to the nuances of policy (and politics) and a potential for the creative application of the tools of policy analysis. In fact, many of the problems faced by government require substantial creativity because little is known about the problem areas. Nevertheless, governments may have to react to a problem whether or not they are sure of the best, or even a good, course of action. In many instances, the routine responses of an agency to its environment will be sufficient to meet most problems that arise, but if the routine response is unsuccessful, the agency will have to search for a more innovative response and involve more actors in policy formulation. In other words, a routine or incremental response may be sufficient for most problems, but if it is not, the policymaking system must initiate some form of conscious search behavior. Making policy choices that depart radically from incremental responses will require methods of identifying and choosing among alternatives.

Two major barriers may block government's ability to understand the problems with which it is confronted. One is the lack of some basic factual information. A number of situations can arise in which government lacks information about the basic policy questions at hand. Most obviously, in defense policy, governments often lack information about the capabilities and intentions of the opposing side. Similarly, in making risk assessments about dangers from various toxic substances or nuclear power plants, there may not be sufficient empirical evidence to determine the probabilities of undesirable events or the probable consequences of those events.[59] Perhaps even more difficult for government is that frequently there are no agreed-upon indicators of the nature of social conditions, and that even widely accepted indicators for economic variables, such as Gross National Product and unemployment rates, are somewhat suspect.[60]

Perhaps more important, government decision makers often lack adequate information about the underlying processes that have created the problems they are attempting to solve. For example, to decide how to solve the poverty problem one should understand how poverty comes about and how it is perpetuated. But despite the masses of data and information generated, there is no accepted model of causation for poverty. This dearth of a causal model may be contrasted with decisions about epidemic diseases made by public health agencies using well-developed and accepted theories about how diseases occur and spread. Clearly decision making to attempt to solve these two kinds of problems should be different.

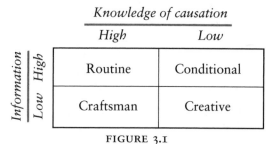

FIGURE 3.1
KINDS OF POLICY FORMULATION

Figure 3.1 demonstrates possible combinations of the knowledge of causation and basic factual information about policy problems. The simplest type of policy to make is a *routine* policy, such as Social Security. Making policy in such areas, with adequate information and an accepted theory of causation, requires primarily routine adjustment of existing policies, and for the most part the policies made will be incremental.[61] This relative simplicity could change if the basic theories about creating a desirable retirement situation or the mechanism for financing such a system were altered.

Creative policy formulation lies at the other extreme of information and knowledge held by decision makers. In this instance, they have neither an adequate information base nor an adequate theory of causation. Research and development operations, such as in the National Institutes of Health or in numerous agencies within the Department of Defense, provide important examples of policy formulation of this type in government.[62] Another example may be the formulation of policies for personal social services, such as counseling. In these instances, a great deal of creativity and care must be exercised in matching the particular needs of the individual with the needs of the agency for efficient management and accountability. Such policies require building in reversibility of policy choices so that creative formulations that may be unworkable can be corrected.

In some situations there may be sufficient information but an inadequate understanding of the underlying processes of causation. These policy-making situations require the formulation of *conditional* policies, in which changes in certain indicators would trigger a policy response of some sort, even if that response is only the reconsideration of the existing policy. It may well be that government can know that certain policies will produce desired results, even if the underlying processes are not fully understood. With the declining faith in Keynesian theories of economic management, it may be that macroeconomic policy is made in this manner. There are several accepted indicators of the state of the economy—unemployment, inflation, and economic growth rates, for example—and changes in these indicators may trigger relatively standard reactions, even if the policymakers cannot always specify, or agree upon, the underlying logic behind those policy responses.[63] Also, it generally is advantageous to build a certain amount of automaticity into the policy response, or at least to provide some insulation against political delay or interference. In economic management, for example, countries with relatively independent central banks have been more successful than those with more politicized central banks.[64]

Finally, in some policy areas governments may have a model of causation for the problem, but may lack sufficient information to have confidence in any policy response they may formulate. Defense policies may fit this category of *craftsman* policies. Governments appear to understand quite well how to respond to threats and how to go to war, but frequently they have only limited, and possibly distorted, information about the capabilities and intentions of their adversaries. Formulating policies of this type depends on identifying a number of contingencies and possible forms of response, as well as developing means of assessing the risks of possible occurrences. The complex policy deliberations of the American government regarding the possible nuclear capability of North Korea illustrates the "craftsman" nature of defense and foreign policy. In other words, formulating such policies involves building a probabilistic basis for response, instead of relying on the certainty that might be taken for granted in other policy areas.

Aids for Policy Formulation

Given the difficulties of formulating effective policy responses to many problems, it is fortunate that some techniques have been developed to assist in that formulation. In general, these techniques attempt to make the consequences of certain courses of action more apparent to decision makers and to provide a summation of the probable effects of policy along a single scale of measurement, usually money, so that different policy alternatives can be more effectively compared with one another. I discuss two of these techniques only briefly here, reserving a more detailed exposition and discussion of cost-benefit analysis for chapter 15. It is important, however, to understand at this point something about the considerations that one might take into account when selecting a policy alternative.

Cost-Benefit Analysis

The most frequently applied tool for policy analysis is cost-benefit analysis. The utilitarian methodology underlying this technique is to reduce all costs and benefits of a proposed government program to a quantitative, economic dimension and then to compare available alternative policies. In this mode of analysis economic considerations are almost always paramount. As the methodology has been developed, it involves attempts to place economic values on factors that might be primarily non-economic, but the principal means of evaluating programs remains utilitarian.[65]

Cost-benefit analysis is in some ways deceptively simple. The total benefits created by the project are enumerated, including those that would be regarded as externalities in the private market (amenity values, recreation, etc.). The costs of the program are also enumerated, again including social costs (e.g., pollution). Long-term costs and benefits are also taken into account, although they are discounted or adjusted because they will occur in the future. Projects whose total benefits exceed their total costs are deemed acceptable, and then choices can be made among the acceptable projects, generally by adopting the projects with the greatest net total benefit (total benefits minus total costs), and then all others that fit within the total available budget.

Some of the more technical problems of cost-benefit analysis are discussed later (see chapter 15), but it is important to talk about some of the ethical underpinnings of the technique here, as they have a pronounced effect on the formulation of policy alternatives. The fundamental ethical difficulties arise from the assumptions that all values are reducible to monetary values and that economic criteria are the most important ones for government when making policy. There may well be other values, such as civil liberties or human life or the environment, that many citizens would not want reduced to dollars and cents.[66] Even if such a reduction of values were possible, it is questionable whether the primary goal of government should be maximizing economic welfare in the society.

Decision Analysis

Cost-benefit analysis assumes that certain events will occur. A dam will be built; it will produce X kilowatts of electricity; Y people from a nearby city will spend Z hours boating and water-skiing on the newly created lake; farmers will save Q dollars in flood protection and irrigation but lose N acres of land for farming. Decision analysis, in contrast, is geared toward making policy choices under conditions of less certainty.[67] This method assumes that in many or most instances government, with inadequate information, is making probabilistic choices about what to do. In fact, many times, government may be almost playing a game, with nature or other human beings as the opponent. As pointed out, governments often do not have a very good conception of the policy instruments they choose, and that lack of knowledge, combined with inadequate knowledge about patterns of causation within the policy area, is a recipe for disaster. However, if we have some idea about the probabilities of certain outcomes (even without a model of causation), there is a better chance of making better decisions.

Take, for example, a situation in which a hurricane appears to be bearing down on a major coastal city. On the one hand, the mayor of that city can order an evacuation and cause a great deal of lost production, as well as a predictable number of deaths during the rush to escape the city. On the other hand, if he or she does not order the evacuation and the hurricane actually does strike the city, a far larger loss of life will occur. Of course, the hurricane is only forecast to be heading in the general direction of the city, and it may yet veer off. What should the mayor do?[68]

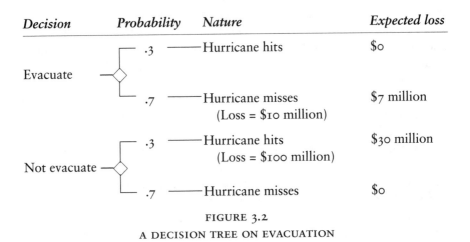

Decision	Probability	Nature	Expected loss
Evacuate	.3	Hurricane hits	$0
	.7	Hurricane misses (Loss = $10 million)	$7 million
Not evacuate	.3	Hurricane hits (Loss = $100 million)	$30 million
	.7	Hurricane misses	$0

FIGURE 3.2
A DECISION TREE ON EVACUATION

This decision-making problem can be organized as a "decision tree" in which the mayor is essentially playing a game against nature (see figure 3.2). The mayor has two possible policy choices: evacuate or not evacuate. We can assign a probability of the two occurrences in nature—hit or miss the city—based on the best information available from the weather bureau, and we have estimates of the losses that would occur as a result of each outcome. In this analysis we assume that if the hurricane does strike, the loss of property will be approximately the same whether or not the city is evacuated. As the problem is set up, the mayor makes the smallest possible error by choosing to evacuate the city. By so doing, he or she might cause an expected unnecessary loss of $7 million ($10 million multiplied by the probability of the event of .70) if the hurricane does not hit, but would cause an expected unnecessary loss of $30 million if the evacuation is not ordered and the hurricane strikes.

In such a simple situation, the decision is easy to make if there is sufficient information available. In more complex situations, when many facts need to be considered simultaneously, the decision-making process becomes more difficult. The process becomes even more difficult when one faces a human opponent, rather than nature. Even in those more complex instances, as in cost-benefit analysis, the technique is only an aid to decision making and policy formulation. Decisions still must be made by individuals who consider ethical, economic, and political factors before making a judgment about what should be done. And as the results of policy formulation will be felt in the future, the exercise of judgment is especially important. When an issue is newly placed on the agenda, the first formulation of a solution will to some degree structure subsequent attempts at solution and therefore will have an enduring legacy that must be considered very carefully.

Policy Design

All the aids that government can utilize when formulating policy still do not generate an underlying approach to policy design. That is, no technical means of addressing public problems relates the characteristics of those problems to the instruments that might be used to solve them or to the values that would be used to evaluate the success of the policy.[69] Without such a comprehensive approach to design, much policy formulation in government is accomplished by intuition or inertia, or by analogy with existing programs. This inertial pattern produces frequent mistakes and often much wasted time and effort. Thus, one of the many tasks of policy analysis is to develop a more comprehensive approach to the problems of formulating effective policies. This would require not only some idea of what "good" policies are but also some ideas about developing policymaking processes that might produce the more desirable policies.

In the United States, any more comprehensive approach to policy design is likely to be resisted. In the first place, the generally antistatist values of American politics make such a planned and rationalistic approach unacceptable to many politicians and citizens. In addition, as pointed out earlier, for institutional as well as ideological reasons American politics tends toward incremental solutions to problems rather than imposition of comprehensive frameworks or use of design concepts for policy.[70] Attempting to impose a design on a policy area may threaten the interests of agencies and committees that have been responsible for the development of the existing policy over time and believe that they "own" the problem. Third, for many of the most important policy problems that American government now faces, there is yet inadequate agreement on the nature of the problem, much less on the nature of the solution to the problem. Important policy problems such as poverty, crime, and mal-education still lack clear definitions of causes, much less of solutions. These important political realities should not, however, prevent policy analysts from attempting to understand social problems in a less haphazard fashion than is sometimes encountered in government or from advocating innovative program designs for solving those problems.

Summary

This chapter has taken the policymaking process through its first stages: considering problems and then developing some mechanisms for solving them. Both activities—and indeed the entire activity of policymaking—are political exercises, but they can also involve the application of techniques and tools for analysis. The tools for agenda setting are largely political and require the "selling" of agenda items to authorized decision makers who may believe that they already have enough to do. Agenda setting also requires a detailed knowledge of the issue in question so that it can be related first to the known preferences of decision makers and second to existing policies and programs. Agenda setting is in some ways the art of doing something new so that it appears old.

The techniques that can be applied to policy formulation are more sophisticated technically, but they also require sensitive political hands that can use them effectively. To a great extent, the use of old solutions for new problems happens in formulation as well as in agenda setting. For both agenda setting and policy formulation, incremental solutions appear to be favored in the United States. Incrementalism produces a great deal of stability in the policy process, but it makes rapid response to major changes in the economy and society difficult. The solutions that emerge from these first stages of the policy process, then, are designed to be readily accepted by legislators and administrators who must authorize and legitimate the alternative policies selected. A more comprehensive approach to design might well produce better solutions to problems but would face the barrier of political feasibility. The task of the analyst and advocate then becomes stretching the boundaries of feasibility to produce better public policies.

4. Legitimating Policy Choices

Once it has been decided that a certain program is required, or is feasible, as a response to a policy problem, that choice must be made a legitimate choice. No matter what course of action is decided on, some citizens will almost certainly believe themselves disadvantaged by the choice. At a minimum, any public program or project will cost money, and citizens who pay taxes and receive (or perceive) no direct benefits from the new program will frequently consider themselves to be harmed by the policy choice. Because policy choices inevitably benefit some citizens to the detriment of others, a great deal of attention must be given in a democratic government to the process by which decisions are made. It is by means of the official process of government that substantive policy decisions are legitimated; that is, the policies have the legitimate authority of the state attached to them by the process.

Legitimacy is a fundamental concept in the discipline of political science and is important in understanding policymaking. Legitimacy is conventionally defined as a belief on the part of citizens that the current government represents a proper form of government, and a willingness on the part of those citizens to accept the decrees of the government as legal and authoritative.[1] The vast majority of Americans regard the government of the United States as the appropriate set of institutions to govern the country. And most Americans consequently accept the actions of that government as authoritative (as having the force of law) as long as they are in accordance with the processes set forth in the Constitution or implemented through procedures derived from the processes described in the Constitution. It is understood that all policies adopted must be within the powers granted to the federal government by the Constitution. The boundaries of what is considered "constitutional" have expanded during the history of the United States, but the limits current at the time establish the boundaries of legitimate action.

Several things should be understood about legitimacy as it affects contemporary policymaking. First, legitimacy is largely a psychological property. It depends on the majority's acceptance of the appropriateness of a government. A government may come to power by all the prescribed processes, but if the population does not willingly accept that government or the rules by which it gained power, then in practice it has no legitimacy. For example, many constitutions (including those of France and Britain) give governments the right to suspend civil liberties and declare martial law, but citizens accustomed to greater freedom may find it difficult to accept such decrees.[2] Further, changes in a government may cause some citizens to question the legitimacy of a new government's actions.

Legitimacy has substantive as well as procedural elements. It matters not only how issues are decided but also what is decided. The government of the United States might decide to nationalize all oil companies operating in the country. (It will not do this, but just imagine so for a moment.) The decision could be reached with all appropriate deliberation as prescribed by the Constitution, but it would still not be acceptable to the majority of citizens. In a more realistic example, the war in Vietnam was conducted according to the procedures of the Constitution, but its legitimacy nevertheless was rejected by a significant share of the population. In addition, that conflict evoked a response from Congress, in the form of the War Powers Act, that would change the procedures by which the United States could become involved in any future foreign conflicts. The substantive question of legitimacy therefore produced a procedural response. At a somewhat less dramatic level, the attempts on the part of Congress to increase its own pay during 1989 and 1990 were procedurally correct but raised such an outcry from the public that they could not be implemented; the American public clearly regarded those actions as illegitimate.

Legitimacy is both a variable and a constant. It differs among individuals and across time. Some citizens of the United States may not accept the legitimacy of the current government. For example, some African American leaders have rejected the legitimacy of the U.S. government and have called for the formation of a separate African American country within the United States. On the other side, white supremacists have organized settlements in parts of the West that reject the authority of the constituted governments, and they even have engaged in armed conflict with federal agents. Citizens also appear more willing to accept the actions of state and local governments than those of the federal government.

A general decline in confidence in American institutions has been occurring, and that decline has been especially pronounced for government institutions other than the military (see table 4.1).[3] There was some upturn in confidence in the early 1980s but that has decayed, and Americans now have less confidence in government than they have had in the past. In particular Congress now is one the least respected institutions in the United States. Interestingly the various scandals during the second Clinton administration do not appear to have had much real impact on the confidence of citizens in the presidency.[4] The ability of the president to hold on to popularity and posi-

TABLE 4.1

PUBLIC CONFIDENCE IN AMERICAN INSTITUTIONS, 1973–96

(PERCENTAGE SAYING "A GREAT DEAL" OR "QUITE A LOT")

Institution	1996	1994	1993	1991	1990	1989	1988	1987	1986	1985	1983	1981	1979	1975	1973
Military	66	64	68	85	68	63	58	61	63	61	53	50	54	58	n.a.
Organized religion	57	54	53	59	56	52	59	61	57	66	62	64	65	68	66
Supreme Court	45	42	44	48	47	46	56	52	54	56	42	46	45	49	44
Presidency	39	38	43	72	n.a.	n.a.	n.a.	n.a.	n.a.	n.a.	n.a.	n.a.	n.a.	n.a.	n.a.
Public schools	38	34	39	44	45	43	49	50	49	48	39	42	53	n.a.	58
Newspapers	32	29	31	32	39	n.a.	36	31	37	35	38	35	51	n.a.	39
Organized labor	25	26	26	25	27	n.a.	26	26	29	28	26	28	36	38	30
Big business	24	26	22	26	25	n.a.	25	n.a.	28	31	28	20	32	34	26
Congress	20	18	18	30	24	32	35	n.a.	41	39	28	29	34	40	42

SOURCE: *Gallup Poll Monthly*, April 1994, 6; April 1997, 25.

tive evaluations indicates in large part the role that the performance of the economy has on citizens' perceptions.[5]

In societies that are deeply divided ethnically or politically the rejection of the sitting government by one side or another is a constant fact of life. Even a government that is widely accepted may lose legitimacy or strain its legitimate status through its activities and its leaders. The Vietnam War and the Watergate scandal illustrate the low points to which the legitimacy of even a widely accepted political regime may fall. Nevertheless, the regime was able to survive those problems, as well as such subsequent problems as the Iran-*contra* controversy, and continue to govern with legitimate authority.

Because of the variability of legitimacy, a fully legitimated government may gradually erode its status through time. A series of blatantly unpopular or illegal actions may reduce the authority of a government. That government may then become open to challenge, whether of a revolutionary or more peaceable nature. Or a government may lose legitimacy through incompetence rather than unpopular activities. Citizens in most countries have a reservoir of respect for government, and governments can add to or subtract from that stock of authority. As a result, governments are engaged in a continuing process of legitimation for themselves and their successors.

Finally, government must somehow legitimate each individual policy choice. No matter how technically correct a policy choice may be, it is of little practical value if it cannot be made to appear legitimate to the public. For example, the decision to correct the over-indexing of Social Security pension benefits once the mistake was discovered was absolutely correct, but it created a huge political controversy and a sense of betrayal among some elderly citizens.[6] Policy analysts, in their pursuit of elegant solutions and innovative policies, frequently forget this mundane point, but their forgetfulness can present a real barrier to their success.[7] To design a policy that can be legitimated, a policy analyst must understand the political process, for that process will define the set of feasible policy alternatives in a more restrictive fashion than does the economic and social world. That is, more programs could work than could be adopted within the political values of the American system. Thus, the task of the policy analyst is to be able to "sell" his or her decisions to individuals who are crucial to their being legitimated. This does not mean that the analyst must advocate only policies that fit the existing definitions of feasibility, but it does mean that the analyst must have a strategy for expanding that definition if a highly innovative program is to be proposed.[8]

In general, legitimation is performed through the legislative process, through the administrative process designed for the issuing of regulations (secondary legislation), through the courts, or through mechanisms of direct democracy. As shown in figure 4.1, these modes of legitimation can be seen as combining characteristics of decisions—majoritarian and nonmajoritarian —and the range of actors involved. The nonmajoritarian-mass cell is empty in this table, but it might be filled by revolutionary or extreme interest-group activities. Indeed, the current political controversy over abortion policy may fall into this cell given that there is apparently no popular majority for the policies being pushed by an intense and active minority, and that minority has been successful in some states. We next discuss each type of legitimation and its implications for the policy choices that might be feasible as a result of each process.

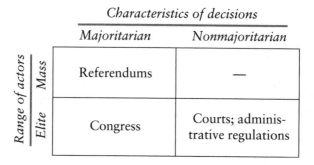

FIGURE 4.1
MODES OF LEGITIMATION

Legislative Legitimation

In the United States we traditionally have equated lawmaking with Congress, the principal legislative body at the federal level, or with similar bodies at the state level. As this section points out, that notion is now excessively naive, for the workload and technical content of many subjects on which decisions have to be made have overwhelmed Congress. This loss of capacity to legislate effectively is true despite the massive growth of legislative staffs and the increased availability of policy advice for congressmen. Governments are simply too large and involved in too many issues to permit a large legislative institution such as Congress, with all its intricate procedures, to make the full range of decisions required to keep the society functioning (from a public policy perspective).

Of course, Congress remains the crucial source for primary legislation. That is, although administrative bodies are responsible for writing regulations in large numbers, Congress must supply the basic legislative frameworks within which other bodies can operate. Congress tends to pass legislation written in relatively broad language, allowing administrators latitude for interpretation. Thus, despite the resurgence of congressional power in opposing the "imperial presidency" in the 1970s and the Reagan administration in the 1980s, it is best to think about legitimation in Congress as the legitimation of relatively diffuse statements of goals and structures. Those broad statements are then made operational by the executive branch, which fills in the details by writing regulations and by using the implementation process.

Congress also retains its supervisory powers—oversight—so that if the executive branch strays too far in writing regulations (see pp. 86–87), Congress can reassert its powers to explain what its intentions were when it constructed the legislation.[9] Until 1983, Congress had virtually unlimited access to the "legislative veto," which required agencies issuing certain types of regulations to submit those regulations to Congress for approval. The Supreme Court, however, declared the legislative veto was excessive meddling by one branch of government into the affairs of another.[10] Despite the Court decision that the legislative veto in the one instance was not constitutional, Congress has continued to utilize similar instruments in other policy areas.[11] If nothing else, Congress can always pass amendments to the previous law to clarify its intentions.

Congress places a great deal of emphasis on procedural legitimation and has established elaborate sets of procedures for processing legislation.[12] In fact, its institutions and procedures have become so well developed that it is difficult for legislation to be passed. Typically, a bill must be passed by a subcommittee, by a full committee, and by floor action in each house. And as one house is unlikely to pass a bill in exactly the same form as the other house, conference committees will be necessary to reconcile the two versions. Given the possibility of using more arcane procedural mechanisms, such as filibusters, amendments, and recommitals, legislation can be slowed down or killed at a number of points by failure to attract the necessary majority at the proper time. Or, to put it the other way around, all that the opponents of a bill have to do is to muster a majority at one crucial point to prevent the passage of legislation.[13]

Legislative procedures are important as mechanisms to prevent unnecessary or poorly formulated legislation from becoming law, but they can also frustrate good and needed legislation. The ability of the opposition to postpone or block civil rights legislation during the 1950s and 1960s demonstrated clearly the capacity of legislative procedures to thwart the apparent majority will of Congress. More recently, the continuing inability to produce a national health insurance bill, or to pass a strong bill to control tobacco, indicates the difficulties of passing legislation even when a significant portion of the population favors some change from the status quo.[14]

Legitimation through the legislative process is majoritarian. It depends on building either simple or special majorities at each crucial point in the process. The task of the policy analyst or the legislative leader is to construct such majorities. In addition to appealing on the basis of the actual qualities of the proposed legislation, the needed majorities can be formed in several other ways. One method has been referred to as *partisan analysis*.[15] This involves convincing members of Congress that the piece of legislation that the analyst wants is also something that the members of Congress want. The trick here is to design the legislation in such a way that it will appeal to a sufficient number of interests to create a winning coalition. For example, the National Defense Education Act of 1958 was passed by a coalition of congressmen interested in education and defense. The title of the bill indicates that it was intended to serve those two purposes, and it affects those two areas. It brought together liberals favoring a stronger federal role in education with conservatives favoring a stronger defense posture. Also, many social and housing programs have been "sold" to conservatives as benefiting business—as urban renewal certainly did—or as providing employment.[16]

Another strategy for forming coalitions that is not dissimilar to partisan analysis is *logrolling*.[17] In logrolling, coalitions are formed not around a single piece of legislation but across a set of legislative initiatives. In the simplest example, Congressman A favors bill A but is indifferent toward bill B. Congressman B, on the other hand, favors bill B but is indifferent to bill A. The logical thing for these two congressmen to do is to trade their votes on the two pieces of legislation, with A voting for bill B and B voting for bill A. The real world may not be so convenient, however, and several bills may be involved in vote trading across time. In some ways, logrolling is a rational activity because it allows the passage of legislation that some congressmen, and presumably their constituencies, favor intensely and that might not otherwise be able to gain a majority. But logrolling also has the effect of passing a great deal more legislation than would otherwise be passed, thus affecting public expenditures and taxation. It enables relatively narrow interests in the nation to develop coalitions for their legislation that may not be justifiable in terms of the broader "public interest."

As well as being a majoritarian body, Congress has universalistic norms that promote the spreading of government expenditures very broadly.[18] This is commonly referred to as *pork-barrel* legislation, or as the parochial imperative in American politics. Pork-barrel legislation often concerns capital expenditures, with the classic examples being river and harbor improvements. Obtaining capital projects such as these has become a measure of the success of congressmen; some argue that it, instead of policymaking on broad national issues, has become the dominant activity of Congress.[19] Congressional representatives must demonstrate to their constituents that they can "bring home the bacon" and produce tangible benefits for the voters of the district. Thus the tendency in designing legislation of this kind is to spread benefits as broadly as possible geographically and to create a majority by benefiting virtually anyone who wants a piece of the "pork." As with logrolling, this pattern of decision making tends to increase the costs of government. Douglas Arnold is quite correct in pointing out that pork-barrel legislation costs very little when compared with national defense or Social Security.[20] It may, however, stand as an example of how government misuses money by funding projects with relatively low social benefit in order to ensure the reelection of incumbent congressmen. Politically, the importance of this style of decision making may outstrip the actual amount of money spent.

The description of legitimation through the legislative process does not give the most favorable impression of Congress. Actually, a good deal of congressional decision making is based on the merits of the legislation. To the extent that partisan analysis, logrolling, and pork-barrel legislation characterize the actions of Congress, however, the legislative process has certain effects on the kinds of rules that can be legitimated. It can be argued that the legislative process almost inevitably will produce broad and rather diffuse legislation. The necessity of building a coalition requires that one take care not to offend potential members and that the legislation produce benefits for individual congressmen and their districts. As a consequence, legislation must be designed to be amenable to partisan analysis and yet not so clearly worded as to reduce the number of possible coalition members. This, of course, allows administrators to make difficult, politically charged decisions on cases, thus deflecting criticism from Congress.

Legislative decision making also is associated with an expanding government. Both logrolling and pork barrel legislation are perhaps related to the expansion of government beyond the bounds that could be set if there were no possibility of vote trading. There is a tendency to adopt public projects that are marginal in terms of social productivity if there is a possibility of trading votes and building coalitions across pieces of legislation. We know quite well that the world of policymaking is by no means perfectly rational, but these patterns of institutional decision making seem to exacerbate the irrational character of much of politics and to produce programs that benefit the few at the expense of the many.[21]

Logrolling and the pork barrel also make reducing the size of unneeded programs difficult. For example, the only effective way that Congress could find to accomplish the closing of redundant military bases in the early 1990s was to adopt, in advance, a rule that an independent commission recommend the closings and that they then be voted on as a group. Without that rule, logrolling might have meant that no bases would have been closed. This self-denying restraint appears to have broken down in 1998, with Congress wanting to have more of a say in retaining bases that the Department of Defense itself wants to close.[22]

These difficulties in congressional decision making suggest more general points concerning problems of social decision making. In its simplest terms, the problem is this: how can a set of social preferences best be expressed in a single decision? Congress faces this problem when it attempts to combine the preferences of its members and their constituents in a single decision whether or not to adopt a piece of legislation; the same general problem arises in club, committee, and college faculty meetings.

One underlying problem facing decision makers is the issue of intensity of preferences. We faced this problem in discussing the logic of logrolling. In a majoritarian system, it may be possible to construct a majority composed of individuals who are not much interested in a proposal and who do not feel intensely about it. This is in part a function of having only one vote per person, whereas in the market setting, individuals have more than one dollar and can apply their resources differentially depending on their preferences and the intensity of those preferences. Logrolling is one means of attempting to overcome the intensity problem, but it can be successful only in a limited set of circumstances with a certain distribution of preferences.

In majoritarian institutions with one vote per member, it is difficult to reflect accurately the preferences of the participants in a decision in a manner that creates the greatest net satisfaction for the participants. Generating such an optimal decision is made more difficult if in a number of successive decisions (e.g., voting on amendments) the order in which options are eliminated affects the final preferences.[23] In examining problems about making choices of this type, the economist Kenneth Arrow argued that it is impossible to devise a social-choice mechanism that satisfies the logical conditions for rationality.[24] The only way in which such decisions can be arrived at, in Arrow's framework, is to impose them, which he rejects on philosophical grounds. But the imposition of administrative regulations as another means of legitimating decisions has some characteristics of imposed solutions, although the procedures for adopting regulations have been sanctioned legally.

Oversight

Once Congress has enacted legislation, it has played its major role in legitimating policy, but its involvement is not over. We have already pointed out that the administrative agencies play a major role in translating legislation into specific regulations. Congress then exercises some degree of oversight over the actions of the agencies.[25] The committees that initially adopted the legislation monitor the way in which the agencies implement that legislation and then can act legislatively to correct anything the agencies may do incorrectly. Congress may not even have to do anything directly, but can rely on its implicit authority over legislation and budgets to gain compliance from the agencies.

Oversight is in essence a second round of legitimation by Congress, which passes the initial legislation and then can look over the shoulders of the implementors to try to ensure that its intentions are followed. That having been said, Congress cannot be wholly effective in this oversight activity. This is in part a function of the scarcity of time and the need for congressional attention to go forward with the next round of legislation. Further, even the well-staffed Congress may have a scarcity of the necessary expertise to judge the numerous complex and technical regulations issued by administrative agencies and the even more numerous administrative decisions taken by the agencies. This means that oversight tends to be more "fire alarm" (reaction to crises) than "police patrol" (routine scanning of the relevant environment).[26] The decision of the Republican Congress to reduce the number of committees and subcommittees has perhaps further limited the capacity to exert oversight, given that there is less focused expertise.[27]

Regulations and the Administrative Process

Most rulemaking in the United States and other industrialized societies is now done through the regulatory process.[28] Here we are referring to the regulatory process in a rather broad context to include the rulemaking activities of executive branch agencies as well as those of independent regulatory commissions. We will be discussing the process by which administrative or independent regulatory bodies can issue binding regulations that are subsidiary to congressional legislation. These regulations are sometimes referred to as *secondary legislation,* and issuing such regulations is definitely a legislative or legitimating activity because it makes rules for the society. Nevertheless, those rules must be pursuant to primary legislation already adopted by Congress.

The volume of regulation writing in the federal government is immense. It can be judged by the size of the *Federal Register,* a weekly publication containing all regulations and proposed regulations (approximately 70,000 pages per year), and by the size of the *Code of Federal Regulations (CFR),* containing all the regulations currently in force. One example of the volume of regulatory activity is provided by the Occupational Safety and Health Administration (OSHA) in the Department of Labor. OSHA, a frequent target of the critics of government regulation, issued 4,600 regulations during the first two years of its existence and continues to issue hundreds of new regulations each year. As of 1997 these regulations amounted to almost 4,000 pages of rather fine print in the *CFR.* Taken together, three areas of public policy—agriculture, labor, and the environment—have rules equalling approximately 25,000 pages in the *CFR.*[29]

Although conducted through a legal process, the decision making required for adopting regulations is not majoritarian. If it were, many of the regulations adopted by OSHA and other regulatory bodies might never be adopted. Decision making in the regulatory process can be more technical and less tied to political considerations than can decision making in Congress, although political considerations cannot be neglected entirely. This is especially true for agencies that are a part of executive branch departments. Executive branch agencies are directly responsible to the president and consequently must issue regulations that address the political priorities of the president. Presidents Ford, Carter, and their successors have taken greater pains than previous presidents to know what regulations are being issued and to ensure that they match presidential priorities. Even the regulations issued by independent regulatory agencies cannot afford to stray too far from the basic political and ideological norms of the public; if they do, the agency threatens its own survival or at least its latitude to issue further regulations.

One of the ways in which government has attempted to keep regulatory activity in check is through regulatory analysis. President Carter, for example, required agencies to justify their choice of any one particular regulation against others, largely on economic grounds. President Reagan went further and required executive agencies to submit all new regulations for review by the Office of Management and Budget (OMB), and later to submit their plans for regulatory activity for the subsequent year. These regulatory reviews were as much political as economic, and they resulted in critics referring to the OMB as the "regulatory KGB."[30] The Republican Congress first elected in 1994 took regulatory analysis even further by mandating, through a formal regulatory review statute (PL 104-208), that OMB submit to Congress an economic assessment of each new regulation so that the magnitude of the impact on the economy could be assessed.

Although the OMB review of regulations was in many cases political and ideological, it also has served a legitimation function. In the first place, the elected presidency does have greater legitimacy than does the unelected bureaucracy, especially given the usual view that Americans have of the bureaucracy. Further, as the techniques used in regulatory analysis are "rational," the argument can be made that any regulations that survive it are perhaps more likely to make a positive contribution to the well-being of society.[31]

Even by the time of the Bush administration some analysts were arguing that deregulation had gone too far. So, for example, during that administration the Environmental Protection Agency began to issue a number of important new regulations, including imposing significant new air pollution standards on five northeastern states. The Clinton administration has taken a somewhat more positive view of regulation and its impact on the economy and society. While proclaiming themselves to be "New Democrats," officials in this administration adopted a more activist position in environmental and economic regulation. They have, however, attempted to write those regulations with even greater amounts of consultation and negotiation than has been common in the past. For example, there are plans for substantially more public involvement and public disclosure during the regulatory processes than in the past, even though some of the tools of regulatory analysis will remain in place.[32]

Public Access to the Regulatory Process

The process of making regulations is open to the public's influence as well as that of the president and OMB. The procedures of the Administrative Procedures Act and several other laws affecting the issuing of regulations require that agencies accept advice and ideas from interested citizens as the process goes forward and call for time at each stage for affected interests in the society to respond to the agency initiatives.[33] For some segments of the economy, in fact, the regulatory process may be more democratic than decision making in Congress. The regulatory process permits direct access of affected interests to decision makers, whereas in Congress those affected interests may be excluded from effective involvement, especially if they represent an interest not widely considered "legitimate" by congressmen. Furthermore, the legislative outcomes may be more "in the public interest" than those in Congress, given that special interest influences are funneled through an administrative process and frequently subject to judicial review.[34]

Access to the process does not, of course, mean that the ideas of the affected interests, or "public-interest groups," will be dominant in the decisions finally made. Simply granting access does not protect the interests of segments of the society that are not sufficiently well organized or alert to make their presentations to the agency. Access to agency decision making is by no means costless, so many less-well-funded groups may be excluded. This has led some agencies, such as the Federal Trade Commission, to provide funding for interests that might not otherwise have the lawyers and other resources needed to participate effectively.[35] Again, there are no guarantees of success, but the procedures do indicate the openness of the regulatory process to a range of ideas and opinions.

The Processes of Writing Regulations

There are two principal ways, referred to as formal and informal rulemaking, in which regulation writers collect ideas and opinions. Formal rulemaking has some of the appearance of a court proceeding, with a formal hearing, the taking of oral testimony from witnesses, and the use of counsel.[36] Formal rulemaking is a time-consuming and cumbersome process, but it is deemed necessary when the social and economic interests involved are considered sufficiently important. Examples of formal rulemaking are the approval of new medications by the Food and Drug Administration and the licensing of nuclear power plants by the Nuclear Regulatory Commission. The written records generated in formal rulemaking are important, given that these rulings are important to many elements in society and may be the subject of subsequent discussion and litigation.

Informal rulemaking proceeds through three basic steps. First, the agency is required to publish (in the *Federal Register*) a notice of its intent to issue a certain regulation. Then a period of several months is allowed, during which individuals and groups who believe themselves potentially affected by the rule can offer opinions and make suggestions about the content of the regulation. After the designated time has passed, the agency may issue a draft of the regulation that the agency would ultimately like to see put into effect. The draft may be based on the suggestions received from affected interests, or it may be what the agency had been planning all along. Then there is another waiting period for responses to the draft regulation. Those responses may be made directly to the agency, or they may be indirect—by having a friendly congressman contact the agency with proposed alterations. Then, based on responses from interests, as well as its own beliefs about the appropriateness of the regulation, the agency issues the final regulation that will have the force of law.

In addition to the two principal forms of rulemaking, administrative law has been developing to include two other ways of adopting regulations. *Hybrid rulemaking* represents an attempt at compromise between the thoroughness of the formal process and the relative ease of the informal process.[37] This form of rulemaking came about in part because of the courts[38] and also was required by some acts of Congress, especially for environmental policy.[39] Although full-scale judicial proceedings are not called for, there may be requirements for the opportunity to cross-examine witnesses in order to create a full judicial record, which can then be the basis for an appeal if further judicial proceedings are demanded.

The other emerging form of rulemaking is *negotiated rulemaking.* Given the complexity of many of the policy areas into which government must now venture, and the number of interests involved in each policy, it may be easier to negotiate rules than to attempt to make them administratively.[40] This process can save a great deal of future ill will among the affected interests and also perhaps actually create superior policies to those that might emerge from a more centrally directed process. Congress has now recognized the validity of this form of rulemaking by passing the Negotiated Rulemaking Act of 1990 to specify the conditions under which this procedure can be used and the procedures required. It has also included language about negotiated rulemaking in the authorizing legislation for several executive agencies.[41]

While negotiated rulemaking is an attempt to open the process to a variety of actors and to make it somewhat more democratic, there are also pressures to make the process more technocratic. In particular there has been increasing interest in regulatory analysis, or the attempt to apply cost-benefit analysis and other forms of economic analysis to regulations before they are adopted.

The legitimate force of a regulation is derived from a statute passed by Congress and from following correct procedures (as specified in the Administrative Procedures Act) in issuing the regulation. In general, issuing a regulation takes about eighteen months from beginning to end of the process and allows for substantial representation of affected groups and individuals. Attempts to short-circuit the process will probably result in the regulation's being rejected, no matter how reasonable on its face, if appealed through the court system. The law does authorize, however, some provisions for emergency rulemaking for some agencies.

The role assigned to affected interests in responding to issues in the regulatory process brings up another point about social decision making. In part as a means of justifying slavery, John C. Calhoun argued that a proper democracy would take into account not only the majority of individuals but also a majority of interests in society. His idea of "concurrent majorities" would have assigned greater importance to the role of pressure groups than is true in most of American political thought and would have made the opinions of the groups more central in the process of writing regulations.

The role permitted to interest groups in decision making about regulations also is similar to the development of "neocorporatism" in Western Europe.[42] The principal difference is that interest groups in the United States usually are not granted the quasi-official status as representatives of the economic or social group that they have acquired in much of Europe. Further, the affected interest groups are rarely brought together to negotiate a compromise decision, as they might be in many European systems.[43] One contrary example is the 1993 conference held in the Pacific Northwest to discuss differences between logging interests and conservationists over protection of the spotted owl.[44] Decision making in the United States is still done largely within the agency itself, with interest groups involved primarily as sources of information for making superior decisions. In addition to protecting the interests of their members, the interest groups frequently make substantive points about proposed regulations and can help prevent agencies from making serious substantive errors in their rules.

Finally, regulatory decision making is also threatened by the classical problem of the capture of regulatory agencies by the very interests they were designed to regulate.[45] Agencies that regulate single industries have tended to become advocates of their industries, rather than impartial protectors of the public interest. Capture results from the agency's need to maintain political support when, especially in the case of an independent regulatory commission, the only logical source of such support is the regulated industry itself. The public is usually too amorphous a body to offer the specific support an agency may need in defending its budget, or its very existence, before Congress. Thus, reforms intended to remove political pressures from regulatory decision making by making the agencies independent only succeeded in making the agencies independent of one source of political pressure while making them dependent on another. In Lowi's terminology, the public interest is appropriated for private gain.[46]

The capture argument is less applicable to newer regulatory agencies, which operate across a number of industries, than it is to single-industry regulatory bodies.[47] For example, either the Consumer Products Safety Commission or the Occupational Safety and Health Administration regulates virtually every industry in the country; their advocacy and protection of any one industry might injure other industries. It is generally too difficult for an industry to capture these cross-cutting regulators, and they are therefore more likely to operate "in the public interest." Even then, however, the agency itself is permitted to define the public interest.

Though many citizens would challenge it, regulation is a central process in the legitimation of policies. Many popular and academic writers comment negatively on laws being made by bureaucrats without direct congressional involvement, which those writers consider an essential processes for legitimation.[48] The procedures used are "due," however, and have been ordained by several acts of Congress. In addition, each regulation adopted must have a legislative peg to hang on. But unlike acts of Congress, these regulations tend to make specific judgments and decisions and by so doing to affect individual interests more directly. Many regulations issued through this process have been criticized as impractical and unnecessary; everyone has his or her favorite silly regulation. Presidents have also been concerned about the effects of regulation on the economy and society and, beginning with at least President Ford, have sought to have more deregulation than regulation.[49] But there is still the possibility of greater objectivity and the application of more scientific "rationality" in the regulatory process than in the more politicized arena of Congress. It may be, in fact, that the very attempt to apply strict criteria for decisions is the source of many objections.

The Courts

Another nonmajoritarian means of legitimating policies is through the courts. Along with the increasing role of the administrative process in legitimation, there has been an increasing involvement of the courts in issuing legitimate policy statements. Some critics have argued that public policy in the

United States is indeed dominated by the court system, and not to the benefit of the types of policies generated.[50] Further, along with complaints against the administrative process, there have been complaints about "judge-made law" as being an illegitimate usurpation of congressional prerogatives. Of course, the courts have been involved in legitimating actions and issuing law-like statements in the United States for some time. However, perhaps because of the increasing litigation involving social issues (e.g., abortion) and the willingness of the courts to make declarations about remedies to remove violations of the Constitution from federal laws, there is a greater popular awareness of the role of the courts in making rules for society.

The courts have as their constitutional basis for making legitimating decisions the supremacy clause, which says that all laws and treaties made in pursuance of the Constitution are the supreme law of the land. In *Marbury v. Madison* (1803), Chief Justice John Marshall decided that it was incumbent on the courts to decide whether or not a law conformed to the Constitution and to declare, if it did not, that the law was void. Following from that basic declaration of judicial power, the courts have been able to make rules based on their interpretation of the Constitution. Particularly crucial to their role in legitimating actions is their ability to accept or reject the remedies proposed by parties to particular disputes. If an action is declared unconstitutional, the courts frequently become involved in determining the actions needed to correct that unconstitutionality.

The most obvious examples of courts prescribing remedies to situations they find unconstitutional have been in cases involving school desegregation and prison overcrowding. In several cases, for example *Swann* v. *Charlotte-Mecklenburg Board of Education* (1971), the courts declared that the existence of boundaries between school districts constitutes an intent on the part of local governments to maintain or create racial segregation of the schools; they then ruled that cross-district busing was the logical remedy for the problem. In other cases, the courts declared that seriously overcrowded prisons constituted cruel and unusual punishment, violating the Eighth Amendment to the Constitution. Judges then decided that they would take over the prison systems and run them directly in order to correct the situation, or they made very specific policies that state administrators were obliged to follow.[51] These decisions represent greater involvement of the courts in mandating state and local government actions than many citizens consider proper.

The role the courts have accepted for themselves in legitimating action is twofold. In its simplest sense, the courts may further legitimate the actions of other decision makers by declaring that their actions are acceptable under the Constitution. As mentioned, American society appears to be becoming increasingly litigious, so more and more issues are not fully decided until they have been ruled on by the courts. Litigation presents an important means of protecting individual rights in the policymaking process, but it can also slow down greatly the implementation of policy. Putting an issue into the court system is sometimes a means of winning a conflict simply by delay, as the largely successful attempts to block construction of nuclear power plants indicate.

In a second sense, the courts take part in policy legitimation by deciding that certain conditions existing in the society are in contradiction to the Constitution and then offering a solution to those problems. The role of the courts in school desegregation is an example of this kind of legitimation. This role was manifested not only in busing cases but also in the entire process of desegregation beginning with *Brown* v. *Board of Education* (1954). The courts have acted relatively independently of other political institutions and have been active in making decisions and offering remedies that they believe are derived from sound constitutional principles. Just as administrative agencies need a legal peg on which to hang their rulemaking, so too do the courts need a constitutional peg on which to hang their interventions. Such phrases as "due process" and "equal protection" are sufficiently broad, however, to permit a wide scope for judicial involvement in legitimation activity.

Because the role of the courts is to judge the constitutionality of particular actions and to protect individual liberties against possible incursions by government or other individuals, decision making in the courts can be expected to be different from decision making through a legislative body. In many ways, the decisions made by courts are more authoritative than are other legitimating decisions, both because of the courts' connection to constitutional authority and because of the absence of any ready avenue of appeal once appeals through the court system are exhausted. The courts leave less room for compromise and vote trading than does a legislative body, and they have a less clearly defined constituency, if they have any constituency at all. Finally, a court decision is narrowly addressed, generally speaking, to the particular case in question rather than offered as a general principle of policy to be implemented in other specific cases. Court decisions legitimate certain actions but leave future decisions somewhat ambiguous, whereas decisions taken by both legislatures and administrative agencies are attempts to develop more general principles to guide subsequent actions and decisions.

Popular Legitimation

The three methods of legitimation discussed so far share a common feature: all are performed by elites through political institutions. Several American

Lawyers George E.C. Hayes, Thurgood Marshall, and James M. Nabrit leave the Supreme Court on 17 May 1954, after announcement of the court's decision declaring school segregation unconstitutional. (AP/Wide World Photos)

states provide mechanisms for direct democracy that allow voters to legitimate policy decisions.[52] The referendum constitutes in part a device for state legislatures to "pass the buck" to the people on issues that the legislators believe might be too hot to handle for the good of their political futures. Also, in some instances the public can use these mechanisms to bypass legislatures entirely or to prod them into action. Despite some agitation, these mechanisms for direct democracy have not been adopted at the federal level.

The majority of states in the United States employ referendums for some policy decisions. Typically, approval of the voters is required to pass bond issues and to change the state constitution. A *referendum* is a vote of the people on an issue put to them by the legislature or some other authoritative body. Approval by popular vote is required before the measure in question can become law. In some states, in addition to passing bond issues and constitutional changes, referendums are used to enact other legislation. An issue thought by the legislature to be sufficiently important, or highly charged politically, may be put to the voters for a decision. This practice certainly satisfies the tenets of democracy, but it may lead to small numbers—turnout in referendums is low—of relatively uninformed voters deciding about issues of great importance that might be better decided in more deliberative bodies.

The *initiative* is an even more extreme means of involving the public in policymaking. It allows voters not only to pass on an issue put to them by government but also to place the issue on the ballot themselves. If the requisite number of signatures is obtained, an item can be placed on the ballot and, if approved by the voters, will become law. A number of significant policy decisions—most notably Proposition 13 limiting property taxes and several important environmental laws in California—have been adopted through the initiative process. The initiative and the referendum have many of the same problems. One difficulty is that complex policy issues such as nuclear power become embroiled in political campaigns so that the complex issues involved become trivialized and converted into simple yes-no questions. The initiative does provide an avenue for the expression of popular opinion, however, and it gives real power to the voters, who often think of themselves as absent from representative policymaking institutions.

In addition to these established mechanisms for popular involvement, there is a continuing discussion of additional means of citizen involvement that would go beyond mere voting or public hearings. These mechanisms are usually discussed under the term "discursive democracy," or sometimes "strong democracy."[53] The basic idea is that a true democracy would not confine the role of citizens to selecting their leaders but should extend to the debate and selection of policies. This model has worked in the traditional New England town meeting, and the advocates of expanded participation would like to make it more general. The difficulty is in making it work in a country of 250 million people.

Even if it cannot work for such a large aggregation, deliberative democracy could perhaps be applied to smaller settings when making public policy. For example, there is a tradition of public hearings in the policy process at all levels of government in the United States. The typical pattern has been for citizens to make statements of their views to a decision-making body. In some areas, however, this basic pattern is being revised to allow citizens to discuss policy among themselves, and perhaps even to make the final decisions themselves.

Summary

Legitimation is at once the most difficult and the simplest component of the policymaking process. On one hand, it generally involves the least complex and technical forms of policy analysis, and the number of actors is relatively constrained, unless the initiative and referendum are used. On the other hand, the actors involved are relatively powerful and have well-defined agendas of their own. Consequently, the task of the policy analyst seeking to alter perceptions and create converts to new policies at this stage is difficult. The type of formal evidence used at other stages of the process may not carry much weight at this stage, while political factors become paramount.

The barriers that the policy analyst faces in attempting to push through his or her ideas are sometimes individual and political, as when congressmen must be convinced through partisan analysis or vote trading to accept the analyst's concept of the desirable policy alternative. Conversely, the task may be one of altering substantial organizational constraints, and turf wars, on a decision that would facilitate the appropriate policy response to a particular problem or a whole set of problems. Alternatively, the problem may be a legal one of persuading the courts to respond in the desired fashion to a set of facts and to develop the desired remedy for the perceived problem. Or, finally, the problem may be political in the broadest sense of persuading the voters (through the political mastery of the analyst) to accept or reject a particular definition of an issue and its solution. This is a wide range of problems for the analyst, demanding an equally wide range of skills.

No individual is likely to have all these skills, but someone must make strategic choices as to which skills are the most appropriate for a particular problem. If the problem is to get a dam built, Congress is clearly the most appropriate arena; if the problem is a civil rights violation, the best place to begin is probably the court system; if the problem is a specialized environmental issue, the regulatory process is the appropriate locus for intervention. Policies do not simply happen: they must be made to happen. This is especially true given the degree of inertia existing in American government and the number of points at which action can be blocked. As with so many problems, the major task of the policy analyst may be to define clearly the problem that must be solved. Once that is done, the solution may not be simple, but it is at least potentially analyzable, and a feasible course of action may become more apparent.

5. Organizations and Implementation

Once a piece of legislation or a regulation has been accepted as a legitimate public law, in some ways the easiest portion of the policymaking process has already transpired, for government must then put the legislation into effect. This requires the development of organizations that will apply the principles of the legislation to specific cases, monitor the performance of the policies, and, it is hoped, propose improvements in the content and method of administration of the policy. Even policies that are primarily self-administered, or that rely on incentives rather than regulations, require some organizational basis for administration, although the organizations can certainly be smaller than those needed for implementing programs that depend on direct administration and supervision. For example, the collection of the income tax, which is largely self-administered, requires many fewer persons for each dollar collected than does collecting revenues from customs duties, even leaving aside the role of customs agents in controlling smuggling.

Traditional American political thinkers have denigrated the roles of public administrators and bureaucrats in policymaking. The traditional attitude has been that policy was made by legislatures and then the administrators were merely to follow the guidelines set forth in the legislation. Such an attitude fails to take into account the important role of administrative decision making and especially the importance of decision makers at the bottom of the organization in determining the effective policies of government.[1] The "real" criminal justice policy of the nation or city is to a great extent determined by the way in which the police enforce the laws, just as the "real" social welfare policy is determined by decisions made by caseworkers or even by receptionists in social service agencies. We have noted that bureaucrats play an important role in interpreting legislation and making regulations to put that legislation into effect; they also play an important role in making decisions while applying laws and regulations to individual cases.[2]

It is also customary to consider government as an undivided entity and to regard government organizations as monolithic. In fact, this is not the case at all. We have mentioned that American government is divided horizontally into a number of subgovernments and vertically into levels of gov-

94

ernment in a federal system. But within the federal bureaucracy, and even within single cabinet-level departments, there exist a number of bureaus, offices, and sections, all competing for money, legislative time, and public attention. Each of these organizations has its own goals, ideas, and concepts about how to attack the public problems it is charged with administering. As in the making of legislation, these ideas will influence the implementation of legislation. Implementation involves conflicts and competition, rather than neat coordination and control, and struggles over the content of policy go on long after Congress and the president have enacted legislation. Policies, as operating instruments, commonly emerge from these conflicts, as much as they do from the initial design of legislation. This does not mean that policies should necessarily be designed initially in order to be implemented easily, but rather that anyone interested in policy outcomes must monitor implementation as well as formulation activities.

Dramatis Personae

The organization of the federal government is complicated not only because of the number of organizations but also because of the number of different kinds of organizations. There is no single organizational format for accomplishing the work of government, and the various organizations exist in different relationships to elective officials and even to government authority as a whole. In addition to the three constitutionally designated institutional actors—the president, Congress, and the courts—there are at least eight different organizational formats existing within the federal government (see table 5.1, p. 96).[3] One of these categories is a catchall containing organizations that are difficult to classify within the other major types.

The absence of a basic organizational format tends to lessen central coordination and to contribute to the incoherence of the policy choices made by the federal government. Further, the eight forms of organizations themselves have a great deal of internal variation. As shown in table 5.1, the organizations differ greatly in size; they can also differ greatly in their internal organization. For example, the Department of Agriculture is structured with almost fifty offices and bureaus, while the Department of Housing and Urban Development is structured more around several assistant secretaries and their staffs, with few operating agencies within the Department.

The most familiar forms of organization are the *executive departments*, such as the Department of Defense and the Department of Health and Human Services. Each of these fourteen departments is headed by a secretary who is a member of the president's cabinet and who is directly responsible to the president. These executive departments should not, however, be regarded as uniform wholes. Instead, they are collections or "holding compa-

TABLE 5.1

EXAMPLES OF EMPLOYMENT IN FEDERAL ORGANIZATIONS

Kind of organization	Employment
Executive departments	
Department of Defense (civilian)	795,813
Department of Education	4,721
Executive Office of the President	
Office of Management and Budget	518
Office of National Service	1
Legislative organizations	
General Accounting Office	4,342
Biomedical Ethics Board	1
Independent executive agencies	
Social Security Administration	64,095
Appalachian Regional Commission	29
Independent regulatory commissions	
Nuclear Regulatory Commission	3,148
Consumer Products Safety Commission	468
Public corporations	
U.S. Postal Service	852,208
Neighborhood Reinvestment Corporation	226
Foundations	
National Science Foundation	1,249
National Endowment for the Arts and Humanities	337
Other	
Smithsonian Institution	5,168
Office of Government Ethics	96

SOURCE: Office of Management and Budget, *Budget of the United States,* FY *1998.*

nies" of relatively autonomous agencies and offices.[4] Departments vary in the extent to which their constituent agencies respond to central direction. Some, such as the Department of Defense, have relatively high degrees of internal coordination; others, such as the Department of Commerce, are extremely decentralized.[5]

Although the cabinet departments are important, in some instances, the individual agency may have more political clout than does the department as a whole. One such agency is the Federal Bureau of Investigation (FBI), which is part of the Department of Justice but often can operate as if it were independent. And in some instances it is not entirely clear why agencies are located in one department rather than another, for example, why the U.S. Forest Service is located in the Department of Agriculture rather than in Interior, or why the U.S. Coast Guard is now located in the Department of Transportation rather than in Treasury or Defense.[6]

Although the executive departments are linked to constituencies and provide services directly to those constituencies, the organizations within the *Executive Office of the President* exist to assist the president in carrying out his tasks of control and coordination.[7] The most important units within the Executive Office of the President are the Office of Management and Budget, the Council of Economic Advisers, the National Security Council, the Domestic Policy Council, and the White House Office. The first two assist the president in his role as economic manager and central figure in the budgetary process. The National Security Council provides advice and opinion on foreign and defense issues independent of that provided by the Departments of State and Defense, while the Domestic Policy Council performs a similar role for domestic policy. The White House Office manages the everyday complexities of serving as president of the United States and employs a number of personal advisers for the president. The units within the Executive Office of the President now employ almost 1,600 people—an insignificant number compared with a total federal civilian workforce of more than 2 million, but quite large when compared with the personal offices of the chief executives of other nations.[8]

Congress has also created organizations to assist it in its role in policymaking. The three most important *legislative organizations* are the General Accounting Office (GAO), the Congressional Budget Office (CBO), and the Congressional Research Service. Legislatures in democratic political systems generally audit the accounts of the executive to ensure that public money is being spent legally. The General Accounting Office, for most of its existence, had been strictly a financial accounting body. In the 1970s, however, the organization began to expand its concerns to the cost effectiveness of expenditures.[9] For example, in one report the GAO agreed that the Internal Revenue Service (IRS) had been acting perfectly legally in the ways it sought to detect income tax evaders, but recommended changing the IRS program to one the GAO considered more efficient. The CBO has its major policy impact on the preparation of the budget; its role is discussed thoroughly in chapter 6. The Congressional Research Service, located within the Library of Congress, assists Congress in policy research and prepares background material for individual congressmen and committees.

In addition to the executive departments responsible to the president, there are a number of *independent executive agencies,* which perform executive functions such as implementing public programs but are independent of

NASA's Space Shuttle program benefits from the enhanced flexibility of its status as an independent executive agency in pursuing a highly technical mission. (National Aeronautics and Space Administration)

the executive departments and generally report directly to the president. There can be several reasons for this independence. Some independent executive agencies, such as the National Aeronautics and Space Administration (NASA), are mission agencies created outside existing departmental frameworks so as to have enhanced flexibility in completing their missions. Others, such as the Environmental Protection Agency and the Small Business Administration, are organized independently to highlight their importance and in recognition of the political power of the interest groups supporting them. Moving the Social Security Administration out of the Department of

Health and Human Services in April 1995 was a recognition of the importance and size of this organization, which spends close to one-quarter of the federal budget. Other organizations, such as the General Services Administration and the Office of Personnel Management, provide services to a number of other government departments, and locating them in any one department might create management difficulties.

The fifth form of organization is the *independent regulatory commission.* Three such organizations are the Interstate Commerce Commission, the Federal Trade Commission, and the Consumer Products Safety Commission. These commissions are different from independent executive agencies in that they do not perform executive functions but act independently to regulate certain segments of the economy.[10] Once the president has appointed the members of a commission, the application and formulation of regulations are largely beyond his control. The absence of direct political support often results, however, in the "capture" of the regulatory commissions by the interests they were intended to regulate.[11] Over time, lacking ties to the president or Congress, the independent agencies may seek the political support of the regulated interests in order to obtain their budgets, personnel, or legislation from the other institutions in government. The tendency toward capture is not so evident in agencies that must deal with several industries—the Federal Trade Commission or Consumer Products Safety Commission, for example.[12] Also, it must be remembered that not all economic regulation is conducted through the independent commissions, and some of the more important regulatory agencies, such as the Occupational Safety and Health Administration (OSHA) and the Food and Drug Administration (FDA), are in executive departments—OSHA is in the Department of Labor, and the FDA is part of Health and Human Services.

The government of the United States has generally avoided becoming directly involved in the economy other than through regulations, but there are a number of *public corporations* in the federal government.[13] For example, since 1972 the U.S. Postal Service has been a public corporation rather than a part of the executive department, as it was before; it employs over 800,000 people, or almost one-third of all federal civilian employees. Another public corporation, the Tennessee Valley Authority, controls about 6 percent of the total electrical generating capacity of the United States. Some public corporations are very small, however. The Overseas Private Investment Corporation, for instance, employs only 100 people.

Public corporations are organized much like private corporations, with a board of directors and stock issued for capitalization. The principal difference is that the board members are all public appointees and the stock is generally held entirely by the Department of the Treasury or by another executive department. There are several reasons for choosing the corporate form of organization. One is that these organizations provide marketed goods and services to the population and hence can be better managed as commercial concerns.[14] Also, this is a means of keeping some government functions at arm's length so that the president and Congress are not held directly responsible for the actions of these organizations.

There are also several *foundations* within the federal government, the principal examples being the National Science Foundation, the National Endowment for the Humanities, and the National Endowment for the Arts. The foundation is intended primarily to separate the organization from the remainder of government. This is done because of a justifiable fear of creating a national orthodoxy in the arts or in science and thereby stifling creativity. The use of the more independent foundation enables government to support the activities while being removed from the decisions. This isolation is far from complete, as Congress has not been reluctant to intervene in the decisions of foundations, most notably in criticizing decisions of the National Endowment for the Arts that conservatives alleged supported "pornography."[15] The Endowment responded by issuing a "general standard of decency" for funding, a provision that has been upheld by the Supreme Court as not violating the First Amendment.[16]

In addition to the wholly owned government corporations described here, there is also a group of organizations described as *quasi-governmental* or as being in the "twilight zone." Examples of these organizations are the National Railroad Passenger Corporation (AMTRAK), the Corporation for Public Broadcasting, and the Federal Reserve Board. These organizations have some attributes of public organizations—most important, access to public funding—but they also have some attributes of private organizations. They are similar to public corporations except that a portion of their boards of directors is appointed by private-sector organizations; the board of AMTRAK is appointed in part by the member railroad corporations. Also, not all their stock may be owned by the public sector, as is true for wholly owned corporations; some may be owned by the cooperating private-sector organizations. For example, up to half the stock of COMSAT (Communications Satellite Corporation) may be held by communication common carriers.[17] Finally, employees of these quasi-governmental organizations generally are not classified as public employees, and they generally are not subject to other public-sector regulations such as the Freedom of Information Act.

The justification for the formation of quasi-governmental organizations such as these is, again, to allow government to become involved in a policy area without assuming any real or apparent direct control. The federal government clearly subsidizes certain activities—passenger railroad service would almost certainly have vanished in the United States without the formation of AMTRAK—but this intervention is not as obvious as other forms of intervention. Also, intervention by an organization of this sort gives the public a greater role in decision making and provides greater representation of private interests such as the affected corporations. And, as with the Corporation for Public Broadcasting, this form of organization permits the federal government to become involved in an area from which it has traditionally been excluded.

It is important to understand just how vital these quasi-governmental organizations are to the federal government. For example, the Federal Reserve Board fits comfortably into this twilight zone, given its isolation from executive authority and its relationship to its member banks. But the Federal Reserve Board is responsible for making monetary policy for the United States and thereby has a significant—if not the most significant—influence on this nation's economic conditions. Similarly, AMTRAK has received massive subsidies, and the public sector has no firm control over its policies, yet it is a significant element in national transportation. Similarly the Corporation for Public Broadcasting is a significant complement to commercial radio and television broadcasting, although Congress often fails to support public broadcasting with anything like the funds available to the commercial channels.[18]

Finally, there is a catchall category of *other organizations.* This category contains several regional commissions that coordinate economic or environmental policy in several parts of the country. Other organizations, including various claims commissions and the Administrative Conference of the United States, operate on the fringes of the judicial process. Finally, organizations such as the Smithsonian Institution, the National Academy of Sciences, and the American Red Cross are mentioned in federal legislation and receive subsidies, but they are far removed from the mainstream of government action.

We should note several other points about the complexity of the organizational structure of the federal government. One is the redundancy that has been built into the system of organization. First, both Congress (through the Congressional Budget Office) and the Executive Office of the President (through the Office of Management and Budget) have organizations to deal with budgeting and with many other economic aspects of government. Because of the doctrine of separation of powers, such duplication makes a great deal of sense, but this still conflicts with conventional managerial thinking concerning eliminating duplicative organizations.

Second, within the federal executive branch itself, we have seen that some units within the Executive Office of the President duplicate activities of the executive departments. Most notably, presidents appear to demand foreign policy advice other than that provided by the Departments of State and Defense, and they get it from the National Security Council. This demand may be justified, as those departments have existing policy commitments and ideas that may limit their ability to respond to presidential initiatives in foreign policy. But, as has happened during at least every administration since that of Richard Nixon, conflicts may arise between the two sets of institutions, and the management of foreign policy may suffer as a result. In most instances, this conflict has been perceived as a conflict between experienced professionals in the Department of State and committed amateurs in the National Security Council.

In other areas more than one federal organization may exercise a regulatory function. For example, both the Federal Trade Commission and the Antitrust Division of the Department of Justice are concerned with antitrust policies and monopolies.[19] Some redundancy can be rationalized as a means of limiting error and providing alternative means for accomplishing the same tasks.[20] But if the redundant institutions are occupied by ambitious men and women, the potential for conflict, "gridlock," or perhaps excessive regulation is substantial.[21]

It is also interesting to note that not all central management functions of the federal government are located in the Executive Office of the President. Several important central functions—monetary policy, personnel policy, debt management, and taxation—are managed by agencies outside the president's office and, in one instance, by an organization in the "twilight zone." This diffusion of duties and responsibilities is a definite limitation on the ability of the president to implement his policy priorities and consequently to control the federal establishment for which he is responsible.

Third, we have mentioned the variations in the "publicness" of organizations in the federal government. Some organizations are clearly public: they receive their funds from allocations in the federal budget; their employees are hired through public personnel systems; and they are subject to legislation such as the Freedom of Information Act, which attempts to differentiate public from private programs.[22] Other organizations described appear tied to the private sector as much as to government: they receive some or all of their funds as fees for service or interest on loans; they have their own personnel policies; and they are only slightly more subject to normal restrictions on public organizations than is General Motors. Again, for a president—who is held accountable to voters and to Congress for the performance of the federal government—this presents an immense and perhaps insoluble problem. How can the president really take responsibility when so many of the organizations charged with implementing his policies are beyond effective control? This is but one of many difficulties a president encounters when he attempts to put his policies into effect; it also serves as a bridge to our discussion of implementation.

Implementation

All the organizations described earlier are established to assist in some way the execution of legislation or the monitoring of that execution. Once enacted, laws do not go into effect by themselves, as was assumed by those in the (presumed) tradition of Woodrow Wilson, who discussed "mere administration."[23] In fact, one of the most important things to understand about government is that it is a minor miracle that implementation is ever accomplished.[24] There are so many more ways of blocking intended actions than there are of making results materialize that all legislators should be pleased if they live to see their pet projects not only passed into law but actually put into effect. Although this is perhaps an excessively negative characterization of the implementation process, it should underline the extreme difficulties of administering and implementing public programs.

Policies do not fail on their own, however, and a large number of factors may limit the ability of a political system to put policies into effect. Rarely will all these factors affect any single policy, but all must be considered when designing a policy and attempting to translate that policy choice into real services for citizens. Further, any one of these factors may be sufficient to cause failure, or suboptimal performance, by a policy while all may have to be in good order for the policy to work. In short, it is much easier to prevent a policy from working than it is to make the policy effective.

The Legislation

The first factor that affects a policy's effective implementation is the nature of the legislation. Laws vary according to their specificity, their clarity, and the policy areas they attempt to influence. They also differ in the extent to which they bind the individuals and organizations charged with implementing them to perform in the way the writers intended. Unfortunately, both legislators and analysts sometimes overlook the importance of the legislation. Also, laws that are easier to implement are, everything else being equal, more difficult to pass. Their specificity may make it clear who the winners and losers are and make building the necessary coalitions for passage that much more difficult.

Policy Issues

Legislators frequently choose to legislate in policy areas where there is not enough information about causal processes to enable them to make good policy choices. Although they may have the best intentions, their efforts are unlikely to succeed if they make only stabs in the dark in attempting to solve difficult problems. If we refer to the illustration used in discussing policy formulation (figure 3.1, p. 67), we can estimate the likelihood of effective implementation of a policy. We anticipate that the highest probability of effective implementation will occur when we have both sufficient information about the policy area and adequate knowledge of the causes of the problems. In such situations, governments can design legislation to solve, or at least ameliorate, the problem under attack. Likewise, we would expect little likelihood of effective implementation in policy areas where there is inadequate information and little knowledge of the causes of the problem.

The other two possible combinations of knowledge of causation and information may differ very little in their likelihood of effective implementation, although we would expect a somewhat better probability of implementation when there is a knowledge of the patterns of causation as opposed to more basic information. If the underlying process is understood, it would appear possible to formulate policy responses based on poor information, even if those responses involve a certain amount of overkill and excessive reaction. If the underlying process is misunderstood or is not understood at all, there is little hope of effectively implementing a policy choice, except by pure luck. In this instance, governments often wind up treating the symptoms, as they do with the problem of crime and delinquency, instead of dealing with the underlying social processes.

Perhaps the best example of a large-scale policy formulation and implementation in spite of inadequate knowledge of patterns of causation was the War on Poverty in the United States several decades ago. There were (and are) as many theories about the causes of poverty as there were theorists, but there was little real understanding even of the basics of the economic and social dynamics producing the problem.[25] Thus, war was declared on an enemy that was poorly understood. Daniel P. Moynihan put it this way:

> This is the essential fact: The Government did not know what it was doing. It had a theory. Or rather a set of theories. Nothing more. The U.S. Government at this time was no more in possession of a confident knowledge as to how to prevent delinquency, cure anomie, or overcome that midmorning sense of powerlessness than it was the possessor of a dependable formula for motivating Vietnamese villagers to fight Communism.[26]

Not only was it a war, but it was a war that appeared to be based on something approaching a dogma about the plan of attack—for example, the use of large-scale and rather expensive programs involving direct services to clients. Arguably, these programs were doomed to fail as soon as they were adopted because they were based on dubious assumptions about the operations of society and the mechanisms for approaching such problems. But they had the political appeal and visibility that smaller-scale efforts would have lacked.

An even more extreme example of a policy made without adequate knowledge was the Clean Air Act of 1970 (see chapter 13). The sponsors of this legislation were, in fact, quite sure that they did not understand the processes and that the technology for producing the environmental cleanup they legislated did not exist. This legislation was designed to force the development of the technology for improving the environment. To some extent, the same was true of the space program, which did not have a sure technology for accomplishing its goals when President John Kennedy pledged to place an American on the moon by the end of the decade. More recently, the Strategic Defense Initiative and subsequent attempts to build an antimissile defense have required development of technologies that may be at least as important for domestic as for defense purposes.[27]

Technology forcing is an interesting if somewhat novel approach to designing public programs, but it is not one that can be recommended as a strategy for policymaking. It has been successful in some policy areas, in part because the problems being dealt with were aspects of the physical world, rather than the more complex social and economic realities that governments often face.[28] These potential difficulties should not be taken to mean that governments should just keep to their well-worn paths and do what they have always done in the ways they have always done it. Instead, they caution that if one expects significant results from programs based on insufficient understanding of the subject matter of the legislation, one's hopes are likely to be dashed.

Political Setting

Legislation is adopted through political action, and the political process may plant within legislation the seeds of its own destruction. The very compromises and negotiations necessary to pass legislation may ultimately make it virtually impossible to implement. The implementation problem becomes especially evident when the construction of the necessary coalition forces logrolling and tradeoffs among competing interests and competing purposes in the legislation.

The effects of the political process of legislation are manifested in different ways. One is the vagueness of the language in which the legislation is written. This lack of clarity may be essential to developing a coalition for the passage of legislation, as every time a vague term is made specific, potential coalition members are lost. But by phrasing legislation in vague and inoffensive language, legislators risk making their intent unclear to those who must implement the laws and allowing the implementors to alter the entire meaning of the program substantially. Phrases such as "maximum feasible participation," "equality of educational opportunity," "special needs of educationally deprived students," and that favorite vague term, "public interest," are all subject to a number of different interpretations, many of which could betray the true intent of the legislators. For example, the rather vague language of Social Security legislation from 1962 to 1972 provided for open-ended grants for "improved services" for citizens.[29] The assumption was that additional services would be provided with this money. Instead, quite contrary to the intent of the drafters of the legislation, the money was used to subsidize existing programs and provide fiscal relief for state budgets. These grants also grew much more rapidly than had been anticipated when states found ways of using them to shift a substantial portion of their social service expenditures to the federal government. Even words about which most citizens can agree may be sufficiently vague to produce problems during implementation, as when the Reagan administration attempted to include ketchup as a "vegetable" under the School Lunch Program.[30]

In addition to coalitions formed for the passage of single pieces of legislation, other coalitions may have to be formed across several pieces of legislation—the classic approach to logrolling. In order to gain support for one favored piece of legislation, a coalition-building legislator may have to trade his or her support on other pieces of legislation. In some instances, this may simply increase the overall volume of legislation enacted. In others, it may involve the passage of legislation that negates or decreases the effects of desired legislation. Some coalitions that must be formed are regional, so it may become virtually impossible to give one region an advantage that may be justified by economic circumstances without making commensurate concessions to other regions, thereby nullifying the intended effect. It is also difficult to make legislative decisions that are redistributive across economic classes; either the legislation will be watered down to be distributive (giving everyone a piece of the pie) or additional legislation will be passed to spread the benefits more broadly. The Elementary and Secondary Education Act and Medicare are examples of this tendency.

Similar problems of vagueness and logrolling can occur when other institutions make rulings that must be implemented. In a number of instances a judicial decision intended to mandate a certain action has been so vague as to be difficult or impossible to implement. One of the best examples of this lack of clarity is the famous decision of *Brown* v. *Board of Education*, which ordered schools to desegregate with "all deliberate speed." Two of those three words, "deliberate" and "speed," appear somewhat contradictory, and the decision did not specify exactly what the phrase meant. Similarly, the police are prohibited from searching an individual, an automobile they stop, or a home without "probable cause," but that term is left largely undefined. Further, the process of writing regulations in administrative agencies, intended to clarify and specify legislation, can itself create ambiguities that require more regulations to clarify and more delay in implementing the decisions.

In summary, politics is central to the formulation of legislation, but the results may be such that the legislation cannot be implemented effectively. The compromises necessitated by political feasibility may result in just the reductions in clarity and purpose that make laws too diffuse to be implemented so as to have a real effect on society. The vagueness of legislation may make room for another type of politics dominated more by interest groups than by elected officials.

Interest-group Liberalism

Related to the problems of vagueness and of government involvement in policy areas about which it lacks knowledge of causation is Theodore J. Lowi's concern regarding government involvement in the more abstract aspects of human behavior.[31] Lowi's argument is that the United States has progressed from concerted and specific legislation such as the Interstate Commerce Act of 1887, which established clear standards of practice for the Interstate Commerce Commission, to abstract and general standards, such as "unfair competition" in the Clayton Act of 1914. This tendency has been extended through even more general and diffuse aspects of human behavior, in the attempts of social legislation following the 1960s to regulate what Lowi refers to as the "environment of conduct." It is simply more difficult to show that a person has discriminated against another person on the basis of race, color, or sex than it is to show that a railroad has violated prohibitions against discriminatory freight rates.

Lowi believes that the problems in these vague laws arise not from their commendable intentions but from the difficulties of implementing them. The diffuseness of the targets specified and the difficulty of defining standards subject policies attempting to regulate those behaviors to errors in interpretation during implementation. Further, it becomes more difficult to hold government accountable when it administers ambiguous legislation. The interest-group liberalism inherent in American politics, in which the public interest tends to be defined in terms of many private interests, means that implementation of legislation will generally differ greatly from the intentions of those who framed the legislation. Implementation will be undertaken by agencies that are themselves tied to clients and to particular definitions of the public interest and that will not want to be swayed from their position by a piece of legislation. The difficulties in accountability and the deviations of policies in practice from the intentions of their framers can only alienate the clients and frustrate the legislator, and perhaps the administrators as well.

The Organizational Setting

As noted earlier, most implementation is undertaken by organizations, especially organizations in the public bureaucracy. Given the nature of public organizations, and organizations in general, the probability that such an organization will effectively implement a program is not particularly high—not because of any venality on the part of the bureaucracy or the bureaucrats but simply because the internal dynamics of large organizations often limit their ability to respond to policy changes and implement new or altered programs.

To begin to understand what goes wrong when organizations attempt to implement programs, a model of "perfect" administration may be useful. Christopher Hood points to five characteristics "perfect" administration of public programs would have:

1. Administration would be unitary; it would be one vast army all marching to the same drummer.
2. The norms and rules of administration would be uniform throughout the organization.
3. There would be no resistance to commands.
4. There would be perfect information and communication within the organization.
5. There would be adequate time to implement the program.[32]

Clearly these conditions are often absent in organizations attempting to implement programs, and almost never are all of them present. Governments depend on large organizations to implement their policies, and consequently, difficulties arise in administration and implementation. These difficulties need not be insurmountable, but they do need to be understood and if possible anticipated, if successful implementation is to occur. Just what characteristics and difficulties in organizations lead to difficulties in implementation?

Organizational Disunity

Organizations are rarely unitary administrations. Instead, a number of points of disunity are almost inherent in organizational structures. One aspect of organizational disunity that affects implementation is the disjunction between central offices of organizations and their field staffs. Decisions may be made by politicians and administrators sitting in national capitals, but those decisions must be implemented by field staff members who may not share the same values and goals as the administrators in the home office.

This disjunction of values may take several forms. A change in central values and programs may occur, perhaps as a result of a change in presidents or in Congress, and the field staff may remain loyal to the older policies. For example, the field staff, and indeed much of the central staff, of the Department of Health, Education, and Welfare regarded the Nixon administration as a temporary phenomenon and remained loyal to the more liberal social values of previous Democratic presidents.[33] This was true despite pressures from above for changes in policies. Much the same was true of the staffs of the Environmental Protection Agency and the Department of the Interior under the Reagan and Bush administrations' apparent retreats on environmental issues.[34] More recently, the Clinton administration inherited a government shaped for twelve years by Republican presidents.[35] Such problems with field staffs over policy changes produce frustration for politicians nominally in control of policies and make the implementation of policies that violate the norms of the existing field staffs extremely difficult.

A more common disparity between the goals of field staffs and those of the home office may occur as the field staff is "captured" by clients. Field staff members are frequently close to their clients, and they may adopt the perspectives of their clients in their relationships with the remainder of the organization.[36] This is especially true when the clients are relatively disadvantaged and the organization is attempting either to assist them or to exercise some control over them. The identification of staff members with their clients is fostered by frequent contact, sympathy, empathy, and quite commonly by genuine devotion to a perceived mission that is in contrast to the mission fostered by the central office. This pattern is emerging as welfare reform (see pp. 304–6) begins to have negative impacts on clients and social workers try to protect their clients.[37] For whatever reason, this identification does make the implementation of centrally determined policy difficult.

In many ways, government in recent years has promoted its own difficulties when using field staffs to implement policy. The requirement for community participation in decision making in many urban social service programs further lessens the control of central organizations over the implementation of programs.

Developing community organizations that fulfill the requirements for participation is a major focus for pressures to divert the program toward more locally determined priorities, including successful efforts to say "Not in My Backyard" (NIMBY).[38] Even when community organizations are not used to implement programs, requirements for local participation can make it more difficult for agencies to do what they had planned.[39] Further, the ethos of local control is being spread sufficiently widely that even without formal requirements for participation there may be movements for involvement.[40]

Arguably, community participation has been less effective than was intended and at worst has been a facade for control by bureaucracies, but to the extent that it has been successful, it may well have made implementation less successful. Further, even in policy areas where community participation has not been so directly fostered by government, either the lessons learned from community participation elsewhere or the general climate favoring participation has produced greater activity by individuals and communities affected by policies. A whole range of programs—including decisions by the Army Corps of Engineers about project siting, the construction of portions of the Interstate Highway System, and most dramatically the siting of nuclear waste facilities—have been seriously affected by local participation.[41]

Field staffs may also find that if they are to perform their tasks effectively, they cannot follow all the directives coming to them from the center of the organization. In such instances, in order to get substantive compliance the organization members may not comply with procedural directives. For example, in a classic study of the FBI, Peter M. Blau noted that field agents frequently did not comply with directives requiring them to report the offering of a bribe by a suspect.[42] The agents had found that they could use the offer of a bribe to gain greater cooperation from the subject because at any time they could have the person prosecuted for offering the bribe. Their performance of the task of prosecuting criminals was probably enhanced, but it was done at the expense of the directive from the central office.

Eugene Bardach and Robert A. Kagan have argued that regulatory enforcement could be improved if field staffs were granted greater latitude for independent action.[43] They believe that rigidities resulting from strict central controls actually produce less compliance with the spirit of the regulations than would a more flexible approach. This interest in enhancing regulatory latitude can, however, be contrasted with the continuing (and strengthening) interest in control over bureaucracies, especially regulatory bureaucracies. Congress is concerned with efficient enforcement, but it is often more concerned with ensuring that what is being implemented corresponds with its intentions.[44]

Standard Operating Procedures

Organizations develop standard operating procedures (SOPs) to respond to policy problems. When a prospective client walks into a social service agency, the agency follows a standard pattern of response: certain forms must be filled out, designated personnel interview the prospective client, specific criteria are used to determine the person's eligibility for benefits. Likewise, if a "blip" appears on the radar screen of a defense installation, a certain set of procedures is followed to determine if the blip is real and, if so, whether it is friendly or hostile. If it should be hostile, further prespecified actions are taken.

Standard operating procedures are important for organizations. They reduce the amount of time spent processing each new situation and developing a response. SOPs are the learned response of the organization to certain problems; they represent to some extent the organizational memory in action. SOPs may also be important for clients, as they are adopted at least in part to ensure equality and fairness for clients. Without SOPs, organizations might respond more slowly to each situation, they might respond less effectively, and they would probably respond more erratically.

Although SOPs are certainly important and generally beneficial for organizations, they can act as barriers to good implementation. This is most obvious when a new policy or a new approach to an existing policy is being considered. Organizations are likely to persist in defining policies and problems in their standard manner, even when the old definition or procedure no longer helps fulfill the mission of the agency. For example, when the Medicare program was added to the responsibilities of the Social Security Administration, the agency was faced with an entirely new set of concerns in addition to its traditional task of making payments to individuals. In particular, it assumed responsibility for limiting the costs of medical care. It chose, however, to undertake this responsibility in much the same way that it would have attempted to manage problems arising from pensions—by examining individual claims and denying those that appeared to be unjustified. It took the Social Security Administration some time to focus attention on more fundamental and systemic problems of medical cost inflation and to develop programs such as Diagnostic Related Groupings (DRGs) (see chapter 10). This agency even took some time to cope with adding the Supplemental Security Income program, which was much closer to its original portfolio of income-maintenance policies, although more similar to a means-tested program.[45]

Thus there is a need for designing programs and organizations that will more consistently reassess their goals and the methods that they use to reach those goals. In some instances, for example, the number of births and the future need for schools, the response should be programmed to be almost automatic; other situations will require more thought and greater political involvement. Organizations do not like to perform these reassessments; they threaten both the employees of the organizations and their clients. One reason for creating organizations with standard operating procedures is to ensure some stability and predictability, but that stability can become a barrier to success when problems and needs in the issue area change.

SOPs also tend to produce inappropriate or delayed responses to crises. Many stories about the slowness or apparent stupidity of the military came from the Cuban missile crisis, and similar stories probably would have come from other military encounters if they had been as well documented. The military, perhaps more than any other organization, tends to employ SOPs and to train its members to carry through with those procedures in the absence of commands to the contrary. In this way, the military can be sure of a certain reaction even when there is no direct link to the command structure. John Kennedy found that although he was nominally in charge of the armed forces of the United States, many things occurred that he had not ordered, and he realized that they were happening simply because they were standard procedures. The brief invasion of Grenada in 1983 encountered difficulties when the communication SOPs of the navy and army did not correspond, and soldiers on the island could not communicate with the ships providing them support. Soldiers found the best way to communicate was to use their telephone credit cards to call the Pentagon, which would then communicate with the navy. More recently, the predictability of the intelligence gathering activities of the CIA enabled India to prepare its nuclear tests without alerting the American government.[46]

One standard means of avoiding the effects of SOPs in a new program is to create a new organization. When the Small Business Administration was created in 1953, it was purposely not placed in the Department of Commerce, whose SOPs tended to favor big business. The Office of National Drug Control Policy was established within the Executive Office of the President to ensure both its priority and its independence from other organizations, such as the Drug Enforcement Agency and the Customs Bureau. There are, of course, limits to the number of new organizations that can be set up, for the more that are created, the more chance there will be of interorganizational barriers to implementation replacing the barriers internal to any one organization. Drug policy, for example, suffers from coordination problems among the numerous agencies (the three mentioned above as well as the Coast Guard, the Department of Defense, the FBI, and so forth) all involved in the policy area.

Paradoxically, although SOPs aid in the implementation of established programs, they are likely to be barriers to change and to the implementation of new programs. Likewise, procedures may be too standardized to allow response to nonstandard situations or to nonstandard clients, thereby creating rigidity and extremely inappropriate responses to novel situations. Organizations tend to try to classify new problems as old problems as long as they can do so and to continue to use familiar responses even when the problems are, to an outsider, demonstrably different.

Organizational Communication

Another barrier to effective implementation is the improper flow of information within organizations. Because government organizations depend heavily on the flow of information—just as manufacturers rely on the flow of raw materials—accurate information and the prevention of blockages of information are extremely important to the success of these public organizations. Unfortunately many organizations, particularly public organizations, are subject to inaccurate and blocked communication.

In general, information in bureaucracies tends to be concentrated at the bottom of the hierarchies.[47] The field staff of an organization are in closer contact with the environment of the organization, and technical experts tend to be clustered at the bottom of organizations, with more general managers concentrated at the top. This concentration means, then, that if the organization is to be steered by changes in its environment, and if it is to make appropriate technical decisions, the information at the bottom must be transmitted to the top and then directions must be passed back down to the bottom for implementation. Unfortunately, the more levels through which information has to be transmitted, the greater is the probability that the information will be distorted when it is finally acted on.

This distortion may result from random error or from *selective distortion*, which occurs when officials at each stage attempt to transmit only the information they believe their superiors wish to hear or the information they think will make them look good to their superiors. And the superiors, in turn, may attempt to estimate what sort of distortion their subordinates may have passed on and at least try to correct for that distortion.[48] The result of this transmitting of messages through a hierarchical organization frequently is rampant distortion and misinformation that limits the ability of the organization to make effective implementation decisions.

Certain characteristics of the organization may improve the transmission of information through its hierarchy. Clearly, if all members of an organization "speak the same language," less distortion of communication should occur. In other words, if organization members share common technical or professional backgrounds, their communication with one another should be less distorted. Their ability to communicate effectively with other organizations, however, may be diminished. In addition, attempts on the part of the organization to create internal unity through training and socialization should also improve internal patterns of communication.[49] Finally, the "flatter" the organization (i.e., the fewer levels through which communication must go before being acted on), the less distortion is likely to occur.[50]

Another way to improve communication in organizations is to create more, and redundant, channels. For example, President Franklin Roosevelt developed personal ties to lower-level members of organizations and placed his own people in organizations to be sure that he would receive direct and unvarnished reports from the operating levels of government.[51] Alternatively, a president or manager might build in several channels of communication in order to receive messages and to serve as checks on one another. Again, Franklin Roosevelt's development of parallel organizations (e.g., the Works

Progress Administration and the Public Works Administration) provided him with alternative channels of information about the progress of his New Deal programs. In more contemporary times, the development of several channels of advice and communication to the president about national security policy and drug policy may be a way of ensuring that the information he receives is more accurate and complete.

One particularly interesting threat to effective organizational communication is secrecy.[52] While a certain level of secrecy is understood to be important for some government organizations, secrecy also may inhibit both communication and implementation. Secrecy frequently means that a communication may not be transmitted because it has been classified; other parts of the organization or other organizations are consequently denied needed information. Again, the Cuban missile crisis offered numerous examples of how the military's penchant for secrecy prevented a rapid response to situations. Also, secrecy may produce inefficiency, as when FBI agents must spend a great deal of time reporting on one another when they infiltrate subversive organizations such as the Ku Klux Klan. Of course, to make themselves more acceptable to the organizations they have infiltrated, the agents tend to be among the most vociferous members and consequently are the subjects of a disproportionate share of reports from other agents. More recently, the CIA's identification of spies within its midst was slowed because different parts of the organization were unwilling to share information with other parts. Finally, secrecy may be counterproductive even when it is justified. For example, one argument holds that the interests of military deterrence are best served by fully informing an adversary of the extent of one's arsenal, instead of masking its strength—uncertainty may only create a willingness to gamble on the strength of the opponent. Openness may thus prevent war. This logic may be particularly applicable in a nuclear age, when every major power has the ability to destroy the world several times over.

In modern organizations knowledge is power, and the inability of an organization to gather and process information from its environment will certainly be a serious detriment to its performance. Clearly the management of communication flows within an organization is an important component of taking raw information and putting it into action. Most organizations, however, face massive problems in performing even this (apparently) simple task and as a consequence do not implement their programs effectively. Their own internal hierarchical structures, the differential commitment to goals, and the differences in professional languages all conspire to make organizational communication more difficult than it may appear from the outside.

Time Problems

Related to the problem of information management in the implementation of policies is the problem of time. Christopher Hood points to two time problems that inhibit the ability of public organizations to respond to situations in their policy environments. One is a linear time problem in which the responses of implementing organizations tend to lag behind the need for the response.[53] This often happens in organizations that have learned their lessons too well and that base their responses on previous learning rather than on current conditions. This problem is somewhat similar to the problem of standard operating procedures, but it has less to do with processing individual cases and more to do with designing the mechanisms for putting new programs into effect. Organizations frequently implement programs to deal with a crisis that has just passed, rather than with the crisis they currently face or might soon face. To some degree the American armed forces in Vietnam used the lessons they had learned, or thought they had learned, in World War II and in Korea. Unfortunately for them, a highly mechanized, technologically sophisticated, and logistically dependent fighting force broke down in a tropical, guerrilla war.

Another example of this problem is the slow reaction of American elementary and secondary school systems to the baby booms that followed World War II and the Korean conflict. Virtually everyone knew that increased numbers of children had indeed been born and would have to be educated, but few educators attempted to prepare for their arrival in the school systems or to construct the physical facilities or train the teachers they would require. Government also has allowed this large generation to proceed through the life cycle without making adequate plans for the burdens that it will impose on the Social Security retirement system (see pp. 293–95).

Other time problems are cyclical, and delayed implementation, instead of solving problems, may actually contribute to them. This is especially important in making and implementing macroeconomic policy in which, even if the information available to a decision maker is timely and accurate, a delay in response may exaggerate economic fluctuations. If a decision maker responds to a threatened increase in inflation by reducing money supplies or reducing expenditures, and if that response is delayed for a year, or even for only a few months, it may only increase an economic slowdown resulting basically from other causes. Thus, it is not sufficient merely to be right; an effective policy must be both correct and on time if it is to have the desired effect.

Horse-Shoe-Nail Problems and Public Planning
The final organizational problem in implementation arises when organizations plan their activities incompletely or inaccurately. Hood calls these "horse-shoe-nail" problems because the failure to provide the nail results in

the eventual loss of the horse and, eventually, the battle.[54] And because government organizations often must plan for implementation with limited access to information and no cues about the necessary choices, problems of this kind are likely to arise in the public sector. Examples of this problem abound: passing requirements to inspect coal mines but failing to hire inspectors; requiring clients to fill out certain forms but neglecting to have the forms printed; forgetting to stop construction of a $160 million highway tunnel leading to nowhere. There are countless examples of this political and policy version of Murphy's law.[55]

To ensure effective management and implementation, planners must identify the crucial potential blockages, or "nails," in their organization and allow for them in their planning. Clearly, with a new program or policy, this planning may be extremely difficult, as the problems that will arise are almost impossible to anticipate. Some planners use these difficulties to justify using incrementalism or experimentation when introducing new policies. Instead of undertaking large projects with the possibility of equally large failures, they may undertake smaller projects for which any failures or unanticipated difficulties would impose minimal costs but would help prepare the organization to implement full-scale projects. The problem, of course, is that the programs often are not permitted to grow sufficiently to reach an effective level but may remain small and "experimental."

But some programs will be effective only if they are on a large scale and comprehensive. Paul R. Schulman's analysis of NASA points out that a venture such as the space program—designed to reach a major goal within a limited amount of time and with an engineering as opposed to a pure research focus—must be large scale in order to be effective.[56] Similarly, it has been argued that the War on Poverty, instead of being the failure portrayed in the conventional wisdom, actually was never tried on a scale that might have made it effective. In contrast, the so-called war on cancer was implemented as if it were a program that required a centralized, mission format. In reality, it required a more decentralized structure to allow scientific research to pursue as many avenues as possible.[57] Those who design programs and organizations must be very careful to match them to the characteristics of the problem and the state of knowledge concerning the subject. Even if perhaps objectively correct, a strategy may still provoke political criticism, as has the failure to launch a "war on AIDS" in many circles.[58]

Interorganizational Politics

Few if any policies are designed and implemented by a "single lonely organization" in the 1990s.[59] Certainly individual organizations have their problems, but many more problems are encountered in the design of implementation structures or the pattern of interactions among organizations as they attempt to implement a policy. The problems of organizational disunity and communication become exaggerated when the individuals involved are not bound even by a presumed loyalty to a single organization but have competing loyalties to different organizations, not all of which may be interested in the effective implementation of a particular program.[60] This tendency may be exaggerated when private contractors are a central element in implementation, and their goals of profit and contract fulfillment conflict with goals of service delivery and accountability in the public sector.

Jeffrey L. Pressman and Aaron Wildavsky, who popularized the concern for implementation several decades ago, speak of the problems of implementing policies through a number of organizations (or even within a single organization) as a matter of "clearance points." These are defined as the number of individual decision points that must be agreed to before any policy intentions can be translated into action.[61] Even if the decision makers at each "clearance point" are favorably disposed toward the program in question, there may still be impediments to reaching agreement for implementation. Some problems may be legal, some may be budgetary, and others may involve building coalitions with other organizations or interests in the society.

Statistically, one would expect that if each decision point is independent of the others and if the probability of any individual decision maker's agreeing to the program is 90 percent (.9), then the probability of any two agreeing is 81 percent (.9 x .9); and for three points, the probability would be 73 percent (.9 x .9 x .9); and so forth. Pressman and Wildavsky determined that there were at a minimum seventy clearance points in the implementation of the Economic Development Administration's decision to become involved in public works projects in Oakland, California.[62] With this number of clearance points, the probability of all of them agreeing, given an average probability of 90 percent for each clearance, is less than one in a thousand. Only if there were a probability greater than 99 percent at each clearance point would the odds in favor of implementation be greater than 50-50. Of course, implementation is not just a problem in statistics, and the political and administrative leaders involved in the process can vastly alter the probabilities at each stage. With so many independent clearance points and limited political resources, however, a leader may well be tempted to succumb to the inertia inherent in the implementation system.

Judith Bowen has argued that the simple statistical model proposed by Pressman and Wildavsky may understate the probabilities of successful implementation.[63] She points out that if persistence is permitted, and each clearance point can be assaulted a number of times, the chances for a successful implementation increase significantly. She also explains that the clearance points may not be independent, as assumed, and that success at one clearance point may produce an increased probability of success at subsequent steps. Similarly, the clever implementer can make strategic choices about which clearance points to try first and how to package the points so that some success can be gained even if the whole campaign is not won. Thus, while successful implementation is still not perceived to be a simple task, it is subject to manipulation, as are other stages of the policy process. The clever policy analyst therefore can improve his or her probabilities of success by understanding how to intervene most effectively.

The administrative reforms of the 1990s have tended to exacerbate these problems of implementation by building in more actors, especially private-sector (both for-profit and not-for-profit) organizations, into the process. One of the common admonitions is now that governments should "steer but not row."[64] That is, governments should make policy but depend upon others who may be more efficient to handle the actual implementation. This is presumed both to reduce cost (and public employment) and to boost service quality. Whether those goals are achieved or not, it is clear that the new style of administration does build in more clearance points and hence more opportunities for policies to go astray in the process of being implemented.

Vertical Implementation Structures

One problem in implementation occurs vertically within the hierarchical structures of government. I have described some problems of intergovernmental relations in the United States associated with the several levels of governments, all of which may well be involved in the implementation of a single piece of legislation. The impact of intergovernmental relations is especially evident for federal social and urban legislation in which all three levels of government may be involved in putting a single piece of federal legislation into effect. For example, Title XX of the Social Security Amendments of 1972 called for the availability of day-care services for poor working mothers. These services were to be funded through the Social Security Administration in Washington but implemented through state and local governments. For the typical poor child to receive day care supported by the federal government, the Social Security Administration must agree to give a grant for the proposed program to a local government. But this money is channeled through the state government, which issues regulations to carry out the intentions of the program within the structure of the particular state government. The grant money is then transferred to the local government. But the local government can rarely provide the day care itself; instead, it contracts with day-care providers (usually private) to provide the services. The local government has to monitor the standards and contract compliance of the private-service providers and ensure that no federal policy guidelines are violated. Even that regulation may differ substantially from state to state or local government to local government.[65] More recently, welfare reform in the 1990s depends on the same mixture of state governments, local governments, and private contractors to move poor citizens off public assistance and into productive work, and that multiplicity of actors has produced an immense implementation problem.[66]

Such a vertical implementation structure can give rise to several possibilities for inadequate implementation or no implementation. One problem could result from simple partisan politics, when the local government and the federal government are controlled by different political parties and consequently have different policy priorities. Or localities may, for other reasons, have different policy priorities than does the federal government and may choose to implement programs differently than the federal government desires. Two good examples of these differences can be seen in the resistance of local governments to federally mandated scattering of public housing projects in middle-class neighborhoods and in the resistance of most state and local governments to federal proposals to locate nuclear waste disposal facilities in their territory.

Even if local governments want to do what the federal government would have them do, they sometimes lack the resources to do so. For example, local governments have attempted to resist various federal mandates, such as the Water Pollution Control Act of 1972 and day-care quality standards, claiming they lacked the funds to meet the standards imposed.[67] Also, the states and localities may have few incentives to comply with federal directives. For example, in the Elementary and Secondary Education Act of 1965 the states were to receive grants merely for participating in the program, without having to do anything in particular to improve education. When easy money is available, there is little or no reason, other than good faith and a desire to encourage good government, to comply with federal regulations.

The increasing emphasis on the use of the private sector to achieve public purposes means that implementation is increasingly being performed by private groups as well as by subnational governments. For example, tenants organizations have begun to manage public housing projects, and churches and other charitable organizations are the contractors for services under the Americorps volunteer program in the Clinton administration. This pattern of implementation can easily create the problems of "capture" described above. For example, some regulations of the amount of fish that can be caught in the Atlantic have been implemented by the affected parties (fishermen and processors, among others) through eight management councils, with the result that over-fishing has been permitted and fish stocks seriously depleted.[68]

Horizontal Implementation Structures

In addition to difficulties in producing compliance across several levels of government, difficulties may occur in coordinating activities and organizations horizontally. That is, the success of one agency's program may require the cooperation of other organizations, or at least the effective coordination of their activities. As one simple example, the Department of Health and Human Services's successful Women, Infants and Children's (WIC) program, which provides nutritional support for the groups named in its title, has been assisted by the Department of Agriculture, which has bargained to keep the price of infant formula lower so that the funds provided by WIC can go farther.

The breakdown of essential coordination can come about in several ways. One is through language and encoding difficulties. Individual agencies hire certain kinds of professionals and train all their employees in a certain manner. As a result, the housing experts in the Model Cities program decided that the problems of residents resulted from substandard housing, whereas employment experts thought that the problems arose from unemployment. Psychiatric social workers, however, perceived the problems as resulting from personality problems. Each group of professionals, in other words, was unaware of the perspectives of the other groups and consequently found it difficult to cooperate in treating the "whole client"—one of the stated objectives of the program. This was strongly demonstrated in the pattern of referrals among agencies; the vast majority of referrals of clients from one agency to another occurred within policy areas, rather than across policy areas.[69] A client who visited an agency seeking health-care services would frequently be referred to another agency, most commonly another health-care agency. Clients would much less frequently be referred to social welfare agencies for assistance in receiving funds to provide better nutrition, which might have been as effective as medical care in improving clients' health. Agencies tend to label and classify clients as belonging in their own policy areas; they often do not refer clients broadly or provide services for the client's whole range of needs. The perceptual blinders of organizations and their members prevent them from seeing all the client's needs, and their training as professionals makes it difficult for service providers to shake off their blinders.

The lack of control among agencies and the consequent deficiencies in the implementation of programs may also occur because the objectives of one organization conflict with those of other organizations. Agencies have to live, and to live they require money and personnel. Thus, at a basic level an organization may not be willing to cooperate in the implementation of a program simply because the success of another agency may threaten its own future prospects. On a somewhat higher plane, organizations may disagree about the purposes of government and about the best ways to achieve the goals about which they do agree. Or an agency may simply want to receive credit for providing a service that inevitably involves the cooperation of many organizations and, by insisting on receiving credit, may prevent anything from happening. For example, several law enforcement agencies knew about a major drug shipment, but they allowed it to slip through their fingers simply because they could not agree about which of the "cooperating" agencies would make the actual arrest and receive the media attention.

Finally, a simple failure to think about coordination may prevent effective implementation. This is the result of oversight and failure to understand linkages among programs; it is not a result of language problems or an attempt to protect an organization's turf. Even if a program can be implemented without adequate coordination with other agencies, its effectiveness may be limited, or substantial duplication of efforts may result. Most citizens have heard their share of horror stories about the same streets being dug up and repaired in successive weeks by different city departments and private utilities. Equally horrific stories are told of reporting requirements issued by a variety of federal agencies that use contradictory definitions of terms or that involve excessive duplication of effort by citizens. Venality is rarely at the root of these problems, but that does not prevent the loss of efficiency nor make citizens any happier about the problems of management in their government.

Coordination of programs appears to have become more difficult during the 1980s and 1990s. As the public sector has begun to rely more on the private sector to deliver public programs, and also to use state and local governments to deliver these services, it becomes more difficult to provide integrated services. This is true despite widespread pressure to make the public sector more "user friendly" and "customer oriented."[70] Further, effective coordination is becoming increasingly important as the interactions of programs become more evident. For example, social programs are becoming increasingly dependent on effective job training programs, and economic success is becoming increasingly dependent on educational policy.

From the Bottom Up?

It has been argued that many of the problems encountered with implementation are a function of their being considered from a "top-down" perspective.[71] That is, the person providing evaluation looks at what happens to a law and considers that the bureaucracies have failed because they have not produced outcomes exactly like those intended by the framers of the legislation. The assumption here, rather like Hood's, is that bureaucracies should march to a single drummer, and that the drummer should be Congress or the president. Expecting such an orderly approach to governance and implementation may be expecting too much from American government, given its complexity and the multiple and competing interests organized into the system. Indeed, the appropriate questions may be these: In what policy areas can we accept the slippage between goals and outcomes? and What can be done to produce greater compliance in the most sensitive areas?[72]

An alternative to the "top-down" perspective is to think of implementation from the "bottom up," or through "backward mapping."[73] This concept holds that the people who design public programs should think about the ease, or even possibility, of implementation as they design the program. Also, programs should take into account the interests of the lower echelons of the bureaucracy, their contacts with the program's clients, and indeed the values and desires of the clients themselves. With these factors in mind, policymakers should then design a set of policies that can be readily implemented. Such a program may not fulfill all the goals that the policy formulators had originally, but it will be able to gain a high degree of compliance and, in the eyes of the advocates of this approach, ultimately yield more than a program based on strict legal norms of compliance and autonomy of policy formulators.

The "bottom-up" concept of implementation and program design is appealing. It promises rather easy victories in the complicated wars involved in making programs work. Even if these promises could be fulfilled—and there must be some reasonable doubts—there are important problems with this approach, however. The most important is the normative problem that political leaders and their policy advisers have the responsibility (and usually the desire) to formulate programs that meet their political goals and to fulfill the promises made in political campaigns.[74] Programs that are easily implementable may not meet those goals. This is perhaps especially true when conservative administrations attempt to implement changes in social programs through field staffs committed to more liberal goals, or when liberals attempt to implement expansionary economic policies through more conservative economic institutions inside and outside government. Governments may wind up doing what they can do, or what they have always done, rather than what they want to do.

In addition, the ability of agency field staffs to define what is "feasible" may allow them substantially greater control over policy than may be desirable within a democratic political system. Their definition of feasibility also may be excessively conservative; with proper design, the options available for government may be much greater. Finally, there is as yet little reliable evidence about what is really feasible in implementation terms and what is really impossible.[75] Too-facile definitions of feasibility may undervalue the abilities and leadership of politicians and administrators alike.

The Third Generation?

After the original top-down and bottom-up implementation studies, and some attention to political factors in implementation, there might be said to be a third generation of thinking about the problem.[76] This generation attempts to replace these relatively simple models with more complex understandings of the relationships involved in the process of implementation. Much of the earlier literature on implementation tended to provide a single answer regardless of the question. This new approach, in contrast, tends to answer most questions about implementation with the accurate, if somewhat unsatisfying, answer "it depends."

The real task for understanding implementation then is to identify the factors that serve as contingencies for the success or failure of implementation. Some of these factors are expressly political, while others are a function of the type of policy being implemented. Still others may be a function of the organizations that are used as the agents of implementation. Specifying why a program succeeds or fails, therefore, involves the identification of all these factors and their interactions. This is a complex research task, just as it is a complex practical task to design an implementation structure that can actually make the program function in a manner close to what was intended by the people who designed it.

Summary

American government is a massive, complex, and often confusing set of institutions. It contains numerous organizations but lacks any central organizing principle. Much of the structure of American government was developed on an ad hoc basis to address particular problems at particular times. Even with a more coherent structure, many of the same problems might still arise when there is an attempt to implement a program. Many problems are inherent in any government, although they certainly are exacerbated by the complexity and diffusion of the structure of American government. For public policy, implementation is a vital step in the process of governing because it involves putting programs into action and producing effects for citizens. The difficulty in producing desired effects, or indeed any effects, then, means that policy is a much more difficult commodity to deliver to citizens than is commonly believed. The barriers to effective implementation commonly discourage individuals and organizations from engaging in the activities devised for their benefit. Public management then becomes a matter of threatening or cajoling organizations into complying with stated objectives, or a matter of convincing those organizations that what they want to accomplish can best be accomplished through the programs that have been authorized.

6. Budgeting

To implement public policies, government requires money as well as institutional structures. The budgetary process provides the means of allocating the available resources of government among the competing purposes for which they could be used. In principle, all resources in the society are available to government, although in the United States a politician who openly advocated such a position probably would not last a day. Likewise, all the purposes for which politicians and administrators wish to spend the money have some merits. The question is whether those purposes are sufficiently meritorious to justify using the resources in the public sector instead of putting those resources to use in the private sector. Finding answers to such questions requires economic and analytical judgment, as well as political estimates of the feasibility of the actions being approved.

Two different aspects of budgeting sometimes merge. One is the question of system-level allocation between the public and private sectors: How many activities or problems justify government intervention into the economy for the purpose of taxing and spending?[1] Could the best interest of society be served by keeping the money in the hands of businesses or individuals for investment and allowing some potentially beneficial programs in government to go unfunded? Or do the equity, equality, and economic growth potentially produced through a public project justify the application of political capital by officials to pass and collect an additional tax or to increase an existing one? During much of the 1980s and 1990s, the system-level questions also came to include the extent to which government should finance its expenditures with taxes and fees, or in other words, how large a deficit could the United States afford to run?[2]

The second major budgeting question is this: how should available public-sector resources be allocated among competing programs? When they devise a budget, decision makers function within resource constraints and must base their decisions on the assumption that no more revenue will come in (or that no larger deficit will be accepted). Decision makers must therefore attempt to allocate available money for the greatest social, economic, and political benefit. This is not an easy task, of course, because of differing opinions about what uses of the money would be best. In addition, decision makers are often constrained by commitments to fund existing entitlement programs, such as Social Security, before they can begin to allocate the rest of the funds to other worthy programs. Because money can be divided almost infinitely, however, it offers a medium for resolving social conflicts that indivisible forms of public benefit, such as rights, often do not. Therefore, although there are a number of possible justifications for budgetary decisions, we must be aware that political considerations tend to dominate and that many of the most effective arguments revolve around votes and coming elections.

Characteristics of the Federal Budget

Before we discuss the budget cycle through which the federal budget is constructed each year, several fundamental features of that budget should be explained. These features offer some benefits for decision makers in the federal government but also constrain them and at times help create undesirable outcomes. There are, therefore, attempts at one time or another to reform almost all these features of the budgetary process. Those reform efforts encounter resistance from the interests advantaged by the status quo, so that the process, as well as the content, of budgeting is part of the political debate.

An Executive Budget

The federal budget is an executive budget, prepared by the president and his staff, approved by Congress, and then executed by the president and the executive branch. This has not always been the case; before 1921, the federal budget was a legislative budget, prepared almost entirely by Congress and then executed by the president. One major tenet of the reform movement in the early twentieth century was that an executive budget was a necessity for more effective management in government.[3] According to that doctrine, no executive should be required to manage a budget that he or she had no part in planning.

The passage of the Budget and Accounting Act of 1921 marked a new stage in the conflict between the executive and legislative branches over their respective powers in the budgetary process.[4] In general, budgetary power has accumulated in the executive branch and in the Executive Office of the President, in large part because of the analytical dominance of the Office of Management and Budget (OMB; it was called the Bureau of the Budget until 1971). The excesses of the Nixon administration, and to some degree those of the Johnson administration during the Vietnam War, led to the development of the Congressional Budget Office (CBO) as a part of the Congressional Budget and Impoundment Control Act of 1974. The CBO provides Congress with much of the analytical capability of the executive branch, just as the development of the budget committees in both houses gives Congress greater control over budgeting than before the passage of the act in 1974. The negotiations with President Bush over the fiscal year 1991 budget appeared to give Congress much greater responsibility in framing budget options. Congress also played a major part in the 1997 budget settlement that was to contribute to attaining a balanced budget as early as fiscal year 1998.[5] Congress, however, remains essentially in the position of responding to budgetary initiatives from the White House.

Line Item

Despite several attempts at reform, the federal budget remains a line-item budget. That is, the final budget document appropriating funds allocates those funds into categories such as wages and salaries, supplies, travel, equipment, and so forth. These traditional categories are extremely useful in that they give Congress some control over the executive branch. Moneys are appropriated for agencies and are allocated for specific purposes within the agency. It is then rather easy for the legislature, through the General Accounting Office, to make sure that the money is spent under legal authority.[6] But it is difficult to determine if the money was spent efficiently and effectively. Also, the rigidities of the line-item budget may prevent good managers in government from managing effectively by limiting how they can spend the money. It may be that more equipment and less personnel can do the same job better or more cheaply or both, but managers generally are not given that option.

Critics have argued that it would be better to give a manager a relatively unrestricted budget and then judge him or her on the achievement of program goals with that money. Congress, however, tends to want to maximize its oversight over the executive instead of offering managerial flexibility. In the late 1990s Congress, through the Government Performance and Results Act of 1993, has attempted to overlay the fundamental line-item nature of the budget with a more performance-based system of assessment and allocation. That system has yet to be implemented, and it may well be that the older patterns of emphasizing financial control rather than performance will come to dominate even a reformed budget process.

An Annual Budget

The federal budget is primarily an annual budget. Agencies are now required to submit five-year expenditure forecasts associated with each of their expenditure plans, but this is primarily for management purposes within the Office of Management and Budget. The budget presented to Congress and eventually the appropriations bills of Congress together constitute only a one-year expenditure plan. The absence of a more complete multiyear budget makes planning difficult for federal managers and does not necessarily alert Congress to the long-term implications of expenditure decisions made in any one year. A small expenditure in one year may result in much larger expenditures in subsequent years and create clientele who cannot be eliminated without significant political repercussions. Conversely, a project that would have to run several years to be truly effective may be terminated after a single year. Many state and local governments in the United States now operate with multiyear budgets, but the federal government still does not. The annual advice from OMB to the agencies as a guide for preparing budgets provides some information about expectations for five years, but the information for the four "out years" is speculative at best.

One of the several recommendations of the Gore Commission (the National Performance Review) was to move toward a biennial budget.[7] The logic behind such a move would be to enable organizations to plan more effectively and therefore to deliver services more efficiently. Further, this reform might enable Congress to reduce the amount of time that it has to spend on the budget and enable it to spend more time performing its other legislative duties. Again, however, Congress does not appear to be very excited about this reform, which might lessen its control over the organizations within the executive branch. Likewise, there has been little enthusiasm for capital budgeting and better identification of the investment aspects of federal expenditures.[8]

The Budget Cycle

Each year there must be a new budget, and an annual cycle has evolved for the appropriation and expenditure of available public moneys. The repetitive nature of the budget cycle is important, for the agency officials involved might behave differently if they did not know that they have to come back year after year to obtain more money from the same OMB officials and the same congressmen. In addition to the emphasis this repetition places on trust and dependability, it allows policy entrepreneurs multiple opportunities to build their cases for new programs and changes in budgetary allocations. If they fail one year they can try the next, and if they fail in one institutional setting they can try in another.

Setting the Parameters:
The President and His Friends

Most of this chapter discusses the micro-level allocation of resources among programs, rather than the setting of broad expenditure and economic management policy. It is necessary, however, to begin with a brief discussion of decisions concerning overall levels of expenditure and revenue. The budget process is initiated by a number of decisions about total spending levels, and those decisions about parameters influence subsequent decisions about programs. Inevitably changes in particular programs and socioeconomic conditions (wars, recessions, and the like) will influence the overall spending levels of government, so this stage is largely one of setting targets rather than making final decisions.

The first official act of the budget cycle is the development, each spring, of estimates of the total size of the federal budget to be prepared for the fiscal year. Although agencies and the OMB will already have begun to discuss and prepare expenditure plans, the letter from the president through the OMB (usually in June) is an important first step in the formal process. This letter is a statement of overall presidential budgetary strategy and of the financial limits within which agencies should begin to prepare their budgets. In addition to setting the overall parameters, this letter presents more detailed information on how those parameters apply to individual agencies. Also, the past experience of budgeting officials in each agency gives them some idea of how to interpret the general parameters. Defense agencies, for example, knew during the Cold War era that they were not necessarily bound by those parameters, whereas planners of domestic programs with little client support and few friends on Capitol Hill could only hope to do as well as the letter had led them to believe they might.

The overall estimates for spending are prepared some sixteen months before the budget goes into effect. For example, the fiscal year 1999 budget went into effect on 1 October 1998, but the planning for that budget began in June 1997 or earlier. For any budget, this means that the economic forecasts on which the expenditure estimates are based may be far from the prevailing economic reality when the budget is actually executed. Any deviations from those economic forecasts are significant. The recession of 1991, for example, meant a reduction in revenues and an increase in expenditures; people who are out of work do not pay income and Social Security taxes and they demand unemployment insurance payments and perhaps welfare. These important economic forecasts are not entirely the product of technical considerations; they are also influenced by political and ideological considerations. For example, during the first years of the Reagan administration the belief that "supply-side" economics would produce larger revenues through increased economic activity led to a serious overestimation of the amount of revenue to be expected. This, in turn, was the beginning of the large federal deficits that were a feature of American public finance for over fifteen years.[9] In the early 1990s the Bush administration's belief that the recession would be short-lived also produced larger actual deficits than those promised in budget documents.

The preparation of economic and expenditure estimates is the result of the interaction of three principal actors: the Council of Economic Advisers (CEA), the OMB, and the Treasury. Collectively, these three are referred to as the "troika."[10] The CEA is, as the name implies, a group of economists who advise the president. Organizationally, they are located in the Executive Office of the President. The role of the CEA is largely technical, forecasting the state of the economy and advising the president on the basis of these forecasts. They also mathematically model the probable effects of budgetary choices on the economy. Of course, the economics of the CEA must be tempered with political judgment, for mathematical models and economists do not run for office, although presidents must. One chairman of the Council of Economic Advisers in the Reagan administration said that he relied on his "visceral computer" for some of the more important predictions.[11]

The OMB, despite its image as a budget-controlling organization, comes as close to being an agency representative of the expenditure community as exists within the troika. Even though the agencies whose budgets OMB supervises find it difficult to perceive the OMB as a benefactor, some of its personnel may be favorably disposed toward expenditures. They see the huge volume of agency requests coming forward, and they are aware of the large volume of "uncontrollable" expenditures (e.g., Social Security benefits) that will have to be appropriated regardless of changes in economic circumstances. These considerations of commitments and inertia were not as important under the Reagan and Bush administrations as during previous administrations, in part because of the political commitment of several directors of the OMB to reducing federal expenditures. The Clinton administration has also grappled with the problem of entitlement spending,[12] reflecting in part the fear that these programs will swamp the entire budget process, and in part the administration's desire for some latitude to launch new programs.

Finally, the Treasury represents the financial community, and historically it has been the major advocate of a balanced budget within the troika. The Treasury, through issuing government bonds, must cover any debts created by a deficit. The principal interest of the Treasury in troika negotiations often is to preserve the confidence of the financial community at home and abroad in the soundness of the U.S. economy and the government's management of that economy. Some particular (and increasing) concerns of the Treasury may be relationships with international financial organizations, such as the International Monetary Fund, that are important for maintaining international confidence.

Even at this first step in the budgetary process, a great deal of hard political and economic bargaining occurs. Each member of the troika must compete for the attention of the president as well as protect the interests of the particular professional, organizational, and political community it represents. But this is just the beginning of a long series of bargains, as agencies attempt to get the money they want and need from the budgetary process.

Agency Requests

As in so much American policymaking, the agency is a central actor in the budgetary process.[13] Whether working independently or in a cabinet-level department, the agency is responsible for the initial preparation of estimates and requests for funding. The agency makes these preparations in conjunction with the OMB and, if applicable, with the agency's executive department budgeting personnel. During the preparation of estimates, OMB provides guidance and advice about total levels of expenditure and particular aspects of the agency's budget. Likewise, the agency may have to coordinate its activities with those of other agencies within the executive department in which it is located. Accomplished through a departmental budget committee and the secretary's staff, this coordination is necessary to ensure that the agency is operating within presidential priorities and that the secretary will provide support in defending the agency's budget to OMB and Congress.

The task of the agency in the budgetary process is to be aggressive in seeking to expand its own expenditure base but at the same time to recognize that it is only one part of a larger organization.[14] In other words, the agency must be aggressive but reasonable, seeking more money but realizing that it operates within the constraints of what the federal government as a whole can afford. Likewise, the executive department must recognize its responsibilities to the president and his program and to agencies under its umbrella. The cabinet secretary must be a major spokesperson for his or her agencies at higher governmental levels, but at the same time agencies often have more direct support from interest groups and perhaps from Congress than does the department as a whole. Thus, a cabinet secretary may not be able to go far in following the president's program if that seriously jeopardizes ongoing programs, and their clienteles, in the department. This problem reflects the general fragmentation of American government, with much of the power and the operational connections between government and the interest groups being at the agency, rather than the departmental, level.

An agency may employ a number of strategies in seeking to expand its funding, but the use of these strategies is restrained by the knowledge that budgeting is an annual cycle. Any strategic choice in a single year may preclude the use of that strategy in later years and, perhaps more important, may destroy any confidence that OMB and Congress have had in the agency.[15] For example, an agency may employ the "camel's nose" or "thin wedge" strategy to get modest initial funding for a program, with the knowledge that the program will have rapidly increasing expenditure requirements. Even if that strategy is successful once, the agency may be assured that any future requests for new spending authority will be carefully scrutinized. Therefore, agencies may be well advised to pursue careful, long-term strategies and to develop trust among the political leaders who determine their budgets.

Executive Review

After the agency has decided on its requests, it passes them on to the OMB for review. The OMB is a presidential agency, and one of its principal tasks is to amass all the agency requests and conform them to presidential policy priorities and to the overall levels of expenditure desired. This may make for a tight fit, as some spending programs are difficult or impossible to control, leaving little space for any new programs the president may consider important. The more conservative presidents of the recent past also have found it difficult to make overall spending levels conform with their views that government should tax and spend less.

After OMB receives the estimates, it passes them on to its budget examiners for review. In the rare case in which an agency has actually requested the amount, or less than the amount, that OMB had planned to give it, there is no problem. In most cases, however, the examiners must depend on their experience with the agencies in question, as well as whatever information about programs and projected expenditures they can collect, to make judgments about the necessity and priority of any requested expenditure increases. And, as with so many decisions about public finance, much depends on the trust that has developed among individuals across time. In this case, the examiners spend a great deal of their time in the agencies they supervise, and they may adopt a stance more favorable to the agency than might be expected, given the image of OMB as a tough budget-cutting organization.

On the basis of agency requests and the information developed by the examiner, OMB holds hearings, usually in October or November. At these hearings the agency must defend its requests before the examiner and other members of the OMB staff. Although OMB sometimes seems to be committed to cutting expenditures, several factors prevent it from wielding its ax with excessive vigor. First, it is frequently not difficult for an agency to pull an "end run" on the hearing board by appealing to the director of OMB, the president, or ultimately to its friends in Congress. Also, some budget examiners tend, over time, to favor the agencies they are supposed to control, so at times they may be advocates of an agency's requests rather than the fiscal conservatives they are expected to be. This is a pattern not dissimilar to that of regulatory "capture," described in chapter 4.

The results of the hearing are forwarded to the director of OMB for the "director's review," which involves all the top staff of the bureau. At this stage, through additional trimming and negotiation, the staff tries to pare the final budget down to the amount desired by the president. After each portion of the budget goes through the director's review, it is forwarded to the president for final review and then for compilation into the final budget document. This stage necessarily involves final appeals from agency and department personnel to OMB and the president as well as last-minute adjustments to take into account unanticipated changes in economic forecasts and desired changes in the total size of the budget. The presidential budget is then prepared for delivery to Congress within fifteen days after it convenes in January. Presidents differ in the amount of time they devote to budgeting, but the budget is perceived as a statement of the priorities of the president and his administration, even if it is really prepared by OMB.

In this way the presidential budget is made ready to be reviewed for appropriations by Congress, but the two branches will already have begun to communicate about the budget. By 10 November of each year the president must submit to Congress the "current services budget," which includes "proposed budget authority and estimated outlays that would be included in the budget for the ensuing fiscal year ... if all programs and activities were carried on at the same level as the fiscal year in progress."[16] This is a form of "volume budgeting," for it budgets for a constant volume of public services.[17] Given the rate of inflation in the 1970s and early 1980s, this constant-service budget gave Congress an early warning of the anticipated size of current expenditure commitments if they were to be extended. But such estimates are subject to substantial inaccuracy, either purposive or accidental, and they provide Congress only a rough estimate for planning purposes.

Congressional Action

Although Congress is specifically granted the powers of the purse in the Constitution, by the 1960s and 1970s it had clearly ceased to be the dominant actor in making budgetary decisions. Congress then attempted a counterattack, largely through the Congressional Budget and Impoundment Control Act of 1974. Among other provisions, this act established in each house of Congress a budget committee to be responsible for developing two concurrent resolutions each year outlining fiscal policy constraints on expenditures, much as the troika does in the executive branch. The act also established the Congressional Budget Office to provide the budget committees a staff capacity analogous to that which OMB provides the president.[18] This

House Speaker Newt Gingrich leads Republican congressional leaders in announcing that they have reached agreement with the president on a compromise plan to balance the budget. (AP/Wide World Photos)

enhanced analytic capacity is important for Congress in understanding its budgetary activity, but the need to implement somewhat more immediate and less analytic expenditure reforms has tended to make these changes less important than they might otherwise have been.

Decisions on how to allocate total spending among agencies and programs are made by the appropriations committees in both houses.[19] These are extremely prestigious and powerful committees, and those serving on them are veteran members of Congress. Members tend to remain on these committees for long periods, thereby developing not only budgetary expertise but also political ties with the agencies they supervise in addition to their ties to their own constituencies.[20] These two committees, and especially the House Appropriations Committee, do most of their work in subcommittees. These subcommittees may cover one executive department, such as Defense, or a number of agencies, such as Housing and Urban Development and independent executive agencies, or a function, such as public works. Most important, the whole committee does not closely scrutinize the decisions of its subcommittees, nor does the House of Representatives as a whole frequently reverse the decisions of its appropriations committee.

Scrutiny by the whole House has increased, in large part because of the general opening of congressional deliberations to greater "sunshine," or public scrutiny. In addition, the politics of deficit reduction has tended to place greater restraints on committee and subcommittee autonomy. The committees must now submit appropriation levels that correspond to the total spending levels permitted under the joint resolutions on taxing and spending. Provided that the committees can stay within those predetermined levels, they have substantial autonomy; once an agency's budget has been agreed to in a subcommittee, that budget has, in all probability, been largely decided.[21]

Beginning with the presidential recommendations, each subcommittee develops an appropriations bill, or occasionally two, for a total of thirteen or fourteen bills each year. Hearings are held, and agency personnel are summoned to testify and to justify the size of their desired appropriation. After those hearings, the subcommittee will "mark up" the bill—make such changes as it feels are necessary from the original proposals—and then submit it, first to the entire committee and then to the House of Representatives. In accordance with the Congressional Budget Act, appropriations committees are expected have completed mark-ups of all appropriations bills before submitting the first for final passage, so as to have a better overall idea of the level of expenditure that would be approved. The Senate follows a similar procedure, and any differences between the two houses are resolved in a conference committee.

This procedure in Congress needs to be finished by 15 September in order for the budget to be ready to go into effect on 1 October; but the Congressional Budget Act also requires the passage of a second, concurrent resolution setting forth the budget ceilings, revenue floors, and overall fiscal policy considerations governing the passage of the appropriations bills. Because there will undoubtedly be differences in the ways in which the two houses make their appropriations figures correspond with the figures in the concurrent resolution, the reconciliation bill, in which both houses agree on the spending totals, must be passed by 25 September.

While the reconciliation bill appears to be a technicality, the Reagan administration used this opportunity to impose its budgetary will at the beginning of the administration;[22] the 1996 welfare reforms also technically came about as a part of a reconciliation bill. Further, the need to pass a single reconciliation bill tends to move power away from the appropriations committees and subcommittees and to centralize it in the leadership, especially in the House of Representatives.[23] After all these stages, the budget (in the form of the various appropriations bills) is ready to go to the president for his signature and execution.

Budget Execution
Once money has been appropriated for the executive branch, the agencies

must develop mechanisms for spending that money. An appropriations warrant, drawn by the Treasury and countersigned by the General Accounting Office, is sent to each agency. The agency then makes plans for its expenditures for the year, on the basis of this warrant, and submits a plan to OMB for apportionment of the funds. The funds appropriated by Congress are usually made available to the agencies on a quarterly basis, but for some agencies there may be great differences in the amounts made available each quarter. For example, the National Park Service spends a very large proportion of its annual appropriation during the summer because of the demands on the national parks at that time. Two principal reasons for allowing agencies access to only a quarter of their funds at a time are to provide greater control over spending and to prevent an agency from spending everything early in the year and then requiring a supplemental appropriation (see pp. 144–45). This still happens, but apportionment helps to control any potential profligacy.

The procedures for executing the budget are relatively simple when the executive branch actually wants to spend the money appropriated; they become more complex when the president decides he does not want to spend the appropriated funds. Prior to the Congressional Budget Act of 1974, a president had at least a customary right to impound funds, that is, to refuse to spend them.[24] Numerous impoundments during the Nixon administration (e.g., half the money appropriated for implementing the Federal Water Pollution Control Act Amendments of 1972 was impounded from the 1973 to 1975 budgets) forced Congress to take action to control the executive and to reassert its customary powers over the purse.

The Congressional Budget and Impoundment Control Act of 1974 was designed to limit the ability of the president to use impoundment as an indirect means of overruling Congress when he has not been able to achieve this through the normal legislative process (the water-pollution control legislation had been passed over a presidential veto). The 1974 act defined two kinds of impoundment. *Rescissions* are cancellations of budgetary authority to spend money. A president may decide that a program could reach its goals with less money or simply that there are good reasons not to spend the money. The president must then send a message to Congress requesting the rescission, and Congress must act positively on this request within forty-five days; if it does not, the money is made available to the agency for obligation (see table 6.1, p. 136). Congress can, however, also rescind money on its own by passing a resolution in both houses withdrawing the agency's authority to spend.

Deferrals, in contrast, are requests merely to delay making the obligational authority available to the agency. In this case, if either house of Congress does not exercise its veto power, the deferral is granted. The comptrol-

TABLE 6.1

RESCISSIONS PROPOSED AND ENACTED, BY PRESIDENT

President	Number proposed	Number accepted	Amount proposed (in millions)	Amount enacted (in millions)
Ford	152	52	$ 7,935.0	$ 1,252.2
Carter	89	50	4,608.5	2,116.1
Reagan	602	214	43,436.6	15,656.8
Bush	169	34	13,293.0	2,354.0
Clinton[a]	125	82	6,153.9	3,308.5

SOURCE: General Accounting Office, *Frequency and Amount of Rescissions*, OGC-97-59 (Washington, D.C.: GAO, 26 September 1997).

a. Through 1996.

ler general (head of the General Accounting Office) is given the power to classify specific presidential actions, and at times the difference between a deferral and a rescission is not clear. For example, attempting to defer funds for programs scheduled to be phased out is, in practice, a rescission. These reforms in the impoundment powers of the president have substantially increased the powers of Congress in determining how much money will indeed be spent by the federal government each year.

Budget Control

After the president and the executive branch have spent the money appropriated, Congress must check to be sure that the money was spent legally and properly. The General Accounting Office (GAO) and its head, the comptroller general, are responsible for the postexpenditure audit of federal expenditures. Each year the comptroller general's report to Congress outlines deviations from congressional intent. Requests from individual congressmen or committees may produce earlier and perhaps more detailed evaluations of agency spending or policies. Each year the GAO provides Congress and the interested public with hundreds of evaluations of expenditures.

The GAO has undergone a major transformation from a simple accounting organization into a policy-analytic organization for the legislative branch.[25] It has become concerned not only with the legality of expenditures but also with the efficiency with which the money is spent. Although GAO reports on the efficiency of expenditures have no legal authority, any agency that wishes to maintain its good relations with Congress would be well advised to take those findings into account. Congress will certainly be cognizant of those recommendations when it reviews agency budgets the following year and will expect to see some changes. These GAO recommendations also form one part of the ongoing process of congressional oversight of administration. The problem with GAO controls—whether of an accounting or a more policy-analytic nature—is that they are largely ex post facto, meaning that the money will probably have been spent long before the determination is made that it has been spent either illegally or unwisely.

Summary

A long and complex process is required to perform the difficult tasks of allocating federal budget money among competing agencies. The process takes almost eighteen months and involves many bargains and decisions. From all this bargaining and analysis emerges a plan for spending billions of dollars. But even this complex process, made more complex by numerous reforms of congressional budgeting procedures and deficit fighting procedures, cannot control all federal expenditures as completely as some would desire, nor can it provide the level of fiscal management that may be necessary for a smoothly functioning economic system. Let us now turn to a few problems that presidents and congressmen face in making the budgetary process an effective allocative process. Because it is inherently political as well as economic, the process may never be as "rational" as some would like, but there are identifiable problems that cause particular difficulty.

Problems in the Budgetary Process

The major problems arising in the budgetary process of the federal government affect the fiscal management function of budgeting as well as the allocation of resources among agencies. It is difficult, if not impossible, for any president or Congress to make binding decisions as to how much money will be spent in any year, or even as to who will spend it for what, and this absence of basic controls makes the entire process subject to error. Those elected to make policy and control spending frequently find themselves incapable of producing the kinds of program or budgetary changes they campaigned for, and this can result in disillusionment for both leaders and citizens.

The Deficit

The deficit has been a major driving force for budget reform in the United States, and deficits and public debt are very negative symbols in American political discourse. Given the ideological baggage associated with these terms, it has been difficult at times to discuss them rationally. The definition of the deficit at the federal level is itself something of an artifact of a number of decisions made about the nature of the public sector and its budget. The most obvious is that we tend to discuss the federal deficit in isolation from state and local governments (see p. 143). Given the ability of the federal government to shift some of its burdens to lower levels of government, looking at only one level of government may give a false impression of the state of public finance (see table 2.3, p. 38).

A less obvious problem in calculating the federal deficit is the role that Social Security funds now play in reducing the deficit. At present the Social Security Trust Fund is receiving substantially more (roughly $38 billion per year) in tax income than it is having to pay out to retirees, but this situation will change around 2010, when large numbers of "baby boomers" begin to retire. In the meantime, the extra income has enabled the Clinton administration to balance the budget (see table 6.2).[26] This definition of the budget as including Social Security funds helps government leaders in the short term, but it presents immense long-term challenges.

TABLE 6.2

ESTIMATED FEDERAL BUDGET DEFICITS
WITH AND WITHOUT SOCIAL SECURITY
(IN BILLIONS OF DOLLARS)

	With Social Security	*Without* Social Security
1997	−21.9	−103.3
1998	−10.0	−106.3
1999	9.5	−95.7
2000	8.5	−104.9
2001	28.2	−94.1
2002	89.7	−44.6
2003	82.8	−62.8

SOURCE: Calculated from Office of Management and Budget, *Budget of the United States* (annual).

Another less obvious definitional problem in the federal budget is the absence of a separate capital budget. All state governments in the United States save one (Vermont) must, according to their state constitutions, run balanced budgets. They do, however, place capital projects—roads, bridges, schools, and the like—into a separate capital budget, and they can borrow money, through issuing bonds, to build those projects. The federal budget does not separate capital from current expenditures in this way. A good deal of federal borrowing is for projects for which borrowing funds is surely reasonable; even good fiscal conservatives borrow money to buy houses or automobiles. With that in mind, the usual (if inaccurate) analogy with the private household can be maintained even if government borrows extensively. Removing the amount of federal spending that reasonably could be labeled "capital" from the total budget would produce a very different picture of the deficit; indeed, the federal government could be seen to have been running a surplus, or at least a much smaller deficit, for a number of years.

This discussion about Social Security funds and capital budgeting should make it clear that many of the terms used in public policy have no single, accepted definition. In fact, definitions, like all other parts of the process, are constructed politically. It pays for incumbent politicians to calculate the deficit with Social Security revenues counted in, although some fiscal conservatives argue that this is actually a misuse of these funds and that the entire system should be privatized to prevent just such "abuses" (see chapter 11). Likewise, it pays for conservatives to calculate the deficit with capital expenditures included, while liberals would argue for excluding those figures from the totals.

Uncontrollable Expenditures

Many expenditure programs in the federal government cannot be controlled in any one year without policy changes that may be politically unpalatable.[27] For example, a president or Congress can do very little to control the level of expenditure for Social Security in any one year without either changing the criteria for eligibility or altering the formula for indexation (adjustment of the benefits for changes in consumer prices or workers' earnings) of the program. Either policy choice would produce a major political conflict and might well be impossible. Some minor changes, such as changing the tax treatment of Social Security benefits for beneficiaries with other income, may be entertained, but the basic expenditure level for the program is essentially uncontrollable.

Much of the federal budget is uncontrollable in any one year (see table 6.3, p. 140). The most important uncontrollable expenditures are the large entitlement programs of social welfare spending such as Social Security, Medicare, and unemployment benefits. These expenditures are uncontrollable both because they cannot be readily reduced and because government cannot accurately estimate while planning the budget exactly how much money will be needed for the programs. The final expenditure levels will depend on levels of inflation, illness, and unemployment, as well as on the number of eligible citizens who actually take advantage of the programs. In addition, outstanding contracts and obligations constitute a significant share of the uncontrollable portion of the budget, although these can be altered over several years, if not in a single year. The major controllable component of the federal budget is the defense budget. The end of the Cold War has made this a particularly attractive target for budget cutting, although the ap-

TABLE 6.3

CHANGES IN "UNCONTROLLABLE" FEDERAL EXPENDITURES

(IN PERCENTAGES)

	1976	1980	1990	1991	1992	1993	1995
Controllable	63.7	46.8	40.0	40.4	38.7	37.2	34.6
Uncontrollable	36.3	53.2	60.0	59.6	61.3	62.8	65.4

SOURCE: Office of Management and Budget, *Special Analyses of the FY 1995 U.S. Budget* (Washington, D.C.: Government Printing Office, annual).

parent shift from large strategic forces to tactical (personnel-intensive) forces may reduce the overall savings.

The uncontrollable element of the budget has meant that even a president committed to the goals of reducing federal expenditures and producing a balanced budget (without figuring in a short-term Social Security surplus) will find it difficult to determine where the expenditure reductions will come from. Congress has begun to grapple with these expenditures but finds the political forces of entitlements difficult to overcome.[28] Some discretionary social expenditures have been reduced in recent years, but the bulk of federal expenditures have continued to increase and are likely to continue to increase. Thus, any president coming into office with a desire to balance the budget by reducing federal spending will soon find it difficult to do so.

Back-Door Spending

Linked to the problem of uncontrollable expenditures is "back-door spending"—expenditure decisions that are not actually made through the formal appropriations process. These expenditures to some degree reflect an institutional conflict within Congress, between the appropriations committees and the substantive policy committees. They also reflect the difficulties of coordinating the huge number of spending decisions that must be made each year through formal, and somewhat recondite, procedures. There are three principal kinds of back-door spending: borrowing authority, contract authority, and permanent appropriations.

BORROWING AUTHORITY

Agencies are sometimes allowed to spend public money not appropriated by Congress if they borrow that money from the Treasury—for student-loan guarantees, for instance.[29] It has been argued that these are not actually public expenditures because the money will presumably be repaid eventually. In many instances, however, federal loans have been written off, and, even if the loans are repaid, the government may not know when that repayment will occur. Further, the ability of government to control expenditure levels for purposes of economic management is seriously impaired when the authority to make spending decisions is so widely diffused.

The pressure of all these contingent obligations is becoming more evident to government, and it is reducing some of the glee about the apparent end of the federal deficit.[30] The federal government has been able to reduce directly budgeted expenditures, but there are few effective controls over loans, loan guarantees, or insurance obligations. For example, there are a dozen major federal insurance programs with authority to borrow over $60 billion.[31] As much as some decision makers would like to impose firmer budget ceilings for these programs, finding the way to do so and preserve all their insurance coverage is difficult.

CONTRACT AUTHORITY

Agencies also may enter into contracts that bind the federal government to pay a certain amount for specified goods and services without going through the appropriations process. Then, after the contract is let, the appropriations committees are placed in the awkward position of either authorizing the funds to pay off the debt or forcing the agency to renege on its debts. While this kind of spending is uncontrollable in the short run, any agency attempting to engage in this circumvention of the appropriations committees probably will face the ire of those committees when attempting to have its annual budget approved. Also, Congress has been developing rules that make it increasingly difficult for agencies to engage in spending of this type.

PERMANENT APPROPRIATIONS

Certain programs have authorizing legislation that requires the spending of certain amounts of money. The largest expenditure of this kind is payment of interest on the public debt, which constituted over 12 percent of total federal expenditures in 1997. Likewise, federal support of land-grant colleges is a permanent appropriation that began during the administration of Abraham Lincoln. In the case of a permanent appropriation, the appropriations committees have little discretion unless they choose to renege on these standing commitments of the government.

The Overhang

Money appropriated by Congress for a fiscal year need not actually be spent during that fiscal year; it must only be obligated. That is, the agency must contract to spend the money, or otherwise make commitments about how it will be spent, with the actual outlay of funds coming perhaps some years later. In 1997 there was a total budget authority of about $2.71 trillion (see figure 6.1, p. 142) with only $1.6 trillion being appropriated during that

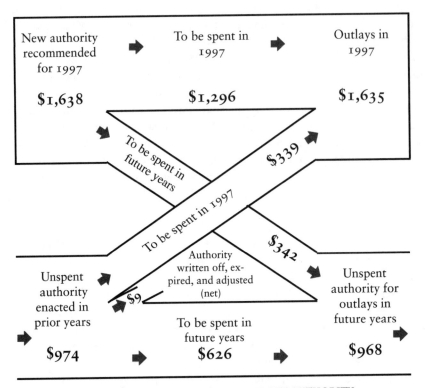

FIGURE 6.1. RELATIONSHIP OF BUDGET AUTHORITY
TO OUTLAYS FOR FY 1997
(IN BILLIONS OF DOLLARS)

year.[32] Thus, the "overhang" was almost two-thirds as large as the amount of money appropriated by Congress during that fiscal year. The president and the executive agencies could not actually spend all that overhang in the single fiscal year (a good deal of it is in long-term contracts), but it represents a substantial amount in unspent obligations for the agencies and the government as a whole.

The major problem is that the overhang makes it difficult for a president to use the budget as an instrument of economic management. One principal component of economic management, even in a post-Keynesian era, is the amount of public expenditure; because of the overhang, the president and Congress cannot always control the actual outlay of funds. The agencies may have sufficient budget authority, convertible into actual outlays, to damage presidential forecasts of outlays. They would do this, not out of malice, but out of a perceived need to keep their programs operating as they thought best, especially if the president was seeking to restrict the creation of new obligational authority.

Intergovernmental Budget Control

Although it does not specifically affect the federal budgetary process, the lack of overall fiscal control in the public sector of the United States makes it impossible for the federal government to control total public expenditures and hence to exercise the kind of fiscal management it might like. Just as a president cannot control the overhang within the federal government, he cannot control the taxing and spending decisions of thousands of state and local governments.

The federal government itself spends only about two-thirds of the total amount of money spent by governments in the United States. It has the capacity to stimulate state and local government expenditures through matching grants, but encouraging reductions in expenditures is more difficult. The federal government has even less control over revenue collection. For example, in 1963 the Kennedy administration pushed through a tax cut for the federal government, only to have almost the entire effect of that cut negated by state and local tax increases. The federal tax cut in the 1980s was also offset (albeit somewhat more slowly) by increases in state and local taxation.[33]

The principles of federalism would appear to reserve to state and local governments a perfect right to decide on their own levels of revenues and expenditures. However, in an era in which the public budget is important for economic management as well as for the distribution of funds among organizations, there may be a need for greater overall control of expenditures. This control need not be imposed unilaterally by the federal government, but it could perhaps be arranged through "diplomacy" among representatives of the several levels of government as it is in Germany and to some extent in Canada.[34] The potential effects on economic performance of uncoordinated fiscal policies were to some degree reflected by the presence of large state and local government surpluses in the mid-1980s, at the same time that the federal government was running large deficits.[35] Depending on one's point of view, this was either a good thing (helping to reduce total public borrowing) or a bad thing (counteracting the economic stimulus of the deficit). In either case, it represented the absence of an integrated fiscal policy within the United States.

Reprogramming and Transfers

The first four problems we have identified in the federal budgetary process affect primarily the total level of expenditures. The next two problems, reprogramming and transfers, affect levels of spending by individual agencies and the purposes for which the agencies spend their money.

Reprogramming is a shifting of funds within a specific appropriations account. When Congress passes an appropriations bill, that bill contains a number of appropriations accounts, which in turn contain a number of program elements. For example, the appropriations bill for the Department of Agriculture contains an appropriations account for crop supports, with separate program elements for cotton, corn, wheat, and so on. Reprogramming involves shifting obligational authority from one program element to another. The procedures for making reprogramming decisions has been thoroughly developed only in the Department of Defense. In general, there is a threshold (variable by agency) below which agencies are relatively free to reprogram funds, but above which they require approval from appropriations committee or subcommittee personnel, although not from the entire Congress. There are also requirements for reporting reprogramming decisions to the appropriations committees.

Transfers are more serious actions, for they involve moving funds from one appropriations account to another. In the Department of Agriculture, this might involve shifting funds from crop supports to the Farmers Home Administration or to rural electrification. Transfer funds have been subject to significant abuse and circumvention of congressional authority, especially during the Nixon administration and the Vietnam War. And, as with reprogramming—outside the Department of Defense—few established procedures exist for controlling the use of transfer funds other than those that specifically forbid the use of such funds for certain functions.

Both reprogramming and transfer funds are important in providing the executive branch with some flexibility in implementing its programs and in using public funds more effectively. These opportunities have been the subject of many abuses, however, and they are ripe for reform and improvement. In particular, they frequently allow an agency to circumvent the judgment of the entire Congress through an appeal to the appropriations committee, or perhaps even to its chairman.

Supplemental Appropriations

Even with the apportionment of funds mentioned earlier, agencies may require supplemental appropriations—those made outside the normal budget cycle—to cover shortfalls during the fiscal year. Agencies sometimes simply run out of money. This can result from improper management, but more often it happens because of changes in the demand for services or because of poor estimates of demand for a new service. For example, during a recession, the demand for unemployment assistance will naturally increase, and supplemental funding will be required. Likewise, a year of poor weather may force additional funding for crop insurance in the Department of Agriculture. Or a new program, such as food stamps, may acquire more clients than anyone anticipated during the early years of its existence.

Supplemental appropriations are not insignificant amounts of money. In

1996 a net of some $3.52 billion was appropriated through supplementals. While a few supplemental actions were to reduce the amounts appropriated, the additions to agency obligational authority ranged from $1.8 million for land acquisition for the U.S. Fish and Wildlife Service to almost $500 million for the Department of Defense (for additional expenses incurred in operations in Somalia and Bosnia). There was also $225.5 million for the Soil Conservation Service to help recovery from disastrous floods in the Midwest. The changes in budget procedure required by deficit reduction strategies (see pp. 156–57) have reduced the size of supplemental appropriations, but they still constitute a potential avenue for additional funding.

The request for supplemental appropriations may be a useful strategy for agencies attempting to expand their funding. An agency may be able to initiate a program with minimal appropriations through the usual budgetary process, anticipating a wide acceptance of its program by prospective clients, and then return to Congress for supplemental appropriations when clients do indeed materialize and demand benefits. Supplemental appropriations frequently are not scrutinized as carefully as are regular appropriations, and this relative invisibility may permit friendly congressmen to hide a rapidly expanding program. The level of scrutiny has increased because of recent requirements for expenditures proposals to be "deficit neutral," but supplementals still are usually easier to push through than are regular appropriations. But obvious and frequent abuse of the supplemental appropriations process will damage the relationship between the agency and Congress. In the long run, that may hurt more than help the agency in expanding its expenditure base, given the importance of trust in the politics of the budgetary process.

Assessing the Outcomes: Incrementalism or What?

One standard description of changes in budgetary allocations in the United States is *incremental*. Any number of meanings are attached to this word.[36] Broadly, incrementalism means that changes in an agency's budget from year to year tend to be predictable. More specifically, incrementalism has taken on several additional interpretations. First, incremental decision making is described as a process that is not "synoptic," or not fully "rational."[37] That is, it does not involve examining sweeping alternatives to the status quo and then making a decision about the optimal use of budgetary resources. Rather, incremental decision making involves "successive limited comparisons," or the sequential examination of marginal changes from the status quo and decisions about whether to make these marginal adjustments to current policies.[38] An incremental decision-making process tends to build on earlier decisions by seeking means to improve the existing situation rather than altering current policies or budgetary priorities completely. In budgetary terms this means that an agency can expect to receive in any year approximately what it received the previous year, plus a little more to adjust for inflation or expanded services.

Advocates of incremental decision making argue that this method of making policy choices is actually more rational than the synoptic method. Because it provides an experiential base from which to work, the incremental method offers a greater opportunity to make good policy choices than does the apparently more rational synoptic method. In addition, errors made in an incremental decision-making process can be more easily reversed than can major changes made in a synoptic process. In many ways incremental decision making is a cost-minimizing form of rationality rather than a benefit-maximizing approach. Incrementalism reduces costs, first, by limiting the range of alternatives and thereby limiting the research and calculation costs for decision makers; and, second, by reducing the costs of change, particularly of error correction. Because in an incremental world few choices involve significant deviations from existing policies or appropriations, there is little need to make major adjustments either in the actual programs or in the thought patterns of decision makers about the policies. Given the limited calculative capacity of human beings, even with the aid of modern technology, and the resistance of most individuals and organizations to change, incrementalism can be argued to be a rational means for making choices.

The term incrementalism also is used to describe the pattern of outcomes of the budgetary process. In particular, Otto A. Davis, M.A.H. Dempster, and Aaron Wildavsky demonstrated a great deal of stability in the increases in agency appropriations from year to year.[39] The changes in budgets are not only small but also quite stable and predictable, so the best estimate of an agency's budget in one year is the previous year's budget plus a stable percentage increase. Some agencies grow more rapidly than others, but each exhibits a stable pattern of growth.

Several factors contribute to the persistence of incremental budgeting in the United States. One is that such a large percentage of the budget is uncontrollable that few significant changes in appropriations can be made from year to year. Also, most empirical examinations of incremental budgeting have been made during periods of relative economic stability and high rates of economic growth; under less favorable economic conditions, the incrementalism appropriate for rich and predictable budgeting systems becomes less applicable.[40] Such a change in the economic climate of budgeting is to some degree reflected in the reform efforts described later (pp. 155–58).

Most important, the repetitive and sequential nature of budgeting tends to produce incremental budget outcomes. A budget must be passed each year, so minor adjustments can be made from year to year as the need arises, thus avoiding the need to attempt to correct all the problems of the policy area at once. Also, the annual cycle prevents an agency from trying to "shoot the moon" in any one year—trying to expand its budget base greatly, perhaps with flimsy evidence. Agency leaders know that they will have to return for more money next year, and any attempt to deceive only invites future punishment. The sequential nature of the process, in which several actors make their own decisions one after another, also tends to produce incremental outcomes. Many decisions have to be made, and many bargains must be struck. The incremental solution not only provides a "natural" choice but also helps minimize bargaining costs among institutions. Once a decision rule of a certain percentage increase for a particular agency each year has been established, it is far simpler to honor that rule than to seek a "better" decision for one year and then have to do the same hard bargaining and calculation in each subsequent year.

Critiques of Incrementalism

A number of criticisms have been leveled at incrementalism, both in its prescriptive capacity (decisions should be made incrementally) and in its descriptive capacity (decisions are made incrementally). The basic argument against incrementalism as a prescription for policymaking is that it is excessively conservative; the status quo is perpetuated long after better solutions are available. This is true for some program decisions as well as for expenditure decisions. Incrementalism may be a perfectly rational means of policymaking so long as all parties agree that a policy or program is functioning well and is well managed. But how many policies currently fall in that happy category in the United States? In addition, even the incrementalist might agree that at times (e.g., during periods of crisis) nonincremental decisions are required, but the approach provides no means of identifying when and how those nonincremental decisions should be made.[41] If one uses the incremental approach to provide a prescriptive model of governmental decision making, then one must be able to specify what a "big" change would be, when it would be appropriate, and how it might be made.

Several other problems relate to incrementalism as a description of budgetary decision making. In the first place, the majority of empirical examinations of incremental budgeting have been performed at the agency level. This is certainly justifiable, given the importance of those organizations in American public policy, but it is perhaps too high a level of aggregation for examining incremental budgeting.[42] When other researchers have disaggregated agency budgets into program-level budgets, they have found a great deal of nonincremental change, although, as pointed out, it is sometimes difficult to define just what an incremental change is or is not.[43] Thus, while a public agency may have a stable pattern of expenditure change, its managers may drastically alter priorities among the operating programs within the agency and produce more rapid shifts of fortune for the programs.

In addition, when the uncontrollable elements of public expenditures are removed from the analysis, the pattern of expenditure change for the controllable portion is anything but incremental.[44] As budgets have been squeezed by inflation and citizen resistance to taxation, and by presidents committed to reducing the public sector, budgetary increments have not been granted as usual, and at times the base has also been cut—that is, there have been real reductions in the amount of new obligational authority for an agency as compared with the preceding year. Incrementalism may therefore now be descriptive of only certain kinds of expenditures, and not of the budget process as a whole. Of course, since uncontrollable expenditures accounted for approximately 80 percent of total federal expenditures in 1998, the incrementalist description may still be useful.

Also, incrementalism may apply only to certain kinds of agencies and programs, such as those whose existence has been fully accepted as a part of the realm of government activity; it may not apply to newer or more marginal programs. For example, the budgets of programs such as food stamps are always more subject to change than are programs such as veterans' benefits or Social Security, although all would be broadly classified as social service expenditures. The food stamps program has been in existence for a number of years, but it still does not have the legitimacy that other programs have developed. In addition, incrementalist theory does not explain how and when programs make big gains—or big losses—in their appropriations. Even if the approach is successful in explaining a great deal of the variance in normal times, it seems incapable of explaining the most interesting and most important aspects of budgeting—who wins and who loses.

Finally, the prescriptive appeal of incrementalism is based in part on the reversibility of small changes. In the real world of policymaking, many changes are not reversible.[45] Once a commitment is made to a client, or a benefit is indexed, it is difficult to go back and take away the benefit. This is especially true of programs that have a "stock" component, that is, they involve the development of a capital infrastructure or a financial base.[46] Once a program such as Social Security is introduced, individuals covered under the program take the benefits under the program into account when making their financial plans for retirement; thus, any reduction or elimination of benefits may create a hardship.

Whether or not incrementalism accurately characterizes the budget process in the United States or its results, it has certainly become the conventional wisdom to believe that it does. And that belief has prompted a number of proposals for reform of the budgetary process to make it more "rational" and to try to reduce the tendency of programs, once authorized, not only to remain in existence forever but to receive steadily increasing appropriations. It is to those attempts at reform that we now turn our attention.

Reforming Budgeting

Numerous criticisms have been directed at the budgetary process in the United States. For most of our contemporary history these criticisms have focused on the incremental, "irrational," and fragmented nature of the process. More recently, however, the focus has shifted from imposing rationality toward finding somewhat simplistic means of correcting the negative results of the process, including both the incremental nature of the decisions made and, more directly, the huge federal deficits of the 1980s and early 1990s. During the first stage of reforms, several methods were proposed to make the consideration of expenditure priorities more comprehensive and to facilitate government's making the best possible use of its resources. The two most important budgeting reforms were program budgeting and zero-base budgeting. We discuss those two reforms briefly, for even though they were implemented several decades ago, the ideas in these reforms remain important. After that, we discuss the less rational but perhaps more effective reforms of the 1980s and 1990s.

Program Budgeting

Program budgeting was largely a product of the Johnson administration, although in some agencies it had been tried previously. Whereas traditional budgeting allocates personnel costs, supplies, equipment, and so forth among organizations, program budgeting allocated resources on the basis of the activities of government and the services that government supplies to society.[47] It also placed a pronounced emphasis on the analysis of programmatic expenditures and the most efficient use of scarce resources.

Underlying program budgeting—more specifically known as the planning, programming, budgeting system (PPBS)—was a systems concept. That is, it assumed that the elements of government policy are closely intertwined, so that a change in one type of policy may affect all others. For example, if one wants to improve the health of citizens in the United States, it may be more efficient to improve nutrition and housing than to invest money in medical care. Program budgeting was always looking for interactions among policy areas and for means of producing desired effects in the most efficient manner.

There were six basic characteristics of PPBS as practiced in the federal government. First, the major goals and objectives of government were to be identified; it was necessary to specify what government was attempting to do, and this identification was to be made high in the hierarchy of government, usually by the president and Congress. Whereas traditional line-item budgeting is initiated by the agencies, the concept of program budgeting began with a specification of the central goals and priorities of government, which could be supplied only by the principal political leaders.

Second, programs were to be developed according to the specified goals. How would government attempt to attain its goals? These programs were analytically defined and might not exist as organizational entities. For example, when Robert McNamara—who, with his "whiz kids," was largely responsible for introducing program budgeting into the Defense Department and thence into the federal government as a whole—developed the program structure for Defense, one of the programs developed was "strategic deterrence." This program was spread among three services: the air force had its manned bombers and some missiles, the navy had Polaris submarines, and the army had Intermediate Range Ballistic Missiles located in Europe. Strategic deterrence certainly described a set of activities of the defense establishment, but no organization was specifically responsible for that program.

Third, resources were to be allocated among programs. Although many traditional line items were used in developing the program budget, the final budget document was presented as overall costs for the achievement of certain objectives. These costs would then be justified as efficient and effective means of reaching the desired goals. PPBS, then, emphasized the costs of reaching certain objectives, whereas line-item budgeting emphasizes the costs of keeping organizations or programs in operation.

Fourth, organizations were not sacrosanct in program budgeting, and there was no assumption that each program would be housed within a single agency, or that each agency would provide only a single program. As in the defense example mentioned earlier, program budgeting attempted to expand the framework of budgeting to include all actors who contributed to the achievement of the goals. This was obviously a realistic attitude toward the interaction of activities and organizations in producing the final effects on the society, but it did make budgeting more difficult in an environment composed of many organizations, each attempting to sustain its own interests.

Fifth, PPBS extended the time limit on expenditures found in line-item budgeting. It attempted to answer questions about the medium- and long-term implications of programs. Programs that appeared efficient in the short run might actually be less desirable when their long-term implications were considered. For example, most publicly supported health programs concentrate on curative medicine, while it may be more efficient in the long run to emphasize prevention.

Sixth, alternative programs were systematically analyzed. Agencies examined alternatives to existing program structures hoping to find more effective and efficient programs. Agencies were expected to present their justifications for programs—to show, in other words, that a chosen program was superior to alternatives investigated. This aspect of program budgeting relates to our previous discussion of policy formulation, for agencies were expected to develop alternatives and to examine their relative merits, using techniques such as cost-benefit analysis.

CRITICISM OF PROGRAM BUDGETING

Advocates of program budgeting pointed with pride to the enhanced rationality and analytic rigor associated with this form of budgeting and to the way that it broke down organizational control over budgetary outcomes. Despite these apparent advantages, PPBS was not especially successful in most of its applications. There were some technical reasons for these apparent failures, but the most severe problems in the implementation of program budgeting were political.

Technically, applying PPBS successfully required a great deal of time and effort; it also required an almost certain knowledge of unknown relationships of spending to program success. The systems concept inherent in the method implies that if one aspect of the system is altered, the entire system must be rethought. This in turn may mean that program budgeting actually institutionalizes the rigidity that it was designed to eliminate. Also, it is difficult if not impossible to define programs, measure their results, and evaluate the contributions of individual agencies and activities to the achievement of those results. One major problem in public policy analysis is the difficulty of measuring the effects of government, and such measurement occupies a central place in program budgeting.[48]

PPBS also had several political disadvantages. First, as mentioned, the method forced decisions to a higher level of government.[49] Agencies disliked this centralizing tendency, as did congressmen who had invested considerable effort in developing relationships with clientele groups supporting an agency. Likewise, the assumption that organizations are not the most appropriate objects of allocation ran counter to all the folkways of American government. Finally, the need to analyze systematically alternative strategies for achieving ends forced the agency to expose its program to possible attack, as it might develop and eliminate alternative programs that others might prefer, and the explicit nature of the process brought those alternatives up for active consideration. The discussion of alternative policies reduced the agency's maneuverability, as it had to justify its policy choices in writing and consequently could not play games with OMB, or with Congress if information developed from the program budgeting system was passed on to the legislative branch.

In short, PPBS was a dagger pointed at the central role of the agency in policymaking in the federal government, and it should not have been expected to succeed, except perhaps in organizations such as the Department of Defense. That organization had a strong leader committed to the concept of program budgeting, and it produced extremely nebulous results that could be tested only against simulations or scenario-building exercises; it also had few potent political enemies. For other agencies, with considerably greater political opposition and with real clients demanding real services, PPBS was doomed to failure from the beginning.

THE REBIRTH OF PROGRAM BUDGETING?

Although it has been declared dead as a formal device, the ideas of program budgeting continue to appear in thinking about the budgetary process. The basic idea of making the most efficient allocation of money among competing resources is an extremely alluring one, and politicians and analysts will attempt to pursue that rationalistic goal, even in the face of masses of evidence that it may not be attainable in the rough world of politics.

The latest rebirth of the basic idea of making the allocation of funds more rational is the Government Performance and Results Act of 1993 (GPRA).[50] The basic idea behind this legislation is to shift the focus in assessing organizations in the budgetary process away from inputs toward outcomes and "results." Each organization in the federal government is therefore required to develop a strategic plan and a set of operational indicators of attaining the goals specified in that plan. The degree of success or failure in attaining those goals is then to play a significant role in determining the budgetary success of the organization. This process involves neither the direct linkage to expenditures nor the level of analysis inherent in program budgeting, but it does depend upon some of the same assumptions.

Zero-Base Budgeting

If program budgeting required an almost superhuman analytical capability and rafts of data, the conceptual underpinnings of zero-base budgeting (ZBB) were extremely simple. The idea was that, whereas traditional incremental budgeting operates from the assumption that the previous year's budget was justified (the "base") and possible increments are all that need examination, a more comprehensive examination of all expenditures should be made. That is, there should be no base, and the entire spending plan should be justified. It was assumed that weaker programs, which were being extended largely through inertia, would be terminated or at least severely cut, and more meritorious programs would be fully funded. This form of budgeting came to Washington with the Carter administration, having been tried by President Carter while he was governor of Georgia.

Zero-base budgeting was carried out on the basis of decision units, which might be agencies but which frequently were smaller components such as operating programs within an agency. Each budget manager was expected to prepare a number of decision packages to reflect his or her priorities for funding. These packages were presented in rank order, beginning with a "survival package" that represented the lowest level of funding on which the unit could continue to exist. On top of the survival package were additional decision packages, reflecting, first, the continuation of existing programs at existing levels of service and then expansions of services. Each decision package was justified in terms of the services it would provide at an acceptable cost.

Decision packages prepared by lower-level budget managers were then passed up the organization to higher-level managers who prepared consolidated decision packages that ranked priorities among the several decision units that they supervised. These rankings were then passed up and consolidated further, ending in the Office of Management and Budget. All the rankings from the lower levels were passed along with the consolidated packages so that higher levels could examine the preferences of lower-level managers and their justifications for those preferences. Like program budgeting, ZBB was geared toward multiyear budgeting to better understand the implications of budget choices made during any one budget cycle.

Zero-base budgeting, again like program budgeting, had several apparent advantages. Obviously, the method would eliminate incremental budgeting. The agency's base was no longer protected, but must be defended— although in practice the survival level might function as a base. Also, ZBB focused on cost effectiveness in the justification of the rankings of decision packages and even of the survival level of funding. One principal advantage of zero-base budgeting was the involvement of managers at relatively low levels of the organization in the consideration of priorities and goals for the organization. Also, this method considered the allocation of resources in package terms, whereas the incremental budget assumes that any additional money can be effectively used. It makes substantially greater sense to think of adding meaningful amounts of money that can produce additional services, rather than simply adding more money without regard for the threshold values for service provision and efficiency.

There were, however, a number of glaring difficulties with zero-base budgeting. For example, this form of budgeting threatened the existence of some agencies. In practice, a number of factors, such as clientele groups and uncontrollable expenditures, could negate the concern that many administrators might have had about the method, but it was nevertheless clear that the intent of the method was to bring the existence of each program into question each year.

To some degree the enormity of the task of examining each program carefully each year was a major weakness of this method. There is no means by which OMB, held to a reasonable size, or a Congress with its other commitments, can carefully consider the entire budget each year. Therefore, there would be either a superficial analysis of each program under the guise of a zero-base review—probably with incremental results—or a selective review of a number of more controversial programs. Either would be an acceptable means of reducing the workload, but neither would constitute a significant departure from the incremental budget or justify the massive effort required to prepare the necessary documents.

In addition, ZBB threatened established programs by allowing the reopening of political conflicts during each budget cycle. One virtue of traditional incremental budgeting is that, once a program is agreed to, it is accepted and is not again subject to significant scrutiny unless there are major changes in the environment or serious administrative problems in the agency. With zero-base budgeting, however, the existence of the program became subject to question each year, and the political fights that authorized the existence of the agency might have to be fought again and again. This was, of course, no problem for well-established and popular programs, but it was certainly a problem for newer and more controversial programs. Also, ZBB tended to combine financial decisions with program decisions and to place perhaps an excessive burden on budgetary decision makers.

From Scalpels to Axes: Budget Reform in the 1980s and 1990s

To a greater degree than the analytic methodologies proposed in program budgeting and (to some extent) zero-base budgeting, the fundamental incrementalist patterns have been challenged by the continuing fiscal problems of government. These problems have spawned a number of "solutions,"[51] some of which have already been implemented, including the Gramm-Rudman-Hollings Act (technically the Balanced Budget and Emergency Deficit Control Act of 1985), the 1990 budget agreement between Congress and President Bush, and the Balanced Budget Act of 1997. Other proposed reforms include a balanced-budget amendment and the partially implemented line-item veto. Most of these reforms are simply incrementalism turned around, featuring the same tendency to substitute minimization of decision-making costs for maximization of benefits resulting from expenditures. They are, for the most part, "no-think solutions," just as incrementalism has been a nonanalytic means for making budgetary decisions. But, even as incrementalism has been successful and acceptable, these methods for dealing with complex problems have been proposed primarily because of their simplicity. Simple policies are not always—and perhaps only rarely—the best solutions for complex problems, but they are very often the most acceptable in the political world.

Gramm-Rudman-Hollings

As the deficits created by the Reagan tax cuts grew, Congress began to find means to stanch the budgetary "hemorrhaging." This was difficult to do by traditional means because of the logrolling and pork-barrel legislative styles so typical of Congress. Therefore Congress adopted a method, commonly referred to as "Gramm-Rudman-Hollings" after its sponsors, that removed some of its discretion and forced spending cuts if Congress and the president could not reach agreement on how to do so. The initial idea was to reduce the federal deficit to zero within five years (fiscal year 1991). This goal was indicative of the totemic status of a balanced budget in American thinking about public finance,[52] but it soon proved to be an unattainable and perhaps unwise target.

The basic idea behind Gramm-Rudman-Hollings was that in order to meet the declining deficit target in any year, Congress and the president could cut spending, raise taxes, or arrive at some combination of the two. If no agreement could be reached on those actions, then automatic cuts in spending (called sequestrations)—half from defense and half from domestic programs—would be imposed. Certain types of expenditures (interest on the federal debt, Social Security and veterans' benefits) were excluded, so the automatic reductions would have to come from only 30 percent of the budget. That, in turn, meant that those cuts would have to be severe. The scorekeeper in the process was to be the General Accounting Office.

The role assigned to the GAO proved to be the downfall of the initial version of the process. In 1986 the Supreme Court ruled[53] that the GAO, as a legislative organization, could not perform an executive act—ordering budget cuts for specific executive agencies. After considerable discussion, the scorekeeper was changed to the Office of Management and Budget in the Executive Office of the President. Although Congress feared that its interests might be slighted by this change, it appeared to be the only possible compromise if the original mechanisms of the act were to be maintained.

But the original intentions of the act proved to be extremely difficult and painful politically, so Congress agreed to several changes in 1987 and 1988. First, the time period for reducing the deficit to zero was extended to fiscal 1993. Second, Congress postponed most of the truly significant cuts until after the 1988 presidential and congressional elections, thereby confirming the adage that future budget cuts are always more acceptable than current ones, especially for incumbents. Congress then attempted to restore deficit reduction to its trajectory after the election but was deterred by economic and political circumstances.

The principal factor hampering the ability of the president and Congress to reach their targets was the sluggish, then decelerating, economy. President Bush proposed a budget that would meet the Gramm-Rudman-Hollings target of a $64 billion deficit for fiscal 1991, but as the budget process progressed in 1990 it became clear that the actual deficit would be closer to $300 billion because of the slowed economy. The sense of crisis emerging from these negotiations produced a new program for deficit reduction, or at least deficit management. Adopted in the Budget Enforcement Act of 1990 (BEA), the legislation provided for

1. Separation of mandatory spending from discretionary spending.
2. Differentiation of three types of discretionary spending: defense, international, and domestic, with separate spending targets for each.
3. A "pay as you go" plan for mandatory spending and revenues, requiring that any increase in spending or reduction in revenue must be associated with another spending reduction or tax increase in order to keep the package deficit neutral.
4. Elimination of overly optimistic or unrealistic targets for deficit reduction.
5. Inclusion of loan programs (previously excluded) in the budgetary calculations.
6. The Office of Management and Budget was to be scorekeeper.[54]

Gramm-Rudman-Hollings and all the other legislative manifestations of fiscal control represent major efforts at reform of the budgetary process to eliminate the federal deficit and to force government to live within its revenues. They also demonstrate the extreme difficulties of making and implementing such reform measures. Not only were unrealistic future targets set and then dismissed, but important segments of federal financial operations, such as credit (initially) and the savings-and-loan bailout, were ignored. Further, cuts were imposed on a relatively small proportion of the budget and therefore fell very heavily in those areas.

The other effect of Gramm-Rudman-Hollings and its sequels has been to add a new level of analysis to the budget process. One of the crucial elements of budgeting in the 1990s is "scorekeeping" in the PAYGO—pay as you go—system. Any spending bill now must be scored to determine whether it is revenue neutral; if it does not meet this criterion, the legislation must be redesigned so that it will. Making these determinations is by no means simple, for it often involves a number of economic assumptions and a variety of ways to do the calculations; politics enters here as well as in the rest of the budget process.[55] In many ways, the Gramm-Rudman-Hollings and BEA enterprises helped add to the already high level of cynicism displayed by the American people toward government.[56]

The incoming Clinton administration used the provisions of the Budget Enforcement Act to begin to implement its own budgetary and economic strategy. Changes in timing contained in the BEA allowed the new administration to submit that year's budget. The first proposed Clinton budget contained a very modest increase in expenditures over that previously projected, but a much larger increase in revenues, thereby producing some reduction in the deficit.[57] Congress did modify that budget but left intact much of the administration's plans for economic change and some reduction in the deficit.

The Balanced-Budget Amendment

The size of the federal budget deficit has elicited a number of proposed solutions in addition to the Gramm-Rudman-Hollings machinery and its sequel. Among the most commonly discussed solutions has been the balanced-budget amendment to the Constitution, which would require Congress to pass a balanced budget each year, unless an extraordinary majority in Congress declared that a sufficient economic emergency existed to justify running a deficit.[58] Somewhat like the PAYGO budgetary process, the amendment would force a more explicit comparison of revenue and expenditure figures, and it would further require those involved in the budgetary process to be responsible for the amount of money they appropriate. The difference, of course, is that this arrangement would be constitutional and therefore permanent.

The balanced-budget amendment has substantial political appeal and has gained some support. It was voted on in 1993 and came close to receiving enough votes in Congress to send it to the states. Like many simple "solutions" to complex problems, however, it presents some major difficulties. First, as already noted, the planning for a budget begins more than a year before the start of its execution, and more than two years before the completion of the budget year. Further, both revenue and expenditure projections on which a budget is based are to some degree influenced by the condition of the economy and the projected state of the economy during the time the budget is to be executed.[59] It is easy to get the projections wrong—over the past twenty years, the official figures have overestimated revenues by an average of 3.9 percent and underestimated expenditures by an average of 4 percent.[60] Even if Congress acts in good faith and attempts to comply with the spirit of the amendment, it could easily miss the target of a balanced budget badly—by an average of almost 8 percent.

As well as the potential economic problems caused by such mistaken projections, an unplanned deficit itself may appear to be a violation of the Constitution and may further undermine already weakened public respect for Congress. A more cynical scenario would have Congress passing a budget that, although balanced on paper, would be known to have little chance of being balanced when executed. In either case, there could be substantial political damage to the legitimacy of Congress and to government as a whole. The difficulties already encountered in implementing Gramm-Rudman-Hollings to limit spending give some idea of how a balanced-budget agreement would, or would not, work.

In addition, deficits are not necessarily a public evil. When adopted for economic reasons, as opposed to those caused by political unwillingness to impose the true costs of government on citizens, budget deficits can be an important tool for economic management, following the Keynesian tradition. Passing a balanced-budget amendment would in fact remove one important tool of economic management from the federal government, without any certainty of generating economic benefits sufficient to justify that loss.

The Line-Item Veto

In his 1985 budget submission, President Reagan proposed that a presidential line-item veto be adopted, especially for use on appropriations bills. Similar to the powers that governors in forty-three states already have, the line-item veto would allow the president to veto a portion of a bill, while permitting the rest to be put into effect.[61] Reagan was not the first president to make this recommendation—Ulysses Grant had done so—nor was he the last. Bill Clinton also advocated this instrument of presidential power, and it was a part of the Republicans' Contract with America. In 1996 Congress, seemingly against its own institutional interests, passed legislation giving the president the line-item veto.[62]

This selective veto was seen as a weapon for the president in dealing with the tendency of congressmen to add their pet projects to appropriations bills, thus placing the president in the awkward position of having to refuse money for a large segment of the federal government in order to prevent the funding of one or two small, and often wasteful, projects. Also, as noted earlier, the majority of appropriations for the federal government are contained in a dozen or so appropriations acts. In order to eliminate a few items, the president would have to veto the entire act and create disruption and hardships for citizens and federal employees. For example, the federal government was shut down in 1995 because of a conflict over a few items in the budget.

One of the justifications for this change in the budgetary process was that it attacked the problem of growing federal deficits. This might be so, but the veto could not be applied to many uncontrollable programs, such as debt interest and Social Security. Further, through the powers of rescission the president can achieve some of the same ends, although he needs the agreement of Congress (see pp. 135–36). In 1992, for example, President Bush attempted to rescind $7.9 billion, but by the time Congress had finished with the proposal there was a rescission of $8.2 billion containing few of the items the president had proposed to cut.[63] Congress also had the option of overriding a presidential line-item veto, first by a simple majority and then by a two-thirds majority if the president maintained his convictions about eliminating the expenditure.

The line-item veto might actually have encouraged Congress to add more pet projects onto appropriations acts, placing the onus of removing those projects on the president. Indeed, in his first use of the veto (before the courts intervened) President Clinton singled out some spending items that were apparent "pork," concentrated in a few congressional districts.[64] It might also have given the president independent powers over public spending not intended by the framers of the Constitution nor desired by the public. Thus, as with the balanced-budget amendment, the line-item veto proposal suggests there are few magic solutions for solving deficit problems, but there is a continuing need for political will and courage to solve them.

After the first use of the line-item veto, several lawsuits were brought by affected parties and by members of Congress. The courts then ruled that the act was indeed unconstitutional, given that it violated the basic separation of powers provisions of the Constitution by conferring legislative powers on the president in enabling him to make selective decisions about what would be spent and what would not. The Constitution does give the president the veto, but it is to be used over entire bills and not over the particular parts he dislikes. The line-item veto provision now appears to be dead, but the debate over its suitability and its constitutionality is likely to continue.

Decrementalism

The preceding discussion of the balanced-budget amendment and the line-item veto is indicative of a general problem facing American government and the governments of other industrialized countries: the control of public expenditures. While incrementalism has become the conventional wisdom for describing budgeting, large numbers of politicians are looking for means of enforcing decrementalism, or the gradual reduction of expenditures, on government.[65] The majority of these political leaders are from the political right—as exemplified by President Bush—but even some on the political left are seeking to reduce expenditures while maintaining levels of service. The word *reform* has been heard often from national capitols, but there has been little agreement on how much reform is needed and whether simple procedural reforms will be sufficient to address the deep and abiding difficulties faced in budgeting.[66]

In addition to the rationalistic approaches to budgeting and the Gramm-Rudman-Hollings machinery already discussed, somewhat more blunt instruments have been employed to try to reduce federal expenditures. One attempt, made in the 1980s, was the president's Private Sector Survey on Cost Control (the Grace Commission). This survey, similar to those that had been conducted in most state governments, brought to Washington some 2,000 volunteers from business and other private-sector organizations to examine the management of the federal government. The volunteers prepared 2,478 distinct recommendations that were projected to save the government $424 billion a year if all were implemented.[67] Many of these proposals for cost reduction were criticized as politically naive or simply impossible, given the political realities of Washington and the connection of the agencies with powerful clientele groups.[68] The survey did, however, give those in Washington something to think about.

Other, even more crude, efforts at controlling the costs of government have included across-the-board reductions in staffing levels and budgets and moratoriums on the implementation of new programs and regulations. In addition, President Reagan and his advisers decided to attempt to reduce the pay of public employees to a level of 94 percent of that of comparable employees in the private sector—the 6-percent difference was to be offset by the greater job security and fringe benefits associated with federal employment.[69] The Clinton administration offered few suggestions for changing the mechanisms of budgeting, other than the familiar arguments for a line-item veto and the proposals for a biennial budget contained in the National Performance Review.[70]

Reaction to these reform efforts has been almost opposite that of proposals such as program budgeting and zero-base budgeting. In contrast to the large-scale analytic exercises required to implement PPBS or ZBB, the more recent across-the-board reform efforts (such as those contained in the Gramm-Rudman-Hollings procedures) have been criticized as mindless, as simply attacking government without regard to the real benefits created by some agencies and the real waste created by others. Perhaps sadly, the across-the-board exercises have a much greater chance of being implemented than do the more analytic methods.

Is Budget Change Its Own Reward?

All the attempts at budget reform we have mentioned have had some impact on the way in which the federal budget is constructed. Both program budgeting and zero-base budgeting were significant rationalistic efforts at reforming the budgetary process but, although both methods had a great deal to commend them, neither was particularly successful in producing changes in the behavior of budgetary decision makers. The less rationalistic methods such as Gramm-Rudman-Hollings have had a greater impact on the budget, in part because they did not attempt to change the basic format of the process or the outcomes. Despite the real problems in both the budget process and budget outcomes, why does the traditional line-item incremental budget persist?[71]

There appear to be several reasons for the persistence of traditional budgeting. One is that the traditional budget gives the legislature an excellent means of controlling the executive branch. It allocates funds to identifiable organizations for identifiable purposes (personnel, equipment, etc.), not to nebulous "programs" or "decision units." Those who manage the real organizations can then be held accountable for the expenditure of the money appropriated to them. The blunt instruments now tacked onto the process, such as the Budget Enforcement Act, can enhance the control elements of the budgetary process without altering its basic elements.

More important, while the benefits promised by both PPBS and ZBB were significant, so too were the costs, both in terms of the calculations required to reach decisions and the political turmoil created by nonincremental changes. Incremental budgeting provides ready guidelines for those who must make budget decisions, minimizing the necessity for them to engage in costly analysis and calculation. In addition, as most political interests are manifested through organizations, the absence of threat to those organizations in incremental budgeting means that political conflicts can be confined to marginal matters instead of repeated battles over the very existence of those organizations.

In short, although incremental budgeting does nothing very well, neither does it do anything very poorly. Incrementalism is a convenient means of allocating resources for public purposes. It is not an optimal means of making policy, but it is a means that works. It is also a means of making policy in which policymakers themselves have great confidence. These factors are in themselves sufficient to explain perpetuation of the incremental budgetary processes in the face of so many challenges by presumably superior systems of budgeting. There are always proposals for change, but there is rarely sufficient agreement on any of the possible changes to move the system away from the status quo. There have been some successful reforms, yet the system remains firmly incremental.

7. Evaluation and Policy Change

The final stage of the policy process is to assess what has occurred as a result of the selection and implementation of public policy and, if it is found necessary, to produce some change in the current policies of government. Critics of government tend to believe that these evaluative questions are extremely easy to answer, that the activities of government are rather simple, and that inefficiencies and maladministration could be corrected easily, if only government really wanted to do so. As this chapter points out, however, producing a valid evaluation of government programs is a difficult and highly political process in itself. That evaluation is much more difficult than for most activities in the private sector.[1] Further, if the evaluation determines that change is necessary or desirable, the policymaking process involved in making the change is perhaps even more difficult to implement successfully than is the process of policy initiation—the first adoption of a policy. Government organizations have a number of weapons to protect themselves against change, so any attempts to alter existing policies and organizations are almost certain to engender conflict.

However, we must not be too quick to assume that government organizations are always wedded to the status quo. Change is threatening to any organization, but most organizations also know their own strengths and weaknesses and want to correct those weaknesses. The difficulties these organizations encounter in producing change arise as often from Congress and from the organizations' clients as they do from internal conservatism. Most organizations, public as well as private, are engaged in continuous evaluation of their performance. What they must find is the means to bring out effective change in that performance when they detect shortcomings.

Problems in Evaluating Public Programs

Evaluation is an important need of government programs and organizations, which, like other enterprises, need to know how they are performing. In its simplest form, evaluating a public program involves cataloging the goals of the program, measuring the degree to which these goals have been achieved, and perhaps suggesting changes that might bring the performance of the organization more in line with the stated purposes of the program. Although these appear to be simple things to do, it is actually difficult to produce unambiguous measurements of the performance of a public organization. Several barriers stand in the way of anyone who attempts to produce such valid evaluations.

Goal Specification and Goal Change

The first step in an evaluation is to identify the goals of the program, but even this seemingly simple task may be difficult, if not impossible.[2] The legislation that establishes a program or organization should be the source of goal statements, but we have already seen (chapter 4) that legislation is frequently written in vague language to avoid offending potential members of the coalition necessary to pass the legislation. As a result, it may be difficult to attach any readily quantifiable goals to programs or organizations. In addition, the goals specified in legislation may be impossible or contradictory. For example, one program had as its goal to raise all students to the mean reading level (think about it), while the expressed aim of one foreign aid program was to assist those nations in greatest need, provided that they were the most likely use the money to produce significant developmental effects. When an organization is faced with merely impossible goals, it can still do something positive, but when it is faced with contradictory goals, its own internal political dynamics become more important in determining ultimate policy choices than any legislative statement of purpose. Further, as organizations do not function alone in the world, the contradictions existing across organizations—as when government subsidizes tobacco production and simultaneously discourages tobacco consumption—make identification of the goals of government as a whole that much more difficult.

Of course, internal political dynamics remain significant even in organizations with clear and unambiguous goals stated in their legislation. An initial statement of goals may be important in initiating a program, but once that program is in operation, the goals may be modified. These changes may be positive, as when programs adapt to changing environmental conditions in order to meet new societal needs. Positive changes in goals most often have been noted in the private sector, as when the March of Dimes shifted its goal from serving victims of polio to helping children with birth defects, but they also occur in the public sector.[3] For example, the Bureau of Indian Affairs has been transformed from an organization that exercised control over Native Americans into one that now frequently serves as an advocate of the rights and interests of those people.[4] Also, the Army Corps of Engineers transformed its image from one of gross environmental disregard to environmental sensitivity and even environmental advocacy.[5]

Goal transformations are, of course, also negative at times. The capture of regulatory bodies by their regulated industries is a commonly cited example of negative goal change.[6] A more common example is the "displacement of goals" among the employees of an organization,[7] who, although they may have been recruited on the basis of public service goals, may over time become more focused on personal survival and aggrandizement (see figure 7.1). Similarly, the goals of an organization as a whole may shift reflexively toward its own maintenance and survival (empire building). Employees' goals may also shift in the operational field as they begin to skirt legal requirements in order to provide new and better types of services to clients (street-level bureaucracy).

Anthony Downs describes organizations (as well as the individuals within them) going through a life cycle, beginning as zealots or advocates of certain social causes, but over time becoming more interested in surviving and maintaining their budgets than in doing anything for clients.[8] In these instances the operating goals of the program deteriorate, even if the stated goals remain the same. The organization may not even realize that the change has occurred, but the clients almost certainly will.

Actors exhibiting transformation

	Individuals	Organizations
Reflexive	Displacement	Empire building
Operational	Street-level bureaucracy	Adaptation

Modes of goal transformation

FIGURE 7.1

TYPES OF GOAL CHANGE

We should be aware that organizational transformation of goals and individual transformations have very different implications for policy and for evaluation. If an individual member of the organization attempts to impose his or her own goals, whether in implementing policy or in attempting to protect his or her own position, the evaluative problem becomes that of identifying the personal deviations. The task then is motivating or sanctioning the individual rather than assessing the performance of the organization (other than in its management). When the organization itself makes such deviations, there is more reason to evaluate the policies of the organization and the actual goals that undergird them.

Among the managerial changes in the public sector over the past several decades has been an attempt to develop ways to prevent goal displacement. One common change has been to make managers more directly responsible for the performance of their organizations, with rewards for those whose organizations perform well and possible dismissal for the managers of poorly performing organizations.[9] At lower levels, performance pay schemes are designed to produce the same results.[10] In addition, there have been attempts to make the public sector more "consumer driven," with a variety of mechanisms developed to permit clients, and the general public, to know what is going on in an organization and to have some influence over the outcomes.[11]

Even when the goals are clearly expressed, they may not be practical. The Preamble to the Constitution, for instance, expresses a number of goals for the American government, but few, if any, are expressed in concrete language that would enable a researcher to verify that these lofty goals are or are not being achieved. Specifying such goals and putting them into operation would require further political action within the organization or the imposition of the values of the researcher in order to make it possible to compare performance with aspiration. For example, the Employment Act of 1946 pledged the government of the United States to maintain "full employment." At the time the act was passed, full employment was declared to be 4 percent unemployment. Over time the official definition crept upward to 4.5 percent and then to 5 percent unemployed, and some economists have argued that 6 percent is an appropriate level of unemployment. Obviously, political leaders want to declare that full employment has been achieved, and in order to justify doing so, they apply pressure to change the definition of "full employment." In this case, an admirable goal has been modified in practice, although the basic concept has remained a part of policy. This is but one instance of government playing the "numbers game" to attempt to prove that goals have been reached.[12]

In addition, most public organizations serve multiple constituencies and therefore may have different goals for those different groups in society. For example, the Comprehensive Employment and Training Act (CETA) performed a number of different functions for different segments of society and was differentially successful at serving those constituencies. For people employed by the program, it was a source of employment and potentially of training for a better job. For individuals concerned about unemployment and whose political careers may have depended on addressing the problem, it was a means of reducing unemployment without undertaking the more difficult task of stimulating the entire economy or altering the economic structure to supply more jobs for unskilled and semiskilled workers. Finally, for mayors and other local government officials, the program was a source of cheap labor that enabled them either to balance their city budgets or to prevent even more rapid tax increases than otherwise would have been necessary to maintain services. To the extent that the program pleased mayors by providing cheap labor in unskilled jobs such as garbage collection, it could never fulfill the goal of training the program participants for better private-sector jobs. Thus, when programs are being evaluated, it is important to ask whose goals, as well as what goals, are being achieved.

Finally, it should be noted that goals may be either straitjackets or opportunities for an organization. In addition to telling an organization what it should be doing, specific goal statements tell it what it is not supposed to be doing. This may limit the creativity of the organization and may serve as a powerful conservative force within the organization. Further, the specification of goals may limit the efficiency and effectiveness of government as a whole. It may divide responsibilities in ways that are less meaningful, given an expansion of knowledge and information or a change in values. So, for example, locating the U.S. Forest Service in the Department of Agriculture may mean that trees are treated more as a crop than as a natural resource, as they might be if the agency were located within the Department of the Interior. Giving one program or organization a goal may mean that other, more efficient means of delivering the same service will not be explored or that existing duplication of services will not be eliminated.

Measurement

Once goals have been identified and expressed in clear, concrete language, the next task is to devise a means to measure the extent to which those goals have been attained. In the public sector, measuring results or production is frequently difficult. In fact, one fundamental problem that limits the efficiency and effectiveness of government is the absence of any ready means of judging the value of what is being produced.

One of the clearest examples of this measurement problem occurs in one of government's oldest functions: national defense. The product called "defense" is, in many ways, the failure of real or potential enemies to take certain actions. Logically, the best defense force would never do anything, for there would be no enemy willing to risk taking offensive actions; in fact, to some degree, if a defense force is called into action, it has already failed. But measuring non-events and counterfactual occurrences is difficult, so defense is frequently assessed by surrogate measures. Thus, the mega-tonnage of nuclear weapons available and capable of being launched within fifteen minutes and the number of plane-hours of flight time logged by the Strategic

Air Command have been used as measures of defense. In a post–Cold War era, the indicators of an effective defense policy are even less clear, involving as much the capacity to enforce peace settlements as the ability to wage war.[13]

The illustration from defense policy helps make the point that activity measures are frequently substituted for output measures when attempting to evaluate performance in the public sector. Some scholars, as well as some politicians and analysts, despair of finding more adequate means to measure the benefits of many public-sector programs. For example, I.C.R. Byatt argues that "it is not possible to measure benefits from defense by any known techniques, nor is it easy to even begin to see how one might be developed." He goes on to say that "it is quite impossible to allocate costs to the final objectives of education."[14] He might well have extended the list to include most of the functions of the public sector.[15]

Scholarly pessimism aside, the perpetuation of activity measures serves the interests of existing organizations. First, it can shield them from stringent evaluations on nonprocedural criteria. Perhaps more important, action becomes equated with success, which will have a predictable upward impact on levels of government expenditure. It may have the less obvious effect of giving program personnel incentives to keep their clients on programs when they might be able to survive without the benefits. Despite such skepticism and organizational politics, governments continue to express interest in measuring what their organizations actually deliver for the public, and reforms of the past decade attempt to focus more clearly on the impacts of government (see p. 175).

Several factors inhibit the adequate measurement of government performance. One is the time span over which the benefits of many programs are created. For example, although the short-term goal of education is to improve reading, writing, and computation, the ultimate and more important goals of education can be realized only in the future. They cannot be measured or even identified during the time in which a child is attending school. Among other things, education is supposed to improve the earning potential of individuals, make society more stable, and simply improve the quality of life for the individuals who receive it. These are elusive qualities to measure when an evaluation must be done quickly. The time problem in evaluation is also illustrated by Lester Salamon's analysis of the "sleeper" effects of the New Deal programs in the rural South, where these programs were widely believed to be failures while in operation although significant results became apparent thirty years after the programs were terminated.[16]

The other side of the time problem is that any effects produced by a program should be durable.[17] Some programs, for example, produce effects only after they have been in existence for years, whereas other programs produce demonstrable results in the short term but have no significant effects in the long run. It has been argued that the latter is true of the Head Start program. Participants in the program do tend to enter school with skills superior to those of non–Head Start children. After several years, however, no significant differences can be discerned between those who were in the program and those who were not. It seems that without reinforcement in later years, the effects of Head Start decay.[18] The program per se therefore may not be unsuccessful or ineffective; it simply is not carried through for a sufficient amount of time.[19]

The time element in program evaluation also produces significant political difficulties. Many individuals responsible for making policy decisions are short of time, and they must produce results quickly if their programs are to be successful. Congressmen, for example, have a tenure of only two years before facing reelection, and any program they advocate should show some "profit" before those two years have passed. Thus, the policy process tends to favor short-term gains, even if they are not durable, over long-term successes. Some actors in the policy process, notably the permanent public bureaucracy, can afford to take a longer time perspective, but most politicians cannot. Thus, time itself is crucial in evaluation.[20] The policymaking cycle is largely determined by the political calendar, but the effects of policies have their own timetables. Part of the job of the analyst and evaluator is to attempt to make the two coincide.

The evaluation of public programs is also confounded by many other factors affecting the population. If we are to evaluate the effectiveness of a health-care program on a poor population, for example, we may find it difficult to isolate the effects of that program from those of a nutrition program or those of a housing program. All these programs may have the effect of improving the health of the population, and we may find it difficult to determine which program caused the observed changes. In fact, all the programs mentioned may be related to those changes, in which case it becomes difficult to determine which program is the most efficient means of affecting the health of that community. We might be able to isolate the effects of an individual program with a more controlled social experiment, but few people would want to be the subjects of such an experiment. Further, it is difficult to hold constant all the social and economic factors that might affect the success of a public program independent of any policy; health may have improved because more people are employed and can afford more nutritious food for their families. All these problems point out that measurement in policy analysis is not as simple as the measurement that a scientist can make of a passive molecule or an amoeba.

In addition, measurement of the effects of a public program can be confounded by the history of the program and of the individuals involved.[21]

Few truly new and innovative policies are initiated in industrialized countries such as the United States, and programs that have existed in the same policy area for several years may jeopardize the success of any new program. Clients may well become cynical when program after program promises to "solve" their problems. Likewise, administrators may become cynical and frustrated after changing the direction of their activities several times. Any number of policy areas have gone through cycles of change and contradiction, with inevitable effects on the morale and cooperation of clients and administrators alike. The numerous attempts to address the problems of the poor are the best example of endless change and confusion.[22] In addition to creating frustration over the inability of government to make up its collective mind, one policy may not be successful after another policy has been in place. For example, if a policy of lenient treatment and rehabilitation has been tried in a prison, it may be difficult for jailers to return to more punitive methods without disruption. Interestingly, the reverse may also be true.

Another problem in the measurement of policy effects is that the organizational basis of much evaluation limits excessively the scope of the inquiry, and many unintended consequences of the program may not be included in the evaluation. For example, highway engineers probably regard the interstate highway system as a great success. Many miles of highways have been built in a relatively short period, and these highways have saved many lives and many millions of gallons of gasoline, assuming that Americans would have driven the same number of miles if these superhighways had not been built. The mayor of a large city or members of the Department of Energy, however, may regard the program as a colossal failure. They realize that the building of highways in urban areas has facilitated urban sprawl and the flight of whites to the suburbs, which in turn reduced the tax base of the city and resulted in social and economic problems for the city (and the costs of urban programs) while the surrounding suburbs grew affluent. Likewise, the rapid automobile transportation promised by the highways encouraged people to move to the suburbs and consequently to consume millions of gallons of gasoline each year in commuting to their jobs. This one example demonstrates that measures defined by any single agency to evaluate its programs may be too narrow to detect many important unintended social or economic effects.

Finally, if experimentation is used as a means of gauging the possible utility of a program, the danger that the "reactive effects of testing" will influence the results becomes an important consideration.[23] If citizens are aware that a certain policy is being tried "as an experiment," they may well behave differently than they would if it were declared to be "the policy." In other words, those who favor the policy may work especially hard to make the program effective, whereas those who do not support the program may attempt to make it appear ineffective. Even those who have no definite opinions on the policy may not behave as they would if the policy was thought to be a true attempt at change instead of an experiment. For example, if a voucher plan for educational financing is being experimented with, neither parents nor educational providers are likely to behave as they would if a voucher plan were said to be fully in operation. Parents may be reluctant to place their children in private schools for fear the voucher program will be terminated, and providers are unlikely to enter the marketplace if the number of parents capable of paying for their services is apt to decrease soon.

The simple knowledge that a policy initiative is considered to be a test will alter the behavior of those involved and consequently influence the results of the experiment or quasi experiment. There have been some very successful experimental evaluations of programs, such as the New Jersey Income Maintenance Experiment, but most require some strong incentives to gain the effective participation of the subjects.[24] Researchers then may have difficulty knowing if the participants are behaving "normally" or simply responding to the unusual, and often exciting, opportunity to be guinea pigs.

In evaluation research, problems are encountered with research designs, experimental or not, that reduce the analysts' ability to make definitive statements about the real worth of policy. The importance and expense of public programs have led to more experimental evaluations of programs before they are implemented; nearly 100 have been instituted since 1991.[25] These experiments are concentrated very heavily in the area of social policy, in part because of the controversy surrounding many programs in that area. These experiments are expensive, but not as expensive perhaps as implementing poorly designed programs. Conversely, not using an experimental method means that a large number of mainly unmeasured social and economic factors, not the program in question, may be the cause of any observed effects on the target population.

Targets

Related to the problem of goals is the question of the targets of a program.[26] It is important for the evaluator to know not only what the program is intended to do but also on whom it is intended to have an impact. A program that has significant effects on the population as a whole may not have the desired effects on the more specific target population. For example, the Medicare program was intended, among other things, to benefit less affluent older people, although all the elderly were declared eligible for the program. But, although the health of the elderly population in general has improved, probably at least in part as a result of Medicare, the health of the neediest portion of the elderly population has not improved commensurately.[27] As the program has been implemented, substantial coinsurance has been required, along with substantial deductibles if the insured enters a hospital. As a consequence, it is difficult for the neediest elderly citizens to participate in the Medicare program.

A similar problem has been developing with the Head Start program mentioned earlier. Conceived as a component of the 1960s War on Poverty, Head Start was meant to serve primarily lower-income families by enabling their children to participate and learn effectively once they entered school. Head Start is, however, only a part-day program, while in most low-income families all the adults who can will be working all day. These families, therefore, tend to find day-care providers for the full day. The educational advantages of Head Start are largely absent from those day-care programs, but the parents must go to work. As a result, Head Start tends to be used by higher-income families than was intended, and the "target population" has been largely missed.[28]

One problem in defining a target population and the program's success in reaching that population is that participation in many programs is voluntary and depends on individuals who are potential beneficiaries "taking up" the benefit. Voluntary programs directed at the poor and the less educated frequently face difficulties in making the availability of the program widely known among the target population. Even if it is made widely known to potential beneficiaries, pride, real and perceived administrative barriers, and real difficulties in consuming the benefits produced may make the program less effective than intended. An extreme example may be taken from the experience of the United Kingdom with its National Health Service (NHS). One ostensible purpose of the National Health Service was to equalize access to medical care for members of all social classes, but the evidence after four decades does not indicate that such equalization has taken place.[29] Instead, the disparities in health status that existed before the adoption of the NHS and that in fact existed in the early twentieth century have not been narrowed by an almost completely free system of medical care. Noneconomic barriers such as education, transportation, free time, and simple belief in the efficacy of medical care have served to ensure that although there has been a general improvement in health status among the British population, little or no narrowing of class differentials has occurred. The less affluent simply have not availed themselves of the services offered to the extent that they might, especially given their relatively greater need for medical services. Although the evidence is less dramatic, it appears that social programs in the United States have suffered many of the same failures in equalizing access, and especially utilization, of some basic social services.

Programs may create a false sense of success by "creaming" the segment of the population they serve.[30] Programs that have limited capacities to serve clients and that use stringent criteria for eligibility may select clients who actually need little help instead of those who have the greatest need. This can make the programs appear successful, although those being served did not need the program in the first place, and a large segment of the neediest go unserved. This pattern has been observed, for example, in many drug-treatment programs that take addicts who are already motivated to rid themselves of their habits. These programs can show a high rate of success when they argue for additional public funding. Such programs are successes, but only of a limited nature. Further, it would be a mistake for policymakers to generalize from the "successes" of such programs and assume that similar programs would work if applied to a general population, many of whom would not have the same level of motivation. Of course, excessively negative results may be produced by including too many people, many of whom may be inappropriate, as members of the population selected for treatment.[31]

As with so much of policy evaluation, defining the target population is a political exercise as much as an exercise in rational policy analysis. As we noted when discussing legitimation, one tendency in formulating and adopting policies is to broaden the definition of the possible beneficiaries and loosen eligibility requirements for the program. This helps to build the political coalition necessary to adopt the program. This political broadening frequently diffuses the target population of the program and consequently makes the program more difficult to evaluate. It is therefore often unfair to blame program managers for failing to serve the target population when those who constructed the legislation provided broad and unworkable definitions of that target. Further, with increasing strains on the public budget, it may become politically feasible to target programs more tightly simply to reduce program costs.

Efficiency and Effectiveness

A related problem is the search for the philosopher's stone of efficiency in government, a search that often leads to a dead-end street. Measuring efficiency requires relating the costs of efforts to results and then assessing the ratio of the two. As noted, measuring results is difficult in many policy areas; it is often equally difficult to assign costs to particular results, even if those results were measurable. For much the same reasons, equal difficulties may arise in attempting to measure effectiveness. Surrogate measures of the intended results are frequently developed for public programs and policies, but all require the suspension of disbelief to be accepted as valid and reliable descriptions of what is occurring in the public sector.

As a consequence of these difficulties in measuring the substantive consequence of government actions, much of the assessment of performance in government depends on the evaluation of procedural efficiency. That is, what is assessed is not so much what is produced as how the agencies go about producing it. Some of this proceduralism depends on the legal requirements for personnel management, budgeting, and accounting; but attempts to assess procedural efficiency go beyond those formal requirements. The efficiency of public agencies may be assessed by determining the speed with which certain actions occur or by ensuring that every decision goes through all the appropriate procedural stages specified for a process. The important point here is that goals may be displaced when evaluations are made on a basis that posits the process itself, rather than the services that it is intended to produce, as the measure of all things.[32] The concern with measuring efficiency through procedures may, in fact, actually reduce the efficiency of the process in producing results for citizens, because of the proliferation of procedural safeguards and associated "red tape."

Values and Evaluation

The analyst who performs an evaluation requires a value system to enable him or her to assign valuations to outcomes. However, value systems are by no means constant across the population, and the analyst who evaluates only a single program may perceive very different purposes and priorities within its policy area. Thus, there may be no simple means of determining the proper valuation of the outcomes of a program. This is especially true when the program has significant unintended effects (usually negative) that must be weighed against the intended consequences.[33]

One point for consideration is that the analyst brings his or her own values to the evaluation process. Despite their rational and neutral stance, most analysts involved in policymaking have proceeded beyond the "baby analyst" stage to the point at which they have values they wish to see manifested through the policy process.[34] And as the analyst is in a central position in evaluation, he or she may have a substantial influence over the final evaluation of outcomes. However, the analyst's values will be but one of several sets of values involved in making that final assessment of a program or policy. The organizations involved will have their own collective values to guide them in evaluating outcomes, or at least their own activities. The professions with which members of the organization or external service providers identify will also provide sets of well-articulated values that may affect the assessment of policies. Frequently, all these different sets of values conflict with one another, or with the values of clients or of the general public. Thus, assessing a policy is not a simple matter of relating a set of known facts about outcomes to a given set of values. As in almost all aspects of the policy process, the values themselves may be the major source of conflict, while rational argumentation and policy analysis are merely the ammunition.

Politics

Finally, we must always remember that evaluations of public programs are performed in a political context. Therefore, there may well be a sharp difference between the interpretation that an analyst might make about the success or failure of a program and the interpretation that political officials might make of the same data. Most evaluation schemes, for example, may be based on total benefits for the society, but political leaders may be interested only in the benefits created for their constituents; if that benefit is significant, the overall inefficiency of a program may be irrelevant. Political leaders may also be supportive of programs that their constituents like, whether or not the programs have any real impact on the social problems for which they were intended.

It is also important to remember that an evaluation may not be done for the purpose of evaluating a program. Its ultimate purpose may be to validate a decision that has already been made for very different reasons. Thus, evaluations are often performed on very short notice, and the evaluators may be given little time to do their work. The purpose then may be simply to produce some sort of a justification for public consumption, not to produce a "real" answer about the quality of the program. That is, in part, why institutionalized forms of evaluation, such as the General Accounting Office, are so important in the public sector.[35]

Summary

Policy evaluation is a central political process, and although it is also an analytic procedure, the central place of politics and value conflict cannot be ignored. As increasing pressures are brought to bear on the public sector to perform its role more effectively and efficiently, evaluation will probably become even more a center of conflict. Negative evaluations of the effectiveness and efficiency of a program now will be more likely to lead to the termination of the program than would have been true in more affluent times. The content of an evaluation, the values that are contained in it, and even the organization performing the evaluation will all affect the final assessment. Evaluation research is now a major industry involving numerous consulting firms ("beltway bandits"), universities, and organizations within government itself. Even these evaluative organizations will have their own perspectives on what is right and wrong in policy and will bring those values with them when they perform an analysis.

The latter point is demonstrated clearly by the evaluation of a CETA program performed by both the John F. Kennedy School of Government at Harvard University and the School of Public Policy at the University of California, Berkeley. The two schools stressed different values and approaches in their evaluations of the program. The JFK researchers concentrated on the costs and benefits of the program in strict economic terms, reflecting more utilitarian values. They found the program to be failing, with the costs surpassing the value of the benefits created. The Berkeley researchers, in contrast, stressed the political and participatory aspects of the program.[36] They found the program to be a great success, with the participants being pleased with the outcomes. The difficulty is, of course, that both evaluations were right.

Increasing Requirements for Evaluation

One component of the wave of managerial change that has swept government over the past several decades[37] is a focus on the outputs of government, as opposed to the inputs (budgets, personnel, etc.). The conventional means of controlling organizations in the public sector is to control their budgets and their personnel allocations stringently (see chapter 6). Evaluations based on outputs, in contrast, examine what government organizations do and the effects of their programs. This approach to evaluation is presumed to be a superior means of understanding the real contribution of the programs to public welfare.

In 1993 Congress passed the Government Performance and Results Act (GPRA), the basic idea of which is to appraise government organizations on the basis of their strategic plans and on the quantitative indicators that are developed as a part of those plans.[38] As noted earlier, this act was an attempt to make programs justify their existence on the basis of their outputs and to use changes in these outputs as a means of judging the continuing performance of those organizations. This emphasis on outputs will, of course, enhance the need for evaluation within the federal government. The danger, as with many other exercises in evaluation, is that Congress will focus attention on a few simple quantitative indicators and fail to understand the complexity of both evaluation and the programs that are being evaluated.

Other initiatives in the federal government also require greater emphasis on evaluation than was present during the Reagan and Bush years.[39] The Gore Report contains some of the same emphasis on outputs as does GPRA.[40] Regulatory review (see pp. 83–84) will require the economic evaluation of all new regulatory initiatives, although this will only touch the surface of the type of evaluation that would be required to understand fully the impact of these rules on the economy and society. The continuing debate over educational quality also appear to require an extensive effort at evaluation, although again there appears to be a narrowing of the debate to simple standardized tests rather than a broader assessment of quality in education.[41]

Policy Change

After evaluation, the next stage of the policy process is policy change. Rarely are policies maintained in exactly the same form over time; instead, they are constantly evolving. This change may be the direct result of an evaluation, but more often it is the result of changes in the socioeconomic or political environment, learning on the part of the personnel administering the program, or simple elaboration of existing structures and ideas. Further, a great deal of policymaking in industrialized countries such as the United States is the result of attempts at policy change rather than the result of new issues coming to the public sector for the first round of resolution.[42] Most policy areas in industrialized democracies are already populated by a number of programs and policies, so that what is usually required is change rather than totally new policies. Policy succession, or the replacement of one policy by another, is therefore an important way of examining the development of contemporary public policies.

When a policy or program is reconsidered or evaluated, three outcomes are possible: policy maintenance, policy termination, or policy succession.[43] Policy maintenance rarely occurs as a conscious choice; more often it is a result of simple failure to make decisions. It is possible, but unlikely, that a policy will be considered seriously and then maintained in exactly the same form. In the first place, politicians make names for themselves by advocating new legislation, not by maintaining existing programs. Less cynically, we acknowledge that few policies or programs are so well designed initially that they require no changes after they have begun operation. The implementation of a program frequently demonstrates weaknesses in the original design that then require modification. Through what might be considered almost continuous experimentation, programs can be made to match changes in society, in the economy, and in knowledge, and can thus be made to work more effectively.

It is also unlikely that many public programs will be terminated. Once begun, programs have a life of their own. They generate organizations, and those organizations hire personnel. Programs also develop clienteles, who come to depend on the programs for certain services. Once clients use the services of a program, they may find it difficult ever to return to the market provision of goods or services, or to do without. This is especially true for programs that create a "stock" of benefits, as opposed to those that are merely a flow of resources. For example, Social Security created a stock of future benefits for its recipients, so once the program was initiated, future recipients began to plan differently for their retirement. Any reduction in benefits would thus create a severe hardship that the participants in the program could not have anticipated. Programs such as AFDC or food stamps,

President Clinton appears with cabinet members and task force representatives to celebrate the signing of an executive memorandum extending provisions of the Americans with Disabilities Act. (AP/Wide World Photos)

which involve no such planning by recipients, create hardships if they are reduced, but the planning or "stock" element is not involved, and so it may be possible to move clients back into the market system. Public programs, policies, and organizations may not be immortal, but relatively few are ever fully terminated.[44] Even the Reagan administration, which came into office making promises to terminate organizations such as the Department of Education and the Small Business Administration, found those promises difficult to keep because the support for existing programs tends to keep them running.[45] The Republican Congress's desire to eliminate other federal organizations such as the Department of Commerce also has run afoul of strongly entrenched interests.

Dismissing the other two options leaves policy succession as the most probable outcome for an existing policy or program. Policy succession may take several forms:

1. *Linear.* Linear successions involve the direct replacement of one program, policy, or organization by another, or the simple change of location of an existing program. For example, the replacement of earlier manpower programs by the Comprehensive Employment and Training Act is an example of a linear succession.

2. *Consolidation.* Some successions involve combining several programs that have existed independently into a single program. The rolling together of a number of categorical health and welfare programs into a few block grants in the Reagan administration, as well as reflecting a change in the delivery system, was a consolidation.

3. *Splitting.* Some programs are split into two or more individual components in a succession. For example, the Atomic Energy Commission was split in 1974 into the Nuclear Regulatory Agency and the Energy Research Development Agency, reflecting the contradictory programs of regulation and support of nuclear energy that had existed in the earlier organization.

4. *Nonlinear.* Some policy and organizational successions are complex and involve elements of other kinds of successions. The complex changes involved in creating the Department of Energy from existing programs (including the two nuclear energy agencies mentioned above) are examples of nonlinear succession.

Although they entail much of the same process described for making policy (chapters 3–6), policy successions are processed in a distinctive manner. First, the agenda-setting stage is not so difficult for policy succession as it is for policy initiation. The broad issue at question has already been accepted as a component of the agenda and therefore needs only to be returned to a particular institutional agenda. Some issues, such as debt ceilings and annual reauthorizations of existing programs, automatically return to an agenda every year or even more frequently. More commonly, dissatisfaction with the existing programs returns an issue for further consideration. But returning the issue to the institutional agenda is easier than its initial introduction, because there are organizational manifestations of the program and identified clients who are in a better position to bring about the consideration. Furthermore, once organizations exist, it is more likely that program administrators will learn from other similar programs and will find opportunities for improving the program, or that they will simply think of better "solutions" to the problems.

The legitimation and formulation processes will also be different from those used in policy initiation. But instead of fewer obstacles, as in agenda setting, there are likely to be more barriers. As noted, the existence of a program produces a set of client and producer interests that may be threatened by any proposed policy change. This is especially true if the proposed succession involves a "policy consolidation" (combining several programs) or a change in the policy instrument delivering the program in a direction that will demand less direct administration. For example, using policy consolidation to combine a number of categorical grants into block grants during the Reagan administration provoked outcries from both clients (primarily big-city mayors) and producers (administrators who had managed the categorical programs). And part of the conflict over the negative income tax proposed in President Nixon's Family Assistance Plan, as well as over some of President Carter's welfare reforms, concerned changes in the instruments used to deliver the benefits, as well as ideological conflicts over the level of benefits.[46] Thus, once a policy change of one of these kinds enters an institutional arena, it is quite likely to encounter severe resistance from the affected interests. This may be true even if the threat to those interests is not real. The mere threat of upsetting established patterns of delivering services may be sufficient to provoke resistance.

Of course, some policy successions may be generated within the organization administering the program rather than imposed from the outside. An array of external political forces may be strong enough to effectuate the change, and the organization and the clientele will "gladly" accede. They may even publicly cosponsor the change. Also, some program managers may be risk takers, rather than risk avoiders like most public bureaucrats. They may be willing to gamble that the proposed change will produce greater benefits for the organization, so they need not attempt to hang on to what they have. Finally, some programs may have expanded too far; their personnel may wish to pare off some of the peripheral programs to target their clientele more clearly and protect the organizational "heartlands."[47] This does not necessarily imply that the pared-off programs will be terminated, only that they will change their organizational locations.

Clientele groups may seek to split a program from a larger organization in order to develop a clearer target for their political activities. Pressures from the National Educational Association and other educational groups to divide the Department of Health, Education, and Welfare (HEW) and establish an independent Department of Education illustrate this point. It was argued that HEW did not give educational interests the direct attention they deserved. In addition, because the education budget had the greatest flexibility of all the budgets in HEW (the remainder being primarily entitlement programs), any cutting that was done was likely to be in education.[48] Although there were pressures on the Reagan administration to eliminate the Department of Education, once established, its independent status proved difficult to alter. To some degree the Bush administration, by virtue of its increased interest in education, placed the Department of Education in a more central position.

Forming a coalition for policy change requires careful attention to the commitment of individual congressmen to particular interests and to ongoing programs. As with the initial formulation and legitimation of a policy, an attempt at policy succession requires the use of the mechanisms of partisan analysis, logrolling, and the pork barrel, in order to deliver that change (see chapter 4). Again, this stage of the policy process may be even more difficult than it is for policy initiation. While the implications of a new policy are often vague, the probable effects of a change in an existing policy may be more readily identifiable. It may be easy to persuade legislators of the benefits of a new policy on the basis of limited information, but once the program has been running for some time, information will become available to the legislator. Persuading legislators to change a program that is "good enough" may be much more difficult.

There may, however, be many clients, administrators, and legislators who are dissatisfied with the program as it is being implemented, and those individuals can be mobilized to advocate the change. A coalition of this kind may involve individuals from both the right and the left who oppose the existing policy. The coalition built around the 1986 tax reform illustrates this process rather well: liberals who wanted more equitable treatment of the working and middle classes and greater equity in the tax system joined with some conservatives who wanted greater fairness in the tax code for all types of businesses.[49] Managing a policy succession by organizing such a broad coalition runs the risk that termination of the policy may be the only thing on which the coalition can agree as an alternative to the status quo. Therefore, before beginning the process, it is crucial for the analyst to have in mind the particular policy succession that he or she would like to have implemented. Otherwise, allowing political forces to follow their own lead may threaten the existence of the program.

Finally, implementing a policy succession may be the most difficult aspect of the process. That is, of course, much the same as was true for the initiation of the policy, for putting a policy into effect in the intended manner is problematic at best. But several features of policy succession as a process may make it that much more difficult. First, it is important to remember that organizations exist in the field as well as at headquarters.[50] People working in the field may have policy preferences as strong as those of the personnel in the home office, but they may not be consulted about proposed changes. Yet it is the field workers who must put the policy change into effect and ultimately decide who will get what as a result of the change. Thus, if policy change does not involve significant and clear modification of the existing policies, then the field staffs may well be able to continue doing what they were doing prior to the nominal change and subvert the intention of the succession legislation. This subversion need not be intentional; it may be only the result of inertia or inadequate understanding of the intentions of headquarters and the legislation.

In addition, it is important to remember that organizations do not exist alone in the world, nor do policies.[51] Rather, each organization exists within a complicated network of other organizations, all of which must cooperate in order for any of them to be successful.[52] Any change in the policies of one organization may reduce the ability of other organizations to fulfill their own goals. Education and job-training may now be as important for economic performance, especially in the long run, as is formal economic policy. This interaction is perhaps especially evident in the field of social policy, where a variety of programs are necessary to meet the many and interrelated needs of poor families and in which changes in any one program may influence the success of all. Terminating food stamps, for example, would mean that welfare payments would not be sufficient for families to buy the amounts of food they used to buy. As a consequence, housing, education, and even employment programs would be adversely impacted by increasing demands.

As government shifts its focus of activity from direct provision of services to "new governance"—in which it operates through a variety of third-party and indirect mechanisms—the capacity to associate particular outcomes with particular programs may become even more difficult. Further, generating change in this setting implies changing not only the public sector programs and their intentions but also the network that will become responsible for delivering programs.[53] Dependence on a network for service will make the changes all the more difficult, given the resilience that appears to characterize the behavior of both public and private organizations.

Finally, implementing policy succession is almost certain to be disappointing. The massive political effort required to bring about a policy succession is unlikely to be rewarded the first month, or even the first year, after the change. This is almost certain to create disappointment in the new program and perhaps cynicism about the entire policy area. As a consequence, one policy succession may generate enough disruption to engender a rapid series of changes. Further, once a stable set of policies and organizations has been disturbed, there will no longer be a single set of entrenched interests with which to contend, so forming a new coalition in favor of policy change or termination may be easier. The advocate of policy change must be cognizant that he or she may produce more change than was intended once the possibility of reform becomes apparent to participants in the policy area.

Since we now understand that implementing policy succession will be difficult, we should address the problem of designing policy changes that would be easier to implement. The ease with which change can be brought about is a function at least in part of the design of previous organizations and programs. In an era of increased skepticism concerning government and bureaucracy, policies are being designed with built-in triggers for evaluation and termination.[54] The interest in "sunset laws" means that any administrator joining such an organization, or any client becoming dependent on its services, should have reason to question the stability of those arrangements.[55] If the declining conception of entitlement to either employment or benefits from an organization can make future policy successions more palatable to those already connected with the program, one major hurdle to policy change will have been overcome. However, this declining sense of entitlement may be related to a declining commitment of workers to the program that can have negative consequences for the organization that exceed the costs of change.

It is not possible to reverse history and redesign programs and organizations that are already functioning without such built-in terminators. The analyst or practitioner of policy change must therefore be prepared to intervene in existing organizations in order to produce the smooth transition from one set of policies to another. One obvious trigger for such change would be a change in the party in office, especially in the presidency. Until the Reagan presidency, however, the alternation of parties in office had produced little significant policy change.[56] (The Clinton administration in many ways is a return to that pattern, with "New Democrats" being very similar to a moderate Republican such as George Bush.) The Reagan administration, however, injected very substantial doses of ideology and policy change into American politics, leaving the question afterwards whether a subsequent Democratic administration could undo the "Reagan revolution."[57] And indeed it has proven extremely difficult for the Clinton administration to assert a more activist agenda for government, given the legitimation of the antigovernment perspective during twelve years of Republican presidents, the election of a Republican Congress, and the constraints imposed by attempting to balance the budget.[58]

Rapid change in demand and environmental conditions may also trigger attempts at policy succession, but organizations have proved to be remarkably effective in deflecting attempts at change and in using change for their own purposes. At present it is fair to say that no technology is available for implementing policy succession, just as there is no reliable technology for implementation in general. A common finding is that organizations are able to interpret new policy initiatives in ways that fortify their current approaches. As with the discussion of the social construction of issues on the agenda (see pp. 46–48), organizations also socially construct the meaning of policy and law, and they do so in ways that will benefit them.

Summary

Policies must be evaluated, and frequently policies must be changed. But neither task is as easy as some politicians, and even some academicians, make it appear. Identifying the goals of policies, determining the results of programs, and isolating the effects of policies compared with the effects of other social and economic forces all make evaluating public policies tricky, and at times impossible. The surrogate measures that must be used sometimes may be worse than no measures at all, for they emphasize activity of any sort rather than actions performed well and efficiently. The method of evaluation then places pressure on agencies merely to spend their money rather than always to spend it wisely.

Evaluation frequently leads to policy change, and the process of producing desired changes and of implementing those changes in a complex political environment taxes the abilities of the analyst as well as the politician. All the usual steps in policymaking must be gone through, but in this case in the presence of established organizations and clients. The implications of proposed policy changes may be all too obvious to those actors, and they may therefore strenuously oppose the changes. As often as not, these entrenched forces are successful in deflecting pressures for change. American government often then is a great machine that proceeds onward in its established direction without the application of significant and skillful political force. Those whose interests are already being served benefit from this inertia, but those on the outside may continue to be excluded.

PART THREE

Substantive Policy Issues

8. Economic Policy

The performance of the economy in Western societies was once considered something like the weather: everyone talked about it, but no one was able to do anything about it. Economic cycles and fluctuation were considered natural, acts of God, beyond the control of governments or human beings. That concept of the economy was altered during the depression in the 1930s and the postwar economic boom.[1] The magnitude and duration of the depression were such that even conservative governments were forced to pay some attention to its effects.[2] Perhaps more important, the work of John Maynard Keynes, Knut Wiksell, and other economists gave governments the economic tools—and the intellectual justification for using those tools—to control an economy.

The confidence of governments in their ability to manage economies is perhaps best exemplified in the postwar full-employment acts in both the United States and the United Kingdom, pledging the governments of the two nations never again to allow mass unemployment. This confidence was bolstered during the economic miracles of the 1950s, 1960s, and early 1970s in which most Western nations experienced rapid and consistent economic growth, very low levels of unemployment (the United States being a notable exception), and relatively stable price levels. In the early 1960s advisers to President Kennedy spoke of the government's ability to "fine tune" the economy and to manipulate economic outcomes by pulling a few simple economic levers.[3]

In the 1980s and early 1990s anyone reading that account of economic policy would have considered it very curious.[4] The American economy, during the period following the "oil shocks" of the 1970s, was characterized instead by unreliable and usually slow growth, high unemployment, extremely high trade deficits, and relatively high (by American, if not international, standards) inflation (see table 8.1, p. 188). This "stagflation" resulted in diminished public faith in the capacity of governments effectively to manage their national economies; politicians who promised a bright economic future were regarded with substantial skepticism.[5]

The Reagan administration was able to produce some economic growth during part of the 1980s with its "supply-side economics" but did so at the cost of a greater public deficit, increased income inequality, and higher un-employment.[6] Even at those social costs, the administration's efforts produced an average annual rate of economic growth (3.2 percent) that was noticeably lower than the postwar average (3.6 percent). The economic growth rate during the Bush administration (2.1 percent) was even lower, and that fact played a significant role in President Bush's defeat in the 1992 election. Despite their conservatism and appeals to free-market values, those Republican administrations could not escape responsibility for economic policy, and although they attempted to ameliorate economic miseries as much as possible, for many voters in 1992, it *was* the economy.[7]

TABLE 8.1

PERFORMANCE OF THE U.S. ECONOMY
(IN PERCENTAGES)

	1950–59	1960–69	1970–79	1980–89	1990–97
Average unemployment rate	4.5	4.8	6.2	7.2	6.0
Average GNP growth	4.0	4.1	2.8	2.7	2.2
Average price change	2.1	2.3	7.1	5.6	3.0
Average real wage growth	3.6	2.9	0.8	−0.2	0.2

SOURCE: Organization for Economic Cooperation and Development, *Main Economic Indicators* (Paris: OECD, monthly).

The Clinton economic proposals during the campaign were more expansionist, focusing on the creation of jobs and economic growth. Although more interested in using the power of government than his immediate predecessors, candidate Clinton found that his emphasis on growth and "growing down the deficit" did well politically in a country facing numerous uncertainties about its economic future. The Clinton proposals were not explicitly Keynesian, but they depended on somewhat increasing government activity to help move the economy forward. The Clinton economic strategy also depended on microeconomic tools, such as industrial policies and job training, to achieve the desired results.[8] Despite these interventions, however, the "flexible labor market," argued to be so important for recent American economic success, implied a willingness to let the market function with minimal regulation. Finally, the Clinton economic strategy continued unabated from Republican administrations the free-trade policy that included implementation of the North American Free Trade Agreement, placing pressure on countries deemed to be protectionist, and continued advocacy of free trade in a variety of international forums.[9]

Once in office the Clinton administration proved to be even less interventionist than its campaign rhetoric. Other than the micro-level programs mentioned earlier, it pursued an almost "hands-off" approach to economic management. One of the touchstones of economic policy—the flexible labor market—has meant in practice little or no direct public intervention into the market. The economic indicators have been positive throughout much the Clinton administration, and indeed the economy appeared to be soaring during the late 1990s, with the lowest level of unemployment for years. Nevertheless, many underlying structural problems remain in the American economy, perhaps the most important being the continuing trade deficits and continuing, if not increasing, levels of economic inequality.

Economic policy is a central concern of government. One important step that a government must take is to form a more or less coherent set of policies intended to manage the economy. But economic policy is also a by-product of many other policy choices, about matters such as spending for public programs, patterns of taxation, and the interest rate charged by the central bank (the Federal Reserve System in the United States). Even if the federal government chooses to make relatively consistent decisions in these areas, a host of other governmental actors (50 states and more than 85,000 local governments) are also making taxing and spending decisions.

Economic policy also depends heavily on the actions of individual citizens over whom governments have little or no control. In the basic Keynesian paradigm of fiscal policy, an excess of public expenditures above revenues is supposed to stimulate the economy because citizens will spend the additional money, creating additional demand for goods and services. But if citizens do not spend the additional money, the intended stimulation effect will not be created. Only when governments choose to regulate the economy directly through instruments such as wage and price controls can they be reasonably confident that their actions will generate desired behaviors. Even then, policing compliance with a wage and price policy presents severe administrative difficulties of its own, for individuals and businesses have shown themselves to be extremely creative in avoiding attempts at control.

The Goals of Economic Policy

Economic policy has a number of goals, all of which are socially desirable, but some of which are not always mutually compatible. Political leaders frequently must make decisions that simultaneously benefit some citizens and impose burdens on others. For example, although it is by no means as clear as it once was, there is a tradeoff between inflation and unemployment.[10] To the extent that governments attempt to reduce unemployment, they may increase the inflation rate. The results of such a decision may benefit the worker about to be laid off but harm the senior citizen on a fixed income, as well as all citizens who hold fixed-rate investments (bonds, for example). In general, economic policy has four fundamental goals, which German political economists have labeled "the golden quadrangle." These goals are economic growth, full employment, stable prices, and a positive balance of payments from international trade. To these may be added an additional intermediate goal: positive structural change in the economy.

Economic Growth

Economic growth has been a boon both to citizens and to governments. Although it is popular among the ecologically minded to question the benefits of economic growth and to praise smaller and less technologically complex economic systems, most American citizens still want more of everything.[11] They became accustomed to receiving more and more income each year during the postwar period up until at least the mid-1970s. All this economic growth translated into massive increases in the availability of consumer goods, making items such as television sets and automobiles, which were not widely available in 1950, almost universally obtainable today. In material terms, economic growth has produced an average standard of living in 1998 much higher than that in 1950, or in 1980, or even in 1990, and almost all Americans enjoy that affluence.[12]

Economic growth has also been important in the political history of the postwar era, acting as a political "solvent" to ease the transition of the United States from a "warfare state" to a "welfare state." Economic growth was sufficiently great that virtually every segment of the society could be given its own government programs without exhausting all the newly created wealth. Public programs grew along with private affluence, so individuals did not feel particularly disadvantaged by their taxes or by government benefits granted to others.[13] Further, economic growth aided the redistribution of income to the less advantaged. According to one calculation, 90 percent of the postwar improvement in the economic status of African Americans has been the result of economic growth rather than of redistributive public programs. The best welfare program is still a good job with a good salary, a fact emphasized in the 1996 welfare reforms that emphasized working rather than receiving social benefits (see pp. 304–6).

Yet American economic growth did not compare well with that of many of our major trading partners during most of the postwar period. Average annual growth in per capita GNP for the United States from 1960 to 1980 was 2.2 percent, while it was 3.1 percent for Germany, 3.8 percent for Italy, and over 6.3 percent for Japan. In addition, the American economic growth rate was falling (although not as rapidly as that in most other industrialized countries); average economic growth in the 1980s was less than half what it had been during the 1950s, becoming even slower, and even negative, in the early 1990s.

After the first few years of the 1990s, however, American economic performance improved significantly, outstripping that of most of our trading partners. For example, in the period from 1990 to 1997 per capita income in the United States increased by 8 percent in real terms, while that of its trading partners was growing by 4 percent or less. The U.S. economy was particularly productive later in that time period as growth in major economies such as Japan and Germany slackened.

Despite the return to affluence, the United States may be still be facing a "zero-sum society," in which the gains achieved by one segment of the society must come at the expense of some other segment.[14] To some degree that has already happened. During the economic growth of the Reagan years, the middle and upper classes gained at the expense (relatively and in some cases absolutely) of the poor and working classes. The relatively slow rate of growth was reflected clearly in the real (adjusted for price changes) income of the average American worker from 1970 to 1990. This important indicator of individuals' economic well-being hardly changed at all over these two decades, but it did begin to move upward again significantly in 1994 (see table 8.1, p. 188).

Whereas previous generations could expect to do better than their parents economically, the economic future for young people entering the labor market now seems somewhat uncertain, despite good times in the late 1990s. Increasing benefits for the elderly through Social Security may mean a direct loss in the income of working-age citizens, and programs for the poor may require a reduction in the income of the middle and upper classes through higher taxes. Likewise, even in times of economic growth and a balanced budget, there are vigorous conflicts between advocates of tax cuts and advocates of public programs. The continuing uncertainty about economic growth, combined with more ideological politics, may well make economic policymaking more contentious and more difficult as the nation enters the twenty-first century.

Full Employment

The benefits of full employment are obvious. Most adults want to work and utilize their talents. The welfare state has provided a floor for those who are unemployed, so that they and their families are unlikely to starve or do without medical care. These social benefits, however, cannot match the income that can be earned by working, nor can social programs replace the pride and psychological satisfaction that comes from earning one's own living. These psychological benefits are perhaps especially pronounced in the United States, where the social and political culture attaches great importance to work and self-reliance. These values are reflected in the significantly higher rates of family problems, suicides, and alcoholism found among the unemployed than among the employed. Further, changes in social policy now make working almost mandatory, and the relevant question has become whether the economy can provide enough jobs for all the people who want and need them.

In addition to its effects on individuals, unemployment also has some influence on government budgets. When individuals are not working, they do not contribute to Social Security or pay income taxes. Also, they cost the government money in unemployment benefits, Medicaid payments, food stamps, and the services of other social programs. Thus, increasing unemployment may upset the government's best plans to produce a balanced budget or a deficit of a certain size. Even if the level of unemployment is accurately anticipated, revenues are still lost and more expenditures are required. Also, other important public programs may be funded inadequately because of the need to assist the unemployed through public programs.

The good news is that, compared to many of its major trading partners, the United States has achieved relatively low rates of unemployment. During the late 1980s and early 1990s, American unemployment rates began to fall below those of other industrialized democracies, in the late 1990s reaching the lowest levels for decades. Critics argued that many of the jobs being created were for "hamburger flippers" (i.e., low-paid workers in the service sector), but while there certainly were a number of such new jobs, there was also evidence that more highly-paid jobs—many also in service industries such as finance, computers, and the like—were also being created. Indeed, in some urban areas the demand for labor in the late 1990s has meant that even hamburger flippers are earning well above the minimum wage.

What is perhaps more important than the aggregate performance of the United States on this indicator is the concentration of unemployment by race and age. Blacks and young Americans bear by far the highest rates of unemployment; among young blacks, the rate of unemployment still approaches *30 percent*. And even though aggregate employment figures appear very good, there has been a shift in the types of jobs being created in the economy. There were over 29 million more nonfarm jobs in the United States in 1996 than in 1980, 10 million more than in 1990. During the period since 1990 the number of goods-producing jobs has declined by 600,000, while the number of service-producing jobs has increased by almost 11 million. Of the new service jobs, at least one-third were in restaurants, hotels, and other relatively low-wage positions, while the other two-thirds were in a variety of more lucrative service occupations, such as financial services, computer firms, and the like.[15] The same pattern of employment change is projected to continue for at least the next decade.[16]

The changing pattern of job creation to some degree reflects changes in the structure of the U.S. economy, which has been shifting away from manufacturing and toward a service base.[17] Further, the end of the Cold War has meant that industries such as aerospace have not been employing as many people as they once did. Also in the late 1990s, the oil industry has been hit by very low prices and little need for domestic exploitation. These shifts pose problems for some regions of the country (e.g., California and Alaska) as well as for the traditional industrial labor force (see table 8.2). Many dozens of new jobs are created in the United States every day, but these jobs tend either to be suited for those individuals with strong technical skills (computer programming) or to pay relatively little (clerking in fast-food restaurants).

TABLE 8.2

UNEMPLOYMENT IN THE UNITED STATES
(IN PERCENTAGES)

Across time

1970	1980	1990	1991	1992	1993	1994	1995	1996	1997
4.4	7.0	5.4	6.6	7.4	6.8	6.1	5.6	5.4	4.9

By state (October 1997)

High		*Low*	
Alaska	7.4	North Dakota	1.9
West Virginia	6.5	Nebraska	2.3
New York	6.4	Iowa	2.6
California	6.3	South Dakota	2.6
Mississippi	6.1	Utah	3.0

SOURCE: Bureau of Labor Statistics, *Monthly Labor Review,* January 1998.

Industrial workers accustomed to earning high wages in unskilled or semiskilled occupations have found the structural shift in the economy very disturbing, but they have been almost powerless to change it.[18] Labor unions (outside government and some service industries) have been losing large numbers of members, and employees know that business can simply move jobs to lower-wage economies if there is too much pressure on them in the United States. The increased prevalence of low-wage jobs often makes two incomes necessary to maintain a reasonable family lifestyle, even after the economic growth of the Clinton years. This economic shift in turn increases demands on the public sector for improved social (family leave) and educational (early childhood) programs. Here, as in almost any area of social or economic life, it is impossible to contain the effects of change within a single policy area.

Stable Prices

Unlike unemployment, inflation affects all citizens through increases in the prices of goods and services.[19] Increased rates of interest are also a form of inflation because they increase the costs of borrowing money for business, a cost that is then passed on in higher prices. Inflation affects different portions of the community differently, however, and it may even benefit some people. On the one hand, inflation particularly hurts those living on fixed incomes, such as the elderly who live on fixed pensions. It also adversely affects those (such as college professors) who are not sufficiently well organized to gain wage increases equal to increases in price levels.

On the other hand, inflation benefits individuals and institutions that owe money. The significance of a debt is reduced as inflation eats away at the real value of currency. As the biggest debtor in the society, government is perhaps particularly benefited by inflation. The amount governments owe, relative to the total production of their economies, can diminish if inflation makes everything cost more and each unit of currency worth less. Governments with progressive tax structures also benefit from inflation, as people whose real incomes (i.e., incomes adjusted for changes in purchasing power) have not increased see their monetary incomes increase. These people are moved into higher tax brackets where they must pay a larger portion of their income in taxes; as a consequence, government receives a relatively painless (politically) increase in revenues. Many tax reforms adopted during the 1980s were partly aimed at reducing the progressivity of taxation, or requiring governments to relate the thresholds of tax brackets to inflation, so that government would not receive an automatic "fiscal dividend" from inflation.

Inflation is by no means an unqualified boon for governments. Many benefits paid out by governments now are indexed, or adjusted for changes in the price level.[20] As a consequence, much of any increase in revenues from inflation must be paid out directly in increased benefits. The things that a government must buy, most notably the labor of its employees, also increase in price during inflationary periods. This is especially important since government has been more labor intensive than the private economy, so that its costs increase more rapidly than do labor costs for other "industries" in the society.[21] As information technology advances, however, governments tend to be major beneficiaries. More than anything else, governments process information, and computers, e-mail, and the internet have tended to boost productivity in government.[22]

The performance of the American economy in maintaining a stable price level during the postwar period has been better than that of most of its major trading partners (see table 8.3). Only Germany and Japan have been more successful in holding down price increases, while countries such as Italy have had more than double the rate of inflation of the United States over this period. The relatively superior performance of the U.S. economy in this area can be explained by several factors, including its relatively poor record on unemployment during much of the postwar period. It is also argued that the Federal Reserve Board's independence from political interference has allowed it to use monetary policy to regulate the price level effectively.[23] Also, the relative weakness of the labor movement in the United States has meant fewer strong pressures to push wages upward than have been brought to bear in most other Western countries, although the power of large corporations might also have been expected to be related to increasing prices.[24]

TABLE 8.3

INFLATION RATE OF UNITED STATES

AND MAJOR TRADING PARTNERS

(IN PERCENTAGES)

	1988	*1990*	*1991*	*1993*	*1995*	*1997*
United States	4.0	5.3	3.0	2.6	2.6	2.0
Canada	4.0	4.8	1.5	1.2	1.4	1.8
Japan	0.6	3.1	1.7	0.6	−0.5	1.6
France	2.6	3.4	2.4	4.0	1.6	1.2
Germany	1.3	2.7	4.0	2.4	1.7	1.9
Italy	5.1	6.5	5.4	4.4	5.7	2.4
Sweden	6.8	6.9	2.2	2.6	2.7	2.2
United Kingdom	4.9	9.4	3.7	3.2	1.4	2.1

SOURCE: Organization for Economic Cooperation and Development, *Main Economic Indicators* (Paris: OECD, monthly).

For whatever reason, in comparison with other nations the United States has been a low-inflation country during most of the postwar period, although many Americans may be far from pleased with the price increases that have occurred. That position began to weaken relative to the rest of the industrialized world during the late 1980s. This was in part because of the inflationary effects of large-scale budget deficits, but the recession of the early 1990s helped keep prices virtually stable for the first years of the decade. Even with the return to economic growth in the mid-1990s, inflation remained very low, in part because of the active intervention of the Federal Reserve. Indeed, one of the astounding features of the economic system in the late 1990s has been the combination of relatively high growth, low un-employment, and an inflation rate of almost zero—a combination not sup-posed to happen.

In the 1990s inflation has no longer seemed to be the threat that it once was, and central banks, politicians, and businessmen all now run the risk of overreacting to the threat of inflation. If the money supply is restricted too much, economic growth and employment will be threatened. A number of economic factors appear to be interacting to make inflation a less significant economic threat. One factor is the increased number of energy sources, with greater access to oil in the former Soviet Union and a number of new sources, that should stabilize or lower the energy prices that are a major component of costs in industrialized economies (especially the United States). Further, the prices for other raw materials (including agricultural products) are stable or decreasing as many Third World countries are stress-ing exports of primary commodities rather than rapid industrialization. Also, wage rates in the United States dropped (in real terms) from the late 1980s into the 1990s, so a major cost of production has also been decreas-ing. Even with some growth in average real wages during the late 1990s, productivity is higher and labor costs lower than in most competitor coun-tries. In short, continued price stability seems a very real possibility, and de-flation may even be possible.

A Positive Balance of Payments

The U.S. economy is relatively autarkic and relatively less involved in inter-national trade than are the economies of most other industrialized coun-tries.[25] It is, however, still important for the United States to manage its bal-ance of payments from trade. The balance of payments is the net result of the cost of imports and the income from exports. If a country spends more money abroad than it receives from abroad, it has a negative balance of pay-ments, while a country that spends less overseas than it receives has a posi-tive balance of payments. The final figure for the balance of payments is composed of the balance of trade (payment for real goods traded) and the balance on "invisibles"—services such as insurance, banking, and shipping fees.

For the past several decades the United States has generally had a very large negative balance of trade but a positive balance on invisibles, and these have added up to a negative balance of payments. A number of factors were included in the large negative balance of payments. For much of the 1980s world oil prices were low, but prices began to increase in the early 1990s. Having learned little from earlier oil crises, the United States had again be-come heavily dependent on foreign oil (see chapter 13). America's demand for other foreign products, such as Japanese automobiles and electronics, continued to increase. By the mid-1990s the relatively rapid recovery of the American economy (when compared to the rest of the industrialized world) meant that U.S. demand for foreign goods tended to increase more rapidly than did foreign demand for American goods. This latter factor was exacerbated in 1997 and 1998 when many Asian economies suffered massive downturns; they stopped buying almost all foreign goods and dropped prices on their own goods to try to sell more.[26]

The effects of a net negative balance of payments are generally detrimental to a country's economy. In the first place, a negative balance of payments indicates that the country's products are not competitive with those from other countries. This may be because of price, because of quality, or because a country cannot produce a commodity, such as oil. More important, a negative balance of payments tends to reduce the value of the country's currency in relation to that of other nations. If a country continues to trade its money for commodities overseas, the laws of supply and demand dictate that the value of the country's currency eventually will decline, as more money goes abroad than is returned. This has been an especially difficult problem for the United States, because the dollar has been the "top currency" in international trade for some years and because so many dollars are held overseas and used in international transactions.[27] Finally, as in the case of trading for raw materials, a negative balance of payments may indicate a country's dependence on the products of other nations, with the potential for international "blackmail." And holding a great deal of a country's currency abroad may mean that the value of that currency is especially vulnerable to the actions of others—governments and individuals.

For the United States in the late 1990s, international flows of capital have also become a difficulty for several reasons. First, money has flowed into the United States since the early 1990s, in part because of political stability and high interest rates, but this has meant that a number of businesses and a large amount of property are now owned outside the country.[28] These capital flows are in part offset by the large amount of property and industries overseas owned by American firms and individuals. The dependency on foreign capital makes some important industries seemingly difficult to steer toward national policy goals, although firms totally owned domestically are not always amenable to national goals either.

Further, as the world economy becomes less national and more international, large capital flows across borders are becoming a fact of economic life.[29] The ease with which capital now moves places restraints on the ability of national governments to make domestic economic policy as they might like, and also strengthens international businesses that bargain with governments over where to locate.[30] That having been said, however, there is some evidence that capital flows do not totally obviate the capacity of countries to influence the behavior of businesses and individuals. For example, there does appear to be more variance in both tax policy[31] and economic regulations[32] than might be expected if governments had such a limited capacity to control the economy. The United States, given the huge size of its domestic economy and its central position in the world economy, has more capacity than most countries to exercise that control.

Structural Change

The final goal of economic policy is structural change, or changing the industrial and regional composition of production. Some regions of a country may be less developed than others; the South traditionally has been the least developed section of the United States, but it is now relatively prosperous compared to some of the Great Lakes states. In addition, the composition of production makes some regions extremely vulnerable to economic fluctuations. The experience of Michigan during the continuing slump in automobile production and that of Louisiana and Alaska during periods of declining oil prices are graphic evidence of the danger of relying too heavily on a single product. In addition, government may want to alter the structure of an entire economy. The most common manifestation of this is the effort of Third World countries to industrialize their agricultural economies. A similar effort was, of course, also made in the United States in the nineteenth century, and many industrialized countries still attempt to shift the composition of their economies in the most profitable directions possible.

In the United States, the federal government has had relatively little involvement in promoting structural change. Major exceptions have been regional programs such as the Tennessee Valley Authority and the Appalachian Regional Commission. Also, the federal government has been active in supporting and protecting defense industries, and those industries have certainly been crucial for the development of "high-tech" enterprises. If anything, the federal government has attempted to utilize trade policies, including quotas on imported products such as automobiles, as a means of slowing the structural change of the economy rather than accelerating it. Politically the federal government has difficulty in supporting one area of the country over another, and so it tends to use rather general instruments except when trying to protect industry from foreign competition that is perceived to be unfair.

State and local governments, however, have been extremely active in attempting to promote economic development and structural change, particularly through their tax systems.[33] States permit industries moving into their area to take tax credits for their investments and to write off a certain percentage of their profits against taxes for some years. Local governments have fewer tax options (property tax relief being the most important), but

they can provide grants for industrial sites and other infrastructural developments to make themselves more attractive to industries. Building infrastructure, indeed, is an underappreciated mechanism for economic development;
the 1990s have seen a very close relationship between investment in roads
and other economic infrastructure and the growth of jobs in the states.[34]

Southern states have been especially active in promoting economic development through tax incentives; these policies, combined with favorable
climate, more available energy, and low rates of unionization, have tended
to reverse the traditional imbalance in economic growth between the North
and the South.[35] Many Frostbelt states have become economically depressed,
while many Sunbelt states have grown rapidly. The general economic up-
surge of the 1990s has tended to bring the northern industrial states along,
however, and many have again been prospering. These states have been using their own incentives to induce industries to remain where they are instead of moving south, and they have actively sought new investment. Several northern states also have turned their economies around by relying on
their educational and technological resources instead of their industrial labor force.[36] This strategy is likely to remain effective as the United States
continues to lose manufacturing jobs overseas and instead competes primarily through its educational and technological capacities (see chapter 12).

The Instruments of Economic Policy

Governments have a number of weapons at their disposal to try to influence
the performance of their economies. Analysts often speak of a dichotomy
between monetary policy and fiscal policy.[37] These are certainly two of the
more important policy options, but other options are available. This chapter
discusses fiscal policy, monetary policy, regulations and control, financial
supports for business and agriculture, public ownership, incentives, and
moral suasion as instruments of economic management. Most governments
use a combination of all of these tools, but the government of the United
States tends to rely most heavily on the indirect instruments of fiscal and
monetary policy.

There is also a debate about whether the traditional tools of national
economic management will continue to be viable, given the increasing globalization of the economic life. The argument is that capital is now so mobile,
and trade so important, that any attempt to influence the economy (especially through monetary policy) is doomed to failure.[38] Further, a number of
international agreements and arrangements—the General Agreement on
Tariffs and Trade (GATT), the World Trade Organization, and the North
American Free Trade Agreement (NAFTA), for instance—restrict the capacity of American government to make autonomous decisions about economic

policy. The United States has played a major role in negotiating these agreements and in continuing policymaking within them, so that the organizations they support are not totally beyond the control of the American government. Further, trade policy remains controversial politically, because the groups harmed directly by trade do not recognize some of the general economic benefits being created for the United States by trade.[39]

Fiscal Policy

We have discussed the importance of the budgetary process as a mechanism for allocating resources among government agencies and between the public and private sectors of the economy. These decisions are also central to the Keynesian approach to economic management, which stresses the importance of the public budget in regulating effective demand. Simply stated, if government wants to stimulate the economy (i.e., to increase economic growth and to reduce unemployment), it should run a budget deficit. Such a deficit places in circulation more money than the government has removed from circulation, thereby generating greater demand for goods and services by citizens who have more money to spend. This additional money, as it circulates through the economy, multiplies in magnitude to an extent that depends on the propensity of citizens to spend their additional income rather than save it. Likewise, if a government wants to reduce inflation in an "overheated" economy, it should run a budget surplus, removing more money from circulation in taxes than it puts back in through public expenditures. The budget surplus leaves citizens with less money than they had before the government's action, which should lessen total demand.

The theory of fiscal policy is rather straightforward, but the practice presents several important difficulties. Perhaps the most important of these is that deficits and surpluses are not politically neutral. It is a reasonable hypothesis that citizens like to receive benefits from government but do not like to pay taxes to finance those benefits. Consequently, despite the rhetoric in American politics lauding the balanced budget,[40] there were forty-seven budget deficits in forty-eight years from 1950 through 1997. Deficits occurred even during the 1950s and 1960s when the economy performed very well. Politicians have practiced "one-eyed Keynesianism," reading the passages Keynes wrote about running deficits but apparently not reading the passages about running surpluses in good times.[41] The tendency toward running deficits was accentuated during the Reagan administration, when the administration's belief in supply-side economics produced large tax cuts without commensurate reductions in expenditure (see pp. 204–6). Although Keynes has been disavowed by many (or even most) economic policymakers, his ideas are still considered when the budget is made, and the influence of deficits (and at least in theory, surpluses) must be considered.[42]

Also, as noted, estimating the amount of revenue to be received, or the outlays of public programs, is not simple. Even with the best budget planning it is not possible to adjust precisely the level of a deficit or surplus (see table 8.4). The automatic stabilizers built into the revenue and expenditure programs of government help regulate the deficit. For example, when the economy begins to turn downward, government revenues will decline as workers become unemployed and cease paying income and Social Security taxes. Also, the unemployed workers and their families will begin to place demands on a variety of social programs. The decline in revenue and the increase in expenditures will automatically push the budget toward a deficit without political leaders making any conscious choices about fiscal policy. Of course, if the recession is very deep or continues for a very long time, government may have to act with new programs that will further increase the deficits.

TABLE 8.4

FEDERAL DEFICIT AND DEBT, 1965–97

(IN MILLIONS OF DOLLARS)

Year	Deficit	Debt
1965	−1,411	322,318
1970	−2,342	380,921
1975	−53,242	541,925
1980	−73,835	908,503
1982	−127,989	1,136,798
1984	−185,388	1,564,110
1985	−212,344	1,816,974
1987	−149,769	2,345,578
1988	−155,187	2,600,768
1989	−153,477	2,867,537
1990	−220,470	3,206,347
1991	−268,746	3,598,993
1992	−290,160	4,002,669
1993	−255,013	4,351,416
1994	−203,104	4,643,705
1995	−163,899	4,821,018
1996	−145,636	5,207,298
1997	−125,591	5,453,677

SOURCE: Tax Foundation, *Facts and Figures on Government Finance, 1997* (Washington, D.C.: Tax Foundation, 1998).

To assist in making decisions about the right-size budget deficit or surplus to aim for, the "full-employment budget" has been suggested, and to some extent used, as a decision-making aid.[43] The idea is that the budget should be in balance during periods of full employment, defined as 5 percent unemployed. Naturally, during times of higher unemployment, there would be a deficit, given the fundamental Keynesian paradigm. A budget is calculated that would be in balance at full employment, and then the added costs of unemployment in social expenditures and lost revenues are added to determine the full-employment deficit. That deficit is deemed justifiable because it results not from the profligacy of governments but from economic difficulties. Any deficit higher than that is seen as a political decision to spend money that will not be raised in taxes in order to give incumbent politicians an advantage in reelection. A deficit also may be accepted for ideological reasons, as was true of the extremely large deficits of the Reagan/Bush administrations, which resulted primarily from tax cuts. Likewise, as it became apparent that the U.S. budget would begin to run a surplus in the late 1990s, there were calls from the Republican right to reduce taxes immediately rather than wait to see just what the effects of this change would be.[44]

MAKING FISCAL POLICY

Most fiscal policy decisions are made through the budgetary process outlined in chapter 6. When the president and his advisers establish the limits under which expenditure decisions of the individual agencies must be made, they make these decisions with a particular budget deficit or surplus in mind. Given the rhetoric and conventional wisdom of American politics, it appears that most presidents initiate the process with the intention of producing a balanced budget, but few if any actually have done so. They are overwhelmed by the complexity of the calculations and, more importantly, by political pressures to spend but not to tax. They may also be overwhelmed by their own belief in economic policies that are intended to produce rapid economic growth but that cannot do so once they are implemented.[45]

Fiscal policy is primarily a presidential concern, and it is a primary issue for most presidents. Only at the level of the entire budget can global decisions about economic management be made and somewhat shielded from special interests that demand special expenditures or tax preferences. But budgetary decisions cannot be purely presidential. Within the executive branch, the president receives advice and pressures—largely in the direction of spending more. Although the president can attempt to rise above special interests, his cabinet secretaries certainly cannot; they may press on the president and his budget director appeals made to them by special interests in their policy areas.

Furthermore, the president cannot make expenditure and taxation decisions alone. Congress is involved in these decisions, and its involvement has been increasingly important since the mid-1970s. The formation of the Congressional Budget Office, combined with the increasing vigor of the Joint Economic Committee and the Joint Budget Committee, has given Congress a greatly enhanced capacity to compete with the president over fiscal policy decisions.[46] The negotiations between the Bush administration and congressional leaders when coping with a budget crisis in 1990 indicated the extent to which budgetary decisions, and decisions about fiscal policy, have become joint decisions.[47]

Similarly, the negotiations between the Clinton administration and Congress over the FY 1994 budget pointed to the enhanced importance of Congress as an economic policymaker.[48] The Clinton administration began with a budget originally proposed by the outgoing Bush administration and attempted to modify it to conform to the economic proposals made by candidate Clinton during the 1992 campaign. In particular, there was some increase in taxes and other revenues ($36 billion net) and some reduction in expenditures (over $50 billion net) in an attempt—to some degree successful—to reduce the size of the federal budget deficit. This initial round of negotiations was followed by the more significant one in 1997 that laid the groundwork for a more extensive shift in budget priorities and eventually for a balanced budget in 1998.[49]

Despite the competition of Congress, the budget is labeled a presidential budget, and the economic success or failure it produces (or at least with which it is coincident) generally is laid at the president's doorstep politically.[50] As a consequence, even if the budget is not the dominant influence on economic performance it is sometimes made out to be, a president will want to have his ideas implemented through the budget and at least to be judged politically on the effects on his own policies, rather than those of Congress.

Leadership in economic policy has become as much a part of the role of a president as being commander-in-chief of the armed forces. Any president who attempts to avoid responsibility for the economy will find difficulty in doing so and may be perceived as a weak domestic leader. President Bush, for example, attempted to blame Congress for the recession of the early 1990s, but he received most of the blame from the public and the media, and economic problems were a major factor in his loss of the 1992 election. Similarly, the success of the economy in the late 1990s has helped maintain President Clinton's popularity with the public when he was beset by a number of other serious political problems. Presidents do receive some credit (or blame) for other types of policies, but it is fiscal policy that most citizens regard as the source of economic fluctuations.

SUPPLY-SIDE ECONOMICS

With the election of President Reagan in 1980 there came something of a revolution in fiscal policy in the United States, usually referred to as "supply-side economics."[51] Basically, this approach postulated that, instead of inadequate demand in the American economy (the standard Keynesian critique), there was a dearth of supply, especially a dearth of investment. The fundamental idea of supply-side economics was to increase the supply of both labor and capital so economic growth would take place. Further, supporters of this approach argued that government intervention, especially through high taxes, is the major barrier to full participation of labor and capital in the marketplace, and therefore any measures to reduce that role will in the (not very) long run produce rapid economic growth.

Some of the analysis supporting supply-side policies had a great deal of face validity. In particular, the United States economy has had a dearth of savings and investment when compared with other industrialized countries (see table 8.5). Savings are the capital from which business can borrow for new factories and equipment, but Americans have chosen to spend, and to borrow to spend more, rather than to save and invest.[52] This has been a real problem in the economy, and the recent record of tax cuts is that the public simply uses its tax savings to spend more. This emphasizes the point that many tools of economic policy depend on the behavior of the public to be effective, and this supply-side theory does not appear to have had much cooperation from the public. Capital accumulation in the American economy has increased somewhat during the late 1990s, as the soaring level of the stock market has attracted more and more small investors, but it is still lower than in most other industrialized countries.[53]

The major instrument for implementing supply-side economics was the Economic Recovery Tax Act of 1981 (ERTA), which over four years reduced the average income tax of Americans by 23 percent. The tax reductions advantaged those in higher income brackets, presumably those most likely to invest if they had additional after-tax income. The fundamental assumption of ERTA was that if individuals were given increased incentives to work and invest they would do so, and economic growth would result. Keynesian economics argued for providing people (usually the less affluent) with increased income through government expenditures, with the expectation that they would spend the money and create demand for goods and services. The supply-side solution, in contrast, argued for providing the more affluent with greater incentives to work and invest because they could retain more of what they earned.

The Economic Recovery Tax Act produced a massive increase in the federal deficit (see table 8.4, p. 201). Taxes were reduced significantly but, despite efforts by some members of the administration, federal expenditures

TABLE 8.5

FIXED CAPITAL FORMATION AS A PERCENTAGE

OF GROSS DOMESTIC PRODUCT

	1974	*1980*	*1988*	*1993*	*1996*
Australia	23.5	23.5	24.9	14.9	18.0
Belgium	22.7	20.7	17.8	18.0	22.2
Canada	23.7	23.1	22.0	18.9	17.8
France	25.8	22.4	20.1	20.6	18.7
Germany	21.6	21.8	19.9	19.6	20.0
Italy	25.9	22.8	20.7	18.9	20.5
Japan	34.8	31.7	30.5	23.3	31.4
Netherlands	21.9	21.0	21.4	19.9	25.7
Spain	28.0	21.8	22.0	21.9	20.7
Sweden	21.5	19.8	19.7	16.1	16.0
Switzerland	27.6	21.8	26.6	26.5	27.1
United Kingdom	20.9	18.6	19.2	18.3	14.6
United States	18.6	20.4	17.1	15.7	16.6

SOURCE: Organization for Economic Cooperation and Development, *Main Economic Indicators* (Paris: OECD, monthly).

were not reduced nearly as much. The fiscally conservative administration did not worry, however, believing that lower taxes would so stimulate economic growth that, over time, more revenue would come from lower tax rates; this sharp response of government revenues to tax reductions was referred to as the "Laffer curve," after economist Arthur Laffer.[54] Even after it became evident that the optimistic Laffer curve did not work, the Reagan administration did not raise taxes, and low taxation became a central feature of its (and the succeeding Bush administration's) economic policies and political appeals.

The deficit problem came to a head during the construction of the 1990–91 (FY 1991) federal budget in the Bush administration. The deficit projected for that year was a great deal higher than what was permissible under the Gramm-Rudman-Hollings rules (see chapter 6), but neither President Bush nor Congress wanted to take responsibility for raising taxes or reducing popular benefits. Also, congressional Democrats offered a very redistributive plan for increasing taxes that neither the president nor even some conservatives in their own ranks could accept. President Bush was especially reluctant to increase taxes after making a campaign pledge of "No new taxes," but in the end he did have to propose some increased taxation. After several continuing resolutions to keep government operating without passing a formal budget and one failed budget bill, a compromise was finally reached in mid-October 1990. This compromise called for increasing some taxes (largely excise taxes on tobacco, alcohol, and gasoline) and reducing a few spending programs, but nothing that would have eliminated the deficit or even reduced it significantly. Further, the deficit figure being discussed was actually a low estimate of the true federal deficit. It did not include, for example, the costs of "bailing out" failed savings-and-loan institutions insured by the federal government and several other "off budget" expenditure programs.[55]

Budget deficits appear to be, at least in the short run, a thing of the past. The end of large deficits should have a number of potentially positive economic consequences. One is that less foreign capital will be required to fund the debt, and the United States may lose its status as the world's largest debtor nation. Further, lower federal borrowing should help stabilize domestic interest rates. Finally, government debt, like private debt, must be repaid; at a minimum, debt interest must be paid. Paying less debt interest—because of both a lower debt to GDP ratio and lower interest rates—may free some money for new programs. The deepest continuing impact of the Reagan administration may be that debt interest has kept government from spending money on new social programs for years, but there may soon be some financial latitude to make new initiatives.

Monetary Policy

Whereas the basic fiscal policy paradigm stresses the importance of demand management through varying levels of revenues and expenditures, the monetary solution to economic management stresses the importance of the money supply in controlling economic fluctuations. Like additional public expenditures, increasing the amount of money in circulation is presumed to stimulate the economy. Extra money lowers interest rates, making it easier for citizens to borrow for investments or for purchases, and this in turn encourages economic activity. Likewise, reducing the availability of money makes it more difficult to borrow and to spend, thus slowing an inflationary economy.

In the United States, the Federal Reserve Board and its member Federal Reserve banks are primarily responsible for monetary policy. They are intentionally independent from the executive authority of the president and, because their budget is only appended to the federal budget, they are also largely free from congressional control through the budgetary process.[56] The Federal Reserve is independent, so its members exercise their judgment as bankers rather than submit to control by political officials who want to manipulate the money supply for political gain. The Federal Reserve has exercised its independence and refused several times to accede to presidential re-

Federal Reserve Board Chairman Alan Greenspan and Treasury Secretary Robert Rubin testify on a bill reforming the nation's banking system. (Agence France Presse/Corbis-Bettmann)

quests. For example, during the Johnson administration, Federal Reserve Chairman William McC. Martin turned down the president's request to increase the money supply more rapidly to ease financial pressures created by the simultaneous expansion of domestic social programs and the Vietnam War. More recently, the Federal Reserve Board would not cooperate with the Bush administration in its efforts to fund continuing deficits with minimal tax increases, nor with President Clinton in his efforts to keep the economic recovery moving as rapidly as possible during 1994.

The Federal Reserve has a variety of monetary tools at its disposal to influence the economy. Its three principal tools are open-market operations, the discount rate and federal funds rate, and reserve requirements. Open-market operations are the most commonly used mechanisms of monetary policy. These involve the Federal Reserve entering the money markets to buy or sell securities issued by the federal government. If it wishes to reduce the supply of money, the Federal Reserve attempts to sell securities, exchanging the bonds for cash that had been in circulation. If it wants to expand the money supply, "the Fed" purchases securities on the market, exchanging money for the bonds. The success or failure of these operations depends, of course, on the willingness of citizens to buy and sell the securities at the time and at the interest rate the Federal Reserve thinks appropriate.

A more drastic option available to the Federal Reserve is to change the discount rate and the federal funds rate. These rates are the rate of interest at which member banks can borrow money from the Federal Reserve bank or from each other to cover shortages in the reserve requirement. Obviously, these rates affect interest rates in the economy as a whole, as member banks must increase the interest rates they charge their customers to compensate for an increased cost of borrowing money from the Federal Reserve. And with the basic monetary paradigm, making money more difficult (or at least more costly) to borrow will slow down economic activity and, presumably, inflation. In some instances the Fed does not even have to change the discount rate; all its chairman has to do is mention the possibility of a change for the economy to react.[57]

The discount rate changes relatively infrequently and then only by a very small amount. For example, the rate had not changed for months prior to December 1990 when the Federal Reserve reduced the rate slightly to attempt to minimize an apparent recession. As that recession continued well into 1991, the Federal Reserve continued to make downward adjustments in the discount rate to attempt to stimulate investment and growth, and the rate reached its lowest level for over a decade. The discount rate has been very stable, and low, since early 1997. Federal Reserve Chairman Alan Greenspan from time to time warns about the dangers of inflation and excessive demand, but in practice the rate has been kept constant.

Finally, the Federal Reserve Board can change the reserve requirement. Member banks of the Federal Reserve system are required to keep on deposit to cover their outstanding loans a percentage—normally around 10 percent—of the total amount they have out in loans. If the Fed raises the reserve requirement from 10 to 12.5 percent, then for each dollar a bank had out in loans before the change, it can lend only 75 cents. The bank will have to deposit more money, call in some loans, or reduce the pace at which it grants new loans. Any of these measures will reduce substantially the amount of money in circulation and should slow down economic activity. Conversely, reducing the reserve requirement makes more money available for loans and should increase economic activity. Changing the reserve requirement is a drastic action, and it is undertaken only if there is a perceived need to influence the economy dramatically and quickly.

The Federal Reserve Board has been a paragon of conservative economic policy. Its members traditionally have been bankers or businessmen, who have tried to please a constituency of similar composition. The Federal

Reserve's tight money policies have been criticized frequently for producing economic hardship and slow growth, as when it raised interest rates during the early days of economic recovery in 1993. On the other hand, Federal Reserve action has also been defended as appropriate, given threats of inflation fueled in part by fiscal policy. What is most important, however, is the possibility either that a lack of coordination of fiscal and monetary policy will cause the two to cancel each other's efforts and produce little or no effect, or that their coordination may produce an excessive degree of correction to the economy so that changes constantly overshoot the mark and economic fluctuations are exaggerated rather than minimized.

Regulations and Control

In general, regulation has been used not for the purpose of general economic management but for the sake of achieving other economic and social goals. Regulations have been associated with cleaning up the environment, making workplaces safer, or making consumer products safer. Obviously such regulations also have an effect on overall economic growth, because they make it more or less profitable to engage in certain activities. In addition, some regulatory activities, such as antitrust regulation, do have a pervasive impact on the economic structure of the society and perhaps on consumer prices for a range of goods.

Antitrust regulation has been one of the most important forms of government control of the economy.[58] Beginning with the Sherman Act in 1890, the federal government has sought to ensure that a few firms did not control an industry and then extract excessive profits.[59] The criminal nature of the sanctions in the Sherman Act and the vagueness of its definitions of illegal actions made enforcement difficult, and the Clayton Act was passed in 1914 at the same time that the Federal Trade Commission was created. This legislation gave clearer (although still far from unambiguous) definitions of actions that constituted "combinations in restraint" of trade and provided an enforcement mechanism that could act administratively rather than entirely through the courts.[60]

Antitrust regulation as a mechanism for fostering competition has been a significant tool in American economic policy, but it is possible that it has outlived its utility. A major concern in the 1990s has been external *competitiveness*, rather than internal *competition*. It may be that in order to compete with foreign firms American businesses will have to be larger and have a larger market share. Further, there may be a need for greater protection of patent rights and intellectual property rights, which, in turn, may create natural monopolies in certain areas. Consumers and nascent firms still need to be protected from the economic power of big business, but antitrust regulation may not be the best tool in the current global economy.

Antitrust prosecution of Microsoft in 1998 brought some antitrust policy issues into sharper focus.[61] An extremely successful company in international as well as domestic markets, Microsoft had been able to create a virtual monopoly in some areas of software. Should Microsoft be punished for being successful and for making technological advances that put it in a dominant position? Or would the software market be better served by more competition and more options for the consumer, even if there were some problems of compatibility? There were cogent arguments on both sides of this debate, and such issues may be more common in the future as engineering changes and patents for new technology become more crucial for economic success.

The United States has a limited experience with the wage and price controls that have been used in Europe, but the minimum wage has been a source of political contention in recent years. The minimum wage was first adopted during the New Deal as a means of ensuring that workers could earn something like a living wage even in hard economic times. While the minimum rate adopted then may have been a living wage at the time, the need for Congress to act to increase that wage rate has meant that its real value has tended to fluctuate over time. Businesses, especially small businesses, naturally resist having to pay higher wages, and they go to Congress to argue that a higher minimum wage would either put them out of business or force them to lay off workers—neither of which is an option that congressmen like to entertain.[62]

Congress has voted to increase the minimum wage *twice* in the past five years. The minimum wage rate, even after these increases, is lower in real terms than it was in the 1950s, but conservatives continue to argue that it is a deterrent to hiring, especially hiring relatively inexperienced younger people. Current high levels of economic activity and employment make the minimum wage a less pressing issue than it has been in other times, for in many cities the demand for labor means that most jobs—even the "hamburger flipping" jobs—now pay above minimum wage. Any slowdown in activity, however, is likely to raise greater concern about the impact of this form of economic regulation.

The question of economic regulation through control of wages is especially relevant for the implementation of the "flexible labor market" that has been claimed as a major source of the Clinton administration's economic success.[63] The ability of workers to move quickly and easily to follow demand and the flexibility of wage rates to adjust to a "market clearing level" have been crucial for high levels of employment and, secondarily, for high levels of growth. In the eyes of many Europeans, the relative insecurity of the American labor market and the absence of an effective social safety net make working conditions in the United States very harsh, but the system has been more effective in generating jobs than the more regulated labor market structures found in Europe.

Public Support for Business

In addition to regulating the conduct of business and providing support through tax incentives, governments provide a number of more direct subsidies to industry. In the United States the federal government has a share of the action in providing such subsidies, but a great deal of support also comes from state and even local governments. The majority of the direct expenditures benefiting business and industry are for research and development, and for the subsidization of credit. Other forms of support for industry include promotion of inland water transportation by allowing use of locks and dams on rivers at below-market prices, services such as free weather reports and other economic information, and a variety of grants and loans for small business. Federal credit facilities are available for a host of business projects, including the facilitation of international trade through the Export-Import Bank and a variety of supports for agriculture and housing. Taken together, the federal government in 1997 supplied over $75 billion of direct and indirect support for business and industry.[64]

State and local governments tend to provide supports for business and industry in a competitive environment. Just as they compete with one another with tax incentives in order to attract industries to their localities, so too can state governments use direct services and credits to attract industry.[65] In fact, there is some evidence that government services are more important than tax breaks in attracting industries. The services of state and local governments need not be extraordinary; they may need only do things that they usually do, such as supplying transportation, water, sewers, and similar services, and do them well. Of course, some expenditures of subnational governments are more extraordinary; they may even include building plants or more elaborate forms of infrastructure for industries that agree to locate in the area.

All these supports for business must be examined in the context of a continuing "industrial policy debate" in the United States. As the United States was falling behind Japan, West Germany, and even such smaller countries as South Korea and Taiwan in the production of basic commodities such as steel and finished products such as automobiles, the question "What is wrong with American industry?" became a central policy issue.[66] Numerous answers to that question have been offered, including inept management, avaricious unions, and meddlesome government. Another answer is that government does not do enough to support American industry, and what it does is poorly organized. The implication has been that a more comprehensive approach to the problems of American industry and its competitiveness in the international marketplace should be adopted. Such a program might include some or all of the following elements:

1. *Direct government grants for the modernization and expansion of industry.* Despite major improvements, some machinery of American heavy industry is outdated in comparison with its competitors'. Government could help by supplying grants, loans, or both. There is some assistance through the tax system, but little or no direct aid.

2. *Trade policy.* American government has followed free-trade policies during most of the postwar period and has used tariffs and other restrictions on imports infrequently. Another option for government would be to impose tariffs and other trade barriers until American industry "gets back on its feet." There are voluntary arrangements with Japan over the import of automobiles, but some advocate broader use of these powers. The United States continues to debate with the European Union over a number of trade issues, although there are about as many European as American complaints about unfair competition and trade policies. Even the free-trade agreements with neighboring Canada and Mexico are believed by some citizens, and some politicians, potentially to undermine the American economy.[67]

   The increasing importance of international trade for the American economy makes trade policy all the more important. As noted earlier, the United States continues to run massive trade deficits. Indeed, the relative prosperity of the late 1990s has tended to exacerbate the trade deficit, as Americans have more money to spend and choose to spend it on foreign-made products, trips to Europe, and the like.

3. *Deregulation.* Some sections of the business community argue that the numerous safety and environmental regulations issued by the federal government make it difficult for American industry to produce products at a price that is competitive on the world market (see chapter 13). In particular, businessmen and unions alike are concerned with the number of jobs being lost to low-wage and low-regulation countries such as Indonesia, Mexico, and Brazil. They believe that deregulation would improve the competitiveness of business; even after ten years of Reagan and Bush administration policies, American industry remained more heavily regulated than that of many competitor countries,[68] and despite the continuing efforts of the Republican Congress (and to some extent the Clinton administration) it continues to be heavily regulated. In addition, the United States tends to pursue regulatory policies such as antitrust with somewhat greater vigor than does most of the rest of the world, also potentially inhibiting the competitiveness of American industry in world markets.

4. *Research and development.* American industry has a tradition of being among the most technologically advanced in the world. Unfortunately, this has become more of a tradition than a reality; except in a few areas, such as computers, American industry appears to be falling behind. Government could make a major contribution to American industry by making more funds available for research.

5. *Regional policy.* The effects of declining industry have not been spread evenly over the United States, but have been concentrated in older industrial regions, especially the Great Lakes area. More recently, the decline in defense industries has also made Southern California one of the more economically depressed areas of the American economy. Thus, as well as dealing with the direct problems of industry, there is a need to address some of the human problems created by a changing industrial base in many states and localities. In turn, these efforts may make those localities more attractive to industries considering relocation.

Government has been involved in supporting industry for most of the history of the United States. Many of the great industrial ventures in this country, including the westward extension of the railroad, were undertaken with the direct or indirect support of government.[69] There may now be an even greater need for government support for business and industry than in the past, given the declining industrial position of the United States. But too much dependence on government to "bail out losers"—either through direct subsidies or through protectionist trade policy—may mean that American industry ceases to be responsible for its own revitalization and simply waits for the public sector to rescue it.[70] Use of the trade policy option for adjusting the economy is, however, increasingly constrained by international agreements such as NAFTA and GATT.

Public Ownership

Although it is not common in the United States, public ownership of certain kinds of industries may be important for economic management, especially influencing the location of certain industries. Even in the United States a number of public and quasi-public corporations are involved in the economy. In 1976 there were twenty wholly publicly owned and seven partly publicly owned corporations in the federal government, and the general movement toward managerialism and privatization in government has led to an increased use of corporate forms of organization, even when the mode of organization appears inappropriate (the National Service Corporation, for example).

At the state and local levels numerous public enterprises are organized to carry out economic as well as some social policy functions. These public enterprises range from publicly owned utilities, such as electricity, gas, and transportation, to functions usually associated with the private sector, such as insurance and banking. Although public enterprises ideologically are anathema in the United States, in practice this form of organization is actually increasingly popular, as a means of providing service while at the same time attempting to be as efficient and businesslike as possible.

These public corporations perform a variety of functions for government. One is to provide revenue. For example, local government utilities can buy electricity at commercial rates and then distribute it at rates that yield a profit. Also, public corporations can be utilized to regulate prices and some essential services. Although many publicly owned transportation corporations run with a deficit, they maintain relatively low costs and provide greater service than could be provided by private firms, and local government considers those objectives important. At the federal level, corporate structures have been used for regional development in the Tennessee Valley Authority, a largely successful attempt to transform the economy of an underdeveloped region through public action and public ownership of electrical power production. Also, federal corporations have been active in promoting U.S. foreign trade through the Export-Import Bank and the Overseas Private Investors Corporation (related to the goals of having a positive balance of payments) and in providing transportation to promote economic growth through the St. Lawrence Seaway and AMTRAK.

One interesting variation on public ownership is the use of loan guarantees and insurance to attempt to assure continuing employment and economic growth. One notable example of this policy option was the Loan Guarantee Board, charged with developing financing to keep the Chrysler Corporation in business and its workers in jobs when the automaker faced bankruptcy in the late 1970s. The federal government did not buy one share of Chrysler stock but used its economic powers to keep the company alive. Also, the federal government has spent billions of dollars to make good on its insurance commitments to account owners of failing savings and loans and banks in the early 1990s. These activities helped to preserve employment and enabled one corporation to reverse its economic fortunes. They also protected the savings of millions of citizens and helped preserve confidence in the financial institutions of the country. It can be argued that public involvement in moribund corporations is disguised social policy and may actually slow economic growth. At least for the short term, however, it represents an important economic policy instrument.

Incentives

Governments can also attempt to influence economic change by providing incentives for desired behaviors. Most incentives are made available through the tax system and are directed primarily at encouraging investment and economic change. The tax reforms of the 1980s eliminated many of these incentives, but they still constitute a powerful economic weapon for government. We have already mentioned the role that state government tax incentives play in encouraging structural change in individual state economies, with some contribution to economic development in the country as a whole. The federal government also provides special incentives for selected industries and general incentives for businesses to invest, especially in research and development.

The major incentives for structural change in the U.S. economy have been the oil depletion allowance and similar allowances for other depletable natural resources. These allowances permit investors to write off against profits a portion of the investments they made in searching for oil. The decontrol of "new oil" under President Carter's energy program was another means of encouraging exploration for domestic energy supplies. A variety of provisions of the federal tax code also serve to encourage investment in general by both corporations and individuals. The capital gains provisions of the tax laws now permit profits made on investments held for more than eighteen months to be taxed at 20 percent, or almost half the highest normal tax rate, and that rate is to fall to a maximum 18 percent in 2001.

Industries are also given extensive tax credits for new investments and allowed higher-than-average depreciation on investments during the first year. All these policies make it easier and more profitable for industries to invest and for economic growth to follow that investment, but none mandates that the industry make the investments. The administrative costs of incentive programs are comparatively small when subsidy programs are considered as the alternative, and those programs also are perceived as less intrusive into the market economy than the possible alternatives. Still, the dollar an industry saves from taxes is worth exactly the same as the dollar granted as a subsidy, and perhaps even more, since there are fewer strings and restrictions attached to the dollar saved from taxes.

Moral Suasion

When all else fails, or perhaps before anything else is tried, governments can attempt to influence citizens and industries by persuasion. Persuasion works best in times of national emergency, but economic circumstances may be sufficiently dire to create the perception of an emergency.[71] Presidents, using their power as spokesmen for the nation, are central to the use of persuasion to control economic behavior, for they can employ a variety of symbols to influence citizens. A number of examples illustrate the appeals that presidents can make about economic policy. Lyndon Johnson exerted the power of the office when he used "jawboning" to encourage industries to restrain price increases. Speaking for the nation as president, he appealed to patriotism to get what he wanted. Ronald Reagan used his gifts as the "Great Communicator" to persuade citizens to accept his economic and tax policies. Even George Bush's purchase of a pair of socks in a shopping mall was an attempt, largely unsuccessful, to manipulate symbols to urge Americans to start buying again and to lift the country out of the recession.

The effects of persuasion depend on the nature of the policy problem being addressed and the character of the political leader attempting to employ the persuasion. Industrialists are unlikely to continue to provide jobs for workers in an unprofitable factory simply because they are asked to do so, but citizens may well resolve to "buy American" in order to improve the balance of payments. Political leaders who are trusted and respected will find it relatively easy to influence their fellow citizens, whereas those who are less popular may find more direct mechanisms for economic management more effective. Also, some economic problems—such as a budget deficit—may simply be too big to be attacked with words alone.

Conclusion

The management of the economy is a central concern of government. It is one area of policymaking on which governments are frequently judged by their citizens. This is true not only because of the central importance of economic issues for citizens but also because of the frequent reporting of such standard indicators as the inflation rate and the unemployment rate. Even if an individual has a job and an income that keeps pace with the cost of living, he or she may believe the president is not doing a good job because of the aggregate numbers that regularly appear in the newspapers. It is interesting to notice the extent to which the performance of the economy is laid at the feet of government, especially the president. This is in marked contrast to the era before the depression, when the economy was not believed to be controllable by government. The president clearly plays a crucial role in economic management—because of his role as spokesman for government, because of the central role of his budget in controlling the economy, and because of his leadership in other areas of economic policy such as taxation.

It is also important to understand, however, that the condition of the economy is not solely a presidential responsibility. Congress is involved with the president in determining the budget, which is the central instrument of presidential intervention in the economy. The actions of the Federal Reserve Board are almost totally beyond the control of the president. Furthermore, the federal structure of the United States is such that state and local government taxing and spending decisions have a significant impact not only on the overall stimulative or depressive effects of public expenditures but also on attempts to move industries and labor geographically. Also, the success of national economic policies is increasingly dependent on the decisions made by other nations, by international organizations such as the International Monetary Fund, and by global markets.

Finally, we citizens have a substantial impact on the state of the economy. Many presidential decisions on fiscal policy and some Federal Reserve decisions on monetary policy depend on citizens responding in the predicted fashion. Even major aggregates such as economic growth depend to a great extent on the perceptions and behaviors of citizens. If citizens and businesses believe that prosperity is coming, they will be willing to invest and thus may make their belief a self-fulfilling prophecy. Government can do everything in its power to try to influence the behavior of citizens, but ultimately most decisions are beyond its control. Nevertheless, the success of an economic policy is a major factor in determining whether citizens believe that government is doing a good job.

9. Tax Policy

Tax policy is a major component of economic policy, but it deserves some discussion in its own right. Here we are especially concerned with the choice of revenue instruments used to collect the money needed by government to run its programs. In addition to the basic decisions about raising adequate revenues to meet expenditure demands, taxes are used to address a number of other policy purposes. Raising the same amount of tax revenues by different means may have very different economic and political effects, and those effects should be understood when discussing tax policies.[1] For example, raising money by an income tax is more favorable to the poor than is raising that same amount of money through a sales tax. Also, raising money by different means may be more or less difficult administratively, so governments may choose ease (and certainty) of collection rather than other values—equity or impacts on economic growth—when selecting their tax policies.

Table 9.1 shows the tax profile of the United States in comparison with other major industrialized countries. The table shows the proportion of total tax revenue in each country derived from a number of possible revenue sources. The United States stands apart from its major trading partners in several ways. First, there is substantially less reliance on taxes on goods and services in the United States than in the other countries. Although most states and many localities have sales and excise taxes, there is no national sales (or general consumption) tax comparable to the value-added tax (VAT) used in most European countries.[2] Fiscal pressures, especially on the Social Security system (see chapter 11), may one day make such a tax necessary, but it has been delayed longer in this country than elsewhere.

Second, the United States derives substantially more of its total tax revenue from property taxes than most other countries do. Property taxes are collected by state and local governments and are the principal revenue source for most local governments (see table 12.2, p. 328). This pattern appears to reflect an Anglo-Saxon tradition in revenue collection, for the United Kingdom, Canada, and New Zealand all use the property tax more heavily than do most other industrialized countries.[3] In the late 1980s Britain dropped the local property tax in favor of a per capita "poll tax," but

TABLE 9.1

KINDS OF TAX REVENUES, 1995 (AS PERCENTAGE OF TOTAL)

	Personal income tax	Corporate income tax	Employees' Social Security	Employers' Social Security	General consumption tax	Selective commodity taxes	Property tax	Customs	Other
Australia	40.6	14.7	0.0	0.0	8.7	14.5	8.7	0.6	12.2
Belgium	31.5	6.7	10.9	20.1	15.1	8.6	2.4	1.1	4.6
Canada	37.3	8.1	5.4	11.1	15.2	8.4	10.5	2.0	2.1
Denmark	53.7	4.1	2.5	0.6	19.3	11.4	3.5	0.6	4.5
France	13.9	3.7	13.1	26.8	17.4	9.0	5.2	1.1	9.8
Germany	27.3	2.8	17.1	20.0	17.3	9.4	2.8	0.9	2.6
Italy	26.2	8.7	6.7	20.9	13.9	11.2	5.7	1.3	5.4
Japan	21.4	15.2	14.4	18.3	5.2	8.0	11.6	2.0	3.9
Netherlands	18.9	7.5	27.1	6.7	15.6	9.2	4.0	1.3	9.8
Norway	22.9	9.2	8.2	13.8	21.1	16.3	2.8	2.0	4.7
Spain	23.8	5.5	6.3	25.0	16.0	10.3	5.3	2.0	5.8
Sweden	35.3	6.1	3.5	24.9	15.1	8.6	2.8	1.9	1.8
Switzerland	31.5	5.7	12.0	11.5	10.1	7.1	7.0	4.6	10.6
United Kingdom	27.4	9.5	7.4	9.6	19.0	14.1	10.5	2.0	0.7
United States	36.3	9.4	10.7	13.1	8.0	7.7	11.2	2.1	3.5

SOURCE: Organization for Economic Cooperation and Development, *Revenue Statistics of OECD Member Countries, 1965–1996* (Paris: OECD, 1997).

public opposition rather quickly forced a reversal of that policy innovation by the Thatcher government.[4] The local property tax is especially important as a source of funding for education (see chapter 12), and it tends to be the tax that local governments rely more than any other for their fiscal independence.

Third, there is a relatively high reliance on corporate taxes in the United States. Given the characterization of American politics as dominated by special interests (especially business interests), high levels of corporate taxation may require greater explanation.[5] Corporations rarely bear the full burden of corporate taxation: the real tax burden falls on consumers of firms' products (higher prices), on the companies' workers (lower wages), or on stockholders (lower dividends). Under many economic circumstances, firms can add taxes as a cost of doing business onto the price of their products. This explanation appears to be supported by the extremely high level of corporate taxation in Japan. A more political explanation involves the tradition of populism in many states in the United States; these states place a relatively heavier burden of taxation on corporations than on individuals, and even the most conservative politicians on the national level must remember that corporations do not vote but individual taxpayers do.[6]

One thing that table 9.1 cannot demonstrate easily is the complexity of the tax system in the United States. Some of this complexity is a function of federalism and the numerous different tax systems existing at the state and local levels. At the federal level, there are also a number of different taxes. Further, as the tax system has evolved, even greater complexity has resulted from the numerous deductions, exemptions, and other special treatments ("tax expenditures" or "loopholes") that have been written into the tax laws (see table 9.2).[7]

The tax reforms of the 1980s (see pp. 231–33) closed some of the more egregious loopholes in the tax system, but a number remain. While many of these remaining exclusions have good economic and social justifications (e.g., the deductibility of mortgage interest stimulates homeownership as well as the construction industry), some loopholes (capital gains or oil depletion allowances) appear to benefit primarily the wealthy and the well organized. Further, in almost every revenue bill since the major reform in 1986 some new special tax treatments have appeared, returning the tax system to the same "Christmas tree" it had been prior to reform.[8] One difference is that legislation in 1996 requires that Congress identify "limited tax benefits," that is, tax breaks that go only to a relatively few individuals or firms.[9] Now the creation of these special benefits is more public, while the closed and expert nature of tax policy had been crucial for its ability to confer benefits with a minimum of public awareness or discussion.

The magnitude of the impact of tax expenditures can be seen from the

TABLE 9.2

TAX EXPENDITURES COMPARED WITH DIRECT EXPENDITURES,
FY 1995 (IN BILLIONS OF DOLLARS)

	Tax expenditure	Direct expenditure	Tax as a percentage of direct expenditure
Housing	97.4	24.1	404.1
Social service	30.1	15.5	194.2
Income security	202.7	481.5	42.1
Health	99.3	272.4	36.5
Education	5.7	32.1	17.8
Employment and training	0.4	32.2	1.2

SOURCE: Christopher Howard, *The Hidden Welfare State* (Princeton: Princeton University Press, 1997), table 1.2.

data in table 9.2, comparing the size of tax expenditures with federal spending for the same objective. In at least one policy area (housing), the financial impact of tax expenditures is substantially greater than federal spending, while in most areas direct expenditures are larger. Still, even in two of the federal government's largest expenditure programs—Social Security and health care—tax expenditures equal at least one-third of total spending. Thus there is, as Christopher Howard has argued, a substantial "hidden welfare state" in the United States.[10]

As well as constituting a hidden welfare state, the prevailing structure of tax expenditures also tends to create a welfare state for the middle class. As shown in table 9.3 (p. 222), with the exception of the excludability of Social Security income and the Earned Income Tax Credit, the majority of the benefits of tax expenditures accrue to people earning over $50,000 per annum. Under some provisions of the tax code, the principal beneficiaries earn more than $100,000. If the benefits that go to business are added to these personal benefits for the affluent, the tax system can be seen to produce substantial negative redistribution. The apparent (and real) unfairness of many aspects of the tax system has helped to spawn tax reform in the past, but a number of apparent inequities remain and even more have been created.

Public Opinion and Taxation

Paying taxes is not the favorite public policy activity of the American public, who would much rather consume the benefits produced by those taxes. But

TABLE 9.3

DISTRIBUTION OF TAX EXPENDITURES, 1994

	Percentage of total dollar benefit going to people in each income group				
	<10k	*10–30k*	*30–50k*	*50–100k*	*>100k*
Mortgage interest	0.0	1.9	10.1	43.9	44.2
State and local income taxation	0.0	0.5	5.2	31.9	62.3
Excludability of Social Security	0.3	35.4	46.8	16.3	1.3
Earned Income Tax Credit	26.2	71.0	2.6	0.1	0.0
Charitable contributions	0.0	3.1	10.4	34.3	52.1
Real estate taxes	0.0	2.1	10.3	44.4	43.2
Medical expenses	0.1	9.9	25.6	44.2	20.2
Child and dependent care	0.0	20.7	27.8	42.3	9.2

SOURCE: Joint Committee on Taxation, *Estimate of Federal Tax Expenditures for Fiscal Years 1995–1999* (Washington, D.C.: Joint Committee, 1995).

although they are not keen to pay taxes, Americans are also not unrealistic, and most appear to realize that they do have to pay a good deal of their income in taxes. The major questions that arise in the minds of the public are whether the tax system is fair and whether as taxpayers they are getting "value for money" for what they pay to government. Further, Americans appear to want to be able to control to some extent how tax money is spent, and they prefer taxes linked to specific types of expenditures—usually called "earmarked taxes"—to taxes that go into the general fund.

Citizens tend to have two concerns when thinking about the fairness of the tax system. One is the basic premise that everybody who benefits from government should pay at least something in taxes. Several surveys about taxes have found that Americans appear to be willing to accept the basic principle of progressivity—that the more affluent should pay at a higher rate—so long as even the poor pay something. Indeed, there tends to be little public support for the principle of the flat tax, with everyone paying the same tax rate, a concept that might be considered "fair." Americans do not appear to think that all taxpayers should pay the same rate, so long as everyone is paying something to support government.

The other concern of the public is whether all citizens are paying their "fair share" of taxes. Defining that fair share is difficult to do objectively, given the number of alternative conceptions of fairness that exist.[11] Taxpayers do not, however, appear to have any difficulty in defining fairness subjectively. Table 9.4 contains the results of a survey about the fairness of taxation. In the first place, it appears that although most Americans do think they pay too much in federal income tax, the numbers are not usually much over 50 percent. Further, the number of those who think they pay too much does tend to vary with economic and political circumstances; good examples are the low numbers during the beginning of the Kennedy administration and the very high numbers during the years of the Vietnam War and Watergate. These reactions to taxes may be as much measures of discontent with government as measures of actual resistance to the taxes themselves.[12] Interestingly, after years of declining confidence in government, when asked just before income taxes were due in 1997, over half of a sample of taxpayers maintained that they thought their taxes were fair.[13]

Citizens also have opinions about who else is, and should be, paying taxes. Table 9.5 (p. 224) points out that most people see the need for some progressivity in the income tax structure. On average they think that lower-income and middle-income people pay too much and the upper echelons of

TABLE 9.4

PUBLIC OPINION ABOUT PAYING TAXES

(IN PERCENTAGES)

"Do you consider the amount of federal income tax you have to pay as too high, about right, or too low?"

	Too high	About right	Too low	No opinion
1948	57	38	1	4
1951	52	43	1	4
1957	61	31	<1	8
1961	46	45	1	8
1967	58	38	1	3
1969	69	25	<1	6
1973	65	28	1	6
1990	63	31	2	4
1992	56	39	2	3
1994	56	42	<1	2
1996	64	33	1	2

SOURCE: Gallup poll, various years.

TABLE 9.5
PERCEPTIONS OF PAYING FAIR SHARE OF TAXES

	Fair share	Too much	Too little	No opinion
Lower-income people				
1996	40	48	9	3
1994	43	42	12	3
1992	32	57	8	3
Middle-income people				
1996	34	58	5	3
1994	39	54	5	2
1992	36	57	5	2
Upper-income people				
1996	19	9	68	4
1994	20	10	68	2
1992	16	4	77	3

SOURCE: Gallup poll, annual.

the income ladder pay too little. The large proportion who believe that middle-income people pay too much reflects in part that most Americans think of themselves as middle class, and they also think that they as individuals pay too much federal tax. Indeed, when these figures are broken down by income groups (not shown in this table), a strong element of self-interest comes through in the responses.

Another aspect of who pays what in taxes, and the perceived fairness of the system, is the ability legally to avoid paying through loopholes. What does the public think of the loopholes built into the tax laws? Several surveys point to some similar findings (see table 9.6). One finding is that the more widely used deductions, such as the home-mortgage deduction, are generally thought to be fair and desirable. The other is that exemptions and deductions going to particular classes of people with special needs—the elderly, the blind—are considered fair while those that are used primarily by the affluent, such as business entertainment deductions, are not considered good public policy. Again, the populism of American political culture can be seen in this belief that programs benefiting the average citizen and the "deserving poor" in society are good policies.

Value for Money
Americans also evaluate taxes according to what they believe they receive in return. Is the tax "price" for goods and services provided by government worth it or not? Survey respondents tend to answer that question rather dif-

TABLE 9.6

FAIRNESS OF TAX DEDUCTIONS AND EXEMPTIONS

(IN PERCENTAGES)

A. Perceived fairness of deductions

	Fair	Unfair	Percentage of respondents using this deduction
Charitable contributions	84	16	51
State and local taxes	76	24	32
Capital gains	51	49	12
Mortgage interest on second home	50	50	7
Fringe benefits at work	28	72	30
Business entertainment	22	78	7

B. Perceived legitimacy of deductions and exemptions

	Legitimate	Illegitimate
Elderly exemption	95	5
Blind exemption	95	5
Property tax on homeowners	93	7
Social Security income[a]	92	8
Home mortgage	92	8
Charitable contributions	71	29
Municipal bonds[b]	53	47
Capital gains	48	52

SOURCE: "Tax Americana," *Public Opinion*, February/March 1986, 28.

a. When the question about the legitimacy of deductions was asked, Social Security was totally exempt from tax; it is now 50 percent exempt.

b. Interest on municipal bonds is not taxable by the federal government.

ferently for different levels of government. In most surveys, local governments are perceived to deliver the most for the tax money, while the federal government delivers the least. This is perhaps to be expected, given that the federal government collects the most in tax revenue (almost 56 percent in 1995) and delivers the fewest direct services to the public. The citizen sees local firemen and state workers repairing highways but relatively few federal employees at work. When the citizen does see a federal employee, it may be an Internal Revenue Service employee or a Customs agent going through his or her baggage. The federal government simply is not perceived as providing many direct services to the public.[14]

Citizens also tend to evaluate "sin taxes" positively. They are likely to support taxation on alcohol, tobacco, gambling, and the like even if they would not support other types of taxation. The support for this type of taxation appears to come less from morality than from a sense that people who spend money in that way also have the money to pay in taxes; this feeling is heightened when the tax revenue is earmarked for a popular policy such as education. Further, this is a tax that is easily avoidable, so people have only themselves to blame if they must pay it. Finally, governments tend to like these taxes because the demand for these products appears relatively inelastic—they are able to pile on high levels of tax and the public will still buy the products.[15] There is, however, some backlash against such excise taxes among conservatives, who argue that they are simply another government intrusion on individual freedom to choose behaviors.[16]

Finally, citizens appear to want to have greater certainty about where their tax money is going. There is both survey and behavioral evidence to back up this point. First, in surveys, citizens appear to support earmarked taxes, such as the gasoline tax, the revenue from which is dedicated to transportation needs, more than they do general taxation. Similarly, when they are asked if they would vote to raise taxes, there tends to be a negative majority among respondents, but when the increase is linked to a particular expenditure—especially a popular one such as Social Security or public education—there tends to be a positive majority. It appears that if citizens are made aware of what their taxes will buy, they become more willing to bear the financial pain of paying.

Responding in a survey that one would be willing to pay more taxes is relatively easy. A more pertinent question is whether one would actually behave that way. At the state and local levels, citizens are given the opportunity to vote for or against proposals for tax increases. For some time the outcome of the Proposition 13 vote in California suggested that a "tax revolt" was under way and that citizens would not accept any new taxes.[17] It now appears, however, that voters have been making somewhat more sophisticated policy choices, proving willing to support tax measures that are associated with particular expenditure programs while tending to oppose more general increases in taxes. Citizens appear to want a clear quid pro quo in taxation.

Choices in Tax Policy

The United States obviously has made a number of choices concerning taxation that are different from policy choices made in other industrialized countries, although tax reform in many countries has tended to make their tax policies increasingly similar.[18] Some of the growing similarity represents a response to global economic forces, while some represents more a need on the part of governments to raise all the income they can. The aggregate figures presented earlier (table 9.1, p. 219) represent taxation decisions made by many thousands of individual governments, although the federal government alone accounts for approximately three-quarters of all taxes collected in the United States. What criteria might these governments be employing when they make their decisions about taxes?

Collectibility

One criterion that must be considered is the ability of government to collect a tax, and even more the ability of that tax to yield large amounts of revenue for the investment made in collecting it. The administration of taxes is expensive and has political costs in addition to its economic costs. Therefore, a government should be sure that it can generate sufficient revenue from a tax to justify incurring those costs. One of the many critiques of the tax system of the United States (at the federal level, as well as the problems resulting from multiple levels of taxation) is that it is very difficult to administer, given its complexity. There are therefore very large burdens on citizens, businesses, and government itself that might be alleviated by various alternative tax systems.[19]

The two major tax "handles" for governments of modern, industrialized countries are income and expenditure. By definition, almost all money in an economy is both income and expenditure, and governments can raise revenue by tapping either or both streams of economic transactions. Further, given that in modern economies most income is earned as salaries and wages in relatively large organizations and most purchases are made through relatively large and identifiable organizations, governments can require private bodies to do much of the tax collection for them. Employers typically withhold a portion of their employees' salaries for income and Social Security taxes, and they are required to submit detailed accountings of sales and profits for their own taxes. These collection procedures impose a cost on the private sector—one estimate is that it costs businesses over $7 billion to comply with tax laws—but they make the collection of revenue easier and less expensive for government.[20] Individual citizens also do a great deal of the work for government. The Internal Revenue Service estimates that the average taxpayer requires 9.4 hours a year to keep records and to fill out and file the forms for the federal income tax; this amounts to over 1 billion hours of work a year for all taxpayers.[21]

Fiscal Neutrality

As well as being collectible, a "good" tax is one that does not produce any significant distortions in the economy.[22] That is, the tax system should not give preference to one kind of revenue or expenditure unless there is a very good reason to do so. If the tax system were to advantage certain economic activities, it could direct resources away from their most productive economic use and probably reduce the rate of economic growth in the society. Prior to tax reform in 1986, the tax system in the United States was not fiscally neutral but rather contained a large number of special-interest provisions ("loopholes") that had been written into the law. These provisions provided citizens and corporations alike with incentives to use their money in ways that might be unproductive on economic grounds (investing in racehorses or in loss-making businesses) but that were quite lucrative for some special interests given the character of the existing tax system.

Tax reform in 1986 made the tax system more fiscally neutral, but there are continuing efforts by special interests to gain tax benefits. Every year since the passage of the major tax reform has seen some special preferences creep back into the tax laws.[23] Another attempt at major change in the mid-1990s has actually resulted in more preferences being added to the tax system, and the Republican Congress and Democratic president continue to battle over others, including a tax deduction for tuition to private elementary and secondary schools (see pp. 338–41). Also, state and local tax systems provide a number of additional tax benefits that can distort economic activity; most important are the numerous tax incentives used to attract new industry to one place or another.

Buoyancy

Raising revenue is unpopular politically, so any tax that can produce additional revenue without necessitating any political activity is a valuable tax for government. A buoyant tax is one for which the yield keeps pace with, or exceeds, the pace of economic growth and/or inflation. In principle, the progressive income tax is a buoyant tax. As individuals earn more, they pay not only higher taxes but higher rates of tax, so there is a fiscal dividend from the tax, with government automatically receiving a higher proportion of national income. Taxes that require reassessments or adjustments in rates in order to keep pace with inflation (e.g., the property tax) are not buoyant and hence may generate political difficulties if the real value of their yield is to be maintained. This effect was evident in the "tax revolt" against the property tax in a number of states.

The fiscal dividend that is associated with the progressive income tax during inflationary periods has led to legislation that indexes tax brackets. That is, as inflation increases the monetary income of citizens without increasing their real income, the income levels at which taxes are first charged and at which tax rates change are increased so that tax rates change at the same rate as real income. Everything else being equal, real tax income for government would therefore remain constant without legislative action to increase rates. This kind of change was a major part of tax reform during the first Reagan administration. In addition, the tax reform of 1986 reduced the progressivity of the tax system; the number of tax brackets was reduced from fourteen to five, and then effectively to three (two rates plus a sur-charge) in 1990. The basic system of brackets has remained in place since that time, albeit with some adjustments in the brackets.

Distributive Effects

Another thing that taxes can do for government is to alter the income distri-bution in society. This change is usually thought of as benefiting the less af-fluent at the expense of the more affluent. However, many taxes used by governments are actually regressive, that is, they take a larger proportion of income from the poor than from the rich. These regressive taxes (e.g., the Social Security tax and sales taxes) must be justified on other grounds, such as ease of collection or their similarity to insurance premiums.

The net impacts of taxes on income distribution are difficult to calcu-late, especially if attention is given to the effects of expenditures that the taxes finance. Nevertheless, there does seem to be a general finding in the United States that both the poor—especially the working poor—and the rich pay a higher rate of tax than do the majority of citizens, while the large ma-jority of citizens pay approximately the same rate of tax.[24] This is true when federal, state, and local taxes are added together; the federal tax structure has been at least moderately progressive, although some changes made dur-ing the Reagan years have made it less so.

It is especially interesting that the working poor pay such a high rate of tax. This is explained by their higher propensity to consume, rather than save their income, so almost all their income is subject to sales and excise taxes. All their income also is covered by Social Security taxation, whereas the more affluent can earn substantial amounts of money above the thresh-old rate of Social Security income and pay no additional tax. Finally, the working poor may be unable to take advantage of many of the loopholes in the tax system that the more affluent can use. Even when they are able to do so, the loopholes are worth less for the less affluent at their lower tax rates.

Changes in the federal tax system in recent years have tended to make the system somewhat less progressive. The top rates of income tax were re-duced significantly (from 70 percent to 33 percent) during the Reagan and Bush years, and the tax burden has been shifting slightly away from income taxation and toward excise and Social Security taxes, as well as toward user fees.[25] These changes have been offset in part by eliminating a number of the less defensible loopholes in the tax laws that primarily did benefit the rich. The decreased progressivity of the tax system was in large part effected very consciously. Part of the "supply-side" strategy of President Reagan was to place more money in the hands of the affluent so they would invest. Further, the Bush administration found that its pledge of "No new taxes" meant in practice no new income taxes. Excise taxes were more palatable, both to the administration and to most citizens.[26]

The Clinton administration has reversed somewhat this trend toward a less redistributive tax. Early in his term of office President Clinton put through an economic reform package and a budget bill that shifted some of the tax burden back onto the more affluent, although critics argued that it was not the middle-class tax cut promised in the campaign.[27] This bill increased the tax rate on taxable incomes over $140,000 for couples (over $115,000 for individuals) to 36 percent. While this tax change affected only a rather small percentage of the American public, it did raise additional revenue of approximately $27.5 billion in 1994. Another $7.5 billion was raised by increasing the top rate of corporation tax to 36 percent. The Clinton package was not entirely redistributive, however, for heavier taxes also were imposed on alcohol, tobacco, and energy—taxes that tend to fall disproportionately on the less affluent. Still, an estimated 70 percent of the new tax revenue came from households with incomes over $100,000 a year (4.4 percent of all households).[28]

Visibility

Finally, public officials making political decisions about taxes must be concerned about the political acceptability of taxes. To some degree this factor is crucial, for low taxes are related to the historical traditions of the country or even a state: in many states with populist political cultures, the property tax is regarded as a threat to the "little man" who owns a house. The political acceptability of taxes also may be a function of their visibility. Everything else being equal, the less visible a tax is, the more acceptable it will be.[29] Even though income tax is withheld from employees' checks at each pay period, the citizen is still required to file a statement each year on which he or she must see the total tax account for the year. Similarly, property-tax bills are typically sent to homeowners each year; in states and localities with high property taxes, the bill may seem huge. Both taxes are obvious to the taxpayer and therefore may be resisted. The Social Security tax is less visible. Even though it is deducted from paychecks along with the income tax, there is no annual reckoning that might bring the total tax bill to the citizen's attention, and, in addition, half of the total Social Security bill is paid by the employer.

The lack of a total tax bill is a very important element in a country (such as the United States) with several levels of government, all of which levy taxes. These taxes are levied at different times and in different ways, so only the better-informed citizens are likely to know their total tax bills.[30] Even though the United States is a low-tax country, the division among taxes and taxing units may make the total bill appear even lower. The United States is a low-tax country in part because Americans want it that way, and the maintenance of the "fiscal illusion" created by multiple taxing units helps to make such taxes as do exist more palatable.[31] This is especially true because citizens tend to focus their ire on taxes at the federal level while permitting state and local taxes to creep upward.

The problem of tax visibility is one reason for considering a value-added tax (VAT) for the United States,[32] perhaps as a means of reducing any future recurrence of the deficit. Unlike a sales tax, which is levied as the consumer pays for the commodity and added on as a separate item, the VAT is levied at each stage of the production process and included in the price of the product when sold. As a result, the actual amount of the tax—and even the fact that a tax is being levied—may be largely hidden from the consumer; consequently, there may be less political mobilization opposing the tax. It is just that invisibility, however, that makes many fiscal conservatives extremely wary of the VAT, fearing that government could expand its activities without citizens understanding what the real increases in their tax bill had been.

The Politics of Tax Reform

Taxation is different from other kinds of policy in that it is essentially something that no one really wants and everyone seeks to avoid. Former senator Russell Long of Louisiana, long a power on the Senate Finance Committee responsible for tax legislation, encapsulated the nature of tax politics in this little ditty: "Don't tax you, don't tax me, tax that fellow behind the tree." The nature of tax politics is to try to divert the burden of taxation onto others and to build in special privileges for oneself. Because virtually no one in contemporary economic systems can avoid taxes, the next best strategy is to ensure that everyone pays his or her fair share of the costs of government. This helps to explain why sales taxes are popular among all segments of society even though they are regressive.[33]

Compared with other forms of policymaking, tax policymaking has also been relatively technical and legalistic.[34] The tax code is an extremely complex set of laws, and it is made even more complex by rulings made by the Internal Revenue Service and tax courts concerning just what the tax code really means. In Congress, tax policymaking historically has been the preserve of a relatively few powerful and knowledgeable congressmen and senators (e.g., Senator Long and former congressman Wilbur Mills).[35] Changes in Congress have tended to lessen the power of the tax committees—and the venerable individuals who populate them—but finance committees still possess substantial political power.

The perceived (and real) complexity of tax policymaking allows many special interests to have desired provisions written into the tax code with little awareness on the part of the general public. The many special interests are represented by members of Congress whose constituencies may contain large concentrations of one kind of industry or another. Adding loopholes to a tax law often is an exercise in coalition building through logrolling, with every congressman adding in his or her provision in return for support of the legislation as a whole. All this has resulted in a federal tax system, especially an income tax system, that is perceived as highly unfair by many citizens. Harris surveys taken prior to tax reform indicated that an average 90 percent of respondents thought that the federal income tax was unfair.[36] Polls taken after the 1986 reforms were almost as negative about the tax structure, and the subsequent years have done little to enhance public confidence.

Any number of proposals for tax reform have been made in the United States. It was surprising to most observers that a major tax reform was actually passed in 1986. What is perhaps even more surprising is that the reform passed was as sweeping and as comprehensive as it was.[37] It is relatively easy to criticize the reform and to point out its weaknesses. Still, given the history of tax policy in the United States, and indeed most other countries, the package actually put into effect was remarkable.

The tax system was simplified for the average taxpayer, a large number of the more egregious loopholes were removed, and impact of the tax system on the less affluent was made somewhat more equitable. A year, or even a few months, prior to passage, such a change in the tax laws would have been thought impossible.

What happened to produce this major reversal of tax policymaking as usual? There is no simple answer to that question; instead, there was a confluence of forces, liberal and conservative, business and labor, producers and consumers, who all wanted change. President Reagan wanted to reduce the progressivity of taxes and to allow the more affluent to keep more of what they earned. Some of his conservative allies wanted to eliminate special preferences for certain industries in order to produce a more level playing field for all industries as a means of stimulating economic growth.[38] Liberals also wanted elimination of the special preferences built into the tax laws as a means of attempting to help middle- and low-income groups that could not take advantage of many of these loopholes. In addition, several policy entrepreneurs—Senator Bill Bradley (D-N.J.), Congressman Dan Rostenkowski (D-Ill.), Secretary of the Treasury Donald Regan, and others—made heavy political investments to bring about this major policy change.[39] There was, in fact, a rare "policy window" through which advocates of tax reform could push their proposals and produce significant change in the tax structure.[40]

Naturally, those interests whose particular benefits were affected by tax simplification were skeptical about the legislation. Among the first to question the efficacy of the legislation were mayors and governors, who argued that ending the deductibility of some state and local taxes would make it more difficult for subnational governments to increase taxes. These officials were followed closely by business interests, who argued that the repeal of special investment credits, accelerated depreciation, and other benefits going to investment would further slow the rate of capital formation in the United States and thereby slow economic growth. A standard place to begin any political analysis is to ask "whose ox is gored"—and a large number of oxen would be gored by this tax reform legislation.[41]

Tax Reform in the 1990s

There was also a significant tax reform in the late 1990s, as President Clinton and the Republican Congress finally came to agree on some transformation of the tax code. Unlike the 1986 reform, however, this reform tended to build in more special provisions and loopholes, rather than to eliminate them. The final shape of the bill reflected a good deal of negotiation and logrolling between a conservative Congress and a more liberal president. In that way it represented a return to the old "Christmas tree" style of tax legislation, with something for everybody hung on it. The tax bill was presented as an effort to be fairer to American families, especially those in the middle class, but in reality it tended to benefit as many or more special interests than it disadvantaged.

Perhaps the major change produced in the 1997 legislation was in the treatment of capital gains. If a citizen invests in stocks, bonds, a piece of land, or whatever and then later sells it at a profit, he or she has had a capital gain that is subject to taxes. The major exception is on houses, where, if the sales yield is reinvested in another house, there is no tax; there is also a one-time exclusion designed for aging people who want to move out of the family home into some other type of housing. Any other type of profit from investment (with very minor exceptions) is subject to tax, although the rate of tax on these profits has tended to be lower than that on ordinary income. For example, for much of the postwar period, capital gains were taxed at half the normal rate of income tax.

There has been a great deal of debate among politicians and economists about the desirability and effects of capital gains taxation. On the one hand, the argument is that this is income just like any other type of income and there is no reason to treat it differently. Given that, for the most part, only the better off in society receive capital gains on any investments other than houses, eliminating capital gains taxation would make the federal tax system less progressive than it is. Further, low or non-existent capital gains taxation would encourage speculation in all sorts of assets and might make the stock market and other financial markets more volatile than they already are.

On the other hand, there are good arguments for having low capital gains taxation or for eliminating it entirely. In the first place, as mentioned (p. 204), one problem for the American economy is a low savings and investment rate. High capital gains taxes discourage investment, or at least they do not reward investors for making good choices. Further, investments involve risk, so that having to pay full tax rates if the risk is justified does not seem fair. Also, capital gains are generally counted in current dollar terms and do not take into account the effects of inflation, which could make an apparently large return on an investment actually trivial.[42] Finally, an aversion to paying capital gains taxes may encourage some investors to hold on to assets after they have ceased to be as productive as would alternative uses of the same money; this is another way in which the tax system may distort the use of resources in the economy and lower potential economic growth.

There was a great deal of agitation for reducing or even eliminating the capital gains tax during the Reagan and (especially) the Bush administrations. Little happened, however, until 1997, which reflected in part a change in the structure of investment in the United States. The combination of a soaring stock market and fears about the viability of Social Security as a source of retirement income (see pp. 293–95) led many more people to begin to invest in the stock market; over 40 percent of households now have some money in the market. Capital gains taxation has therefore become a general issue, rather than just a concern for the wealthy.[43]

Despite public discontent with many aspects of the prevailing tax system, adopting a tax reform is a difficult undertaking politically. Making tax policy has traditionally been the preserve of the special interests, and it may be difficult to prevent them from continuing their role in the process. In addition, many of the arguments advanced by those special interests may have social and economic validity. The repeal of credits for business investment contained in the 1997 reform may indeed have some long-term negative impact on economic growth in the United States. In short, tax reform was a desirable policy goal, but like almost any policy change, it was not without its critics and its negative consequences. Further, as American politics has become more ideological, tax policy tends to be an area in which the conflicts between conservative and progressive ideas about good public policy appear very stark.

Proposals for Further Fundamental Reform

The tax reform of 1986 and the less comprehensive reforms of the mid-1990s were significant, but they were all produced in the context of the progressive income tax, which is assumed as the basic source of revenue for the federal government. That assumption is, however, being questioned in a number of proposals for reform, which range from shifting the income tax to a flat rate on all income to shifting away from personal income to either integrated corporate taxation to consumption taxation. All of these reform proposals have some merit, but all also have political and economic costs.

The federal government may want to maintain its fundamental reliance on the income tax, but it can collect that revenue in rather different ways than it has been doing. As we pointed out earlier, the current structure of the income tax imposes different levels of tax on different income levels and also provides a number of deductions and exemptions—the loopholes already discussed. Therefore the tax system is very complicated—the tax code is approximately 10,000 pages long—and requires a large amount of administration (both by government and by private citizens). The current system also may create inequities because some types of expenditures are considered worthy of deductions and others are not.

THE FLAT TAX

One logical alternative to the current system is to have a simple flat tax on all income regardless of its source. Likewise, this form of taxation would eliminate almost all deductions and loopholes for expenditures. The argument of the advocates of this reform, notably the publisher and Republican politician Steve Forbes, is that this system would be fairer, treating all income and expenditure equally and treating all citizens equally. The flat tax also would be simpler and could eliminate a good deal of the employment in the Internal Revenue Service and in the private-sector tax industry, as well as reducing distress over the way in which people believe they are (mis)treated by the IRS.[44] On more technical grounds, the flat tax would be more fiscally neutral, so that decisions about how to invest could be made on economic, rather than tax, considerations.

As might be expected, the flat tax is not without its critics. First, it would almost certainly be a regressive move from the current tax structure, with the more affluent having to pay less than they do now. The flat tax is usually discussed in the range of 17 percent of total income, which is a substantially lower rate than the more affluent now pay on average in income tax (see table 9.7, p. 236). Under this plan the very affluent seemingly would

TABLE 9.7

INCOME TAX RATE AS A PERCENTAGE

OF ADJUSTED GROSS INCOME, 1994

Income group	Percent paid in income tax
<$15,000	2.8
$15,000–24,999	5.8
$25,000–49,999	10.2
$50,000–74,999	12.3
$75,000–99,999	15.0
$100,000–199,999	18.5
$200,000–499,999	25.6
$500,000–1,000,000	30.0
$1,000,000 and above	31.2

SOURCE: *Statistical Abstract of the United States, 1997.*

benefit at the expense of the remainder of the population. Despite the political rhetoric about the ability of the affluent to avoid income tax through loopholes, on average they do pay high taxes under the current system. In addition, the flat tax would eliminate the ability to use the tax system for other public policy purposes. There are certainly problems with some of the loopholes that have been created in the tax system, but the use of tax expenditures has also been a powerful tool for addressing other policy concerns, especially housing and support for charities.[45] Finally, a shift to a flat tax might also require some shifting of state tax structures, given that several states calculate their own income taxes as a percentage of the federal tax.

NATIONAL CONSUMPTION TAX

A more extreme solution to the problems identified in the federal income tax is to move from an income tax to a consumption tax. Americans are used to general consumption taxes (sales taxes) being levied by state and local governments, but the federal government has only levied specific consumption taxes, such as those on alcohol, tobacco, and gasoline. This is in contrast to many other developed economies that raise a large proportion of their tax revenue through a national consumption tax, usually the VAT (see table 9.1, p. 219).

The logic of a consumption tax is, first, that it places the burden on spending, rather than earning, money. If indeed one of problems with the American economy is that there is inadequate savings, then it makes sense to

Senior citizens and others gather on Capitol Hill to express opposition to a Republican-drafted bill to offset proposed income tax cuts by reducing Medicare benefits. (AP/Wide World Photos)

tax spending rather than saving money. Another positive aspect of the consumption tax is that it would require that everyone in the society pay some part of the tax burden. We noted earlier that Americans want to be sure that all citizens "participate" in funding government, and a consumption tax would certainly accomplish that goal. Further, the consumption tax would place the burden of recordkeeping on businesses rather than on the general public, thus eliminating citizen frustrations with the tax system and with government more generally.

No tax is perfect, and there would certainly be some drawbacks to a consumption tax. First, to collect the amount of money now collected by the federal government, the tax rate would have to be roughly 30 percent on all purchases.[46] This is about four times higher than the highest rate of sales tax in the states, and it would produce a huge, if one-time only, increase in prices.[47] Further, this alternative form of taxation would be regressive. On average the poor tend to spend a much higher proportion of their income than do the more affluent. Like state and local sales taxes, a national consumption tax could be made less regressive by excluding items such as food, medicines, clothing, and the like, but then the tax rate on other goods and services would have to be all the higher. Finally, given that businesses rather than individuals would be liable for the consumption tax, government could not use the tax system for other purposes, such as providing the important Earned Income Tax Credit as a means of subsidizing the poor.

Some of the objections to a national consumption tax based on business transactions could be met by adopting a personal consumption tax. The idea here would be that individual taxpayers report all the money they have earned during the year and then subtract the amount they have saved. The difference would be consumption, and that would be subject to tax.[48] This proposal may solve some problems, but it in turn creates others. This form of taxation would require personal filings and, therefore, as large and intrusive an IRS as there is at present. Indeed it might be more difficult for the average citizen to get his or her level of tax withholding through the year correct, so that there would be more refunds and/or large payments due at filing. Further, determination of what "savings" are might be difficult with this form of taxation. Are consumer durable goods savings? A house almost certainly would be, but a car or a washing machine?

Conservatives have several other complaints about the concept of a national consumption tax. One is that it could be more easily hidden from the public than can other types of taxes, given that it probably would be a part of the price of the product rather than a separate item to be paid. At a rate of 30 percent, it would be unlikely to go unnoticed, but at a lower rate, to supplement the income tax, it might. Further, some conservatives argue that taxing consumption is a way of punishing the more affluent for their success, rather than rewarding them for it, and therefore it might be as much or more of an economic disincentive than the income tax.[49]

INTEGRATING CORPORATE AND PERSONAL TAXATION

A more technical recommendation for changing the existing tax code is to integrate corporate and personal taxation—usually called the Comprehensive Business Income Tax. The basic concept is that if most income-earners in the United States work for some sort of organization, then those organizations rather than the individual citizens would make the tax filings. Individual wages might be taxed, but this payment could be collected at source, with only the self-employed having to make individual filings.

This proposal has advantages for at least two reasons. The first is that it would make tax administration easier. If corporations, with their computerized recordkeeping, could be made responsible for most tax filings, the job of collecting taxes would be much easier. If nothing else, that would mean "only" 24 million tax returns to be generated, as compared to the 139 million now being filed.[50] Some individuals would still be responsible for filing tax forms for items such as capital gains, but the bulk of the work of record-keeping and filing would be done by businesses with better capacities for keeping the records.

The other reason for pushing for an integration of personal and corporate taxation derives from concern about the economic effects of the existing tax structure. Under the current system there is some double taxation of business profits—once when the corporation earns the profits and again when they are paid out to individuals as dividends. This duplicate taxation is felt by many economists to tax corporate income excessively and to deter investment. Integration of the two forms of taxation is suggested, therefore, as a means to facilitate investment and savings.

Conclusion

Taxation is one public policy that most citizens would as soon not think about, but one that nonetheless occupies a good deal of their time (and money). Taxation is also the subject of a number of myths, not least of which is that the United States is a high-tax country.[51] Paying taxes may be anathema to most members of the public, but taxation is central for government because it is how government obtains the money it needs to survive and to provide public services. Tax policy is also used to attain a number of policy goals in addition to simply raising adequate revenue for survival and for needed programs. The "tax expenditures" through which those goals are reached are among the most controversial features of tax policy. While in some ways an efficient means of reaching policy goals, by providing benefits to some segments of the society, they appear unfair to those who are not able to take advantage of the same benefits.

Although many citizens are dissatisfied with the existing structure of taxation in the United States, reforming the system remains extremely difficult. There has been one major tax reform in recent history, but that attempt to make the tax system simpler and fairer is being increasingly diluted year after year. The impacts of reforming capital gains taxation in 1997 are yet to be fully understood, and given the wider range of stock ownership, these reforms will have a wider impact than would have been the case even a few years ago. There are few powerful political forces on the side of tax reform, but there are numerous forces that want to utilize the tax system to feather their own economic and social nests. Even though most Americans are not keen on paying taxes, they would be more likely to tolerate, and comply with, a tax system that appeared fair and equitable.

10. Health-Care Policy

One of the great myths about American political life and public policy is that we have a private health-care system. In fact, in 1997, over 44 percent of all health-care expenditures in the United States were made by government agencies of some sort, and many physicians who loudly proclaim the virtues of private medical care receive a substantial portion of their income from public medical programs such as Medicare and Medicaid (see table 10.1). Further, on average 81,000 patients receive treatment in Veterans Administration hospitals every day, and millions of other patients are treated in hospitals operated by state and local governments. Although the public sector makes a much smaller proportion of total health-care expenditures in the United States than in most other industrialized countries, there is still a significant involvement of government in the provision of health care.

The extent of involvement of American government in health care can be seen in part in the health-care programs listed in table 10.2. All three levels of government are to some degree involved in health care, and at the federal level a wide variety of public agencies are involved. Almost all cabinet-level departments of the federal government are to some degree involved

TABLE 10.1

SOURCES OF PAYMENT TO HEALTH CARE PROVIDERS,
1992 (IN PERCENTAGES)

	Hospitals	*Physicians*	*Other*
Government			
Federal	39.9	27.4	20.1
State	15.3	6.7	11.1
Direct payments	5.0	19.1	47.6
Private insurance	35.1	46.8	17.7
Other private payers	4.7	0.1	3.5

SOURCE: Sally T. Sonnefeld et al., "Projections of National Health Expenditures through the Year 2000," *Health Care Financing Review* 13 (Fall 1991).

TABLE 10.2

MAJOR HEALTH PROGRAMS

Federal	State	Local
Department of Agriculture	State hospitals	City hospitals
Meat inspections	State mental	Sanitation and
	hospitals	public health
Department of Health and Human	Substance abuse	
Services	Medicaid	
Food and Drug Administration		
Community Health Services		
Indian Health Services		
National Institutes of Health		
Substance abuse programs		
Health education		
HMO loan funds		
U.S. Public Health Service		
Medicare		
Medicaid		
Department of the Interior		
Territorial health programs		
Department of Veterans' Affairs		
VA hospitals		

with health care, as are a number of independent executive agencies. Their involvement ranges from directly providing medical care to some segments of the population (e.g., through the Department of Defense, the Department of the Interior, or the Department of Veterans' Affairs), through funding medical care for the general public, through regulating some aspects of medical care, to subsidizing medical research.

Without involvement of the public sector, American health care would certainly be very different and probably would not be as good as it is. Without government, health care certainly would not be as accessible for the poor and the elderly, and the overall technical quality would probably not be as high as it currently is for those who nominally pay all their own medical expenses. For one thing, the federal government is a major source of funds for medical research ($15.2 billion in 1995), without which many of the advances in medicine with which the average citizen is now familiar would not have happened or would have been delayed.

Although the role of government in health care is larger than most American citizens believe it to be, that role is still not as great as many people believe it should be. Rather than opt for greater involvement in medical care, however, the Reagan and Bush administrations reduced the federal role, cutting back on federal health-care funding and converting former categorical programs subsidizing health care at the state and local level into block-grant programs. This type of grant program depends much more on the priorities of state governments for implementation, and there is some evidence that health care for the very poor has been significantly reduced in quantity and quality.[1] Medicaid has become an extremely expensive program for the states, and they have been searching for means to limit their financial exposure.[2] By the 1990s even many members of the middle class were encountering difficulty in financing adequate medical care for themselves and their families (see pp. 247–48); in 1998 approximately 40 million Americans had no medical insurance, public or private.

The problems of cost and access to care have helped produce increasing demands for more public involvement in health care, including some continuing interest in national health insurance.[3] Some surveys indicate that well over half the American population would support some form of national health insurance. For example, a survey in mid-1994 indicated that 77 percent of the population wanted some form of universal medical care, although they disagreed on the exact nature of the program.[4] More recent surveys indicate that health care continues to be an area that Americans believe requires substantial rethinking and a strong public role.[5] Health care is one policy area in which the conservative policy ideas of the last decade appear to be encountering substantial skepticism, and over half of the population say that the federal government should have a primary role in financing health care.[6] Yet, with typical ambivalence about the role of government, Americans appear to want universal access to medical care without a large-scale government program.

President Clinton placed health-care reform at the top of his policy agenda when he came to office in 1993. He took a strong personal interest in this policy area and placed Hillary Rodham Clinton in charge of a task force to draft the reform. After a series of consultations around the country and hearings before congressional committees, the administration drafted a bill that proposed a complex arrangement of purchasing organizations ("alliances") that would operate somewhat like existing Health Maintenance Organizations (HMOs, discussed later). For the administration, the most important aspect of the bill was that it guaranteed coverage to all citizens. The Clintons' health-care proposal generated several other proposals, ranging from a single-payer plan similar to that found in Canada (detailed later in this chapter) to very modest extensions of existing public- and private-sector programs relying on voluntary acceptance and tax subsidies.[7]

None of the plans for reform of health care were successful, and the net result of the 1993 effort was that Congress never actually voted on any of the attempts at comprehensive reform. We discuss this failure in some detail later in this chapter (see pp. 274–76), but it is indicative of some broader themes in health-care policy. One is the ambivalence felt by the public toward government involvement; people want health-care reform in general but often oppose specific plans. A second point is the importance of health care not just for patients but also for the economy—one dollar in seven of the GNP is spent on health care, and the lobbying surrounding health-care reform had as much to do with the economy as with caring for patients. Finally, beyond its pervasive effects on the economy, health care also touches every citizen who has been, or will ever be, ill. Thus, health-care politics touches everyone in society.

Although the major political concern is often with creating a *national* program of health insurance, the states have already begun to put their own programs into place (see table 10.3). For example, Hawaii already has a public health-care system that, along with private insurance, covers almost the entire population of the state, and Massachusetts has experimented with a similarly extensive plan.[8] Minnesota also has adopted a health-care program using HMOs that approaches comprehensive coverage, and other states such as Pennsylvania provide some health-care coverage for all children, if not adults.[9] Individual states also have innovated in the manner in which they deliver Medicaid services to improve coverage and lower costs. Many states also have added substantial coverage for children, funded at least in part by the federal government as a part of the reform of the welfare system in 1996.[10] The major question on the public role in health care appears to be the extent of the government's role, rather than whether the public sector will be involved.

TABLE 10.3

PERCENTAGE OF POPULATION NOT COVERED
BY HEALTH INSURANCE, 1995

Low		*High*	
Wisconsin	7.3	New Mexico	25.6
Minnesota	8.0	Texas	24.5
North Dakota	8.3	California	20.6
Connecticut	8.8	Louisiana	20.5
Hawaii	8.9	Arkansas	20.4

SOURCE: Bureau of the Census, *Health Insurance Coverage, 1995* (Washington, D.C.: Bureau of the Census, Department of Commerce, annual).

One ironic outcome of the failure to adopt the Clinton reforms is that the American medical system now has many of the same elements that were perceived to be so undesirable in the Clinton plan, but without the greater equality that would have resulted under that plan.[11] That is, the controls over access to care, the bureaucracy, and the complexity all are components of the managed-care system that has emerged during the 1990s, but the private system (even with the involvement of the public sector) still leaves more than 40 million people without adequate health-care coverage. We may have achieved the worst of both worlds.

Problems in Health Care

The United States is one of the richest countries in the world, and it spends a much larger proportion of its economic resources (as measured by gross national product) on health care than does any other industrialized nation (see table 10.4). The results of all those expenditures, however, are not so impressive. In infant mortality, a commonly used indicator of the quality of medical care, the United States ranks seventeenth in the world, behind most Western European countries as well as Japan, Taiwan, Hong Kong, and Brunei.[12] Depending on one's perspective, these figures are made better or worse if the total figure is disaggregated by race. For the white population in the United States, the infant mortality rate is as low (7.7 per 1,000 live births in 1996) as that of all but a few Western European and Asian countries, but the rate for African Americans (17 deaths) is closer to rates found in the countries of the former Soviet bloc and some South American countries (see table 10.5). Further, the disparity between black and white infant mortality rates has actually increased since 1970.

TABLE 10.4

HEALTH EXPENDITURES AS A PERCENTAGE OF GROSS NATIONAL
PRODUCT, SELECTED COUNTRIES, 1995

United States	14.2	Austria	7.9
Germany	10.4	Italy	7.7
France	9.8	Japan	7.2
Canada	9.6	Sweden	7.2
Australia	8.6	New Zealand	7.1
Belgium	8.0	United Kingdom	6.9
Norway	8.0	Denmark	6.4

SOURCE: Organization for Economic Cooperation and Development, *OECD Health Systems: Facts and Trends* (Paris: OECD, 1997).

TABLE 10.5
INFANT MORTALITY RATES (DEATHS IN THE FIRST YEAR
OF LIFE PER 1,000 LIVE BIRTHS), 1996

Japan	4.4	United States (whites)	7.7
Sweden	4.5	Italy	7.8
Iceland	5.4	United States (total)	8.4
Taiwan	5.7	Slovakia	8.4
Hong Kong	5.9	Greece	8.9
Netherlands	6.2	Bulgaria	9.4
Switzerland	6.6	Czech Republic	9.7
Germany	6.6	Portugal	9.8
Brunei	6.8	Cuba	10.5
France	6.8	Slovenia	10.8
Canada	7.0	Bosnia	12.6
Austria	7.3	Hungary	13.1
Australia	7.4	Chile	15.9
United Kingdom	7.4	United States (blacks)	17.0
Norway	7.7	Belarus	19.0
		Ukraine	21.0

SOURCES: World Health Organization, *World Health Statistics Annual, 1996* (Geneva: WHO, 1997); Bureau of the Census, *Statistical Abstract of the United States, 1996* (Washington, D.C.: Government Printing Office, 1997).

Health care of absolutely the finest quality is available in the United States, but it may be available only to a limited (and perhaps declining) portion of the population. Vast disparities in access exist among racial, economic, and geographical groups in the United States; even with Medicare, Medicaid, and other public programs, the poor, the elderly, and those living in rural areas receive less medical care, and poorer care, than do white middle-class urban citizens. Those groups also report that their own health is poor, as compared to that of more advantaged Americans (see table 10.6, p. 246). Further, an increasing number of middle-class citizens are beginning to be squeezed out of the medical-care market by rapidly increasing prices and by declining insurance benefits provided by employers. The problems that Americans confront in medical care now are basically three: access, quality, and cost.

Access to Medical Care

If any medical-care system is to function effectively, prospective patients must have access to the system. A number of factors can deter citizens from

TABLE 10.6

PERSONAL ASSESSMENT OF HEALTH STATUS

(IN PERCENTAGES)

	Excellent	Very good	Good	Fair or poor
Race				
White	42.8	34.8	21.7	10.1
Black	28.3	21.7	29.8	19.5
Family income				
Under $10,000	28.9	21.7	27.5	21.1
$10,000–14,999	34.0	24.7	27.0	13.7
$15,000–19,999	36.9	26.7	25.5	10.4
$20,000–34,999	43.7	27.1	21.9	6.9
$35,000 or more	52.8	26.1	15.9	4.6

SOURCE: Department of Health and Human Services, *Health Status of the Disadvantaged: Chartbook, 1986* (Washington, D.C.: Public Health Service, 1986).

becoming patients, and one purpose of public involvement in the medical marketplace must be to equalize access for all citizens. Americans still differ on the extent to which they believe that equal access to medical care should be a right of citizenship, but most are willing to accept that all citizens require some form of protection against at least serious illnesses.[13] As it is, a large—and growing—proportion of Americans do not have any health insurance.

The most commonly cited barrier to access to health care is economics. As the majority of medical care in the United States is still paid for privately, those who lack the income or insurance to pay for it may not receive medical care. Even with several public medical-care programs, medicine is still not as available to the poor as it is to the more affluent. As of 1990 almost 30 percent of all the poor (those with incomes below the official poverty line) were not eligible to receive Medicaid benefits. They were poor, but not sufficiently poor to qualify under the means-testing criteria of Medicaid.[14] Only 20 percent of the poor have any privately financed health insurance, and only 10 percent of the poor have any nonhospital coverage.[15] Among all Americans, approximately 40 million people do not have health insurance (see table 10.7). Even the elderly poor, who have access to Medicare because of their age, must still pay for parts of their insurance, and at a rate that may well deter some from taking full advantage of the program.

The middle class now may find that the rising cost of medical care and the possibility of catastrophic illness make all but the very wealthy medically

TABLE 10.7

PERCENTAGES OF GROUPS COVERED BY HEALTH INSURANCE,
1996

Group	Percentage
Total	84.8
Race	
White	86.0
Black	80.3
Hispanic	66.3
Other	80.5
Employment status	
Full-time, full year	86.5
Part-time, full year	73.5
Some unemployment	56.1
Nonworker	77.4
Age	
Under 16	85.8
16–24	72.3
25–34	78.0
35–44	84.0
45–54	87.2
55–64	86.1
65+	99.1

SOURCE: Bureau of the Census, *Current Population Survey*, monthly.

indigent. The federal government made a brief foray into catastrophic coverage for Medicare recipients, but financing, administrative, and political difficulties led to the program's termination in 1989 after only one year.[16] Further, the absence of medical insurance is not a problem just for the poor. In 1992 almost 30 percent of all the uninsured had incomes over $30,000 per year, and one in eight had an income over $50,000. Over 84 percent of the uninsured live in families headed by people who work, usually for small firms in service industries, at least part of the year.[17] Over half the uninsured have someone in the family who works full-time.[18] These facts help to explain why there is a continuing demand to reform the health-care system of the United States (see pp. 271–80).

The problem of inadequate health-insurance coverage is not going away; if anything it is getting worse. From 1990 to 1995 private health-insurance coverage dropped from 75 percent to 70.5 percent of the population; the proportion with coverage in 1979 was 80 percent.[19] This decline in coverage occurred across all economic classes but hit hardest among those earning between $10,000 and $40,000. In addition, workers who are covered by insurance from their employers are currently being required to pay through their own contributions on average more than double the proportion of the total costs that their counterparts paid several years ago.

In the contemporary American medical-care system, having insurance, as well as not having it, can present troubles. Having insurance, for instance, can minimize mobility in the economy. If a person holds a job that provides health-care benefits, it is difficult for him or her to leave that job for one that may be better in other respects but does not offer health-care benefits. In some cases, even if the new job does provide insurance, that insurance will not cover preexisting conditions. If a prospective employee or family member has been diagnosed with any serious condition that cannot be covered by the new insurance, moving between jobs may be impossible. One reform that did follow the failure of the Clinton health-care program was the Kennedy-Kassebaum bill, which mandated increased portability of medical insurance so that fewer people would lose coverage if they changed jobs.[20]

Even if direct economic barriers to access to medical care were removed, there might still be significant noneconomic barriers to equal access. Interestingly, even with the almost entirely free medical-care system of the United Kingdom, the differences in health status by social or economic class have not narrowed significantly.[21] Each social class is on average healthier, but the disparities between the wealthy and the poor have been maintained, indicating that there are other barriers to consuming health care and, perhaps more important, other barriers to creating health that cannot be removed simply by providing free access. Members of the poor and working classes tend to lose hourly wages if they go to the doctor, whereas salaried employees either do not lose pay or take personal-business leaves. Transportation is generally easier for the more affluent, whereas the poor must rely on public transportation.

Perhaps the most important barrier to equal access is becoming communication. The more affluent and educated know better how to get what they want from professional and bureaucratic organizations than do the poor, and they are more likely to be well treated by individuals and institutions than are the less-well-off. A doctor is more likely to pay serious attention to the description of symptoms of a middle-class person than to those of a poor person, and the middle-class person is more likely to demand extra diagnostic and curative procedures. Also, there is some evidence that doctors do not pay adequate attention to the complaints of the elderly. These communication and bureaucratic skills are especially important in managed care, where a number of gatekeepers are used to try to prevent spending money; generally only the articulate and persistent are able to get what they want.[22] So even if all direct economic barriers were removed, there might still be serious impediments to equality in medical care, especially as the poor are generally not as healthy to begin with as the affluent and as a consequence may require more medical care.

These socioeconomic differences in access to health care are manifested in differential health outcomes between racial groups in the United States. The clear differences in infant mortality by race have already been mentioned, but equally large differences are evident in any number of other indicators of health-care quality.[23] For example, maternal mortality among African Americans is over three times higher than for the remainder of the population, as is the incidence of tuberculosis. Deaths from diabetes-related causes in the African American population are double those in the population as a whole. It is clear that there are some extra problems of access to quality care among the nonwhite population.

In addition to economic conditions, geography plays a significant dual role in defining access to medical care. First, urban areas are generally better served with doctors and especially with hospitals than are rural areas. For example, in Standard Metropolitan Statistical Areas (SMSAs) in the United States, the average number of physicians per 100,000 population is 215, and the average number of hospital beds per 100,000 is 459. This contrasts with 97 physicians per 100,000 and 425 hospital beds per 100,000 in the non-SMSA regions of the country. Another example of the disparity in medical-care resources is that eighteen rural counties in Texas alone have not a single physician although there are more doctors in the United States than ever before. The geographical disparities in medical services would be even more pronounced if the areas of specialization of physicians and the standards and equipment of hospitals were also considered. This imbalance in care does not necessarily equate with health outcomes; the District of Columbia has one of the highest numbers of physicians in relation to population (641 per 100,000 population, as compared to a national average of 230) but also has perhaps the worst health outcomes in the country.[24]

Second, there are marked regional imbalances in access to medical care.[25] These can be related in part, but not entirely, to urban-rural differences. The places in the United States best served by physicians and hospitals are the Middle Atlantic states and the states of the Far West. The worst served are the Upper Midwest and the Deep South. There are, for example, 387 physicians per 100,000 in Massachusetts and 362 per 100,000 in Maryland, but only 138 per 100,000 in Mississippi and 137 per 100,000 in Idaho. A variety of programs, public and private, have been tried to equalize the distribution of personnel but these imbalances persist. This maldistribution does not, however, exist so clearly for hospital beds. Many small communities have been able to maintain hospitals, in part as a means of attempting to attract physicians and other health-care workers.[26]

Thus, in some parts of the United States, high-quality medical care may not be available, even for someone who can afford it, without a substantial investment in travel. For any serious emergency, this puts the affected individual at even greater risk. Several pilot programs to encourage young doctors to practice in rural, "underdoctored" areas have been tried, and more are being advocated, but there are still pronounced inequalities. Many rural areas have tried on their own to attract physicians and may be willing to finance the medical education of young persons willing to come to their towns. These issues of access must be addressed along with economic issues if there is to be greater equality in access to health care. The federal government has instituted a program for funding rural health-care clinics, but even those facilities appear to go to the largest settlements eligible for assistance.[27]

Finally, we should note that access alone may not be sufficient to ensure that medical care is successful. The relatively high rate of infant mortality (especially among the minority population) is often taken as an indicator of poor access to medical care, although there is some evidence that other factors may be as important in determining those health outcomes. For example, the highest rates of infant mortality (by state) tend to be less related to the availability of medical personnel and facilities in the state, or even to per capita income, than to the family situations into which children are born. Illegitimate births, for example, tend to have a much higher rate of infant mortality.[28]

Cost

The second fundamental problem that has troubled health-care consumers and policymakers is the rapidly rising cost of medical care; this is the health-care "problem that won't go away."[29] As well as not going away, cost has become the driving force in health-care policy, especially within the private sector. The majority of Americans with health insurance are now in some sort of managed-care plan, with cost-containment as a principal objective of the plan. Indeed, critics of these plans argue that cost concerns have become too dominant, and there is a need to ensure quality as much as to minimize costs (see pp. 266–68).

The total cost of medical care in the United States results from two components. The first is the number of medical procedures performed in the United States, which is tending to increase, in part because of the aging of the population and the increasing number and types of treatments becoming available through advances in medical science.[30] The other element of the total cost of medical care is the price of each procedure and the general increase in prices for all medical activity.

The increase in prices is the component of medical costs that is usually discussed. Table 10.8 shows changes in prices for some components of medical care compared with the overall consumer price index (CPI), and the composite medical-care price index. It is clear from these data that medical costs as a whole have increased more rapidly than have total consumer costs and that, among the components of medical costs, hospital costs have increased most rapidly. These costs have increased 219 percent more over a twenty-seven-year period than have total consumer prices, while those for total medical care have increased "only" 65 percent more rapidly than has the CPI.

The rate of increase in medical costs has been slowing slightly during the 1990s, but it is still outpacing general price increases. Further, many experts expect another surge in medical care costs in the immediate future. Most of the savings from implementing managed care have already been realized, so the underlying dynamics of medical inflation may quickly reassert themselves.[31] Further, the continuing aging of the American population means that there will be more elderly citizens requiring more medical care, and with that, more demand pressures on costs. Finally, because of the political pressures to ensure that patients in managed care have better access

TABLE 10.8

CHANGES IN MEDICAL CARE COSTS COMPARED
WITH CONSUMER PRICE INDEX (1967 = 100)

Year	CPI	Total medicine	Hospital	Physicians	Commodities
1960	88.7	79.1	57.3	77.0	104.5
1965	94.5	89.5	75.9	88.3	100.2
1970	116.3	120.6	145.4	121.4	103.6
1975	161.2	168.6	236.1	169.4	118.8
1980	246.8	265.9	418.9	269.3	168.1
1985	326.6	413.0	722.5	407.9	262.7
1990	421.8	592.9	1,096.1	533.1	388.4
1991	439.5	645.7	1,199.1	565.1	420.2
1992	452.7	694.7	1,309.7	600.7	447.1
1993	465.2	740.0	1,421.0	634.3	463.6
1994	477.3	778.2	1,502.0	662.3	477.1
1995	491.4	817.6	1,577.1	692.5	486.2
1996	512.5	847.8	1,638.6	717.0	500.3

SOURCE: Bureau of the Census, *Statistical Abstract of the United States* (Washington, D.C.: Government Printing Office, annual).

to a full range of treatment options, managed care may no longer be an effective barrier to medical inflation.

The importance of these data on costs is that medical care is becoming more difficult for the average person to afford. Even if an individual's income keeps pace with the consumer price index, it will still fall behind the increase in the costs of even general medical care. With these rapidly increasing prices, few people can afford to pay for a catastrophic illness requiring long-term hospitalization and extensive treatment. Even the best medical insurance available will frequently be exhausted by such an illness. Thus, it has become increasingly possible that even those with substantial incomes will be financially destroyed by a major illness. An additional problem is that all the concern about the cost of medicine may undermine the quality of medical care, an effect that may be especially problematic with "prospective reimbursement," Diagnostic Related Groupings (DRGs, see p. 260), and especially managed care.

Medical-care costs are a problem for government as well as for private citizens, as almost half the total medical-care bill in the United States is paid by governments. But even such a large share of the medical marketplace has not enabled government to exercise any significant control over health-care costs, perhaps because decisions about health-care spending are made, not by one government, but by several governments. And within each government there are several agencies interested in health care. Government's attempts to control medical costs have been diffuse and have encountered difficulty overcoming the technical and political power of health-care providers. As we discuss later, however, government is attempting to move more effectively to assist citizens—both as taxpayers and as patients—to cope with the costs of health care.

To be able to control costs, we must understand why medical costs have been increasing so rapidly. A number of factors have been identified as causing at least part of the increase in medical-care costs.[32] For hospitals, one factor has been a rapid increase in the cost of supplies and equipment. This has been true of large capital investments such as magnetic resonance imaging (MRI) scanners, as well as more mundane items such as dressings and surgical gloves. In addition, labor costs for hospitals have been increasing rapidly, as many professional and nonprofessional employees unionize to bargain for higher wages. Also, there may be too many hospital beds for the number of patients. Empty hospital beds involve capital costs and even some running costs that must be met, and these costs are spread among the patients who occupy beds through increases in the room rates. The same thing may be said for overinvestment in technology; every hospital that buys an MRI scanner, for example, must pay for it whether or not it is used very often. For example, the United States has over 2,500 MRI systems (at several million dollars each), while Canada is able to get by with less than 30.[33] Finally, the complex system of funding medical care in the United States costs a great deal of money. Some studies find that 25 percent of total U.S. hospital costs are administrative—a rate about twice as high as Canada's, with its single-payer public insurance program.[34]

During the 1990s hospitals have reacted to increasing pressures from insurers (including government agencies) and also have begun to anticipate changes from national health-care reform. They have attempted to reduce their operating costs by reducing the number of employees, managing patient loads more efficiently, and consolidating expensive services such as MRIs. Managed-competition programs also have been used to establish maximum payments for certain procedures and to encourage the insured to make the best use of their insurance dollars.[35] Hospital costs continue to increase, but the rate of increase has slowed. Further, the best way to limit hospital costs is to keep patients out of hospitals, so increasing amounts of surgery are done on an out-patient basis, and stays in hospitals are being shortened—at times to dangerous levels.

Physician costs also have been rising, although not as rapidly as hospital costs. In addition to the general pressures of inflation in the economy as a whole, increases in equipment and supply costs, the increasing cost of medical malpractice insurance, and the practice of "defensive medicine" to protect against malpractice suits by ordering every possible diagnostic procedure have all produced increases in doctor's fees.[36] Some of the relatively high cost of physicians' services in the United States results from the high level of specialization of American doctors.[37] Only 14 percent of the private physicians in office-based practice in the United States are in general practice, down from 27 percent in 1970 (see table 10.9, p. 254). When the number of internists (who often function as GPs) is considered, however, the shift away from general practice is not nearly so pronounced. In addition, a higher percentage of American doctors practice in hospitals than is true for many other countries, and hospital care is much more expensive than out-patient care.

Physicians have cooperated increasingly with "preferred provider" programs, in which large insurance carriers such as Blue Cross negotiate fees for their clients below the fees nominally charged by physicians and monitor the charges imposed by physicians. The insurers also require second opinions for expensive procedures and for procedures that are often performed unnecessarily. Physicians sometimes resent interference in their clinical freedom, but the programs ensure them access to large pools of patients, all of whom by definition have insurance and who therefore present fewer problems in collecting fees than might other patients.[38]

The federal government has undertaken another program to attempt to

TABLE 10.9

DISTRIBUTION OF PHYSICIANS BY TYPE OF PRACTICE

(IN PERCENTAGES)

	1980	1990	1992	1995
General medicine	17.6	17.0	15.1	14.0
Internal medicine	14.9	17.5	16.8	17.0
Obstetrics and gynecology	7.2	7.4	7.0	6.6
Surgery	16.0	15.2	13.3	12.4
Pediatrics	6.4	8.1	7.5	7.9
Other	38.9	34.8	40.3	44.1

SOURCE: American Medical Association, *Physician Characteristics and Distribution* (Chicago, Ill.: AMA, annual).

control physician costs for Medicare patients, called the "resource-based relative value scale" (RBRVS).[39] This plan assigns reasonable costs to procedures based on the time involved, as well as the physician's direct costs and malpractice premiums. Medicare then reimburses 80 percent of those "reasonable costs." As designed, this program assigns somewhat higher relative values to services provided by general practitioners than it does to those offered by specialists, which should also tend to reduce medical costs. This program has had limited impact on costs in Medicare,[40] and government is increasingly moving Medicare recipients into managed-care programs as a more effective mechanism for controlling its health-care costs.[41]

Finally, the method of payment for most medical care, especially hospital care, may influence increasing costs. Well over 90 percent of all hospital costs and approximately 80 percent of all medical expenses are paid by third-party insurers.[42] These third-party payers may be private (e.g., Blue Cross) or public (Medicaid or Medicare). As a result, neither doctors nor patients have had an incentive to restrict their consumption of medical care; it is perceived as "free." Individuals may, in fact, want to use all the insurance benefits they can in order to recover the amount they have paid as premiums over the years. This is a "tragedy of the commons," in which the rational behavior of individuals creates a pattern of irrationality for the society as a whole.[43] To rectify some of the problems with third-party payment, the Reagan administration included in the 1985 budget a program to tax employer-financed health insurance above a certain value. This made it more expensive to have so-called first-dollar coverage (i.e., coverage from the first dollar spent for treatment and all subsequent dollars). Managed-care programs also provide first-dollar coverage for some types of care, but they often require co-payments of some sort to deter consumption or at least make the consumer conscious of the costs.

The states have the primary responsibility for administering Medicaid, the public medical program for the poor, and they have been encountering large increases in their costs. In addition to the usual programs for managed care and scrutiny of costs, at least one state, Oregon, adopted a more radical plan for cost containment. The state government decided that it wanted to be able to continue to provide care to all persons who could not afford private care, rather than lowering the income level at which individuals lost eligibility for the program. But the state also concluded that it could not pay for everything for everybody.[44] It therefore decided that Medicaid in Oregon would pay only for a range of diseases—selected by cost, seriousness, and effectiveness of treatment—that fell above a line determined by the amount of money available; the program would not pay for treatment of other conditions. So, for example, in 1991 Medicaid would pay for inflammation of the stomach (no. 587 on the list of disorders) but not for lower back pain (no. 588).[45] Also, the program would not pay for "heroic treatments" in extremely difficult cases, such as babies born weighing less than 500 grams.

This policy had its critics, who argued that this program of rationing prevented the poor from getting equal treatment and that the selection of the cutoff point in care was arbitrary.[46] It was particularly attacked by groups representing the disabled and chronically ill. Advocates, however, argued that this program enabled the state to continue serving all the poor and to continue providing routine and cost-effective diagnostic procedures free of charge. At least in the short run, critics of the program were able to win, and the program was curtailed because it was alleged to violate legal protections for the disabled.[47] This is but one of many difficult choices that rising medical costs may soon impose on American society and its government, as the specter of rationing continues to hang over medical care, whether it is done implicitly or explicitly.

Quality

Finally, both citizens and government must be concerned with the quality of medical care being provided. Citizens' clearest expressions of concern about quality have been the increased number of malpractice suits and complaints against physicians and hospitals. Governments' concerns about quality extend from the general social responsibility for regulating the safety and effectiveness of medicines and medical devices on the market, to the quality of care provided to Medicare and Medicaid patients, to perhaps a more philosophical concern with the efficacy of modern medical care as a remedy for the health problems of American citizens.[48] Medical care is, however, a difficult product for which to judge quality.

When a patient—regardless of whether the resulting bill will be paid by Blue Cross–Blue Shield, by Medicaid, or out of pocket—enters a physician's office, he or she has the right to expect, at a minimum, competent medical care that meets current standards. Unfortunately, many patients do not receive such care. Many patients complain about receiving poor-quality care or medical treatment that they believe is delivered without any genuine humanity. The American Medical Association's own statistics document a significant rate of error in diagnosis and treatment. A more subtle manner in which the quality of treatment is eroded is through either overtreatment or undertreatment of patients. Overtreatment appeared in a number of studies documenting excessive use of medical technology and drugs as a means of earning more money for physicians and hospitals. For the public sector, complaints of overtreatment mean increased costs for Medicare and Medicaid patients, as well as the more human costs for the patients. This problem in quality appears to be declining as fewer and fewer patients have indemnity insurance that pays providers on a fee-for-service basis.

The rise of managed care in the health-care industry has raised even more questions about quality. Are patients being denied beneficial, or even necessary, treatments simply to minimize costs? Are patients being moved in and out of hospitals—so-called drive-through surgery—in order to maintain profit margins? Government has begun to make some regulatory interventions to address these issues, including regulating length of stay for some procedures. The current quality problem in health care is one of undertreatment, rather than the overtreatment found in fee-for-service medicine, as managed care places pressures on providers not to provide services. HMOs and other managed-care providers have an economic interest in not providing services, and they employ screening devices to prevent patients from consuming certain types of care. One mechanism, for example, has been to prohibit doctors from informing patients about expensive treatments that might be beneficial. Such "gag rules" have now been largely eliminated through pressures from government and the medical providers.[49] Indeed, some states are beginning to make insurance companies and HMOs liable if they do not provide information and needed care.[50]

The medical profession itself is supposed to be the first line of defense in the quality of medical care. State medical associations and their review boards are supposed to monitor the practice of medicine and handle complaints about incompetent or unethical practitioners. Other professional organizations are supposed to perform the same task for their members. While these organizations do have an interest in maintaining the integrity of medicine, they also find it difficult to discipline their fellow professionals and friends.

A more important philosophical question has been injected into the discussion of the quality of care. This resulted in part from the comment by former Colorado governor Richard Lamm that "we all have the duty to die," meaning that the terminally ill perhaps should not be kept alive by heroic means when that intervention only "prolongs dying" rather than saves life.[51] Is it high-technology medicine that sustains a semblance of life that has lost most human qualities, or is it a high-technology ego trip for the physician? The physicians' first commandment, *primum non nocere* (first, do not harm), has always been taken to mean preserving life at all costs; modern technology has made that an expensive and possibly inhumane interpretation. Some patients' families have gone to court to have their loved ones removed from life-support systems, but the techniques available to sustain life appear to have outpaced the ethical, legal, and policy capacity to cope with the changes.[52]

The question of what care is appropriate for the very elderly and the terminally ill again raises the issue of rationing of health care (see chapter 16). While this is sometimes discussed primarily as a problem of cost, it also has a number of implications for a definition of quality. Some countries have already begun to impose rather strict rationing of care—not performing organ transplants for patients over certain ages, for example.[53] Rationing in other systems has, in turn, produced fears that a more extensive public role in American medical care will also mean a greater possibility of rationing. For consumers used to being able to purchase what they want (provided they have good insurance) in the medical marketplace, the imposition of rationing is prima facie a reduction of quality.

Public Programs in Health Care

Government is deeply involved in health-care services, despite the rhetoric about a free-enterprise medical-care system in the United States. Existing public programs provide direct medical services to some segments of the population, offer health-care insurance for others, and support the health of the entire population through public health programs, regulation, and research. Many citizens question the efficacy of these programs, especially regulatory programs, but they are evidence of the large and important role of government in medicine. We now discuss several major government programs in medical care, with some attention to the policy issues involved in each, and the possibilities of improving the quality of health care through public action.

Medicare

The government medical-care program with which most citizens are familiar is almost certainly Medicare, adopted as part of the Social Security Amendments of 1965. The program is essentially one of medical insurance for the elderly and the disabled who are eligible for Social Security or Railroad Retirement benefits. The program has two parts. Part A, financed principally through payroll taxation, is a hospitalization plan, covering the first 60 days of hospitalization but requiring the patient to pay the first $764 (1998). The program also covers hospitalization during the 61st to 90th days, but requires a co-payment of $191 per day. This portion of the plan also covers up to 100 days in a nursing-care facility after release from the hospital, with this coverage being subject to a $95.50 co-payment by the insured after the first 20 days.[54]

Part B of Medicare is a supplementary insurance program covering doctors' fees and other outpatient services. These expenses are also subject to deductibles and to coinsurance, with the insured paying the first $100 each year, plus 20 percent of allowable costs. This portion of the Medicare program is financed by the insured, who pay a monthly premium of $43.80 (1998). Insured persons bear a rather high proportion of their own medical expenses under Medicare, given that it is a publicly provided insurance program. The program is, however, certainly subsidized and it is still a bargain for the average retired person, who might not be able to purchase anything like the coverage provided in the private market because the elderly have, on average, significantly higher medical expenses than the population as a whole.

Medicare is a better program than would be available to most of the elderly under private insurance programs; it requires no physical examination for coverage, covers preexisting health conditions, is uniformly available throughout the country, and provides some services that might not be available on private plans. The program does have some problems, however, perhaps the greatest of which is that it requires those insured to pay a significant amount out of their own pockets for coverage, even when they are hospitalized. Purchasing Part B of the plan requires an annual outlay of $525.60 (1998), which, although it is not much money for health insurance, may be a relatively large share of a pensioner's income. In addition, the costs of deductibles and coinsurance in both parts of Medicare may place a burden on less affluent beneficiaries of the program.

In addition to the costs to the recipient of covered expenses, Medicare does not cover all the medical expenses that most beneficiaries will incur. For example, it does not pay for prescription drugs, eye or dental examinations, eyeglasses or dentures, preventive examinations, or immunizations. Nor does the program cover very extended care. In short, Medicare does not cover many medical problems that plague the elderly population the program was intended to serve, and as a result it does not really meet the needs of the elderly poor, who are most in need of services. In fact, at least one study shows that the gap between the health status of rich and poor elderly people widened initially after the introduction of Medicare.[55] The more affluent can use the program as a supplement to their own assets or private health insurance programs, while the less affluent are still incapable of providing adequately for their medical needs, even with Medicare.

One attempt to solve the "medigap" problem has been the introduction of a number of private health insurance programs to fill in the lacunae of Medicare coverage. Unfortunately, most existing policies of this type do not cover the most glaring deficiencies of Medicare—for example, the absence of coverage for extended nursing-home care. In addition, the policies do not cover preexisting health problems and frequently have long waiting periods for eligibility. In short, these policies often cost more money without providing the protection required. The 96th Congress passed legislation in 1980 imposing some standards on such insurance policies, but the law was directed more at outright fraud than at providing policies that truly cover the gaps in Medicare coverage. Additional legislation in 1990 tightened controls on insurers, but often there is still duplication and waste.[56]

On the government's side of the Medicare program, the costs of funding medical insurance for the elderly impose a burden on the working-age population and on government resources. Basic hospitalization coverage under Medicare is financed by a payroll tax collected as a part of the Social Security tax, taking 1.45 percent of each worker's salary in 1991. Since 1995, the health insurance portion of the Social Security tax has been extracted on all earned income, unlike the pension and disability portion, which is extracted on earnings only up to $65,400 per year (1997). With increasing opposition to the Social Security tax have come suggestions to shift the financing of Medicare to general tax revenues such as the income tax, leaving the entire payroll tax to fund Social Security pensions.[57]

With the increasing costs of medical care and the growing number of Americans eligible for Medicare, difficulties are likely to arise in financing the program for some years to come. Congress attempted to address these difficulties as a part of the balanced-budget bill in the summer of 1997.[58] A number of options are now available to Medicare recipients, including traditional fee-for-service medicine, managed care, preferred-provider plans, and medical savings accounts. Any of the shifts from fee-for-service medicine will provide some savings, but some, such as the medical savings account, involve the recipient's taking a chance that he or she will remain relatively healthy during a particular time period, a very risky gamble for most elderly people.[59]

Finally, problems of quality and fair pricing for Medicare patients are also likely to persist. Medicare regulations allow the Health Care Financing Administration to pay "reasonable" costs to physicians and hospitals for

...es rendered to beneficiaries and, of course, also require that the providers give adequate and "standard" treatment. In some instances physicians have charged more than the amount designated as "reasonable," thereby imposing additional costs on the patient. In other instances physicians have employed tests and procedures generally unnecessary, knowing that the costs would be largely covered by Medicare.

The 1982 Tax Equity and Fiscal Responsibility Act created PROs (Peer Review Organizations), now called Quality Improvement Programs, to augment and then replace the earlier Physician Service Review Organizations (PSROs). These organizations are concerned with quality and attempt to work with providers to improve outcomes. They are, however, also increasingly involved in detecting and exposing outright fraud on the part of a few physicians who bill for patients whom they do not see, or who otherwise abuse the system.[60] Their actions have been supplemented by the efforts of private insurance firms, which also lose money through fraud.[61] But fraud is but one of many factors increasing costs of medical care, and the need for effective cost control will remain an important issue for some time to come.

One move to control costs for public medical programs is Diagnosis Related Groupings (DRGs), a form of prospective reimbursement. This program, adopted 1 October 1983, has hospitals reimbursed for Medicare and Medicaid patients according to one of over 400 specific diagnostic groups (e.g., appendicitis).[62] The hospital is guaranteed a fixed amount for each patient according to the DRG to which his or her complaint is assigned. A hospital that is able to treat a patient for less can retain the difference as "profit," but if the hospital stay costs more than allowed under the DRG, the hospital must absorb the loss. This system is in large part responsible for hospital stays in the United States being the shortest in the world.

Despite some experience with DRGs, a number of questions remain about how they affect medical care. For example, the doctor, more than the hospital, determines how much a course of treatment will cost, and there has been increased conflict between hospital administrators and physicians over patient care. Also, this program may tend to reduce the quality of care provided to Medicaid and Medicare patients or cause too-early dismissals of patients, with associated cost-shifting onto home medical-care programs and community medicine; patients are discharged "quicker and sicker," and too often they must be readmitted soon after discharge. Also, DRGs do not easily accommodate the multiple diseases and infirmities characteristic of so many Medicare patients. Nevertheless, the DRG program is an interesting attempt to impose greater cost consciousness on hospitals and physicians that has been copied by some private health-care insurers. This approach to cost control may be preferable to rationing approaches such as that imposed for Medicaid patients in Oregon.

Medicaid

While Medicare is directed toward the elderly and disabled, Medicaid, the second major public health-care program, is directed toward the indigent. Medicaid was passed at the same time as Medicare, to provide federal matching funds to state and local governments for medical care of welfare recipients and the "medically indigent," a category intended to include those who do not qualify for public assistance but whose income is not sufficient to cover necessary medical expenses. Unlike Medicare, which is a uniform national program, Medicaid is administered by the states, and as a consequence benefits, eligibility requirements, and administration vary considerably. But if a state chooses to have a Medicaid program (two states do not), it must still provide medical-care benefits for all welfare recipients and for those who receive Supplemental Security Income because of categorical problems—age, blindness, or disability.

Medicaid regulations require states to provide a range of services to recipients of the program: hospitalization, laboratory and other diagnostic services, X-rays, nursing-home services, screening for a range of diseases, and physicians' services. The states may also extend benefits to cover prescription drugs and other services. For each service, the states may set limitations on the amount of care covered and on the rate of reimbursement. Given increasing costs, states have tended to provide little more than the minimum benefits required under federal law. Federal laws, however, are becoming increasingly stringent and are imposing additional costs on the states that the states are finding difficult to fund.[63] Some are reacting by using alternative service systems such as HMOs for their Medicaid clients—by 1996 almost one-third of Medicaid recipients were in managed care.[64]

In addition to the problems of variance in the coverage and benefits across the country, Medicaid has other policy problems. Those most commonly cited are fraud and abuse. It is sometimes estimated that up to 7 percent of total federal outlays for Medicaid are accounted for by abuse.[65] Almost all of this abuse is perpetrated by the service providers, rather than by the beneficiaries of the medical treatments, in part because of the complex eligibility requirements and procedures for reimbursement. Still, this fraud presents a negative image of the program to the public.[66] With a continuing strain on public resources, any program that has a reputation for fraud is likely to encounter difficulties in receiving its funding. This is true whether the fraud is committed by respected providers such as physicians or by their indigent clients.

The general strain on fiscal resources at all levels of government and increased medical costs also have produced serious problems for the Medicaid program. States have been forced to cut back on optional services under the program and to reduce coverage of primary (physician) care in order to be

finance hospital care for recipients. Also, some states have set limitations on the amount of physicians' reimbursements for each service. These
reimbursements are significantly lower than what doctors would receive
from private or even Medicare patients; the result is that an increasing number of physicians refuse to accept Medicaid patients. In part because of these
trends, Medicaid has increasingly become a program of institutional medical
care—paradoxically, this is the most expensive way of delivering medical
services. As with Medicare, however, institutional care through hospitals,
hospital emergency rooms, and nursing homes is the one kind of medical
care almost sure to be covered under the program. So, today less than 2 percent of all Medicaid spending goes to home health-care services, while over
40 percent of all expenditures goes to extended-care facilities, many of
which do not meet federal standards.

Like Medicare, the Medicaid program has done a great deal of good in
making medical care available to people who might not otherwise receive it.
Nevertheless, some significant Medicaid problems—notably costs and coverage—will be political issues for years. Proposals for solving those problems
range from the abolition of both programs to the establishment of national
health insurance, with a number or proposals for internal readjustments of
the programs or the use of private health insurance in between the more radical alternatives. There is a special drive to ensure that as many children as
possible are included in the program.[67]

Health Maintenance Organizations

A fundamental criticism frequently made of American medical care is that it
is, or at least has been, fee-for-service medicine. Medical practitioners are
paid for each service they perform and, as a consequence, they have an incentive to practice their skills on patients; surgeons make money by wielding
their scalpels, and internists make money by ordering diagnostic procedures.
Furthermore, critics charge that American medical care is primarily acute
care. The system is oriented toward treating the ill rather than toward preventing illness. The most money is to be made through curing illness, not
through promoting good health. This point is to some degree substantiated
by the relatively low levels of immunizations found among American children (see table 10.10). Despite all the money spent on medical care in the
United States, there are still millions of children who are not fully immunized against common childhood diseases.

The health maintenance organization was developed as at least a partial
attack on these two characteristics of the health-care system.[68] First, the
HMO provides prepaid medical care. Members of an HMO pay an annual
fee, in return for which they receive virtually all their medical care. They
may have to pay ancillary costs (e.g., a small set fee for each prescription),

TABLE 10.10

PERCENTAGE IMMUNIZED, CHILDREN AGES ONE TO FOUR
YEARS, 1997

	Total	*White*	*Nonwhite*
Diphtheria-pertussis-tetanus	70.0	70.7	64.2
Polio	79.1	80.1	72.9
Measles, etc.	67.3	68.3	60.5
Haemophilus B	75.2	76.7	67.8

SOURCE: Bureau of the Census, *Statistical Abstract of the United States, 1997* (Washington, D.C.: Government Printing Office, 1998).

but the vast majority of medical expenses are covered through the HMO by the annual fee. Under this prepayment scheme, doctors working for the HMO have no incentive to prescribe additional treatments. If anything, given that the doctors commonly share in the profits of the organization or frequently own the HMO themselves, they have an incentive not to prescribe treatments. Any surgery or treatment that costs the organization money without providing additional income reduces profits. By the same reasoning, doctors in an HMO have an incentive to keep the members healthy and to encourage preventive medicine. A healthy member is all profit, while a sick member is all loss. It is argued that, by reversing the incentives usually presented to physicians, HMOs can significantly improve the quality of health care and reduce the rapid escalation of medical-care costs.

The formation of HMOs has been supported by the federal government. In 1973 President Nixon signed into law a bill directed at improving choice in the health-care marketplace.[69] The legislation provided for planning and development grants for prospective HMOs, but at the same time placed a number of restrictions on any HMO using federal funding. Most important, all HMOs had to offer an extensive array of services including psychiatric care. Any employer offering group insurance to employees had to make the same amount of money available to any employee who wanted to join an HMO. The federal involvement in HMOs was reauthorized in 1978 for another three years, with additional support for the development of outpatient care facilities—important in eliminating expensive hospitalization. The HMO movement has also been assisted by federal efforts restricting the actions of physicians and private insurers who sought to reduce the competition offered by HMOs.

HMOs and other forms of managed care now operate in the United States, the most successful being the Kaiser-Permanente organization, with over 4.5 million members and 5,000 physicians. A good deal of skepticism continues about the quality of medical care provided by HMOs, and some citizens appear unwilling to adopt this rather significant departure from the traditional means of delivering health services. Although the concept does have critics—most of them members of the medical profession—it also has supporters. HMO plans have been supported by organized labor as one means of reducing medical inflation, and they appear to be increasingly acceptable to businesses as a means of reducing costs, a mechanism that is more palatable than direct government regulation. In one vote of confidence, the Reagan administration in 1984 allowed Medicare and Medicaid patients to opt to join HMOs for their medical care, believing that this option could reduce the government's costs for these programs with no loss of medical quality.[70] As the pressures on medical costs have increased, and employers and individual consumers have sought lower-cost alternatives, an increasing proportion of the medical profession has moved into HMOs and similar organizations.[71]

HMOs were the first step in creating the concept of managed care. The basic idea of managed care is that doctors do not make all decisions about what sort of care to provide, nor do patients (or their primary-care physicians) make their own decisions about what specialists to consult. Physicians, hospitals, and other providers are connected in "networks" or "organizations," and referrals are made within those constraints. Further, health-care managers make decisions about what sort of care is appropriate and can prevent a patient's receiving the kind of care that he or she, or even the physician, wants. The patient may still go to the emergency room, but the service generally will not be covered by insurance.

The managed-care system has been successful in reducing the rate of increase in health-care costs, although pressures are beginning to drive the prices upward. The most important is that the system of insurance is becoming so general that many poorer and sicker people are being brought into managed care.[72] There is also some political pressure to require managed-care plans to permit greater clinical freedom for physicians and to ensure that patients can make their own decisions about some aspects of care, especially visits to the emergency room. President Clinton, for example, has advocated a "patient's bill of rights"[73] that would give patients much greater control over their own medical care, with the probability of higher costs, and the Republican Congress is pressing its own ideas for ensuring that patients receive adequate care.[74]

Health-Care Regulation

Perhaps the most pervasive impact of government on the delivery of health-care services in the United States has been through regulation. There are

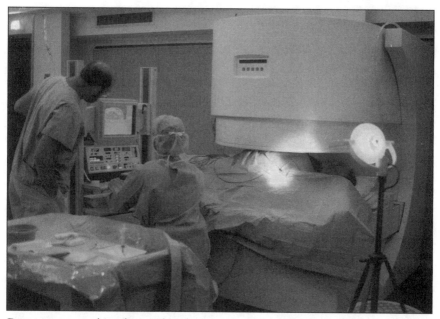

Doctors at a teaching hospital make use of a combination of advanced technologies, monitoring their progress on an MRI screen as they burn a patient's cancerous tumor with radio waves. (AP/Wide World Photos)

many kinds of health-care regulations, and this chapter now briefly discusses three: costs, quality, and pharmaceuticals.[75]

Hospital Costs

Cost increases are a major consideration in health care, and hospital costs have been the most rapidly increasing component of medical costs. Further, as hospitals constitute a major component of the total health-care bill (44 percent) and are readily identifiable institutions with better recordkeeping than the average physician, it appears sensible to concentrate on them as a locus for controlling medical-care costs. Approaches to controlling hospital costs have been varied. The Carter administration proposed direct regulation of hospital costs, which sufficiently frightened the hospital industry that it introduced its own voluntary effort (VE) program to slow increases in costs.

Another major approach to controlling hospital costs, begun in New Jersey, has been prospective reimbursement. The federal version of this approach for Medicare patients is Diagnostic Related Groupings (see p. 260). In essence DRGs constitute a market approach to cost containment, for they allow hospitals that are efficient to make a profit, while those that are not well run can sustain losses. As such, they are more in line with the thinking of the Reagan administration than the direct price controls proposed by the Carter administration.

Although both the Carter program and DRGs attack the problem of hospital costs, neither attempted to address some fundamental problems causing prices to escalate. One problem was the fundamental principle of fee-for-service medicine, which gives hospitals and doctors an incentive to provide more services. Related to that is the tendency of the medical profession to use high-cost hospital treatment when lower-cost options would be as effective. This is done for the convenience of the physician and because many health insurance policies will pay for hospital treatments but not for the same treatments performed on an outpatient basis. The regimen of DRGs and preferred provider plans limiting costs in private insurance have helped to change this somewhat, but American medical care remains more centered on the hospital than that of many other countries. Finally, it is important to remember that hospitals do not have patients, doctors do; and hospitals must compete for doctors in order to fill hospital beds. This competition takes place largely through the acquisition of high-cost technology (CAT scanners, MRI systems, etc.), which must be amortized through the higher price of hospital care.

Health-Care Quality

The regulation of health-care quality is one of the most controversial areas of government intervention in the health-care field. First, regulation operates directly against long-established canons of clinical freedom and the right of members of the medical profession to regulate their own conduct. The medical profession, and probably most of the public, assume that the only person qualified to judge the professional conduct of a physician is another physician. The specter of bureaucrats intervening in medical care is not comforting to the average American.

In addition, private mechanisms for rectifying harm done by a physician in the conduct of his or her profession are well established. There are, of course, tort and malpractice lawsuits, which generate their own problems for medicine and have been cited as one factor causing rapid increases in medical-care costs. Some effects of malpractice litigation are direct, as physicians pass the doubled or tripled malpractice insurance costs on to patients in higher fees. The direct impact of malpractice insurance fees on medical costs appears minimal, but indirect effects, including the practice of "defensive medicine," are more substantial. A doctor, fearing a malpractice suit, may prescribe additional diagnostic procedures, extra days in the hospital, or extra treatments to lessen his or her chances of being legally negligent, and the costs of these extra procedures also are passed on to consumers. Other effects of malpractice as a quality control are more systemic, as doctors in specialties such as obstetrics and neurosurgery that are subject to frequent suits simply change to other specialties. This condition is leaving small towns and even small cities without certain types of medical care.

Despite some earlier opposition from the medical and legal professions, there is now a strong drive for increased quality regulation of medical care. As noted, much of this has come about because of the apparent abuses of HMOs. Several surveys have found that significant majorities of the population want some protection from the economic power of HMOs.[76] Even some conservative Republican congressmen have sought a stronger role for government in the regulation of the managed-care industry.[77]

As we mentioned when discussing Medicare, the major public instruments for regulating the quality of medical care are the Quality Improvement Programs. These organizations are designed in part to monitor costs of services provided to Medicare patients, but they necessarily become involved in the issue of appropriate and effective treatment as well. Treatments that are ineffective or dangerous can also be costly. Some quality organizations have gone so far as to establish standard profiles of treatment for common conditions and then to question physicians whose treatment differs significantly from those patterns. Physicians who use more extensive treatments may be imposing additional costs on the program, while those who are using unusual or less extensive treatments may be threatening the health of the patient.

The growth of managed care is placing more pressure on government to regulate health care. As we have noted several times, patients often believe that they are being denied adequate care by their HMO or other form of managed care. These complaints have generated a number of regulatory interventions, or proposals for regulations. For example, at least one state has enabled patients to sue HMOs for malpractice when care is inadequate, rather than placing all the onus on the individual physician.[78] Eighteen states have attacked one of the most infamous of the practices of managed-care programs—the so called "gag rules" that prevent physicians from informing patients about more expensive, and perhaps more effective, treatments. The federal government also has become involved, as in President Clinton's proposal of a "patient's bill of rights," as a means of ensuring that patients in managed care have some protections.

Such attempts to regulate the managed-care industry are to some extent impeded by the early protection given to HMOs and similar organizations. When these forms of providing care were first being considered, they were seen as a way of combatting the dominance of fee-for-service medicine, and they were expected both to limit costs and to place greater emphasis on preventive medicine.[79] They were, in fact, made immune from legal action for their actions in restricting access to some types of care. One of the proposals for boosting the quality of service in these organizations now is to eliminate this immunity and use the legal system as the mechanism for quality control, as is done with most other aspects of the medical system, and to extend its reach to insurers as well as practitioners.[80]

Drug Regulation

The federal government is also deeply involved in the regulation of the pharmaceutical industry and in the control of substances in food and water that are potentially harmful to health. The government began to regulate food and drugs in 1902, with extensive increases in its powers in 1938 and again in 1962. The issues surrounding drug regulation have been more heated since the early 1980s than at any time since the initial passage of the legislation. The Food and Drug Administration (FDA), which is responsible for most drug regulation, has been under attack from all sides. Some argue that its regulations have been excessively stringent and have prevented useful drugs from coming to the market. The AIDS epidemic has brought this complaint to the fore and has actually produced some changes in the procedures for licensing new drugs.[81] Other critics of the FDA believe that its regulations have been too lax and excessively dominated by the pharmaceutical industry and that, as a result, potentially dangerous drugs have been certified for sale.

The basic regulatory doctrine applied to pharmaceuticals is that a drug must be shown to be both safe and effective before it can be approved for sale. Several problems arise from this doctrine. First, almost any drug will have some side effects, so proving its safety is difficult, and some criteria must be established for weighing the benefits of an individual drug against the side effects it may produce. The example commonly cited here is that because of a range of known side effects, common aspirin might have considerable difficulty being certified for use under standards prevailing in the 1990s. The safety and effectiveness of a drug must be demonstrated by clinical trials that are often time-consuming and expensive, and potentially important drugs are thereby delayed in coming to the public.

Critics of the drug industry point to other problems in drug regulation and in the pharmaceutical industry as a whole. For example, there are the problems of look-alike drugs and the use of brand names as opposed to generic drugs.[82] It is argued that a great deal of attention in drug research is directed toward finding combinations of drugs that can be marketed under a brand name or in reproducing findings of already proven drugs so that they can be marketed with a different brand name. Brand-name drugs are invariably more expensive than generic drugs, and critics argue that the licensing of brand names actually aids the pharmaceutical industry by promoting the sale of its higher-priced products. They also argue that drugs are sold and prescribed without adequate dissemination of information about possible side effects. Some states have intervened to reduce the problem of drug costs, allowing pharmacists to substitute a generic drug for a brand-name drug unless the physician specifically forbids such substitution. Many drugstores attempt to make their customers aware of this opportunity, so unless physicians believe that the generic drug would not be effective (some would argue for other, less noble reasons as well), citizens can get generic drugs.

A major attempt to modify drug regulations was made in 1979 in a Senate bill proposed by Senator Edward Kennedy (D-Mass.). Among the most important issues in the proposed legislation was the shortening of the review periods required prior to marketing new drugs, especially so-called breakthrough drugs that offer great promise for serious illnesses and seem greatly superior to existing drugs. The proposed legislation also mandated that more information on drugs be disseminated to physicians and patients so that more informed decisions could be made about the drugs' use, and it attempted to limit certain drug-company promotion practices. Through skilled political management, the bill passed the Senate easily, but it did not pass the House of Representatives. The legislation represents, however, some possible directions for future drug regulation.

Associated with drug regulation in the FDA has been food regulation, especially the prohibition of carcinogenic substances in food. The Delaney Amendment requires the FDA to remove from the market foods containing any substance that "induces" cancer in human beings or animals. An issue developed over this amendment during the late 1970s in regard to the attempt to ban the sale of the artificial sweetener saccharin. In April 1977 studies in Canada showed that large amounts of saccharin tended to produce bladder cancer. Under the Delaney Amendment (passed in 1958), the FDA was then required to propose a ban on saccharin. The ban would have removed saccharin from the market as a general food additive but would have allowed its sale as an over-the-counter drug with a warning label. The proposed regulations were opposed by diabetics, the food and soft-drink industries, and weight watchers, among others. The outcry was sufficient to cause Congress to pass a bill in 1977 delaying for eighteen months the removal of saccharin from the market, requiring the labeling of items containing saccharin, and demanding more testing of the effects of saccharin, both as a carcinogen and as an aid in weight control.

The studies during the eighteen-month period did not provide any conclusive evidence on the safety of saccharin, but they did point to possible changes in the regulation of possibly carcinogenic or otherwise harmful substances. The reports of the National Academy of Science recommended that the government, instead of prohibiting all such substances, establish categories of risk with attached regulations ranging from complete prohibition to warning labels to no action at all. It suggested also that such decisions take into consideration the possible benefits from the continued sale of the substance. Because many believed that saccharin was highly beneficial for some people and presented only a low risk, they suggested that it be allowed to remain on sale. These risk-benefit or cost-benefit considerations are a common aid to decision making (see chapter 15) in the public sector, although they are perhaps less valid when applied to risks of the occurrence of a disease such as cancer. For whatever reasons, Congress reauthorized the continuing sale of saccharin.

Another issue related to the regulation of pharmaceuticals is the regulation of tobacco, and especially cigarette smoking. The surgeon general determined some years ago that smoking cigarettes is harmful and required warning labels on packages and forbade advertising through electronic media. Since that time state and local governments have imposed bans on smoking in public places. The surgeon general and the FDA also have developed evidence on the thousands of deaths caused by smoking. In congressional hearings in 1994 the FDA presented evidence on the addictive nature of nicotine and began movements to strengthen regulations on the sale, advertising, and use of cigarettes. In particular, if it declared nicotine to be a drug, the FDA could regulate cigarettes as the delivery system for that drug.

Cigarettes and their regulation also figure prominently in the discussion of financing health care. Several of the plans for national health insurance (see pp. 274–77) depended on an increased tax on cigarettes for at least a part of the financing. For example, under the Clinton plan, taxes on cigarettes would have increased to $1 per pack, while the health-care reform package developed by the House Ways and Means Committee would have added an additional 45 cents to the existing 24-cent tax. This tax would in essence function like a regulation if it encouraged people to stop smoking, but that too would provide a benefit by reducing the estimated $65 billion spent on diseases caused by smoking. After the demise of these health-care proposals, there are continuing demands for higher cigarette taxes.

Summary

Regulation is a common and pervasive form of public intervention into the health-care industry in the United States. It is not without controversy, and almost all forms of regulation are under active review and reconsideration. Under Republican administrations many regulations were replaced by competitive mechanisms using market forces to produce changes in the health-care industry. The Clinton administration has been by no means as negative about public intervention, but more regulations may be replaced. Even with the increasing public concern over health care in the 1990s, some conservatives want to reduce further public attempts to control this industry, while liberals seek to maintain and expand regulations.

The Pursuit of National Health Insurance

The United States is the only Western industrialized nation without a significant program of national health insurance or direct health-service delivery by the public sector. As we have seen, this does not mean that the government has no role in medical care. In fact, approximately 14 percent of the American people now depend directly on the federal government for their health care, another group of the same size receive Medicaid funded jointly by the states and the federal government, and still others receive most or all of their care from emergency rooms in municipal hospitals. What the absence of national health insurance does mean is that citizens who do not fit into the particular categories eligible for public insurance—for example, the aged, veterans, the medically indigent—must rely on private health care, or the often substandard and usually slow care available through emergency rooms in public hospitals.[83] With rising medical expenses, the ever-present possibility of catastrophic illnesses with equally catastrophic economic consequences, and declining availability of health insurance as an employee benefit, there have been increasing pressures to extend the public role in medicine to the entire population.

The idea of a national health insurance program for the United States goes back at least to the Truman administration. Indeed, Theodore Roosevelt, aware of health-care programs then beginning in European nations, had proposed something like a national health-care program at the beginning of the twentieth century. But in 1945 President Truman's proposal of a comprehensive national health insurance program as a part of the Social Security program met with relentless opposition from the American Medical Association (AMA) and conservative business organizations, who labeled the plan "socialized medicine." The AMA spent millions of dollars in its successful campaign against national health insurance, and most Americans appeared to want to retain the private medical system. The adoption of Medicare in 1965 represented a first partial success for advocates of a national health insurance program, but pressures have continued to grow for a plan that would insure the entire population.

Interestingly, public opinion about health care has also changed. Although the AMA's arguments against socialized medicine were persuasive in the 1940s and 1950s, by 1973 a majority of Americans polled favored some system of public health insurance. By the mid-1990s as many as two-thirds of respondents in polls said they favored national health insurance of some sort.[84] The political importance of health care as an issue was highlighted in a 1991 senatorial election in Pennsylvania in which a relatively unknown Democrat (Harris Wofford), campaigning heavily on the issue of national health care, soundly defeated a popular ex-governor and ex–U.S. attorney general (Richard Thornburgh). Democrats quickly identified the health insurance issue as a possible avenue to the White House in 1992, and Bill Clinton seized on this policy as a centerpiece of his campaign.

One major difficulty in the drive for some sort of national health insurance in the 1990s was that there were several alternative plans available. Some of the plans had the backing of powerful interests in the medical establishment (a plan has even been proposed by the AMA), some had the backing of the Republicans in Congress and others of the Democrats in Congress, and still others were proposed by health-care advocacy groups. The Clinton administration began the most recent active discussion of national health insurance, but its plan was but one among many. The political problem, therefore, was to get enough support coalesced around any one plan to have it adopted and then implemented successfully.[85] As we have already pointed out, the Clinton administration, as well as advocates of other plans, failed in that effort.

We now look at several broad alternative approaches to national health insurance[86] and then more specifically at several of the plans that have been under active consideration at one time or another.

"Play or Pay"

One approach to national health insurance is commonly referred to as "play or pay." The idea is that all employers would have to provide at least a minimum of health insurance for their employees ("play") or contribute to a public insurance program that would cover their employees and everyone else not covered by private health insurance ("pay"). Most plans call for a payroll tax of 7 or 8 percent for companies that do not provide health-care benefits. These plans also depend to a great extent on the actions of the private sector, but they include a public insurance program (usually an expanded Medicare program) to provide a safety net for the unemployed. A program like this is already in place in Hawaii; a more extensive program was tried in Massachusetts, but it encountered substantial financial difficulties when the economy in that state sustained a number of serious reverses.[87]

The play-or-pay system largely would preserve the existing insurance system, although probably with more extensive regulation. It would also preserve the existing, fee-for-service medical-care system, again perhaps with greater regulation of costs. In addition, it would allow companies to provide better benefits to their employees than the minimums mandated under the law, although those benefits might be treated as taxable income for the recipients. The principal difficulty with this plan is that many small employers argue that health insurance costs would force them out of business, much as many small employers have been forced in the 1990s to drop medical coverage of their employees because of the costs.

The reform plan proposed by the AMA contains most elements of the play-or-pay system and would require all employers, over time, to provide medical care to their employees. Combined with this fundamental change in the status quo would be reform of existing public programs to ensure greater equality of coverage (Medicaid) and greater financial soundness (Medicare). Further, the plan would impose several cost-cutting ideas, such as limitation of malpractice claims. While this proposal is to some degree self-serving on the part of the medical-care profession, it does demonstrate the pervasiveness of concern about access and cost issues in medical care in the United States.

Canadian-Style Comprehensive Coverage

The most extreme proposal for public medical care would adopt something like the plan currently in operation in Canada—generally referred to as the "single-payer" system.[88] Such a program would change the medical industry in the United States rather fundamentally and would place the public sector, not the private providers (doctors and hospitals), in the driver's seat in medicine. The simplest proposal of this type would extend Medicare, with its deductibles and co-payments, to cover the entire population. Other plans involve issuing to all legal residents cards that they would present to providers, who would then receive their reimbursement from government. Fees would be set or maximum reimbursements established, although doctors and hospitals could charge more if the patient were willing (and able) to pay.

Critics argue that this program would mean large tax increases and would put existing health insurance providers out of business in favor of large public bureaucracies. Further, the critics claim that the experience of Canada has been that health-care innovation has been slowed and that there is some waiting for elective procedures. Advocates of the Canadian system, in contrast, argue that the claims of waiting lists and slower introduction of new technologies are exaggerated and have had little real impact on the quality of care. Indeed, they assert that Americans are receiving too many needless tests and treatments because that is the only way that doctors earn money in a fee-for-service environment. Further, the advocates argue that some costs may be necessary for those better served under the old system if a more equitable system of medical care is to be introduced.

The Bush Administration

The Bush administration began an initiative on national health-care reform toward the end of its term in office, in part as a means of preventing the Democrats from capturing this issue entirely. Several plans were broached by the White House and its allies, all quite minimal and depending largely on the private sector to provide most of the coverage and on reduction of medical costs to make insurance plans affordable for individuals and small businesses. The most basic proposal coming from the administration was a simple refundable tax credit to assist individuals who purchase private insurance.

A more complete plan favored by some in the Bush administration was labeled "managed competition."[89] This plan would have had people working for firms sufficiently large to provide cost-effective medical insurance continue to receive insurance as they had in the past. But these large companies would receive tax write-offs of only 80 percent of the average current cost of providing similar medical care and would therefore be motivated to pressure medical providers to give preferential rates if those providers wanted the large volume of business they could offer. "Preferred provider plans" such as this are already used by insurers such as Blue Cross–Blue Shield, and this plan would have extended that idea to most private insurance.

The remainder of the population, whether employed or not, would receive health insurance from newly created agencies called "public sponsors." Individuals would be offered several prepaid plans (HMOs) and perhaps a conventional insurance plan, but the assumption was that the insurance plans would cost more and that the difference would have to be paid by the insured. This would mean that most people would choose to be covered through HMOs, which therefore would have a great deal of market power, like the insurers for large firms, and could bargain with providers for lower rates. This plan would have provided medical care to all citizens and might have stabilized or lowered medical-care costs, assuming the market worked as expected.

The Clinton Administration Plan and Its Alternatives

The Clinton administration placed health-care reform at the top of its domestic agenda when it took office in January 1993. Almost immediately Hillary Rodham Clinton began a series of meetings with "stakeholders" and with ordinary citizens to collect ideas for reform. The plan that she and the administration proposed was a complex one, depending on "alliances" of health-care providers. Very much as HMOs have done for years, these alliances would supply all the health-care needs of their members for a set annual fee, although fee-for-service plans also would be available. According to the provisions of the Clinton plan, those fees would be fixed at an average of $1,800 for an individual and $4,200 for families, below existing private insurance rates for much of the population. Individuals would also be required to pay deductibles and co-payments for services on the fee-for-service plans. Businesses would be mandated to pay for their employees (up to 7.9 percent of their payrolls), with subsidies available for small business.

Universality was the central tenet of the Clinton proposals, and this was the issue over which the president has said he would never compromise. The employer mandates were a central element of this universality but also a focus of much criticism. For the unemployed or for people working for very small employers, there would be insurance paid for by the federal government, with the funds coming from cigarette taxes and perhaps other additional taxes. Employers could provide insurance better than the national minimums, but that might be treated as taxable income for the employee or made not deductible as a business expense for the employer. The program therefore would tend to create much greater equality in access to medical care than is currently found in the United States. The program also had provisions for cost containment, initially through competitive incentives but later through regulated prices, if necessary to reduce medical inflation to the general rate of inflation (see pp. 251–52).

As might be expected, the Clinton plan met with a good deal of opposition from a number of directions. A number of critics, even those who favored universality and mandates, regarded the plan as excessively complex and too heavily reliant on the alliances both to provide care and to minimize costs. These critics often advocated a single-payer plan such as the Canadian system. Other critics disagreed with the concept of universality, believing that it was too costly and imposed excessive costs on employers to provide medical insurance. They sought to find an alternative more like that proposed by the Bush administration, relying more on voluntary efforts and the private sector. They also saw the Clinton plan as requiring a huge and costly federal bureaucracy.

One of the principal alternatives to the Clinton plan was devised and championed by then-senator Robert Dole (R-Kans.), whose plan relied heavily on voluntary compliance and private insurance. Dole's plan did not seek universal coverage—the target was 91 or 92 percent of the population—but it did provide for subsidies for the less affluent for purchasing insurance, to be paid for by cost containment in Medicare and Medicaid. Further, this plan attempted to address the problem of people being locked into jobs by mandating portability of health insurance. There was also a "fail-safe" provision to prevent the program from adding to the federal deficit. Although supported by numerous Republican senators, this plan was prevented from emerging from the committee system by Democratic control of Congress.

Several other plans also emerged from Congress, including one from the Senate Labor and Human Resources Committee, chaired by Senator Edward

Kennedy. This plan provided a number of alternative means for acquiring medical insurance, including private insurance, purchasing cooperatives at the state level, and participation in the existing Federal Employees Health Benefit Plan. This plan had many elements of "play or pay," with employers not providing insurance for their employees having to pay a substantial payroll tax, and it relied on a substantial tax on cigarettes to help fund the additional costs of the program.

The Senate Finance Committee chaired by Daniel Patrick Moynihan (D-N.Y.) prepared another health insurance plan. This plan was less universal than either of those advocated by the president or Senator Kennedy; it offered no employer mandates, and participation in insurance-purchasing alliances was voluntary. This plan promised to increase rates of coverage of the population gradually over seven years, with a national commission making policy recommendations to Congress if 95 percent of the population were not covered by 2002. The plan was financed by increased cigarette taxes and by taxes on higher-priced private insurance plans.

The House Ways and Means Committee also authored a plan for national health insurance. Its plan relied on the existing Medicare program (but with a new Part C) as a basis for providing health insurance to the currently uninsured and to Medicaid recipients, with most employees remaining on private insurance.[90] Thus, unlike the Clinton plan, it did not require the creation of a new federal bureaucracy but only the extension of an existing one. The bulk of insurance (80 percent) would be still be private, provided by employers, with small employers eligible for subsidies of up to half the cost of insurance. Low-income insured workers would also be eligible for subsidies for their part of the premiums. This proposal also would have strong elements of cost-control, with each state and the nation having a limit for health-care spending. The additional costs of the program would be financed by a gradual increase in the cigarette tax to 69 cents a pack and a tax on private insurance programs.

Finally, the House Education and Labor Committee developed its own plan for national health-care reform. This proposal offered many of the same features as the Clinton plan, but it contained expanded benefits and did not involve the mandatory alliances. Instead there would be purchasing cooperatives formed at the state level, with employers of more than 1,000 workers allowed to opt out and create their own insurance plans. The financing of this program was rather similar to that in the Clinton plan, with an additional tax on large employers that opted out of the basic plans.

After the various committees in both houses had acted, the majority leadership of both houses of Congress attempted to blend their several proposals into two plans. In the House of Representatives Congressman Richard Gephardt (D-Mo.) presented a plan that had many of the features of the

Clinton proposal, most notably the demand for universal coverage and employer mandates to cover 80 percent of the cost of the average individual policy. It differed in requiring a range of options for all citizens, and in providing subsidies to people with much higher incomes (as well as a number of other technical details).

In the Senate, Majority Leader George Mitchell (D-Maine) developed a plan that attempted to reconcile the basic intentions of the Clinton plan with the criticisms of it. In the first place, the Mitchell plan dropped the goal of immediate universality and replaced it with a goal of 95-percent coverage by the year 2000. If that goal were not reached by voluntary means, a system of mandates might be imposed by 2002. Most of the other features of the Mitchell plan were somewhat simplified versions of the Clinton plan.

Summary

In the end none of the proposals for reforming health care could be passed by Congress in 1994. As the debate wore on during the year, more questions than answers emerged about health care.[91] Many citizens and many politicians began to raise a wide range of questions about the impacts of the various proposals for reform. The politicians also worried about the impact on their political careers of voting for one or another proposal, especially just before midterm elections. This fear was exacerbated by the vast amounts of lobbying, especially from the insurance and health-care industries.[92] Further, it was impossible for liberals and conservatives to put aside their ideological differences to find a compromise that all could accept. For all sides, the pursuit of a perfect plan was the enemy of selecting an acceptable plan.

All the reform proposals faced insurmountable obstacles to adoption and perhaps even greater barriers to effective implementation. All the plans considered were complex, grafting on top of an already complex system of medical-care provision one or another means of financing a program that could become universal. Universality was intended to address the problem of access. The plans all involved increases in the amount of money flowing through the public sector, although almost all were likely to reduce the total amount of money spent on medical care over what would be spent under the existing system. All the plans also involved imposing some costs on the private sector, although the degree of mandating varied substantially. These plans also all proposed to maintain choice for consumers, but many opponents of the Clinton plan and more comprehensive plans feared rationing and a decline in the quality of care available, especially for those with the resources to pay for it.[93]

Choosing among these alternative plans for health-care reform demonstrates a good deal about the politics of public policy in the United States. The continuing conflict pits a number of special interests and their resources against the interests of the uninsured and even the general public who might benefit from lower medical-care costs. Further, it demonstrates very clearly the conflicts that can arise between the president and Congress over both the substance of policy and the relative power of their two branches of government. It also reflects the degree of fragmentation that exists within the individual institutions, with a number of congressional committees drafting their own health-care reform plans.[94] Finally, this reform effort points to the importance of policy entrepreneurship. In this case several players—Hillary Rodham Clinton and Senators Dole and Moynihan—were all attempting to be successful entrepreneurs, although only one could succeed. In this case, despite their skills, none of them succeeded.

The failure of comprehensive health-care reform did not end attempts at implementing some reforms. In particular, the federal government began to consider some regulatory reforms that could address some of the most egregious problems of the current health-care system. For example, there were proposals to require insurers to cover illnesses clients already have at the time they acquire insurance (preexisting conditions) and to make insurance portable when people change jobs.[95] Some thought was also given to extending the federal employees' health-care plan to more Americans, and many Americans began to ask why they can't have health-care coverage as good as that of the people who voted down reform.[96] Conservatives are discussing converting the system to one with more individual choice and more options, albeit under significant regulation.[97]

Although the federal government in 1994 failed to generate comprehensive reforms, there are still attempts at changing health care. One is a series of incremental reforms at the federal level.[98] Also, individual states have returned to making innovations in health care for their citizens, and they are again serving as laboratories for a variety of reforms.[99] Already twenty states are experimenting with the idea of alliances for small business and individuals to purchase insurance at rates lower than they could obtain individually. Other states (Washington and Oregon) have attempted to mandate that employers provide, and pay half the cost of, health insurance for full-time workers, but they are currently blocked by federal regulations from doing so. While all these efforts are encouraging, they risk creating a patchwork of laws and regulations that may make it more difficult for companies to do business, and that may give some states competitive advantages over others.

Conclusion

Reforming existing policies is always difficult, and health care is a particularly difficult policy field in which to produce change. A number of powerful interests—doctors, hospitals, pharmaceutical companies, and insurers—are involved in the area. Further, as issues of universal coverage arise, business interests become concerned about the costs that may be imposed on them. Citizens are also concerned that by attempting to provide better medical care for the entire population, government may undermine the existing high-quality medical care available to the most fortunate segments of the society.

Although restoring or encouraging competition in the medical-care industry is appealing to many Americans as a solution to the problems we have identified in the health-care industry, there may be difficulties in implementing this concept. The health-care industry differs from other industries in important ways that reduce the utility of competition as a remedy for its problems. In particular, the dominance of professionals in determining the amount and type of care consumed by patients makes standard competitive mechanisms less applicable. Those characteristics of the industry may, in turn, require a stronger role for the public sector if effective control over costs, quality, and access is to be attained.

First, very little information on the price or quality of medical care is available to the consumer. Prices for health-care services are rarely advertised; frequently the consumer does not even consider them when making decisions about care. In fact, in a perverse way, consumers often choose a higher-priced rather than a lower-priced service in the belief (often correct) that the more expensive service will be superior. And, beyond hearsay, little information is available to patients about the quality of services provided by individual physicians or hospitals. The public sector has been intervening to try to make more information about health-care quality available, but it is still difficult for the average consumer to make choices.

In addition, the provision of health care is, in many ways, a monopoly or cartel. Entry into the marketplace by potential suppliers is limited by licensing requirements and further controlled by the professions themselves, that is, by limiting the number of places available in medical schools. Thus, unlike some industries, the health-care field makes it difficult for competition to develop among suppliers. One possible means of promoting competition would be to break down the monopoly of the medical profession by giving nurse practitioners and other paraprofessionals greater opportunities to practice. The medical profession, however, resists such changes. Hospitals do compete increasingly for patients, however, and with that competition has come greater attention to the quality of care.

Bringing about any significant reforms in the delivery of health care in the United States will be difficult because of the power of the professions, large medical organizations such as hospitals, and, increasingly, managed-care organizations. The strongest pressures are to preserve the status quo, although physicians are becoming increasingly concerned about the control that insurers are exerting over services in the name of cost containment. It may well be that only a large-scale program such as national health insurance will be sufficient to break the existing system of finance and delivery, and to provide better and more equitable medicine to most Americans.

11. Income Maintenance Policies: Social Security and Welfare

The United States has frequently been described as a welfare state "laggard" because its levels of expenditures on social policies are low compared with those of other industrialized nations and because it has not adopted certain public programs (e.g., child benefits and sickness insurance) that are common in other countries.[1] Although this is true, the gap between the United States and other Western democracies has narrowed as American expenditures for social programs increased dramatically during the 1960s and 1970s and as program services and expenditures in almost all countries were reduced in the 1980s. The increased level of expenditures reflected both new programs, especially during the Johnson administration's War on Poverty, and increasing expenditures for established programs, particularly Social Security. U.S. social programs, broadly defined, in 1995 cost over $650 billion and provided services to millions of clients. These social expenditures now account for approximately *one-third* of all federal expenditures; social expenditures are approximately *40 percent* of total public expenditures.

The Reagan administration reduced the rate at which social expenditures expanded at the federal level. The amount spent on social programs in 1988 was at least as great as when that administration took office, although the amount spent was approximately 10 to 12 percent less than would have been spent under pre-1981 laws.[2] The gradual erosion of spending for social benefits continued during the Bush administration, with social spending less as a percentage of total federal spending in 1992 than before 1985.

President Clinton placed welfare reform on the agenda during his presidential campaign and pressed Congress for those reforms after his election.[3] He and Congress agreed on a major reform in 1996, with the new program beginning to be implemented in 1997. Despite their political visibility, welfare programs account for a relatively small proportion of total social spending, much less of total public spending, and the reformed welfare program almost certainly will be more expensive than the previous program.[4] It was hoped that these costs would be short-term, however, and that over time the new program would move people off public assistance and into productive jobs.[5] Interestingly, the United States and Europe are continuing to come together in this new policy direction, as a number of European countries are beginning to implement welfare reforms similar to those (see pp. 304–6) of the United States.[6]

Despite their apparent vulnerability to political pressures, social programs, especially social insurance programs such as Social Security, have some characteristics that make it difficult to cut them and even produce some demands for increases. Too many people (and/or their aging parents) depend on social insurance programs for politicians to be anxious to cut spending on these programs, despite the rhetoric. Pressures to preserve and enhance the programs are especially strong as the population continues to age and as the full range of effects of welfare reform become evident. Social programs are likely to remain a major battleground for forces of the political right and left in the United States.

What are these social programs that cost so much and touch the lives of so many citizens? Leaving aside programs such as public housing, education (see chapter 12), and health care (see chapter 10), all of which have obvious social importance, we are left with an array of programs that themselves provide a broad range of services and benefits. The largest programs, in terms of costs and number of beneficiaries, are social insurance programs such as Social Security (old-age and disability pensions), unemployment insurance, and workers' compensation (see table 11.1). Means-tested benefits such as "workfare," food stamps, and Supplemental Security Income also are significant in terms of expenditure. These programs are available only to individuals willing to demonstrate that their earnings fall below the level of need designated by the program. Finally, there are personal social services directed toward improving the quality of life for individuals through services such as counseling, adoption, foster care, and rehabilitation. The three major kinds of social programs address different needs and usually benefit different clients. Likewise, each has its own particular programmatic and political problems, which we address in this chapter.

Social Insurance

The largest single federal program of any type is Social Security. Although generally thought of as providing pensions for retired workers, the program actually offers other protections to its clients. It provides benefits, for example, for the survivors of workers who die before retirement. Thus the program provides benefits for children of a deceased worker until they reach the age of eighteen, if they are not employed. The program also offers disability

TABLE II.I

COSTS OF INCOME MAINTENANCE PROGRAMS
(IN MILLIONS OF DOLLARS)

	1960	1970	1980	1990	1991	1993	Percentage increase
Social Security	$11,032	$29,686	$117,118	$244,100	$264,100	$302,200	2,743
Unemployment	2,830	3,819	18,327	37,400	38,600	40,700	1,454
Public aid[a]	7,410	16,800	73,400	160,100	181,000	221,000	2,986
Food stamps	0	577	9,100	23,400	24,100	24,500	3,274[b]
Public housing	177	702	7,200	16,300	20,100	20,100	10,356
Other	6,591	19,660	73,200	48,800	49,770	46,900	694
Total	$28,100	$71,300	$298,200	$496,100	$577,600	$655,400	1,647
Percentage of public expenditure	18.2	20.1	28.2	37.4	37.9	38.1	—

SOURCE: Bureau of the Census, *Statistical Abstract of the United States* (Washington, D.C. Government Printing Office, annual).

a. AFDC plus some minor programs.
b. From 1970.

protection so that, if a worker becomes incapable of earning a living, he or she and any dependents can receive benefits. Finally, Medicare is linked with Social Security for financing purposes, as is discussed in chapter 10. In addition to Social Security, there are two significant social insurance programs in the United States. One, unemployment insurance, is managed by the states with a federal subsidy. The other, workers' compensation, is managed by the states, with employers bearing the major financial burden for the program. This program is the American equivalent of the industrial accident insurance common in other industrialized countries.[7]

Table 11.2 provides information on the recipients of social insurance benefits. By far the largest number of recipients are retired workers, although significant numbers of citizens receive benefits under other social insurance programs. Likewise, the largest share of social insurance goes to retired persons, although the highest average benefit paid is for the unemployed, followed closely by disabled workers. Many social changes are responsible for the growing number of social insurance recipients. Most important is that the average age of Americans is increasing, making more people eligible for retirement benefits. Also, the passage of the Americans with Disabilities Act in 1991 made other citizens more conscious of their right to benefits. The Social Security program is an entitlement program, meaning that citizens who have paid for their social insurance cannot be denied benefits once they meet the criteria for eligibility.

TABLE 11.2

SOCIAL INSURANCE RECIPIENTS, 1995

Program	Number
Social Security	
Retired workers and families	30,139,000
Disabled workers and families	5,852,000
Survivors	7,379,000
Railroad retirement	
Workers	551,000
Survivors	272,000
Unemployment insurance	8,035,000
Workers' compensation	2,314,000 (est.)
Total	54,542,000

SOURCE: Social Security Administration, Social Security Bulletin, *Annual Statistical Supplement, 1997.*

We must understand several important characteristics of social insurance programs, especially Social Security, if we are to comprehend the programs and the political debates that sometimes surround them. First, social insurance programs do relatively little, given the volume of expenditure, to redistribute income across economic classes.[8] Instead, they tend to redistribute income across time and across generations. Unlike a private annuity, in which an individual pays in money that accumulates in a personal account, Social Security is not an actuarially sound insurance program but a direct transfer program that taxes working people and their employers and pays out that money to the beneficiaries. The major purpose of Social Security is to distribute income across time; workers and their employers pay into the fund while employed, thereby reducing their income at that time, but receive benefits when they retire or if they become disabled.

Second, despite not being actuarially sound, this program is conceived as insurance rather than as a government "giveaway" program. Citizens believe they are purchasing an insurance policy when they pay their payroll taxes. Defining the program as social insurance has been crucial in legitimating it, as many citizens would not have been willing to accept a public pension to which they had not contributed; they would think it was charity. Further, most congressmen in 1935 (when the program was enacted) would not have been willing to vote for the program if it had not been defined as insurance. The insurance element is also important because of the implicit contract between the citizen and the government. More than any other public program, Social Security is an entitlement program; citizens believe themselves entitled to benefits and believe they have a legal and moral claim to receive those benefits in large part because they have contributed throughout their working lives.

The insurance nature of the program also helps explain its financing. Social Security is financed by payroll contributions, paid equally by employers and employees.[9] These payroll taxes are paid not on all earnings, but on only the first $68,100 (in 1998) of earnings each year; the health insurance component is now paid on all earnings. As shown in table 11.3 (p. 286), rates of tax and the threshold at which individuals stop paying social insurance taxes increase in order to pay for the rising costs of the program. Thus, instead of being a general tax, Social Security "contributions" are limited in much the same way as are premiums for a private insurance policy, although not all workers will pay the same amount for social insurance if they earn below the threshold. Because it was envisioned as an insurance program and not a vehicle for redistributive social policy, the Social Security tax has been a flat-rate, rather than progressive, tax.

Finally, Social Security is an earmarked tax: all the money collected is devoted to Social Security benefits, and only Social Security taxes are avail-

TABLE 11.3

INCREASING RATES OF SOCIAL SECURITY TAXATION

	Tax rate		On earnings	Maximum
	OASDI[a] (%)	HI[b] (%)	up to ($)	tax[c] ($)
1960	3.00	n.a.	4,800	144
1965	3.625	0.35	4,800	174
1970	4.20	0.60	7,800	374
1975	4.95	0.90	14,100	825
1980	5.08	1.05	25,900	1,588
1985	5.70	1.35	39,600	2,792
1988	6.06	1.45	45,000	3,380
1990	6.20	1.45	51,300	3,924
1991	6.20	1.45	53,400	4,085
1992	6.20	1.45	54,300	4,154
1993	6.20	1.45	57,600	4,406
1994	6.20	1.45	60,600	4,636
1995	6.20	1.45	61,200	n.a.
1996	6.20	1.45	63,000	n.a.
1997	6.20	1.45	65,400	n.a.
1998	6.20	1.45	68,100	n.a.

SOURCE: Social Security Administration.

a. Old Age, Survivors, and Disability Insurance.
b. Health insurance (Medicare).
c. Prior to 1995, the health insurance component was capped at the same level as the OASDI component; since 1995, the health insurance component has been charged on all earnings, so there is now no maximum tax.

able for financing the benefits.[10] The restrictiveness of the financial system makes the tax, and the program in general, more palatable to many citizens, but it also severely constrains its financial base. There has been much speculation about the Social Security system "going bankrupt," but given the political importance of the program, it is unlikely that Congress would allow that to happen.

Social Security now includes almost all working people. In 1997 over 90 percent of employed Americans were covered by the program. This figure includes a large number of self-employed individuals, who pay a self-employment tax instead of having their contributions matched by an employer. The principal groups now excluded from the program are federal government employees hired before 1984, employees of many state and local governments, and some farm workers. These exclusions are made for administrative convenience or because of constitutional inhibitions on the federal government to tax state or local governments, but many employers who could avoid the system opt into it to provide protection for their employees.

Finally, the benefits of the program are only partially related to earnings.[11] Those who pay more into the program during their working lives receive greater benefits when they retire, although those at the bottom of the income ladder receive a larger rate of return on their contributions and have a higher replacement of their earnings on retirement than do those with higher earnings (see table 11.4). Social Security is not intended to be a welfare program, but it is slightly redistributive in that it attempts to ensure that those at the bottom of the earnings ladder have something approximating an adequate retirement income—although it is difficult to argue that anyone living entirely on Social Security, even at the full-benefit level, receives enough money to live comfortably. The average worker and his or her family under Social Security receive about 76 percent of preretirement income; at the threshold level of Social Security tax, the family receives a 43-percent replacement.[12]

The redistributive element of Social Security has been reinforced by increasing taxes on benefits paid to more affluent recipients. For most of the program's history, the pensions paid to retired Americans were not taxable, regardless of the recipient's income. Beginning in 1984, however, 50 percent of Social Security income became taxable for recipients with taxable incomes and tax-free interest income over $25,000 (individual) or $32,000 (couple).[13] One part of a more radical reform (see p. 296) would make all benefits taxable. These current and proposed changes make the system more redistributive, but in the process they are making the system more like a welfare program.

TABLE 11.4
REPLACEMENT RATIOS OF EARNINGS IN SOCIAL SECURITY,
BY INCOME GROUPS
(IN PERCENTAGES)

	Monthly earnings					
	$100	*$500*	*$1000*	*$1387*	*$1800*	*$2033*
Worker alone (aged 65+)	167	74	60	51	44	41
Worker with spouse (aged 65+)	250	112	80	77	66	62

Problems in Social Security

Although Social Security is widely accepted by, and generally very popular with, the public, several problems arise when the program is considered for renewal or modification, and they were central to the work of the 1996 commission that reviewed the program. These policy problems, of course, have political ramifications that affect the way in which the program is treated in Congress and by the president. They also reflect the difficulties encountered in adjusting a successful program that is being affected by social and demographic changes.[14] Social Security has been maintained with incremental adjustments for over sixty years, but at the end of the century there may be a need for more fundamental reform.

THE RETIREMENT TEST

One policy problem is the retirement test—the penalty imposed on recipients of Social Security who wish to supplement their benefits by working. As the program is currently managed, if a recipient earns a certain amount of money (excluding income from private retirement funds or investments), a penalty is imposed on the benefits paid to him or her. In 1998 a recipient of Social Security up to the age of sixty-four lost $1 in benefits for every $2 earned over $8,640 a year. From age sixty-five to seventy, a worker earning over $13,500 a year lost $1 for every $3 earned; over seventy, earnings were unlimited.[15] For the person younger than sixty-five, there was, in effect, a 50-percent tax on earnings over the level allowed, a tax rate higher than that imposed on any individual paying the federal income tax.

There are several good reasons for removing, or at least relaxing, this retirement test. First, if the program is conceived as social insurance rather than as a means-tested benefit, then recipients should receive benefits as a matter of right, much as do recipients of private annuities. The retirement test in many ways gives the lie to the idea of Social Security as an insurance program. Additionally, that test may make the program more expensive and more of a donation from the young to the old. As it becomes unrewarding for retirees to work, they will stop working and cease paying Social Security taxes, whereas if they continued to work they could pay some of their own benefits through taxes. The higher tax cost for the program borne by the working-age population becomes especially troubling as the population ages and there are fewer active workers to pay for retirees.

There are also humane reasons for eliminating or modifying the retirement test. With the increase in life expectancy of American citizens, many individuals are capable of continuing to work after the usual retirement age. In a society that frequently defines an individual's worth on the basis of his or her work, retirement and the inability to work without paying a penalty on that work may impose severe psychological as well as economic burdens on the retiree. More flexible or unlimited earnings would allow Social Security recipients to participate in the labor market, perhaps not to the extent they did previously, and would permit phasing out employment rather than a sudden and often traumatic retirement.

On the other side of the argument, allowing retirees to continue working would have significant effects on other potential employees, especially those just entering the labor market. Every retiree who continues to work means one less job for a young person. Youth unemployment (especially for minority groups) is a significant problem, and the needs of the elderly must be balanced against needs of younger people. Additionally, allowing the retiree to continue working while still receiving benefits would amount to a direct transfer of income from the young to the old, based simply on age rather than on participation in the labor market. With a strong economy in the late 1990s, however, the economy may need the skills and abilities of workers who might otherwise retire under the Social Security system.

FIXED RETIREMENT AGE

Related to the problem of the retirement test is the question of a fixed retirement age. Under existing laws, the standard retirement age is sixty-five; it is being increased gradually to sixty-seven. Under the Social Security system, individuals receive little additional benefit for working after this age, although they must continue to pay Social Security taxes. In addition, individuals who choose to retire before reaching sixty-five have their benefits reduced, even if they have been paying into the system for years. These rules provide an incentive for workers to retire at the official age, and now all individuals are expected to retire at that age regardless of health or financial situation.

Good reasons can be found both for raising and for lowering the retirement age. One main reason for raising the age would be cost containment in a system that is facing severe financial problems; other reasons involve humane considerations. By raising the retirement age, total program costs can be reduced, because people will not be living on the program as long. When Social Security was adopted in 1935, only about half the male population could expect to live to age sixty-five, and those who reached sixty-five could expect to live only about twelve years. By 1990, however, over 72 percent of the male population would live to sixty-five, and they would live on average fifteen years on Social Security. By 2010, 78 percent are expected live to sixty-five and to remain on the program for an average of sixteen years.[16] Thus, there are more retirees and each retiree costs more today, and total program costs are increasing. In addition, the health status, the nature of work, and the educational levels of workers have all been improving. As the baby-boom generation begins to retire around 2010, there will be an additional 77 million recipients; delaying their retirement could help retain the solvency of Social Security—one preliminary recommendation of the National Commission on Retirement Policy was to raise the retirement age to seventy.[17] Also, the absence of private pension plans for some workers may mean that they cannot maintain their lifestyles if they are forced to retire.

On the other side of the argument are some reasons to lower the retirement age. Many people who have retirement incomes in addition to Social Security may want to retire while they are still in good health and capable of enjoying more years of leisure.[18] And at the systemic level, the lowering of the retirement age may create additional job openings for unemployed youths. In addition, the availability of a flexible retirement age may make it easier to modernize the nation's workforce. Workers with obsolete skills may move to Social Security more readily, and as a consequence, some human costs of modernization and economic change may be reduced.

Some policies for determining benefits and appropriate retirement ages may have to be retained, but there are good reasons for making this policy more flexible and for balancing different needs. Such flexibility could benefit individuals as well as the economy and society as a whole. Nevertheless, care would need to be taken that this flexibility took into account the needs and wishes of workers as well as administrative convenience and the financial problems of government.

THE TREATMENT OF WOMEN AND FAMILIES

The treatment of women under the Social Security system is another continuing issue. The system was designed in an era when the vast majority of women were housewives who did not work outside the home and who remained married to the same men for their entire lives. Those characteristics would hardly describe the average woman in the United States today, and as a consequence some aspects of the treatment of women under Social Security now appear outdated and blatantly discriminatory. Several aspects of Social Security substantiate the claim of unfairness. For example, if a woman is married to a covered employee for fewer than *ten years* (twenty years until the 1977 amendments were added), a divorce takes all the husband's benefits away from her, and for Social Security purposes it is as if they had never been married. And, as we have noted, the benefits an individual receives are roughly based on contributions, so even if a woman returns to work or begins to work after the divorce, she will find it difficult to accumulate sufficient credits for a significant retirement benefit.

Also, if both husband and wife work, as is now true for many if not most married households, the pair receive little additional benefit. This is true even though they may pay twice as much in Social Security contributions as a couple with only one worker. Benefits are based on each partner's individual work record, and there is no spousal benefit unless one worker would receive more from a spousal benefit than from her or his own work. Therefore, on average, the replacement rate for a one-worker couple with average earnings is 61 percent; for two-earner couples the replacement rate is 44 percent. The penalty at high rates of income is even more severe.[19]

An even broader question is whether a woman, or a man, who chooses not to work outside the home should not in fact receive some Social Security protection based on his or her contributions to the household and to society through this work in the home. The idea of a "homemaker's credit" in Social Security has been advanced so these individuals would have their own protection within Social Security. This protection may be especially important for disability insurance, for if the homemaker should become disabled, especially with children still in the home, this would impose additional financial burdens on the family. Other family members would have to do the work he or she had once performed in the home, or pay to have it done. With the current financial pressures on Social Security, however, there is little likelihood of homemakers' benefits being expanded; if anything, the treatment of women under Social Security may be even less generous. For example, the Reagan administration reduced extra spouses' benefits and surviving spouses' benefits over the course of its years in office.

THE DISABILITY TEST

In addition to providing benefits in retirement or if a breadwinner in a family dies, Social Security also protects families whose breadwinner is unable to work because of sickness or injury. The "substantial gainful employment" test in the program is an important problem. The test, as administered, is rather harsh and requires a person to be totally disabled before he or she can receive benefits.[20] The individual must be disqualified from any "substantial gainful employment," if such employment is available within the area of the potential beneficiary and if the applicant has the requisite skills. These standards are much more stringent than those applied in private disability programs, which require only the inability to engage in one's customary occupation, or for other public programs such as the Black Lung program or veterans' programs. At present, well under 50 percent of all applicants for disability receive benefits. In addition, the Social Security Amendments of 1980 mandated frequent reexaminations of the eligibility of program claimants, with the result that significant numbers of people have been removed from the program.[21] Also, there has been a movement to tighten eligibility for people with substance-abuse problems, but programs to reduce eligibility even further often have problems with implementation.[22]

The stringency of the disability test requires workers who have any disability to leave the workforce almost entirely in order to qualify for disability benefits. A situation may well arise in which an individual is too unhealthy to earn an adequate income but too healthy to receive benefits under the existing disability program. For both social and financial reasons it would appear beneficial to have a more graduated disability test to assist those who have a partial disability but who wish to continue to be as productive as they can be. A person could be assigned a percentage disability and compensated accordingly: such a test is already used in the Veterans Administration.

Workers' compensation is another accident and disability program in the United States, although it is managed by the states rather than by the federal government (except for the program covering federal employees). The disability tests employed in this program vary markedly from state to state, but generally they are less stringent than the Social Security test.[23] Further, there are provisions for permanent partial disability payments that enable a person to continue working, even if not in his or her original occupation. Workers' compensation programs now cover almost 90 percent of the American workforce but provide different levels of benefit in the several states.[24]

Social Security and the Economy

Social Security also affects the American economy. The most commonly cited effect is the reduction of individual savings and the consequent reduction in the amount of capital available for investment, compared with the situation if there were no public insurance program. Because individuals know that their retirement will be at least partly financed by Social Security, they do not save as much during their working lives as they might otherwise. Further, because Social Security as it is currently managed does not accumulate large reserves to pay future benefits but tends to be a direct intergenerational transfer program, there is less capital accumulation in the U.S. economy than there might otherwise be. Estimates of the magnitude of savings lost as a result of the Social Security program vary widely, but most experts agree that there has been some reduction in savings as a result of Social Security. Most also think that the disincentive effects are less than many conservative critics of the program have argued.[25]

The second major effect of Social Security on the economy is lessening labor market participation by older workers. As noted, the retirement test and the standard retirement age tend to provide disincentives for potential workers over sixty-five to continue working. As with the economic effect of reduced savings, it is difficult to estimate the magnitude of this effect on total growth and productivity, although several empirical studies have documented its existence. Also, as the number of young workers entering the labor market decreases, the skills of the older workers become increasingly valuable to the economy.

Financing Social Security

We now come to the most frequently discussed question concerning Social Security: how can the program be financed? Periodically since the 1960s, there have been reports that Social Security was going bankrupt, raising the specter that many elderly people would be left with no income from their contributions. In 1984 President Reagan said that he did not believe that those currently making contributions to the system would ever receive that much back in benefits.[26] Many citizens came to believe that negative prognosis, and by the mid-1980s less than half of all Americans expressed confidence in Social Security; in one survey only 36 percent of working Americans said they expected to receive any significant help with their retirement from Social Security.[27] The lack of confidence was especially noticeable among the young. This may appear foolish, given that the system is running a surplus and has accumulated a significant trust fund. In the late 1990s, however, the impending retirement of a huge age cohort—the "baby boomers" born between 1945 and 1952—threatens to send the system into deficit and to exhaust the reserve fund by 2025.

Given the entitlement nature of the program, such dire outcomes are extremely unlikely. Indeed, at other times the Social Security system has run large surpluses that politicians have sought to use to balance an otherwise unbalanced federal budget.[28] But the Social Security system as a program financed entirely by payroll taxes may be in difficulty, and the trust fund created to back the program may be in danger of being exhausted by the middle of the twenty-first century as the number of retirees increases relative to the number of workers.[29] Younger workers may be called on to finance the program with ever higher payroll taxes but may be reluctant to do so if they fear that they will not receive the benefits themselves. Indeed, the projections are that to continue to finance the system through payroll taxes would impose extremely high payroll taxes on workers—approximately 15 percent by 2020.

There are several reasons for the financial difficulties of the Social Security program. The most obvious problem is the increasing number of aging Americans, a trend that began in the 1960s and is projected to continue if the birth rate continues to be low. In 1960 only 9 percent of the American population was over sixty-five. By 1990 that figure had increased to almost 13 percent, and it is expected to increase to almost 20 percent by 2025. Phrased differently, in 1984 each Social Security beneficiary was supported by the taxes of approximately three active workers. By 2030, it is estimated that each beneficiary will be supported by only 2.3 workers, and by 2050, by less than 2.2 active workers.[30] This obviously implies either an increasing burden on active workers or a modification of the existing financial structure of the program.

Another factor increasing the difficulties in financing Social Security has been indexing benefits to match increases in prices and wages. Under existing arrangements, the initial benefit levels paid retirees are adjusted annually to reflect changes in the average wages paid in the economy. In addition, in every twelve-month period during which prices increase more than 3 percent, benefits are adjusted so that retirees have approximately constant purchasing power from their pensions. This indexing of benefits (a cost-of-living adjustment, or COLA) is an obvious target for those seeking to control social program costs. As Social Security faced one more crisis in 1983, legislation was passed that imposed a one-time delay of six months in the COLA. Another possibility suggested by a group of economists at the usually moderate-to-liberal Brookings Institution would be to eliminate the COLA in a year in which inflation was less than 5 percent; if inflation were greater than 5 percent, the correction would be the rate of inflation less 5 percent. Another suggestion would have the COLA pegged several percentage points lower than the inflation rate.[31] All these suggestions encounter opposition from the expanding and active lobbying organizations for the elderly.

The reasons for attacking the indexing of benefits as a means of reducing some financial problems in Social Security are twofold. First, it is a relatively simple change to make. Second, it has the potential to save significant amounts of money. For example, it is estimated that the six-month COLA delay in the 1983 legislation saved $40 billion from fiscal 1983 to 1988. But such measures may well place serious hardships on some of the elderly. One study has estimated that a COLA set 3 percentage points below inflation would put over a million elderly below the official poverty line within several years; many people wonder why the federal budget and the Social Security system have to be made solvent on the backs of the elderly.[32] President Reagan, despite his open skepticism about the future of Social Security, agreed in July 1984 that even if inflation fell below the 3-percent figure, the COLA adjustment would still be made. Congress rapidly agreed with the president (especially given that there was an election soon) and there is every reason to expect future administrations to continue to index Social Security.

With the financial pressures on Social Security, there is a question whether the system can afford to continue financing itself entirely through payroll taxes. There are also problems with the payroll tax, perhaps the most important being that the tax is basically regressive, exacting a higher percentage from low-paid workers than from the more affluent. This regressive character of the tax is the result of the threshold above which individuals earning additional income do not pay additional tax. In 1998 individuals paid a payroll tax of 7.65 percent on the first $68,100 of covered employment for a maximum tax of $5,210; after that amount, they paid no more taxes for the old age, survivors, or disability programs.[33] Thus, everyone who earned the threshold amount or less paid the same 7.65 percent of their income, while those earning $100,000 paid only about 5 percent of their income as Social Security taxes.

In addition, the Social Security tax is applied only to salaries and wages, not to earnings from dividends or interest. But because the system is conceptualized as providing insurance and not as providing benefits directly proportional to earnings, these disparities are justified; once you have paid your annual "premium" on the insurance policy, there is no need to pay more. The payroll tax for Social Security is regressive in another way as well. Most economists argue that workers actually bear the burden of the employers' contributions (the same 7.65 percent of salaries and wages up to the threshold) to Social Security because employers count their contributions as a part of the costs of employing a worker and reduce wages accordingly.[34]

The payroll tax also has the disadvantage of being relatively visible to employees.[35] They see the money deducted for Social Security from each paycheck, and they have some idea of how much money they pay into the system. This visibility also means that the level of payroll taxation may be limited by real or potential taxpayer resistance. Although the payroll tax is a visible one, its use in combination with the personal income tax makes the total tax "bite" on wages less obvious than if there were a single tax on income to be used for social benefits as well as general government purposes.

The earmarked payroll tax does have one advantage that some people believe is worth retaining. Because the receipts from this tax are relatively limited, politicians are prevented from using the Social Security system for political gains. That is, as general tax revenue (the income tax primarily) is not used to finance the system, it is difficult for a president or Congress to increase rates of benefits just before an election to attempt to win votes from the elderly. The COLA adjustment of benefits, however, may have some of the same effects because changes in benefits tend to go into effect shortly before election time in November. Further, the earmarked tax makes the system appear to most citizens to be a contributory insurance program instead of a welfare program.

Reforming Social Security

Several proposals have been made to alleviate some of the financial problems of Social Security. Among the simple, incremental changes would be to remove the financing of Medicare from the payroll tax and finance that program through general revenues. This would provide Social Security more money while retaining the existing rates of payroll taxation; in 1995, 1.45 percent of the 7.65 percent paid in payroll taxation was used to finance Medicare. Another mechanism, already mentioned, is to change the COLA adjustment and timing, although in a period of high inflation such a change might work a considerable hardship on the elderly. Raising the retirement age, or at least making it more flexible, is another possible solution to the costs of Social Security, as would be a reduction of some of the welfare-like benefits attached to the program (e.g., spouses' benefits). One such minor benefit—the burial allowance—has in some cases already been eliminated.

These proposals represent rather minor tinkering with the program, but more significant modifications have been proposed. One would be to make the program truly comprehensive so that it would include all workers; new federal government employees are now in the system but state and local government employees can still opt out. Expanding membership in the program would provide a larger financial base of white-collar workers who earn better-than-average incomes. This change might also provide a psychological benefit: it would point out that all citizens are a part of the same Social Security system. A large majority of Americans support the idea of making the system totally inclusive, but there are legal barriers that may prevent that happening.[36]

Others have suggested that the entire basis of Social Security financing be changed from payroll contributions to general revenue, through either the income tax or a value-added tax (VAT) like that used in Europe.[37] The VAT is a tax levied on businesses at each stage of production, based on the value that each business adds to the raw materials used to create the product it sells. The VAT has the advantage of being virtually invisible, its cost reflected only in the price of a product. It also has the advantage of being somewhat less regressive than the payroll tax, especially if some commodities (food, prescription drugs, etc.) are untaxed. The invisibility of the VAT would be an advantage for those managing Social Security, although many citizens might not regard it as such; VAT would allow Social Security income to expand with less restraint than the present system of finances.

Social Security finance is likely to remain an important policy issue. As the average age of the population continues to increase, program costs keep growing, and they will probably increase more rapidly than will the yield from the payroll tax. Unfortunately for the program's managers, the form of finance is now entrenched and may be difficult to modify without changing the insurance concept of the system and perhaps thereby reducing general support for the program. Also, it has been suggested that all Social Security benefits should be counted as taxable income. The 1983 amendments to the Social Security Act permitted the taxation of benefits received by retirees with incomes at the higher end of the scale: $25,000 for individuals, $32,000 for a couple. The passage of any provision to tax benefits indicates a perceived crisis in Social Security financing and may in effect make Social Security a means-tested program.

Radical Reforms

All the reforms of Social Security discussed so far amount to tinkering. Some reformers, however, are proposing an almost complete overhaul of the system. One of the more prominent proposals is to begin to move the population away from social insurance as we have known it toward something resembling a private annuity program. For example, Senators Daniel Patrick Moynihan (D-N.Y.) and John Kerry (D-Mass.) have proposed a "2 percent solution" to the long-term problems of Social Security, with Social Security taxes reduced by 2 percent and participants in the system being able to invest that savings in private retirement accounts.[38] Other congressmen have proposed diverting even more money into private accounts. Benefits for recipients with private accounts would then be scaled back, saving public money.

Support for this partial privatization of the system was spurred in part by the boom in the stock market during the late 1990s; people saw what might have been if they had put their money in the stock market instead of in government bonds, perhaps not recognizing the risks associated with that type of investment.[39] During the Thatcher period, the United Kingdom adopted just such a partially private pension system, albeit as a supplement to the regular pension, and this program was implemented with some success.[40] The assumption of such a partial privatization is that the average retiree will have more money for retirement, and the public sector will be relieved of a potential financial burden. Even with this change, however, there are questions about the solvency of the system, and the same reformers call for raising the retirement age and making all income taxable.

Moving from a fully public system to a more private one would cause some transitional problems and perhaps some inequities among different age groups, but advocates argue that the system would be improved by the shift. In the short term there would be uncertainty about the reliability of the new system, and indeed there should be some concern whether a privatized system would be able to provide the level of pensions expected by the reformers, or even the rate of return available under the existing social insurance scheme. Certainly it would be difficult to guarantee any level of pension if there were any significant reliance on the movements of the stock market. Therefore, many longtime supporters of the program (including many advocacy groups for the elderly) are at best skeptical and seek to assure that they, and future retirees, will have at least comparable benefits to those now available.

Summary

Social Security is a large, complex, and expensive program. As a result, several important policy issues exist concerning its effects on citizens and on the economy. What is more fundamental, however, is that the program will persist, albeit in modified form. Some way must be found to finance the program so it will provide an adequate or at least minimal income for pensioners without bankrupting the working-age population. Likewise, there are increasing demands that we remove some of the rigidities and discrimination from the system and make it more humane and responsive. The system, in all probability, will continue to be a major success story in public policy but one that will remain on the policymaking agenda.

Means-Tested Programs

The second major kind of social program is the means-tested program. To qualify for benefits under such a program an individual must satisfy a means test, or, more accurately, an absence-of-means test. Individuals cannot earn more than a specified amount or have any major assets if they are to qualify for a means-test program. Rather obviously, then, these programs benefit groups of people, defined by economic criteria, who are generally neither the most influential in society nor the easiest to mobilize politically. Also, the means testing involved in the program tends to stigmatize and to some extent degrade individuals who must apply for the benefits. These programs are not entitlements in the strict sense of the term, although political and judicial actions have tended to make them more matters of right than in the past.[41]

These programs are the locus of a good deal of ideological debate, even in a country that tends to have more pragmatic than ideological politics.[42] Some citizens regard means-tested benefits as handouts or giveaways, and they describe recipients of such benefits as "lazy welfare cheaters" and sing songs about "welfare Cadillacs." President Reagan once referred to AFDC recipients as "welfare queens." Polls showed that Americans definitely wanted the AFDC (Aid to Families with Dependent Children) system reformed, but were willing to spend to improve the system and did not want to punish the truly needy (see table 11.5). More intellectual critics of the programs blame them for social disintegration, family breakups, and rising rates of urban crime. Racial issues are also involved in means-tested benefits, for although the majority of welfare recipients are white, a disproportionate share of blacks and Hispanics receive welfare benefits. Supporters note, however, that the means-tested benefits—welfare payments, food stamps, Supplemental Security Income, and a variety of other programs—provide the only livelihood for many citizens, and they have been criticized by some as both inadequate and demeaning.[43] What is clear is that these programs raise several important social, political, and economic issues.

TABLE II.5

ATTITUDES TOWARD THE WELFARE SYSTEM

1. *Is welfare in need of reform?*	Fundamental reform	81%
	Minor reform	16%
	No answer	3%
2. *Would you pay more taxes*	Yes	68%
for a system that would get	No	27%
people off welfare?	No opinion	5%

3. *Do you agree with the following welfare reforms?* (% yes):

Take money from paychecks and tax refunds of fathers who refuse to make child support payments.	95
Require all able-bodied people on welfare to work or learn a job or skill.	92
Spend money to provide free day care to allow poor mothers to work or take classes.	90
Reduce welfare with a system of guaranteed public jobs.	74
End increases in welfare payments to women who give birth to children while on welfare.	42
Cut the amount of money given to all people on welfare.	25
Require women to get a job and get off welfare within two years; if they can't take care of their children at that time, give them to an orphanage.	17
Eliminate all welfare payments entirely.	7

SOURCES: Questions 1 and 2, *USA Today*, 22 April 1994. Question 3, Yankelovich poll, reported in *Time*, 20 June 1994.

AFDC

The largest means-tested program, and the one that generated the most political controversy, was AFDC, or "welfare." This program benefited more than 14 million Americans, including approximately 8 million children, in 1994. The program cost the federal government over $14 billion, or less than 1 percent of all its expenditures and less than 5 percent of the federal deficit that year. AFDC took a larger share of state governments' expenditures, especially as the welfare rolls increased substantially during the early 1990s.[44] AFDC was expensive, although perhaps not so expensive as some believed, and because the program provided benefits on the basis of need rather than contributions, it was controversial in a market-oriented society.

In addition, AFDC was growing in numbers and expense, and that produced even more pressure for reform.

It is especially interesting that the controversy over AFDC arose in the 1960s and 1970s rather than in the 1930s, when it was adopted. The program was part of the package that produced Social Security, and at that time the major controversy was over Social Security rather than AFDC.[45] It was assumed that AFDC would be used by a relatively small number of widows with children, rather than by women who were remarried, divorced, or separated. Social Security, however, would become a widely accepted feature of American life, while AFDC was increasingly perceived as a problem by the taxpayers who funded the program, as well as by its recipients. Changing family patterns, with many more women working in the economy, also played a part in the low status of AFDC recipients.

Before we discuss the 1996 reform of the program, it is important to understand why the reform was so important. In general, AFDC recipients were women with children and virtually no income, and with no one living in the household capable of supporting the children. Actually, some males also qualified for AFDC; an increasing number qualified for assistance under the Family Support Act (see p. 303). In 1988 fewer than 15 percent of the recipients were widowed, spouses of disabled workers, or unemployed—those for whom the program was intended. Most AFDC recipients were in fatherless families; approximately half of those were families in which the parents were never married, and the other half were headed by separated or divorced mothers.

AFDC, although a national program, was administered by states and localities. Despite several attempts at reform and "nationalization" of the program, its administration remained decentralized. The federal government provided a small subsidy to the states for the program, and the remainder of the benefits came from state and local funds. The level of benefits varied widely across the states. In 1994 the highest average monthly benefit for a family of three was $740, in Alaska. If we leave aside Alaska and its extremely high cost of living, however, the highest payment was $553, in Connecticut. The lowest AFDC payment for a family of three was $123, in Mississippi; the average across the nation was $378 per month. None of these levels of benefits was particularly munificent, and substantial differences existed, even taking into account differences in the cost of living in the various localities. In addition, a number of states sought to reduce AFDC benefits during the fiscal problems of the early 1980s. In some instances this meant just failing to increase benefits in line with inflation, while in others it meant real cuts in program benefits.

In addition to general benefit cuts, states began to use AFDC payments to regulate the behavior of recipients.[46] The image of the "welfare mother" having illegitimate children in order to qualify for benefits was one that gave supporters of the program difficulties when they attempted to improve funding and benefits. Indeed, several states reacted against this common image by refusing to continue to increase payments for mothers on AFDC who had additional children, with one state actually reducing benefits if there were an additional child.[47] Likewise, at least one state eliminated general assistance payments that had been paid to individuals not eligible for AFDC, and others reduced the size and duration of payments. Other states gave lower AFDC benefits to recipients who had just moved in from out of state. There were a number of other regulations on the behavior of AFDC recipients. For example, several states reduced benefits if the children of AFDC recipients did not attend school regularly. Other regulations included reducing or eliminating benefits for teenage recipients who did not attend school regularly. Other states cut off AFDC payments to teenage mothers who did not live with a parent or legal guardian. In a more general move, some states required all welfare recipients to be fingerprinted to help reduce fraud.[48]

The AFDC program was not without major problems, but those problems were exaggerated in the popular mind. First, as was established earlier, AFDC was not a big spending program; it actually cost the federal government relatively little. Further, once on welfare, most recipients did not remain on the program throughout their lives. In 1994 over one third of AFDC recipients had been on the program one year or less, and over 78 percent had been on it for five years or less; the median time on the program was 22 months. Also, almost as many whites as African Americans were on AFDC. Finally, as might be expected from the transitional nature of the program, divorce and separation, rather than having a child without benefit of marriage, were the major reasons for accepting AFDC.

Problems with AFDC

As mentioned, both taxpayers and the recipients of AFDC recognized numerous problems in the program. Naturally, the problems seen by the two groups were rarely the same, although to some extent they may have been different ways of saying the same thing about certain aspects of the program.

MEANS TESTING

Programs that require recipients to prove that they are indigent create problems for the recipients, who become stigmatized, especially in a society that places a high value on success and income as symbols of personal worth. Most recipients of welfare benefits were relatively powerless anyway, and the stigma attached to being on a program such as AFDC tended to lessen their feelings of self-worth and power. That stigmatization might, in turn, have helped to perpetuate the problems that caused them to go on AFDC in the first place. Unfortunately, the program as designed tended to perpetuate indigence rather than allow people to work their way out of poverty.

PUNISHMENT FOR WORKING

One aspect of the older AFDC program that appeared to make the least sense was that individuals who attempted to work their way out of poverty were penalized. An individual could work no more than 100 hours per month, no matter what rate of pay was received. After a certain amount was earned each year (the sum varied by state), the recipient was required to return $2 in benefits for every $3 earned.[49] This was, in effect, a tax higher than any tax rate in the regular income tax system. Rather obviously, such a high rate of "tax" on earnings provided little incentive for individuals to work their way out of poverty; despite that, beginning with the Work Incentives Program in 1967, AFDC recipients without children were required to work. Once people went on AFDC they could find it difficult to get off, and the system seemed to perpetuate both itself and the poverty it was intended to address. In addition, because other benefits, such as food stamps and Medicaid, might be tied to receiving AFDC, taking a job meant the loss of a great deal more than the AFDC check.[50]

FAMILY STRUCTURE

The AFDC program also had severe effects on family structure. As noted, under most circumstances, a woman with children could not receive benefits if there was an able-bodied male in the home. This meant that traditional families, the virtues of which were stressed by politicians such as Bill Clinton and Dan Quayle, usually were not eligible for AFDC. This stipulation made it more difficult for women on AFDC to work, requiring that they either care for the children themselves or find suitable day-care facilities. It also had deleterious effects on the children, who must then grow up in fatherless households. As single-parent families became more common in the United States, growing up in a single-parent home became less stigmatizing than it once was, but problems of social adjustment remained. And yet, as more women began working outside the home, the image of the welfare mother staying home grew more negative than ever.[51]

COSTS AND BENEFITS

Depending on whom you asked, the benefits of AFDC were either too high or too low. Those concerned about the costs of the program argued that the generous benefits encouraged recipients to stay on welfare rather than find jobs, and they simply did not want to pay taxes so that other people could refuse work. On the other side of the argument, most recipients of AFDC benefits would point out that even the highest monthly state benefit of $740 was hardly sufficient for a life of leisure, and that the average benefit across the country was only $378. The recipients and their supporters also argued that in fact the benefits were too low to provide a decent living for the recipients and their children, who inherited poverty along with the substandard housing, low-quality education, family disruption, and poor diet commonly associated with AFDC households.

Even before major reforms, advocates of stringent controls on welfare spending were winning, as a number of states began to limit, or even reduce, the benefits offered under AFDC. Indeed, these are only the most visible examples of a long-term erosion of the value of AFDC payments. One study by the Congressional Research Service found that the average purchasing power of maximum welfare payments across all states declined 42 percent from 1970 to 1991.[52] The program may have appeared expansive, but its recipients were becoming increasingly impoverished.

The Family Support Act

The problems inherent in the AFDC program did not go unnoticed by lawmakers, and one reaction was the Family Support Act of 1988.[53] This act, associated especially with Senator Moynihan, addressed a number of important issues in AFDC. It attempted to break the "cycle of poverty" that had led to several generations of family members following one another as recipients of AFDC. Among the provisions of the act were:

1. *Greater help for families with two parents.* The act required the states to amend their AFDC programs to provide at least six months' benefits per year (AFDC-UP) to families with both parents unemployed.
2. *Improved child support enforcement.* This was intended to reduce the number of children requiring assistance from AFDC, as well as to have some impact on strengthening parental responsibility toward children.
3. *Job training.* States were mandated to provide enhanced job training and child-care services so that AFDC recipients would be able to get and keep reasonable jobs in the economy.[54]
4. *Enhanced Medicare benefits.* People who left welfare for work would not automatically lose medical insurance, a major impediment to leaving AFDC, given that a declining number of jobs for which most people leaving welfare were qualified offered health benefits.[55]

The Family Support Act certainly was not a cure-all for the problems of the AFDC program, nor did it eliminate poverty in the United States. Further, the requirement for implementation by the states produced substantial variations in the generosity of the benefits and the speed of their adoption.[56] Still, the adoption of this program was a recognition of the kinds of changes that were needed to cope with problems inherent in the basic system of providing financial support for the indigent.

The 1996 Reforms

As noted earlier, there was a major reform of the welfare system in 1996. Building on reforms that were already underway in several states, these changes—usually referred to as "workfare"—have fundamentally altered the nature of welfare policy in the United States. There are six basic provisions of workfare, which is more formally entitled the Personal Responsibility and Work Opportunity Reconciliation Act of 1996 (PRWORA).[57]

ENDING AFDC

This act terminated AFDC as it had been developed during the New Deal, substituting in its place a short-term, work-oriented program. The bill also brought together the funding for a number of other means-tested benefits such as Supplemental Security Income, food stamps, and child support enforcement.

RESTRICTION OF ELIGIBILITY

One of the most important elements of the reform was restricting the time period for which an individual was eligible for benefits. A standard critique of the prereform AFDC system was that people never left the program once they were on. This was actually not the case,[58] but it was certainly the stereotype of the program and it became an important part of the politics of reform. PRWORA limited benefits to two years at any one time, and to a total of five years over a lifetime. Further, food stamps benefits were limited to three months in any three years.

DEMANDS FOR WORK

The basic rationale for the reform was that if recipients could not remain on the program indefinitely, they would have to find some other source of income. The reform tends to hasten the recipients along the path to self-sufficiency by requiring that they either get a job or prepare themselves for a job in order to receive benefits. This requirement may mean that state and local governments will have to develop new job opportunities, but the assumption is that people will have to work. The Clinton administration has proposed giving tax breaks to businesses that provide job opportunities for former welfare recipients and the long-term unemployed.[59]

TREATMENT OF IMMIGRANTS

Another provision of PRWORA was a limitation on the welfare benefits allowed to immigrants, even legal immigrants, who were made ineligible for food stamps. There has been some rethinking of this last provision in the course of implementation, but the basic provisions should save money, especially for states such as California that have large numbers of immigrants.[60]

VIGOROUS ENFORCEMENT OF CHILD SUPPORT

One means of saving government money would be to force fathers (or, in a few cases, mothers) to provide for their children. The Family Support Act of 1988 had also stressed enforcement, but PRWORA placed even more pressure on the states to find "dead-beat dads" and get child support money from those who could provide it.

IMPLEMENTATION BY THE STATES

Like AFDC, the new welfare program is implemented by the states. Unlike AFDC, however, it is meant to be interpreted and implemented with a good deal of latitude.[61] Indeed, some states are working with private firms as agents for implementation[62] or are decentralizing the implementation even further to local governments.[63] The legislation also funds the program through a limited block grant rather than an open-ended subsidy so that, in addition to being given more latitude in implementation, states are relieved of the requirement to match federal funding as in the previous regimen. The states, however, will begin to lose part of this block grant in 2002 if they do not meet work participation targets for their program recipients.

The provisions of PRWORA appear extremely punitive, and in some ways they are. That having been said, the final legislation is not as severe as some of the other proposals that were made, especially in the Republican Congress, where one zealous reformer proposed to deny benefits to teenage mothers and to encourage them to put their children up for adoption. Interestingly, the very politicians who generally talk most about individual autonomy were central in placing so many controls on personal behavior in this bill.[64] There remains some question whether this program is really the best thing for welfare recipients, and especially the children. There is some evidence that children do better—in school, socially, and ultimately, economically—when they have at least one parent at home regularly to care for and nurture them.[65] This point has been stressed by conservatives such as Dan Quayle, but it has also been recognized by more liberal child-advocacy groups. The emphasis on work is appealing to most Americans for ideological and financial reasons, but in the long run it may actually exacerbate the cycle of dependency that the reforms are intended to break. While

AFDC had negative consequences for family life, workfare may prove to have even more negative consequences for children.

It is far too early to say what the impacts of this legislation will be.[66] It is too soon to say whether people with relatively few job skills can support themselves and their families adequately. What is certain is that it has changed the nature of American social policy in a rather fundamental way. Also, it is clear that this one policy change will require further policy interventions to provide child care as well as programs for chemical dependency, job placement, and a number of other needs that arise out of this one change.[67] The success of the policy change, as well as the overall substitution of work for welfare, will depend very much on the ability of the economy to provide the needed jobs. Otherwise, the program may simply push the poor into short-term public-sector jobs rather than meaningful work in the private sector. Getting people off welfare may be much easier than keeping them off.[68]

Alternatives for Further Reform of the Welfare System

With the one major reform already in place, there are still options for additional reforms. Several alternatives to the existing programs have been seriously proposed in the United States, and some are in operation in Europe. These alternative programs might provide benefits for poor citizens without the stigma, or the administrative complexity, of the existing programs. Most alternatives would, however, require a significant change in the contemporary mind-set about the poor and social policy in the United States.

FAMILY ALLOWANCES

One alternative, used in virtually all other democratic, industrialized societies, is the family allowance.[69] Under this program, families receive a monthly benefit check from the government, usually based on the number of children. For the more affluent, this simply becomes additional taxable income, while for the poor it may be a major source of income. But the most important aspect of the program is that it includes everyone, or at least all households with children. The stigma of receiving government benefits is therefore removed, and the program is substantially easier to administer than PRWORA. The level of benefit for each child would have to be sufficient to match the current level of benefits, which would mean that a great deal of money would have to pass through the public sector as taxes and expenditures, but the effects would perhaps justify that decision, given the negative consequences of means-tested programs.

THE NEGATIVE INCOME TAX

A second alternative to the existing program is the negative income tax.[70] Under such an arrangement, a minimal level of income would be determined, based on family size. Each family would then file its tax statement, and those earning below the established minimal level would receive a rebate or subsidy, while those above that minimal level would pay taxes much as usual. This program would provide a guaranteed annual income for all citizens and would be administratively simpler than AFDC or PRWORA. The recipients themselves would provide a good deal of the information necessary to calculate benefits, instead of having to rely on state and local welfare offices. In addition, this program would establish equal benefits across the United States, with perhaps some adjustments for different costs of living in different parts of the country. The negative income tax, as it is usually conceptualized, also makes it easier to work one's way out of poverty because it imposes only one-third or one-half reduction of benefits for any money earned.

Interestingly, President Nixon's 1969 proposal for a family assistance plan was much like a negative income tax.[71] If this program had been enacted, it would certainly have been the most sweeping reform of the welfare system ever made, providing a guaranteed annual income for all citizens. The program was not adopted by Congress, however. A coalition of liberals, who thought its benefits were too meager, and conservatives, who were ideologically opposed to the concept of a guaranteed minimum income, defeated the bill. In addition, social workers and other professionals believed that their jobs were threatened by a program that placed the major burden of proving eligibility on the individual citizen.

Although the concept has never been adopted in its entirety, there have been some movements toward a negative income tax in the United States. Most importantly, the Earned Income Tax Credit operates through the tax system to benefit low-income taxpayers with at least one child in the family. The ideas behind this program (introduced in 1975) were to offset the effects of the Social Security tax on low-income individuals and to encourage people to work rather than take AFDC. This program now provides benefits (reduced taxes, or in some cases direct cash transfers) to over 54 million Americans, and therefore ranks as by far the most widely used means-tested benefit in the country. Implemented through the tax system, it also is very inexpensive to administer and less intrusive than many other social programs.

CHILD SUPPORT

Although the popular image of the AFDC recipient was of a woman who had had one or more children out-of-wedlock, in reality almost half of AFDC recipients went on the program because of divorce or separation. These women were left with children to support and often lacked significant job skills and work experience. Even in cases in which the legal divorce or separation decree awarded child support to the mother, many men did not pay this support regularly, if at all. Several studies found that a large percentage of the children whose families received AFDC had fathers who were not paying child support.

The federal government has now undertaken (with the assistance of the states) to enforce child support, especially in cases in which the mother otherwise would be receiving benefits such as monthly welfare payments and food stamps. The Family Support Act of 1988 required the states to establish enforcement plans, and in 1994 employers were required to deduct child support payments from the wages of fathers who were not in compliance with the law. These efforts have been somewhat successful, making recoveries of over $10 billion in 1995 from almost 4 million absent parents.[72]

This approach to the problem of poor children is not without its difficulties, however.[73] First, the delinquent fathers must be identified and located. Further, a federal study has found that these fathers tend to be relatively poor themselves, with 29 percent below the poverty line, and there may be little income to extract from them.[74] Still, states have adopted increasingly vigorous programs of enforcement and now are able to collect 80 percent of in-state support.[75] Some go so far as to confiscate the property as well as garnishee the wages of fathers who violate support orders.[76] Other states have begun to impose other penalties, such as loss of drivers' licenses, on fathers who fail to provide support.[77]

FULL EMPLOYMENT

Perhaps the simplest means of eliminating many of the problems of the existing system would be to guarantee citizens jobs rather than social benefits. The federal government has been involved in a number of programs for job training and subsidized employment, the most prominent being the Comprehensive Employment and Training Act (CETA) in the 1970s and early 1980s and then J.O.B.S in the later 1980s.[78] The purpose of these programs was to enable people to acquire job skills by working with local private contractors and then to subsidize the employment of those trainees for several years. After that time they were expected to have improved their productivity sufficiently to be able to earn a decent wage in the labor market. Although CETA continued in operation until 1981, it was severely criticized on several grounds—using inefficient and corrupt prime contractors, for example, and training people to do nonexistent jobs. Some critics charge that the CETA program placed too many trainees in the public rather than the private sector, that it swelled the size of local government employment rolls, and that it created problems for local government when the trainees' eligibility for CETA expired.

The combination of an economy in recession and continuing pressures to find an answer to the problems of poverty and welfare led the Bush administration to place renewed emphasis on jobs and job training. The president announced "Job Training 2000" as part of his economic program for the reelection campaign in 1992. As announced initially, the details were far from clear, but the idea that jobs were superior on almost all counts to welfare was clearly stated. The difficulty the president faced at that time, as would have any other welfare reformer, was a shortage of good jobs in the American economy even for workers with well-developed skills and ample job experience—qualifications that most welfare recipients lack.

The Clinton administration continued to place a significant emphasis on the development of jobs as perhaps the best means for addressing social problems. Robert Reich, President Clinton's first secretary of labor, as both an academic and practitioner analyst of changing employment patterns in the world, pressed the need for the U.S. economy to adjust to the globalized economy.[79] The welfare reforms implemented by the Clinton administration (discussed earlier in this chapter) emphasize work as a solution to the problem of welfare, but they have not relied entirely on the private sector to develop those jobs. The federal government already has a number of jobs programs in place, but these have multiple (and often competing) goals, and their effects are not as positive as they might be.[80] The emphasis of these programs is on education and training, and many are targeted at young people.

Job-training programs have not had a positive image in the United States, although they are gaining additional importance under "workfare" programs. The training programs have been argued to be beneficial in the long run, but in the short run they do not appear to be addressing the immediate needs of many poor citizens. Also, in the early days of PRWORA, there is evidence of widely differing use of the funds made available for job training, as many white recipients have been using the money for college, while many nonwhite recipients have opted for trade schools or more vocational programs. In an era of full employment this may make little difference in the short run, but it may well produce major differences in earnings in the long run.

The War on Poverty

An earlier attempt at a comprehensive solution to the problems of poverty and means-tested benefits was the Johnson administration's War on Poverty. During the administration of John F. Kennedy, poverty was "rediscovered"

Rediscovery of the depressing economic plight of families with children in the 1960s gave rise to a comprehensive series of programs intended to break the cycle of poverty. (AP/Wide World Photos)

in the United States, and it became a popular political issue, especially among liberals. After President Kennedy's assassination, Lyndon Johnson used his formidable political talents and the memory of the slain president to implement legislation attempting to break the cycle of poverty, which, as we have seen, tends to be perpetuated by most social programs. The War on Poverty differed from other social programs of the time in that it was less directed toward the short-term amelioration of deprivation than toward changing long-standing patterns and conditions of the very poor.[81]

War on Poverty programs did more than just hand out money—although they certainly did a good deal of that—but attempted to attack the cultural and social conditions associated with poverty. They also sought to involve the poor in the design and implementation of the programs more directly than had the more paternalistic programs common at the time. The umbrella organization for the programs of the War on Poverty was the Office of Economic Opportunity, created as a separate agency outside the Department of Health, Education, and Welfare. It was feared that the bureaucratic nature of HEW, and its commitment to social insurance programs as the mechanism for solving social problems, would hinder the activism envisioned for the War on Poverty, and consequently an independent organization was established.

One aim of the War on Poverty was to attack poverty by educating the children of the poor so that they could compete successfully in school and in the economy. One of the most popular programs for children was Head Start, which attempted to prepare poor children to compete with other children when they entered school. The program tried to provide the skills that middle-class children generally have when they enter kindergarten but that children from economically deprived households frequently lack. Despite the popularity of Head Start, its demonstrable effects have been rather modest. Children who participated in the program were better prepared to enter kindergarten than children who had not been in the program, but their "head start" rapidly vanished. Without continuing extra assistance after several years, the Head Start children were not significantly different from children who had not participated.[82] Of course, depending on one's point of view, this could be an argument that the program had failed or that it needed more follow-up once children reach elementary school. Additionally, a college work-study program was initiated to try to make it more possible for students from low-income families to attend college, a program that has been expanded and continues after the demise of the War on Poverty.

For adults, the War on Poverty initiated a variety of programs primarily intended to provide employment or to prepare people from poor households for productive employment. These programs commonly involved cooperation between the federal government and either state and local governments or private businesses. In addition to the employment-related projects, many of the smaller programs provided counseling, loans for small businesses, family planning, and a whole range of other social services. In general, the War on Poverty provided something for almost everyone who needed and wanted work or help.

By the early 1980s most of the programs of the War on Poverty had been dismantled, reduced, or modified. What happened? Several events reduced the emphasis that government originally placed on the programs. The escalation of the Vietnam War diverted both attention and money from domestic programs, especially those lacking a solid political base and an institutionalized bureaucracy. Also, the goals of the War on Poverty were so lofty, and perhaps so unrealistic, that it was easy for critics to argue that the programs had not been successful and to question their continued funding. Further, the prospect of ever-increasing wealth that had fueled many public programs began to become less certain, and governments began to face real fiscal problems.[83]

On the other hand, it would be difficult to argue that many of the programs of the War on Poverty were really seriously tried. So many programs were begun that some were funded only as pilot programs and others, such as Head Start, may have lacked the funds necessary to pursue their goals through to a successful conclusion. Further, to argue that even a large array of programs intended to change generations of poverty and deprivation could actually work miracles in a few years is unrealistic, and therefore the "trial" given the programs may not have been a fair trial at all. Finally, with the election of Richard Nixon as president in 1968, the political climate that had spawned the programs changed, and since the impetus for the programs had so clearly been presidential, Congress had few strong advocates to defend the War on Poverty programs.

But were the programs of the War on Poverty, and the whole war itself, a massive failure or at best a noble experiment? These programs represented a major departure from the traditional means of attempting to solve, or at least ameliorate, poverty in the United States, and their impact may actually be more enduring than short-term evaluations indicate. Certainly the need to address the problems of poverty in the midst of affluence remains as pressing today as it was in 1965 when the programs were initiated. Whether the change is to come through better jobs in the private sector or through public programs, at least 30 million Americans live below the official poverty line, still waiting to enter the economic mainstream of American life.

Other Means-Tested Programs

Although AFDC has been the most common topic of discussion when the issue of means-tested benefits arises, there are also a number of other benefits available to less-privileged citizens. For example, food stamps are generally available to people on welfare as well as to other people who are working but whose income falls below certain levels. Participants purchase the stamps at a discount and then use them to buy food. Unlike most other social programs, food stamps cannot be used legally other than for food (and some other necessities) so that some of the common complaints against "welfare"—the misuse of the funds for alcohol, gambling, and so forth—can be controlled. In addition, this program helps to create more demand for American agricultural products, so it gains support from those interests as well as from the interests that support social assistance. A similar program, WIC (Women, Infants, and Children), provides specified nutritional benefits to women and children. As noted, however, these programs have been impacted by the general move to reform welfare, making them much less available to the poor than in the past.

Supplemental Security Income is another important means-tested program. As of 1995 it provided benefits to 6.4 million people. The largest number of these recipients qualify by falling into the categories of aged, blind, or disabled. These were the categories in earlier state assistance programs, but in 1974 these programs were federalized, thus removing them from the (then) weaker financial position of the states. These benefits have been indexed since the time that they were federalized, so that the assistance now offered to these groups is probably substantially superior to what it would have been if the program had remained at the state level.

The Persistence of Poverty in the United States

We began our discussion of agenda setting with a discussion of the impact of Michael Harrington's book *The Other America* on the development of a poverty program in the United States.[84] Despite the attention brought to the issue and programs such as the War on Poverty, the problem of poverty continues. In fact, poverty in the late 1990s is nearly as great a problem as it was in the mid-1960s when the War on Poverty was beginning. Poverty had been declining during the 1960s and 1970s, but it began to increase again in the early 1990s. Further, the poverty rate is not uniform across the population, with female-headed households, blacks and native Americans, and children being particularly likely to live in poverty (see table 11.6, p. 314). Over 20 percent of all children under the age of eighteen now live under the official poverty line; 41 percent of all black children and over 39 percent of Hispanic children lived in poverty in 1995. Both of these rates of poverty reached their height in the early 1990s, and although they have decreased slightly since then, they remain higher than during the 1970s. In contrast, the poverty rate for the elderly has improved substantially over the decades since poverty became an issue; that poverty rate is now less than half what it was in 1970, despite a growing elderly population.

In general, the social policies of the Reagan and Bush administrations seem to have forced more people to live in poverty than if earlier social policies had been continued. A number of other factors, such as slower economic growth and changing demographics may have had some impact on the increasing poverty rate,[85] but public policy has been an important element. The Clinton administration has returned to some of the social activism of previous Democratic administrations, although in a somewhat more restrained manner. The emphasis for the most part has been on developing more jobs and preparing people for those jobs than on direct grants to improve the situation of the poor.

There may, however, need to be more than just jobs if poverty is to be eliminated. As we pointed out earlier, a minimum-wage job will not pull a

TABLE 11.6

CHANGES IN THE POVERTY RATE, 1960–95

(IN PERCENTAGES)

	1960	1970	1975	1980	1985	1988	1991	1995
Total	22.2	12.6	12.3	13.0	14.0	13.0	14.2	10.8
Blacks	55.1	33.5	31.3	32.5	31.3	31.3	32.7	26.4
Children[a]	n.a.	14.9	16.8	17.9	20.1	19.0	21.1	20.2
Female-headed households	n.a.	38.1	38.1	36.5	40.2	32.1	34.8	33.6
Over 65 years of age	n.a.	24.5	24.5	15.7	14.1	11.4	11.9	10.5

SOURCE: Bureau of the Census, *Current Population Reports,* Series P-60, annual.

a. Fifteen and younger.

family of three or four above the poverty line, and in most areas it will not do so even for an individual.[86] The minimum wage was raised in 1996, but it still is lower than in 1955 when inflation is considered, and an increasing proportion of jobs in the United States are at the minimum-wage level. Given that many if not most of the families involved have a single wage-earner (usually female), there is little possibility of combining incomes to bring a family above the poverty line. There may be a need to link social benefits—food stamps, energy assistance, Medicaid—with work more than in the past. This effort is a part of the welfare-reform movement, but it may need to be extended to families already working as well as those receiving welfare.[87]

Poverty is a symbolic issue, but it is also a matter of careful counting.[88] How do we know who is poor and who is not? The official definition of poverty for 1996 was a family of four living on an income of $15,589 or less; adjustments are made for family size, urban versus rural areas, and so on. This definition does not include as income all noncash public benefits, such as food stamps, Medicare or Medicaid, and housing subsidies (see table 11.7). In addition, no allowance is made for levels of taxation that could reduce income below poverty levels.

Because of the availability of numerous public benefits and the relationship of poverty status with eligibility for other public programs, conservative economists during the Reagan and Bush years argued for a change in the definition of poverty.[89] Such a change in the definition would have indicated that many fewer people were in poverty (see table 11.8) and would thereby have benefited an administration that consistently argued that its policies had not harmed the poor. In addition, such a change in definition might have had the effect of a "reverse Harrington"; if the problem could be defined out of existence, it would be much easier to eliminate from the public agenda. The Clinton administration and Congress are also concerned about the definition of poverty and its current level. They have chosen, however, to

TABLE 11.7

POVERTY RATES USING ALTERNATIVE DEFINITIONS
OF INCOME, 1995 (IN PERCENTAGES)

	Cash only	Cash less transfers	Plus non-means-tested benefits	Plus Medicaid	Plus imputed rent
Total	13.8	21.8	14.1	11.7	9.4
Whites	11.2	19.4	11.3	9.5	7.6
Blacks	29.3	37.2	30.4	24.7	19.6

SOURCE: Bureau of the Census, *Current Population Reports,* P60-194 (1995).

TABLE 11.8

POVERTY RATES USING ALTERNATIVE DEFINITIONS
OF POVERTY, 1987 (IN PERCENTAGES)

	Cash only	Cash plus food and housing benefits		Cash plus food, housing, and medical benefits	
		a	b	a	b
Total	13.0	12.0	12.4	8.5	11.0
Female-headed households	38.3	32.8	34.2	21.6	30.9
Elderly	12.2	10.2	10.7	2.1	6.4

SOURCE: Patricia Ruggles, *Drawing the Line: Alternative Poverty Measures and Their Implications for Public Policy* (Washington, D.C.: Urban Institute Press, 1990), table 7.2.

a. Benefits valued according to prices in market.

b. Benefits valued according to income beneficiaries willing to give up to receive benefits. Given that noncash benefits are not available for any other use, they tend to be considered less valuable than a cash benefit.

address the problem indirectly—through employment programs and welfare reform—rather than directly.

The Homeless

In addition to the large number of people living in poverty in the United States, there are also an increasing number of people who are homeless. Often the homeless are not included in the official poverty figures because they are not caught in the statistical nets used to calculate those figures. Rather, they live on the margins of society, often without government benefits of any sort, sleeping in shelters or on the streets, and eating in soup kitchens.[90] Were it not for their visibility in many urban areas, the homeless might not really be counted as a part of society at all.

The reasons for homelessness are numerous. Government policies have reduced the number of subsidized low-income housing units available and forced many people—including families—onto the streets.[91] Further, changes in mental health laws requiring minimal possible restraint led to the release of many patients from institutions to poorly prepared community mental-health programs, and some of those patients have since found their way to the streets.[92] Increases in chemical dependency have also made their contributions to homelessness in the United States. Finally, the declining number of jobs at which a person with a low level of education can earn a wage sufficient to support a family, or even him- or herself, has had an impact on homelessness.

For whatever reason, there is now a significant social policy problem that is not being addressed effectively. The federal government has little or no policy for coping with the issue of homelessness. The only federal program of any consequence is the McKinney Act, authorizing several types of emergency assistance such as housing, food, health care, and drug and alcohol treatment. The federal government appropriated $4.2 billion for such assistance from 1987 to 1993, most of it being spent through state and local governments.[93] Although this appears to be a significant amount of money, it is rather meager amount compared with the magnitude of the need, and the program does not address the fundamental causes of the social problem.[94] More homeless persons now are being assisted by private organizations than by governments at any level. This emphasis on the private sector corresponds well with the emphasis on volunteerism during both the Reagan and Bush administrations, as well as in the post-1994 Republican Congress, but it has done little to solve the underlying problems. Further, city governments have begun to crack down on the homeless as a part of programs such as "zero tolerance" policing that have sought to eliminate all forms of perceived antisocial behavior.

There is little evidence that approaches to homelessness have been altered significantly after a return to a Democratic administration. This is in part because of an absence of a clear policy solution to a multidimensional problem. People are homeless for a variety of reasons, so that addressing the problem will require an equally broad and probably expensive strategy. Further, many of those reasons, such as addiction and mental illness, may be difficult for public officials to "solve" through conventional policy instruments. The Clinton administration has concentrated on a number of other domestic policy priorities—such as health-care and welfare reform—and has largely relied on state and local governments, and especially the charitable private sector, to address the problem of homelessness.

Personal Social Services

The final category of social-service programs delivered by the public sector receives less attention than either Social Security or welfare assistance, largely because these programs cost much less and deliver benefits that do not depend on either age or income. The term "personal social services" applies to a range of services, such as adoption, foster care, suicide prevention, counseling, and the like, that are definitely not for the poor alone. In fact, some services, such as adoption, are used primarily by middle-class families. Eligibility for most personal social services is determined by citizenship or by definition of need based on attributes other than lack of income rather than by means testing. Again, unlike many other social services, personal social services—adoptions, for example—are viewed positively and carry no stigma. Even for services not so positively regarded (e.g., suicide prevention or alcoholism counseling), the client receives greater sympathy than does the poor person on welfare.

Personal social services, more perhaps than even the welfare system, are dominated by professional social workers. As a consequence, these programs can appear formidable to a poorly educated potential client. It may, in fact, be virtually impossible for the poor or the poorly educated to use these programs effectively. This, in turn, may mean that additional economic benefits may have to be provided when personal counseling might have been sufficient. This, in terms of policy analysis, may be a situation in which too much of one service (PRWORA or other means-tested benefits) is being provided as a substitute for a less expensive, and ultimately superior, service.

Private Social Programs

Finally, we should point out that although most Americans tend to think about social programs as benefits provided directly by government, a large number of social benefits are conferred by the private sector, usually with the indirect support of government. Pensions are a good example. We discussed earlier the very large and important program for public pensions provided through the Social Security Administration. There are, however, a huge number of private pensions—some 64.7 million workers in 1994 had pension rights through their employers or through their unions, and millions of others have purchased private annuities or have contributed to Individual Retirement Accounts (IRAs) that are designed generally to supplement other forms of retirement income.

The federal government supports these private social benefits in at least two ways. First, the employee can deduct from his or her taxable income most contributions made to these programs, and the contributions made by the employer are not taxable until the employee begins to receive the pension. In addition, the federal government now supervises and guarantees pensions through the Pension Benefit Guaranty Corporation, much as it does bank deposits through the Federal Deposit Insurance Corporation. Pension schemes also are regulated through the Employee Retirement Income Security Act (ERISA). Given that most recipients of private programs are members of the middle class, these supports amount to a major social benefit for that segment of the population. Much the same economic distribution holds true for federal support for private medical insurance, disability insurance, and owner-occupied housing through the tax system.

Conclusion

The disjuncture between the poor and the non-poor is not evident in Social Security, but it is in almost all other elements of social policy in the United States—and in most other countries as well.[95] Especially in the United States, this dual pattern makes the politics of social policy very difficult for reformers. The political struggle quickly is translated into a conflict of "us versus them," or the "haves" versus the "have nots." This struggle is exacerbated when the economy is not growing and any benefits granted the poor are perceived as directly reducing the standard of living of the middle classes. Even during periods of affluence there are alternative uses for money that might be spent for social programs.

The social services are composed of a large number of rather diverse programs. What holds them together is an overriding concern with individual needs and conditions, some economic and some personal. The programs that have been tried and that are still in operation represent attempts by government to improve the conditions of its citizens, although the programs in operation by no means represent entirely satisfactory solutions to the problems. Several of the programs are as unpopular with their clients as they are with the taxpayers who fund them. This chapter has pointed to some approaches to modifying existing programs, as well as some more sweeping changes in program structure that may benefit government finances as well as program clients. These social problems will not go away; if anything, the 1980s and 1990s brought increasing demands for services, especially for the elderly and the homeless. What must be found is a means of providing adequate benefits through a humane mechanism that taxpayers will agree to support. This is no easy task, but it is one that policymakers must address.

The emerging globalized market and its effects on wages, earnings, and employment will place even greater pressures on social policy in the United States. One of the enduring problems likely to be exacerbated by internationalization is the number of people who work full-time but who still earn wages that keep them in poverty. Further, if average real wages continue to fall as they have, the amount of money available to fund retirement benefits will also decrease and financial pressures on Social Security will increase. After at least a decade of neglect it may be time for some serious analysis and reform of social policy.

12. Educational Policy

Education traditionally has had a central position among American public policies. Although the United States as a nation has been slow to adopt other social programs—pensions, unemployment insurance, national health insurance, and the like—we have always been among the world leaders in public education. Some 17 percent of all public spending and over one-third of all public employment in the United States are devoted to education. Most public involvement in education has been at the state and local levels, and the federal government has become directly involved in elementary and secondary education only relatively recently. Still, by the late 1990s the federal government has become a major actor in educational policy at all levels, exerting its influence through direct expenditures as well as through a variety of indirect instruments.

The Clinton administration has sought to make the federal government an even more important player and has placed a great deal of emphasis on expanded funding and regulation of all areas of education. The adequacy of American education continues to be questioned, as American students perform at or near the bottom of some international standardized tests, and poor education has become identified as a major problem in American economic competitiveness.[1] President Clinton has argued for the federal government to play a more significant role in addressing these deficiencies, and the American public appears to agree. In a 1998 survey when asked what should be done with any budget surplus that might become available, almost a quarter mentioned education as the first priority—it was the most frequently mentioned use.[2]

Congressional Republicans, in contrast, continue to argue that education is a local, family issue and that the federal government should not expand its activities in this area. Recalling that the Reagan and Bush administrations' plans to terminate the U.S. Department of Education hurt the electoral fortunes of their party, Republicans have not recently called for the federal government to get out of education entirely, but they do fight expansion of its role. In the late 1990s the Republican Congress chose not to challenge the existence of the Department of Education directly, but they have opposed administration efforts to impose more federal controls over teacher competence and to provide more support for educational facilities. Given the electoral appeal of education, however, Republican leaders in Congress have advanced some programs of their own, mostly involving vouchers or tax credits supporting private education.

Background

The public role in education began very early in the United States, with the State of New York adopting free public education in 1834. Education later became compulsory in all states until a student reached a certain age (this provision was temporarily revoked in some southern states as a means of avoiding racial integration). Even in the early years of the Republic, the federal government had some role in education. The Northwest Ordinance of 1787, in planning the organization of the Northwest Territories of the United States, divided the land into townships and the townships into sections. One of the sixteen sections in every township was to be set aside for supporting free common education. In 1862 Congress passed the Morrill Act, granting land and a continuing appropriation of federal funds to establish and maintain in each state a college dedicated to teaching "agriculture and mechanical arts." From this act grew the system of land-grant colleges that has produced such major educational institutions as Cornell, Texas A&M, and the Universities of Wisconsin, Illinois, and Minnesota. The research and extension activities of these institutions have been important for the expansion of American agricultural productivity in addition to their broader educational activities.

In the 1990s the federal government has developed a large-scale involvement in education,[3] spending approximately $70 billion on education in 1996. This appears to be a huge amount of money, but it actually represents a smaller share (4.5 percent) of total federal spending than was devoted to education in 1980 (5.8 percent). In addition to the amount of money being spent, a wide variety of federal organizations provide assistance for education. In 1997 all cabinet departments except one (Commerce) had some involvement with education, as did a variety of other federal agencies such as the National Science Foundation, the National Aeronautics and Space Agency, the Agency for International Development, and the National Endowments for the Arts and Humanities.

There have been several important characteristics of American education and educational policy. First, the emphasis on education is indicative of the general attitude the United States has taken toward social mobility and social change, the belief that education is important because it gives people "chances, not checks."[4] The prevailing American ethos is that government should attempt to create equal opportunity through education rather than equal outcomes through social expenditure programs. Individuals who have the ability are presumed to be able to better their circumstances through education and to succeed no matter what their social or economic backgrounds. It is perhaps important to note that, despite the evils of segregation, blacks in the South prior to *Brown v. Board of Education* were given access to public schools and public educational opportunities through the level of the Ph.D. degree. One cannot realistically argue that the opportunities were equal, but education was more easily available to African Americans than might be expected, given their social status in those states. The norm of educational opportunity appeared to cover even social groups that were systematically discriminated against.

Related to the role of education in social mobility is the importance of American public schools for social integration and assimilation. The United States has absorbed a huge number of immigrants, 8 million of whom arrived in the first decade of the twentieth century alone. The institution that was most important in bringing those new arrivals into the mainstream of American life was the public school system. This was certainly true for adults who learned English and civics in "Americanism" classes in the evenings. Also important in this regard is that the public schools in the United States traditionally taught all the children living in the community. Only a very few wealthy families sent their children to private schools; everyone else in the community went to the same school, often all the way through their elementary and secondary years.[5] The tradition of comprehensive schools that provided a variety of educational opportunities, from college preparatory through vocational, was important in reinforcing the ideology of a classless society and in at least promoting social homogeneity, if not achieving it.

The 1980s and 1990s also were a period of large-scale immigration to the United States, and the public schools have continued to play a role in assimilating the children of those millions of new Americans. But the social and economic realities of the 1980s and 1990s appear to have broken down some of the homogenizing impact of the public schools, and education has become increasingly ethnically and economically segregated.[6] To some degree the lack of homogenization has been by choice, as "multiculturalism" has become a rallying cry for those who want a more diverse society and a more diverse educational system to support that society.[7] Deciding how to manage increasing social diversity and still meet the educational needs of all segments of the society is a major question now facing American education. Bilingual education is another part of the battle, especially in states, such as California and Florida, with large immigrant populations.

Despite the centrality of public education at the elementary and secondary levels, there has never been a state monopoly on education. Alongside the public schools have existed religious schools—almost 10 percent of the elementary students in the United States in 1995 attended parochial schools —and other private schools. This diversity is especially evident in postsecondary education, with over 22 percent of all college students attending private institutions.[8] Almost anyone can open a school, provided it meets the standards set by government or other accrediting bodies. If anything, the diversity of options for students in American education has been increasing over the past several decades. The sense that the public schools are not doing an adequate job of education has spawned a variety of new educational providers, ranging from very strict schools concentrating on the "Three Rs" to unstructured attempts to promote greater creativity and free exploration of ideas.

Finally, the emphasis in American education has always been on local and parental control. Of all the major activities of government, education is the one clearly retaining the greatest degree of local control and local funding. In fact, the largest single category of public employment in the United States is made up of public school teachers who are employed by local governments. And the control that government exercises over education is generally also local. There are 14,422 local school boards in the United States, as well as over 22,000 counties and cities that frequently play a substantial role in providing public education. Despite all those opportunities for local political action, there have been pressures for even greater local control and parental involvement. These pressures have come from white suburbanites, from inner-city minority parents, and from ideologues, all of whom believe that the public schools should be doing things differently.

Although the local school has traditionally been a positive symbol of local government and the community, there are now a number of doubts about education and pressures for change. These problems are to some degree reflected in the evaluation Americans give their schools. When asked to grade schools, respondents to national polls have tended to give their own community schools a grade of C, while they give schools nationally a very low C—barely passing (see table 12.1, p. 324). In another poll less than half of respondents said they were satisfied with the quality of education in the United States.[9] It should be noted, however, that parents with children in public schools offer substantially higher evaluations of public schools than do people with no children in school or with children in private schools. The assessment of education appears to be another aspect of public life that is being affected adversely by publicity and negative media coverage.

The negative feelings about public schools are reinforced by numerous findings that American students do not do as well on standardized tests as do students in Western Europe, Taiwan, Korea, or Japan. Even here, how-

TABLE 12.1
PUBLIC'S GRADES FOR PUBLIC EDUCATION,
1974–96

	School in own community	Schools nationally		School in own community	Schools nationally
1974	2.63	—	1986	2.36	2.13
1975	2.38	—	1987	2.44	2.18
1976	2.38	—	1988	2.40	2.10
1977	2.33	—	1989	2.35	2.02
1978	2.21	—	1990	2.44	2.11
1979	2.21	—	1991	2.47	2.08
1980	2.26	—	1992	2.41	2.01
1981	2.20	1.94	1993	2.37	2.05
1982	2.24	2.01	1994	2.31	2.00
1983	2.12	1.91	1995	2.28	1.97
1984	2.36	2.09	1996	2.31	1.98
1985	2.39	2.14			

SOURCE: *Phi Delta Kappan,* annual.

NOTE: 4.0 = A; 3.0 = B; 2.0 = C; 1.0 = D; <1.0 = F.

ever, the evidence is not as bleak as it sometimes appears. Students in some states, especially those in the Upper Midwest, do as well or better than students overseas.[10] Further, American students have been improving in their performance of these tests, and they already tend to do better on other types of testing. The perceived problems and the reforms proposed to deal with them are discussed later in this chapter.

The Federal Government's Role in Education

The involvement of the federal government in education has been controversial, and it was thought that the Reagan administration might further reduce federal involvement. President Reagan's first secretary of education, Terrel Bell, came into office pledging to dismantle the then recently created Department of Education. But the need for improved education and educational funding became more apparent during the first four years of the administration, and not only was the Department of Education saved but it launched new initiatives for improving American education. President Reagan's second secretary of education, William Bennett, reversed the initial direction of the administration and launched a federal effort to improve what he considered to be the deplorable state of American education. That campaign was based on that one individual's view of good education—a highly structured curriculum stressing basic skills and the canon of Western civilization.[11] The campaign was waged more with rhetoric than with resources, but it did point to the importance of a national educational policy in a postindustrial and highly competitive world. By most objective indicators, however, the quality of education did not improve under Bennett's leadership.

The Bush Administration

George Bush campaigned in 1988 as the "educational president." That campaign pledge was vague, and the first several years of his administration provided little clarification. Bush promoted several programs for magnet schools and rewards for schools that improved student achievement, but until 1991 very little happened in education policy. The education issue remained important nationally, but the immense federal budget deficit and the generally conservative nature of the Bush administration did not permit substantial federal funding for education during the first half of Bush's term, despite pleas from state and local officials for assistance. The Bush administration advocated better education for the United States at every opportunity but did relatively little to provide local school districts with additional resources to meet those educational goals.

In 1991 President Bush and his then new secretary of education, Lamar Alexander, unveiled an ambitious plan, entitled "America 2000: An Education Strategy," to meet his campaign pledges on education. The plan had four major elements:

1. *National testing.* Unlike competency testing (see pp. 341–43), the national tests proposed were to be diagnostic and public. The openness of testing was proposed to enable communities to judge how well their local schools were doing and to exert political pressure for better education. The scores on the tests (in principle voluntary) could also be used by prospective employers, thereby pressing both students and schools to do better.
2. *New schools.* The federal government would fund 535 new schools (one for the district of each congressman and senator) that would serve as models of what could be done with public education. Federal funding was to be supplemented by funds from business so that the new schools could "break the mold" of existing educational programs.
3. *Improving teachers.* "America 2000" included several recommendations for improving the quality of teachers, including merit pay and alternative means of certifying competency for teaching (especially in

subjects such as mathematics and science), rather than depending upon state certification.

4. *Choice.* Consistent with the market-oriented philosophy of many Republicans, President Bush proposed creation of a market in education, so parents would have more opportunity to choose and schools would feel more pressure to perform (see pp. 338–40).

It was an ambitious plan, but in practice almost nothing actually happened in education at the federal level during those four years.

The Clinton Administration

Education, unlike health-care reform and welfare reform, was not a central element of President Clinton's campaign for office. But he and his administration hardly ignored the need for addressing the educational needs of the society. During the first Clinton administration, education policy addressed three principal concerns. One was the role of education in economic competitiveness and in sustaining the place of the United States in the world economy. A second concern was the role of education in coping with the social and economic disparities existing within the United States. Finally, the administration focused on early childhood education and sought to increase funding for programs such as Head Start.[12]

Several major pieces of legislation were indicative of the Clinton administration's approach to education issues.[13] One of the first was "Goals 2000," a linear descendant of the Bush administration's education efforts. This was a broad-scale reform act promoting state and local efforts for improving American education and making it equal to that in other industrialized democracies. There was a great deal of emphasis on testing and improving the qualifications for teaching in the schools. The administration also advocated reauthorization of the 1965 Elementary and Secondary Education Act, the major source ($10 billion) of federal support for education.

Another important educational initiative of the Clinton administration was the School-to-Work Opportunities Act.[14] The program created by this act attempts to coordinate the activities of the Department of Education and the Department of Labor to enable those students who do not get a college degree (almost three-quarters of the total) to prepare themselves for good jobs in a rapidly changing economy. As well as an educational program, this act was an attempt to cope with the global competitiveness problem. Implementation of this ambitious program, to be carried out by state and local governments, however, requires an unusual degree of cooperation between two bureaucracies that have not always seen eye-to-eye on how best to meet the education and training needs of the society.[15]

The Clinton administration also has emphasized the need to reduce class size and to improve the general standards of teaching in schools.[16] Few people would dispute that these measures would improve the quality of education, but questions remain about whether the states or the federal government should play the major role in improving education. The anti-Washington education agenda of the Republican Congress, for example, continues to emphasize the role of states, local governments, and families. The Clinton administration, in contrast, asserts that only by working at the national level can real educational progress be made for the country as a whole. Relying on state and local governments, it is argued, may only perpetuate the inequalities that exist among the programs offered by those governments.

Local Financing and the Federal Role

We should discuss one aspect of local control in education because it conditions the need for federal involvement. This is the traditional means of funding public education through the local property tax, which has in recent years presented two significant problems. One is that property tax revenues generally have not kept pace with inflation (see table 12.2, p. 328). The administration of the property tax involves assessing property values and applying a rate of tax to the assessed value. In an inflationary period, assessments may not reflect the real value of the property, and certainly not the costs of goods and services, unless revaluation is done very frequently. Thus, many local school boards find that their funding is no longer adequate for their needs. The second problem is that, even if there were no inflation, the tax base available to some school districts would be markedly different from that available to others. To provide the same quality of education, parents living in poorer districts have to tax themselves at higher rates than those in more affluent areas. This is an extremely regressive way to finance a basic public service, requiring the poor to pay a higher rate of tax to provide the same level of education.

The usual result of this pattern of funding is that the education provided to poorer children is not as good as that provided to wealthier students.[17] Thus, it is argued that the local property tax is an inequitable means of financing education and that some alternative, such as federal or state general revenues, should be used to equalize access to education. Both federal and state contributions have been declining slightly over the past decade (see table 12.3, p. 328), however, leaving localities to bear an increasing responsibility for funding education. As we discuss later, the court system has already begun to bring about some changes in school finance in the direction of greater equality and greater state funding, but the inadequacy of local taxation remains an important reason for federal involvement in education.

TABLE 12.2

PROPERTY TAX REVENUES OF LOCAL GOVERNMENTS, 1960–94

(IN MILLIONS OF DOLLARS)

	Current	Real[a]	Percentage of total revenues
1960	15,798	17,851	47.8
1970	32,963	28,367	40.7
1975	50,040	31,061	34.2
1980	65,607	26,594	28.2
1985	99,772	32,825	28.2
1988	127,191	35,909	25.3
1990	149,765	38,116	29.2
1991	161,706	39,180	26.7
1992	172,334	49,876	25.9
1993	182,452	58,659	26.6
1994	188,864	63,928	26.2

SOURCE: Bureau of the Census, *Statistical Abstract of the United States* (Washington, D.C.: Department of Commerce, annual).

a. Converted to constant (1967) prices using consumer price index.

TABLE 12.3

SOURCES OF EDUCATIONAL FUNDING

(IN PERCENTAGES)

	1970	1980	1985	1990	1994
All education					
Federal government	10.7	11.4	8.6	8.2	8.8
State governments	31.5	38.8	38.8	37.2	34.4
Local governments	32.1	26.1	25.6	27.1	26.1
All other	25.7	23.6	27.0	27.4	30.7
Elementary and secondary education					
Federal government		9.1	6.1	5.6	6.5
State governments		43.3	44.7	43.6	41.7
Local governments		40.3	40.7	40.7	41.7
All other		7.3	8.5	10.1	10.1

SOURCES: National Center for Educational Statistics, *Digest of Education Statistics* (Washington, D.C: Department of Education, annual); Bureau of the Census, *Statistical Abstract of the United States* (Washington, D.C.: Department of Commerce, annual).

Higher Education

It has traditionally been more acceptable for the federal government to be involved with higher education, perhaps because the students are almost adults and are assumed to have formed their basic value systems free of influence by the central government, or perhaps simply because of the higher per student expense. At any rate, the federal government began to assist institutions of higher education somewhat earlier than elementary schools. During the Lincoln administration, the federal government initiated the land-grant college system that continues to receive substantial federal support, especially for its agricultural extension activities. The federal government also runs or supports several of its own institutions of higher education—the service academies, Gallaudet College (for the deaf), and Howard University. In addition to the direct funding of nearly eighty colleges and universities, the federal government provides substantial indirect support for almost every college and university in the United States.

The major form of indirect federal subsidy for colleges and universities comes through funding individual students. These funding programs obviously benefit students directly, but without the federal funds many students could not attend college and many colleges might close. A variety of federal programs have aided college students. The largest has been the GI Bill, enabling veterans of World War II, Korea, and, to a lesser extent, Vietnam and the Gulf War to attend college with the government paying virtually all the costs. For nonveterans, one of the largest programs of student aid was also justified as a defense program—the National Defense Education Act. Passed in 1958, soon after the Soviet Union launched *Sputnik I,* this act was intended to help the United States catch up in science, although students in the social sciences and foreign languages benefited as well.

Federal assistance began to reach beyond defense-related concerns during the 1960s and 1970s. The college work-study program was adopted as part of the Johnson administration's War on Poverty but was moved from the Office of Economic Opportunity to the Office of Education and began to benefit a wider range of students. Likewise, the Education Amendments of 1972 instituted something approaching a minimum income for college students. The Basic Educational Opportunity Grant (or Pell grants), the centerpiece of the program, gave students $1,800 minus what the student's family could be expected to contribute, a figure later increased slightly to account for inflation. While this was not much money if the student wanted to attend Harvard or Yale, it provided the means to attend at least some institution of higher education. In the 1990s Pell grants have been subject to considerably stricter eligibility requirements and lower levels of funding per student.

The federal government also assists students by guaranteeing student loans (Stafford loans) and even providing some student loans for very low-income students (Perkins loans). The guaranteed loans are particularly important because they permit government to leverage a great deal of private money for students in higher education with minimal direct federal outlays. The federal government agrees to guarantee a private lending institution that the money the institution lends a student will be repaid even if the student reneges—as many have done. In turn, the money is offered to the student at a lower interest rate than would otherwise be available and repayment does not have to begin until after the student leaves higher education. The failure of many students to repay their loans and the fraudulent use of the loans by some trade schools (whose students are also eligible for loans) have brought this program into question, but it remains a major source of funding for students in higher education; some 5.1 million received some benefit from the guaranteed loan program in 1996, with an average loan of $3,690.

All these programs primarily benefit students entering college just out of high school. One federal program, however, benefits more mature students. Provisions of the income tax code that provide students deductions if they go to school to maintain or improve their job skills support a variety of trade and technical schools as well as academic institutions. For colleges and universities, the tax program stimulates attendance, especially among a segment of the population that might not otherwise attend college, although the university never sees the money. The 1997 tax act permits parents to develop educational savings accounts for future expenses and provides some limited tax deductions for tuition payments made by lower- and middle-income parents. The benefits are rather small in comparison to rising tuition costs, but they do provide parents some relief.

Finally, the federal government supports higher education in other, indirect ways—for example, by providing aid for facilities through the Higher Education Facilities Act of 1963 and for dormitories through the Department of Housing and Urban Development. Federal research money (almost $13 billion in 1996) helps institutions of higher education meet both direct and indirect costs, and there are specialized federal grant programs for such fields as public service and urban studies. In short, the federal government has become central to the maintenance of American higher education as it has developed in the late twentieth century.

The large amounts of federal money invested in higher education give the federal government a substantial amount of control over the policies of the universities. This has been manifested primarily through efforts to promote the hiring of women and members of minority groups as faculty members. In the *Grove City College* case,[18] however, the Supreme Court diminished the influence of the federal government to some degree in ensuring greater equality in higher education programs. Before that decision, if a college was found to be discriminating, all its federal money could be with-drawn. In its 1984 ruling the Court found that only money directly support-ing the activity in which the discrimination occurred could be withdrawn. So, for example, if discrimination was found in the programs covered by Title IX (athletics and student activities), the government could not with-draw money from student support or from federal research grants. Given the generally conservative policies of the Bush administration, discrimina-tion was not pursued vigorously either by the Department of Education or the Department of Justice. In fact, one member of the administration argued against scholarships being given on the basis of race to needy students even in private institutions, although he was forced to recant. Later the adminis-tration offered a moderate plan to eliminate most race-specific scholarship aid.[19]

This conservative policy thrust was to some extent modified by the Clinton administration, which supported a more vigorous program of af-firmative action and attempts to improve the status of minority populations. Those intentions of the administration were in some ways voided when the Supreme Court overturned practices promoting admission and scholarships awarded on the basis of race.[20] This decision has required universities to re-think how they cope with achieving greater diversity in their student bodies without the assistance of large numbers of dedicated scholarships.

Funding for Higher Education

Since 1980 federal funding for students in higher education has not fared well. The Reagan administration cut back on federal support, reducing the base level of the Pell grant by $80 and tightening the income restrictions; this resulted in approximately 100,000 fewer Pell grant recipients in 1983 than in 1981. There was also a drop of some 460,000 in the number of new guaranteed student loans. There were reductions in federal funding of social science and humanities research through cuts in the budgets of the National Science Foundation and the National Endowment for the Humanities. Clearly the policy of the Reagan administration was that higher education is primarily a state and local government function, if government is to be in-volved at all, and that the federal government should be only minimally in-volved.

The general commitment of the Bush administration to education was manifested in a somewhat more supportive attitude, but it only slightly in-creased funding for programs such as the National Science Foundation. Edu-cation was claimed to be a central priority in the Bush administration, al-though federal funding was only slightly improved over that in the Reagan administration.[21] The Clinton administration has reversed that trend some-what, but it had to face severe budget restraints while attempting to fund a variety of other policy priorities such as welfare and health-care reform. The Clinton budget for education has sought to increase the level of direct federal support for higher education and to provide more money for current and prospective students. One of the more creative of these efforts has been the "Americorps" program, which provides scholarship money for students who spend several years in service positions. They receive small salaries while in those positions, but a good deal of the reward for participation comes when they go on to pursue educational opportunities.

Elementary and Secondary Education

The role of the federal government in secondary and elementary education has been less significant historically and is less significant today than its involvement in higher education. However, there is definitely a federal role in precollegiate education. Other than the planning provisions of the Northwest Ordinance, the first involvement of the federal government in elementary and secondary education resulted from the passage of the Smith-Hughes Act (1917), which made funds available for vocational education. In the 1930s surplus commodities and money were provided to school districts for hot lunch programs, and those programs were expanded during the War on Poverty to include breakfasts for children from poor families. Then the Lanham Act of 1940 made federal funds available to schools in "federally impacted areas," which was understood to mean areas with large numbers of government employees and especially areas in which tax-exempt government properties reduced the tax base used to fund education. In 1958 the National Defense Education Act authorized funds to improve science, mathematics, and foreign language teaching in the elementary and secondary schools as well as at the college level.

The major involvement of the federal government in elementary and secondary education currently is through the Elementary and Secondary Education Act of 1965. This act was the culmination of efforts of a number of education and labor groups to secure more extensive federal funding for education.[22] This legislation was passed along with a number of other social and educational programs during the Johnson administration, and like so much of that legislation, it could not have been passed without the substantial legislative skills of Lyndon Johnson and the memory of John Kennedy. But before it could become law, legislators had to remove the barriers that had blocked previous attempts at federal aid to education.

One of these barriers was the general belief that education should be controlled locally. The federal aid that had already been given to schools had been peripheral to the principal teaching functions of the schools—the exception being the National Defense Education Act—in the belief that such aid should not influence what was taught in the classroom. The Elementary and Secondary Education Act (ESEA) involved direct, general subsidies for education, and it was feared that this would influence what was taught. But, as the federal government was already becoming increasingly involved in many aspects of education and social life through other mechanisms, such as the courts, this fear of federal control diminished.

Another issue that arose about federal subsidies to education was the availability of funds for parochial schools. Any aid of that sort involved constitutional questions about the separation of church and state. Most Protestant groups opposed aid to parochial schools as a violation of that separation, while Catholic groups opposed any federal aid to education that did not provide assistance to parochial schools. ESEA funds eventually went to parochial as well as public schools, although the money could not be spent for teaching religious subjects. The legislation specified that the federal money was to go to the students, not to the schools directly, which helped defuse any significant criticism based on separation of church and state.

Federal aid to education also encountered opposition prior to the 1965 act because of the possibility that the money might be used by segregated school systems in the South. The passage of the Civil Rights Act of 1964 had already prohibited using federal funds in any program that discriminated on the basis of race. This provision meant that this issue was largely decided by the time the 1965 legislation was considered. On the other side, southern school systems had been afraid that federal subsidies would be used to enforce desegregation, using a carrot instead of a stick. However, these school systems were already under pressure from the courts to desegregate, and so accepting ESEA money was a minor additional step toward their eventual desegregation.

The 1965 ESEA legislation was part of the War on Poverty, but as implemented it provided assistance to almost all school districts in the United States; only 5 percent of all school districts in the country received no ESEA money.[23] The legislation provided funds for hiring teachers' aides, stocking libraries, purchasing audiovisual materials, and developing compensatory programs. The basic intention of the program was to enable students from poor families to perform better in school and to learn to compete more effectively in the labor market. Federal funds from ESEA were allocated to the states according to a formula, as is true of a number of federal programs. The formula adopted for ESEA in 1965 allocated to each state federal funds equal to one-half of its annual per pupil educational expenditure multiplied by the number of low-income children. These funds were to be used for remedial programs (Title I) and to purchase materials, but the principal policymaking and programming came from the federal government rather than from the local school boards. The 1965 formula aided high-income states more than low-income states, as it was based on the amount of money already being spent, and so it quickly came under attack and was amended in 1967 to provide greater assistance to the poorer states. Under the new formula, a state received half of its own per pupil expenditures or half of the national mean per pupil expenditure, whichever was higher. Also, the definition of low-income students was eased so that school districts could claim more students and receive more federal funding. The 1967 amendments equalized funding between richer and poorer states and produced rapid increases in ESEA expenditures.

During the Nixon administration the categorical nature of the funds allocated through ESEA came under severe attack, as a part of the "new federalism."[24] Efforts to convert ESEA funding into another of the block grants that characterized that administration's approach to federal grants did not succeed, however, and the federal government retained nominal control over the ways in which money was to be spent. What did change was the formula for computing aid. In 1974 a new formula was adopted that put both rich and poor states at a disadvantage, as measured by their per pupil expenditures. That formula narrowed the range of allowable per pupil grant funds from 80 to 120 percent of the national mean. In other words, the very wealthy states could claim only 120 percent of the national average per low-income pupil when computing aid, while the very poor states could claim only 80 percent of the national average (not the national average). And instead of receiving 50 percent of the per pupil figure, the states could receive only 40 percent. These changes reduced the amount a state would probably receive from ESEA funding, although amendments to the legislation did specify that no state would receive less than 85 percent of what it had received under the previous formula.

As with so many public programs, implementation was crucial to the success of the ESEA programs. And in many ways ESEA represents a classic example of a program being modified through implementation. The U.S. Office of Education, which was charged with implementing ESEA, was quite passive in ensuring the attainment of the stated goal of the program: equalization of educational opportunity for economically deprived children. The tendency of those who implemented the program at the state and local levels was to pork-barrel the funds, spreading them around among all school districts regardless of the concentration of low-income students. As a result, wealthier suburban school districts used ESEA funds to purchase expensive "frills," while many inner-city and rural school districts still lacked basic materials and programs that might compensate for the poorer backgrounds of the pupils.[25]

The initial failure in implementation of ESEA resulted in part from the close ties between the U.S. Office of Education and local school districts and in part from the misinterpretation of the intention of Congress, which had

First Lady Hillary Clinton visits a Harlem elementary school to highlight a program aimed at developing after-school programs for children in need. (Reuters/ Brad Rickerby/Archive Photos)

established the program not as general assistance to education, but strictly as a compensatory program. With some changes in the Office of Education and greater concern about the use of the funds, the implementation of ESEA has been improved, although a number of questions remain about the ways in which the funds are being used. The Title I money—or that portion of the program that is most directly compensatory (now part of the Compensatory Education Program)—is now targeted more clearly on the poorer districts, but money available under other provisions of the act is widely distributed and used by wealthier schools and school districts to supplement their programs.

In addition to its impact on education through its spending programs, the federal government also has a substantial impact through numerous regulations and mandates. Among the most important of the legal mandates is the Education for All Handicapped Children Act of 1975, which mandated that all handicapped or "exceptional" students be educated in a manner suitable to their special needs. This legislation was intended primarily to as-

335

sist children with learning disabilities and physical handicaps in receiving education through the public schools. The meaning of the act, however, has been extended to include educationally gifted children, so that school districts are now required to provide a variety of special programs for a variety of different students. Bilingual education has also been mandated in some circumstances for minority students. All of these programs add to the costs of providing public education but impose most of the costs on state and local governments.

Has all this federal aid to education and regulation of education really improved the quality of American education? There is some evidence that ESEA Title I reading programs have been successful in raising the reading levels of low-income students.[26] Further, to the extent that additional funding can aid education in any number of ways, some of which are difficult to quantify, these programs have certainly produced benefits. It is ironic, however, that in spite of all the federal money directed at it (more than $11 billion in 1994), the issue of the quality of American education has been as prominent in the 1990s as at any time since the launching of *Sputnik I* in 1957. As was true then, much of the concern centers on education in science, mathematics, and engineering. The difference is that in the 1990s the perceived need has been to improve competitiveness with the Japanese and West Europeans rather than to protect the country against a Soviet military threat. In that competition, there is a strong sense that education is failing and that the American workforce is decreasingly capable of competing. Some of the blame for these failures is placed on families that do not nurture students sufficiently, and some on the students themselves, but a great deal of the blame is directed at the public schools.

Issues of Educational Policy

Even with the victory of advocates of federal funding for elementary and secondary education, a number of problems remain in public education, and some new ones are arising. In general, the public schools and their teachers have lost some of the respect with which they were traditionally regarded, and educational policy has been the subject of more heated discussion than was true during most of our history. In fact, it has not been uncommon for politicians or analysts in the 1990s to charge that the public schools have failed and to call for significant change. President Bush's program for improving the schools was but one statement of this sentiment. Some would counter this argument by pointing out that it is perhaps not that the schools have failed but that too much has been demanded of them and that the schools cannot be expected to solve all of the society's problems. These analysts would argue that the resources and tasks given the schools have not been equal and that too much has been expected for too little money. Several specific issues illustrate both sides of this argument, but what may be most important is that education, which has been regarded as one of the great success stories of American public policy, is no longer considered quite so successful.

Quality of Education

One common complaint against the schools that has continued since the 1950s is that "Johnny can't read"—that is, that the schools are failing in their fundamental task of teaching basic skills such as reading, writing, and computation. In addition to reading, this criticism has extended to progressive teaching techniques such as the "new math." Substantial evidence that would appear to support this point includes the decline of SAT scores since the early 1960s (see table 12.4). It should be noted, however, that an increasing proportion of high school students were taking the SATs in the early 1980s, so the reduction in scores may reflect to some degree the performance of a number of students who were not intending to go to college but who were required to take the test solely to judge the quality of their education. Test scores since the early 1980s registered small changes up and down, but in the late 1990s an upward turn in scores gave rise to some sense that perhaps investments in education, and some school reforms, were beginning to have a real impact on the quality of education.

The complaint about the schools' failure to teach basic skills can be contrasted to the complaints of other critics who regard the existing educational system as excessively rigid and stultifying. These critics believe that public schools destroy the innate creativity of children; they would prefer

TABLE 12.4

SCHOLASTIC ACHIEVEMENT TEST SCORES

	Verbal	*Mathematics*
1967	543	516
1970	537	512
1975	512	498
1980	502	492
1985	509	500
1990	500	501
1993	500	503
1994	499	504
1995	504	506
1996	505	508

more "open" education with fewer rigid requirements and greater emphasis on creativity and expression. Other critics believe that the existing public schools are excessively rigid in teaching a single class or racial perception of the world, instead of providing a broader perspective on the human experience. They demand a broader curriculum, or perhaps different schools for minority children. Quality in education, therefore, is not a self-evident attribute but may have definite class and racial components, and it may include creativity as well as the ability to solve math problems.[27]

Even if the school systems were doing a good job for the majority of students, they still might not be doing a good job for disadvantaged students. Those students have a number of special needs that are not met through many conventional classrooms. Title I of the Elementary and Secondary Education Act sought to meet those needs, but its widespread distribution and uncertainty about methodologies has limited its success.[28] When ESEA was reauthorized in 1994, a number of suggestions were made for making the program more effective at producing change for poor students. Unfortunately for those goals, it will be difficult to keep this act from distributing funds as widely as it has in the past, given the tendency of Congress to convert any legislation possible into "pork-barrel" programs.

Vouchers and "Choice"

While the various complaints about education sometimes appear worlds apart, they have in common a desire to modify the type of education offered through the public schools. One way to respond to these complaints is to decentralize the school system. This is in the tradition of local control over education but merely alters the definition of what the appropriate local area is. In New York City the conflict between parents in Ocean Hill–Brownsville and the city's public schools represented one of the most explosive events of this movement. Later, Chicago and then Milwaukee decentralized much of their school systems to the individual school level, giving parents a great deal of direct managerial authority over teachers and curriculum. These experiments in local control have been judged by many to be successes, but for most pressing problems in public education decentralization may not be the answer in all situations.[29] If a local school does not have the right leadership (professional and parental) it may be disastrous to decentralize.[30]

Related to the idea of decentralization of public schools is the possibility of choice among schools within a given school system. In almost any school system some schools have the reputation, and perhaps the reality, of being better than others. These schools are often in middle-class neighborhoods, with parents who place pressure on the school board, principal, and teachers for high-quality education. Some school systems also utilize magnet (specialized or selective) schools to promote educational quality and to achieve racial integration. One solution to general problems of quality in education is to allow any student in a public school system to attend any school in the system. This proposal creates something approaching the market system implied in voucher plans (discussed later in this chapter) but keeps all the funds in the public school system.

A more common policy option proposed to address the problem of quality education is the use of educational vouchers.[31] The voucher plan would give each parent a "check" equal to some specified amount of money but good only for education. The parents could spend that voucher either in the public schools, where it would pay the entire cost of the child's education, or at some other school where the voucher might not cover the entire cost and the parents would have to spend some of their own money. Under the voucher plan, parents would have significantly greater control over the kind of education their children would receive: they could choose an open school, a fundamental school stressing basic skills and discipline, a religiously oriented school, or any other school that met state standards. One voucher or choice program implemented in Milwaukee was specifically targeted for low-income students and did not require additional parental funds.[32]

The idea of educational vouchers has been around for several decades, but it received a large boost from the work of John Chubb and Terry Moe, published by the Brookings Institution.[33] These scholars argued that the fundamental problem with public education was organizational; schools and school systems were too bureaucratic to provide good education. They argued that the only way to remedy that problem was to create competition and choice for parents and students. Although Chubb and Moe argued that they would not be necessary, vouchers came to be considered a part of their proposed reforms. The Bush administration's advocacy of choice in education placed voucher plans in the center of the debate over improving American education.

More recently the Republicans in Congress have been placing a great deal of emphasis on vouchers as a means of improving education, in particular for students in the District of Columbia. In April 1998 they proposed giving a limited number (2,000 of 78,000 students) vouchers to attend private or suburban schools. The logic was that the financially strapped schools in the nation's capital are among the worst-performing schools in the United States and children should be given the opportunity to escape them. President Clinton responded by arguing that this proposal would only divert needed money from the public schools, and he promised to veto the legislation.[34]

Although the voucher plan is appealing as a means of improving choice in education and thereby improving education, a number of questions have been raised.[35] Perhaps the most fundamental question is whether the voucher plan would increase stratification in education; one of the fundamental virtues and goals of American education, after all, has been its promotion of social homogeneity and integration. If a voucher plan did not cover the full price of a child's education, many low-income parents would not be able to make up the difference between the value of the voucher and the tuition of private schools, especially the better private schools. The voucher plan might therefore only subsidize the tuition costs of middle-class parents and not improve the quality of education for the poor, who need that improvement the most—plans like that in Milwaukee are an obvious exception. In fact, the voucher plan might well undo the racial integration that resulted from years of effort and policymaking. All these questions are reinforced by the Coleman report and numerous other studies of education pointing out that the home background of children is crucial to educational success.[36] A voucher plan would tend to benefit children who would probably succeed anyway, and it might divert funds from schools and children who need the most help.

Also, although the educational vouchers could be used only for schools that met established state standards, there are still questions about the propriety of spending public money for education over which the state has no control and about the possibility that the voucher system might actually lower the quality of education. It is not entirely clear where the capital —both human and physical—required to implement this reform of the education system would come from. As a consequence, a full-scale voucher plan might result in the formation of a number of small and inadequate schools, none of them providing the quality of education that could be offered by large, comprehensive public schools. It may be that education is a service that is not amenable to market logic and competition.

The idea of the voucher plan is, however, often justified by market ideology. Some analysts think that the introduction of competition into the education marketplace would improve the quality of education by increasing the choices available to consumers and by placing competitive pressures for improvement on existing public schools. For this education marketplace to function effectively, however, the consumer must have access to information about the "product" being offered. This may be difficult if a number of new schools are started in response to a voucher plan. After all, even in established systems of public and private education, it is difficult to assess quality, especially because much of the difference in educational success of students is accounted for by family backgrounds, and much of the effect of education may not be evident until far in the future.

"Charter schools" are a means of providing choice more on a collective than an individual basis. Charter schools are organized by parents or by providers as a means of opting out of the local schools, albeit with local government support.[37] Many states have passed legislation providing for funding for these schools provided they meet standards for accreditation.

Finally, schemes to provide "tuition tax credits" for parents sending their children to private schools are similar to vouchers. These credits were actively supported by the Reagan administration as a means of providing better education and education in line with the "cultural and moral values" of the parents, and the proposals surfaced several times in the Bush administration and again in the 1997–98 Republican Congress. The credits would provide tax credits for tuition paid to a private school (up to some maximum amount). The political, and educational, arguments for tuition tax credits are similar to those for vouchers. They would promote greater pluralism in education and allow parents greater choice. In addition, as many minority students have performed better in private (especially Roman Catholic) schools, this program could be of substantial benefit to minorities.

Those opposed to tuition tax credits, such as the National Education Association, the Parent-Teacher Association, and the American Federation of Teachers, argue that these tax credits would only undermine public education and create a two-class educational system. Even though some minority students seem to do better in private schools, their parents must still have the means of paying any tuition over the specified amount of the tax credit, so the students who benefit would be middle-class students, who may not need the assistance. Finally, programs such as this that would tend to benefit parochial and other religiously based schools raise the continuing question of the separation of church and state in education.

Thus, while few educators or policy analysts would claim that education is currently what most citizens want it to be, it is not entirely clear that a voucher plan, or other plans promoting choice, would improve it all that much. The benefits of the voucher plan may be as much psychological as real: it would appear to offer parents more choices and to allow them greater control over their children's education, although the effects on the general quality of education may be difficult to discern. This is especially true if one effect of the programs is to siphon significant amounts of money away from public education to private schools. For most students, the effect of "choice" would be less money for their public schools to spend and likely, therefore, poorer quality education.

Competency Testing

Another means of addressing issues of educational quality is competency testing,[38] which is intended to address claims that students are being promoted who have not mastered the material required at each grade level, that they are being promoted simply to get them through the school system, and that students who cannot read and write are graduating from high school.

Competency testing would require a student to pass a test on basic educational skills—reading, writing, and computation—before being awarded a high school diploma. This program is intended to ensure that at least minimal standards of quality are enforced. Advocates of competency testing also argue that it would provide more incentives for students to learn and for teachers to teach.

Although many leaders of minority communities have argued that the public schools do not adequately prepare minority students, they have not been supporters of competency testing. The program has been attacked as racist, however, because a disproportionate share of the students who fail the tests in states where such programs are in operation (most notably in Florida) are nonwhite. These competency tests, now being challenged in the courts, are said to be biased against nonwhites because the tests employ standard English and are based on values and concepts that are derived from white middle-class culture and thinking. The tests are, at best, a minimal demonstration of educational quality. The low scores on the tests are, however, indicative of the concern over the poor quality of education being offered some students.

The federal government has been an advocate of various forms of competency testing for the public schools. It has supported the National Assessment of Educational Progress, a test given in the fourth, eighth, and eleventh grades, for twenty years.[39] In addition, the Bush administration's 1991 proposals for improving education were based heavily on the efficacy of standardized testing and something close to a national curriculum. The proposed tests would not prevent a student from graduating from high school, but they could be used to compare student performance so that, in essence, poor performers might as well not have graduated in the eyes of prospective employers. These tests are also intended to provide parents and taxpayers with a measure of the effectiveness of their schools that could be used to generate political pressures on poorly performing school systems. More recently the Clinton administration has also stressed national testing as a means of promoting educational quality, while Republicans have tended to oppose it, favoring more decentralized forms of accountability.[40]

Even without national testing, or the use of standardized testing as a means of determining whether a student can graduate, educational testing has become an issue in education. On the one hand parents and state legislatures want some way to hold teachers and educational officials accountable for their activities. They argue that standardized tests offer a means of seeing if their schools are doing a good job and, if not, trying to find out why. On the other hand, critics argue that students are already spending too much time on these tests, to the detriment of other types of learning. For example, eighth-graders in thirty-nine states will take some state-wide tests, as will eleventh graders in thirty-five states.[41] Further, some critics charge that teachers now teach to have students do well on the tests, rather than to give them the skills they will need in future life. As these issues continue to be fought out in Washington, they make it clear that education has become an important topic of national politics, not just a local issue.

Testing Teacher Competence

In addition to testing the quality of the product of the schools—the students—a number of reformers in education have argued that the producers—the teachers—should also be tested. The tradition in education had been that once a teacher graduated from a school of education he or she would be given a certificate, usually renewable after additional coursework, and he or she would soon receive tenure and could then teach for life. Numerous parents and education experts thought that the traditional system was insufficient to guarantee that teachers could indeed educate students effectively. The teacher-testing policy is widely supported by the public (85 percent in one poll), and some form of competency testing for teachers has been adopted in forty-four states.

Initial scores on the teachers' tests appeared to justify the arguments from the critics of the existing educational system. In several southern states, only about half the teachers who took a test passed it the first time. As the testing became more general across the United States, the failure rate has dropped significantly, and testing has become a standard part of the certification process for new teachers. Even though it is now widely used, there are still a number of complaints about the use of testing. First, just as for pupil competency testing, it is argued that the tests are discriminatory; indeed, a much higher proportion of nonwhites fail the test than do whites. Also, teachers' unions argue that the tests—especially if given to established classroom teachers—do not adequately measure all the things a teacher must do to be effective. Finally, testing is seen as just one more hurdle that can keep teachers out of the classroom where they are needed.

Competency testing itself certainly cannot guarantee a supply of good teachers in the United States. There appear to be other problems. One is low teachers' salaries, a problem that the Reagan administration identified as a major part of its efforts to improve education. Another problem is the declining interest in teaching among young women. Once the major source of talent in elementary and secondary education, young women now have numerous other, more lucrative, careers open to them. Another problem is the working conditions found in many schools, especially problems of discipline and personal safety.[42] Finally, teachers no longer appear to command the respect that they traditionally had in American society, and many of the psychic rewards of teaching are gone for much of the teaching profession. Un-

343

less the public schools can attract enough qualified and dedicated teachers, all the other reforms in educational policy may be to little avail.

School Facilities

Americans are fond of saying they will do anything for their children, but an impartial observer walking into many of America's schools would have to doubt the sincerity of those statements. Many American schools look dilapidated and appear to be unlikely places in which to find excellence in education. The General Accounting Office conducted a survey concluding that one school in three in the country was inadequate, and almost six in ten had at least one inadequate feature, such as a leaking roof.[43] There were, however, marked differences (see table 12.5) across the country in the condition of school buildings, for half of the school buildings in the District of Columbia were labeled inadequate, while less than 19 percent of school buildings in Iowa were found to be so. In the District of Columbia, 91.1 percent of schools had at least one inadequate feature, compared to only 37 percent of

TABLE 12.5

INADEQUATE SCHOOL BUILDINGS, BY STATE,

1995 (IN PERCENTAGES)

A. School buildings

Least		Most	
Iowa	18.8	District of Columbia	49.3
New Jersey	19.1	Alaska	44.6
Montana	20.4	Washington	44.2
South Dakota	21.3	California	42.9
Vermont	21.4	Arizona	40.8

B. Building features

Least		Most	
Georgia	37.2	District of Columbia	91.1
Nevada	41.8	Ohio	76.1
Arkansas	41.9	Massachusetts	75.0
Pennsylvania	41.9	California	70.8
Nebraska	44.5	Delaware	69.5

SOURCE: General Accounting Office, *School Facilities: America's Schools Report Differing Conditions*, GAO/HEHS-96-103 (Washington, D.C.: GAO, June 1996).

schools in Georgia. In addition to the variations by state, there are intra-state differences, with inner cities having generally worse school facilities.

In 1998 President Clinton began to press a national campaign to improve the quality of the facilities available to school children.[44] The federal government already had begun to be involved with school building issues through a number of mandates, especially access for the disabled. The president argued that there was a pressing need to improve facilities, in some cases for basic safety and in many others to ensure that students had a positive learning environment. This campaign produced a number of favorable public relations events for the administration, and although the Republican Congress refused to provide funds for this purpose in the 1998 budget agreement, it may yet produce some real improvements in facilities. In the concern for facilities it is important to remember that schools now need a range of electronic equipment and access if they are to be adequate for the task of educating for the emerging economy and society.

The Separation of Church and State

The First Amendment to the Constitution both forbids the establishment of a religion and ensures the free exercise of religion. In public education, these two clauses have caused a number of controversies about education and government's role in education. The two clauses may, in fact, be interpreted as being in conflict. For example, if schools require a prayer, this is deemed an establishment of religion.[45] Conversely, prohibiting prayer is seen by some as a limitation on the free exercise of religion.

Questions about the separation of church and state in education arise over two areas. The first is the issue of school prayer. Since 1962, when the Supreme Court outlawed official school prayer, there have been attempts on the part of religious groups to have prayer returned to the schools, either through a constitutional amendment permitting prayer or through mechanisms such as silent meditation and voluntary attendance at prayers. The issue of prayer in school resurfaced in 1984 when a Reagan administration proposal directed at improving the quality of American education contained a provision allowing local school boards to permit a moment of silent meditation at the beginning of the school day; this was presumed to promote discipline as well as moral education. When individual states have attempted to impose such plans, they have been struck down by the Supreme Court.[46] In 1990 the Court did, however, permit religious groups formed by students to use school facilities for their meetings after school hours, and this may be an entering wedge for greater use of the public schools for religious exercises.[47]

If the Supreme Court followed election returns, the justices would have sided with President Reagan, President Bush, and their fundamentalist supporters on the issue of school prayer. Large majorities of the American population have expressed opinions in favor of permitting prayer in schools. As with many other issues, elite groups tend to be more sensitive to the civil liberties issues involved in school prayer, and attempts at passing a school-prayer amendment in Congress have been unsuccessful. The usual tactic has been to block consideration of the issue by procedural mechanisms rather than by a vote that would make it clear to constituents how congressmen felt about school prayer.

The second area of controversy concerning the separation of church and state is public support for religious schools. In deciding this issue, the Supreme Court has been forced to make a number of difficult decisions, but over the years it has been tending to allow greater public support for religious education. For example, in 1930 the Court upheld the right of states to provide textbooks to children in parochial schools on the same basis as books are provided to students in public schools.[48] In 1947 the Court upheld bus transportation for parochial school students at public expense. Both rulings were upheld on the grounds that these expenditures benefited the students, not the church.[49]

In contrast, in 1971 the Court struck down a Pennsylvania law that had the state pay part of parochial school teachers' salaries, arguing that this was of direct benefit to the church and created excessive entanglement between church and state.[50] The Court has permitted states to provide teachers for exceptional students in parochial schools, but not on the premises of these schools. In a somewhat contradictory fashion, the Court in 1976 upheld general grants of public money to church-affiliated colleges.[51] Most recently, the Court has ruled that the State of New York violated the separation principle by creating a school district that served only the disabled children of a Hasidic Jewish sect that did not want its children to attend public schools.[52]

The reasoning behind all these decisions may appear tortuous, but three principles do stand out. The first is that aid to students and their families is more acceptable than aid to institutions. Second, institutions of higher education are permitted more entanglement between church and state than are elementary and secondary schools. Finally, the public sector should not have to spend additional money on education because of the special religious demands of a group, but neither should it impose additional financial burdens on the religious groups.

Unionization and Management

The image of the American "schoolmarm" is ingrained in the popular mind. Leaving aside any sexist stereotypes about all elementary and secondary schoolteachers being female, the point here is that the popular image of the schoolteacher has been a positive one. The image was that of a person dedicated to education and to her students, even in the face of adverse circumstances. The teacher and the school were considered integral parts of the American community.

The image of the teacher is now changing, partly because of increasing unionization and a growing number of teachers' strikes.[53] No longer the representatives of culture and learning in small towns, teachers are now more likely to be employed by large school districts and to be members of an organization that bargains collectively for improved wages and benefits. One of the two major teachers' organizations is the American Federation of Teachers, which is affiliated with the AFL-CIO. This organization is clearly a union and has been quite willing to employ the strike weapon in its dealings with school districts. The second major teachers' organization, the National Education Association, is a professional organization, but its local chapters operate as collective bargaining units. The NEA has been more reluctant to use the strike to gain its ends, although certainly a number of its local chapters have struck. As of 1993 approximately 73 percent of the teachers in the United States were members of these organizations or of local teachers' unions. In almost any year there will be several hundred strikes by public school teachers. The sight of teachers picketing and of children out of school until October and even November has changed the once-positive image of the teacher. As local government budgets have been squeezed in the 1990s, there have been demands for more students in each classroom and less money for raises, and the teacher's strike has become an even more common phenomenon.

In addition to forcing parents to make arrangements for their children during strikes, labor unrest in education has other, more important consequences. We have mentioned that many Americans believe that the quality of American education is not as high as it should be. The sight of educators on strike tends to erode the public image of education even further. Of course, those who favor the more militant actions by teachers quite rightly point out that good teachers will not work for the salaries they are sometimes offered and that fewer good students will be attracted into careers in teaching. There are, however, still important problems of symbolism and public image when teachers go on the picket line.

Equalization of Resources

As mentioned earlier in this chapter, most public education is financed by local property taxes, and this basis of finance can produce substantial inequities in education. Local school districts with poor resource bases must either tax their poorer constituents more heavily or, more commonly, provide inferior education to the district's children.[54] Further, given that poorer school districts frequently have concentrations of minority-group families, this form of education finance also affects racial and cultural integration and the perceived fairness of government. These inequalities in educational opportunity may, in turn, perpetuate racial differences in economic and social opportunities.

Reliance on the local property tax to finance public schools has been challenged successfully in the courts. In two early cases the courts have entered this policy area, but they have not provided any definite answers to the questions involved. In *Serrano* v. *Priest* (1971), the California Supreme Court ruled that the great economic disparity between school districts in the Los Angeles area violated provisions of both the state and the federal constitutions. In particular, this disparity constituted a denial of equal protection for the residents of the poorer districts. The court did not, however, make any direct recommendations on how this disparity could be ameliorated to meet constitutional standards. One common assumption was that the state might have to either take over educational finance entirely or alter the formula for distributing state equalization payments.

In a similar case, *San Antonio School District* v. *Rodriquez* (1973), the U.S. Supreme Court ruled that the differences between two school districts in Texas were not so great as to constitute a violation of the equal protection clause. The Court did not say how much of a difference would constitute such a violation. This decision left the constitutionality of the continuation of these disparities between school districts up in the air, but the problems of local school districts attempting to provide decent education with low taxable property remained quite tangible.[55]

In the 1990s the answer to the enduring questions came when the Texas courts decided that the existing system of school finance violated the state constitution's requirements for "an efficient system for the general diffusion of knowledge." The Texas Supreme Court ordered the State of Texas to find some means of redressing the differences among its 1,044 school districts.[56] Those school districts displayed massive disparities: the 5 percent of richest school districts spent $11,801 per pupil, while the poorest 5 percent spent $3,190 per pupil.[57] The state legislature first opted for regional tax sharing, but the voters rejected this amendment to the state constitution in a referendum.[58] The final plan called for wealthier school districts to transfer some of their taxable property to poorer districts so that those poorer districts could provide a better education for their pupils.[59]

The question was settled in Texas through the courts, and it has been in the courts in seventeen other states, but this is a general problem for all fifty states.[60] Some states have begun to address questions of equality of funding for education without direct court intervention. The most important example is Michigan, which has decided to substitute a 2-percent sales tax and a tripling of the cigarette tax for the property tax as the source for educational finance. Voters were given the choice of this option or an increase in the state income tax; they chose the consumption taxes.[61] The courts did not mandate this change, but it did follow several embarrassing incidents, such as the closing of a school district in northern Michigan several months before the scheduled end of the term. The new revenue sources are statewide, and proceeds are divided according to the relative needs of the school districts. The states have a variety of mechanisms for equalizing the access to funding, and ESEA money can also be used for that purpose.[62] One state—Kentucky—that historically had one of the most unequal and least effective school systems in the country attacked this problem directly, centralizing the funding of schools, with a great deal of apparent success.[63]

Disparities in funding and quality persist across the country, however, and many children continue to receive substandard education because of the state, county, or neighborhood in which their parents happen to live. As a part of its "Goals 2000: Educate America Act," the Clinton administration has proposed some equalization funding for poorer districts.[64] This plan has been supported by many educational groups, but naturally has been opposed by both more affluent districts and by a Republican Congress that wants to preserve or enhance local control. While generally more concerned with content than with funding, congressional emphasis on local power in education does tend to preserve inequalities.

The school district in which a student lives may affect the quality of his or her education, but the state in which that school district operates may also make a difference. There are pronounced variations in the level of funding for public education by state (see table 12.6, p. 350); a student in New York has 176 percent more spent on his or her education than does a student in Mississippi. There are also substantial variations in the average salaries offered to teachers in different states; the highest average salary (Connecticut) is 96 percent higher than that in South Dakota. The relatively poor states of the South and Upper Midwest do the worst in terms of support for public education, while the industrial states of the Northeast tend to do the best.

These data illustrate that there is yet no national policy or national standard for education, and a child's life chances may depend on where he or she grows up. The differences in actual educational outcomes, however, may not be as disparate as the amounts of money being spent. Some states with very low levels of per pupil expenditure, such as Iowa, South Dakota, and Utah, actually have very good results on standardized tests such as the SAT.[65] In fact, there is actually a slight negative statistical relationship between the amount of money spent per pupil and scores on the SAT.[66] Some of this success may be attributed to relatively homogeneous populations in these states, while some of the observed outcomes may be a function of the smaller schools in rural America and the closer personal attention the pupils receive in those settings. Further, students in small rural schools do not have to cope with as much crime and social disruption as is found in urban areas where more money is spent.

TABLE 12.6

INEQUALITIES IN EDUCATIONAL FUNDING, 1996

Per pupil expenditures
National average = $4,960

High		Low	
Alaska	$10,156	Utah	$3,909
New Jersey	9,967	Mississippi	4,185
New York	9,535	Arizona	4,232
Connecticut	8,216	Arkansas	4,353
Rhode Island	7,733	Alabama	4,479

Average annual teacher salaries
National average = $37,700

High		Low	
Connecticut	$50,300	North Dakota	$27,600
Alaska	48,600	Mississippi	27,700
New York	48,100	South Dakota	28,300
New Jersey	47,900	Louisiana	28,800
Pennsylvania	46,100	Arkansas	29,300

SOURCE: Tax Foundation, *Facts and Figures on Government Finance, 1996* (Washington, D.C.: Tax Foundation, 1997).

Desegregation and Busing

Finally, we come to the issues of desegregation and busing. The important educational question here is whether the school system can be expected to solve all of society's problems or whether it should concentrate more narrowly on education. This question is frequently raised with respect to desegregation, particularly in regard to busing. The argument is that little is being done to change the underlying causes of segregation, especially segregated housing, and that the only institution in society that works under such stringent requirements for desegregation is the public school system. Frequently busing affects popular support for public education. The decline of public education after desegregation becomes a self-fulfilling prophecy as white parents either remove their children from the integrated school and send them to private school, or move their families out of the affected area. The latter move is probably more destructive because it erodes the financial basis of the schools.

The Bush administration began to remove some federal pressure for desegregation in 1992, as it joined with a Georgia school district to seek release from court-directed desegregation. The courts in general have been less active in forcing desegregation, and the Clinton administration has demonstrated no particular activism on the part of the Department of Justice or the Department of Education in pushing for new efforts at desegregation.

On the other side of the argument is the central importance of education in the formation of the values and attitudes of students. Desegregation appears to benefit black children by improving not only the quality of their education but also their own self-image. It may also be important in reducing the social isolation of white children from black children. Social integration has traditionally been one purpose of American public education, and it may be important for the society to continue to pursue that goal through desegregation. After years of fighting for an end to segregation, somewhat paradoxically some minority groups now have come to favor a resegregation of students. The advocates of separate minority schools argue that the curriculum of most public schools does not reflect the interests or needs of their community and that students can learn better without racial tensions and when taught by teachers of their own race. This resegregation may be occurring de facto, especially in northern cities, as residential patterns become increasingly segregated.[67]

The new and old issues surrounding desegregation can be, and have been, debated at length, but the issue of busing has been so emotionally charged that rational discourse is frequently impossible. The connection between educational quality and racial equality is an important one for the society that must be pursued within both policy domains.[68] Some argue that education is too central to the formation of the social fabric of the United States to be allowed to become isolated from other social concerns. However, education also may be too important in a highly technological society to be compromised in any way in an attempt to solve other social problems, and it may be that too many social responsibilities are being placed on schools and their teachers. How this debate is resolved may say a great deal about the future of American society and the American economy.

If busing is the most divisive issue in desegregating elementary and secondary schools, affirmative action policies for admission and the awarding of scholarships are its analogues at the level of higher education. Under pressure from the federal Department of Education and the Department of Justice as well as from their own state legislatures, a number of state university systems were providing preferences for minority students. In 1997, however, California and Texas courts found that the states were unlawfully discriminating on the basis of race in providing these preferences and enjoined the state universities from doing so in the future. The initial results were some reductions, albeit not so great as expected, in minority enrollments (especially in the "flagship" campuses in each system).[69] This may be just one more event in the ongoing struggle to reconcile different interpretations of the word *equality* as it applies to education and other public policies.

Conclusion

Education has been and remains a central issue in American public policy. While traditionally the concern of state and local government, it has become increasingly influenced by federal policy, in part because of education's close connection to other goals such as economic growth. But while education has been an important and highly respected public function, it is currently under attack. The quality of education, the competence of school personnel, and the place of education in social change are all topics of vital concern to many Americans. Several policy instruments have been proposed in the attempt to rectify perceived difficulties in these areas, the most commonly discussed being the voucher plan, but few initiatives in educational policy have gained wide public acceptance.

The debate over educational policy is in part a result of the absence of a widely accepted theory of causation in education. Unlike science policy, educational policy is a subject about which reasonable people often disagree radically. Voucher plans are intended in part to allow people to make individual choices concerning education without having to pay too great an economic price. The role of government as the funding agent for these programs, however, requires greater attention to the real benefits of certain forms of education and a decision about just how far the use of vouchers can be allowed to extend. This is a task for rational policy analysts who recognize that such judgments must be subjected to serious political and social scrutiny. This is especially true because education is an issue about which almost everyone has an opinion; and because the students involved are the children of those opinion-holders, there will be controversy.

13. Energy and the Environment

As it prepares to enter the twenty-first century, the United States faces two significant problems that affect the relationship between its economy and the physical world. One is a demand for energy that has become virtually insatiable and is much higher per capita than that of almost any of the other industrialized economies. The other policy problem is the need to manage the effluents of an industrialized society and to preserve as much of the natural environment as possible. These two policy areas are discussed together here, in part because they interact in several crucial ways.

First, the high consumption of energy, especially the use of fossil fuels, produces huge quantities of pollution, and the periodic shortage and high prices of petroleum and natural gas place pressures on industries to burn cheaper coal, at the cost of even higher levels of pollution. Even the transportation of fossil fuels, especially oil, presents several well-known and politically visible threats to the environment—the *Exxon Valdez* spill being one of the more infamous examples. Failure to address the energy problem with nontraditional sources will almost certainly exacerbate the environmental problem.

Also, some regulations issued by the Environmental Protection Agency to reduce pollution (e.g., emission controls on automobiles) have tended to require using more energy than would otherwise be used. Both energy and environmental issues also have a large technical and scientific element, and governments have required the development of new technologies to meet their environmental demands. Ultimately, however, changes in human behavior—including such simple ones as energy conservation and recycling—may be more important than technological change in producing improvements in the environment.

Both energy and environmental policy are also closely linked with the continuing concerns about the American economy. Uncertainty about energy supplies, including those arising from frequent political instability in the Persian Gulf, and the potential for rising energy prices make investment decisions more difficult for businesses and contribute to inflation. Likewise, critics charge that strict environmental controls make economic development projects more expensive and in some cases impossible. Contrarily, when the economy picks up, all the more pollution is produced.

Finally, both energy and environmental policies are linked increasingly to global considerations. Pollution is no longer a national question about clean water and clean air. It has taken on a pronounced international dimension with concerns about global warming, ozone depletion, transborder pollution, and decreasing biological diversity.[1] Meanwhile, as the economy is increasingly affected by international competition, the argument is being made that weaker environmental standards in other countries give them an advantage over American firms. Also, energy is an international concern not only because the United States imports so much of its energy supply but also because the immense demand of the United States and other industrialized countries tends to increase the price and to lower availability for the developing countries. This chapter examines energy and environmental problems, the responses of governments to these problems, and some possible alternative policies.

Energy: Problems and Policies

Energy is a crucial component of the American way of life. We are accustomed to using, and squandering, energy to a degree unimaginable even in other affluent industrialized societies. The large American automobile has been a symbol of that attitude toward energy usage, as is the single person driving an automobile to work each day. Car sizes tended to decrease when energy was expensive in the 1980s and early 1990s, but more recently Americans have opted for even larger and heavier vans and "sports utility vehicles." The United States consumes over 4 percent of all the energy used in the world. This country uses 90 percent more energy per capita than does Sweden, although it does use slightly less per capita than does Canada—both countries having standards of living similar to that of the United States.[2] While energy usage is related to industrialization and higher standards of living, the United States appears to use much more than required to maintain the comfortable standard of living to which most of its citizens have been accustomed.

Energy was not perceived as a problem for the United States until the 1973 OPEC (Organization of Petroleum Exporting Countries) embargo on export of oil to the United States demonstrated our dependence on imported oil.[3] The rapidly escalating price of oil that resulted from OPEC price-fixing, restricted production, and then a second embargo further emphasized the dependence of the United States on foreign oil to supplement relatively large quantities of domestic oil, natural gas, and coal. On the basis of the experiences of the 1970s, it is clear that we need seriously to examine American energy policies and probably to alter some of those policies. That policy lesson does not appear to have been learned, however, and cheaper oil in the 1980s and 1990s has produced more relaxed attitudes toward energy use. These relaxed attitudes continue even after alarms during the Iran-Iraq war and later the Gulf War. In addition, the policies of the Reagan and (especially) the Bush administrations stressed exploration and exploitation rather than conservation as the best way to eliminate energy difficulties.

Energy Sources

In spite of the importance of foreign petroleum and the American love affair with the automobile, petroleum is not the only energy source for the United States, and other available sources of energy could be more highly developed. Oil is, however, the major energy source for the United States, accounting for 43 percent of all energy consumed, a percentage that has fluctuated little in recent years. Approximately 46 percent of the oil the United States consumes is imported. A little simple arithmetic reveals that almost 20 percent of the total U.S. energy supply is imported oil.[4] Again, the total amount of oil we import has been increasing as domestic supplies have become more difficult (and expensive) to extract and as demand has continued to increase. This situation has produced political pressures to open exploration in more environmentally fragile parts of the United States, such as the Alaska Wildlife Refuge and off the Florida coast.

The reliance on imported oil produces a number of problems for the United States. First, it makes energy supplies extremely uncertain and places the American economy in the position of a hostage to foreign powers. Second, the money we pay for foreign oil goes outside the United States and is difficult to match with exports. The U.S. negative balance of payments has increased in the 1990s, which has negative consequences for the domestic economy (see chapter 8). Over 11 percent of U.S. imports are energy, without which the balance-of-payments deficit would be approximately half what it actually is.[5] Also, oil is a finite resource, and proven world reserves of oil are sufficient only for a limited number of years at current rates of consumption. This means that eventually the American economy will have to convert to some other form of energy, and continued reliance on foreign oil may only delay the hard economic, social, and technological choices we will have to make when this particular energy resource is depleted. Finally, although other energy sources pose environmental risks as well, oil is particularly hazardous in that an average of almost a million gallons of oil is spilled into the waters of the United States each year. Most oil spills are not nearly as destructive as that of the *Exxon Valdez* in Alaska, but all have some environmental consequences.

Natural Gas

The United States has been more blessed with reserves of natural gas than with petroleum. Currently, almost all natural gas used in this country comes from domestic sources. Natural gas is also a limited resource, however, with something between thirty-five and sixty years' worth of proven reserves available at current and predicted rates of consumption.[6] Therefore, natural gas does not constitute a long-term alternative for the United States. In addition, natural gas is so valuable for its industrial uses—in the fabrication of plastics and synthetic fibers, for example—that it may be inefficient to use it to heat buildings and cook meals.

Alternatives to domestically produced natural gas include importing gas in liquid form from Algeria or the former Soviet Union. These sources would extend the availability of natural gas supplies but would present the same political and economic problems as imported oil. In addition, the technology involved in transporting liquid natural gas is still being developed, and massive explosions could occur if great care were not exercised. Given the environmental difficulties already encountered with oil spills, it may not be politically acceptable to develop a new technology for transporting natural gas that may produce even greater difficulties simply to preserve an energy supply for a relatively short period.

Coal

America's most abundant energy resource is coal. The United States has enough coal to last approximately 200 years, and it exports substantial quantities of coal to Japan and to parts of Europe. In addition to supplying relatively cheap energy, coal can be used as a raw material for industrial purposes, as is natural gas. If coal usage were developed more fully, the demand for natural gas and petroleum might be reduced. Coal has several disadvantages as an energy resource, however. First, there is the environmental problem. Coal does not burn as cleanly as does oil or natural gas, and a good deal of American coal is rather high in sulfur. When this coal is burned, it forms sulfur dioxide (SO_2), which then combines with water to form sulfuric acid ($H_2 SO_4$). This is a major source of the "acid rain" that threatens forests and wildlife in the northern United States and Canada. Also, the extraction of coal presents other environmental difficulties, since much coal is most efficiently extracted by strip mining, a process that may deeply scar the landscape and render the land unusable for years. Improved methods for reclaiming strip-mined land have been developed, but this recovery still takes time and money, and the original natural landscape is lost forever.[7] Alternatively, mining coal by building tunnels presents major health and safety problems for the miners.[8]

In addition to the environmental problems it presents, coal use is limited by the lack of any technology for using coal to power automobiles or trucks. The "synfuels" project that was one component of President Carter's energy plan was intended to find a way to extract a liquid fuel from coal ("gassification"), but no such technology yet exists at a reasonable price.[9] Thus, coal can be used to generate electricity and heat, but not for transportation, which accounts for 26 percent of energy used in the United States. The development of other technologies (e.g., improved storage batteries and better electric cars) may help to expand its utility, but at present the usefulness of coal for transportation remains limited.

Finally, there are massive logistical problems in using coal as a major energy source. Coal is more difficult to transport than is petroleum or natural gas, which are readily movable through pipelines. Furthermore, at present, American railroads do not have sufficient rolling stock or suitable roadbeds to manage major increases in coal shipments, and a good deal of the available coal is located a substantial distance from the points of principal energy demand. Increased use of water transportation might help, but even that possibility would require investment in boats or barges to make greater use of coal a more practical option than it is at present.

Nuclear Power

As of 1998 the United States had 110 nuclear power plants that produced approximately 8 percent of the total energy used in this country and almost 22 percent of all electricity. In several states two-thirds of electrical power comes from nuclear power. At one time it was believed that nuclear power would meet future energy needs as, particularly with fast-breeder reactors, the supply of energy appeared almost endless. But after the near-disaster at the Three Mile Island nuclear plant in 1979, and the very real 1986 disaster at Chernobyl in the former Soviet Union, the possibility of a nuclear future appears less likely. In part this is true because, without the breeder reactor and its potential dangers, the United States must deal with a limited supply of fissionable uranium. More important, safety and environmental problems, and the very real problems of disposing of nuclear waste, have called the feasibility of nuclear power into question in the minds of the public as well as of many experts.[10]

The Three Mile Island and Chernobyl incidents pointed to the possibility that nuclear power plants might present health and safety hazards for citizens living near them and possibly even for people living hundreds of miles away. If the "China syndrome" had occurred and the reactor core had melted, the extent of damage to the health of citizens is difficult to estimate. If a nuclear power plant has no incidents of this sort, the additional radioactivity in its vicinity is indeed negligible, but there is the possibility—although advocates of the technology argue that it is remote—of a serious accident.

The accident at Chernobyl caused at least 330 deaths during the first four years after it occurred, and there are estimates of up to a half million additional deaths as a result of this one nuclear accident.[11] The American nuclear industry points to the inadequate design of the Soviet reactor and the ever safer designs available in the United States, but many Americans can see only the atomic horrors produced in the Ukraine.

Even if there were no danger of accidents, the environmental and health problems associated with nuclear waste disposal would present difficulties. Some nuclear wastes lose their radioactivity very slowly: the half life, or the time required for half the nuclear activity to be exhausted, of plutonium-239 (one of the by-products of nuclear reactors) is 24,000 years. This means that the nuclear industry (and ultimately government) must find a means of disposing of these wastes so as to prevent contamination of the environment. There are proposals for burying these wastes, but almost no one wants the facilities near their home—the NIMBY (Not-in-My-Backyard) phenomenon is very strong in this field.[12] Government must also find a means to prevent terrorists from gaining control of the radioactive material, which could constitute a powerful instrument for blackmail. The disposal of nuclear wastes presents environmental problems and potential problems in guarding large areas against possible terrorist attacks and thefts.

Finally, the construction of nuclear power plants has been so slow, and so expensive, that many electrical utilities have become frustrated and abandoned the projects. Requirements for extensive inspection and reinspection of the plants as they are built, because of the dangers of accidents and contamination, have slowed construction significantly, as have the lawsuits filed by opponents of nuclear power. Operating costs of nuclear power plants will certainly be less than those of fossil-fuel plants, but the initial capital investment and the relatively short operating life of nuclear plants (often 30 years or less) have caused many private utilities to cancel plans to build these facilities; no new plans have been initiated in almost two decades. These problems put much of the burden for energy production back on to fossil fuels, with their associated pollution and finite global supply.

The regulatory difficulties of coping with nuclear power in the United States are indicated by the long controversy over the Seabrook nuclear plant in New Hampshire.[13] The Public Service Company of New Hampshire originally announced plans to build twin reactors at Seabrook in 1972. A series of legal disputes and demonstrations, as well as rising costs, caused the cancellation of one of the reactors in 1984, even after $800 million had been spent on it. Construction of Unit 1 was completed in July 1986, but the Chernobyl accident in that year led the surrounding states and their utility companies to withdraw their cooperation in building the plant. After investing $2.1 billion in Seabrook without generating a single kilowatt, Public

Service of New Hampshire filed for bankruptcy protection in 1988. After intervention by the Reagan administration, the Nuclear Regulatory Commission (NRC) permitted testing of the plant beginning in June 1989, and on 1 March 1990, the NRC granted an operating license to the new owner, Northeast Utilities.[14] While this scenario represents the extreme case, it is little wonder that all nuclear power plants ordered since 1974 have now been cancelled.

Other Energy Sources in Use

Several other energy sources are currently being used in the United States, although none accounts for a significant percentage of total energy capacity. They include hydroelectric power, wood, and some solar and geothermal power. To date, with the exception of hydroelectric power, these have not offered much hope for rapid development, although a great deal is promised for solar power, and geothermal power (produced by the heat from natural sources in the earth) is apparently successful in Iceland and parts of Europe. Wood is perhaps our oldest power source, and it is an energy source that is renewable. But the constraints on the amount of wood available, its cost, and the pollution problems it presents limit its usefulness, in spite of a growing number of Franklin stoves and wood-burning furnaces in the northern United States.

Unconventional Energy Sources

As the problem of America's energy future has become more apparent to citizens, politicians, and scientists, a number of alternatives to fossil fuels and nuclear power have been explored. The search has been for energy sources that are renewable, clean, safe, and compatible with the American lifestyle. Of the four criteria, the last has appeared least important, as some understanding of the uniqueness of that lifestyle has begun to penetrate our collective consciousness. At present, there appear to be five major possible alternative energy sources, two of which are variations on existing power sources. These two variations are the extraction of oil from the shale found in Colorado and Wyoming, and nuclear fusion (rather than fission). The oil-shale technology, if developed, would have an immense environmental impact, much like that of strip-mined coal. Further, extracting the shale oil would produce a number of undesirable effluents in areas that are both beautiful and environmentally fragile. In addition, the extraction of oil from shale would require huge amounts of water in an area already short of water. And all of these environmental problems would produce a relatively small amount of oil, when compared with current levels of consumption and other modes of production.

Power generating windmills line a California highway, offering one of several kinds of pollution-free energy sources available to that state's electricity consumers. (AP/Wide World Photos)

The technology of fusion power is still in the beginning stages despite significant research and development expenditures. The idea of this power source is to approximate, in a laboratory or power station, the processes that produce the energy of the sun, which would require temperatures of tens of millions of degrees and the technology to create and then contain a superheated "plasma" of charged particles.[15] In other words, fusion would necessitate massive technological developments, but it might someday produce cheap and virtually limitless supplies of energy, with much less radioactivity than is caused by nuclear fission. European researchers have been able actually to produce some limited amounts of power using a fusion technique, and American researchers also have produced a brief sustained fusion.[16]

Limited amounts of solar power are also in use in the United States, heating some houses and businesses and heating water for home use. But the use of solar power to produce electricity for mass distribution ("big solar") would require technological breakthroughs as well as answers to some environmental questions. Although theoretically we have a limitless source of solar power, many areas of the United States may not receive sufficient amounts of sunlight when they need it most. For example, northern cities need energy most for heating during the winter, when they receive little sunlight; one more likely use for solar power, therefore, might be to take care of peak-loading periods caused by air-conditioning use in the summer.

The photovoltaic cell—the means of converting sunlight into electrical energy—is at present underdeveloped and inefficient. Thus, to make sufficient quantities of electricity with "big solar" projects would require large land areas devoted to solar panels, and some environmentalists might regard this as just another form of pollution. Solar power is, however, also being developed for automobiles, one of the major uses of energy in the United States. There are engineering contests for solar-powered vehicles, although none of the winners—most of them extremely small and slow—appears likely to be available in automobile showrooms any time in the foreseeable future.

There has also been a great deal of discussion about using wind power to generate electricity. The windmill, which used to dominate rural landscapes, is to many people also the symbol of the energy future. Again, like solar power, wind power is already in use in small and decentralized ways, but the unreliability of the source and the mental vision of thousands of windmills dotting the American plains and coasts have reduced the attractiveness of this alternative.[17] With the development of better means of storing electricity, wind power may become a more practical means of meeting at least some of America's future energy requirements, but in the short term it does not appear a viable alternative.

Finally, there is the possibility of using the agricultural productivity of the United States as a means of addressing energy needs. Gasohol, a combination of gasoline and methyl (wood) alcohol produced from plants, is already sold in some areas of the United States as a fuel for automobiles. The same plant material used for gasohol could be converted into methane gas and used like natural gas to heat homes. There are also a number of options for using the substantial forest reserves of the United States and the by-products of timber production, as alternative energy resources.

The production of energy from biomass has several advantages. One is that it is renewable. Use of rapidly growing plants—or agricultural by-products such as cornstalks—would have less impact on the environment than some other energy sources. The methane gas that is one usable product of the biomass process, however, has been demonstrated to be at least as much a culprit in the "greenhouse effect" as carbon dioxide. In addition, great expanses of land would have to be cultivated to produce the necessary quantities of organic material. This means of energy production has the decided advantage for Americans of producing a product that—unlike solar, wind, or fusion power—can be used to fuel automobiles. Of course, more efficient electric automobiles and storage batteries may be developed, but gasohol or even pure methanol already can be burned in a modified internal combustion engine. The technology for burning methane gas in automobiles is also being developed. Thus, biomass production may serve the American lifestyle better than other alternative forms of energy production. At present, price is a major barrier to the production of significant quantities of methanol; the price of alcohol has been higher than the price of gasoline. However, with higher and uncertain petroleum prices and increased methanol production, methanol may become a more competitive energy source.

Policy Options

Broadly speaking, there are two ways of addressing the energy problems of the United States (and the world). One strategy is conservation, or discouraging energy consumption by citizens and industry, and the other strategy is producing more energy. The conflict between these two approaches can be seen easily in the history of American energy policy following the crises over oil supplies in the 1970s. It also reflects some fundamental ideological differences in approaches to energy, with liberals tending to favor conservation and conservatives more likely to support increased production.

Conservation was the Carter administration's principal approach to the energy problem. For example, there were orders specifying the temperature range in public buildings and tax incentives for insulation and other energy-saving modifications for homes. But more than anything else, the issue of conservation was highlighted by controversies over deregulation of oil and natural gas prices, especially for so-called new oil and gas. The idea was that any gas and oil discovered after the passage of the legislation would be priced at a rate determined by the market, rather than at the controlled price of domestic oil and gas, which was then below world prices. This would allow the price of oil and gas to rise, thereby encouraging conservation. But it would also mean huge "windfall" profits for oil and gas companies. To attempt to make the impacts of decontrol more equitable across the society, a windfall profits tax on oil companies was part of the Carter energy package.

Another important aspect of the Carter approach to energy problems was the Synthetic Fuels Corporation, intended to develop substitutes for petroleum from coal and other resources. As noted earlier, this research has yet to bear fruits that are economically feasible, but still there have been some significant advances. Finally, there was to be a stockpile of petroleum—the Strategic Petroleum Reserve—that would delay the effects of any future oil embargoes on the United States. The mere mention by President Bush that this reserve could be used, for example, served to stabilize petroleum prices during the Gulf War.

The Reagan administration's approach to energy was more market and production oriented. During his 1980 campaign, candidate Reagan stressed the need for the market to deal with energy problems and condemned the Department of Energy as a "wasteful bureaucracy."[18] Reagan's first administration assumed that price deregulation would encourage the market to produce more energy and that price increases would make some energy sources (e.g., oil in old wells) profitable to exploit. Also, the administration—with the special attention of Interior Secretary James Watt—sought, largely unsuccessfully, to exploit energy resources on public lands, such as the Alaska lands "locked up" under the Carter administration. There was some leasing of federal lands for coal mining—some 16,000 acres in the Powder River Basin of Montana and Wyoming, for example—but the favorable prices offered to private coal companies when the coal market was glutted were condemned as poor resource management and as a national "fire sale." This sale was especially vulnerable to criticism because of the environmental sensitivity of the area leased. The declining price of petroleum on the international market, however, has made the planned exploitation of shale oils in equally sensitive areas of the West less attractive, and that development has ended.

The lowered price of oil had other effects on national energy policy in the 1980s. First, it facilitated the development of the Strategic Petroleum Reserve, which by January 1984 had reached 360 million barrels (almost a month's supply). Further, as shale oils became less attractive, so too did synthetic fuels, and the Synthetic Fuels Corporation had a difficult time maintaining any interest in the private sector.[19] President Reagan was successful in 1984 in having Congress rescind funding for the Synthetic Fuels Corporation.[20] Stable energy prices also made the continued deregulation of oil and natural gas feasible, with this policy continuing in the 1990s to include competition among home suppliers.

In summary, during the Reagan administration energy policy was not a major concern. Energy prices were relatively stable, and the international market had plentiful oil. Also, energy consumption in the United States declined; existing supplies and sources were more than adequate, and the market-oriented strategies of the administration were largely successful. Not surprisingly, the Bush administration continued a similar approach to energy policy. In general, President Bush pursued a policy of finding and exploiting new fossil fuel resources. In his National Energy Strategy announced in early 1991, however, Bush offered a more diversified approach to energy policy. He advocated increasing domestic oil production to 3.8 million barrels a day but also called for a research and development program on alternative energy sources such as biomass and solar power.[21] Many critics—even some in business—argued that the president did not place adequate emphasis on energy conservation.

The Clinton administration has proposed no major initiatives in energy policy. Coming to office at a time of relatively plentiful energy and bringing a host of other agenda items with him, President Clinton has invested little political capital in energy issues. His first secretary of energy, Hazel R. O'Leary, was a very visible figure, but not because of any bold initiatives in new policy. Rather, she received high marks from the public and from Washington insiders for opening numerous files on U.S. atomic testing during the height of the Cold War. These files pointed to a number of severe abuses by government, and she then set out to try to compensate the victims of some of the most egregious of those abuses.[22] Clinton's second secretary of energy, Bill Richardson, arrived at the time of the Starr report and had little chance for bold initiatives.

It once was popular to talk about the energy "crisis" in the United States, and indeed in the 1970s a crisis seemed to loom as prices soared and supplies dwindled. Those fears now appear exaggerated because energy is not an immediate problem. Yet there is reason to believe that the current halcyon period may only be a short respite from an ongoing energy problem. Supplies of fossil fuels in the world are finite. The fading of immediate problems in energy therefore provides a false sense of security and prevents the search for viable long-term energy sources. This is especially true in view of the fact that many citizens are suspicious of technological solutions (e.g., nuclear power) to energy problems. Further, the continuing dependence of the United States on foreign oil may make the economy and society hostage to forces over which we have no control. It may require yet another energy "crisis" for citizens and government to be willing to return to the active consideration of alternative energy futures for the United States.

Hard and Soft Energy Options

One of the best presentations of policy options facing the United States with respect to energy is Amory Lovins's discussion of "hard" versus "soft" energy paths.[23] Although there have been numerous criticisms of the apocalyptic conclusions reached by Lovins, his analysis of the alternative routes is important. The hard route would continue to increase energy consumption as fast as or faster than national economic growth and to rely on fossil fuels, especially coal, or on nuclear power to supply that energy. This option is both production oriented and centralized in its use of large-scale energy production and distribution, primarily through existing electrical utilities. The soft route, on the other hand, would allow energy use to grow less rapidly than national economic growth and would stress conservation. The soft route would also stress decentralized production of energy, with each family or small community having its own power source, usually of a renewable variety.

Lovins's analysis is important for several reasons. First, economic growth is often linked with energy consumption. In fact, the usual assumption has been that these two are inextricably linked, but they need not be in Lovins's decentralized vision of the future. Second, he stresses the connection between environmental issues—he is an environmental activist—and energy issues, as we have been doing here. Finally, he stresses the links between political decision making, political structures, and energy sources. He fears the centralization that might occur in politics as a result of large-scale use of nuclear power, with the attendant need to protect waste storage sites and even the power plants themselves.

The energy "crisis" implies a need to change our lifestyle so as to conserve energy, to live more frugally and with different forms of energy, or to locate additional sources of petroleum, natural gas, and uranium. Or all three. There are few clear answers to the problems posed for the country by its expanding need for energy and the eventual exhaustion of our traditional sources. Americans tend to believe that technological solutions can be found to the problems that face the country, but the application of technology has yet to make a significant dent in the continuing problems of energy.

Also, it is important to discuss the political and social effects of the energy crisis and not just its technical aspects. As mentioned, the choices made about energy supplies may well be so basic that they affect the manner in which governments function, or in more extreme versions they may affect the level of government that citizens regard as most important. In a future characterized by highly decentralized energy production, a centralized federal government may be less important than the community government. The community, as opposed to the large urban area, may become the appropriate unit of social organization. Like so many other policy areas, energy policy may be too important to be left to the experts; there must be active citizen understanding and involvement to shape a humane as well as technologically feasible politics.

Environmental Policies

Just as Harriet Beecher Stowe's *Uncle Tom's Cabin* is alleged to have helped initiate the Civil War and as Michael Harrington's *The Other America* is said to have helped initiate the War on Poverty, so it is sometimes said that Rachel Carson's *The Silent Spring* helped to launch the environmental movement in the United States. Her description of the horrors of a spring without the usual sounds of life associated with that season helped to make citizens and policymakers understand the possible effects of the pollutants—especially insecticides—being poured into the air and water of the United States.

The environment remains no small problem. Even after several decades of increased environmental awareness, tons of pollutants are still being dumped into the air and water or stored in rusting barrels with the potential to poison the land for years. It is difficult to determine the amount of disease and the number of deaths that result from this pollution or to estimate the amount of property damage it causes, but the effects produced in each of these categories would be substantial. The economic damage, however, may be minimal compared to the human and aesthetic damage caused by uncontrolled pollution. Against the scenes of natural beauty in the country can be set scenes of wastelands made by unthinking human activities.

America does have widespread pollution problems. Further, we have found that these problems are not confined to our own air and water but rather that they are global. Scientific research published during the 1980s pointed to a gradual warming trend in the earth's atmosphere—the "greenhouse effect"—that could alter climates and even produce massive coastal flooding if the polar ice caps were to melt. This warming appears to be largely the product of carbon dioxide put into the atmosphere by burning fossil fuels.[24] Many people have raised doubts about the validity of these theories, but the excessively hot summer of 1998 in some parts of the country, and the numerous floods in other parts, convinced many Americans that something is upsetting the weather and that it may well be global warming.

Other scientists have pointed to the destruction of ozone in the earth's atmosphere that will permit more ultraviolet radiation to reach the surface and increase the risk of skin cancers. Much of this atmospheric change is a result of the release of chlorinated fluorocarbons (CFCs) into the atmosphere from aerosol cans, refrigeration units, and numerous industrial applications. Still other scientists have pointed to the destruction of the tropical rain forests that supply not only much of the world's oxygen but also a large number of as yet undiscovered useful plants.[25] Also, the United States exports acid rain to Canada and imports some water and air pollution from Mexico and Canada. It no longer appears sufficient to address environmental problems within the context of a single country; concerted international action and policies are needed.

Within the context of the United States, environmental problems have been addressed through a variety of statutes now enforced largely by the Environmental Protection Agency (EPA).[26] Few people now question the desirability of a clean environment, but some would like to see that value balanced more carefully with other important values, such as economic growth, jobs, and controlling inflation. The slowdown of the American economy during the late 1980s and early 1990s led many citizens to question whether the nation could afford stringent controls on pollution, especially when many U.S. jobs were going to countries with less stringent environmental controls on manufacturers. It is also argued that environmental controls could contribute to inflation by making some commodities, such as automobiles, more expensive than they would otherwise be. Great progress has been made in environmental policy, but the challenges have changed to some extent, and the connections with energy policy and economic policy have become ever clearer.

The Politics of Pollution

It would be difficult in the 1990s to find a group that actively favors environmental degradation. Rather, the politics of pollution is generally phrased in terms of tradeoffs between environmental values and other values. There is sufficient public concern about the environment that it would be almost impossible to make wholesale retreats from existing environmental programs. For example, in 1990, 71 percent of the respondents to a national poll said they would support environmental protection laws regardless of the costs, while only 21 percent disagreed with that proposition. This unequivocal support for environmental protection is up from less than 50 percent in the early 1980s; in 1997 over two-thirds of Americans considered themselves environmentalists.[27] At the same time, individuals who want to preserve their own jobs and firms that want to preserve their industries are willing to sacrifice at least part of the environment for those ends.

One recent example was the conflict between logging interests and environmentalists in the Pacific Northwest, first over the spotted owl and then over more general concerns about the "old-growth" forests in that region. Environmentalists sought to save the forests to protect that endangered species, while loggers saw primarily the loss of their livelihoods if the owl were saved.[28] Both sides had powerful reasons to support their positions, and the resolution of that controversy has slowed, but by no means ended, logging in old-growth forests.[29] Other emerging conflicts between the environment and the economy will require equally careful decision making by government.

Some tradeoffs have to be made. As the U.S. economy slowed during the 1980s, some of the blame for the slowdown was placed on more stringent environmental controls in the United States than in other countries. Similarly, a portion of inflation was blamed on regulations of all kinds, including environmental regulations; the cost of the average American automobile increased by several hundred dollars because of environmental controls.[30] These same environmental controls made the automobile somewhat less energy efficient, so in this case energy conservation and environmental concerns constituted another tradeoff. A similar energy versus environment tradeoff can be seen in coal mining. The cheapest means of mining coal, strip mining, is extremely destructive of the environment. Further, potential petroleum reserves have been found in environmentally sensitive areas in

Alaska and along the Florida coast. Even if all Americans are to some degree in favor of a clean environment, it will be difficult to find much agreement on how individual tradeoffs among values are to be made.

The stakeholders in the environmental arena are obvious. Industry is a major actor, for many environmental regulations restrict the activities of businesses. Local governments are also the objects of environmental controls, for much water pollution is produced by poorly treated sewage from local government sources, and federal and state governments have imposed expensive mandates on local governments requiring them to clean up water supplies. Again, most of the interests affected by pollution legislation have not opposed the legislation so much on ideological grounds as on technical or economic grounds, arguing that many of the regulations are technologically infeasible or are so expensive that enforcing them would make the cost of doing business prohibitive.[31] Local governments in particular have argued that they simply do not have the money to comply with all the rules being imposed on them.

On the other side of the debate are the environmental interest groups, such as the Sierra Club, the National Wildlife Federation, and the Friends of the Earth. A few of these organizations—most notably the Sierra Club—have been in existence for years, but the majority are the products of the environmental mobilization of the late 1960s and 1970s. By the mid-1990s there were approximately 9 million members of national environmental groups, with more members of local organizations.[32] Yet there are disagreements among members of these groups as to the tactics that they want to follow and their willingness to make tradeoffs with other values, such as economic growth. Some environmental groups have been highly confrontational, placing large spikes in trees to make them dangerous to cut with power saws, and harassing hunters and the wearers of fur coats. Environmentalists no longer all fit the image of the mild-mannered bird watcher; some are militant advocates of their political and moral positions.

Finally, government itself is an active participant in environmental politics. The major actor in government is the Environmental Protection Agency (EPA), organized in 1970 to take the lead in environmental regulation for the federal government. Given its mission and the time at which it was formed, many employees of the EPA were, and are, committed environmentalists. This commitment put them into conflict with political appointees of the Reagan administration who did not share those values. Before her ouster, for example, Reagan's EPA director, Anne Burford Gorsuch, had numerous conflicts with employees who did not accept her values and thought she was too much in league with industry. Given the commitment to environmental politics by Vice-President Al Gore[33] among others in the Clinton administration, there has been a return to a stronger commitment to environmental protection, although by no means as strong as environmentalists would like.[34]

The EPA is not, however, the only federal agency with environmental concerns; one enumeration found almost thirty federal organizations with some environmental regulatory responsibilities. Some, such as the Department of the Interior, which manages federal lands, have a substantial impact on federal policies but may have their own ideologies that are not purely environmental. The Forest Service in the Department of Agriculture, for example, tends to regard forests as crops rather than as natural assets, and therefore it seeks to make a profit by harvesting them. The Department of Defense also has massive environmental responsibilities, including cleaning up large-scale pollution on military bases.[35] The number of agencies involved in the environmental arena has meant some lack of coordination, but consequent attempts to coordinate their activities and to produce greater uniformity in regulation have enjoyed little success because of the diverse interests in this policy community.[36]

Also, although most attention in environmental policy is focused on the federal government, the states have become major players in the field, as was to some extent intended by the major environmental laws that depend in part upon the states for implementation. The states, however, often have incentives to be relatively permissive in their enforcement, in order to attract industry. During the Clinton administration there has been a greater level of conflict between state and local governments and the EPA, even though both the president and his leading EPA administrators have had experience as state officials.[37] For example, the states have become increasingly aggressive in using the courts to oppose the interventions of the EPA.[38]

Making environmental policy is in part a technical exercise. There are numerous complex technical questions about the nature of environmental problems and about the feasibility of solutions offered for problems. Making environmental policy is also an ideological exercise on the part of many of those involved—especially the environmental groups. Most fundamentally, making environmental policy means finding tradeoffs among environmental values, technical feasibility, and economic growth that can satisfy the multiple constituencies involved.

Given the complex tradeoffs required in this policy area, there has been increased interest in risk-based decision making. The logic of this approach is that rather than focusing on absolute prohibitions against all hazards, government should concentrate on the most dangerous pollutants and seek to reduce those hazards to levels that are deemed to be "safe."[39] Further, this approach calls for balancing the costs and benefits of the production of potentially dangerous substances. Of course, this approach offends committed defenders of the environment who would prefer to retain the traditional "command and control" regulatory regimens.[40] The EPA has been attempting to tailor its regulatory interventions more closely to the characteristics of particular industries. Also, beginning in the Bush administration and continuing in the Clinton administration, the EPA has sought to be more cooperative in its approach to regulation.[41]

Finally, as in so many other areas of federal policy, the courts are important decision makers. This role has been manifested on some substantive issues, as in the implementation of the Endangered Species Act, but it has been particularly important in defining the procedural rules under which the EPA must function. In particular, the Supreme Court has been tending to minimize some of the procedural requirements in environmental laws, such as Environmental Impact Statements, and to permit somewhat more rapid decisions on implementing other types of environmental policy actions. The courts also have been important in defining the standing to sue of environmental groups, with the Rehnquist Court tending to diminish the capacity of those groups to bring suits in federal court.[42]

The Legislation

Except for some older regulatory initiatives, the principal pieces of environmental legislation were passed in the 1960s and 1970s. Most of this legislation had built into it specific guidelines so that authorization would expire after a certain number of years. Reauthorizations of these acts have subsequently been passed, each with some variations on the original legislation, and these were the cause of major political and ideological battles in the mid-1990s.[43] Even among those very committed to environmental protection, there is some interest in developing alternatives to direct regulation as the means of reducing pollution.[44] The need to build policy regimens that produce greater compliance, less impact on economic performance, and lower administrative costs is recognized by many people in the field. We now discuss each area of legislation and the enforcement of environmental policy, as well as the alternatives proposed to the existing system of regulation.

WATER POLLUTION

Federal interest in water pollution goes back to the Refuse Act of 1899, which was intended to prevent the dumping of refuse in navigable waters and was enforced by the Army Corps of Engineers. This legislation provided the principal federal means of attacking water pollution until more stringent legislation was passed in the 1970s. The Water Pollution Control Act of 1956 was another piece of relatively early federal legislation. This act allowed interested parties around a polluted body of water to call a conference concerning that pollution. The recommendations of the conference would be passed on to enforcement officials in the states involved. If the states did not act within six months, the federal government (through the Department of the Interior) could intervene and seek an injunction to stop the polluting. Although there were possibilities of more stringent enforcement through the court system, only one injunction was issued during the fifteen years the 1956 law was in effect. But by making federal matching funds available for the construction of sewage treatment facilities, the act did encourage cities and towns to clean up their water.

The early legislation on water pollution proved ineffective, and the federal government took a major step forward in 1965 with the Water Quality Act. This act relied on the states, as had the 1956 act, but it made the first steps toward establishing criteria for water quality. Each state submitted to the Department of Health, Education, and Welfare—after 1970 to the Environmental Protection Agency—standards for water quality. These standards were to be in measurable quantities (e.g., the number of bacteria per unit of water). After HEW or the EPA approved these quality standards, they were to be translated into specific effluent standards (e.g., an industry would release only so many tons of pollutants each month). It was then anticipated that the states would enforce these standards; if they did not, the secretary of HEW was given the authority to enforce the standards approved by the state within that state's boundaries.

The state basis of the Water Quality Act proved to be its undoing. States were competing with one another to attract industries, and those that adopted more stringent water-quality standards might scare industries away; therefore, the standards tended to converge on the lowest common denominator. Even then, the states rarely if ever enforced their own standards. Also, the federal government did little to encourage more vigorous enforcement by the states and nothing to enforce the standards themselves. It became clear that the states had little incentive to enforce pollution standards or to clean up their own water, and, as a consequence, more effective national standards would be required.

Those national standards were developed through the 1972 Clean Water Act (CWA). Technically amendments to the Water Pollution Control Act, this legislation established national goals, with 1983 established as the deadline for all streams to be safe for fish and for human swimming, and 1985 as the date when all harmful discharges into navigable streams must stop. Those goals had to be abandoned after a flood of lawsuits and an enumeration of the costs persuaded government that they were too optimistic. Still, the requirements said that all private concerns were to adopt the "best practicable technology" by 1977 and the "best available technology" by 1983. Standards for public sewage treatment were less demanding, with all wastes to receive some treatment by 1977 and the "best practicable technology" standard to be applied by 1983 as the policy guidelines.[45] As the regulatory regime for water quality has developed, risk assessment has become a more important tool for analysis.

This legislation established a nationwide discharge permit system, enabling the EPA to specify the amount of effluents that could be released and to monitor compliance with the technology requirements. As noted, this legislation established nationwide standards, although a good deal of the implementation actually was done at the state level. The states could not use low water-quality standards as a means of competing for industry, but their implementation of the standards continued to differ substantially in severity.

President Reagan vetoed the reauthorization of the CWA in 1986, arguing that compliance was too expensive for industry and local governments. Congress overrode the veto, however, with the perhaps unexpected support of many industrial organizations. Industry appeared to accept the existing set of standards as a reasonable compromise between what it might want and what more militant environmentalists might want.[46] As a part of the general pattern of devolution of authority in the federal system, the Reagan administration placed greater reliance on the states.[47] Further amendments and rewriting during the Clinton administration have strengthened some aspects of the legislation but also weakened some important regulations, such as those on control of chlorine and the various compounds formed from chlorine in water.[48]

Also in 1986 amendments were made to the Safe Drinking Water Act that added eighty-six contaminants to the list of substances prohibited from public drinking water. This act, originally passed in 1974, had, like a good deal of all environmental legislation, faced implementation difficulties because of its reliance on state and local governments, as well as suits by citizens as means of bringing problems to the attention of the EPA. Despite continuing enforcement problems and some degree of vagueness in the legislation itself, some progress has been made in cleaning up the water in the United States (see table 13.1).

AIR POLLUTION

Air pollution did not become a matter of federal concern as early as did water pollution, perhaps because of the lack of a clear constitutional peg on which to hang any attempt at enforcement. Federal control over navigable streams provided such a legal peg for water pollution legislation. In addition, the effects of air pollution failed to produce much public attention —even though twenty people died during severe air pollution in Donora, Pennsylvania, in 1948 and even though an obvious smog problem plagued the Los Angeles area as early as the 1950s.

TABLE 13.1

IMPROVEMENTS IN WATER QUALITY (PERCENTAGE OF TESTED
WATERSHEDS EXCEEDING PERMISSIBLE STANDARDS)

	1975	*1980*	*1985*	*1989*	*1995*
Coliform bacteria	36	31	38	20	35
Dissolved oxygen	5	5	3	3	1
Phosphorus	5	4	3	3	4
Lead	n.a.	5	< 1	< 1	< 1

SOURCE: Bureau of the Census, *Statistical Abstract of the United States,* annual.

The first federal legislation against air pollution was the Clean Air Act of 1963. This legislation was similar to the 1956 Water Pollution Act in that it relied on conferences, voluntary compliance, and possible HEW enforcement. Only once during the seven years in which the original act was in effect did HEW attempt to force a firm to cease polluting. Also, in 1965 the act was amended to authorize the secretary of HEW to set standards for automobile emissions, using measurable standards like those of the Water Pollution Control Act Amendments of 1972.

The Clean Air Act was significantly amended in 1970, directing the EPA to establish ambient ("surrounding") air-quality standards. There were to be two sets of standards, primary and secondary. Primary standards were those necessary to protect public health and were to be attained by 1975. Secondary standards, those necessary to protect vegetation, paint, buildings, and so forth, were to be attained within "a reasonable time." Also, the EPA was given the authority to establish emissions standards for certain new facilities, such as cement and sulfuric acid factories and electrical generating stations fired by fossil fuels ("point sources"), that had greater-than-average potential for significant air pollution. In 1977 further amendments to the Clean Air Act required developing state plans for controlling new point sources of pollution and for higher standards of protection for certain areas, such as parks, within a state.

The Clean Air Act amendments also addressed emissions from automobiles, which continue to constitute the principal air pollution problem for most American cities. The 1970 standards superseded the weak standards obtained in the 1965 Motor Vehicle Air Pollution Control Act, mandating a 90-percent reduction in the level of hydrocarbons and carbon monoxide emissions by 1975, with similar reductions in oxides of nitrogen to be achieved by 1976. Although the standards set by the amendments were tough, a variety of factors slowed their implementation. Primarily, the technology for achieving these reductions was difficult and expensive to develop, and some of it, such as the catalytic converter, had side effects perhaps as dangerous as the emissions it was designed to eliminate. In addition, many pollution controls reduced gasoline mileage, and increasing energy shortages brought the conflict between environmental concerns and energy problems to the attention of citizens and policymakers alike. This conflict began to place a great deal of unwelcome pressure on automobile manufacturers to create more fuel-efficient and cleaner-running automobiles. After some delays, those standards have been largely met. The success of one round of "technology forcing" standards has produced demands for even greater reductions in automobile emissions. These demands from environmentalists, and the countervailing resistance from industry, caused changes in air pollution legislation to stall from 1977 to 1990. Despite the stagnant legislative scene, however, the quality of air in the United States was improving, in large part a function of the old legislation (see table 13.2).

The legislative impasse over air-pollution legislation was broken in 1990 with a major set of amendments to the Clean Air Act. These amendments addressed some of the traditional concerns over air quality within the United States, but they also began to address larger, global issues such as the greenhouse effect and acid rain. The provisions of the amendments included

1. Protection of the ozone layer by banning use of CFCs in aerosol sprays and regulation of their use as refrigerants.
2. Plans to reduce acid rain by halving emissions of sulfur dioxide and oxides of nitrogen. Environmental requirements on fossil-fuel power plants strengthened considerably.
3. Further emissions requirements on automobiles and requirements for oil companies to create cleaner-burning fuels.[49]
4. Increased restriction on "toxic air pollutants," with the EPA given the power to control emissions of over 200 substances from a variety of sources, ranging from coke and steel mills to dry cleaners, and to demand installation of new technologies to limit or eliminate emissions.

The 1990 amendments to the Clean Air Act depended largely on traditional "command and control" regulation. These regulations were not well received in the Bush administration, which despite being led by the "environmental president," sought to maximize use of market mechanisms to solve social and economic problems. The Environmental Protection Agency, in contrast, received something of a new lease on life from this legislation and the 1990 Pollution Control Act and is now capable of exerting greater pressures to clean up America's air.

TABLE 13.2

IMPROVEMENTS IN AIR QUALITY

(MILLION METRIC TONS EMITTED)

	1970	*1980*	*1985*	*1988*	*1995*
Particulates	19.0	9.1	7.9	7.9	3.1
Sulfur oxides	28.4	23.8	21.7	21.5	18.3
Nitrogen oxides	19.0	23.6	22.9	23.0	21.8
Carbon monoxide	123.8	115.6	114.9	115.8	92.1
Lead	199.1	66.0	18.3	5.9	4.9

SOURCE: Environmental Protection Agency, *National Air Quality and Emission Trends Report,* annual.

In line with the general movement of environmental controls away from strict hierarchical regulatory regimens, there is an increasing emphasis on negotiation and accommodation in air pollution policy. For example, in late 1994 the EPA negotiated an agreement with ten northeastern states to reduce air pollution from factories (especially electrical power plants).[50] This followed a similar agreement (among twelve states) to reduce significantly the amount of air pollution coming from automobiles. The outcomes of these negotiations were not all that either industry or environmentalists would have wanted, but the bargaining that was involved in making these pacts produced agreements that all affected interests, including the states that must implement the agreements, could live with.

GENERAL ENVIRONMENTAL LEGISLATION

In addition to the legislation addressing specific kinds of pollution, the National Environmental Policy Act (NEPA) of 1970 established guidelines for environmental controls for projects involving the federal government. The principal component of this legislation was the Environmental Impact Statement, which was required for any federally funded project that might have an effect on environmental quality. Before a project can be approved, the Environmental Impact Statement must be filed, detailing the environmental impact of the project, its potential negative consequences, and possible alternatives. These statements must be prepared well in advance of the proposed starting date of the project to allow citizen participation and review and then are filed with the Council on Environmental Quality in the Executive Office of the President.

The NEPA also allows citizens to challenge a project on environmental grounds, and over 400 court cases were filed during the first five years that the legislation was in effect. The legislation requires that environmental considerations be taken into account when a project is planned, but it does not indicate the weight that is to be attached to these considerations as compared with other costs and benefits of the project. This ambiguity in the legislation has been the source of many court cases and has made decisions difficult for the judges involved. In the case of the Alaska pipeline, the court challenges required special legislation to allow the project to continue in the face of determined opposition by conservation groups. That case also pointed to the increasing conflict between energy needs and environmental protection. Similar conflicts continue over proposals to open the Alaska National Wildlife Refuge to oil exploration.

Toxic Waste

Toxic wastes are one of the by-products of a society that has become dependent on synthetic products for its way of life. The usual estimate of the volume of hazardous waste in the United States, used by the EPA, is that around 250 million tons is created each year—one ton per citizen in the United States.[51] Only about 10 percent of this waste is disposed of safely.[52] In addition to the hazard itself, the problem with hazardous wastes is that they tend to be persistent chemicals that have to be stored for years or even centuries and have to be kept away from people and their water and food supplies. Such storage is expensive, and before there was a full understanding of the dangers of these wastes, or proper regulation, industries disposed of these wastes in a very haphazard manner, thus endangering many citizens.

The issue of hazardous wastes first came to widespread attention in 1977 when the Love Canal dump near Buffalo, New York, spilled wastes into a nearby residential neighborhood. Eventually several hundred residents had to be moved out of their homes, and most have never returned. Hazardous wastes again came to widespread attention in 1982 when it was found that the town of Times Beach, Missouri, had been contaminated with the extremely toxic chemical dioxin. The town had to be evacuated. Although these have been the most obvious manifestations of the toxic waste problem, there are approximately 30,000 toxic waste dumps across the United States, and several thousand of them pose serious threats to the health of citizens. It is estimated that up to $50 billion would be required to clean up existing waste dumps and dispose of all the chemicals stored in them in an environmentally safe manner.

The federal government adopted two major pieces of legislation to address the problem of toxic wastes. The first was the Resource Conservation and Recovery Act (RCRA) of 1976, which was reauthorized in 1980, and allowed to continue in effect since then. This act required the EPA to determine what chemicals were hazardous and what was the appropriate means of disposing of them and to establish a system of permits to ensure that hazardous chemicals were indeed disposed of properly. Because of the technical complexity of the task and the low priority attached to the exercise during the Carter administration, the necessary regulations were not promulgated until 1980.[53] The regulations then were attacked by industry as being too stringent and by environmentalists as being too lenient. By the time President Carter was ready to leave office, toxic waste issues were beginning to be assigned a high priority in the EPA.

When the Reagan administration came into office in 1981, it began almost immediately to attack the "regulatory excess" believed to be characteristic of the RCRA. Specifically, using the authority of the Paperwork Reduction Act and an executive order promoting deregulation, the Office of Management and Budget sought to dismantle some of the reporting and permit regulations of the RCRA. The OMB also cut funding for the RCRA by almost 25 percent.[54] The attempts by the Reagan administration, under the leadership of then EPA director Anne Burford Gorsuch, met strong opposition from environmental groups and some congressmen, and the EPA did not achieve the degree of deregulation desired. When scandals within the EPA forced Gorsuch from office, the new EPA administrator, William Ruckelshaus, began to restore some teeth to a law that had become almost unenforced. Under the Bush administration, the "Quayle Commission" was established to review and eliminate regulations, and it tended toward weakening the provisions of the RCRA.

The second major program for dealing with toxic wastes is the Superfund, which applies funds derived from a tax on oil and chemical companies to the cleaning up hazardous waste sites. This program, as first proposed by the Carter administration, contained regulations requiring industry to clean up its own sites, as well as directly funding the cleanup of particularly hazardous sites. The program was finally adopted just before the Reagan administration came into office, with substantially weaker penalties for industries violating the act than had been proposed, but the act did provide a means of addressing some of the worst hazardous waste sites in the United States.

The Reagan administration quickly moved away from the regulatory strategy and rapid timetable of the Carter administration and toward "negotiated settlements" between the industries and the Office of Waste Programs Enforcement in the EPA. There was a great deal of emphasis during this time on having industries clean up their own sites and on avoiding conflict with industries. Members of Congress grew increasingly impatient with what they regarded as a slowing of the planned cleanup schedule and a change in the intended mechanisms for achieving cleanups. They investigated the Superfund for alleged mismanagement and removed its head from office. They also passed the Superfund amendments of 1986 (SARA), requiring the manufacturers of toxic chemicals to monitor the types and releases of those chemicals.[55]

The EPA under Ruckelshaus soon began to pursue cleaning up dumps more actively. Even with that increased activity, only about a third of the 1,600 hazardous sites on the "National Priority List" had been cleaned up by 1998.[56] This slowness has been in part a function of the costs. It cost on average over $21 million to clean up one site in the late 1980s, and those costs were escalating rapidly; by the early 1990s the cost had increased to over $30 million.[57] Against that level of need Congress has been appropriating in the vicinity of $9 billion over five years. Indeed, an increasing number of sites requiring cleanup continue to be discovered, and with them an increasing demand on the limited resources available.

Both the RCRA and the Superfund are potentially important for addressing the problem of a massive amount of toxic waste threatening the environment. The implementation of these programs has been slowed by difficulties in writing the necessary regulations and by partisan and ideological opposition during the Reagan and Bush administrations. Also, somewhat paradoxically, the "strict liability" provisions of the legislation, which make the producers of toxic wastes responsible for it over its entire lifetime, have deterred enforcement. It is often cheaper for producers to take the risk of criminal prosecution and to dispose of wastes illegally than to identify the wastes to the EPA and then bear the costs of their safe disposal.[58] The delays and the enforcement difficulties have only made the toxic waste problem more serious.

There is a need for a large-scale effort to identify existing waste sites, clean them, and devise regulatory mechanisms for the safe disposal of such wastes in the future. The government has a number of policy tools at its disposal for addressing these tasks, including prosecution, accommodation and negotiation, and direct federal action to remove the toxic materials.[59] All of these approaches have some advantages and disadvantages for coping with problems arising from private-sector wastes. The problem is, however, being confounded by the large volume of toxic wastes generated by the federal government itself, especially the Department of Defense.[60] Emissions of toxic wastes have been slowed, but they will remain a serious environmental problem in the United States for decades to come.

The Endangered Species Act

One of the more controversial pieces of environmental legislation is the Endangered Species Act, originally passed in 1973. This act depends more on the Department of the Interior than the EPA for enforcement. The act enables the Fish and Wildlife Service (FWS) to designate species as endangered or threatened (over 300 have been so labeled since the act was passed) and then permits the FWS to protect the crucial habitats of the species. There have been a number of famous (and infamous) instances in which a seemingly insignificant species (such as the snail darter) blocks a major public or private project. As noted, however, the most famous case involving endangered species was that of the spotted owl in the Pacific Northwest and its impact on the logging industry.

The Endangered Species Act has produced some significant results, including bringing back the bald eagle population from its formerly depleted state. Despite those accomplishments, however, the act remains controversial. The legal and philosophical concept of "takings" has been applied particularly to this act, although other environmental legislation has some aspects of takings. The idea is that these acts deprive landowners of the use of their property without just compensation.[61] There is little doubt that there has been procedural due process, given that the takings result from an act of Congress, but there is some doubt as to whether the substance of these acts is indeed legitimate. The courts have begun to examine environmental legislation from this perspective, and to find in favor of landowners.[62]

Implementation of Environmental Controls

The principal organization charged with the implementation of environmental control legislation is the Environmental Protection Agency, organized in 1970 as an executive agency, responsible to the president but independent of any cabinet department. The agency was charged with implementing a variety of air, water, and toxic waste programs, but its rather broad set of responsibilities and wide field of action inevitably brought it into conflict with other federal and state agencies. When the EPA sought to flex its environmental muscles, it regularly encountered difficulties with agencies that wanted to build dams, roadways, or waterways and with the heads of private industries who believed that the standards imposed on them by the EPA were too stringent and lessened their ability to compete in the marketplace, especially the world market. The EPA was given an unenviable task to perform, and because it was made up mostly of people committed to the environmental movement, it set out to accomplish that task with some zeal. The difficulties it encountered were intensified because many of the projects it sought to stop were pet projects of some congressman or senator, and the agency's reputation on Capitol Hill was not the best.

The EPA was also given a difficult administrative task. Congress was relatively specific about the dates by which certain levels of pollution reduction were to be achieved, which gave the agency little latitude and little opportunity to bargain with polluting industries. Also, in attempting to specify so precisely the conditions for alleviating pollution, Congress often wrote into the legislation contradictory paragraphs, which only created more implementation difficulties for the EPA. Finally, the strategy adopted for a good deal of the program—technology-forcing regulations—caused substantial difficulties for implementors and for industries seeking to comply with the legislation.[63] When standards were adopted to reduce air pollution by 1975 to 10 percent of what it was in 1970, the technology to produce that improvement in air quality simply did not exist. It was believed that passage of the legislation would result in the development of the technology, but the result was a delay in implementation rather than any technological breakthroughs. Certainly a number of improvements have been made, especially in the internal combustion engine, as a result of this legislation, but the major innovations anticipated have not materialized.

One major implementation problem associated with environmental policies has been standard setting. We noted that such terms as "primary and secondary standards of air quality" and "best available technology" were not clearly defined in the legislation. Even if they had been, it would still have been necessary to convert those standards into permissible levels of emissions from individual sources of pollution (e.g., for each factory and municipal waste treatment facility). Overall goals for pollution reduction are relatively easy to establish, but great difficulty is encountered in translating those goals into workable and enforceable criteria. And the criteria developed must be applicable to polluters, not just to pollution, if any significant improvements in environmental quality are to be achieved. At times the difficulty of setting those standards has forced the EPA to adopt a "best practice" doctrine: if a plant is doing things like every other plant, then it must be doing things right. Also, the standard setters have been under pressure to accept more risk and to ease the strictness of environmental controls for the sake of economic growth and competitiveness.[64]

The enforcement of established criteria has presented several interesting questions. First, should a mechanism exist for making tradeoffs between environmental protection and economic growth? For example, the Sierra Club succeeded in obtaining a court ruling that air pollution legislation did not allow any degradation of existing air quality, an interpretation resisted by the EPA. This ruling meant that people living in an area with very clean air —probably an area with little or no industry—might be forbidden to bring in any industry. A related question is how to allocate any proposed reductions in effluents among industries or other polluters. For example, should there be across-the-board percentage reductions, with each polluter reducing pollution by 20 percent or whatever, or should attention be given both to the level of emissions and the technological feasibility of reducing pollution at each source? For some industries even minor reductions in effluents might be very difficult to attain, while others might be able virtually to eliminate their effluents with only a limited investment. How should these considerations be taken into account?

Second, although environmental protection legislation is replete with legal weapons to force compliance from polluters, including the authority to close down an offending industry, in reality the enforcement of the legislation has been much less draconian. Politically, the EPA cannot afford to close an industry that provides a major source of employment, either nationally or in a single community. Thus, frequently the agency's hands are tied, and the level of compliance desired or mandated has not been achieved. This element of political vulnerability may be functional in some ways, given the evidence that cooperation is more effective than adversarial relationships in generating compliance.

Finally, although the Environmental Protection Agency has been given a number of legal and administrative mechanisms for improving air and water quality, its efforts are frequently hampered by the complex systems for standard setting and implementation. State governments, for example, are essential in devising plans for reducing pollution, and local communities have to become involved in building new waste-treatment facilities. And the EPA itself is not responsible for distributing federal matching funds for those treatment facilities, so instead of being distributed on the basis of the severity of the pollution problem, the funds are allocated on a first-come, first-served basis. Consequently, instead of developing definitive standards and practices, the enforcement of environmental legislation is frequently only a by-product of compromise, negotiation, and bargaining.[65] This characteristic does not, of course, distinguish environmental policy from most other policy, but it does run counter to some of the rhetoric about the EPA "running roughshod" over the interests of industries and local communities.

Alternatives to Regulation

As we have been demonstrating, the principal means of addressing environmental problems has been through direct regulation—the mandating of certain actions or the attainment of certain standards—enforced through legal penalties or possible closings. It has been argued that a more efficient means of producing improvements in the environment would be to impose effluent charges or taxes.[66] In other words, instead of telling an industry that it could emit only a certain number of tons of effluents each year, government would allow it to emit as much as it desired. The polluter would, however, have to pay for the amount of pollution discharged, and the greater the quantity, the higher would be the cost. And some means of graduating the charges could also be devised so that the greater the volume of effluents, the higher the rate of payment.

The presumed advantage of effluent charges is that they would allow more efficient industries to pollute, while less efficient industries would either have to close down or improve their environmental standards. The more efficient industries could afford to pay the effluent tax and still make a profit, while less efficient industries could not. This market-oriented solution to the pollution problem would be compatible with economic growth and efficiency.[67] It is argued that it would be a definite improvement over direct regulation as a means of forcing the tradeoff between those competing values, and it would give most industries a real incentive to improve their environmental performance, as well as their economic efficiency.

Another component of the market-oriented approach to environmental regulation is to issue tradeable permits to pollute. The 1990 amendments to the Clean Air Act allow utility firms to trade rights to pollute, particularly in sulfur dioxide and later in chlorinated fluorocarbons. The initial allocation of these allowances was related roughly to the amount of pollution the firms emitted in 1987. These amendments required the firms to begin to reduce their total emissions by 1995, with the choice for each firm being to invest in pollution control devices or to buy pollution rights from other utilities that were reducing their emissions.[68] Again the assumption was that this mechanism would produce an efficient allocation of resources as well as reduced pollution; it is too early to say if this assumption is correct.[69]

Effluent taxation and tradeable permits also have been criticized, however, especially by environmentalists. They are regarded by some critics as mechanisms for buying the right to pollute, and even to kill. To those critics the value of a clean environment is greater than the value of economic growth in almost any circumstance, and they cannot accept the idea of balancing the two. In addition, enforcing a pollution tax might be even more difficult than enforcing existing regulatory standards. Effluents would have to be monitored almost continuously to determine the total amount of discharge, whereas under the present regulatory system more infrequent monitoring often is sufficient, as is less exact measurement.

The air and water of the United States are much cleaner than they were before the passage of the environmental legislation. Fish have returned to streams that were once biologically dead, and cities such as Pittsburgh, which were once constantly shrouded in smoke and grit, now can be seen from a distance. Despite these successes, the EPA and its legislation have come under a great deal of criticism. The agency has been attacked from both sides—for being insensitive to the needs of industry and for being too soft on polluters. And questions about the role of the EPA are likely to recur whenever scarce resources and slow economic growth raise the average citizen's concern about national priorities. During the recession of the 1980s, for example, the Reagan administration began early during its term of office to question the efficacy of many standards and to soften environmental regulations, especially on automobile-caused pollution. This was intended to assist the depressed automobile industry and allow American automobiles to compete with imported automobiles, at least on price. Subsequent administrations have reinstated older rules and added some new ones, but they could do so easily when American products became more competitive.

Decisions in one policy area often impinge on many other areas. Environmental policy cannot be discussed apart from energy policy, or from policies concerning economic growth. The institutions of government, however, frequently do not provide mechanisms for rectifying these conflicts of values. Each policy area is treated separately, according to its own constellation of interests and professional standards, and seeks to maximize the returns from political activities for the participants in the policymaking. As both natural resources and government resources dwindle, however, decisions by "subgovernments" may be a luxury we can no longer afford. There is a need for enhanced policy coordination between these areas as well as many others, but Washington tends to work better *within* policy areas than across them, and conflict rather than cooperation is the common outcome.

The early years of the twenty-first century may be the era during which some important questions about the relationship between Americans and their physical environment are decided. We as a nation must decide how much value to attach to a clean and relatively unspoiled environment, as compared with the value we attach to the mastery of that environment through energy exploration and economic growth. Although renewable energy resources and some shifting of attitudes about the desirability of economic growth may soften these hard choices, the choices must still be made. These choices will arise with respect to specific issues, such as the opening of more Alaskan lands to energy exploration or the management oil shale in the West, as well as the disposal of increasing quantities of toxic industrial wastes and the need to develop cleaner means of producing the goods to which we have become accustomed. In the process, Americans will be asked what they are personally willing to give up for a cleaner environment. Are styrofoam cups worth the emission of CFCs into the environment and the swelling of solid-waste dumps? Are we willing to spend an hour or so each week recycling materials to prevent pollution and conserve energy? The sum of such individual choices, along with the regulatory choices made by government, will say a good deal about the quality of life in the United States for years to come.

14. Protective Policies: Defense and Law Enforcement

The U.S. Constitution lists "to provide for the common defense" as the second purpose of the government of the United States. Going back to Lexington and Concord and the Minutemen, military defense has been a visible and sometimes extremely expensive function in a country favoring small government and few government employees.[1] Not all threats to peace and order are foreign, and from the beginning of government, policing and law enforcement have been a major public function. In the United States policing has been largely a state and local function but, like education, has seen an increasing involvement of the federal government. Some of that involvement has been purely financial, but increasingly the federal government is directly concerned with enforcing the law.

This chapter examines these two government functions. Interestingly one (defense) now appears to be of less concern to the average citizen, while the other (law enforcement) has been a growing concern. Indeed, in many surveys during the 1990s crime and personal safety were ranked as the most pressing problems of government (see table 14.1). The two policy areas are alike in some ways (e.g., the use of force in the name of the public), but they also have some more subtle similarities (e.g., potential threats to civil liberties). We also explore some obvious and important differences between these policy areas.

Defense Policy

Providing for the common defense is now a much more complex and expensive task than it was when an effective military force could be raised by each man in the community taking down the rifle from over the fireplace. Military spending accounted for 25 percent of federal spending in 1994, down from 35 percent in 1980. In 1995 military spending was 3.6 percent of gross national product—$3.60 out of every $100 in the economy went for defense—down from 6.5 percent of GNP in 1985. (For a comparison of U.S. military spending with that of some other countries, see table 14.2.) In some

384

TABLE 14.1

MOST IMPORTANT ISSUES FOR AMERICANS

(IN PERCENTAGES, UP TO THREE MENTIONS RECORDED)

	Nov. 1991	*Aug.* 1992	*Jan.* 1993	*Sept.* 1993	*Jan.* 1994	*Jan.* 1997
Unemployment	23	27	22	20	18	} 21
Economy (general)	32	37	35	26	14	
Drugs	10	6	6	6	9	17
Health care	6	12	18	28	20	7
Crime	6	7	9	16	37	23

SOURCE: *Gallup Poll Monthly,* September 1992, 11; January 1994, 43; January 1997, 20.

TABLE 14.2

MILITARY EXPENDITURES AS A PERCENTAGE OF

GROSS DOMESTIC PRODUCT, 1995

North Korea	28.6	United States	3.8
Saudi Arabia	13.5	France	3.1
Russia	11.4	United Kingdom	3.0
Israel	9.6	Sweden	2.8
Jordan	7.7	Germany	1.9
Taiwan	5.0	Japan	1.0
Sri Lanka	4.6	Mexico	1.0

SOURCE: U.S. Arms Control and Disarmament Agency, *World Military Expenditures and Arms Transfers,* annual.

parts of the United States such as Norfolk, Virginia, and Southern California, defense (whether the military itself or civilian defense contractors) is a dominant component of the local economy.

Defense policy has become even more controversial after the end of the Cold War and the short Gulf War. The demands placed on the defense establishment now involve even greater complexity, and planning for even greater uncertainty than when the adversary was clear and the types of weapons needed, at least for deterrence, were largely agreed upon. Further, although many Americans expected a "peace dividend" from the end of the Cold War, most government leaders have not been as anxious to dismantle the military establishment as were their more optimistic citizens. Even military leaders, however, accept the necessity of reducing defense expenditures in the present political and financial climate; the questions are how fast and what components of defense spending should be cut. If the federal budget continues to decline at the projected rate, this will reduce defense spending to "only" about 20 percent of federal spending.

Some current budget estimates, however, also call for an *actual* increase in defense spending within a very few years as a number of weapons systems under contract begin to be delivered and existing systems are modernized, with the obvious question whether those weapons are still necessary.[2] Also, the shift from nuclear deterrence to conventional warfare and peacekeeping may make defense more expensive. A missile can sit in a silo for some time with minimal maintenance costs, but soldiers and sailors have to be paid every month and fed every day. They may cost even more when the economy is good and recruits are difficult to attract. Deciding on defense policy has never been easy, but it is likely to be even more difficult because most of the former certainties have changed in a very short period of time and there is little certainty about the future.

The Environment of Defense Policy

A number of factors condition the manner in which defense policy is made and the likely outcomes of the policy process. Unlike many other policy areas, defense is to a great extent subject to influences beyond the control of officials in government making the decisions. In part because of the uncertainty involved in making defense policy, there may be greater perceptual differences among individuals involved in the process than is true for other policy areas.[3] For example, the degree of threat that any decision maker perceives in the international environment will affect his or her willingness to allocate resources to defense. These perceptual differences may have actually been exacerbated since the clear threat of the Soviet Union has ended, leaving the United States to make policies to contend with the possibility of smaller-scale, yet still dangerous, conflicts around the world. Further, terrorism and unconventional threats to American security now loom larger and require a different military posture.

These smaller-scale threats also raise questions of whether the role of the United States should be that of global policeman or merely one more nation in the international community, albeit the only remaining superpower.[4] Further, if the United States is to act as an international policeman, should it do so alone or in concert with international organizations such as the United Nations, NATO, and the Organization of American States?[5] An even more basic question is whether the national interests of the United States are really served by using its military forces for these peacekeeping and relief functions around the world, no matter how desirable those tasks may be on humanitarian grounds.[6]

ADVERSARIES AND POTENTIAL ADVERSARIES

For most of the past half-century the fundamental factor that shaped defense policy was the international climate and the relationship between the United States and the Soviet Union. Almost as soon as the two superpowers ceased being allies after World War II, they became adversaries on a global scale. Early stages of that adversarial relationship included the Berlin blockade and the Korean War, followed by the U-2 incident, the Cuban missile crisis, Vietnam, and Afghanistan, not to mention hundreds of more minor incidents.[7] None of these incidents involved direct conflict between troops of the two superpowers, although clashes between the troops of one superpower and those of allies or surrogates of the other occurred several times. The degree of hostility expressed between the United States and the Soviet Union varied, however; periods of détente ameliorated the tensions of the Cold War, and some important negotiated agreements (e.g., the nuclear test ban treaty and the SALT agreements) lessened tensions, at least for a while.

In addition to conventional conflicts, the nuclear arms race had each country developing massive stockpiles of nuclear weapons, capable of destroying the world several times over. Nuclear weapons have not been used since World War II, and there were several successful attempts to reduce their numbers (or at least reduce their rate of growth) even during the peak Cold War years. As more historical materials from the Cold War period become available to scholars and analysts, it is even clearer that the nuclear threat did serve as a major deterrent to conflictual behavior, but also that the number of near-disastrous accidents made the world a very dangerous place indeed.[8]

The remaining stockpiles of these weapons represent a crucial factor that defense policymakers must always take into account, especially after the former Soviet Union has disintegrated into a number of smaller states. Several of these new states retain large stockpiles of weapons and have national ambitions that may lead them to rattle the nuclear saber, if not actually use the weapons.[9] In 1993 Russia's president, Boris Yeltsin, made a proposal to reduce stockpiles severely in Russia and the United States, and President Clinton accepted an accelerated reduction of atomic stockpiles, despite continuing instability in the world. Russian leaders say that their weapons are no longer aimed at the United States, but it is not clear where they are aimed.

Thus, although the world was a dangerous place during the Cold War when the two superpowers were stockpiling their nuclear weapons, it may actually be more dangerous now that "peace" has broken out. Instead of one Soviet Union with nuclear weapons, a handful of smaller republics now possess those weapons. The Gulf War also pointed to the presence of nuclear, chemical, and biological weapons in a number of other countries and the apparent willingness of those countries to use force to attain their political and economic goals. Some potential adversaries, such as North Korea,[10] still appear to be fighting the Cold War, while others such as Iraq are pursuing more nationalistic or economic goals. Further, there is some evidence that the new nuclear powers are not nearly as cautious as the former Soviet Union in how they develop and deploy weapons.[11] India and Pakistan have both developed and exploded nuclear weapons, and although their primary target is not the United States, the existence of more nuclear powers adds another variable to an already difficult set of strategic calculations.

Although many potential adversaries are small and relatively weak militarily, they are widely dispersed around the globe, and the American defense establishment must decide how quickly, and in how many simultaneous situations, it must be prepared to respond.[12] Further, those planners must decide how much force both we and the potential adversaries can, and should, bring to bear in these potential conflicts. There is a danger that the United States military has been so attuned to large-scale international conflicts that it will not be capable of coping effectively with seemingly mundane low-level conflicts that appear more probable in the post–Cold War era. The "bottom-up review" of defense policy in 1994, an attempt to develop new strategic doctrine, was premised on the possibility of several smaller conflicts, such as the Gulf War.[13] The question then became how many of these "major regional conflicts" should the American military be able to cope with simultaneously? The basic answer was two, with one to be contained while the other was being won.

There is ongoing debate within the military policy community over (1) whether this is indeed the right force structure to plan for, and (2) whether the existing forces of the United States are adequate for these demands. The experience of the Gulf War indicated that the United States was capable of mounting a major effort at an extreme distance from its own borders, but could it simultaneously have handled another such conflict, even to contain it?[14] There has been some reordering of force structures in an attempt to make divisions capable of responding more quickly to threat, but concern remains about whether the forces are still geared for more intense conflicts than those with which the immediate future may challenge them.

ALLIES

The United States also has friends in the world, although its allies do not always agree with the United States on defense and foreign policy issues. The most important alliance has been the North Atlantic Treaty Organization

(NATO), which has linked nations in Europe and North America for their mutual defense since the late 1940s. NATO has been responsible for the defense of Western Europe and the North Atlantic, and the United States has committed by far the largest share of men and matériel to the alliance.[15] The Soviet Union also had allies, and its equivalent to NATO was the Warsaw Pact. The United States also has important defense agreements with Japan, South Korea, Israel, and Australia.

The events of the late 1980s have made many people—defense analysts and ordinary citizens alike—question the continuation of NATO, at least in its traditional format. The Warsaw Pact has disintegrated, and there is little likelihood of an invasion of Western Europe. In fact, several former Warsaw Pact members (Poland, Hungary, and the Czech Republic) are attempting to join NATO. Further, economic pressures at home and the continuing economic and political integration of Western Europe mean that there is less need for a large American military presence in Europe, and almost all of the divisions stationed in Germany since the end of World War II have come home. Similarly, the United States was willing to give up major military bases in the Philippines, in the belief that they will be much less valuable in a world without direct East-West confrontations.

Although these alliances are apparently now less valuable, the experience of the Gulf War indicated that Western nations, and even some former adversaries from the Warsaw Pact, could band together to confront a perceived common threat. The United Nations stamp of approval on their actions in the Persian Gulf made the alliance more viable, but there is a sense that the United States does have friends around the world that can be counted on in many military situations. The alliances may be ad hoc arrangements rather than continuing treaty commitments, but they can still generate collective action to maintain international security. Further, economic and social issues (including human rights) may become more important in defining security arrangements in the near future, so the United States needs to adjust its own thinking about how to make and maintain international alliances.[16]

The importance of U.S. involvement in NATO was evident in the effort to maintain the peace in the former Yugoslavia. A variety of European members of NATO had made attempts to control the violence in Croatia and Bosnia but to little avail until American troops became involved.[17] The deployment of these troops as a NATO activity helped to legitimate the operations of the peacekeeping forces, but the American troops remained crucial. The initial commitment of troops for one year had to be extended for an indefinite period in order to maintain the uneasy peace. Again, these activities indicate the extent to which the traditional role of the U.S. military has been altered.

Technology

The technology of modern warfare has advanced far beyond that available even during the Vietnam War or the more recent conflict in the Persian Gulf.[18] Nuclear armaments are a major part of the technological change, but systems for delivering weapons have improved even more rapidly. In the 1950s it took hours for a plane to fly from the former Soviet Union to the United States; a missile can now make a comparable journey in fifteen minutes, and a missile launched from a submarine offshore could arrive in a few minutes. There even are plans for war in space, with "killer satellites" and orbiting weapons as part of an antimissile system ("Star Wars").[19] The technology of conventional warfare also has advanced and now includes the laser-guided weapons, infrared night-vision scopes, stealth airplanes, computers, and antimissile defenses featured prominently during the Gulf War. There is also discussion of a whole new generation of weapons, such as those extending the potential for laser weapons, that would have been only science fiction a few years ago.

Advancing weapons technology has several implications for defense policy. One is that defense is a constant activity; there is no longer time to raise an army and then go to war. A standing army historically is something of an anathema to many Americans, but in the 1990s the U.S. military has numbered approximately 2 million uniformed personnel plus almost 1 million civilian employees in the Department of Defense. The technology for modern warfare is now widely dispersed, and many smaller countries can bring sophisticated weapons to the battlefield. The need to have the most modern technology in order to be effective implies that the former "citizen soldier" model is increasingly less viable.

Another feature of the increased technological component of modern warfare is cost. This is in part a function of having to maintain a large standing military establishment, but it goes beyond that. One new air force B-1 or B-2 bomber costs almost $1 billion; one army tank now costs approximately $10 million, and one proposed new carrier for the navy could be several billion dollars.[20] Therefore, any discussion of improving the technical quality of American military forces must be conducted within the context of very high costs. Indeed, as the need to control public spending is combined with the declining threat from the Soviet Union, new strategies of weapons procurement may be devised to keep American forces armed well but as inexpensively as possible.[21] One of the most important cost-containment strategies will be the modernization of existing weapons instead of the development of whole new systems.

Public Opinion

Finally, American defense policy is made in a relatively open political arena

and is definitely influenced by public opinion. As is true for many public issues, public opinion about defense is ambiguous. There are few committed
advocates of unilateral disarmament in the United States, even after the apparent end of the Soviet threat, and virtually all politicians advocate a strong
defense for the United States. Nevertheless, there are a sufficient number of
questions about program costs, about whether many of the high-technology
weapons purchased actually contribute much to the security of the United
States, and about the manner in which the military power of the United
States should be used (e.g., in the Caribbean, Central America, or other
parts of the Third World). All of these questions are political as well as technical military issues that will be fought out in Congress and the media as
well as in the Pentagon.

Nuclear weapons constitute an even greater public opinion problem. A
significant portion of the population, although favoring a strong defense,
were opposed to the nuclear arms race between the United States and the
Soviet Union. The public generally applauded the negotiated freezes on nuclear weapons and the reduction in the numbers of such weapons stockpiled
by both sides. There is virtual unanimity on one point: the United States
should never be the first country to use nuclear weapons in a conflict.[22] This
is true whether the conflict is one among superpowers or a more limited
confrontation such as the Gulf War.

With the negotiated reduction in nuclear forces in the United States and
the former Soviet Union, the issue of nuclear weapons did not, however,
vanish. The one remaining superpower, and the successor states to the former one, still possess substantial stocks of nuclear weapons, as well as the
means to deliver those weapons. Further, despite the existence of the nuclear
nonproliferation treaty, and the efforts of the United Nations to enforce that
treaty, nuclear weapons appear to be spreading around the globe, potentially
to terrorist groups as well as to legitimate governments such as India and
Pakistan.[23] The threat of nuclear weapons will be something that the United
States must live with for the foreseeable future. Simple agreement among
Americans that the weapons are an immense danger will not eliminate the
fact of their existence.

U.S. Force Configurations

Table 14.3 (p. 392) lists the nuclear weapons holdings of the United States
and the new states of the former Soviet Union. With the end of the Cold
War and the dismantling of the Soviet Union, much of this vast arsenal appears to be dinosaurs left from the earlier age. Pledges from Boris Yeltsin,
then leader of the Russian federation, and from President Bush to dismantle
much of the strategic forces indicated that these weapons would follow the
path of intermediate range weapons in Europe and be destroyed. Each coun-

TABLE 14.3

NUCLEAR WARHEADS IN POSSESSION OF UNITED STATES
AND MAJOR POTENTIAL ADVERSARIES

Deliverable by	United States	Russia	China
Bombers	2,900	1,374	150
ICBMs	2,000	2,000	110
Submarine launched missiles	3,520	2,600	24

SOURCE: International Institute of Strategic Studies, *The Military Balance 1997–98* (London: Oxford, 1998).

try still retains a nuclear arsenal, but neither will be of the magnitude that characterized them for several decades. In particular, most of the missiles are being fitted with a single warhead, rather than the multiple warheads now on many missiles. In downsizing, the United States is likely to hold on to its submarine-launched weapons most dearly, and to be more willing to trade away other parts of its "triad."[24] As promising as these developments are, the uncertainty about whose "finger is on the button," and indeed how many buttons there are, in the former Soviet Union leaves the world still a dangerous place and makes maintaining some nuclear deterrent an important part of American defense policy.

The balance in nonstrategic forces in the world is less easy to define. Table 14.4 gives the balance of conventional forces between the United States and the former Soviet Union, as well as those of some other potential adversaries. The countries formed out of the former Soviet Union have a very large military force, but their own fragmentation (among and within them) may make those forces less dangerous than they might otherwise be. Still, the actual force levels of the United States are smaller than those of some other countries. In any conflict with those countries, it is hoped that the superior technical capabilities of some of the American weapons, as well as superiority in the number of attack aircraft, will level the balance.

Table 14.5 shows the balance of naval forces between the United States and the former Soviet Union, as well as several other countries. The United States has fewer surface ships and far fewer general-purpose submarines, but numerical superiority may in fact underestimate the strength of the U.S. Navy, given the capabilities contained in one attack-carrier battle group. In addition, superior detection equipment and satellite tracking makes submarines of other countries relatively less effective. Thus, despite reduction in naval construction, and the far-flung missions that the U.S. Navy must serve, on balance the edge seems to go to the naval forces of the United States.

TABLE 14.4

CONVENTIONAL LAND FORCES OF UNITED STATES
AND MAJOR POTENTIAL ADVERSARIES

	United States	*Russia*	*China*	*North Korea*
Personnel	670,000	500,000	200,000+	950,000
Main battle tanks	8,200	16,800	8,500	2,500
Artillery	8,200	18,400+	14,500+	10,200

SOURCE: International Institute of Strategic Studies, *The Military Balance 1997–98* (London: Oxford, 1998).

TABLE 14.5

NAVAL FORCES OF UNITED STATES AND MAJOR
POTENTIAL ADVERSARIES

	United States	*Russia*	*China*	*North Korea*
Submarines	95	133	63	25
Carriers	12	1	0	0
Other major surface vessels	132	165	54[a]	3

SOURCE: International Institute of Strategic Studies, *The Military Balance, 1997–98* (London: Oxford, 1998).

a. Excludes numerous patrol craft.

If nothing else, toting up personnel and weapons systems demonstrates the huge destructive potential that can be unleashed in a few moments by a number of countries in the world. Such great power carries with it great responsibility and the need for effective strategic doctrines to prevent the use of nuclear weapons—or, indeed, any weapons. The doctrines of a bipolar world (e.g., mutually assured destruction) are no longer valid, and because of that there is perhaps less security than even during the height of the Cold War.

Problems of Defense Policy

Maintaining the defenses of the United States presents several significant policy problems, none of which can be solved readily. One of these is how to manage nuclear strategy in a multipolar world. Other problems are more specific, such as the interaction of specific defense issues (e.g., the acquisition of weapons and manpower) with either fundamental features of the economic system or fundamental American values. These problems have only grown more complex as the uncertainty about the military future of the United States makes the choices more difficult and more risky.

Military Procurement

The first major defense problem is that of acquiring new weapons systems.[25] In a modern, high-technology military force, new weapons are not bought "off-the-shelf," but represent years or even decades of research and development. This in turn presents several problems for the military managers who seek to acquire the weapons. One problem is attempting to predict years in advance just what sort of weapons will be required to secure American national security. For example, during the Reagan years a great deal of money was funneled into the Strategic Defense Initiative.[26] Given changes in the strategic environment, that program now appears to be of limited utility. There is now relatively less chance of strategic missiles being launched at the United States, and much greater chance of terrorism or small, limited wars.

Another problem for procurement officials is deciding what form of competition to demand among potential suppliers of the weapons. One option is to have possible competitors develop full-scale, operating systems and then test those weapons against each other. The other option is to settle on one or a limited number of vendors for a weapons system very early in the development process and then work with the contractor to develop it. Although the former option corresponds to the usual ideas about bidding for contracts and getting the most "bang for the buck" from the Department of Defense's money, it may ultimately produce more expensive and less effective weapons. If a firm must develop fully operational weapons in order to compete for a program, it may choose simply not to compete; hence many potentially useful ideas (especially from smaller firms) will be lost. Second, if this kind of competition is carried out, any firm competing for government contracts may have to amortize its failures across winning contracts in order to make a profit, and consequently the costs of weapons systems as a group will increase. Another option is to sell the weapons to other countries, a strategy that came back to haunt several countries, including the United States, during the Gulf War and that may not be the best strategy of reducing the level of military tension in the world.

Awarding contracts for major weapons systems on the basis of only prototypes and engineering projections, however, may produce numerous disappointments and cost overruns. Despite screening by skilled military and civilian personnel in the Department of Defense, ideas that look good on the drawing board may not work when they are brought to full-scale production and deployment. There are numerous examples in recent weapons systems: the Sergeant York (DIVAD) antiaircraft cannon, the Bradley fighting vehicle, the C-17 aircraft, and several missile systems, for example, have not performed as expected.[27] Even if a manufacturer is capable of making the system work as promised, there may be large cost overruns; the delivered price of the C-5A military transport plane was several times the projected price.

Given that most weapons contracts are "cost plus" and virtually guarantee the manufacturer a profit, manufacturers have a strong incentive to bid low on projects and allow costs to escalate. The Department of Defense has instituted controls to try to prevent the most flagrant violations of its contracting system, but it is difficult to control genuine cases of cost underestimation when a project is well into production. If a workable product can be attained, it will almost certainly be better to go ahead with the project and permit cost overruns rather than to begin again.

Another problem arising from the procurement process is that a manufacturer awarded a contract for a particular weapons system becomes the "sole source" for that system and for the parts that go along with it. This allows firms to charge exorbitant prices for spare parts and tools; simple wrenches costing a dollar or less have been billed to the Department of Defense for several thousand dollars. Some of these apparent excesses were more media events than real cost problems, and curbs have been instituted to stop some of the greatest abuses, but the underlying problem in weapons procurement remains.

The division among the armed services may also produce problems in procuring weapons, or at least may make weapons cost more than they should. Again, there are two options. One would be to attempt to force the services to use the same weapons, if at all possible; the other would be to allow the services to acquire systems more suited to their individual needs. For example, both the air force and the navy fly airplanes that perform similar missions; why can they not use the same planes? In addition to the long-standing rivalries between the services, there may be a danger that weapons resulting from an integrated procurement process would be neither fish nor fowl. For example, the weight added to a plane to make it strong enough for carrier landings for the navy may make it less suitable as an air-superiority interceptor for the air force.

On the other hand, procurement of a number of different weapons may produce higher costs, for the research and development costs of each can be amortized across fewer units of production. In addition, the budgetary process of the United States presents problems for weapons procurement. Unlike the large majority of countries, the United States has an annual defense budget, and there is a possibility (as well as some real examples) that an ongoing weapons system may not be funded. This, of course, presents problems for both contractors and the military. To date, proposals for a multiyear procurement process have been adopted only in part, because Congress wishes to maintain its control over the public purse.[28]

The continuing fiscal constraint on the federal government and the end of the Cold War have introduced other budget problems into the procurement process. Some procurement plans continue to develop prototypes of new weapons systems and to test these prototypes, but not to produce the systems in any quantity.[29] The idea is that the armed forces could remain technologically modern, yet do so at limited expense. If there were an outbreak of hostilities, then the weapons systems could go into production. On the one hand, this approach to procurement appears to violate some of the assumptions about contemporary military preparedness mentioned earlier, in which speed of response is an essential element. On the other hand, this may be the only way to maintain the technological edge demonstrated during the Gulf War while also reducing the amount of money spent on the military.

The process of equipping a modern army is a difficult one, and it is made more difficult by the budgeting process and the budget constraint of the United States. It is made even more difficult by the close ties between the Department of Defense and their defense contractors—the military-industrial complex, or the fifth branch of the armed forces—that may make an independent evaluation of some proposed weapons systems more difficult. These problems are harder to solve because Congress wants to preserve its budgetary powers, while the defense establishment needs the cooperation and capabilities of contractors; given the importance of hardware and technology for the modern military, however, significant attention must continue to be given to these questions.

Updating the Strategic Deterrent

Much of the strategic deterrent force of the United States is aging; in some cases, it already may be obsolete. The B-52 bomber entered service in the 1950s and, despite updates and modifications, it is a very old weapon. The Minuteman missile is by no means obsolete, but it was vulnerable to a Soviet first strike. These problems with existing weapons led to the development of three new weapons systems—the B-1 and B-2 bombers and the MX missile—all of which have been at the center of controversy.

The B-1 bomber was designed as a supersonic penetrating intercontinental bomber that can fly to the target and return, depending on speed and electronic countermeasures for its survival. After several prototypes were built and tested, the Carter administration canceled the project in 1977, arguing that bombers may not be as efficient as Cruise missiles and that the development of the "stealth" technology that makes an airplane less visible to radar would make the B-1 obsolete quickly. This decision caused a great deal of negative reaction in the military—especially in the air force—and was reversed by the Reagan administration, which called for a force of 100 B-1 bombers. Continuing problems with the prototypes of the B-1, and the rapid development of stealth technology incorporated into the B-2, however, eventually led to the end of the B-1. B-2 production has been stopped after only 20 planes, a victim of the end of the Cold War and tightened Pentagon budgets.

Updating the U.S. missile fleet presents an even more difficult problem. The MX was designed to reduce the vulnerability of Minuteman missiles, as well as to upgrade the accuracy and number of warheads in the U.S. nuclear arsenal. While existing Minuteman III missiles had three MIRVed warheads, the MX could carry ten. The Reagan administration decided to produce 100 MX missiles and appointed a bipartisan Commission on Strategic Alternatives (the Scowcroft Commission) to make suggestions for basing the MX. This commission recommended the development of a new, small, and highly mobile missile that could be fired from a mobile launcher and therefore moved almost anywhere, much as Cruise missiles can be. This suggestion soon came to be known as the "Midgetman" missile. The Midgetman would have only a single, rather small warhead, but given its relatively low cost and its relative invulnerability, it could present a serious deterrent, especially given the destructive capacity of even a small warhead. This missile was not purchased, despite plans for up to 600, and only 50 MXs have been purchased. Instead, there has been a rapid development and deployment of less expensive Cruise missiles.

While all these advances in weapons technology were once of tremendous importance for the defense of the United States, their importance is not now clear. Are they really necessary for the threats that may be posed by smaller nuclear powers, or will these weapons and a host of other strategic weapons become merely rather quaint relics of the past? Already the long journeys of Trident submarines have an element of the Flying Dutchman about them,[30] and in late 1991 the B-52s that had been on constant alert since the 1950s stood down. Again, there is need for a thorough and careful examination of just what military purchases of the future should be.

The All-Volunteer Military
During the Vietnam War, the use of conscription to provide manpower for the armed forces became increasingly unpopular in the United States. Therefore, in 1975, the draft was phased out and replaced by an all-volunteer force. While this was politically desirable at the time, and almost certainly is still so today, that policy decision presents several problems for the armed

forces.[31] These problems will be reduced but by no means eliminated by the "build-down" of forces now being implemented.[32]

The most obvious problem is that the military must now compete directly with civilian employers for the same pool of young people, instead of being able to train young people in the military for a short time and perhaps induce some of them to remain in the service. Given the risks associated with serving in the military, it is not surprising that there have been difficulties at times in filling enlistment quotas. Special difficulties have been encountered in attracting educated and skilled personnel to the armed forces, for these are the people whose services are most in demand in the civilian labor market. Thus, for much of its history, the all-volunteer force has been plagued by stories of low-quality recruits.

These recruitment problems diminished during the recession of the early 1980s and again in the 1990s, when any job seemed attractive, and there were long queues of potential enlistees waiting to enter the armed forces. But the quality problem began to resurface as the economy recovered. The military has lessened its demand for young men somewhat by placing women in jobs formerly filled by males (although still not in all combat positions) and by using civilians in jobs once filled by uniformed personnel. There are still problems, however, in attracting enough highly skilled personnel to a military increasingly dominated by technical weapons systems. There seems to be an increasing disparity between the skills required to function effectively in the modern armed forces and the personnel generally available to the military, although performance of the all-volunteer forces and reserves in the Gulf War allayed these fears somewhat.

Associated with the general problem of attracting personnel is the problem of compensating them. An obvious means of attracting and retaining people in any job is to pay them adequately; this is especially true for the military, given the dangers and hardships associated with serving in the armed forces. Unfortunately, however, military pay is generally not competitive with private-sector pay, even when the value of allowances and benefits is included in the comparison. Military pay is much better than it was before the introduction of the all-volunteer military, but it is not yet capable of attracting as many of the best personnel in the labor market as the armed forces require. With the end of the Cold War patriotism and the appeal of defending the United States also have been less effective in recruitment. Nevertheless, military pay has become more expensive in the aggregate and now accounts for a larger percentage of the defense budget than it did before the all-volunteer force. An increased reliance on reserve forces has helped to reduce the financial burden, but adequate compensation for military employment is likely to remain an issue.

Related to the general problem of pay for military personnel is the especially difficult problem of retaining people whom the armed forces have trained. For example, an individual trained as a pilot in the air force is frequently able to command at least twice his military pay by working for a private airline. Even skilled enlisted personnel, such as machinists and radar operators, have found that the private sector offers them much greater economic rewards than does continuing in the military. The economic slowdown of the early 1990s made military employment appear more attractive, but that was only a short-term phenomenon. As military pay failed to keep pace with wages in the private sector, many military personnel found themselves in a difficult economic position.[33] The retirement option available to military personnel (full retirement benefits after thirty years) may make staying in the service more desirable, but the loss of crucial skilled personnel continues, and there are some pressures to make military retirement less generous.

Finally, there are philosophical and constitutional questions about the development of an all-volunteer military. Given historical patterns and perhaps continuing discrimination in the labor market, an all-volunteer force may be composed increasingly of members of minority groups. This may be seen as imposing an excessive cost of national defense on these groups. More generally, the traditional ideal of the U.S. military has been that of the "citizen-soldier"; customarily we have rejected the idea of a professional standing army. The policy of maintaining an all-volunteer force makes it more likely both that we will have a professional military force and that we will not have large numbers of young Americans serving for a time in the armed forces.

This pattern of recruitment, in turn, may make the military more of a group apart from the rest of society and may make it less amenable to civilian control. Thus, paradoxically, although we may need a professional military to be able to handle the highly sophisticated weapons in the contemporary arsenal, and even to develop the skills needed for covert actions,[34] we may thereby lose some control over those weapons and their potential for massive destruction. In addition, the end of the Cold War, and the resultant sense that the military is not so necessary any longer, may (again, paradoxically) make the military a more distinctive element of the society. There is little evidence to support a claim that a "warrior caste" has developed in the United States, but the current personnel system of the armed forces may make that development more possible than it would be under the former system of conscription.

Other Personnel Issues

The military of the United States cannot be isolated from the social issues that influence life in the country as a whole. In particular, the issues of how to integrate women into the armed forces and how to deal with the issue of homosexuality have become importance concerns for the military. Women have been involved unofficially in the military for the entire history of the United States,[35] but they have been an official part of the military only since 1942. For most of this involvement, women have been assigned to support roles, including clerical duties, nursing, and a variety of other activities far removed from actual fighting. Further, men and women were kept apart as, for example, women were not allowed to serve on ships in the navy.

During the late 1980s and early 1990s, the military began to place women in more positions. The navy already had begun to allow women on some ships, but it has now extended that to include all ships except submarines. The air force has begun to allow women to train for combat positions, and the army now permits women to serve in all capacities except front-line combat positions. As the Gulf War demonstrated, women will be involved more directly in any future armed conflicts than they were in the past, and there will almost certainly be more women casualties than ever before.

A number of highly publicized sexual harassment and "fraternization" cases in the military have elevated attention to the issue of the role of the two sexes in the military. Some critics claim that harassment of women is endemic in the military,[36] while others argue that the issue has been blown out of proportion.[37] Whatever the reality, the military has a public relations problem on this issue. One of the solutions has been to return to training in single-sex units, a policy the Marine Corps alone retained in the 1990s. Training and constant monitoring are also offered as remedies, but there appear to be no quick and easy answers.[38] Fraternization between men and women, especially between officers and enlisted personnel, is hardly new, but there again are issues about how to maintain discipline and how to enforce military codes of conduct. To some critics, especially women's groups, these rules are being implemented unfairly, citing the female air force pilot who was forced out of the service for a relationship with an enlisted man, while a male general was not punished nearly as severely.[39]

The issue of the rights of homosexuals to serve in the armed forces has been even more controversial than the integration of women into the combat arms. President Clinton promised during his first presidential campaign to give homosexuals full rights to serve, but once in office he faced strong pressures from within the military to modify that stance. The suggested compromise position was referred to as "Don't ask, don't tell," meaning that recruiters would not inquire about sexual preference and recruits would not volunteer that information. Sexual orientation would not in itself be a cause for release from the armed forces. The criteria for dismissal instead would be involvement in homosexual acts or causing disruptive incidents.[40]

This compromise position satisfied neither side in the dispute.[41] Members of the homosexual community believed that the president had reneged on his promise and that this compromise still did not accord homosexuals the same rights to military service as those of the heterosexual community. In contrast, opponents of the compromise in the military services and in Congress believed that this decision conceded too much to a group that they believed would undermine military discipline and reduce the effectiveness of the armed forces. In addition, the courts have become involved in the controversy and issued a number of rulings, most of which have tended to increase the rights of homosexuals to serve in the military. For example, a ruling in 1994 reinstated a homosexual officer who had been dismissed earlier for publicly stating that he was homosexual.[42] Other cases, however, have been resolved in favor of the military and its needs to maintain discipline. This continues to be a controversial and potentially harmful area of conflict in personnel policy.

Conventional Forces and Strategies

With all the concern about nuclear weapons and nuclear disarmament, it is easy to forget that the most likely use of force by the United States is by conventional forces. These forces were used twice under the Reagan administration—in Lebanon and in Grenada—and three times during the Bush administration—in Panama, in the Persian Gulf, and finally in Somalia. The Clinton administration decided to use military forces to deal with problems in Haiti, in the Balkans, and then in Afghanistan and the Sudan in response to terrorism. In addition, the navy has been used frequently to "show the flag" in the Caribbean, the Mediterranean, and the Persian Gulf. While these activities were taking place, American troops remained on duty in Western Europe, South Korea, Okinawa, Guantanamo Bay in Cuba, and several other places around the globe. The ability of the United States to respond to threats to its national interests around the world with conventional forces remains an important element in defense planning.

One of the important elements in the ability of the United States to project its presence around the world is the Rapid Deployment Force, troops ready to be deployed by air on very short notice. Matériel has been positioned around the world so that troops can be supplied during the time that might be required to have seaborne equipment delivered to them. The Carter and then the Reagan administration positioned supplies for up to six divisions (a program called POMCUS) in Western Europe and the Persian Gulf region; in the event of a confrontation, troops can be flown in without the need to airlift heavy equipment and munitions. Both these programs are designed to make the U.S. armed forces more flexible and mobile.

Technology plays a major role in that flexibility and mobility. For example, the deployment of the M-I tank during the Gulf War indicates that it is an extremely reliable, fast, and effective weapon despite its technological sophistication. The problem then becomes acquiring enough of these weapons to meet the needs of the armed forces. But what are those needs? What should the armed forces be preparing for? The current doctrine is that the armed forces should be preparing for one-and-a-half wars; that is, the armed forces should be preparing for one major and one minor conflict to occur at any one time.[43] Even that level of conflict might strain the available resources, especially if the conflicts involved the logistical problems of the Gulf War and did not include a convenient friendly power such as Saudi Arabia.

Planning to meet contingencies with conventional forces is important not only for the ability to implement national policy, but also because strong conventional forces make the use of weapons of mass destruction, meaning primarily theater nuclear weapons, less likely. Plans still exist for using such weapons in the event of apparent defeat by conventional forces; once the use of those weapons begins, it will be difficult to contain their escalation. The problem of escalation has largely been eliminated in Europe, but it would definitely be present in dealing with smaller powers and might also escalate to include chemical and biological weapons. Thus, the availability of nuclear weapons makes conventional forces that much more important.

Having an effective conventional deterrent also depends upon the readiness of those forces to fight when needed. There is some fear among military leaders, as well as military analysts, that reductions in military spending will reduce military capacity to meet the demands that may be placed upon it. There is the fear that American defense forces have become "hollow"—that they do not have sufficient readiness to meet another crisis on the order of the Gulf War.[44] Given the numerous crises around the world, such as the Balkans, several places in the former Soviet Union, and Africa, those fears may be more than academic even if the role of the United States is only that of peacekeeper.[45]

Defense and/or Jobs
As the Cold War ended and many if not most Americans anticipated a significant cut in the defense budget, we found that cutting back is not as simple as it appears. In part the economic prosperity of the United States is built on its military-industrial complex, and reducing defense expenditures means reducing employment. This is true for the men and women in the armed services and for employees in defense industries. As of early 1998 there were somewhat less than 2 million personnel in the armed forces, another 900,000 civilian employees in the Department of Defense, and an additional million people employed in defense industries.[46] While the defense establishment will not shrink to nothing, or anything close to it, the likely cuts mean the loss of employment for a large number of people.

Economically, the end of the Cold War arrived at a difficult time for the United States. Unemployment was already high without soldiers returning to the domestic labor force or workers in aircraft factories or tank factories being laid off. Even when the economy is better, job losses have a major impact on the politics of the defense budget. Most congressmen are in favor of reducing the budget in principle but are much less interested in the idea when it directly impacts their own districts. In an interesting Freudian slip, Senator Dianne Feinstein (D-Calif.) once argued that the B-2 bomber did not deliver a "big enough payroll." Thus, to a great extent, defense spending has been reconceptualized as a means of providing jobs and as a (thinly) disguised industrial policy.[47] Also, the United States is a successful exporter of arms when it wants to be, so promoting defense industries may be one way to address our balance of payments problem.

In addition to general economic problems, downsizing the armed forces may have other costs as well. For the military it may mean the loss of a great deal of talent, especially in the officer corps and in career nonenlisted personnel, that could be important for any future military activities. For the individuals who may have joined the all-volunteer military (see pp. 397–99) in the hope of building a career, it may mean a huge adjustment of life plans and career prospects. Even for military personnel who remain in the service, reductions will mean very slow promotions and probably some career frustration.[48]

Another strategy for the armed forces to ensure continued employment for its personnel and continued funding from Congress may be to find new tasks on which to employ its capabilities. The most obvious opportunity for the use of the military is in the "war" on drugs. It is obvious that the rhetoric of the issue is already suited to use of the military, and some missions in that war may be as well. There are, however, questions about the desirability of military involvement in this policy area. For example, do we want to use American military might to attack the problem in other countries, especially those of Latin America which have many unpleasant memories of previous U.S. military expeditions? Finally, is the military really capable of doing the police work necessary to be effective in drug control? As right as such involvement may seem for supporting the military budget, it may be wrong for a variety of other reasons.

As we have noted several times, another use of the military has been in peacekeeping. This is in some ways only thinly disguised military action, with the hope that the weapons do not actually have to be used. In other ways peacekeeping is police work, such as attempting to detect violations of cease-fires or of agreed borders, and perhaps arresting alleged war criminals. This is difficult and dangerous work, given that it generally places the troops between opposing sides, neither of which may particularly want them to be there. Still, it is a crucial role in a world that is still divided by numerous ethnic hostilities and national divisions, if no longer by the Cold War.

Making defense policy is exceedingly difficult, requiring planning for an uncertain future that involves adversaries whose strength and strategies are not readily predictable as well as allies whose commitments to a common purpose and a common set of policies are uncertain. Defense policy also requires making decisions about weapons that may take years or even decades to develop and that may not perform as well as (or perhaps even better than) intended. Finally, defense involves huge costs that may be politically unpopular even when the public strongly supports a strong military posture. Defense policymaking is a series of gigantic gambles about the future, gambles on prospective actions that most of those involved hope never actually have to be taken.

Defense policy was the subject of intense and sustained political debate during the Reagan administration. Although Ronald Reagan came into office promising to modernize and strengthen America's armed forces and then won reelection stressing the same themes, his ambitious program of military procurement and expansion came into conflict with the increasing federal deficit. After Reagan left office some programs were delayed, while others had to be scaled down and a few eliminated. President Bush's use of the military in the highly successful Gulf War renewed its confidence and its sense of mission, but even that may not be enough to save the military budget in an era of declining resources and declining threat. The Clinton administration came to office seeking to cut defense further, but it has found both conventional military and more novel humanitarian tasks for the armed forces to perform. Further, members of Congress can be expected to protect military bases and weapons systems manufacturers located in their home districts.

Law Enforcement

Defense involves the use of force, or the threat of the use of force, outside the borders of the United States. Law enforcement involves the legitimate use of coercion within the borders of the country. Most of the policies we have talked about (taxation is a notable exception) confer benefits on citizens. Law enforcement tends to be directed at penalizing certain citizens, while at the same time providing significant benefits to other citizens. Policing traditionally has been a concern of state and local governments in the United States, but as in most other policy areas, the federal government has begun to play a larger and larger role. This is true in terms of financial support for the subnational governments, as well as in the direct provision of police protection to the American population.

Crime has been a very salient policy issue in the United States in the past several decades. Politicians have competed with one another over who could be the toughest on crime, and one presidential candidate, Michael Dukakis, suffered badly when he was perceived as being too soft on crime while governor of Massachusetts. Public concern about crime has remained high even after crime began to decline significantly in the late 1990s. This decline—due to very good economic conditions, more effective policing (including "zero tolerance" in cities such as New York[49]), and demographic change[50]—reduced crime in the United States to levels not much greater than those found in Western Europe (the major exception to that generalization is murder, especially murder involving firearms). An uninformed observer, however, would not have known that reduction to have taken place, either from political advertisements or from public opinion polls (see table 14.6).

TABLE 14.6
VICTIMIZATION RATES[a]

	Rape	Burglary	Robbery	Assault	All violent crimes
1973	2.3	110.0	6.9	38.3	48.6
1975	2.3	110.0	7.0	39.1	48.9
1980	2.3	101.2	6.8	40.3	49.6
1985	1.8	75.2	5.3	38.0	44.7
1990	1.5	64.6	5.9	39.2	44.1
1991	2.3	64.7	6.1	40.5	48.0
1992	1.8	58.6	6.1	40.0	49.0
1993	1.5	59.9	6.1	42.9	51.3
1994	1.5	54.4	6.1	42.7	50.8
1995	1.1	47.4	5.3	37.6	44.5

SOURCE: Bureau of Justice Statistics, *Criminal Victimization*, annual.

a. Instances reported in surveys per 1,000 persons 12 years old or older; slight changes in reporting techniques in 1991.

Federal Law Enforcement

The role of the federal government in police protection is not entirely new. Indeed, the first organization formed in the federal government—the United States Coast Guard—was established primarily to catch smugglers. Countless western movies and television programs have portrayed the role of the U.S. marshall as the principal peace officer in the territories of the American West before they gained statehood. In less dramatic settings federal marshalls have been responsible for the implementation of the orders of federal courts. The military has also served this function in our history, especially when there is a threat of major violence or civil disorder. One of the most notable examples was President Eisenhower's use of federal troops to prevent violence when Central High School in Little Rock, Arkansas, was integrated in 1957.

Perhaps the most familiar law enforcement organization in the federal government is the Federal Bureau of Investigation (FBI). A component of the Department of Justice, this organization is responsible for enforcing a number of federal laws (e.g., those against kidnapping and bank robbery). During the Cold War the FBI also had major responsibilities for finding and apprehending foreign agents. That function now continues, albeit directed against the agents of different countries, and especially in protection against terrorism; flying dozens of FBI agents to Africa after the American embassy bombings in 1998 was indicative of their current role in combating terrorism. This organization gained a reputation for efficiency and incorruptability during the many years in which J. Edgar Hoover was its director.[51] That reputation has declined somewhat, but the FBI remains a very effective law enforcement organization.

In addition to the FBI, the Coast Guard and federal marshalls, there are a number of other law enforcement bodies in the federal government. The Secret Service in the Department of the Treasury is responsible not only for protecting the safety of the president and the vice-president, but also for catching counterfeiters of U.S. currency. Also within Treasury, the Bureau of Alcohol, Tobacco, and Firearms (BATF) is responsible for enforcing a variety of federal taxes and other laws having to do with the three commodities in its title.[52] The Drug Enforcement Administration (DEA) enforces federal laws concerning selling and possessing illegal drugs. Postal Inspectors are responsible for enforcing laws concerning the use of the mails for fraudulent or other illegal purposes. The Customs Bureau is responsible for enforcing laws about imports into the United States, including some aspects of drug laws and the protection of endangered species. Finally, the Immigration and Naturalization Service and the Border Patrol are responsible for enforcing immigration laws. This is a rather long list of organizations for a government presumably having a minimal role in law enforcement.[53]

The role of the federal government in law enforcement is predicated upon several of the powers given to it in the Constitution. One of these is the power to tax, and the roles of the BATF and Customs are derived largely from that very basic power. Many of the powers of the FBI are based on the responsibility of the federal government to deal with issues that transcend state borders. For example, kidnapping became a federal concern after the kidnapping of the Lindbergh baby and the interstate flight of the criminal in the 1920s. The federal government also exercises its authority over interstate

President Clinton and Mayor Rudolph Giuliani celebrate the provision of federal grant money to fund the hiring of additional police officers for New York City. (Agence France Presse/Corbis-Bettmann)

commerce to regulate the sale and distribution of certain drugs, with the DEA obviously deriving most of its powers from that source. Finally, the federal government obviously has the duty to protect its own officials and the value of its currency, and that gives the Secret Service its constitutional justification.

Federal Support to State and Local Government

In addition to providing police protection directly, the federal governmental supplies some support to state and local governments that bear the major burden of policing. The kind and amount of this support has tended to vary across time, but there is some ongoing support for this important activity coming from Washington. Fighting crime is not often a controversial issue, so politicians usually can feel safe in spending on this function even when there are pressures to reduce the size of the federal budget.

John DiIulio has argued that there have been two federal "wars on crime," with a third being initiated in the 1990s.[54] He (like the founders of the programs) argued that the first was the War on Poverty (see pp. 309–12), whose programs were an attack on the root causes of crime as well as of poverty. This war was also fought with a number of more direct weapons, such as the Omnibus Crime Control and Safe Streets Act of 1968, which provided a substantial amount of federal funding for local governments through the Law Enforcement Assistance Administration (LEAA)—greater funding than the entire Department of Justice budget by 1968.

The second federal "war on crime" was a more direct attack on crime and criminals. This initiative, occurring during the Reagan administration, was spearheaded by the Comprehensive Crime Control Act of 1984 and the Anti–Drug Abuse Act of 1988. The LEAA was phased out and with it much of the federal support for local law enforcement (other than for antidrug programs). This war focused on providing stiffer sentences for perpetrators of federal crimes and especially on the linkage between illegal drugs and other crimes.

As we discuss later in this chapter, the third "war" against crime contains some elements of the strategies of the two previous ones. Like DiIulio's first war, it provides a good deal of money for local law enforcement—100,000 more police officers were placed on the streets because of the 1994 Crime Control Act. That legislation also contained a strong element of crime prevention and social policy.[55] Like the second, this war focuses attention on federal crimes and federal law enforcement and specifies new death penalties for sixty federal crimes. Given public fear of crime in 1994, there was little question that the federal government should be taking an active role in fighting crime; the policy question was what form that assault should take.

Issues in Law Enforcement Policy

As in most policy areas, there are a number of enduring issues that illustrate the complexity of law enforcement policy. It is easy to think that, because government has long been in the business of enforcing laws and policing, the issues and approaches to the issues must be well established. This is not the case, however, in part because this policy area involves the intersection of a number of issues and interactions with a number of other policy areas, and the complexity of the issues is becoming more apparent all the time.

The Causes of Crime

The most fundamental issue is identification of the root causes of crime. On the one hand there is the belief that crime results from the failure of society to enforce its values on people who do not share those values. The advocates of this position insist that the best and perhaps the only way to address problems of crime is to ensure that convicted criminals receive swift, sure, and perhaps harsh punishment.[56] Supporters of this view argue that current programs of parole and pardon put criminals back on the streets too quickly. For example, there has been a move in several states and at the federal level toward a "three strikes and you're out" approach to sentencing—that is, an individual who is convicted of three felonies must be imprisoned for life without the possibility of parole.[57]

The contrary position is that crime results from social and economic problems, including problems in family structure. From this perspective, the best and most efficient means of dealing with crime is to address those socioeconomic issues.[58] It is argued that instead of punishing the criminal after he or she has already decided to commit a criminal act, attacking the social roots of crime would help prevent crime. In addition to programs for improving socioeconomic conditions, advocates have stressed the need for programs that would help parents learn how to raise their children without the violence that appears to breed additional violence.[59] Even some police forces have begun to think of their role as dealing with "problems" rather than clearing up crime "incidents."[60] Part of the Clinton crime-control program, for example, was to emphasize "community-oriented policing," which attempts to develop more a positive social fabric as well as enforcing the law.

The selection of one model of causation or another for crime initiates a series of choices about how to spend public money. If the punishment route is selected, government must spend its money on police protection and on prisons. This latter choice is often expensive—it costs approximately $60,000 per year to keep a prisoner in jail, which is nearly double what it costs to send a student to an expensive private university for a year.[61] In contrast, focusing on the social roots of crime requires heavy expenditures on education, social services, family support, and many similar programs, as well as on rehabilitative services for prisoners already in jail.

Neither policy choice is without its costs and benefits, and selection of one or the other approach involves fundamental value decisions. Some of these values will be expressed by professional policy analysts and policymakers. Like education, however, crime and punishment are issues about which the average American is likely to have an opinion, as can be seen in the responses to polls about the basic purpose of prisons (table 14.7, p. 410). The American public has tended to think that criminals can be rehabilitated and deserve a second chance, but the spate of violent crime in the 1990s has reversed that opinion dramatically, and now most Americans are seeking retribution rather than rehabilitation in the prison system. Likewise, states are passing legislation removing educational and recreational facilities from prisons, simply as a means of punishing prisoners as much as possible.[62]

Gun Control
The problem that many citizens now identify as most important in their lives

TABLE 14.7

ATTITUDES TOWARD PUNISHMENT AND REHABILITATION,

1971–93 (IN PERCENTAGES)

"Is the primary task of prisons to punish criminals or re-habilitate them?"

	1971	*1976*	*1980*	*1989*	*1993*
Punish	15	21	32	38	61
Rehabilitate	76	65	53	48	25

SOURCE: George Pettinico, "Crime and Punishment: America Changes Its Mind," *Public Perspective*, September 1994, 30–31.

is violent crime. Probably the major instrument of that violence is the firearm. There are an estimated 60 million handguns in the United States, with millions of other firearms, including semiautomatic assault weapons, in the hands of private citizens. The Second Amendment to the Constitution gives citizens the "right to bear arms," although that right is phrased in the context of the need for a militia.[63] The advocates of gun control point to the number of murders by handguns each year (approximately 11,500 in 1997 —well over half the total number of murders[64]) to argue for regulation of handguns, especially the cheap "Saturday Night Specials" that are bought and used in the heat of the moment. Critics of gun control, however, argue that criminals will always find a way to get guns and that law-abiding citizens need some means of protecting themselves, their families, and their property.

State and local governments have already begun to regulate the ownership and sale of firearms. Almost all large local governments require that handguns be registered. Some also require a waiting period between application for purchase of a handgun and the delivery of the weapon. This is to allow the police time to check on the reliability of the purchaser. Further, the federal government has regulated automatic weapons and other especially dangerous weapons since the days of Prohibition and the fight against gangsters. More recently, the federal government began to regulate sales of weapons through the mails and then adopted the "Brady bill" in 1993, which imposes a federal requirement for a five-day waiting period between application to purchase a handgun and its delivery.[65] The states have their own laws on gun sales, making firearms more available in some states than in others; guns are often purchased in one state and then used in another.

Clearly there is no absolute right for a citizen to own any type of gun he or she wants, or to get it anytime he or she wants. The questions, then, are what sort of restrictions are permissible under the Constitution and what specific restrictions are politically possible. The National Rifle Association (NRA) has developed into an active, well-financed, and usually successful lobbying organization opposing gun control. The passage of the Brady bill, however, was seen by some as a signal of the declining influence of the NRA,[66] and that power appeared to wane even further when NRA lobbyists were ultimately unsuccessful in removing the ban on assault weapons from the Clinton crime bill (see pp. 414–16).

Despite the lobbying by the NRA, gun control tends to be popular among the American population. For example, in a poll taken in late 1993, some 87 percent of Americans (and 79 percent of gun owners) favored the Brady bill. Seventy-seven percent of respondents (and 66 percent of owners) favored a ban on cheap handguns and 72 percent a ban on all handguns. The only question for which there was not majority support was an absolute ban on guns, although 39 percent of respondents did favor a measure of that sort.[67] There has been little change in public opinion since that time, despite NRA efforts to improve its image by sponsoring more programs for children and in 1998 electing as its president the popular actor Charlton Heston, whose celebrity is put to effective use in its political advertisements.

The Death Penalty

Related to the issue of punishment of criminals is whether government should impose the ultimate sanction, the death penalty. If the answer to that general question is yes, that raises the subsidiary question, under what circumstances it should be imposed. The most common answer given to the general question is indeed yes, and fourteen states now impose the death penalty. Some, such as Florida and Texas, do so vigorously, while in other states the penalty is rarely imposed. The federal government also specifies the death penalty for certain federal crimes, and the 1994 crime bill increases dramatically the number of crimes for which that penalty can be applied. The increase in the use of the death penalty appears to suit most Americans: 72 percent of respondents favored the death penalty in a 1993 survey.[68] The Texas execution in 1997 of a woman who seemingly had reformed significantly prompted further discussion about the justification of the death penalty, but the public continues to support the ultimate penalty for many major crimes.

The arguments centered on this issue are practical, constitutional, and moral.[69] The basic practical question is whether the death penalty is really an effective deterrent to violent crime. Advocates believe that it is, although some of the states with the highest murder rates are also among those that impose the penalty most readily. Advocates also argue that it is a certain deterrent to the possibility of the criminal in question committing any more crimes. Opponents of the death penalty argue that it is not really a deterrent, and that most of the acts for which it is now imposed are often not calculated choices by the perpetrators but products of the passion of the moment. The opponents further argue that the legal work now required to implement the penalty is monumental, often costing a government more than might be spent in keeping the convicted criminal in jail for life.

The constitutional questions revolve around the issue of whether the Eighth Amendment to the Constitution, which outlaws "cruel and unusual punishment," does in practice prohibit the death penalty. Supporters of the penalty argue that at the time this amendment was written, the death penalty was widely used, so it would not be "unusual" under the amendment; they believe that the phrase referred instead to practices such as torture. Opponents of the death penalty, however, argue that it is indeed cruel under contemporary interpretations of that word. For a long period of time the Supreme Court tended to side with the opponents and in effect outlawed the execution of prisoners.[70] The Court, however, reversed its stand in 1976 and began to permit the use of the penalty in certain defined situations.[71]

A second constitutional question concerning the death penalty is whether the act as currently administered violates the "equal protection" clause of the Fourteenth Amendment. Opponents of capital punishment argue that African Americans and other minorities are much more likely to be put to death than are whites, even when they have committed roughly comparable crimes.[72] They also point to a pronounced economic bias in the imposition of the penalty, with poor defendants having difficulty in securing adequate legal counsel to prevent their being sentenced to death.[73] Supporters of the death penalty argue, however, that there are per capita more violent crimes by members of minority groups and that the differential rate of executions may merely reflect an unfortunate social reality.

Finally, there is a moral question about the use of the power of the state to put people to death. Critics of the death penalty argue that this makes government and society little better than the criminals that they are punishing. The critics further argue that the finality of the sentence poses the risk of executing innocent people who then have no meaningful recourse. As we discussed in the section on decision theory (pp. 69–71), the possibility (even if small) that the decision to execute is incorrect may exact social costs greater than any benefits to be realized. The supporters of the death penalty recognize the severity of the punishment, and few if any take the imposition of the death penalty lightly. They argue, however, that individuals who commit extremely brutal crimes and crimes involving certain categories of victims (children, for example) have forfeited the right to live in a civilized society.

The debate over the death penalty continues. Its supporters received some comfort from the inclusion of a large number of new crimes requiring the death penalty in the Clinton crime bill. In addition, the Supreme Court has reduced the capacity of convicts on death row to receive stays of execution.[74] Opponents of capital punishment in turn received some good news when Justice Harry Blackmun, near retirement, wrote a dissenting opinion declaring that he would no longer take part in any decisions to execute prisoners, despite the fact that he had voted a number of times previously to permit states to impose the death penalty.[75] This statement by a respected justice did cause some reassessment, but there have been no shifts in the legality or use of this punishment.

The Rights of the Accused

In addition to the prohibition of cruel and unusual punishment, the Bill of Rights provides a number of protections to the accused. For example, those accused of crimes are protected against self-incrimination (Fifth Amendment) and against unlawful search and seizure of their persons and property (Fourth Amendment). They are assured a trial by a jury of their peers and guaranteed that the writ of habeas corpus is available to them so that they will know why they are being arrested and so that they cannot be held for long periods of time without the filing of some formal charge against them (Article I, section 9). Finally, accused citizens have a right to legal counsel when they go to court (and now as soon as they are arrested).

This an impressive list of protections. In fact, some critics believe that the list is too long and that the police are being "handcuffed" in their attempts to arrest and convict criminals. This feeling has become all the more pronounced over the past several decades as the courts have tended to interpret the rights of the accused more broadly and to require the police to be more careful in how they treat the accused. For example, when arrested, a suspect must now be advised of his or her legal rights, including the right to counsel.[76] Also, the courts have tended to interpret the protections against unreasonable search more strictly, so the police must have sound reasons to obtain a search warrant, and even stronger justification if they search without first receiving a warrant. (Still, in the media event that was the O.J. Simpson trial, the judge admitted some crucial evidence gathered before a search warrant had been issued because its discovery was incidental to other proper police activities.)[77] All these protections for the accused have produced a number of cries that too many criminals are able to escape conviction on mere "technicalities."

The defenders of the current restrictions on police behavior argue that civil liberties are not mere "technicalities" but are fundamental to the nature of the American political system and the judicial process. They argue that if the police and prosecutors cannot make sustainable cases against defendants within these restrictions, they are not doing their jobs properly. The defenders of the restraints on police and prosecutorial behavior argue that the police now have a number of powerful scientific tools, such as DNA testing, that should enable them to justify convictions without having to resort to more suspect means of investigation. These defenders, in fact, would be willing to trade off a few convictions in order to ensure that the fundamental civil liberties of all Americans are protected.

Associated with the perceived difficulties in prosecuting accused criminals is the issue of pardon and parole. There are frequent newspaper accounts of paroled convicts committing further crimes, sometimes within days of having been released from prison. But the possibility of parole is often a motivating device for cooperation by prisoners in what could otherwise be extremely dangerous settings.[78] In addition, prisons in most states in the United States are filled to capacity—the United States has the highest per capita rate of incarceration of any industrial democracy. Without the option for early release, even more prisons would have to be built, imposing a further drain on state and local resources. As with most policy problems, there is no quick and easy answer.

Youth Crime

A final issue in law enforcement became more evident in the late 1990s—the problem of violent crimes committed by children. A number of instances of children taking guns to school and attacking their classmates and teachers in 1997 and 1998 produced real feelings of shock and made the public very aware of this issue, although the evidence is that there has always been a much higher rate of crime by children than is generally understood.

In light of the earlier discussion of gun control, it is important to note that all of these notorious incidents of juvenile violence involved guns. This in turn has led to calls for requirements for locking all guns away from access by children or others who may want to use them unwisely. Not surprisingly, this proposal has been opposed by the National Rifle Association and other pro-gun groups. The other question raised by these killings was how to treat crimes committed by the young. Should they be prosecuted in the same manner as any other crimes, or should they, as is true in almost all instances, be subject to separate legal standards? The two boys who killed four people in Arkansas, for example, can only be kept in jail (or other institutions) up to the age of twenty-one.

The Clinton Crime Bill

In response to the high degree of public concern about crime, and particularly violent crime, the Clinton administration developed and advocated a major federal crime bill in 1994. The nature of this bill and the politics that surrounded it illustrate a number of points we have been making about the policy process in the United States. The first point has to do with the social and political construction of the issue of crime.[79] While the majority of the efforts and money in the Clinton bill were dedicated to direct law enforcement, the legislation also contained some recognition of the socioeconomic roots of crime. Approximately one-third of the expenditures in the original bill were to go for social and educational programs designed to prevent crime—especially among the young. These proposed expenditures permitted opponents of the bill to describe it as a social welfare program rather than a "tough" anticrime bill and eventually to force some reductions in social spending.[80]

A second point is that the crime bill was designed to provide state, and especially local, governments with large amounts of new money for hiring additional police and a number of other purposes. Critics of the bill characterized these provisions as "pork-barrel legislation" rather than an attempt to address the fundamental problems of crime.[81] The bill did require a distribution of benefits, with a large proportion of spending—perhaps larger than might be justified by their relative rates of violent crime—going to rural and suburban communities rather than to the large central cities. That windfall for their constituents somehow did not stop conservative critics from rural areas from arguing that the bill really was no more than a subsidy for the cities.

A third point about the Clinton bill is that it tended to anger a range of groups in the society. As it was finally written, the bill offended many members of minority groups, as well as the congressmen who represented them. One of the original drafts of the bill had contained a strong racial justice provision that would have addressed the perceived disparities in sentencing, especially in the application of the death penalty, between white and non-white criminals.[82] Negotiations over the final version of the law deleted these provisions, however, and several potential supporters then abandoned the bill, although the leadership of the Congressional Black Caucus maintained its support. On the other side of the ideological spectrum, the National Rifle Association lobbied extremely hard against the bill because it contained provisions banning the sale of certain types of weapons, mostly semiautomatic assault rifles. As noted earlier, this once omnipotent interest group had recently lost a major battle over the Brady bill and felt that it could not lose another.

A final point is that the crime bill illustrates the tendency of problems to float upwards in a federal system, despite the construction of the Constitution reserving powers to the states. The crime bill gave the federal government a role in investigating a number of crimes, especially domestic violence, that previously had been almost the exclusive preserve of state and local governments. In part it was good politics for federal legislators to be seen as concerned about the rising crime rate, so they agreed to intervene. Also, the perception that the federal government has more resources than the other levels of government to "solve" these problems has tended to push the problems upward.

Given all the objections, the bill could not be passed as first proposed, and that failure illustrates another very important point about the process of legitimating public policies. The bill's critics appeared to fix their attention on the one or two features they could not support, rather than on those they might have approved. Adopting legislation almost invariably involves compromise, and the failure to do so may be a major barrier to effective government action. This is perhaps especially true in the United States, given the inherent tendency of the system toward gridlock.[83] In the end, a more acceptable compromise was forged and the bill could finally be passed by Congress and signed by the president.

The legislation that was passed still contained a mixture of punishment and prevention.[84] Of the $30.2 billion allocated over six years, the bulk of the money went to hiring local police officers ($8.8 billion), building prisons ($7.9 billion), incarcerating criminal aliens ($1.8 billion), and other programs directed at catching and punishing criminals ($4.8 billion). After cuts, there was still $6.9 billion for prevention programs such as fighting violence against women ($1.6 billion), noncriminal "drug courts" ($1 billion), and recreation opportunities for inner-city children ($562 million).[85] The act also had a number of regulatory features, the most important being the outlawing of the sale of nineteen kinds of assault rifles and gun clips holding more than ten bullets, extension of the federal death penalty, and provision for adult treatment of thirteen-year-olds charged with major crimes.

Whether because of the Crime Control Act or not, substantial reductions in crime (especially violent crimes) soon made it appear that crime was becoming less of a problem for American society than it once had been. This meant politically that candidates would find it more difficult to play the crime card, a device that has been especially useful for more conservative politicians, and that some money might be saved from policing and from jailing convicted criminals. Open questions remained as to whether this reduction in crime could survive welfare reform and its potential for creating more poverty and whether it would survive any economic downturn of consequence. In the short term, however, there did appear to be some good news in this area.

Conclusion

We have been discussing the ways in which governments in the United States attempt to protect their citizens from "enemies, domestic and foreign." This is one of the defining duties of any government,[86] and it is one in which governments have been engaged since their inception. The issues involved in this policy area have, however, become more complex in recent years. First, in defense, there is no longer a clearly identifiable enemy against which to plot strategy. Instead the task is one of preparing for a wide range of threats to national security, including some for which the military is not particularly well adapted. Further, there are demands for use of the military for a number of purposes that go well beyond conventional national defense and require it to fulfill virtually a social mission on the international scene. Finally, domestic social and political concerns have invaded the world of the armed forces, requiring some rethinking of the values and mores of that world.

Crime is an equally complex policy and political problem. It is perhaps even more complex than defense given that the United States attempts to combat crime while maintaining an open and free society. Police measures that might be effective in curtailing the growth of crime are simply not possible if the tradition of the open society is to be maintained. Even without the complications of civil liberties there would be other difficulties for a government attempting to solve a serious crime problem, not least of which is understanding the root causes of this social pathology and therefore the means of best addressing the problem.

PART FOUR

Policy Analysis

15. Cost-Benefit Analysis

Much of this book has been concerned with the process through which policies are adopted in the United States and with the characteristics of those policies. This chapter extends that discussion by discussing the principal method of policy analysis used when making policy choices: cost-benefit analysis. Because governments operate with limited resources and limited ability to predict the future, they must employ some techniques to help them decide how to utilize those scarce resources. Cost-benefit analysis is the most commonly employed technique, other than the informal techniques arising from intuition and experience. The fundamental principle of cost-benefit analysis is that any project undertaken should produce a benefit for society greater than the cost of the project.[1] Second, when several projects promise to yield positive net benefits and when all cannot be undertaken because of limited resources, then the project that creates the greatest net benefit to the society should be selected. This technique is perhaps most applicable to capital projects, such as building highways or dams, but it can also be applied to other public programs. In fact, cost-benefit analysis was adopted as a means of assessing all proposed regulations during the Reagan administration in an attempt to curb the growth of government involvement in the economy.

Obviously there is a decided utilitarian bias underlying cost-benefit analysis.[2] The costs and benefits of a project are all collapsed onto the single measuring rod of money, and those that create the greatest net benefit are deemed superior. This implies that the dominant value in society is economic wealth and, further, that more is always better. The importance of total wealth is presumed to be dominant even if rather perverse distributional consequences arise from the program. I discuss the philosophical and practical issues that arise with cost-benefit analysis later in this chapter. These implications may be sufficiently troubling, especially in a democratic political system, for some critics to argue for alternative means of evaluating policies. But cost-benefit analysis does have the advantage of reducing all the costs and benefits of public programs to that single dimension, whereas other forms of analysis may produce apparent confusion by lacking such a common dimension. Within that single dimension, cost-benefit analysis can give an answer as to whether a project is desirable or not, while other methods tend to produce more ambiguous results.

Principles of Cost-Benefit Analysis

In the world of cost-benefit analysis, more is always better. Although it does have serious intellectual foundations, which we explore in a moment, the method is in many ways no more than a systematic framework within which to collect data concerning the merits and demerits of a public program. And it is not a new idea: the Army Corps of Engineers used the technique as early as 1900 to evaluate the merits of proposed improvements to rivers and harbors. The basic idea is to enumerate the positive features of a program and attach a monetary value to them, and at the same time to enumerate the negative features and attach a monetary value to those features. The net balance of costs and benefits will then determine if a program is economically feasible, although many other questions about its desirability may remain.

One principal idea underlying cost-benefit analysis comes from the tradition in welfare economics that has sought to develop an acceptable social welfare function, or a socially desirable means for making collective policy decisions.[3] That is, how can societies take the numerous and often conflicting views of their citizens and generate the policy choice that is the most acceptable to the society? One of the first welfare criteria of this sort was the Pareto principle, which argued that a policy choice was optimal if no move away from it could be made to benefit someone without hurting someone else.[4] Stated another way, a Pareto optimal policy move would be one that benefits at least one person without hurting anyone. Clearly, in the real world of political decision making, policies of this kind are rare indeed, and politics is frequently about who gets what at the expense of whom. Therefore, using the Pareto principle would be extremely conservative, supporting very few public interventions.

A substitute welfare criterion was advanced by Nicholas Kaldor and John Hicks. They argued that a policy change was socially justified if the winners gained a sufficient amount to compensate the losers and still had something left for themselves.[5] This does not imply that those winners necessarily *will* compensate the losers, or that government could even identify the losers, but the idea is that the society as a whole is better off because of the overall increase in benefits. This welfare criterion, then, is a justification of the reliance of cost-benefit analysis on the production of the greatest possible net benefit. It can perhaps be hoped that at least part of the benefits created will somehow find their way to the individuals who may have been harmed by the policy choice, but greater weight is given to the fact that those benefits have been created. Intellectually, this approach poses another problem. It requires aggregating utilities across a range of individuals, and that requires doing the nearly impossible—making interpersonal comparisons of utility.[6]

A second fundamental idea underlying cost-benefit analysis is that of the consumer's surplus.[7] Stated simply, this is the amount of money a consumer would be willing to pay for a given product, minus the amount he or she must actually pay. Consumers tend to value the first unit of a product or service they receive more highly than the second, and the second more than the third; the first quart of milk where there has been none is more valuable than the second. But the units of a product are not priced marginally; they are sold at an average price. This means that the utility of increased production will give consumers a surplus value from the production. Thus, any investment that reduces the cost of the product or service produces a benefit in savings that increases the consumer's surplus. The investment by government in a new superhighway that reduces the cost to consumers of driving the same number of miles—in time, in gasoline, and in potential loss of life and property—creates a consumer's surplus. And as the time, gasoline, and lives saved by the new highway may be used for other increased production, the actual savings represent a minimum definition of the improvement to society resulting from the construction of the new highway.

Also important in understanding cost-benefit analysis is the concept of opportunity costs: any resource used in one project cannot be used in another. For example, the concrete, steel, and labor used to build the superhighway cannot be used to build a new dam. Consequently, all projects must be evaluated against other possible projects to determine the most appropriate way to use resources—especially financial resources. Projects are also compared, implicitly if not explicitly, with taking no action and allowing the money to remain in the hands of individual citizens. Again, the basic idea of getting the most "bang for the buck" is important in understanding cost-benefit analysis.

When identifying and assessing costs and benefits, the analyst must also be concerned with the range of effects of the proposed program and with determining at what point he or she disregards effects as being too remote for consideration.[8] For example, building a municipal waste incinerator in Detroit, Michigan, will have pronounced effects in Windsor, Ontario, Canada, that must be considered, even though that city is outside the United States. Prevailing air currents may mean that some ash and acid from the incinerator also come down in Norway and Sweden, but those effects may be so minimal and so remote that they can be disregarded. Engaging in this form of analysis requires making judgments about what effects are sufficiently proximate and important to include as part of the calculations.

Finally, in evaluating costs and benefits, we must be concerned about time. The costs and benefits of most projects do not occur at a single time but accrue over a number of years. If our superhighway is built, it will be serviceable for fifty years and will be financed over twenty years through government bonds. Policymakers must be certain that the long-term costs and benefits as well as the short-term consequences are positive. This, of course, requires some estimation of the nature of the future. We may estimate that our new superhighway will be useful for fifty years, but oil shortages may so reduce driving during that period that the real benefits will be much less than anticipated. Or, conversely, the value of gasoline may increase so much that the savings produced are more valuable than assumed at present. These kinds of assumptions about the future must be built into the model of valuation for it to aid a decision maker.

In part because of the uncertainty over future costs and benefits, and in part because of the general principle that people prefer a dollar today to a dollar next year, the costs and benefits of projects must be converted to present values before useful cost and benefit calculations can be made. That is, the benefits that accrue to the society in the future have their value discounted and are consequently worth less than benefits produced in the first year of the project. Likewise, costs that occur in future years are lower than costs that occur in the first few years. Thus, cost-benefit analysis would appear to favor projects that have a quick payoff rather than greater long-term benefits but perhaps higher maintenance and operation costs. While there may be a good logical justification for these biases in the method, they do certainly influence the kinds of program that will be selected and that will have definite social implications, not least of all for future generations. Other forms of analytic aids for government decision makers, such as "decision trees" (see p. 70), include probabilities of outcomes as a means of coping with the uncertainties of the future, but cost-benefit analysis tends to rely on discounting future costs and benefits.

Doing Cost-Benefit Analysis

To better understand the application of cost-benefit analysis we now work through the steps required to justify the construction of a new dam on the Nowhere River. This project is being proposed by the Army Corps of Engineers, and we have to determine whether or not the project should be undertaken. We have to decide first if the project is feasible and acceptable on its own, and then if it is preferable to other projects that could be funded with the same resources. Again, this decision is being made initially on economic grounds; we may have to bring other forms of analysis (politics) and other criteria (the environment, which may be a trump card) into the decision process at a later time.

The TVA's multiple hydroelectric projects provide cheap power, stimulate industrialization, and create new recreational opportunities in a remote rural area. (Tennessee Valley Authority)

Determining Costs and Benefits

One of the most important factors to consider when performing a cost-benefit analysis, especially of a public project, is that all costs and benefits should be enumerated. Thus, unlike projects that might be undertaken in the private sector, public projects require an explicit statement of the social, or external, costs and benefits. In the public sector, projects whose strictly economic potential may outweigh their costs may not be adopted because of the possibility of pollution or the loss of external benefits such as natural beauty. In fact, one of the principal logical justifications for the existence of the public sector is that it should take into account these external factors and attempt to correct them in ways not possible in the private sector.[9] Even with that social justification, however, the values of the costs and benefits are usually computed in economic terms just as if they were to accrue in the private market. This reliance on market logic for nonmarket decisions is one of the fundamental ironies in cost-benefit analysis.[10]

Thus, for our dam project, we can think of two lists of attributes (see table 15.1, p. 426). On one side are the costs of the project, the main one

TABLE 15.1

COSTS AND BENEFITS OF DAM PROJECT

Costs	Benefits
Construction costs	Hydroelectric power
Flooded land	Flood control
Relocation of families	Irrigation
Loss of recreation	New recreational opportunities

being the economic cost of constructing the dam, which should reflect the market valuation of the opportunity costs of using the same resources for other purposes. Also, the dam will impose an economic cost by flooding the houses and farmland of present inhabitants of the area. But there are also social, or human, costs involved here, as these farms have been in the same families for generations, and the farmers have resisted the project from the beginning. Finally, there are further social costs in that the proposed dam will impound a river that currently has some recreational value for canoeists and is essentially an unspoiled natural area.

On the other side of the ledger are the benefits of the program. First, the dam will provide hydroelectric power for the region, and, in so doing, it will provide a source of electric power that does not consume scarce fossil fuels and does not create the air pollution that would result from producing the same amount of electricity with fossil fuels. Also, the dam would help control the raging Nowhere River, which every spring overflows its banks and floods a number of towns, cities, and farms downstream from the proposed dam. In addition, the water impounded behind the dam will provide irrigation for the remaining farmers, enabling them to grow crops more reliably than if they had to rely just on rainfall. Finally, although canoeists will lose some recreational benefits as a result of the building of the dam, citizens who enjoy power boating and water skiing will benefit from the large lake formed behind the dam. Thus, although the proposed dam does impose a number of costs on the society, it also provides a number of benefits in return. To proceed with this analysis, we must now begin to attach some quantitative values to these costs and benefits in order to be able to make a decision as to the feasibility and desirability of the project.

Assigning Value

Assigning real monetary values to all the costs and benefits of this mythical project would be difficult. For some costs and benefits the market directly provides a value. We know, or can estimate accurately, the costs of building the dam and the market value of the hydroelectric power it will produce. Although such costs are generally measurable through the market, the market may not fully measure other possible costs and benefits. For example, if our dam is to be built in a remote area with little more than subsistence agriculture, bringing in a large number of highly skilled and highly paid workers may distort prices and increase the costs of building the dam. Similarly, not only is the hydroelectric power salable, but it may produce substantial secondary benefits (or perhaps costs) by stimulating industrialization in this rural and remote area. The experience of the Tennessee Valley Authority and its impact on the Tennessee Valley as a result of the development of cheap electric power illustrates this point rather nicely.[11] We cannot fully predict these secondary benefits, nor can we rely on them to make the project feasible, but they do frequently occur.

Some other costs and benefits of the project, although not directly measurable through the market, can be estimated in other ways. For example, we have to estimate the dam's recreational value to the people who will use the lake to water-ski as well as its cost to those who will no longer be able to use the river for canoeing. We can do this by estimating the people's willingness to pay for their recreation.[12] Just how much time and money are they willing to invest to enjoy their recreation? Evidence for this calculation can be gained from surveys of recreation participants or from their actual behavior in renting equipment and travel to recreation sites. These calculations will provide some measure of the economic value of the lake, and of the free-flowing stream, to the population.

The creation of the dam and the lake behind it help illustrate another point about valuing costs and benefits. The lake will produce lakefront property, which tends to have a higher market value than does other nearby property, so something of the aesthetic value of the impoundment can be calculated. This reckoning is analogous to estimating the value of clean air by comparing prices of similar housing in polluted and less polluted areas of a city.[13]

This method of valuation returns to the concept of the consumer's surplus. The first unit of a particular commodity is valued more highly than any subsequent units, so as production is increased, each unit is marginally less valuable to the consumer. In our dam example, if there already have been a number of impoundments in the area, as there have been in the Tennessee Valley, then a new lake will have less value to recreation consumers, and they will be less willing to pay than if this were the first lake in an area with a large number of free-flowing streams. Likewise, one more hydroelectric power station in an area that already has cheap electrical power is less valuable than it would be in an economically backward area, and consequently citizens will be less willing to pay for that new power plant.

Finally, on some aspects of the project, the market provides little or no guidance about valuation. For the farmers who are displaced by the project, we can calculate the economic value of their land, their houses, and their moving costs. However, we cannot readily assign an economic value to those houses that are the ancestral homes of families and that are therefore more valuable psychologically than ordinary houses.[14] Similarly, there is some value in not disturbing a natural setting, simply because it is natural, and this is a difficult thing to which to assign an economic value. As a result, at times absolute prohibitions are built into legislation to prevent certain actions, so planners cannot depend entirely on net benefit ratios. The Environmental Protection Agency's guideline for preserving the habitats of endangered species, which resulted in the now notorious case of the snail darter in the Little Tennessee River and the more recent case of the delta smelt in California, is an example of the application of regulations to prevent some actions regardless of the relative economic costs and benefits.[15]

The willingness to pay approach to valuation questions the people directly involved with the project about their own valuation of costs and benefits. For some of those costs and benefits the population at large may be equally important as judges of the value. Federal regulators are now under congressional mandate to find ways to assess the value that the public assigns to the costs of environmental problems such as oil spills. These "contingent value" measurements by passive users are now being undertaken by survey methods. The first of these has been conducted by the National Oceanic and Atmospheric Administration and has so far gained broad support from environmental groups.[16] This method of valuation has, however, met general opposition by business concerns and is being contested in the court system.[17]

It is fortunate that the dam we are building does not require any direct decisions about loss of life or injury to human beings. For projects that do—for example, building the superhighway as a means of saving lives—we come to perhaps the most difficult problem of valuation: estimating the value of a human life.[18] Although it is convenient to say that life is priceless, in practice decisions are made that deny some people their lives when that loss of life is preventable. If this is the case, then some subjective, if not objective, evaluation is being made of the worth of lives. One standard method of making such a judgment involves discounted future earnings. In this method the life of the individual is worth whatever the individual could have earned in the course of his or her working life, discounted to present value. Therefore, in this perspective, a highly paid corporate executive's life is worth more than a housewife's or a college professor's. This mechanism for evaluating lives clearly conforms to the basic market valuation, although it could clearly be contested on humane grounds.

Another means of assessing the value of lives as a basis for cost-benefit analysis utilizes the size of the awards to plaintiffs in legal cases of negligence or malpractice that resulted in loss of life. In other words, what do panels of citizens or judges consider a human life to be worth? This method constitutes yet another version of the market criterion, albeit one in which considerations of human suffering and "loss of companionship" have a greater—some would say too great because of the emotionalism involved —impact on the economic valuation than does earning power.

Another means of assessing the value of a human life is somewhat similar to the "willingness to pay" criterion. In theory, individuals would be willing to pay almost anything to preserve their own lives and the lives of their loved ones. However, individuals engage in risky behavior and risky occupations all the time, and when they do so, they make subjective statements about the value of their lives.[19] Because we know how much more likely it is for a coal miner to be killed at work—either in the mines or as a result of black lung disease—than it is for a construction worker we can estimate from any differences in wages how much these individuals would appear to value their lives. This method does, of course, imply a certain level of knowledge that individuals may not have, and it assumes that the collective bargaining process, through which wages of coal miners and construction workers are determined, accurately reflects both individual preferences and the market values of lives. This method does, however, offer another feasible means of estimating the value of life, one that uses the assessment of individual citizens rather than that of the market or the courts.

Discounting

We now return to the problem of time. The costs and benefits of a project do not all magically appear as soon as the project is completed, but typically are stretched over a number of years. Table 15.2 shows the stream of benefits coming from the dam on the Nowhere River over a twenty-year period. This is the projected feasible lifetime of the project, as the Nowhere River carries a great deal of silt and the lake behind the dam is expected to fill with silt after that period. How do we assess these benefits and come up with a single number that we can compare with costs to determine the economic feasibility of the project?

To calculate such a figure, we must compute the present value of the future benefits. We have already decided on the time span of the project; the only task that remains is to determine the discount rate that should be applied to a public investment. And, as with the valuation of costs and benefits, disagreements may arise about what that rate should be.[20] One method is to use the opportunity costs of the use of these funds. Presumably any money used in a project in the public sector will be extracted from the pri-

TABLE 15.2
HYPOTHETICAL COSTS AND BENEFITS OF DAM PROJECT
FOR TWENTY YEARS

Year

	1	2	3	4	5	6	7	8	9	10	11	12	13	14	15	16	17	18	19	20
Costs	5	8	7	2	1	1	1	1	1	1	1	1	1	1	1	1	1	1	1	1
Benefits	0	0	0	3	4	5	5	5	5	5	5	5	5	5	5	4	4	4	3	2

vate sector by some means such as taxation or borrowing, and consequently the rate of return these resources could earn if they were invested in private-sector projects is the appropriate rate of discount for public-sector projects. This is not always a practical solution, however, as rates of return differ for different kinds of investments, and investors apparently choose to put some money into each kind of investment. Is building a dam more like speculative mining investments, building a steel mill, or investing in an insured savings account? Which of the many possible rates of return should be selected?

Several other issues arise with respect to the selection of a discount rate. First, in discussing projects for which most benefits are to accrue in the future, there is an element of uncertainty. In our example we have assumed that the probable life span of the dam will be twenty years, but in reality the lake may fill up with silt in fifteen years. Consequently, it may be more prudent to select a discount rate higher than that in the market because we cannot be sure of the real occurrence or real value of the benefits. And because these benefits are expected to be further away in time, they are less certain; therefore, even higher rates of discount should be applied. Also, with inflation and the uncertainties about the development of new energy sources, we may need to be more conservative about discount rates.

Second, some analysts argue that there should be a "social rate of discount" lower than that established by the market.[21] Such an arbitrarily set discount rate would be justified on the basis of the need for greater public investment and the need to provide a capital infrastructure for future generations. Further, as the size of the public sector is to some degree determined by the rate of discount, that rate should be set not by the market but by more conscious political choices concerning the appropriate level of public activity. But the economic counterargument is that, in the long term, the society will be better off if resources are allocated on the basis of their opportunity costs. If a public project is deemed infeasible because of the selection of a market-determined discount rate, then the resources that would have been used in that project would, it is argued, produce greater social benefit in a project that is feasible under that rate of discount. This would be true regardless of whether the project is in the public or the private sector. If no such project is available, then the money would be better saved until such a project does materialize.

Finally, a question arises about intergenerational equity. What do we owe to posterity or, put the other way around, what has posterity ever done for us? If the discount rate is set lower than that determined by the market, then we will tend to undertake more projects that have an extended time value and that will benefit future generations. But we will also deprive the present generation of opportunities for consumption by using those resources as investment capital. This is as much a philosophical as a practical issue, but it is important for our understanding of alternative consequences arising from alternative choices of a rate of discount for public projects.

Using several discount rates, let us now work through the example of levels of benefit from the dam. Let us assume that the prime interest rate in the United States is approximately 8 percent. If we use this market-determined interest rate, the $100 in benefits produced after one year is worth

$$V = \$100/1.08 = \$92.59.$$

And $100 in benefits produced after two years would be worth

$$V = \$100/(1.08)^2 = \$85.73.$$

And $100 in benefits produced in the twentieth year of the project would be worth only $21.45 in present value. Thus, if we use this market rate of discount in evaluating a public project, the net benefit of that project at present value is positive. This project has a rather high cost during its early years, with the benefits occurring gradually over the twenty years. With a higher discount rate such a project is not feasible. If we use a discount rate of 18 percent, which would have seemed very reasonable in the late 1970s (but absurd in the 1990s), then the net benefit of the dam at present value would be negative and the project would be economically infeasible.

Discounting is a means of reducing all costs and benefits of a project to present value, based on the assumption that benefits created in the future are worth less than those created immediately. Philosophically or ideologically one might desire a low discount rate to encourage public investment but object to the entire process of discounting. Should we simply not look to see if the stream of benefits created is greater than the total costs, no matter how and when they occur? This would, of course, be equivalent to a discount rate of zero. This point might be valid philosophically, but until the argument is accepted by economists, financiers, and government decision makers, public investment decisions will be made on the basis of present value and on the basis of interest rates that approximate the real value of the rate of return in the private sector.

Choosing Among Projects

We have determined that our dam on the Nowhere River is feasible, given that a benevolent deity has provided us a discount rate of 8 percent for this project. But it is not yet time to break ground for the dam. We must first compare our project with alternative projects for funding. Thus, the opportunity cost question arises not only with respect to the single project being considered and the option of allowing the money to remain in private hands, but also with regard to choices made among possible projects in the public sector.

We have argued that the fundamental rule applied is to select the project that will produce the greatest total benefit to society. If we apply the Kaldor-Hicks criterion (see pp. 422–23), we see that this project is justified simply because it will create more benefits to spread around in the society and presumably compensate those who lost something because the project was built. Thus, in the simplest case, if we were to choose to undertake only a single project this year—perhaps because of limited manpower for supervision—we would choose Project D from table 15.3 simply because it creates the largest level of net benefit. By investing less money in Projects A and B we could have produced slightly more net benefit for society, but we are administratively constrained from making that decision and must choose only the one most productive investment.

TABLE 15.3
COSTS AND BENEFITS OF ALTERNATIVE PROJECTS
(IN MILLIONS OF DOLLARS)

Projects	Costs	Benefits	Net benefit
A	70	130	60
B	90	140	50
C	200	270	70
D	150	250	100

More commonly, however, a particular resource—usually money—is limited and, with that limitation in mind, we have to choose one or more projects that will result in maximum benefits. Let us say that the ten projects listed in table 15.4 are all economically feasible and that we have been given a budget of $50 million for capital projects. Which projects should we select for funding? In such a situation, we should rank the projects according to the ratio of net benefits to initial costs (the costs that will be reflected in our capital budget), and then we should begin with the best projects, in terms of the ratio of benefits to initial costs, until the budget is exhausted. In this way, we will get the greatest benefit for the expenditure of our limited funds. And projects that we might have selected if we were choosing only a single project would not be selected under these conditions of resource constraint.

This problem of selecting among projects demonstrates the first of several problems that arise from the application of the basic rule of cost-benefit analysis. Given the budgetary process and the allocation of funds among agencies, we may produce a case of "multi-organizational suboptimization." This is a fancy way of saying that if our agency has been given $50 million, we will spend it, even if other agencies have projects that will produce greater benefits for society but do not have adequate funds in their budgets. Thus, if I had the money, I would continue to fund the projects listed in table 15.4 even though several of them have relatively low net-benefit ratios and even though there were better projects that other government bureaus wanted to fund. Of course, I will have been asked what benefits my proposed projects would produce when the capital budget was being considered, but because of political considerations arising in the process my budget is excessive for the benefits that could be produced from alternative uses of the money. This is not, of course, a flaw in the method; it is a flaw in the application of the method in complex and competitive government settings.

A not unrelated problem is that cost-benefit analysis places relatively little importance on efficiency or cost effectiveness. It looks primarily at total benefits rather than at the ratio of benefits to costs produced. It could be ar-

TABLE 15.4

CHOOSING A PACKAGE OF PROJECTS BY NET BENEFIT RATIO

(IN MILLIONS OF DOLLARS)

Project	Costs	Cumulative costs	Benefits	Net benefits	Net benefit ratio
A	2	2	12	10	5.0
B	4	6	20	16	4.0
C	10	16	40	30	3.0
D	10	26	35	25	2.5
E	8	34	28	20	2.5
F	16	50	51	35	2.2
G	2	52	6	4	2.0
H	15	67	42	27	1.8
I	10	77	26	16	1.6
J	18	95	45	27	1.5

gued that this tends to favor the ax over the scalpel as a cutting tool. In other words, the method tends to favor large projects over small projects. This may be an inefficient use of resources and may also lock government into costly projects, whereas smaller projects might provide greater flexibility and greater future opportunities for innovation. Capital projects are inherently lumpy, so that only projects of a certain size are feasible, but the concentration on total net benefits in cost-benefit analysis may exaggerate the problems of size and inflexibility.

We have now worked our way from the initial step of deciding what costs and benefits our project provides to deciding if it is the best project to undertake, given limited budgetary resources and the competing uses of the money. At each stage of the process we have had to use a number of assumptions and approximations to reach a decision. The cost-benefit analysis does provide a "hard" answer as to whether or not we should undertake a project, but that answer should not remain unquestioned. We now discuss some criticisms of cost-benefit analysis and some possible ways of building greater political and economic sophistication into the application of the methodology.

Extensions

We have so far been discussing a very basic approach to the method of cost-benefit analysis. There are, however, a number of extensions and modifications that are important for thinking about the utility of the method. First, there are other techniques such as cost-effectiveness analysis that have many things in common with cost-benefit analysis but have their own particular perspectives on the analysis. For example, cost-effectiveness analysis does not require the assessment of the value of various outcomes to the extent required in cost-benefit analysis, but rather assumes that an outcome is desirable.[22] Unlike cost-benefit analysis, this technique cannot tell the analyst whether an outcome is beneficial, only what it will cost to achieve a specified quantity of the outcome. Therefore, cost-effectiveness analysis tends to be used frequently in health policy and medicine where curing a disease is a prima facie good; the question is how much will it cost.[23] Even then, however, some physicians do not like the concept of attaching a price to a cure and thinking about efficiency in medical care.[24]

Criticism and Modification

We have discussed some critical problems regarding cost-benefit analysis. Such things as the difficulty of assigning monetary values to nonmonetary outcomes, the choice of time ranges and discount rates, and the reliance on total net benefit as the criterion all introduce uncertainties about the usefulness of the outcome. We now discuss more basic problems that arise concerning the method itself and its relationship to the political process. Perhaps the most important is that some naive politicians and analysts might let the method make decisions for them, instead of using the information derived from the analysis as one among many elements in their decision-making process. If the method is used naively and uncritically, its application can result in decisions that many people would deem socially undesirable. For example, all costs and benefits are counted as equal in the model, and, even if they could be calculated accurately, some individuals would argue that the cost of death might be more important than other costs. Thus, we might wish to reduce deaths to the lowest possible level and then perhaps apply a cost-benefit analysis to other aspects of the project. We might use this "lexicographic preference" as a means of initially sorting projects, when a single dominant value such as life or the preservation of endangered species is involved. That is, we take only projects that "pass" the one crucial test and then subject those to cost-benefit analysis.

Perhaps the most socially questionable aspect of the cost-benefit analysis is that it gives little attention to the distributive questions involved in all policies.[25] All benefits and costs are counted equally in the method, regardless of who receives or bears them. A project that increased the wealth of a wealthy man by several million dollars and was financed by regressive taxation of $100,000 would be preferred to a project that produced a benefit of $900,000 for unemployed workers and was financed by progressive taxation of $200,000. This is an extreme example, but it does point to the distributional blindness of the method. Of course, advocates of the method justify it by saying that the society as a whole will be better off with the greatest increase in benefits, and presumably winners can later compensate losers. In reality, however, winners rarely if ever do so, and usually losers cannot be directly identified anyway. Redistributional goals may be included directly in the analysis by attaching some weight greater than one to positive changes in the salaries of low-income or unemployed persons, or redistributional objectives may be imposed on the analysis after the fact. However, because government exists in part to attempt to redress some of the inequities produced in the marketplace, some attention must be given to redistributional goals when evaluating public projects.

Furthermore, the utilitarian and "econocratic" foundations of cost-benefit analysis may not be entirely suitable for a functioning political democracy.[26] In cost-benefit analysis, money alone is the measure of all things, and decisions made according to the method can be expected to be based on the economic rather than the political values involved. I discuss in chapter 16 some possible ethical alternatives that may be more suitable in a democracy. The difficulty is that these other criteria lack the apparent precision of cost-benefit analysis as well as its ability to provide a definitive answer to questions about the desirability of a policy intervention.

Finally, cost-benefit analysis has been referred to as "nonsense on stilts."[27] This rather rude phrase means that there are so many assumptions involved in the calculations, and so many imponderables about the future effects of projects, that cost-benefit analysis is the functional equivalent of witchcraft in the public sector. Although these criticisms have been phrased in exaggerated language, to some degree they are well taken. It is difficult if not impossible to know the value of eliminating an externality, just as it is difficult to know just how much life, health, and snail darters are worth economically. Cost-benefit analysis can be used to avoid difficult political decisions and to abdicate responsibility to experts who can supply the "correct" answer. Of course, this fundamental abdication of political responsibility is indeed an "insidious poison in the body politick." Only when the results of analysis are integrated with other forms of analysis, such as ethical analysis, and then combined with sound political judgment can the "correct decisions" ever be made.

16. Ethical Analysis of Public Policy

All the mathematical and economic capabilities in the world and all the substantive knowledge of policy areas are of little consequence if we have no moral or ethical foundation on which to base our evaluation of policies. Most of the important questions concerning policy analysis have as much to do with the "should" questions as with the "can" questions. That is, most important policy decisions involve assessment of what should be done by government as much as they involve the feasibility question of what government can do. The range of technical possibilities for action is frequently broader for policymakers than is the range of ethically justifiable possibilities for acting "in the public interest." But, unfortunately, many values that should affect policy decisions in the public sector conflict with one another. Analysts frequently confront choices among competing positive values, rather than clear-cut decisions about options that are either completely right or completely wrong.

In making almost all allocative decisions, policymakers must choose among worthy ends; they do not have the luxury of picking the only acceptable policy. Which is more important, the jobs of 500 loggers or an endangered species of owl? Also, policymakers must choose among alternative means to reach the desired goals, and those means themselves may have substantial ethical implications. Finally, in attempting to make decisions on ethical grounds, decision makers are confronted with an overwhelming utilitarian bias in the discussion of public policy.[1] As noted in our discussion of cost-benefit analysis, the prevailing conception is that government should do what creates the greatest economic value for the society rather than worry too much about the "softer" values we discuss in this chapter.

The basic concept behind utilitarianism—producing the greatest net benefit to society—is in the main admirable, but it can be used to justify actions that violate procedural norms as well as usual conceptions of fair distribution of the benefits of society. Further, this approach tends to reduce all considerations to economic ones, while there are a variety of other values that may be equally important for determining the proper course of government action. This chapter presents several important ethical premises that constitute alternatives to utilitarianism and that can be used to guide policy

437

decisions. It also discusses some of the difficulties of implementing those alternative ethical and moral values in real public-sector decisions.

Fundamental Value Premises

Any number of premises have been used to justify policy decisions, ranging from vague concepts such as "Americanism," "Aryan purity," "the principles of Marxism-Leninism," and that old standby, "the public interest," to well-articulated philosophical or religious principles.[2] The main difficulty in ethical analysis of policy decisions is finding principles that can be consistently applied to a number of situations and that produce acceptable decisions in those situations.[3] Words such as "justice," "equity," and "good" are tossed about in debates over public policies in a rather cavalier fashion. The analyst must attempt to systematize his or her values and learn to apply them consistently to issues. The policy analyst therefore must be a moral actor as well as a technician, or else remain what Arnold Meltsner refers to as a "baby analyst" throughout his or her career.[4] As we pointed out when discussing application of cost-benefit analysis (see chapter 15), values are involved throughout the policy process and are embedded in policy options and in commonly used analytic methods. In order to understand what one wants, one must explicate and examine those values.

In this chapter I discuss five important nonutilitarian value premises for making policy decisions: preservation of life, preservation of individual autonomy, truthfulness, fairness, and desert. These values would probably be widely accepted by the public as important standards for assessing policies, and they have a wide range of applicability across policy issues. As I point out, however, these values cannot be applied unambiguously, and conflicts are embedded in each issue as well as ranging across the several issues. In many cases there are conflicts among the values so that the analyst will have to decide how to weight the different values.

The Preservation of Life

The preservation of human life is one of the most fundamental values that we could expect to see manifested in the policy process. The sanctity of life is, after all, a fundamental value of Judeo-Christian ethics and is embodied in all professional codes of ethics.[5] Despite the importance of preserving human life as an ethical criterion, a number of conflicts arise over its application in real world decision situations. These are "tragic choices" because the resources available often do not permit everyone to be aided, and those not aided are condemned to die earlier than they might otherwise.[6] The ethical question then becomes which lives to preserve.

One obvious conflict over the use of resources to save lives exists

438

between identifiable lives and statistical lives. Here we are faced with the tendency of individuals to allocate resources differently if known lives of specific individuals are at stake from how they would evaluate them if some unspecified persons would be saved at some time in the future. If we know that certain individuals will die in the near future, we tend to provide them the resources they need to save themselves, even though the same resources could save many more unidentified lives in the future if allocated differently.

In medical care this problem is manifested in the conflict between acute and preventive medicine. Preventive medicine is almost certainly the most cost-effective means of saving lives that could be lost as a result of cancer, circulatory diseases, or accidents, but it is difficult to identify the direct beneficiaries. The victims of a disease, however, are clearly identifiable, have identifiable families, and consequently are more difficult to refuse care than the unknown statistical beneficiaries of preventive medicine. This pattern of decision making was referred to earlier (chapter 3) as the "mountain-climber syndrome," in which we may spend thousands of dollars to save a stranded mountain climber, even though we could save many more lives by spending the same amount of money on highway accident prevention. It is virtually impossible to say no to stranded mountain climbers and their families, although if the appropriate ethical criterion is to save as many lives as possible, that is perhaps what we should do.

But even if all the lives at stake in a decision are identifiable, in some instances allocative decisions must be made. Table 16.1, although it concentrates on a relatively small number of individuals who are potential recipients of a liver transplant, points out the broader problem of choice among lives. Each individual in table 16.1 is worthy of receiving the lifesaving treatment simply because he or she is a human being. But because organs for transplants are scarce and because the demand for them far exceeds the supply, decisions must be made that will allow some people to live and leave others to die. What criteria can be applied in making such a choice? One might be the conventional utilitarian criterion: the individuals who will contribute the most to the community (especially economically) should be allowed to live. Another criterion might be longevity: the youngest persons should be allowed to receive the treatment, thus saving the greatest number of person-years of life. Another criterion might be autonomy: individuals who have the greatest probability of returning to active and useful lives after treatment should receive the treatment.[7] Another criterion might be whether the disease requiring the treatment is self-inflicted or not. For example, should chronic alcoholics be given the same preference for receiving a new liver as other patients? At least one state in the United States has ruled that Medicaid should not pay for such treatments for active alcoholics and drug abusers.[8]

TABLE 16.1

WHO SHALL LIVE AND WHO SHALL DIE?

Patient	Sex and age	Occupation	Home life	Medical stability	Civic activities and other considerations
A	M 55	Cardiac surgeon on the verge of a major new technique	Married; two adult children	Bad long-term prognosis, maybe 2 years	Philanthropist with very high net worth; rumors of unfaithfulness
B	F 38	Owner of successful designer shop	Widow; three children, ages 4, 8, and 13	Good	From out of state; excellent violinist in community orchestra
C	M 46	Medical technician	Married; six children, ages 8 to 14	Good	Union boss
D	M 29	Assembly-line worker	Single	Good	Retarded—mental age, 10 years; ward of the state
E	F 36	Well-known historian, college professor; Ph.D.	Divorced; custodian of one son, age 5; ex-husband alive	Fair prognosis, but odd case that would allow perfection of new surgical technique	Excessive eater, drinker, and smoker; very popular professor; other medical conditions
F	M 60	Ex-state senator, now retired	Widower	Good	Criminal record (extortion)
G	M 45	Vice-president of local bank	Happily married; three sons, ages 15 to 25	Good	Deacon of local church; member of Rotary Club

SOURCE: *Washington Post*, 22 March 1981.

A variety of other criteria could be used to justify the choice of one transplant candidate over another, but there is still a choice among real lives to be made. In addition, some even broader allocative questions arise from this example: How many transplant centers should be developed in American hospitals? Should there be sufficient capacity to help all the patients who might need this treatment, regardless of the cost and the underutilization of the facilities most of the time? Or should only enough centers be developed to meet average demands? Should individuals who can afford to pay be allowed to jump ahead of others in line to receive new organs if their payments can fund future surgeries for the less fortunate?

These questions have arisen in a very real way in the debate over the allocation of the limited supply of donor organs among transplant centers around the country. One model of allocation would keep the organ in the catchment area where it was procured and permit the local transplant center to use it. The alternative would have a more centralized system of allocation, providing the organ to the patient who is most in need, that is, the nearest to death.[9] Given that the sicker patients tend to cluster at a few major transplant centers, this might put smaller centers out of business. This in turn raises several ethical questions: Why should an individual's chance of survival depend on where he or she lives rather than on medical criteria? Should there not be some attempt to keep more centers open and promote the technology for longer-term benefits?

Even though the preservation of life may be an important or even dominant value for public policymaking, in many situations the definition of life itself is subject to debate. This is true legally as well as morally. The use of therapeutic abortion as a means of birth control presents one problem of this sort: determining when human life begins.[10] This issue has been fought in the court system and in the streets of many American cities and towns with no resolution that both sides of the issue can accept. Even here, however, the question is not always clear, as many abortion opponents would accept abortions in the case of rape or incest, and many abortion supporters would not accept the procedure as a means of determining the gender of children in a family. Issues concerning artificial means of prolonging life even when a person would be considered dead by many clinical criteria illustrate the problem of defining life at the other end of the life cycle.[11]

Assisted suicide for the terminally ill has raised a possible contradiction between the value of preserving life and the value of preserving autonomy (a concept to be discussed later).[12] If an adult wants to end his or her life, because of a terminal and painful disease, for example, should government have the obligation—or even the right—to prevent that adult from doing so? Should the individual have access to assisted suicide if he or she is simply depressed or despondent? Thus, while all policymakers and all citizens may agree on the importance of preserving human life, serious disagreements arise over just what constitutes a human life and who can dispense with it.

Finally, in some situations the government sanctions and actively encourages the taking of human lives. The most obvious example is war; others are capital punishment and, in some instances, the management of police response to threats to their own lives and safety. The question that arises here is what criteria can governments use to justify the taking of some lives while we deplore and prohibit the taking of others?[13] Obvious criteria that we might apply are self-preservation and the protection of society against elements that could undermine it or take other lives. But to some degree there is a definite inconsistency in the arguments here, and government must justify placing higher values on some lives than on others. Again, the fundamental point is that although there may be broad agreement in society on the importance of preserving human lives as a goal of all public policies, this criterion is not obviously and unambiguously enforceable in all policy situations. We must have a detailed analysis of all such situations and some understanding of the particular application of the criterion in each of those varied situations.

The Preservation of Individual Autonomy

Another important value for public policy, especially in a democracy, is that the autonomy of each citizen to make decisions about his or her own life should be maximized. This principle underlies a considerable body of conservative political thought that assumes that the interests of the individual are, everything else being equal, more important than those of the society as a whole.[14] It further assumes that individuals may at times select alternatives that many other people, and society as a whole acting through government, might deem unacceptable. Thus, child labor, sweatshops, and extremely long working hours with low wages were all justified at one time because they preserved the right of the individual to "choose" his or her own working conditions.[15]

In adhering to an extreme definition of individual autonomy, which includes the right to choose conditions or products that are inherently harmful, the public sector would be excluded from almost all forms of social and economic activity. Even using this extreme version of autonomy, however, the state has been able to intervene to protect individuals against fraud and breach of contract, and it did to some degree protect children and other less competent individuals more than it did adults, who presumably were able to make their own decisions. In contrast, advocates of an enhanced role for the public sector have argued that the welfare state, by increasing the options available to citizens, especially less advantaged citizens, actually enhances individual freedom and autonomy.[16]

Several interesting questions arise in the public sector in regard to individual autonomy. One involves the legitimacy of state intervention. What groups in society should the state attempt to protect, either against themselves or against those who would defraud them or otherwise infringe on their rights? Children have traditionally been protected—even against their own parents—because they have been assumed to be incapable of exercising full, autonomous choice.[17] The state has been empowered to operate in loco parentis to attempt to preserve the rights of children. Likewise, the state has protected mentally incompetent adults who cannot make rational, autonomous choices. Less justifiably by most criteria, the state has operated to limit the choices of welfare recipients (see pp. 298–301), unwed mothers, and individuals who, although they may have full mental capabilities, are stigmatized in some fashion by society and punished for making questionable choices in the past. As Desmond King points out, liberal states such as the United States have at times adopted extremely illiberal policies—policies that limit exercise of free choice of the individual—when some compelling state interest is believed to be involved.[18] Again, the question is what criteria should be used to decide which groups the state should treat as its children?

The state may also intervene to protect the life of an individual who has made an autonomous decision to end his or her life. Legislation that makes suicide a crime and attempts to prevent individuals from purposely ending their lives indicates the apparent belief that the value of preserving life supersedes the value of preserving individual autonomy. In this hierarchy of values, the decision to end one's own life is taken by definition to indicate that the individual needs the protection of the state. The same principle is apparently applied to individuals who have made it clear that they do not wish to be kept "alive" by artificial means when all hope of their recovery to a fully conscious and autonomous life is lost. In such an instance there are several conflicting values, and we return to the question of what actually constitutes a human life. Does it matter that an individual may have declared while in good health that he or she does not want to be kept alive by artificial means?[19] The potentially conflicting principles of preserving life and preserving autonomy become even more confused here because an individual who once made an autonomous choice about how he or she would like to be treated may at the crucial time be no longer able to decide anything autonomously and may, in fact, never be able to do so again.

In less extreme instances, the state may also restrain the autonomy of an individual for the sake of protecting him or her. Consumer protection is an obvious example; government may disregard the traditional principle of caveat emptor and simply prohibit the sale of potentially harmful products in order to protect the citizen. On the one hand, the conservative, or any other person interested in preserving individual choice, would argue that

443

such protections are harmful inasmuch as the paternalistic actions of government prevent citizens from being truly free actors. On the other hand, the complexity of the marketplace, the number of products offered for sale, and the absence of full information may prevent individuals from making meaningful judgments.[20] As a consequence, government is justified in intervening, especially because many of the products banned would affect persons incapable of making their own informed choices—for example, children. In less extreme circumstances, governments require labeling and full disclosure of information so that citizens are able to make rational, informed autonomous decisions about the products they purchase.

At times government also forces citizens to consume certain goods and services because they are presumably for the citizens' own good. Two examples of such "merit goods" that have been of concern recently are requirements that people riding in automobiles wear seat belts and that motorcycle riders wear helmets.[21] These measures have been supported by a number of safety organizations and by many citizens, but other citizens argue that they should be "free to be foolish," to make their own choices, and to assume certain risks.[22] As appealing as that argument sounds within a free society, there are also potential costs from risky decisions that extend beyond the individual who is willing to take the chance. Their families are potentially harmed, both emotionally and economically, by such risky behavior. The society as a whole may also have a stake in the individual decision because public money may well have to pay for a long and expensive hospitalization from a preventable injury. Thus, as with all of the ethical principles that can be applied to public decisions, there tend to be few absolutes and a great deal of balancing of ideas and ethical criteria when government must act to make policy.

Professional licensing and laws that control the licensing of drugs also have been criticized as unduly restricting the free choice of individuals. It is argued that individuals should have the right to select the form of treatment they would like, even if the medical establishment deems it quackery. So, for example, activists for AIDS victims have criticized the Food and Drug Administration for delaying approval of some drugs that may have potential for ameliorating the symptoms of AIDS and slowing the progress of the disease.[23] The criticisms have been particularly pointed because these drugs already are licensed and available in other industrialized countries. Similar arguments were made earlier about the failure of the FDA to approve laetrile as a drug for the treatment of cancer. In both cases, the individual is being denied the right to choose courses of treatment for a deadly disease.

Of course, the counterargument from the FDA is that these restrictions are justified because they increase the probability that the individual will receive treatments that are known to have some beneficial effects. If there were no licensing, the individual might rely on a treatment without any real therapeutic value until it was too late to use other treatments. The question from the perspective of ethics is who should be able to make the choice about the best treatment—the individual affected or a government organization?

Lying

Most systems of ethics and morality prohibit lying.[24] People generally regard lying as wrong simply "because it is wrong." It can also be considered wrong because it allows one individual to deprive another of his or her autonomy. When one person lies to another, the liar deprives the other person of the ability to make rational and informed decisions. In some instances, telling "little white lies" may prevent awkward social situations, but perhaps more stringent criteria should be applied to justify lies told by government, especially in a democracy.

Lying to the public by public officials has been justified primarily as being in the public's own good. Political leaders who accept this paternalistic justification assume that public officials have more information and are unwilling to divulge it either for security reasons or because they believe that the information will only "confuse" citizens. They may therefore lie to the public to get average citizens to behave in ways that they—the public officials—prefer. They also seem to believe that the citizens would behave in that same way if they had all the information available to the political leader. Even if citizens would not behave as public officials want them to, officials think that they *should* behave in that manner, and the lie is therefore justified as a means of protecting the public from itself and its own irresponsibility or ignorance.

Such lying obviously limits the autonomy of the average citizen when making policy choices or evaluating the performance of those in office. Even white lies are questionable—the importance of autonomy in democratic political systems may demand much closer attention to honesty, even though the short-term consequences of telling the truth may not benefit incumbents. In times of war officials may need to lie, or at a minimum withhold information, for security reasons or to maintain morale, but even that largely justifiable behavior will tend to undermine the legitimacy of a democratic system. In part, citizens may find it difficult to know when the lying has stopped, a problem that became very evident during the Cold War.[25]

Other white lies told by officials to the public involve withholding information that might cause panic or other responses that are potentially dangerous. For example, a public official may learn that a nuclear power plant has had a minor and apparently controllable accident that is not believed to endanger anyone. The official may withhold this information from

445

the public in the belief that doing so will prevent a panic; a mass flight from the scene could cause more harm than the accident. But, as with other ethical situations, the decision to lie about one thing and not about others makes it difficult for the official (and government as a whole) to behave consistently. Perhaps the only standard that can be applied with any consistency in this case is the utilitarian criterion: the harm prevented by the lie must outweigh the ill effects caused by the lie. Determining this utilitarian balance is relatively easy when we are balancing the possible few deaths and limited property damage from a minor nuclear accident against probable widespread and violent panic. Continued lying, however, will eventually generate a public loss of trust in government and its officials, and the cost of such skepticism is difficult to calculate.[26]

A special category of lying is the withholding of information by public officials to protect their own careers. This is a problem for the "whistleblowers" who would expose deceit, as well as for the liars, and it happens in the private as well as the public sector.[27] Attempting to act ethically and responsibly has placed many individuals in difficult situations. For example, the man who blew the whistle on government cost overruns on the Lockheed C-5A airplane lost his job; so did the EPA official who exposed the agency's shortcomings under Rita Lavelle; and so did many other conscientious officials in less dramatic circumstances.[28] The problem caused when someone blows the whistle on a lie is especially difficult to analyze when the individual at fault does not lie directly but simply does nothing to expose errors made in government.

The whistleblower must go to some lengths in order to make the information about official lying known to the public and must accept substantial career risks. Because of these difficulties, policymakers may want to devise means to encourage whistleblowers and to protect them against reprisals. The federal government and many state and local governments have devised programs to protect whistleblowers, but there are still substantial risks for the individual who chooses to act in what he or she considers a responsible manner. In conjunction with, or in the absence of, programs encouraging officials to divulge information, legislation such as the Freedom of Information Act can at least make it more difficult for government to suppress information.[29]

Thus, in addition to the general moral prohibition, lying carries a particular onus in the public sector because it can destroy individual citizens' ability to make appropriate and informed choices about their government. Although a lie may be told for good reasons (at least in the mind of the liar), it must be questioned unless it has extremely positive benefits and is not told just for the convenience of the individual official. The long-term consequences for government of even "justifiable" lying may be negative. Citizens who learn that government lies to them for good reasons may soon wonder if it will not lie to them for less noble reasons, and they may find it difficult to believe the official interpretation of anything. In the United States, for example, the Vietnam War, Watergate, and "Irangate" have created a sense of distrust toward government among an entire generation of citizens that manifests itself in somewhat general disaffection with government.[30]

If strictures against lying are to some degree dependent on a desire to preserve the political community and a sense of trust within it, then somewhat different rules may apply in international politics. Although there is a concept of an international community of nations, the moral bonds within that community tend to be weaker than the bonds that exist within a single nation. Further, a political leader's paramount responsibilities are to his or her own citizens. Therefore, lying in international politics may be more acceptable; political leaders regularly face the problem of "dirty hands," which seems to be part of the job of being a political leader in an imperfect world.[31] That is, leaders may be forced to engage in activities that they know to be wrong in most circumstances, such as lying, in order to serve the (largely utilitarian) goals of protecting and preserving the interests of their own country.

Fairness

Fairness is a value to which citizens expect government to assign maximum importance. One standard justification for the existence of government, even for conservatives, is that it protects and enforces the civil and political rights of all individuals and does so with as much equality as possible. Further, it is argued (at least by liberals) that government has the legal and economic capacity to redress inequities in the distribution of goods and services that result from the operations of the marketplace.[32] Government, then, is charged with ensuring that citizens are treated fairly in the political system and perhaps in the economy and society.

But just what is "fair treatment of citizens"? In different schools of social and political thought the word "fair" has had different meanings. To a conservative, for example, fairness means allowing individuals maximum opportunities to exercise their own abilities and to keep what they earn in the marketplace through those abilities. Some conservatives consider it fair that people who cannot provide for themselves should suffer, along with their families, although they disagree about how much suffering is acceptable.[33] Similarly, many conservatives do not consider it fair for government to take property from some citizens in order to benefit others; in this view property, as well as people, has rights.[34]

The familiar Marxist doctrine "from each according to his abilities, to each according to his needs" implies a very different standard of fairness.[35]

Were it not for their visibility in many urban areas, the homeless might not really be counted as a part of society at all. (Agence France Presse/Corbis-Bettmann)

448

That statement implies that all members of the society, provided they are willing to contribute their own abilities (however limited), are entitled to have their material needs satisfied. According to this standard of fairness, those with lower earning capacities need not suffer, although the doctrine does not imply a standard of absolute equality. There is, however, no uncontested definition of "needs," so that this standard could become an open-ended entitlement for citizens were it to be accepted.

The standard of fairness applied in most contemporary welfare states is something of a mixture of the conservative and Marxist standards, although it generally lacks the intellectual underpinnings of either extreme.[36] The mixed-economy welfare state that operates in industrialized societies usually allows productive citizens to retain most of their earnings and at the same time requires them to help build a floor of benefits under the less fortunate so that the less fortunate can maintain at least a minimal standard of living. Unlike the situation in the Marxist state, this redistribution of goods and services to the less fortunate from the more successful is conducted in the context of free and open politics.

As well as being concerned with fairness across classes and among individuals, governments increasingly must be concerned about fairness across generations. The current generation is custodian of the natural resources of the society and must make decisions about the use of those resources. Is it *fair* for the current generation to use such a large share of the proven reserves of resources such as oil, copper, chromium, and the like? Is it *fair* for this generation to incur a massive public (and private) debt that will impose burdens on, and restrain the opportunities of, future generations? What principles can be used to justify choices that have intergenerational consequences?[37] How can those principles be included in the analytic techniques used to make policy decisions?[38]

Can these operating principles of the contemporary welfare state—principles that arise largely from political accidents and a pragmatic evolution process—be systematized and developed on a more intellectual plane? One promising approach to such a systematic justification of the welfare state can be found in philosopher John Rawls's concept of justice in a society. In his essay "Justice as Fairness,"[39] Rawls develops two principles of justice for a society. The first is that "each person participating in a practice, or affected by it, has an equal right to the most extensive liberty compatible with like liberty of all." This is a restatement of the basic right of individuals to be involved in governmental decisions that affect them, a principle not incompatible with the cry "No taxation without representation!" This first principle of justice would place the burden of proof on anyone who would seek to limit participation in political life; it can therefore be seen as a safeguard for procedural democracy in contemporary societies. Thus, Rawls places a pronounced emphasis on the decision-making procedures employed when evaluating the fairness of those decisions and the fairness of the institutions of society. This may present great difficulties for the citizen and the analyst, however, if the decisions reached by participatory means conflict with more substantive conceptions of fairness.

The second principle of fairness advanced by Rawls is more substantive and also more problematic. Referred to as the "difference principle," it states that "social and economic inequalities are to be arranged so that they are both: (a) to the greatest benefit of the least advantaged; and (b) attached to offices and positions open to all under conditions of fair equality of opportunity."[40] This principle places the burden of proof on those who attempt to justify a system of inequalities. Inequalities can be seen as just only if all other possible arrangements would produce lowered expectations for the least-well-off group in society. To help a society that is striving for equality, citizens are asked to think of their own place in society as shrouded behind a "veil of ignorance," so that it cannot be known to them in advance.[41] Would they be willing to gamble on being in the lowest segment of the society when they decide on a set of inequalities for the society? If they would not, then they have good reason to understand the need of the society to equalize the distribution of goods and services. Of course, it is impossible to apply the logic of the veil of ignorance within existing societies, but it is a useful concept for understanding the rational acceptance of redistributive government policies and for justifying such policies politically.

Several interesting questions arise with respect to Rawls's difference principle. One is the place of natural endowments and individual differences in producing and justifying inequalities. Should individuals who have special natural abilities be allowed to benefit from them? This borders on the basic ethical principle of desert—the degree to which any individual deserves what he or she receives in the world (the concept is discussed in the next section). This question is reminiscent of a Kurt Vonnegut story in *Player Piano*, in which individuals' particular talents are balanced by the "great handicapper."[42] Individuals who can run particularly fast, for instance, are required to wear heavy weights to slow them down, and those who have creative gifts are required to wear earphones through which come loud and discordant noises to distract them from thinking and using that creativity. Does Rawls regard such a homogeneous and ultimately dull society as desirable or fair? One would think not, but he does point out that natural endowments are desirable primarily because they can be used to assist those in the lowest segment of society. Thus, noblesse oblige is expected of those who possess natural talents.

Does the same expectation hold true for those whose endowments are economic rather than physical or intellectual? It would appear that in

Rawls's view equality is a natural principle that can be justified by decision making that would occur behind the veil of ignorance, as well as by the co-operative instincts that Rawls believes are inherent in humans. Again, in his view, these economic endowments should exist only to the extent they can be used for the betterment of the lowest segments in society.

Quite naturally, critics point to what they consider the natural rights of individuals to retain their holdings,[43] and to the potential incentives for work and investment that are inherent in a system of economic inequalities. Inequalities are argued to be functional for the society because they supply a spur to ambition and an incentive to produce more, which in turn can be used to benefit the entire society.[44] These incentives should influence artistic as well as economic production. Thus, to critics of Rawls's philosophy, the tendency toward equality may be inappropriate on ethical grounds because it would deny individuals something they have received through either genetics or education, and it may be wrong on utilitarian grounds because it reduces the total production of the society along several dimensions.

Finally, the Rawlsian framework is discussed primarily within the context of a single society, or a single institution in which cooperative principles would at least be considered, if not always followed. Can these principles be applied to a broader context; in particular, should they be applied to a global community? In other words, should the riches accumulated in the industrialized countries be used to benefit the citizens of the most impoverished countries of the world?[45] Such a policy would, of course, be politically difficult to implement, even if it could be shown to be morally desirable. Nevertheless, the ethical underpinnings of foreign aid may be important, especially as the world moves into an era of increased scarcity as well as increased interdependence.

Although we have been discussing issues of fairness primarily in economic terms, increasingly these issues are conceptualized in terms of race, ethnicity, and gender. The same logic of analysis may well be applicable, and fairness could be maximized by assuming the same veil of ignorance for making decisions about these social differences as it is when used for decisions about economic differences. For these social categories, however, issues of compensation for past injustices also arise, along with the perceived need to create structures and programs that will encourage future achievement by members of the previously disadvantaged groups.

This remedy for past ills, in turn, creates resentments by those who feel that their natural endowments of skills and abilities are being devalued. This resentment arises in reference to scholarships granted on the basis of race or gender, hiring quotas, and a variety of other "affirmative action" policies intended to change existing social and economic patterns.[46] In addition, economic inequalities may be justified as providing incentives for individuals to do more for themselves and to change their own conditions, while it is generally not feasible for individuals to change gender or race. No question of equality and fairness is easy to resolve, but these issues of race and gender have proved to be among the most difficult to cope with in the political system.

While opinions may differ as to the applicability of Rawls's ideas in the real world of policymaking, and the desirability of such application if it is indeed possible, his work does raise interesting and important ethical questions for those attempting to design public policies. Many industrialized democracies have been making redistributive economic policy decisions for years. These decisions often have been justified on pragmatic or political grounds rather than on ethical principles.[47] The work of Rawls provides intellectual underpinnings for these policies, even though no government has gone as far in redistributing income and wealth as Rawls's difference principle would demand. These governments are now facing more decisions about race and gender inequalities, and these too require some guidance beyond simple political expediency.

The Concept of Desert

Discussion of the values of the welfare state raises the question of desert. What does a citizen deserve as a member of the society, and what does the individual deserve as an individual with particular needs and virtues? As discussed earlier, the American people enjoy some rights by virtue of the Constitution and the Bill of Rights. The existence of these rights is largely incontestable, although there certainly are multiple interpretations of their meaning. The more interesting cases, however, are benefits from government that have come to be considered rights but which are much less clearly grounded in the basic law of the land.

The concept of *entitlement* is the most important case of desert being constructed by policy and then being accepted by the population.[48] Social insurance programs are the clearest example of entitlements, with the citizen having paid for the program over his or her working lifetime with government making a commitment to provide the benefits when the citizen needs them (e.g., when retired, unemployed, or disabled). These programs were designed so that citizens would consider them neither charity nor a government "handout" but a right. Further, entitlement programs were designed to make it difficult for subsequent generations of politicians to dismantle them.[49]

When we move away from social insurance and other contributory programs, the concept of desert becomes more difficult to sustain within the public sector of the United States. It is clear that young people do have a right to a free public education but only through high school.[50] Why is it not available through college, or even through graduate school? Likewise, the debate over health care in 1994 raised the question whether citizens have a right to health care, and if so, to what level of health care. If there is a right to basic health care, is there also a right to the most advanced and expensive treatments available? If the rights are restricted to basic services, where does the entitlement stop and why? Certain public goods, such as clean air and water, also are often conceptualized as the entitlements of citizens. Why?

Can there be a "negative desert"? Do some citizens deserve certain punishments and sanctions? It is sometimes argued that the perpetrators of certain crimes "deserve" the death penalty[51] and that those responsible for economic or environmental crimes "deserve" certain (less) severe penalties. On what basis can it be said that a person deserves a particular form of punishment, particularly one as final as the death penalty? At a less extreme level, do people who have other perceived failings, such as having to accept public assistance, deserve to be punished or controlled in other ways?[52] Chapter 11 discussed the imposition of an increasing number of restrictions and regulations on welfare clients; do those people "deserve" that treatment, and if so, why?

A final point about desert is that it is often defined in terms of particular communities, with those outside the community being excluded. In a search to find alternatives to big government and utilitarian values a strand of communitarian thinking in the United States has argued for greater devolution of decision making to communities, which would be empowered to make decisions for themselves.[53] This, however, could easily lead to an "us versus them" conception of governing, with (paradoxically) a great deal of mutuality within the community and substantial exclusion of outsiders. For example, would equalization of school funding (see pp. 347–50) be an appropriate policy under communitarian governance? The concept of community has a powerful appeal to many Americans, but its restrictive concept of desert raises a number of questions about membership in the community.

Ethics and Public Policy: Alternatives to Utilitarianism

The ethical system most often applied to public policy analysis is utilitarianism, with actions being justified as producing the greatest net benefit for the society as a whole. As noted in chapter 15, this principle undergirds the dominant analytic approaches in the field, such as cost-benefit analysis. In this chapter we have discussed several ethical questions that arise in making and implementing public policies, as well as some possible answers to these questions. Most of the discussion of these questions presented here reflects a nonutilitarian perspective. Ultimately, however, just as no one can provide definitive answers to these ethical policy questions, public officials may face policy questions that have no readily acceptable answers, economically, politically, or ethically. Values and ethical principles are frequently in conflict, and the policymaker must frequently violate one firmly held ethical position in order to protect another.

Despite these practical difficulties, it is important for citizens and policymakers to think about policy in ethical terms. Perhaps too much policymaking has been conducted without attention to anything but the political and economic consequences. Of course, those economic consequences are important as criteria on which to base an evaluation of a program, but they may not be the only criteria. Both the policymaker and the citizen must be concerned also with the criteria of justice and trust in society. It may be that ultimately justice and trust make the best policies—and even the best politics.

Notes

Chapter 1. What is Public Policy?

1. Bureau of the Census, *1992 Census of Governments* (Washington, D.C.: Government Printing Office, 1993). The number of governments increased by an average of more than 300 per year during the early 1990s.

2. Richard Nelson, *The Moon and the Ghetto* (New York: Norton, 1977).

3. Richard Rose, "The Programme Approach to the Growth of Government," *British Journal of Political Science* 15 (1985): 1–28.

4. Alison Mitchell, "Clinton Promotes Education Testing, Gingrich Opposes," *New York Times,* 8 September 1997.

5. Brian W. Hogwood and B. Guy Peters, *The Pathology of Public Policy* (Oxford: Oxford University Press, 1985); and Craig W. Thomas, "Public Management as Interagency Cooperation," *Journal of Public Administration Research and Theory* 7 (1997): 221–46.

6. Helen Ingram and Anne Schneider, "Improving Implementation Through Framing Smarter Statutes," *Journal of Public Policy* 10 (1990): 67–88; Stephen H. Linder and B. Guy Peters, "The Study of Policy Instruments," *Policy Currents* 2 (May 1992): 1, 4–7; and B. Guy Peters and Frans K.M. Van Nispen, *Tools and Public Policy* (Cheltenham, England: Edward Elgar, 1998).

7. Private actors do, of course, have recourse to law as a means of influencing policy and forcing government action. This is especially true in the United States where the courts are so important for determining policy. For example, in addition to the enforcement activities of the Federal Trade Commission and the Antitrust Division of the Department of Justice, private individuals also bring suit to enforce the antitrust laws.

8. *Bragdon v. Abbott,* 97 SC 156 (1997).

9. B. Guy Peters and Martin O. Heisler, "Thinking About Public Sector Growth," in *Why Governments Grow: Measuring Public Sector Size,* ed. C.L. Taylor (Beverly Hills, Calif.: Sage, 1983). But see Giandomenico Majone, *Regulating Europe* (London: Routledge, 1996).

10. The costing of these regulatory interventions was made popular by Murray Wiedenbaum. See his "The High Costs of Government Regulation," *Challenge,* November 1979, 32–39. These costings were not without their political motivations, e.g., to demonstrate the high costs of government, and they usually failed to include the offsetting value of the benefits of regulation.

11. William T. Gormley, *Privatization and Its Alternatives* (Madison: University of Wisconsin Press, 1991).

12. Penelope Lemov, "Jailhouse, INC," *Governing* 6 (May 1993): 44–48.

13. Donald F. Kettl, *Government by Proxy: (Mis)Managing Federal Pro-*

grams? (Washington, D.C.: CQ Press, 1988); and Patricia W. Ingraham, "Quality in the Public Services," in *Governance in a Changing Environment,* ed. B. Guy Peters and Donald J. Savoie (Montreal: McGill/Queens University Press, 1995).

14. Charles H. Levine and Paul L. Posner, "The Centralizing Effects of Fiscal Austerity on the Intergovernmental System," *Political Science Quarterly* 96 (1981): 67–85.

15. James D. Chesney, "Intergovernmental Politics in the Allocation of Block Grant Funds for Substance Abuse in Michigan," *Publius* 24 (1994): 39–46; and Doug Peterson, "Block Grant 'Turn-Backs' Revived in Bush Budget," *Nation's Cities Weekly* 15 (3 February 1992): 6.

16. Neal R. Pierce, "Bush 'Turnback' Plan Sounds Nice but It's 'Irrelevant,'" *Nation's Cities Weekly* 14 (18 February 1991): 12.

17. Stanley S. Surrey and Paul R. McDaniel, *Tax Expenditures* (Cambridge, Mass.: Harvard University Press, 1985).

18. Aaron Wildavsky, "Keeping Kosher: The Epistemology of Tax Expenditures," *Journal of Public Policy* 5 (1985): 413–31.

19. Charles L. Schultze, *The Public Use of Private Interest* (Washington, D.C.: Brookings Institution, 1977).

20. See, for example, F. Anderson, *Environmental Improvement through Economic Incentives* (Baltimore: Johns Hopkins University Press, 1977); and Richard C. Hula, *Market-based Public Policy* (New York: St. Martin's, 1990).

21. Barry P. Bosworth et al., *The Economics of Federal Credit Programs* (Washington, D.C.: Brookings Institution, 1987).

22. Thomas Anton, *Moving Money* (Cambridge, Mass.: Oelgeschlager, Hain and Gunn, 1980).

23. Johan Fritzell, "Income Inequality Trends in the 1980s: A Five-Country Comparison," *Acta Sociologica* 36 (1993): 47–62; and Sheldon Danziger and Peter Gottschalk, *Uneven Tides: Rising Inequality in America* (New York: Russell Sage, 1993).

24. On taxation, see B. Guy Peters, *The Politics of Taxation: A Comparative Perspective* (Oxford: Blackwell, 1991). On conscription, see Margaret Levi, *Consent, Dissent, Patriotism* (Cambridge, England: Cambridge University Press, 1997).

25. Anthony King, "Ideas, Institutions and Policies of Government: A Comparative Analysis," *British Journal of Political Science* 5 (1975): 418.

26. See Linda L.M. Bennett and Stephen Earl Bennett, *Living With Leviathan: Americans Coming to Terms with Big Government* (Lawrence: University of Kansas Press, 1990).

27. Lloyd A. Free and Hadley Cantril, *The Political Beliefs of Americans* (New York: Simon and Schuster, 1968).

28. David O. Sears and Jack Citrin, *Tax Revolt: Something for Nothing in California,* rev. ed. (Berkeley: University of California Press, 1991).

29. See "Opinion Pulse," *The American Enterprise,* March/April 1997, 92.

30. See pp. 84–87.

31. Peter Bachrach and Aryeh Botwinick, *Power and Empowerment: A Radical Theory of Participatory Democracy* (Philadelphia: Temple University Press, 1992).

32. Michael T. Hayes, *Incrementalism* (New York: Longman, 1992).

33. See, for example, Charles O. Jones, *The Reagan Legacy* (Chatham, N.J.: Chatham House, 1989).

34. Robin Toner, "House Democrats Support Abortion in Health Plans," *New York Times*, 14 July 1994.

35. See William Schneider, "What Else Do They Want?" *National Journal*, 16 May 1998, 1150.

36. See Robert Reich, *The Work of Nations: Preparing Ourselves for 21st Century Capitalism* (New York: Knopf, 1991); and Ann O. Kreuger, *The Political Economy of American Trade Policy* (Chicago: University of Chicago Press, 1995).

37. Andrew Hacker, *Two Nations: Black and White, Separate, Hostile, Unequal* (New York: Scribners, 1992).

Chapter 2. The Structure of Policymaking

1. Charles H. Levine, "Human Resource Erosion and the Uncertain Future of the U.S. Civil Service: From Policy Gridlock to Structural Fragmentation," *Governance* 1 (1988): 115–43.

2. Peter H. Stone, "Tobacco's Road," *National Journal*, 1 January 1994, 19–23. Increasing concern over the health effects of tobacco is making any support less palatable.

3. See Terry Sanford, *Storm Over the States* (New York: McGraw-Hill, 1967), 80.

4. Deil S. Wright, *Understanding Intergovernmental Relations*, 3d ed. (Belmont, Calif.: Brooks/Cole, 1988), 83–86.

5. Ibid.

6. For a somewhat different view, see Jae-Won Yoo and Deil S. Wright, "Public Policy and Intergovernmental Relations: Measuring Perceived Changes in National Influences," *Policy Studies Journal* 21 (1993): 687–99.

7. John Kincaid, "From Cooperative to Coercive Federalism," *The Annals* 509 (1990): 139–52.

8. The Unfunded Mandate Reform Act of 1995.

9. Angela Antonelli, "Promises Unfilled: Unfunded Mandates Reform Act of 1995," *Regulation* 19, no. 2 (1996): 44–52.

10. *New York Times*, 13 October 1991.

11. Bureau of the Census, *Census of Governments, 1992* (Washington, D.C.: Government Printing Office, 1993).

12. Jerry Mitchell, *Public Authorities and Public Policy: The Business of Government* (New York: Greenwood, 1992).

13. During the mid-1980s the states averaged over 11 percent surpluses in their total budgets. See the Tax Foundation, *Facts and Figures on Government Finance, 1991* (Baltimore: Johns Hopkins University Press, 1991), table E2.

14. On the concept of "veto points," see Ellen M. Immergut, *Health Politics: Interests and Institutions in Western Europe* (Cambridge, England: Cambridge University Press, 1992).

15. Mark Peterson, *Legislating Together* (Cambridge, Mass.: Harvard University Press, 1992).

16. See, for example, James Q. Wilson, *Bureaucracy* (New York: Basic Books, 1989).

17. Morris P. Fiorina, "An Era of Divided Government," *Political Science Quarterly* 107 (1992): 387–410; and James L. Sundquist, *Constitutional Reform and Effective Government*, rev. ed. (Washington, D.C.: Brookings Institution, 1992).

18. For example, other Democrats were active in developing and promoting alternatives to the Clinton health-care reform proposals (see chapter 10). See also Viveca Novak, "It Still Takes Two," *National Journal*, 25 September 1993, 2301–3.

19. David Mayhew, *Divided We Govern* (New Haven: Yale University Press, 1991); Charles O. Jones, *The Presidency in a Separated System* (Washington, D.C.: Brookings Institution, 1994); Nelson Polsby, *Policy Innovation in America* (New Haven: Yale University Press, 1984); and John E. Schwartz, *America's Hidden Success*, rev. ed. (New York: Norton, 1988). For a critique, see Alberto Alesina and Howard Rosenthal, *Partisan Politics, Divided Government and the Economy* (Cambridge, England: Cambridge University Press, 1996).

20. Michael T. Hayes, *Incrementalism* (New York: Longman, 1992).

21. Charles E. Lindblom, *The Intelligence of Democracy: Decision Making through Mutual Adjustment* (New York: Free Press, 1965).

22. For example, a poll in late 1993 found that 56 percent of the American populace supported a guaranteed health insurance program even if that program were to mean increased taxes. *Gallup Poll Monthly* 338 (November 1993): 8. In a later poll, 77 percent of respondents supported universal coverage for health insurance. *USA Today*, 30 June 1994.

23. Brian W. Hogwood and B. Guy Peters, *Policy Dynamics* (Brighton, England: Wheatsheaf, 1982); and Robert E. Goodin, *Political Theory and Public Policy* (Chicago: University of Chicago Press, 1986).

24. The classic statement is J. Leiper Freeman, *The Political Process: Executive Bureau–Legislative Committee Relations* (New York: Random House, 1965).

25. The classic statement of this point is Theodore J. Lowi, *The End of Liberalism*, 2d ed. (New York: Norton, 1979).

26. Peter L. Hall and C. Lawrence Evans, "The Power of Subcommittees," *Journal of Politics* 52 (1990): 335–55.

27. See D. Roderick Kiewiet and Mathew D. McCubbins, *The Logic of Delegation* (Chicago: University of Chicago Press, 1991).

28. D. McCool, "Subgovernments as Determinants of Political Viability," *Political Science Quarterly* 105 (1990): 269–93.

29. André Blais and Stephane Dion, *The Budget-Maximizing Bureaucrat* (Pittsburgh: University of Pittsburgh Press, 1992).

30. Peter B. Natchez and Irvin C. Bupp, "Policy and Priority in the Budgetary Process," *American Political Science Review* 67 (1973): 951–63.

31. See Robert H. Salisbury, J.P. Heinz, R.L. Nelson, and Edward O. Laumann, "Triangles, Networks and Hollow Cores: The Complex Geometry of Washington Interest Representation," in *The Politics of Interests*, ed. Mark P. Petracca (Boulder, Colo.: Westview, 1992).

32. Rufus E. Miles, "A Cabinet Department of Education: An Unwise Cam-

paign Promise or a Sound Idea?" *Public Administration Review* 39 (1979): 103–10.

33. See Jack L. Walker, *Mobilizing Interest Groups in America* (Ann Arbor: University of Michigan Press, 1991).

34. Charles O. Jones, *The United States Congress* (Homewood, Ill.: Dorsey, 1982).

35. Try it!

36. Some scholars make a great deal over the differences between these concepts, defining a community as a more unified and tightly knit set of groups than a network. See Martin J. Smith, *Pressure, Power, and Policy* (Pittsburgh: University of Pittsburgh Press, 1993).

37. See Richard Rose and B. Guy Peters, *Can Government Go Bankrupt?* (New York: Basic Books, 1978).

38. William T. Gormley, *Privatization and Its Alternatives* (Madison: University of Wisconsin Press, 1991).

39. See Linda L.M. Bennett and Stephen Earl Bennett, *Living With Leviathan: Americans Come to Terms With Big Government* (Lawrence: University of Kansas Press, 1990).

40. Jonas Prager, "Contracting Out Government Services: Lessons from the Private Sector," *Public Administration Review* 54 (1994): 176–84; and Steven Rathgeb Smith and Michael Lipsky, *Nonprofits for Hire: The Welfare State in the Age of Contracting* (Cambridge, Mass.: Harvard University Press, 1993).

41. B. Guy Peters, "Public and Private Provision of Services," in *The Private Provision of Public Services,* ed. Dennis Thompson (Beverly Hills, Calif.: Sage, 1986).

42. This form of organization has not been typical in the United States. See Robert H. Salisbury, "Why No Corporatism in America?" in *Trends Toward Corporatist Intermediation,* ed. Philippe C. Schmitter and Gerhard Lehmbruch (Beverly Hills, Calif.: Sage, 1979); and Susan B. Hansen, "Industrial Policy and Corporatism in the American States," *Governance* 2 (1989): 172–97.

43. Donna Batten and Peter D. Dresser, eds., *Encyclopedia of Government Advisory Bodies, 1996–97* (Detroit: Gale Research, 1997).

44. See Jonathan R.T. Hughes, *The Governmental Habit Redux: Economic Controls from Colonial Times to the Present* (Princeton: Princeton University Press, 1993).

45. The figures for later years would be somewhat lower, but with a significant number of jobs still being created by defense purchases.

46. Tax Foundation, *Facts and Figures on Government Finance, 1996* (Baltimore: Johns Hopkins University Press, 1997).

47. Howard Banks, "The Costs of the Fed's Ketchup and Other Rules," *Forbes* 151 (15 February 1993): 39.

48. See Thomas D. Hopkins, "OMB's Regulatory Accounting Report Falls Short of the Mark," *Policy Study* 142 (St. Louis: Washington University Center for the Study of American Business, November 1997).

Chapter 3. Agenda Setting and Policy Formulation

1. See Michael Harrington, *The Other America: Poverty in America* (New

York: Macmillan, 1963). The huge number of more recent books explicitly on the topic of poverty include Judith A. Chafel, *Child Poverty and Public Policy* (Washington, D.C.: Urban Institute Press, 1993); Jonathan L. Freedman, *From Cradle to Grave: The Human Face of Poverty in America* (New York: Athenaeum, 1993); and Christopher Jencks, *Rethinking Social Policy* (Cambridge, Mass.: Harvard University Press, 1992).

2. But see Barbara J. Nelson, *Making an Issue of Child Abuse* (Chicago: University of Chicago Press, 1984).

3. James Agee, *Let Us Now Praise Famous Men* (Boston: Houghton Mifflin, 1941). This is a book of photographs and text about the plight of rural America during the depression, funded by the Farm Security Administration. The book clearly had some impact, but that impact was more limited than a comprehensive attack on poverty.

4. Anthony Downs, "Up and Down with Ecology: 'The Issue Attention Cycle,'" *Public Interest* 28 (1972): 28–50; and B. Guy Peters and Brian W. Hogwood, "In Search of the Issue-Attention Cycle," *Journal of Politics* 47 (1985): 238–53.

5. Peter Hennessey, Susan Morrison, and Richard Townsend, "Routines Punctuated by Orgies: The Central Policy Review Staff," *Strathclyde Papers on Government and Politics,* no. 30 (1985). This reference has nothing to do with the sexual harassment issue discussed above.

6. Frank Baumgartner and Bryan D. Jones, *Agendas and Instability in American Politics* (Chicago: University of Chicago Press, 1993).

7. See also Bryan D. Jones, *Reconceiving Decision-Making in Democratic Politics* (Chicago: University of Chicago Press, 1994).

8. Michael D. Cohen, James G. March, and Johan P. Olsen, "The Garbage Can Model of Organizational Choice," *Administrative Science Quarterly* 17 (1972): 1–25; and John Kingdon, *Agendas, Alternatives, and Public Policy,* 2d ed. (Boston: Little, Brown, 1993).

9. Joel Best, *Images of Issues* (New York: Aldine DeGruyter, 1989).

10. Roger W. Cobb and Charles D. Elder, *Participation in American Politics* (Baltimore: Johns Hopkins University Press, 1983), 85.

11. This is what Peter Bachrach and Morton S. Baratz referred to as the "second face of power." See their "Decisions and Nondecisions: An Analytic Framework," *American Political Science Review* 57 (1964): 632–42.

12. Cobb and Elder, *Participation,* 86.

13. Ibid., 96.

14. Jack L. Walker, "Setting the Agenda in the U.S. Senate: A Theory of Problem Selection," *British Journal of Political Science* 7 (1977): 423–45.

15. See A. Grant Jordan, "The Pluralism of Pluralism: An Anti-Theory," *Political Studies* 38 (1990): 286–301.

16. For another, similar setting, see B. Guy Peters, "Agenda-Setting in the European Community," *Journal of European Public Policy* 1 (1994): 9–26.

17. C. Wright Mills, *The Power Elite* (New York: Oxford University Press, 1961); and Charles E. Lindblom, *Democracy and the Market System* (New York: Oxford University Press, 1988).

18. E.E. Schattschneider, *The Semi-Sovereign People* (New York: Holt, Rinehart and Winston, 1969).

19. Lance deHaven-Smith, *Philosophical Critiques of Policy Analysis: Lindblom, Habermas, and the Great Society* (Gainesville: University of Florida Press, 1988). Habermas proposes the development of a more participatory "dialogical democracy" as a means of effectively including all interests. See also John Dryzek, *Discursive Democracy* (New York: Cambridge University Press, 1990).

20. Bachrach and Baratz, "Decisions and Nondecisions."

21. Ibid.

22. Martin J. Smith, *Pressure, Power, and Policy* (Pittsburgh: University of Pittsburgh Press, 1993).

23. K. Beckett, "Media Depictions of Drug Abuse: The Impact of Official Sources," *Research in Political Sociology* 7 (1995): 161–82.

24. J. Leiper Freeman, *The Political Process: Executive Bureau–Legislative Committee Relations* (New York: Random House, 1965).

25. Advisory Commission in Intergovernmental Relations, *The Federal Role in the Federal System* (Washington, D.C.: ACIR, 1980).

26. Nelson Polsby, *Policy Innovation in America* (New Haven: Yale University Press, 1984); and John E. Schwartz, *America's Hidden Successes,* rev. ed. (New York: Norton, 1988).

27. Charles O. Jones, *Separate but Equal Branches: Congress and the Presidency* (Chatham, N.J.: Chatham House, 1994).

28. See Robert S. Gilmour and Alexis A. Halley, eds., *Who Makes Public Policy? The Struggle for Control between Congress and the Executive* (Chatham, N.J.: Chatham House, 1994).

29. See, for example, Baumgartner and Jones, *Agendas and Instability.*

30. Best, *Images of Issues;* and Anne Schneider and Helen Ingram, "Social Construction of Target Populations: Implications for Policy and Politics," *American Political Science Review* 87 (1993): 34–47.

31. Kingdon, *Agendas, Alternatives, and Public Policy;* and Nancy C. Roberts, "Public Entrepreneurship and Innovation," *Policy Studies Review* 11 (1992): 55–73.

32. See James Q. Wilson, *The Politics of Regulation* (New York: Basic Books, 1980).

33. Robert H. Salisbury, "The Paradox of Interest Groups in Washington—More Groups, Less Clout," in *The New American Political System,* ed. Anthony King (Washington, D.C.: American Enterprise Institute, 1990).

34. Theodore R. Marmor, *The Politics of Medicare* (Chicago: Aldine, 1973).

35. Julie Kosterlitz, "All Together Now," *National Journal,* 13 November 1993, 2704–8.

36. Brian W. Hogwood and B. Guy Peters, *Policy Dynamics* (Brighton, England: Wheatsheaf, 1983).

37. See Christopher Howard, *The Hidden Welfare State: Tax Expenditures and Social Policy in the United States* (Princeton: Princeton University Press, 1997).

38. Aaron Wildavsky, "Policy as Its Own Cause," *Speaking Truth to Power* (Boston: Little, Brown, 1979): 62–85.

39. Advocates for the victims of the disease would argue that there were significant delays in responding to the issue, in part because of "homophobia." See Gregory M. Herek and Beverly Greene, *AIDS, Identity, and Community* (Bev-

erly Hills, Calif.: Sage, 1995). On the other hand, the National Institutes of Health now spends $33,513 in research for every AIDS death in the country as opposed to $1,162 for each heart disease death. "Panel Criticizes NIH Spending," *USA Today*, 9 July 1998.

40. One education bill advanced by the Clinton administration, in fact, contained an explicit reference to the need for improving competitiveness through education.

41. But see Peter Self, *Government by the Market? The Politics of Public Choice* (Boulder, Colo.: Westview, 1991).

42. James M. Buchanan, *The Demands and Supply of Public Goods* (Chicago: Rand-McNally, 1958), 3–7.

43. A classic statement of the issue is R.H. Coase, "The Problem of Social Cost," *Journal of Law and Economics*, 1960, 1–44.

44. Charles Wolf Jr., *Markets or Governments?* (Cambridge, Mass.: MIT Press, 1987).

45. The issue remains central to the political agenda, with politicians being evaluated very much on the performance of the economy. See chapter 8.

46. Cohen, March, and Olsen, "Garbage Can Model."

47. Abraham Kaplan, *The Conduct of Inquiry* (San Francisco: Chandler, 1964).

48. On instruments, see Christopher Hood, *The Tools of Government* (Chatham, N.J.: Chatham House, 1986); Lester M. Salamon with Michael S. Lund, *Beyond Privatization* (Washington, D.C.: Urban Institute Press, 1989); and Stephen H. Linder and B. Guy Peters, "Instruments of Government: Perceptions and Contexts," *Journal of Public Policy* 9 (1989): 35–58.

49. Richard F. Elmore, "Instruments and Strategy in the Study of Public Policy," *Policy Studies Review* 7 (1987): 174–86.

50. They are argued to be so by, among others, William Niskanen, *Bureaucracy and Representative Government* (Chicago: Aldine/Atherton, 1971). But see André Blais and Stephane Dion, *The Budget-Maximizing Bureaucrat* (Pittsburgh: University of Pittsburgh Press, 1991).

51. Kenneth J. Meier, *Politics and the Bureaucracy*, 3d ed. (Pacific Grove, Calif.: Brooks/Cole, 1993).

52. Mark A. Eisner, "Bureaucratic Professionalism and the Limits of Political Control Thesis: The Case of the Federal Trade Commission, *Governance* 6 (1992): 127–53.

53. John DiIulio, ed., *Deregulating Government* (Washington, D.C.: Brookings Institution, 1994); and B. Guy Peters, *The Future of Governing* (Lawrence: University of Kansas Press, 1996).

54. See Charles L. Heatherly, ed., *Mandate for Change: Policy Management in a Conservative Administration* (Washington, D.C.: Heritage Foundation, 1981).

55. The conservative end of the dimension of policy advice is also populated by the Cato Institute, which tends to offer advice from an almost philosophical libertarian position. On Bush, see *The Bush Presidency: First Appraisals,* ed. Colin Campbell and Bert A. Rockman (Chatham, N.J.: Chatham House, 1991).

56. See, for example, Robert Reich, *The Work of Nations: Preparing Ourselves for 21st Century Capitalism* (New York: Knopf, 1991); and idem, *Educa-*

tion and the Next Economy (Washington, D.C.: National Education Association, 1988).

57. Again, try it!

58. Michael Malbin, *Our Unelected Representatives* (New York: Basic Books, 1980). For a conservative critique, see Eric Felten, "Little Princes," *Policy Review* 63 (1993): 51–57.

59. See W. Kip Viscusi, "The Value of Risks to Life and Health," *Journal of Economic Literature* 31 (1993): 1912–46; Richard Zeckhauser and W. Kip Viscusi, "Risk within Reason," *Science* 248 (4 May 1990): 559–64; and R. Hahn, *Risks, Costs and Lives Saved* (Oxford: Oxford University Press, 1996).

60. Robert Eisner, *The Misunderstood Economy* (Cambridge, Mass.: Harvard Business School, 1994).

61. There have been a number of books and articles about "crises" in Social Security, but the pattern of decision making tends to be more incremental. See Theodore R. Marmor, *Social Security: Beyond the Rhetoric of Crisis* (Princeton: Princeton University Press, 1988); and Martha Derthick, *Agency under Stress: The Social Security Administration in American Government* (Washington, D.C.: Brookings Institution, 1990).

62. See Richard Topf, "Science, Public Policy, and the Authoritativeness of the Governmental Process," in *The Politics of Expert Advice,* ed. Anthony Barker and B. Guy Peters (Pittsburgh: University of Pittsburgh Press, 1993).

63. R. Kent Weaver, "Setting and Firing Policy Triggers," *Journal of Public Policy* 9 (1989): 307–36.

64. Paulette Kurzer, "The Politics of Central Banks: Austerity and Unemployment in Europe," *Journal of Public Policy* 8 (1988): 21–48.

65. Indeed, reducing values such as clean air, natural beauty, and social equality to dollars and cents (as is necessary to make cost-benefit analysis work) represents an extreme form of utilitarianism.

66. See Henry J. Aaron, Thomas E. Mann, and Timothy Taylor, *Values and Public Policy* (Washington, D.C.: Brookings Institution, 1994).

67. Moshe F. Rubenstein, *Patterns of Problem Solving* (Englewood Cliffs, N.J.: Prentice Hall, 1975).

68. The political risks for the mayor may be different than the actual risks to the city and its people. The mayor does not want to be seen as panicking in the face of a crisis, but unnecessary loss of life may be the most damaging possibility of all for a political leader.

69. Stephen H. Linder and B. Guy Peters, "From Social Theory to Policy Design," *Journal of Public Policy* 4 (1984): 237–59; and Davis Bobrow and John S. Dryzek, *Policy Analysis by Design* (Pittsburgh: University of Pittsburgh Press, 1987).

70. Anne L. Schneider and Helen M. Ingram, for example, argue that policy design runs directly opposite to the pluralistic politics that dominates policy-making in the United States. See their *Policy Design for Democracy* (Lawrence: University of Kansas Press, 1997).

Chapter 4. Legitimating Policy Choices

1. Peter G. Brown, *Restoring the Public Trust* (Boston: Beacon Press, 1994);

and Rodney Barker, *Political Legitimacy and the State* (Oxford: Clarendon Press, 1990).

2. The government of the United Kingdom suspended civil liberties in Northern Ireland in response to the sectarian violence there. For at least a portion of the population this action reduced its legitimacy. For other citizens, the extreme crisis of sectarian violence and terrorism justified the action.

3. See, for example, Alan Brinkley, "What's Wrong with American Political Leadership?" *Wilson Quarterly* 18, no. 2 (1994): 46–54.

4. The very high figure in 1991 appears to be at least in part a function of the Gulf War (see also the figure for the military in that year); the president often gets a popularity boost from a war.

5. Robert Z. Lawrence, "Is It Really the Economy, Stupid?" in *Why People Don't Trust Government,* ed. Joseph S. Nye, Philip D. Zelikow, and David C. King (Cambridge, Mass.: Harvard University Press, 1997).

6. On indexation, see p. 294.

7. This is to some degree what Aaron Wildavsky meant when he argued that policy analysts must engage in *Speaking Truth to Power* (Boston: Little, Brown, 1979).

8. Arnold J. Meltsner, "Political Feasibility and Policy Analysis," *Public Administration Review* 32 (1972): 859–67; and Giandomenico Majone, "The Feasibility of Social Policies," *Policy Sciences* 6 (1975): 49–69.

9. Joel D. Aberbach, *Keeping a Watchful Eye: The Politics of Congressional Oversight* (Washington, D.C.: Brookings Institution, 1991).

10. *Immigration and Naturalization Service* v. *Chadha* 462 U.S. 919 (1983). See also William West and Joseph Cooper, "The Congressional Veto and Administrative Rulemaking," *Political Science Quarterly* 98 (1983): 285–304.

11. Louis Fisher, "The Legislative Veto: Invalidated, It Survives," *Law and Contemporary Problems* 56 (1993): 273–92; and Jessica Korn, *The Power of Separation: American Constitutionalism and the Myth of the Legislative Veto* (Princeton: Princeton University Press, 1997).

12. Walter J. Oleszek, *Congressional Procedures and the Policy Process* (Washington, D.C.: CQ Press, 1988); Sarah A. Binder and Steven S. Smith, *Filibustering: Politics or Principle* (Washington, D.C.: Brookings Institution, 1997).

13. There are, therefore, a number of "veto points," a concept not dissimilar to "clearance points" in implementation theory. See Ellen M. Immergut, *Health Politics: Interests and Institutions in Western Europe* (Cambridge, England: Cambridge University Press, 1992).

14. There have been majorities in favor of reforming medical care for some time, but there is as yet no major change. Likewise, there was substantial political pressure for a tobacco settlement in 1998, but the proposal died under an onslaught of interest-group pressures and concerns about economic impacts. See Barry Meier, "Talks Stall in Efforts to Reach Accord," *New York Times,* 5 August 1998.

15. Charles E. Lindblom and Edward J. Woodhouse, *The Policy-making Process,* 3d ed. (Englewood Cliffs, N.J.: Prentice Hall, 1993).

16. In many ways these programs were more successful in reaching these goals than in reaching the social and housing goals toward which they were nominally directed. See Clarence Stone and Heywood T. Sanders, eds., *The Poli-*

tics of Urban Development (Lawrence: University of Kansas Press, 1987).

17. James Buchanan and Gordon Tullock, *The Calculus of Consent* (Ann Arbor: University of Michigan Press, 1962), 120–44.

18. See John A. Hamman, "Universalism, Program Development and the Distribution of Federal Assistance," *Legislative Studies Quarterly* 18 (1993): 553–68.

19. Morris P. Fiorina, *Congress: The Keystone of the Washington Establishment* (New Haven: Yale University Press, 1981).

20. R. Douglas Arnold, *Congress and the Bureaucracy* (New Haven: Yale University Press, 1979).

21. Many programs will do that; the question is whether there is also a broader public interest involved.

22. James Kitfield, "The Battle of the Depots," *National Journal*, 4 April 1998.

23. William R. Riker and Peter Ordeshook, *Positive Political Theory* (Englewood Cliffs, N.J.: Prentice Hall, 1973), 97–114.

24. Kenneth Arrow, *Social Choice and Individual Values*, 2d ed. (New York: John Wiley, 1963).

25. Aberbach, *Keeping a Watchful Eye.*

26. These terms come from Mathew McCubbins and Thomas Schwartz, "Congressional Oversight Overlooked: Police Patrols versus Fire Alarms," *American Journal of Political Science* 28 (1984): 165–79.

27. "GOP, to its Own Delight, Enacts House Rule Changes," *CQ Weekly Report* 53, no. 1 (7 January 1995): 13–15.

28. Cornelius M. Kerwin, *Rulemaking: How Government Agencies Write Law and Make Policy* (Washington, D.C.: CQ Press, 1994).

29. Ibid., 18–19.

30. Margaret T. Kriz, "Kibitzer With Clout," *National Journal*, 30 May 1987, 1404–8.

31. Thomas O. McGarity, *Reinventing Rationality: The Role of Regulatory Analysis in the Federal Bureaucracy* (Cambridge, England: Cambridge University Press, 1991).

32. Viveca Novak, "The New Regulators," *National Journal*, 17 July 1993, 1801–4.

33. Martin Shapiro, "APA: Past, Present, and Future," *Virginia Law Review* 72 (1986): 447–92.

34. Jerry L. Mashaw, "Prodelegation: Why Administrators Should Make Political Decisions," *Journal of Law, Economics, and Organization* 5 (1985): 141–64.

35. Even then, there was a concentration of participation, with only a few interest groups taking advantage of this opportunity. See Barry Boyer, "Funding Public Participation in Agency Proceedings: The Federal Trade Commission Experience," *Georgetown Law Journal* 70 (1981): 51–172.

36. See Glen O. Robinson, *American Bureaucracy: Public Choice and Public Law* (Ann Arbor: University of Michigan Press, 1991), 139–47.

37. Stephen Williams, "Hybrid Rulemaking Under the Administrative Procedures Act: A Legal and Empirical Analysis," *University of Chicago Law Review* 42 (1975): 401–56.

38. *International Harvester Co.* v. *Ruckelshaus* 478 F. 2nd. 615 (1973).

39. William Gormley Jr., *Taming the Bureaucracy* (Princeton: Princeton University Press, 1989), 94-97.

40. Philip Harter, "Negotiated Rulemaking: A Cure for the Malaise," *Georgetown Law Review* 71 (1982): 1-28; and Thomas McGarrity, "Some Thoughts on Deossifying the Rulemaking Process," *Duke Law Journal* 41 (1992): 1385-1462.

41. David Pritzker and Deborah Dalton, *Negotiated Rulemaking Sourcebook* (Washington, D.C.: Administrative Conference of the United States, 1990).

42. Philippe C. Schmitter, "Still the Century of Corporatism?" *Review of Politics* 36 (1974): 85-131.

43. See Robert Kvavik, *Interest Groups in Norwegian Politics* (Oslo: Universitetsforlaget, 1980).

44. Mike Mills, "President to Stage Timber Summit," *Congressional Quarterly Weekly Report* 51 (13 March 1993): 593.

45. See Colin S. Diver, "A Theory of Regulatory Enforcement," *Public Policy* 29 (1980): 295-96.

46. Theodore J. Lowi, *The End of Liberalism*, 2d ed. (New York: Norton, 1979).

47. Richard A. Harris and Sidney M. Milkis, *The Politics of Regulatory Change* (New York: Oxford University Press, 1989).

48. David Schoenbrod, *Power Without Responsibility* (New Haven: Yale University Press, 1993).

49. Martha Derthick and Paul J. Quirk, *The Politics of Deregulation* (Washington, D.C.: Brookings Institution, 1985).

50. Robert A. Kagan, "Adversarial Legalism and American Government," *Journal of Policy Analysis and Management* 10 (1991): 369-406; and Robert J. Samuelson, "Whitewater: The Law as Bludgeon," *International Herald Tribune*, 8 March 1994.

51. Federal Judge Frank Johnson in Alabama literally took over the prisons and mental hospitals of that state. See *Wyatt* v. *Stickney* 344 F. Supp. 373 (M.D. Ala 1972) and *Pugh* v. *Locke* 406 F. Supp. 318 (M.D. Ala 1976).

52. Thomas J. Cronin, *Direct Democracy* (Cambridge, Mass.: Harvard University Press, 1989). See also Ian Budge, *The New Challenge of Direct Democracy* (Oxford: Polity, 1996).

53. James Bohman, *Public Deliberation: Pluralism, Complexity, and Democracy* (Cambridge, Mass.: MIT Press, 1996); and Benjamin R. Barber, *Strong Democracy: Participatory Politics in a New Age* (Berkeley: University of California Press, 1984). For a less philosophical discussion, see Phil Duncan, "American Democracy in Search of Debate," *Congressional Quarterly Weekly Report* 51 (16 October 1993): 2850.

Chapter 5. Organizations and Implementation

1. Michael Lipsky, *Street-level Bureaucracy* (New York: Russell Sage, 1980).

2. Gary Bryner, *Bureaucratic Discretion* (New York: Pergamon, 1987); and Cass Sunstein, *After the Rights Revolution: Reconceiving the Regulatory State* (Cambridge, Mass.: Harvard University Press, 1990).

3. See U.S. Senate, Committee on Governmental Affairs, *The Federal Executive Establishment: Evolution and Trends* (Washington, D.C.: Government Printing Office, 1980), 23–63.

4. Harold Seidman and Robert S. Gilmour, *Politics, Position, and Power*, 4th ed. (New York: Oxford University Press, 1986).

5. The degree of central control in the Department of Defense can be exaggerated. See C. Kenneth Allard, *Command, Control, and the Common Defense* (New Haven: Yale University Press, 1990).

6. At various times in its history, the Coast Guard has been lodged in those other two departments.

7. John Hart, *The Presidential Branch*, 2d ed. (Chatham, N.J.: Chatham House, 1994).

8. B. Guy Peters, R.A.W. Rhodes, and Vincent Wright, eds., *Administering the Summit* (London: Macmillan, 1998).

9. Frederick C. Mosher, *The GAO* (Boulder, Colo.: Westview, 1979); and Ray C. Rist, *Program Evaluation and Management of Government* (New Brunswick, N.J.: Transaction, 1990).

10. Marc Alan Eisner, *Regulatory Politics in Transition* (Baltimore: Johns Hopkins University Press, 1993).

11. The classic statement is Samuel P. Huntington, "The Marasmus of the ICC," *Yale Law Review*, April 1952, 467–509. For a very different perspective, see Jonathan R. Mezey, "Organizational Design and Political Control of Administrative Agencies," *Journal of Law, Economics, and Organization* 8 (1992): 93–110.

12. In addition, the growth of the consumer movement has placed additional pressures on regulatory agencies to escape capture. See Michael D. Reagan, *Regulation: The Politics of Policy* (Boston: Little, Brown, 1987).

13. Annemarie Hauck Walsh, *Managing the Public's Business* (Cambridge, Mass.: MIT Press, 1980), 41–44.

14. See Peter Passell, "The Sticky Side of Privatization: Sale of U.S. Nuclear Fuel Plants Raises Host of Conflicts," *New York Times*, 30 August 1997.

15. Michael Dorf, "Artifactions: The Battle over the National Endowment for the Arts," *Brookings Review*, Winter 1993, 32–35.

16. On 25 June 1998, the Court held that there is no right to a grant, so artists could not argue that this denied them any fundamental rights. *National Endowment for the Arts* v. *Finley*, SC 97–371.

17. Herman Schwartz, "Governmentally Appointed Directors in a Private Corporation—The Communications Satellite Act of 1962," *Harvard Law Review*, December 1961, 341–65.

18. Seidman and Gilmour, *Politics, Position, and Power*, 274.

19. Marc Alan Eisner, *Antitrust and the Triumph of Economics* (Chapel Hill: University of North Carolina Press, 1992).

20. Martin Landau, "The Rationality of Redundancy," *Public Administration Review* 29 (1969): 346–58; and Jonathan R. Bendor, *Parallel Politics* (Berkeley: University of California Press, 1985).

21. James L. Sundquist, "Needed: A Political Theory for a New Era of Coalition Government in the United States," *Political Science Quarterly* 108 (1988): 613–35.

22. U.S. Senate, Committee on Governmental Affairs, *Federal Executive Establishment* (Washington, D.C.: Government Printing Office, 1980), 27–30.

23. Woodrow Wilson, "The Study of Administration," *Political Science Quarterly* 1 (1887): 197–222.

24. This is perhaps especially true of American government, given the number of "veto points" that exist within the system. See Ellen Immergut, *Health Care Politics: Ideas and Institutions in Western Europe* (Cambridge, England: Cambridge University Press, 1992).

25. See Else Oyen, S.M. Miller, and S.A. Samad, *Poverty: A Global Review* (Oslo: Scandinavian University Press, 1996).

26. Daniel Patrick Moynihan, *The Politics of Guaranteed Income* (New York: Vintage, 1973): 240.

27. The importance of laser technologies is demonstrated in William Broad, *Teller's War: The Top-Secret Story behind the Star Wars Initiative* (New York: Simon and Schuster, 1992).

28. That difference is discussed well in Richard R. Nelson, *The Moon and the Ghetto* (New York: Norton, 1977).

29. Robert B. Stevens, ed., *Income Security: Statutory History of the United States* (New York: McGraw-Hill, 1970), 639–59.

30. That decision eventually was rescinded after a public outcry. However, in 1998, another decision by the Department of Agriculture made salsa a vegetable for school lunches, provided it was made from fresh vegetables.

31. Theodore J. Lowi, *The End of Liberalism,* 2d ed. (New York: Norton, 1979), 42–63.

32. Christopher Hood, *The Limits of Administration* (New York: John Wiley, 1976).

33. Ronald Randall, "Presidential Power Versus Bureaucratic Intransigence: The Influence of the Nixon Administration on Welfare Policy," *American Political Science Review* 73 (1979): 795–810.

34. Paul R. Portney, "Natural Resources and the Environment," in *The Reagan Record,* ed. John Palmer and Isabel Sawhill (Washington, D.C.: Urban Institute Press, 1984).

35. Burt Solomon, "'Twixt Cup and Lip," *National Journal,* 24 October 1992, 2410–15; and Paul C. Light, *Thickening Government: Federal Hierarchy and the Diffusion of Accountability* (Washington, D.C.: Brookings Institution, 1995).

36. A classic description of the dangers of this occurring is found in Herbert Kaufman, *The Forest Ranger* (Baltimore: Johns Hopkins University Press, 1960).

37. Janet Schrader, "Lost on the Road to Reform: Some of My Clients Can't Do the Jobs Out There," *Washington Post,* 11 May 1997.

38. Jan Horah and Heather Scott, *NIMBYs and LULUs: (Not-in-My-Back-Yard and Locally-Unwanted-Land-Use)* (Chicago: Council of Planning Librarians, 1993).

39. See Jack DeSario and Stuart Langton, *Citizen Participation in Public Decision Making* (New York: Greenwood, 1987).

40. See Henry Tam, *Communitarianism: A New Agenda for Politics and Citizenship* (London: Macmillan, 1998).

41. See Ortwin Renn, Thomas Webler, Horst Rakel, Peter Dienel, and

Branden Johnson, "Public Participation in Decision Making: A Three-Step Procedure," *Policy Sciences* 26 (1993): 189–214.

42. Peter M. Blau, *The Dynamics of Bureaucracy* (Chicago: University of Chicago Press, 1955), 184–93.

43. Eugene Bardach and Robert A. Kagan, *Going by the Book: The Problem of Regulatory Unreasonableness* (Philadelphia: Temple University Press, 1982).

44. This is now often phrased in terms of a "principal" controlling its agents. See Dan Wood and Richard Waterman, *Bureaucratic Dynamics: The Role of Bureaucracy in a Democracy* (Boulder, Colo.: Westview, 1994).

45. Martha A. Derthick, *Agency Under Stress: The Social Security Administration in American Government* (Washington, D.C.: Brookings Institution, 1990).

46. Elaine Sciolino, "Nuclear Anxiety: The Blunder," *New York Times,* 16 May 1998.

47. Arthur Stinchcombe, *Information and Organizations* (Berkeley: University of California Press, 1990).

48. James G. March and Herbert A. Simon, *Organizations* (New York: John Wiley, 1958).

49. On the other hand, too much similarity in backgrounds and training enhances the possibilities of "group-think" and an absence of error-correction within the organization. See Paul t'Hart, Eric K. Stern, and Bengt Sundelius, *Beyond Groupthink: Political Group Dynamics and Foreign Policy-Making* (Ann Arbor: University of Michigan Press, 1997).

50. The Gore Commission (National Performance Review) reforms are having the effect of reducing drastically the number of levels in organizations, with the presumed effect of empowering employees at lower levels of organizations and improving internal communications.

51. James McGregor Burns, *Roosevelt: The Lion and the Fox* (New York: Harcourt, Brace, 1956).

52. Harold Wilensky, *Organizational Intelligence* (New York: Basic Books, 1967), 130–45.

53. Hood, *Limits of Administration,* 85–87.

54. Ibid., 192–97.

55. For a good compilation, see Peter Hall, *Great Planning Disasters* (London: Weidenfeld and Nicolson, 1980). We should remember, however, that these failings are as common in large private organizations as in the public sector, but there they tend to be less publicized. See Charles T. Goodsell, *The Case for Bureaucracy: A Public Administration Polemic,* 3d ed. (Chatham, N.J.: Chatham House, 1994).

56. Paul R. Schulman, *Large-Scale Policy Analysis* (New York: Elsevier, 1980).

57. Richard A. Rettig, *Cancer Crusade* (Princeton: Princeton University Press, 1977).

58. This assumes that this disease is similar to cancer in requiring a more decentralized research format.

59. Benny Hjern and David O. Porter, "Implementation Structures: A New Unit of Organisational Analysis," *Organisation Studies* 2 (1981): 211–28.

60. Eugene Bardach, "Turf Barriers to Interagency Collaboration," in *The State of Public Management*, ed. D.F. Kettl and H.B. Milward (Baltimore: Johns Hopkins University Press, 1996).

61. Jeffrey L. Pressman and Aaron Wildavsky, *Implementation* (Berkeley: University of California Press, 1979).

62. Ibid., 145–68.

63. Judith Bowen, "The Pressman-Wildavsky Paradox," *Journal of Public Policy* 2 (1982): 1–22; and Ernst Alexander, "Improbable Implementation: The Pressman-Wildavsky Paradox Revisited," *Journal of Public Policy* 9 (1989): 451–65.

64. See David Osborne and Ted Gaebler, *Reinventing Government* (Reading, Mass.: Addison-Wesley, 1992); and B. Guy Peters, "Can't Row, Shouldn't Steer: What's a Government to Do?" *Public Policy and Administration* 12, no. 2 (1997): 51–61.

65. Peter J. May, "Mandate Design and Implementation: Enhancing Implementation Efforts and Shaping Regulatory Policy," *Journal of Policy Analysis and Management* 12 (1993): 634–63.

66. Rochelle L. Stanfield, "Between the Cracks," *National Journal*, 11 October 1997.

67. William T. Gormley, "Regulating Mr. Rogers's Neighborhood: The Dilemmas of Day Care Regulation," *Brookings Review* 8 (1990): 21–28.

68. Barry Meier, "Fight in Congress Looms On Fishing," *New York Times*, 19 September 1994.

69. R. Lewis Bowman, Eleanor C. Main, and B. Guy Peters, "Coordination in the Atlanta Model Cities Program," Department of Political Science, Emory University, 1971, mimeo.

70. Jon Pierre, "The Marketization of the State: Citizens, Consumers and the Emergence of Public Markets," in *Governance in a Changing Environment*, ed. Donald Savoie and B. Guy Peters (Montreal: McGill/Queens University Press, 1995).

71. Richard F. Elmore, "Backward Mapping and Implementation Research and Policy Decisions," in *Studying Implementation*, ed. Walter Williams (Chatham, N.J.: Chatham House, 1984).

72. M. Kiviniemi, "Public Policies and their Targets: A Typology of the Concept of Implementation," *International Social Science Quarterly* 108 (1986): 251–65.

73. Elmore, "Backward Mapping"; Paul A Sabatier, "Top-Down and Bottom-Up Models of Policy Implementation: A Critical Analysis and Suggested Synthesis," *Journal of Public Policy* 6 (1986): 21–48; and Stephen H. Linder and B. Guy Peters, "Implementation as a Guide to Policy Formulation: A Question of 'When' Rather Than 'Whether,'" *International Review of Administrative Sciences* 55 (1989): 631–52.

74. Linder and Peters, "Implementation as a Guide."

75. Giandomenico Majone, "The Feasibility of Social Policies," *Policy Sciences* 6 (1975): 49–69.

76. Malcolm L. Goggin, Ann O'M. Bowman, James P. Lester, and Laurence J. O'Toole, *Implementation Theory and Practice: Toward a Third Generation* (New York: Harper/Collins, 1990).

Chapter 6. Budgeting

1. Jan-Erik Lane, *The Public Sector: Concepts, Models, and Approaches* (London: Sage, 1994).

2. Rather than a matter of the efficient division of resources between the public and private sectors, this is an intergenerational equity question.

3. Charles Stewart III, *Budget Reform Politics* (New York: Cambridge University Press, 1989).

4. Louis Fisher, *Presidential Spending Power* (Princeton: Princeton University Press, 1975).

5. "After Years of Wrangling, Accord Is Reached on Plan to Balance Budget by 2002," *New York Times*, 3 May 1997.

6. Frederick C. Mosher, *The GAO: The Quest for Accountability in American Government* (Boulder, Colo.: Westview, 1979), 65–96.

7. General Accounting Office, *Biennial Budgeting for the Federal Government*, GAO/T-AIMED-94-4 (Washington, D.C.: GAO, 7 October 1993). See also Louis Fisher, "Biennial Budgeting in the Federal Government," *Public Budgeting and Finance* 17, no. 3 (1997): 87–97.

8. "Federal Capital Budgeting," *Intergovernmental Perspective* 20 (1994): 8–16; and Beverly S. Bunch, "Current Practices and Issues in Capital Budgeting and Reporting," *Public Budgeting and Finance* 16, no. 2 (1996): 7–25.

9. Charles L. Schultze, "Paying the Bills," in *Setting Domestic Priorities,* ed. Henry J. Aaron and Charles L. Schultze (Washington, D.C.: Brookings Institution, 1992).

10. Paul E. Peterson and Mark Rom, "Macroeconomic Policymaking: Who Is in Control?" in *Can the Government Govern?* ed. John E. Chubb and Paul E. Peterson (Washington, D.C.: Brookings Institution, 1989).

11. This official was Murray Weidenbaum. See David Stockman, *The Triumph of Politics* (New York: Harper & Row, 1986), 104.

12. David E. Rosenbaum, "Answer: Trim Entitlements. Question: How Do You Do It?" *New York Times,* 8 June 1993.

13. See Roy T. Meyers, *Strategic Budgeting* (Ann Arbor: University of Michigan Press, 1994), 52–60.

14. Aaron Wildavsky, *The New Politics of the Budgetary Process* (Glenview, Ill.: Scott, Foresman, 1986), 100–118.

15. Ibid., 81–82.

16. Office of Management and Budget, *Preparation and Submission of "Current Services" Budget Estimates,* Bulletin 76-4 (Washington, D.C.: OMB, 13 August 1975), 2–4.

17. Maurice Wright describes volume budgeting in "From Planning to Control: PESC in the 1970s," in *Public Spending Decisions,* ed. Maurice Wright (London: Allen and Unwin, 1980), 88–119.

18. See Thomas W. Wander, F. Ted Hebert, and Gary W. Copeland, *Congressional Budgeting* (Baltimore: Johns Hopkins University Press, 1984); and Robin Toner, "Putting Prices on Congress's Ideas," *New York Times,* 21 August 1994.

19. John W. Ellwood and James A. Thurber, "The Politics of the Congressional Budget Process," in *Congress Reconsidered,* 2d ed., ed. Lawrence C. Dodd

and Bruce Oppenheimer (Washington, D.C.: CQ Press, 1981). There has been some tendency to disperse this power, with appropriations committees now handling only about two-thirds of the total budget; see John F. Cogan, "Congress Has Dispersed the Power of the Purse," *Public Affairs Report* 35 (September 1994): 7–8.

20. Paul Starobin, "Bringing It Home," *National Journal*, 27 March 1993.

21. D. Roderick Kiewiet and Mathew D. McCubbins, *The Logic of Delegation* (Chicago: University of Chicago Press, 1991).

22. John R. Gilmour, *Reconcilable Differences: Congress, the Budget Process and the Deficit* (Berkeley: University of California Press, 1990), 115–23.

23. See Irene Rubin, *The Politics of Public Budgeting*, 3d ed. (Chatham, N.J.: Chatham House, 1997), 75–76; and James Thurber, "Congressional Budget Reform: Impact on Congressional Appropriations Committees," *Public Budgeting and Finance* 17, no. 3 (1997): 62–73.

24. Fisher, *Presidential Spending Power.*

25. Mosher, *The GAO*, 169–200; and Ray C. Rist, "Management Accountability: The Signals Sent by Auditing and Evaluation," *Journal of Public Policy* 9 (1989): 355–69.

26. Technically, the general fund is borrowing the money from the Social Security trust fund, although the presentation of deficit figures does not make that distinction clear. See General Accounting Office, *Retirement Income: Implications of Demographic Trends for Social Security and Pension Reform*, GAO/HEHS-97-81 (Washington, D.C.: GAO, July 1997).

27. See Robert D. Reischauer, "The Unfulfillable Promise: Cutting Nondefense Discretionary Spending," in *Setting National Priorities: Budget Choices for the Next Century*, ed. Robert D. Reischauer (Washington, D.C.: Brookings Institution, 1997).

28. Jeff Shear, "The Untouchables," *National Journal*, 16 July 1994.

29. A variety of federal loan programs account for over $200 billion in outstanding direct loans and over $700 billion in guaranteed loans. The Tax Foundation, *Facts and Figures on Government Finance, 1993* (Washington, D.C.: Tax Foundation, 1994).

30. Ben Wildavsky, "After the Deficit," *National Journal*, 29 November 1997, 2408–10.

31. General Accounting Office, *Budgeting for Federal Insurance Programs*, GAO/AIMD-97-16 (Washington, D.C.: GAO, September 1997).

32. Office of Management and Budget, *Budget of the United States, FY 1997, Analytical Perspectives* (Washington, D.C.: Government Printing Office, 1997).

33. Peter Passell, "Despite All the Talk about Tax Cuts, People Can Expect to Pay More," *New York Times*, 17 November 1991.

34. For Canada, see Richard B. Simeon, *Federal Provincial Diplomacy* (Toronto: University of Toronto Press, 1974); for Germany, see Russell J. Dalton, *Politics in Germany*, 2d ed. (New York: HarperCollins, 1993), 372–77.

35. These surpluses tended to be, on average, 11 percent of total state revenues, although some 13 percent of total state revenues came from grants from the federal government.

36. William D. Berry, "The Confusing Case of Budgetary Incrementalism:

Too Many Meanings for a Single Concept," *Journal of Politics* 52 (1990): 167–96.

37. M.A.H. Dempster and Aaron Wildavsky, "On Change: Or, There Is No Magic Size for an Increment," *Political Studies* 28 (1980): 371–89.

38. See David Braybrooke and Charles E. Lindblom, *A Strategy for Decision* (New York: Free Press, 1963).

39. Otto A. Davis, M.A.H Dempster, and Aaron Wildavsky, "A Theory of the Budgetary Process," *American Political Science Review* 60 (1969): 529–47.

40. Aaron Wildavsky, *Budgeting: A Comparative Theory of the Budgetary Process,* rev. ed. (New Brunswick, N.J.: Transaction, 1986): 7–27.

41. Michael T. Hayes, *Incrementalism and Public Policy* (New York; Longman, 1992): 131–44. See also Meyers, *Strategic Budgeting.*

42. Peter B. Natchez and Irvin C. Bupp, "Policy and Priority in the Budgetary Process," *American Political Science Review* 64 (1973): 951–63.

43. Dempster and Wildavsky, "On Change."

44. John R. Gist, "'Increment' and 'Base' in the Congressional Appropriation Process," *American Journal of Political Science* 21 (1977): 341–52.

45. Robert E. Goodin, *Political Theory and Public Policy* (Chicago: University of Chicago Press, 1983): 22–38.

46. Brian W. Hogwood and B. Guy Peters, *The Pathology of Public Policy* (New York: Oxford University Press, 1985), 124–26.

47. David Novick, *Program Budgeting: Program Analysis and the Federal Budget* (Cambridge, Mass.: Harvard University Press, 1967).

48. Robert H. Haveman and Burton A. Weisbrod, "Defining Benefits from Public Programs: Some Guidance from Policy Analysts," in *Public Expenditure and Policy Analysis,* 3d ed., ed. Robert H. Haveman and Julius Margolis (Boston: Houghton Mifflin, 1983); and Philip G. Joyce, "Using Performance Measures for Federal Budgeting: Proposals and Prospects," *Public Budgeting and Finance* 13 (1993): 3–17.

49. Aaron Wildavsky, "Political Implications of Budgetary Reform," *Public Administration Review* 21 (1961): 183–90.

50. Lenneal J. Henderson, "GPRA: Mission, Metrics, and Marketing," *Public Manager* 24, no. 1 (1995): 7–10.

51. These solutions are examples of "formula budgeting," which substitutes formulas for political judgment and political will. See Eric A. Hanushek, "Formula Budgeting: The Economics and Politics of Fiscal Policy Under Rules," *Journal of Public Analysis and Management* 6 (1986): 3–19.

52. James D. Savage, *Balanced Budgets and American Politics* (Ithaca, N.Y.: Cornell University Press, 1988).

53. *Bowsher* v. *Synar* 478 U.S. 714 (1986); see also Lance T. LeLoup, Barbara Luck Graham, and Stacey Barwick, "Deficit Politics and Constitutional Government: The Impact of Gramm-Rudman-Hollings," *Public Budgeting and Finance* 7 (1987): 83–103.

54. Congressional Budget Office, *The Economic and Budget Outlook,* 1992–96 (Washington, D.C.: Government Printing Office, 1991).

55. Philip G. Joyce, "Congressional Budget Reform: The Unanticipated Implications of Federal Policy Making," *Public Administration Review* 56 (1996): 317–24.

56. Allen Schick, *The Federal Budget: Politics, Policy, and Process* (Washington, D.C.: Brookings Institution, 1995), 40–41.

57. Karl O'Lessker, "The Clinton Budget for FY 1994: Taking Aim at the Deficit," *Public Budgeting and Finance* 13 (1993): 7–19.

58. Alvin Rabushka, "Fiscal Responsibility: Will Anything Less than a Constitutional Amendment Do?" in *The Federal Budget,* ed. Michael J. Boskin and Aaron Wildavsky (San Francisco: Institute for Contemporary Studies, 1982), 333–50. See also Henry J. Aaron, "The Balanced Budget Blunder," *Brookings Review,* Spring 1994, 41; and James V. Saturno and Richard G. Forgette, "The Balanced Budget Amendment: How Would It Be Enforced," *Public Budgeting and Finance* 18, no. 1 (1998): 33–53.

59. Rudolph G. Penner and Alan J. Abramson, *Broken Purse Strings: Congressional Budgeting 1974–1988* (Washington, D.C.: Urban Institute Press, 1989), 95–100. For more recent figures, see Bill Montague, "New Budget Forecasts 'Solid,'" *USA Today,* 13 December 1995.

60. Updated by author from Rudolph G. Penner, "Forecasting Budget Totals: Why We Can't Get It Right," in Boskin and Wildavsky, *Federal Budget,* 89–110. See also Donald F. Kettl, *Deficit Politics* (New York: Macmillan, 1992), 109–17.

61. U.S. House of Representatives, Committee on the Budget, *The Line-Item Veto: An Appraisal* (Washington, D.C.: Government Printing Office, 1984).

62. See Norman Ornstein, "Why GOP Will Rue Line-item Veto," *USA Today,* 18 November 1997.

63. Viveca Novak, "Defective Remedy," *National Journal,* 27 March 1993.

64. These included one provision that would have provided $84 million to one sugar beet processor in Texas, and another that benefited certain potato growers in Idaho. See Robert Pear, "Justice Department Belatedly Finds New Defense of Line-item Veto," *New York Times,* 26 March 1998.

65. Daniel Tarschys, "Rational Decremental Budgeting: Elements of an Expenditure Policy for the 1980s," *Policy Sciences* 14 (1982): 49–58.

66. Allen Schick, "Micro-Budgetary Reform," *Public Administration Review* 48 (1988): 523–33.

67. President's Private Sector Survey on Cost Containment (Grace Commission), *Report to the President* (Washington, D.C.: PPSSCC, 1984).

68. Charles T. Goodsell, "The Grace Commission: Seeking Efficiency for the Whole People?" *Public Administration Review* 44 (1984): 196–204; and B. Guy Peters and Donald J. Savoie, "Civil Service Reform: Misdiagnosing the Patient," *Public Administration Review* 54 (1994): 418–25.

69. Sar A. Levitan and Alexandra B. Noden, *Working for the Sovereign* (Baltimore: Johns Hopkins University Press, 1983), 85.

70. National Performance Review, *From Red Tape to Results: Creating a Government That Works Better and Costs Less* (The Gore Report) (Washington, D.C.: Government Printing Office, 1993).

71. Aaron Wildavsky, "A Budget for All Seasons: Why the Traditional Budget Lasts," *Public Administration Review* 38 (1978): 501–9. See also Dirk-Jan Kraan, *Budgetary Decisions: A Public Choice Approach* (Cambridge, England: Cambridge University Press, 1996).

Chapter 7. Evaluation and Policy Change

1. For a good summary of the issues involved in evaluating public-sector programs, see Evert Vedung, *Public Policy and Program Evaluation* (New Brunswick, N.J.: Transaction, 1997).

2. J.N. Noy, "If You Don't Care Where You Get To, Then It Doesn't Matter Which Way You Go," in *The Evolution of Social Policy*, ed. C.C. Abt (Beverly Hills, Calif.: Sage, 1976): 97–120.

3. David L. Sills, *The Volunteers* (Glencoe, Ill.: Free Press, 1956), 253–68.

4. To get some idea of the current orientation of the organization, take a look at the Bureau of Indian Affairs website (http://www.doi.gov/bureau-indian-affairs.html).

5. Daniel A. Mazmanian and Jeanne Nienaber, *Can Organizations Change?* (Washington, D.C.: Brookings Institution, 1979).

6. There is a growing literature on the means of minimizing and controlling changes in the mission of regulatory agencies. See Mathew D. McCubbins, Roger G. Noll, and Barry R. Weingast, "Structure and Process, Politics and Policy: Administrative Arrangements and the Political Control of Agencies," *Virginia Law Review* 75 (1989): 431–82; and Jonathan R. Mezey, "Organizational Design and the Political Control of Regulatory Agencies," *Journal of Law, Economics, and Organization* 8 (1992): 93–110.

7. Robert K. Merton, "Bureaucratic Structure and Personality," *Social Forces,* 1940, 560–68.

8. Anthony Downs, *Inside Bureaucracy* (Boston: Little, Brown, 1967), 92–111.

9. See Paul Light, *Tides of Reform* (New Haven: Yale University Press, 1998).

10. Patricia W. Ingraham, "Of Pigs and Pokes and Policy Diffusion: Another Look at Pay for Performance," *Public Administration Review* 53 (1993): 348–56.

11. See Christopher Hood, B. Guy Peters, and Helmutt Wollmann, "Sixteen Ways to Consumerise the Public Sector," *Public Money and Management* 16, no. 4 (1996): 43–50.

12. William Alonzo and Paul Starr, *The Politics of Numbers* (New York: Russell Sage Foundation, 1987).

13. Richard N. Haass, *The Reluctant Sheriff: The United States after the Cold War* (Washington, D.C.: Brookings Institution, 1997).

14. I.C.R. Byatt, "Theoretical Issues in Expenditure Decisions" in *Public Expenditure: Allocation among Competing Ends,* ed. Michael V. Posner (Cambridge, England: Cambridge University Press, 1977), 22–27.

15. This is especially true for the federal government, which delivers few identifiable services to the public, and it explains in part why the federal government is often evaluated as the least effective of the three levels of government in the United States.

16. Lester M. Salamon, "The Time Dimension in Policy Evaluation: The Case of New Deal Land Reform," *Public Policy,* Spring 1979, 129–83.

17. See Robert E. Goodin, *Political Theory and Public Policy* (Chicago: University of Chicago Press, 1983), 26–29.

18. Debra Viadero, "'Fade-Out' in Head Start Gains Linked to Later Schooling," *Education Week* 13 (20 April 1994): 9.

19. For a discussion of this point, see Henry J. Aaron, *Politics and the Professors* (Washington, D.C.: Brookings Institution, 1978), 84–85. More recent research indicates that there may be some more durable effects. See Edward Zigler and Susan Muenchow, *Head Start: The Inside Story of America's Most Successful Educational Experiment* (New York: Basic Books, 1992).

20. Gerald Schneider, *Time, Planning, and Policymaking* (Bern, Switzerland: Peter Lang, 1991).

21. Donald T. Campbell and Julian C. Stanley, *Experimental and Quasi-Experimental Design for Research* (Chicago: Rand-McNally, 1966); and Richard E. Neustadt and Ernest R. May, *Thinking in Time: The Uses of History for Decision-Makers* (New York: Free Press, 1986).

22. See, for example, Edward D. Berkowitz, *America's Welfare State: From Roosevelt to Reagan* (Baltimore: Johns Hopkins University Press, 1991). The welfare reform passed in 1996 (see chapter 11) represents yet another milestone on this long road.

23. Campbell and Stanley, *Experimental and Quasi-Experimental Design for Research,* 44–53.

24. For a discussion of the role of experimentation in assessing social policy, see R.A. Berk et al., "Social Policy Experimentation: A Position Paper," *Education Research* 94 (1985): 387–429.

25. Peter Passell, "Like a New Drug, Social Programs Are Put to the Test," *New York Times,* 9 March 1993. Also, the reforms of Medicare after the 1997 Balanced Budget Act involve an experiment of 300,000 citizens using Medical Savings Plans. See chapter 10.

26. Helen Ingram and Anne Schneider, "The Choice of Target Populations," *Administration and Society* 23 (1991): 149–67; and Anne Schneider and Helen Ingram, "Social Construction of Target Populations: Implications for Politics and Policy," *American Political Science Review* 87 (1993): 334–47.

27. Karen Davis, "Equal Treatment and Unequal Benefits," *Milbank Memorial Fund Quarterly,* 1975, 449–88.

28. See Rochelle L. Stanfield, "Jump Start," *National Journal,* 12 February 1994, 364–67.

29. Peter Townsend, ed., *Inequalities in Health* (The Black Report) (London: Penguin, 1988).

30. Brian W. Hogwood and B. Guy Peters, *The Pathology of Public Policy* (Oxford: Oxford University Press, 1985).

31. Barbara J. Holt, "Targeting in Federal Grant Programs: The Case of the Older Americans Act," *Public Administration Review* 54 (1994): 444–49.

32. Peter H. Rossi and Howard E. Freeman, *Evaluation: A Systematic Approach,* 4th ed. (Newbury Park, Calif.: Sage, 1989), 135–37.

33. Sam D. Sieber, *Fatal Remedies* (New York: Plenum, 1980).

34. Arnold Meltsner, *Policy Analysts in the Bureaucracy* (Berkeley: University of California Press, 1976).

35. Eleanor Chelimsky, "The Politics of Program Evaluation," *Society* 25 (November 1987): 24–32.

36. Michael Nelson, "What's Wrong With Policy Analysis," *Washington*

Monthly, September 1979, 53–60. See also Dan Durning, "Participatory Policy Analysis in a Social Service Agency: A Case Study," *Journal of Policy Analysis and Management* 12 (1993): 297–322.

37. See B. Guy Peters, *The Future of Governing: Two Decades of Administrative Reform* (Lawrence: University of Kansas Press, 1996).

38. General Accounting Office, *Managing for Results: Critical Issues for Improving Federal Agencies' Strategic Plans,* GAO/GGD-97-180 (Washington, D.C.: GAO, 16 September 1997). A full range of information on GPRA can be obtained from the GAO's website.

39. See B. Guy Peters, "The Rise and Fall and Rise of Evaluation in American Government" (unpublished manuscript), Nuffield College, Oxford University.

40. Donald F. Kettl and John J. DiIulio, eds., *Inside the Reinvention Machine: Appraising Governmental Reform* (Washington, D.C.: Brookings Institution, 1995).

41. Rochelle L. Stanfield, "Education Wars," *National Journal,* 7 March 1998, 506–9.

42. Brian W. Hogwood and B. Guy Peters, *Policy Dynamics* (Brighton, England: Wheatsheaf, 1983).

43. Ibid.

44. Peter DeLeon, "A Theory of Policy Termination," in *The Policy Cycle,* ed. Judith V. May and Aaron Wildavsky (Beverly Hills, Calif.: Sage, 1978): 279–300; and Janet E. Franz, "Reviving and Revising a Termination Model," *Policy Sciences* 25 (1992): 175–89.

45. Kirk Victor, "Uncle Sam's Little Engine," *National Journal,* 23 November 1991.

46. Laurence E. Lynn Jr. and David deF. Whitman, *The President as Policymaker: Jimmy Carter and Welfare Reform* (Philadelphia: Temple University Press, 1981).

47. Downs, *Inside Bureaucracy.*

48. Rufus E. Miles, "Considerations for a President Bent on Reorganization," *Public Administration Review* 37 (1977): 157.

49. Gary Mucciaroni, "Public Choice and the Politics of Comprehensive Tax Reform," *Governance* 3 (1990): 1–32; and Timothy J. Conlan, Margaret T. Wrightson, and David R. Beam, *Taxing Choices: The Politics of Tax Reform* (Washington, D.C.: CQ Press, 1990).

50. Jean-Claude Thoenig and Eduard Friedberg, "The Power of the Field Staff," in *The Management of Change in Government,* ed. Arne F. Leemans (The Hague: Martinus Nijhoff, 1976).

51. E.H. Klijn and G.R. Teisman, "Effective Policymaking in a Multi-Actor Environment," in *Autopoeisis and Configuration Theory,* ed. L. Schap et al. (Dordrecht: Kluwer, 1991).

52. On the network concept, see Edward O. Laumann and David Knoke, *The Organizational State: Social Change in National Policy Domains* (Madison: University of Wisconsin Press, 1987); R.A.W. Rhodes, *Understanding Governance: Policy Networks, Governance, Reflexivity, and Accountability* (Buckingham, England: Open University Press, 1997).

53. See Jan Kooiman, "Socio-Political Governance," in *Debating Governance,* ed. Jon Pierre (Oxford: Oxford University Press, 1998).

54. R. Kent Weaver, "Setting and Firing Policy Triggers," *Journal of Public Policy* 9 (1989): 307–36.

55. William T. Gormley Jr., *Taming the Bureaucracy: Muscles, Prayers, and Other Strategies* (Princeton: Princeton University Press, 1989), 205–7.

56. John L. Palmer and Isabel V. Sawhill, *The Reagan Record: An Assessment of America's Changing Domestic Priorities* (Cambridge, Mass.: Ballinger, 1984).

57. Gary Orfield, "Refurbishing a Rusted Dream," *Change* 25 (March 1993): 10–15.

58. Colin Campbell and Bert A. Rockman, eds., *The Clinton Presidency: First Appraisals* (Chatham, N.J.: Chatham House, 1996).

Chapter 8. Economic Policy

1. See Michael Stewart, *Keynes and After* (Harmondsworth, England: Penguin, 1972); and Peter A. Hall, *The Political Power of Economic Ideas: Keynesianism Across Nations* (Princeton: Princeton University Press, 1989).

2. Robert Skidelsky, *Politicians and the Slump* (London: Macmillan, 1967).

3. Walter Heller, *New Dimensions of Political Economy* (Cambridge, Mass.: Harvard University Press, 1966).

4. Paul Ormerod, *The Death of Economics* (London: Faber and Faber, 1994).

5. Ironically, politicians who tell the truth about the economic future, and especially about higher taxes, are regarded with even greater skepticism.

6. Herbert Stein, *Presidential Economics: The Making of Economic Policy from Roosevelt to Clinton,* 3d rev. ed. (Washington, D.C.: American Enterprise Institute, 1994).

7. During the 1992 campaign, Bill Clinton's chief campaign advisor, James Carville, kept a sign visible in his office—"It's the economy, stupid." Substantial survey evidence indicates that the public does reward and punish administrations based on economic performance; see *Economics and Politics,* ed. Helmut Norpoth, Michael S. Lewis-Beck, and Jean-Dominique Lafay (Ann Arbor: University of Michigan Press, 1991).

8. Jonathan Rauch, "The Visible Hand," *National Journal,* 9 July 1994, 1612–17.

9. G. Feketekuty, ed., *Trade Strategies for a New Era: Ensuring U.S. Leadership in a Global Economy* (New York: Council on Foreign Relations, 1998).

10. This trade-off is referred to as the "Phillips Curve." See "A Cruise Around the Phillips Curve," *The Economist,* 19 February 1994, 82–83; and A.J. Hallett-Hughes and M.L. Petit, "Stagflation and Phillips Curve Instability in a Model of Macroeconomic Policy," *Manchester School of Economic and Social Studies* 59 (1991): 123–45.

11. In fairness, they have frequently been promised more of everything by politicians, and often without any associated costs. See Isabel V. Sawhill, "Reaganomics in Retrospect," in *Perspectives on the Reagan Years,* ed. John L. Palmer (Washington, D.C.: Urban Institute Press, 1986).

12. We will point out, however, that although the average has been getting higher, the degree of inequality of distribution of the benefits of growth has also been increasing.

13. For a discussion of this "treble affluence," see Richard Rose and B. Guy Peters, *Can Government Go Bankrupt?* (New York: Basic Books, 1978).

14. Lester Thurow, *The Zero-Sum Society* (New York: Basic Books, 1979).

15. Service industries include a wide range of activities such as insurance, medical care, computer services, and banking, in addition to dry cleaners, restaurants, etc.

16. William B. Johnston and Arnold H. Packer, *Workforce 2000: Work and Workers in the 21st Century* (New York: Hudson Institute, 1987); and U.S. Bureau of Labor Statistics, *Monthly Labor Review*, November 1996.

17. Although employment in manufacturing has been declining, value added has been relatively stable. Industries are finding ways to produce with less labor or are shifting toward high value-added products such as computers and other information technologies.

18. Paul Starobin, "Unequal Shares," *National Journal,* 11 September 1993, 2176–79.

19. Fred Hirsch and John H. Goldthorpe, *The Political Economy of Inflation* (Cambridge, Mass.: Harvard University Press, 1978); and R.C. Burdekin and Paul Burkett, *Distributional Conflict and Inflation: Theoretical and Historical Perspectives* (London: Macmillan, 1996).

20. R. Kent Weaver, *The Politics of Indexation* (Washington, D.C.: Brookings Institution, 1987).

21. This is the so-called Baumol's disease, named after the economist William J. Baumol; see his "The Macroeconomics of Unbalanced Growth: The Anatomy of Urban Crisis," in *Is Economics Relevant?* ed. Robert L. Heilbroner and A.M Ford (Pacific Palisades, Calif.: Goodyear, 1971).

22. See B. Guy Peters, "Public Employment in American Government," paper presented at annual Workshops of European Consortium for Political Research, Bern, Switzerland, March 1996.

23. John T. Woolley, *Monetary Politics: The Federal Reserve and the Politics of Monetary Politics* (Cambridge, England: Cambridge University Press, 1987).

24. Gøsta Esping-Anderson, *The Three Worlds of Welfare Capitalism* (Princeton: Princeton University Press, 1990).

25. In 1996 imports equalled just over 14 percent of gross national product in the United States; they averaged 46.4 percent of GNP in Western Europe and 32.5 percent of GNP in all OECD countries.

26. These factors were further exacerbated by a strong U.S. dollar that made selling goods overseas more difficult. The dollar is seen as a "safe haven" in times of crisis, and the price of the dollar was driven up on international money markets.

27. William S. Harat and Thomas D. Willett, eds., *Monetary Policy for a Volatile Global Economy* (Washington, D.C.: AEI Press, 1991).

28. Martin Tolchin and Susan Tolchin, *Buying into America: How Foreign Money is Changing the Face of Our Nation* (New York: Times Books, 1988).

29. See Susan Strange, *The Retreat of the State: The Diffusion of Power in the World Economy* (Cambridge, England: Cambridge University Press, 1996).

30. Michael M. Weinstein, "Twisting Controls on Currency and Capital," *New York Times,* 10 September 1998.

31. M. Hallerberg and S. Basinger, "Internationalization and Changes in

Tax Policy in OECD Countries: The Importance of Domestic Veto Players," *Comparative Political Studies* 31 (1998): 321–52.

32. David Vogel, *Trading Up: Consumer and Environmental Regulation in a Global Economy* (Cambridge, Mass.: Harvard University Press, 1995).

33. Susan B. Hansen, *The Politics of State Economic Development* (Pittsburgh: University of Pittsburgh Press, forthcoming).

34. Fred R. Bleakley, "Infrastructure Dollars Pay Big Dividends," *Wall Street Journal,* 12 August 1997.

35. Robert J. Reinshuttle, *Economic Development: A Survey of State Activities* (Lexington, Ky.: Council of State Governments, 1984).

36. Fox Butterfield, "New England's Siren Call of the 1980s Becomes Echo of Depression," *New York Times,* 15 December 1991.

37. Paul E. Peterson and Mark Rom, "Macroeconomic Policymaking: Who Is in Control?" in *Can the Government Govern?* ed. John E. Chubb and Paul E. Peterson (Washington, D.C.: Brookings Institution, 1989).

38. See Strange, *Retreat of the State;* and K. Ohmae, *The End of the Nation State* (New York: Free Press, 1995). For a contrary view, see Linda Weiss, *The Myth of the Powerless State* (Cambridge, England: Cambridge University Press, 1998).

39. For one view, see Robert B. Reich, "Trade Accords That Spread the Wealth," *New York Times,* 2 September 1997.

40. James D. Savage, *Balanced Budgets and American Democracy* (Ithaca, N.Y.: Cornell University Press, 1988); and Gary R. Evans, *Red Ink: The Budget, Deficit, and Debt of the U.S. Government* (San Diego: Academic Press, 1997).

41. Rose and Peters, *Can Government Go Bankrupt?* 135–41; and James M. Buchanan and Richard Wagner, *Democracy in Deficit: The Political Legacy of Lord Keynes* (New York: Academic Press, 1978), 38–48.

42. When listening to the debates about the impacts of budgets in most parliaments or central agencies, it is clear that the ideas of Keynesianism are far from dead.

43. Henry Aaron et al., *Setting National Priorities: The 1980 Budget* (Washington, D.C.: Brookings Institution, 1979). For a critique, see William H. Buiter, "A Guide to Public Sector Deficits," *Economic Policy* 1 (1985): 3–15.

44. Richard W. Stevenson, "House Republicans to Seek Big Tax Cuts," *New York Times,* 10 September 1998.

45. President Reagan's belief in supply-side economics is an obvious case in point.

46. G. Calvin Mackenzie and Saranna Thornton, *Bucking the Deficit: Economic Policymaking in America* (Boulder, Colo.: Westview, 1996).

47. See chapter 6; and Lawrence J. Haas, "Deficit Doldrums," *National Journal,* 7 December 1991.

48. "Budget Resolution Embraces Clinton Plan," *1993 CQ Almanac* (Washington, D.C.: CQ Press, 1994), 102–21.

49. "Pact Aims to Erase Deficit by 2002," *1996 CQ Almanac* 53 (1997): 2, 18–23.

50. Douglas A. Hibbs, *The American Political Economy: Macroeconomics and Electoral Choice* (Cambridge, Mass.: Harvard University Press, 1987).

51. Paul Craig Roberts, *The Supply-Side Revolution: An Insider's Account*

of Policymaking in Washington (Cambridge, Mass.: Harvard University Press, 1984), esp. 27–33.

52. B. Douglas Bernheim, *The Vanishing Nest Egg: Reflections on Saving in America* (New York: Twentieth Century Fund, 1991).

53. American industry tends to be financed more by equity capital than do most European and Japanese companies, which depend more on close relationships with banks. Therefore, investment in the stock market does supply business the capital it needs.

54. Bruce Bartlett and Timothy P. Roth, eds., *The Supply-Side Solution* (Chatham, N.J.: Chatham House, 1983). George Bush once referred to this assumption as "voodoo economics."

55. James T. Bennett and Thomas J. DiLorenzo, *Underground Government: The Off-Budget Public Sector* (Washington, D.C.: Cato Institute, 1983); and Bruce R. Bartlett, *The Federal Debt: On-Budget, Off-Budget, and Contingent Liabilities,* Study Prepared for Use of Joint Economic Committee (Washington, D.C.: Government Printing Office, 1983).

56. Donald F. Kettl, *Leadership at the Fed* (New Haven: Yale University Press, 1986). For a more muckraking account, see William Greider, *Secrets of the Temple: How the Federal Reserve Runs the Country* (New York: Simon and Schuster, 1987).

57. In September 1998, when Greenspan mentioned that rates might be lowered to continue the expansion of the economy, markets reacted almost instantly.

58. See B. Guy Peters, "Institutionalization and Deinstutionalization: Regulatory Institutions in American Government," in *Comparative Regulatory Institutions,* ed. G. Bruce Doern and Stephen Wilks (Toronto: University of Toronto Press, 1998).

59. Marc Alan Eisner, *Antitrust and the Triumph of Economics* (Chapel Hill: University of North Carolina Press, 1991).

60. The Department of Justice had been the only enforcement agency. It retained its powers after the passage of the Clayton Act, and now both it and the Federal Trade Commission enforce antitrust legislation.

61. Joel Brinkley, "Strategies Set in Microsoft Antitrust Case," *New York Times,* 14 September 1998.

62. Some of this argument appears specious given that all firms will face the same wage increases.

63. See Stein, *Presidential Economics.*

64. Author's calculation based on federal budget documents.

65. J.C. Gray and D.A. Spina, "State and Local Government Industrial Location Incentives: A Well-Stocked Candy Store," *Journal of Corporation Law* 5 (1980): 517–687.

66. William S. Dietrich, *In the Shadow of the Rising Sun: The Political Roots of American Economic Decline* (University Park: Penn State University Press, 1991).

67. The most famous was Ross Perot, who characterized the predicted large loss of jobs to Mexico under NAFTA as a "large sucking sound." See also G. Bruce Doern and Brian W. Tomlin, *Faith and Fear: The Free Trade Story* (Toronto: Stoddard, 1991).

68. Jonathan Rauch, "The Deregulatory President," *National Journal,* 30 November 1991, 2902–6.

69. Jonathan R.T. Hughes, *The Governmental Habit Redux: Economic Controls from Colonial Times to the Present* (Princeton: Princeton University Press, 1991).

70. That support may come through direct subsidies or through protection from foreign competition. See David B. Yoffie, "American Trade Policy: An Obsolete Bargain," in Chubb and Peterson, *Can the Government Govern?*

71. See Marie-Louise Bermelmans-Videc, Ray C. Rist, and Evert Vedung, eds., *Carrots, Sticks, and Sermons: Policy Instruments and their Evaluation* (New Brunswick, N.J.: Transaction, 1998).

Chapter 9. Tax Policy

1. Henry J. Aaron and William G. Gale, *Economic Effects of Fundamental Tax Reform* (Washington, D.C.: Brookings Institution, 1996).

2. Charles E. McClure, *The Value Added Tax: Key to Deficit Reduction?* (Washington, D.C.: American Enterprise Institute, 1987).

3. B. Guy Peters, *The Politics of Taxation: A Comparative Perspective* (Oxford: Blackwell, 1991).

4. David Butler, Anthony Adonis, and Tony Travers, *Failure in British Government: The Politics of the Poll Tax* (Oxford: Oxford University Press, 1994).

5. See Cathie Jo Martin, "Business Influence and State Power: The Case of U.S. Corporate Tax Policy," *Politics and Society* 17 (1989): 189–223.

6. For a somewhat polemical account of recent developments, see Christopher Lasch, *The Revolt of the Elites and the Betrayal of Democracy* (New York: Norton, 1995). William F. Holmes, *American Populism* (New York: D.C. Heath, 1994) provides a more scholarly treatment of populism.

7. Stanley S. Surrey and Paul R. McDaniel, *Tax Expenditures* (Cambridge, England: Cambridge University Press, 1985).

8. Richard W. Stevenson, "The Secret Language of Social Engineering," *New York Times,* 6 July 1997.

9. Robert Pear, "Now, Special Tax Breaks Get Hidden in Plain Sight," *New York Times,* 1 August 1997.

10. Christopher Howard, *The Hidden Welfare State: Tax Expenditures and Social Policy in the United States* (Princeton: Princeton University Press, 1997).

11. The two standard ideas are "ability to pay," justifying a progressive system of taxation, and "benefits received," which can justify more of a flat-rate system of taxation.

12. See O. Listhaug and Arthur H. Miller, "Public Support for Tax Evasion: Self-interest or Symbolic Politics?" *European Journal of Political Research* 13 (1985): 265–82. See also John T. Scholz and Mark Lubell, "Adaptive Political Attitudes: Duty, Trust, and Fear as Monitors of Tax Policy," *American Journal of Political Science* 42 (1998): 903–20.

13. Gallup poll, 24–26 March 1997.

14. It does, of course. Leaving aside how one counts the protective services delivered by the military, there are the Veterans Administration and its hospitals, the Postal Service, the National Park Service, agricultural extension agents, and a host of others.

15. This is, however, bad news for health advocates who are attempting to use the cigarette tax as a means of deterring smoking. It may be more of a deterrent for the main target group—teen smokers—who have less disposable income.

16. See William F. Shugart, ed., *Taxing Choices: The Predatory Politics of Fiscal Discrimination* (New Brunswick, N.J.: Transaction, 1997).

17. David O. Sears and Jack Citrin, *Tax Revolt: Something for Nothing in California,* enl. ed. (Cambridge, Mass.: Harvard University Press, 1985).

18. Allan M. Maslove, *The Economic and Social Environment of Tax Reform* (Toronto: University of Toronto Press, 1995).

19. Joel Slemrod, "What is the Simplest Tax System of Them All?" in Aaron and Gale, *Economic Effects of Fundamental Tax Reform.*

20. F. Vaillancourt, "The Compliance Costs of Taxes on Businesses and Individuals: A Review of the Evidence," *Public Finance* 42 (1989): 395–414.

21. Even at the minimum wage of $5.15 per hour, this will amount to over $5 billion in free work by citizens.

22. Richard A. Musgrave, *Fiscal Systems* (New Haven: Yale University Press, 1969).

23. For somewhat different views, see Robert S. McIntyre, "Thrown for a Loop," *New Republic* 208 (15 March 1993): 17, 19ff; and Laura Sanders, "The Campeau Coup and the May Maneuver," *Forbes* 142 (31 October 1988): 98–99.

24. Joseph A. Pechman, *Who Paid the Taxes, 1966–85?* (Washington, D.C.: Brookings Institution, 1986).

25. Paul E. Peterson and Mark Rom, "Lower Taxes, More Spending, and Budget Deficits," in *The Reagan Legacy,* ed. Charles O. Jones (Chatham, N.J.: Chatham House, 1988).

26. Peters, *Politics of Taxation,* 166–73.

27. See the extended analysis of the Clinton proposals in the *New York Times,* 18 February 1993.

28. Gwen Ifill, "President Assures Middle Class over Income Taxes," *New York Times,* 17 February 1993.

29. Harold Wilensky, *The "New Corporatism," Centralization, and the Welfare State* (Beverly Hills, Calif.: Sage, 1976).

30. The author, for example, pays four separate income taxes, three property taxes, sales and excise taxes, etc. Some of these taxes are small, but they do add up.

31. W.W. Pommerehne and F. Schneider, "Fiscal Illusion, Political Institutions, and Local Public Spending," *Kyklos* 31 (1978): 381–408.

32. McClure, *Value Added Tax.*

33. Peters, *Politics of Taxation,* 165–67.

34. Sven Steinmo, *Taxation and Democracy* (New Haven: Yale University Press, 1992).

35. J.M. Verdier, "The President, Congress and Tax Reform: Patterns over Three Decades," *The Annals,* 1988, 114–23.

36. Even after reforms, the federal income tax is considered the least fair tax by a plurality of respondents in surveys. See Advisory Commission on Intergovernmental Relations, *Changing Public Attitudes on Government and Taxes* (Washington, D.C.: ACIR, annual).

37. Timothy J. Conlan, Margaret T. Wrightson, and David R. Beam, *Taxing Choices: The Politics of Tax Reform* (Washington, D.C.: CQ Press, 1989); and J.H. Birnbaum and A.S. Murray, *Showdown at Gucchi Gulch* (New York: Random House, 1987).

38. Gary Mucciaroni, "Public Choice and the Politics of Comprehensive Tax Reform," *Governance* 3 (1990): 1–32.

39. Conlan, Wrightson, and Beam, *Taxing Choices*.

40. John W. Kingdon, *Agendas, Alternatives, and Public Policies* (Boston: Little, Brown, 1984).

41. See Cedric Sandford, *Successful Tax Reform* (Bath, England: Fiscal Publications, 1993).

42. For example, if I had invested $100 in a piece of land in 1970, and then sold it in 1998 for $500, there would be an apparent profit of $400. If, however, inflation were taken into account, the "real" profit would be less than $200 (in 1998 dollars). On what basis should I be taxed?

43. In 1995, 82 percent of all returns reporting capital gains cited incomes less than $100,000, although 76 percent of all capital gains income does go to people earning over $100,000.

44. This resentment came to a head in 1997 and 1998 with a series of congressional hearings about the Internal Revenue Service and its treatment of citizens. See Daniel J. Murphy, "IRS: An Agency Out of Control?" *Investor's Business Daily*, 1 October 1997; and "It's April at the IRS," *USA Today*, 2 April 1998.

45. But see Aaron Wildavsky, "Keeping Kosher: The Epistemology of Tax Expenditures," *Journal of Public Policy* 5 (1985): 413–31.

46. See Robert S. McIntyre, "The 23 Percent Solution," *New York Times*, 23 January 1998.

47. Psychologically that might create demands for increases in wages, even though people should have a great deal more take-home pay with the elimination of the income tax.

48. See David F. Bradford, *Untangling the Income Tax* (Cambridge, Mass.: Harvard University Press, 1986); General Accounting Office, *Tax Administration: Potential Impact of Alternate Taxes on Taxpayers and Administrators*, GAO/GGD-98-37 (Washington, D.C.: GAO, January 1998), Appendix VIII.

49. See Thomas J. DiLorenzo and James T. Bennett, "National Nannies Seek Taxes on All We Consume," *USA Today*, 23 December 1997.

50. That is, 24 million business returns plus 115 million personal returns.

51. Ben Wildavsky, "A Taxing Question," *National Journal*, 28 February 1998.

Chapter 10. Health-Care Policy

1. The evidence is that most states have not replaced the health-care money they lost from block grants. See George E. Peterson et al., *Block Grants* (Washington, D.C.: Urban Institute, 1984).

2. Penelope Lemov, "States and Medicaid: Ahead of the Feds," *Governing* 6 (July 1993): 27–28.

3. Marilyn Werber Serafini, "Oh Yeah, the Uninsured," *National Journal*, 15 November 1997, 2300–3.

4. Judi Hasson and Jessica Lee, "Poll: 43% Back Clinton Health Plan," *USA Today*, 30 June 1994.

5. For example, in a 1996 poll, half the respondents said that providing affordable medical care for all was one of the top national priorities, and 22 percent said it was the highest priority. See Robert D. Reischauer, Stuart Butler, and Judith R. Lave, eds., *Medicare: Preparing for the Challenges of the 21st Century* (Washington, D.C.: Brookings Institution, 1997), 300.

6. "Federal, State, Local, or Private Action," *American Enterprise*, November/December 1997, 94.

7. Adam Clymer, "House Bill Asks 8.4% Payroll Tax For Canadian-Style Health Plan," *New York Times*, 28 January 1994.

8. Deane Neubauer, "Hawaii: The Health State," and Camille Asccuaga, "Universal Health Care in Massachusetts: Lessons for the Future," in *Health Policy Reform in the United States: Innovations from the States*, ed. Howard Leichter (Armonk, N.Y.: M.E. Sharpe, 1992); and General Accounting Office, *Health Care in Hawaii: Implications for National Reform*, GAO/HEHS-94-68 (Washington, D.C.: GAO, February 1994).

9. Robin Toner, "Health Care in Minnesota: Model for U.S. or Novelty?" *New York Times*, 9 October 1993. Children and the elderly again can be seen to hold a privileged position, as programs for them are deemed permissible even if more general programs are not.

10. With the loss of welfare also came a loss of Medicaid coverage, but another federal law funded care for children in states that adopted a suitable program. See Peter T. Kilborn, "States to Provide Health Insurance to More Children," *New York Times*, 21 September 1997.

11. See B. Guy Peters, "Is It the Institutions? Explaining the Failure of Health Care in the United States," *Public Policy and Administration* 11, no. 1 (1996): 8–15.

12. World Health Organization, *World Health Statistics Annual* (Geneva: WHO, annual).

13. "The Public Decides on Health Care Reform," *Public Perspective* 5 (September/October 1994): 23–28. A very large proportion support care for the elderly, with Medicare now being highly institutionalized.

14. These are primarily the working poor, who are employed in jobs without health-care benefits and who are not eligible for Medicaid as they would be if they were on welfare.

15. Henry J. Aaron, *Serious and Unstable Condition: Financing America's Health Care* (Washington, D.C.: Brookings Institution, 1991): 47–57.

16. Ibid., 45–47.

17. Robert Pear, "Tough Decision on Health Care If Employers Won't Pay the Bill," *New York Times*, 9 July 1994.

18. *New York Times*, 11 July 1994.

19. General Accounting Office, *Private Health Insurance: Continued Erosion of Coverage Linked to Cost Pressures*, GAO/HEHS-97-122 (Washington, D.C.: GAO, July 1997).

20. Despite its good intentions, the indications are that Kennedy-Kassebaum is not as effective as it might be because the rates at which the portable insurance can be charged are not adequately controlled. See Robert Pear, "High

Rates Hobble Law to Guarantee Health Insurance," *New York Times,* 17 March 1998.

21. Peter Townsend, ed., *Inequalities in Health: The Black Report* (London: Penguin, 1988).

22. Lisette Alvarez, "A Conservative Battles Corporate Health Care," *New York Times,* 12 February 1998.

23. Peter T. Kilborn, "Black Americans Trailing Whites in Health, Studies Say," *New York Times,* 26 January 1998.

24. The infant mortality rate is more than double the national average. In 1995 it was more than 50 percent higher than the next highest unit—Mississippi.

25. Steven Greenhouse, "The States' Stakes in Clinton's Health Plan," *New York Times,* 10 October 1993.

26. Rural areas tend to have a number of hospital beds but very low occupancy rates, thereby driving up costs.

27. *Rural Health Clinics: Rising Program Expenditures Not Focused on Improving Care in Isolated Areas,* Testimony of Bernice Steinhardt, GAO/T-HEHS-97-65 (Washington, D.C.: General Accounting Office, 13 February 1997).

28. Nicholas Eberstadt, "Why Are So Many American Babies Dying?" *American Enterprise* 2 (September 1991): 37–45. This finding, of course, gives comfort to conservatives who stress individual responsibility and minimize the need for government intervention in the medical marketplace.

29. See Henry J. Aaron, *The Problem That Won't Go Away: Reforming U.S. Health Care Financing* (Washington, D.C.: Brookings Institution, 1995).

30. For example, CAT scans and MRIs are now common diagnostic procedures that were used scarcely if at all until relatively recently. Each use of these technologies is billed at over $1,000.

31. Milt Freundenheim, "H.M.O.'s Beginning to Ease the Rules on Specialty Care," *New York Times,* 2 February 1997.

32. Aaron, *Serious and Unstable Condition,* 8–37.

33. The U.S. population is approximately 11 times as large as that of Canada, but we have approximately 100 times as many MRI units.

34. Spencer Rich, "Hospital Administration Costs Put at 25%," *Washington Post,* 6 August 1993.

35. John K. Inglehart, "Health Policy Report: Managed Competition," *New England Journal of Medicine* 328 (22 April 1993): 1208–12; and Joshua M. Wiener and Laura Hixon Illston, "Health Care Reform: Six Questions for President Clinton," *Brookings Review* 11 (Spring 1993): 22–25.

36. Aaron, *Serious and Unstable Condition,* 45–47.

37. Julie Kosterlitz, "Wanted: GPs," *National Journal,* 5 September 1992.

38. Susan Hosek et al., *The Study of Preferred Provider Organizations* (Santa Monica, Calif.: Rand Corporation, 1990). Doctors are beginning to fight back against managed care; see Reed Abelson, "A Medical Resistance Movement," *New York Times,* 25 March 1998.

39. Paul B. Ginsburg et al., "Update: Medicare Physician Payment Reform," *Health Affairs* 9 (Spring 1990): 178–88.

40. Sandra Christenses and Scott Harrison, *Physician Payment Reform Under Medicare* (Washington, D.C.: Congressional Budget Office, 1990).

41. See Stan Jones, "The Medicare Beneficiary as Consumer," in Reischauer,

Butler, and Lave, *Medicare.*

42. These are 1995 figures. Health Care Financing Administration, *Health Care Financing Review,* annual.

43. Garrett Hardin and John Baden, *Managing the Commons* (San Francisco: W.H. Freeman, 1977).

44. This approach was not popular with a number of groups, including the Children's Defense Fund, which has been closely associated with Hillary Clinton. See Timothy Egan, "Oregon Health Plan Stalled by Politics," *New York Times,* 17 March 1993.

45. Susan Ferriss, "Plan in Oregon Would Expand Health Coverage to Poor Citizens," *Pittsburgh Post-Gazette,* 20 December 1991.

46. Susan Feigenbaum, "Denying Access to Life-Saving Technologies: Budgetary Implications of a Moral Dilemma," *Regulation* 16, no. 4 (1994): 74–79.

47. Thomas J. Marzen and Louis W. Sullivan, "ADA Analyses of the Oregon Health Care Plan," *Issues in Law & Medicine* 9 (1994): 397–424.

48. On the latter point, see Ivan Illich, *Medical Nemesis* (New York: Pantheon, 1976).

49. Abelson, "Medical Resistance Movement"; and "The Tricky Business of Keeping Doctors Quiet," *New York Times,* 22 September 1996.

50. As of spring 1997, eight states had comprehensive laws providing managed-care rights to citizens, two others had regulations and were writing legislation, and nineteen others had legislation under active consideration.

51. The same questions arise concerning developments in medical technology, such as artificial hearts. See "One Miracle, Many Doubts," *Time,* 10 December 1984, 10ff.

52. Henry R. Glick, *The Right to Die* (New York: Columbia University Press, 1994).

53. Rudolf Klein and Patricia Day, *Managing Scarcity: Priority Setting and Rationing in the National Health Service* (Buckingham, England: Open University Press, 1996).

54. In addition to the ninety days covered per stay, each participant has sixty "reserve days" during his or her life that can be used after any ninety-day period of hospitalization, although these require a co-payment of $382.

55. Karen Davis, "Equal Treatment and Unequal Benefits," *Milbank Memorial Fund Quarterly,* Fall 1975, 449–88; and Robert Ball, "What Medicare Had in Mind," *Health Affairs,* 14 (1995): 62–72.

56. "Tougher Standards for Medigap Insurance," *Aging* 362 (1991): 44–45.

57. Advisory Council on Social Security, *Report on Medicare Projections by the Health Technical Panel* (Washington, D.C.: Government Printing Office, 1991).

58. Marilyn Werber Serafini, "Brave New World," *National Journal,* 16 August 1997.

59. In a medical savings account, Medicare buys the patient a catastrophic-care policy and covers part of the deductible payments for care under the policy. If there are any savings over the year, i.e., the recipient is healthy and actually spends less than under the standard program, he or she gets to keep the difference.

60. In 1997 the Office of the Inspector General of the Department of Health

and Human Services uncovered $23 billion a year in fraud and waste in Medicare.

61. Julie Kosterlitz, "Health Rip-Offs," *National Journal,* 20 June 1992.

62. Louise B. Russell and Carrie Lynn Manning, "The Effect of Prospective Payment on Medicare Expenditures," *New England Journal of Medicine,* 16 February 1989, 439–44.

63. Jeffrey A. Buck and Mark S. Kamlet, "Problems with Expanding Medicaid for the Uninsured," *Journal of Health Politics, Policy and Law* 18 (1993): 1–25. Medicaid spending now accounts for approximately one dollar in five of state expenditures.

64. Health Care Financing Administration, *Health Care Financing Review,* annual.

65. Paul Jesilow and Gilbert Geis, "Fraud by Physicians Against Medicaid," *Journal of the American Medical Association* 266 (18 December 1991): 3318–22.

66. Leslie G. Aronovitz, *Medicaid: A Program Highly Vulnerable to Fraud,* GAO/T-HEHS-94-106 (Washington, D.C.: General Accounting Office, 25 February 1994).

67. See note 10.

68. Karen Davis et al., *Health Care Cost Containment* (Baltimore: Johns Hopkins University Press, 1990), 222ff.

69. Patricia Baumann, "The Formulation and Evolution of Health Maintenance Organization Policy, 1970–73," *Social Science and Medicine,* 1976, 129–42.

70. This conformed to the general tendency of the Reagan and Bush administrations to use market and quasi-market devices as means of reducing the costs of government.

71. Elisabeth Rosenthal, "Doctors Who Once Spurned H.M.O.'s Now Often Find Systems' Doors Shut," *New York Times,* 25 June 1994.

72. See Lester C. Thurow, "As HMOs Lose Control, Patient Costs Head Skyward," *USA Today,* 16 December 1997.

73. Robert Pear, "Clinton Picks Panel to Draft Bill of Rights in Health Care," *New York Times,* 27 March 1997.

74. "Panel Nears Agreement on Patient's Rights," *USA Today,* 19 June 1998.

75. One of the older forms of health-care regulation, the control of facilities through certificates-of-need has ceased to be of great relevance, given the emphasis on cost containment in managed care.

76. Peter H. Stone, "Ready for Round Two," *National Journal,* 3 January 1998.

77. In particular, Rep. Charles Norwood (R-Ga.) has been leading a campaign for more extensive regulation of HMOs, and this effort has him making common cause with Senator Edward Kennedy (D-Mass.), one of the more liberal members of the Senate.

78. Sam Howe Verhovek, "Texas Is Lowering H.M.O. Legal Shield," *New York Times,* 5 June 1997.

79. There is some evidence that managed-care systems do invest more in preventive care. Steven Findlay, "Survey Shows HMO Care Varies Widely," *USA Today,* 2 October 1997.

80. Tort actions may not be as effective as ex ante controls, but they do at least force the industry to consider the long-run costs of any decisions it may make.

81. Peter S. Arno and Karyn L. Feiden, *Against The Odds: The Story of AIDS Drug Development, Politics and Profits* (New York: Harper/Collins, 1992).

82. A "look-alike" drug is virtually identical chemically with another drug but has some slight modification to avoid patent restrictions.

83. The "substandard" here is a function largely of inadequate preventive care and lack of consistent follow-up, rather than the quality of the individual treatments.

84. Gallup poll, January 1996.

85. For a discussion of these problems, see chapter 4.

86. Julie Kosterlitz, "A Sick System," *National Journal,* 15 February 1992.

87. Howard Leichter, *Health Policy Reform in America: Innovations from the States,* 2d ed. (Armonk, N.Y.: M.E. Sharpe, 1997).

88. Although it is referred to as "Canadian" in the American debates over health care, this type of plan is actually found in most developed democracies.

89. Some aspects of the plan have been implemented in various states, under the same name. See, for example, A.C. Enthoven and S.J. Singer, "Managed Competition and the California Health Economy," *Health Affairs* 15 (1996): 39–57.

90. Robert Pear, "Bill Passed by Panel Would Open Medicare to Millions of Uninsured People," *New York Times,* 1 July 1994.

91. See Peters, "Is It the Institutions?"

92. Katherine Q. Seelye, "Lobbyists are the Loudest in the Health Care Debate," *New York Times,* 16 August 1994.

93. The degree of choice actually existing in the current medical-care system appeared to have been exaggerated by the opponents of reform. See Robin Toner, "Ills of Health System Outlive Debate on Care," *New York Times,* 2 October 1994.

94. Richard E. Cohen, "Into the Swamp," *National Journal,* 19 March 1994.

95. Adam Clymer, "With Health Overhaul Dead, A Search for Minor Repairs," *New York Times,* 28 August 1994.

96. Robert Pear, "Health Care Debate to Shift to Federal Employees' Plan," *New York Times,* 7 September 1994.

97. Marilyn Werber Serafini, "A New Prescription," *National Journal,* 14 March 1998, 572–75.

98. Clymer, "With Health Overhaul Dead."

99. Robert Pear, "States Again Try Health Changes as Congress Fails," *New York Times,* 16 September 1994.

Chapter 11. Income Maintenance Policies: Social Security and Welfare

1. See Harold Wilensky, *The Welfare State and Equality* (Berkeley: University of California Press, 1975), 32–36. For a different view, see Theodore R.

Marmor, Jerry L. Mashaw, and Philip L. Harvey, *America's Misunderstood Welfare State* (New York: Basic Books, 1990).

2. For one analysis, see Fred Englander and John Kane, "Reagan's Welfare Reforms: Were the Program Savings Realized?" *Policy Studies Review* 11 (1992): 3–23.

3. Jeff Shear, "Pulling in Harness," *National Journal*, 4 June 1994, 1286–90. Several of the designers of the original program quit in protest over the program eventually adopted in 1996.

4. In 1995 welfare was 9.1 percent of federal social expenditure and 3.2 percent of total federal expenditure. It was 8.9 percent of total social expenditure and 3.4 percent of total public expenditure.

5. For example, if former recipients are required to find jobs, child care will be needed once they have the jobs, as will training and education before they can qualify. See Rochelle L. Stanfield, "Home Economics," *National Journal*, 4 April 1998, 751–54.

6. See Helen Fawcett, "Workfare: The Politics of Policy Transfer," paper presented at Conference of Structure and Organization of Government Research Committee, Lady Margaret Hall, Oxford University, July 1998.

7. Peter Flora and Arnold J. Heidenheimer, "The Historical Core and Changing Boundaries of the Welfare State," in *The Development of Welfare States in Europe and North America*, ed. Peter Flora and Arnold J. Heidenheimer (New Brunswick, N.J.: Transaction, 1981).

8. Donald O. Parsons and Douglas R. Munro, "Intergenerational Transfers in Social Security," in *The Crisis in Social Security*, ed. Michael J. Boskin (San Francisco: Institute for Contemporary Studies, 1977): 65–86.

9. Self-employed persons pay a rate equal to the combined sum of contributions of employers and employees.

10. This separation of pensions and other social insurance benefits from general taxation is unusual in the rest of the world. See Margaret S. Gordon, *Social Security Policies in Industrial Countries: A Comparative Analysis* (Cambridge, England: Cambridge University Press, 1990).

11. Michael D. Hurd and John B. Shoven, "The Distributional Impact of Social Security," in *Pensions, Labor, and Individual Choice*, ed. David A. Wise (Chicago: University of Chicago Press, 1985).

12. As income goes up, replacement rates go down; at $100,000 per year, the rate would be 28 percent, although that individual would probably have additional sources of retirement income.

13. The actual determination of taxability is somewhat more complicated; see David Pattison and David E. Harrington, "Proposals to Modify the Taxation of Social Security Benefits: Options and Distributional Effects," *Social Security Bulletin* 56 (Summer 1993): 3–13.

14. This program has been, like so many, "path dependent" and its initial formulation has largely determined its development. See Ellen M. Immergut, *Health Politics: Interests and Institutions in Western Europe* (Cambridge, England: Cambridge University Press, 1992).

15. Joseph Bondar, "Beneficiaries Affected by the Annual Earnings Test, 1989," *Social Security Bulletin* 56 (Spring 1993): 20–34.

16. Social Security Agency, Office of the Actuary, *Life Tables for the United*

States Social Security Area, 1900–2080 (Baltimore, Md.: SSA, 1992).

17. "Commission: Raise Retirement Age to 70," *USA Today*, 19 May 1998.

18. There has been a tendency for people to retire earlier, especially for the more affluent who have a retirement income in addition to Social Security.

19. C. Eugene Steuerle and Jon M. Bakija, *Retooling Social Security for the 21st Century* (Washington, D.C.: Urban Institute Press, 1994), 97.

20. Deborah Stone, *The Disabled State* (Philadelphia: Temple University Press, 1985).

21. Bernadine Weatherford, "The Disability Insurance Program: An Administrative Attack on the Welfare State," in *The Attack on the Welfare State*, ed. Anthony Champagne and Edward J. Harpham (Prospect Heights, Ill: Waveland Press, 1984).

22. General Accounting Office, *Social Security Disability: SSA Needs to Improve Continuing Disability Review Program*, GAO/HRD-93-109 (Washington, D.C.: GAO, July 1993).

23. "Workers' Compensation," *Social Security Bulletin* 56 (Winter 1993): 28–31.

24. The maximum payment in Connecticut is $737 per week, while that in Georgia is $225 per week.

25. For a detailed analysis, see Henry J. Aaron, Barry P. Bosworth, and Gary Burtless, *Can America Afford to Grow Old?: Paying for Social Security* (Washington, D.C.: Brookings Institution, 1989), 55–75.

26. Practical politics, however, prevented President Reagan from doing anything to reduce Social Security benefits. See Paul E. Peterson and Mark Rom, "Lower Taxes, More Spending, and Budget Deficits," in *The Reagan Legacy*, ed. Charles O. Jones (Chatham, N.J.: Chatham House, 1988), 224–25.

27. Princeton Survey Research survey reported in *USA Today*, 27 July 1998.

28. Jonathan Rauch, "False Security," *National Journal*, 14 February 1987, 362–65.

29. Aaron, Bosworth, and Burtless, *Can America Afford to Grow Old?*

30. Board of Trustees of the Federal Old-Age, Survivors and Disability Insurance Trust Funds, *Annual Report, 1993* (Washington, D.C.: Government Printing Office, 1993).

31. Linda E. Demkovich, "Budget Cutters Think the Unthinkable—Social Security Cuts Would Stem Red Ink," *National Journal*, 23 June 1984.

32. Ibid.

33. As noted, the health insurance component of the payroll tax (1.45 percent) is applied to all income.

34. George F. Break, "The Economic Effects of Social Security Financing," in *Social Security Financing*, ed. Felicity Skidmore (Cambridge, Mass.: MIT Press, 1981), 45–80.

35. See B. Guy Peters, *The Politics of Taxation: A Comparative Perspective* (Oxford: Blackwell, 1991).

36. See "Americans Want Everyone in Social Security," *USA Today*, 29 July 1998.

37. Charles E. McClure, "VAT Versus the Payroll Tax," in Skidmore, *Social Security Financing*.

38. Ben Wildavsky, "The Two Per Cent Solution," *National Journal*, 11

April 1998, 794–97.

39. As long as it runs at a surplus, the Social Security system has money to invest, but it is required to invest in ultra-safe (but low-yield) government securities.

40. The basic state pension in the United Kingdom is rather low, so there was a felt need to provide an earnings-related pension for the middle classes. See James Midgley and Michael Sherraden, eds., *Alternatives to Social Security: An International Inquiry* (Westport, Conn.: Auburn House, 1997).

41. R. Shep Melnick, *Between the Lines* (Washington, D.C.: Brookings Institution, 1994).

42. Most of these critics are on the political right, e.g., Charles Murray, *Losing Ground* (New York: Basic Books, 1984) and "Stop Favoring Welfare Mothers," *New York Times,* 16 January 1992; and Lawrence M. Mead, *The New Politics of Poverty* (New York: Basic Books, 1992). There are, however, also critics on the left, e.g., David T. Ellwood, *Poor Support: Poverty and the American Family* (New York: Basic Books, 1988); and Frances Fox Piven and Richard Cloward, *Regulating the Poor,* 2d ed. (New York: Vintage Books, 1993).

43. See James L. Morrison, *The Healing of America: Welfare Reform in a Cyber Economy* (Brookfield, Vt.: Ashgate, 1997).

44. Penelope Lemov, "Putting Welfare on the Clock," *Governing,* November 1993, 29–30.

45. Edwin W. Witte, *The Development of the Social Security Act* (Madison: University of Wisconsin Press, 1962), 5–39.

46. Julie Kosterlitz, "Behavior Modification," *National Journal,* 1 February 1992, 271–75; the earlier attempts to control behavior pale in comparison to those of the 1996 reforms.

47. Ibid.

48. Kevin Sack, "Fingerprinting Allowed in Welfare Fraud Fight," *New York Times,* 9 July 1994.

49. Some evidence appearing just as workfare was being implemented placed doubt on the efficacy of permitting greater earnings. See Jason DeParle, "More Questions About Incentives to Get Those on Welfare to Work," *New York Times,* 28 August 1997.

50. As noted, despite those disincentives to leave, the majority of people on AFDC did not stay long. The other problems with the program, and the relatively meager benefits, attracted few long-term beneficiaries.

51. Julie Kosterlitz, "Reworking Welfare," *National Journal,* 26 September 1992.

52. Cited in Isaac Shapiro et al., *The States and the Poor* (Washington, D.C.: Center of Budget and Policy Priorities, December 1991), 8.

53. Michael Wiseman, "Research and Policy: A Symposium on the Family Support Act of 1988," *Journal of Policy Analysis and Management* 10 (1991): 588–89.

54. Kay E. Sherwood and David A. Long, "JOBS Implementation in an Uncertain Environment," *Public Welfare* 49 (1991): 17–27.

55. It was expected, however, that this problem would be rectified if any of the plans for universal health insurance were to be passed.

56. Sherwood and Long, "JOBS Implementation."

57. The title of the bill is a masterpiece of symbol manipulation (see pp. 56–57).

58. For a discussion of this and other myths, see Steven M. Teles, *Whose Welfare?: AFDC and Elite Politics* (Lawrence: University Press of Kansas, 1996).

59. Robert Pear, "Clinton Will Seek Tax Break to Ease Path Off Welfare," *New York Times,* 28 January 1997.

60. Robert Pear, "Governors Limit Revisions Sought in Welfare Law," *New York Times,* 3 February 1997.

61. See Jonathan Rabinowitz, "Connecticut Welfare Law Cuts Hundreds Off the Rolls," *New York Times,* 3 November 1997; and Richard Wolf, "Some States Still at Welfare Impasse," *USA Today,* 2 July 1997.

62. Nina Bernstein, "Giant Companies Enter Race to Run State Welfare Programs," *New York Times,* 15 September 1996.

63. Judith Havemann, "Welfare Reform Still on a Roll as States Bounce It Down to Counties," *Washington Post,* 29 August 1997.

64. Dilys M. Hill, "Social Policy," in *Developments in American Politics 3,* ed. Gillian Peele et al. (New York: Chatham House, 1998).

65. Rochelle L. Stanfield, "Valuing the Family," *National Journal,* 4 July 1992, 1562–66.

66. Rochelle L. Stanfield, "Cautious Optimism," *National Journal,* 2 May 1998, 990–93.

67. See General Accounting Office, *Welfare Reform: States Are Restructuring Programs to Reduce Welfare Dependency,* GAO/HEHS-98-109 (Washington, D.C.: GAO, 18 June 1998). Oregon, for example, has found that half those on the welfare caseload will require treatment for chemical dependency before they are likely to be employable.

68. Stanfield, "Cautious Optimism."

69. Sheila Kammerman and Alfred Kahn, "Universalism and Testing in Family Policy: New Perspectives on an Old Debate," *Social Work* 32 (1987): 277–80.

70. Hermione Parker, *Instead of the Dole: An Enquiry into the Integration of Tax and Benefit Systems* (London: Routledge, 1989).

71. M. Kenneth Bowler, *The Nixon Guaranteed Income Proposal: Substance and Process in Policy Change* (Cambridge, Mass.: Ballinger, 1974).

72. Office of Child Support Enforcement, *Annual Report to Congress.*

73. Irwin Garfinkel, Sara S. McLanahan, and Philip K. Robins, *Child Support and Child Well-Being* (Lanham, Md.: Urban Institute Press, 1994).

74. General Accounting Office, *Child Support Assurance: Effects of Applying State Guidelines to Determine Fathers' Payments,* GAO/HRD-93-26 (Washington, D.C.: GAO, January 1993).

75. Nadine Cohodas, "Child Support: No More Pretty Please," *Governing,* October 1993, 20–21.

76. Mimi Hall, "Child Support: States Pay If Parents Don't," *USA Today,* 28 March 1994.

77. At least one state has already done so; see "In Maine, No Child Support, No Driving," *New York Times,* 28 June 1994.

78. For a general discussion of employment policy, see Margaret Weir, *Politics and Jobs* (Princeton: Princeton University Press, 1992).

79. Robert B. Reich, *The Work of Nations: Preparing Ourselves for 21st Century Capitalism* (New York: Knopf, 1991).

80. General Accounting Office, *Multiple Employment Training Programs: Conflicting Requirements Hamper Delivery of Services,* GAO/HEHS-94-78 (Washington, D.C.: GAO, January 1994).

81. Sar A. Levitan, *The Great Society's Poor Law: A New Approach to Poverty* (Baltimore: Johns Hopkins University Press, 1969).

82. Later research, however, is finding some latent effects of Head Start, much like the "sleeper effects" described in chapter 7. See William Celis III, "Study Suggests Head Start Helps Beyond School," *New York Times,* 20 April 1993. See also Carlotta C. Joyner, "Head Start: Research Insufficient to Assess Program Impact," Testimony to Subcommittee on Early Childhood, Youth, and Families, Senate Committee on Labor and Human Resources, 26 March 1998.

83. Richard Rose and B. Guy Peters, *Can Government Go Bankrupt?* (New York: Basic Books, 1978).

84. For a more recent view, see Michael Harrington, *The New American Poverty* (New York: Holt, Rinehart and Winston, 1984).

85. Paul Starobin, "Unequal Shares," *National Journal,* 11 September 1993, 2176–79.

86. Sar Levitan, Frank Gallo, and Isaac Shapiro, *Working But Poor: America's Contradiction,* rev. ed. (Baltimore: Johns Hopkins University Press, 1993).

87. Ibid., 99–125.

88. Patricia Ruggles, *Drawing the Line: Alternative Poverty Measures and Their Implications for Public Policy* (Washington, D.C.: Urban Institute Press, 1990).

89. John L. Palmer, Timothy Smeeding, and Barbara Boyle Torrey, eds., *The Vulnerable* (Washington, D.C.: Urban Institute Press, 1988).

90. The currently fashionable phrase for these problems, made popular by the Labour government in Britain, is "social exclusion."

91. Maybeth Shinn and Colleen Gillespie, "The Roles of Housing and Poverty in the Origins of Homelessness," *American Behavioral Scientist* 37 (1994): 505–21.

92. Ann Braden Johnson, *Out of Bedlam: The Truth About Deinstitutionalization* (New York: Basic Books, 1990); and Julian Leff, *Care in the Community: Myth or Reality* (New York: John Wiley, 1997).

93. General Accounting Office, *Homelessness: McKinney Act Programs Provide Assistance but Are Not Designed to Be the Solution,* GAO/RCED-94-37 (Washington, D.C.: GAO, May 1994).

94. Ibid.

95. Martin Rein and Lee Rainwater, *Public-Private Interplay in Social Service Provision* (Armonk, N.Y.: M.E. Sharpe, 1988).

Chapter 12. Educational Policy

1. Catherine S. Mangold, "Students Make Strides But Fall Short of Goals," *New York Times,* 18 August 1994.

2. "Poll Readings," *National Journal,* 14 February 1998, 368.

3. National Center for Education Statistics, *Digest of Education Statistics*

(Washington, D.C.: Government Printing Office, 1992).

4. Richard Hofferbert, "Race, Space and the American Policy Paradox," paper presented at 1980 conference of the Southern Political Science Association.

5. In areas in which parochial schools were important, these schools also tended to draw from a wide range of social classes if not religions.

6. Karen De Witt, "Nation's Schools Learn a Fourth R: Resegregation," *New York Times,* 19 January 1992.

7. For diverse views on this topic, see Gerald Graff, *Beyond the Culture Wars: How Teaching the Conflicts Can Revitalize American Education* (New York: Norton, 1992); and Russell Jacoby, *Dogmatic Wisdom: How the Culture Wars Divert Education and Distract America* (New York: Doubleday, 1994).

8. Bureau of the Census, *Statistical Abstract of the United States, 1997* (Washington, D.C.: Government Printing Office, 1998).

9. "Poll Readings," *National Journal,* 19 January 1998. Twelve percent of respondents said they were very satisfied, and 32 percent were somewhat satisfied.

10. Students in Iowa and North Dakota on average scored as well as those in Korea, and better than those in any European country on math and science tests. Tamara Henry, "Math, Science Gains May Spark More School Reform," *USA Today,* 26 March 1996.

11. See his *Our Country and Our Children: Improving America's Schools and Affirming Our Common Culture* (New York: Touchstone, 1988). There have been a number of books advocating such a traditional curriculum for American schools, including Allan Bloom, *The Closing of the American Mind* (New York: Touchstone, 1987).

12. Jeffrey L. Katz, "Head Start Reauthorization," *Congressional Quarterly Weekly Report* 52 (18 June 1994): 1653–55.

13. Rochelle L. Stanfield, "Standard Bearer," *National Journal,* 2 July 1994, 1566–70.

14. *Evaluating the Net Impact of School-to-Work: Proceedings of a Roundtable* (Washington, D.C.: U.S. Department of Labor, 1997).

15. Rochelle L. Stanfield, "Team Players," *National Journal,* 13 November 1993, 2723–27.

16. Anemona Hartcollis, "Educators Say Clinton's Plan on Class Size Faces Problems," *New York Times,* 29 January 1998.

17. Jonathan Kozol, *Savage Inequalities: Children in America's Schools* (New York: Crown Publishers, 1991).

18. *Grove City College v. Bell,* 465 U.S. 555 (1984).

19. Scott Jashik, "Secretary Seeks Ban on Grants Reserved for Specific Groups," *Chronicle of Higher Education* 38 (11 December 1991): A1, A26.

20. See pp. 351–52.

21. Rochelle L. Stanfield, "We Have a Tradition of Not Learning," *National Journal,* 7 September 1991, 2156–57.

22. Norman C. Thomas, *Educational Policy in National Politics* (New York: David McKay, 1975).

23. The figure is now roughly 8 percent.

24. Michael D. Reagan, *The New Federalism* (New York: Oxford University Press, 1972).

25. Jerome T. Murphy, "Title I of ESEA: The Politics of Implementing Federal Educational Reform," *Harvard Education Review* (1971): 35–63.

26. *Title I of ESEA: Is It Helping Poor Children?* (Washington, D.C.: NAACP Legal Defense Fund, 1969).

27. Some recent polls show that minority parents, like majority parents, want good basic education instead of a distinctive curriculum. See "Minority Parents Seek Quality over Diversity," *USA Today,* 29 July 1998.

28. Rochelle L. Stanfield, "Making the Grade?" *National Journal,* 17 April 1993.

29. Robert Guskind, "Rethinking Reform," *National Journal,* 25 May 1991, 1235–39.

30. It appears that in Milwaukee there has been a good deal of effective and committed leadership in the schools.

31. Myron Lieberman, *Privatization and Educational Choice* (New York: St. Martin's, 1989).

32. John Witte, "The Milwaukee Parental Choice Program Third Year Report," *LaFollette Policy Report* 6 (1994): 6–7.

33. John E. Chubb and Terry M. Moe, *Politics, Markets, and America's Schools* (Washington, D.C.: Brookings Institution, 1990).

34. Rochelle L. Stanfield, "Education Wars," *National Journal,* 7 March 1998.

35. Jeffrey R. Henig, *Rethinking School Choice: Limits of the Market Metaphor* (Princeton: Princeton University Press, 1994).

36. James S. Coleman, *Equality of Educational Opportunity* (Washington, D.C.: Government Printing Office, 1966). Since that time Coleman has modified his view to be substantially less supportive of busing.

37. Department of Education, *A Study of Charter Schools* (Washington, D.C.: DOE, 1997).

38. D.M. Lewis, "Certifying Functional Literacy: Competency and the Implications for Due Process and Equal Educational Opportunity," *Journal of Law and Education* (1979): 145–83; also see Chubb and Moe, *Politics, Markets, and America's Schools,* 197–98.

39. John L. Palmer and Isabel V. Sawhill, eds., *The Reagan Record* (Washington, D.C.: Urban Institute Press, 1984), 364–65.

40. Alison Mitchell, "Clinton Promotes Education Testing, Gingrich Opposes," *New York Times,* 8 September 1997.

41. Association of Chief School Officers, reported in Tom Squiteri, "Are Kids Tested to Death?" *USA Today,* 7 October 1997.

42. Jessica Portner, "Educators Keeping Eye on Measures Designed to Combat Youth Violence," *Education Week* 13 (9 February 1994): 21.

43. General Accounting Office, *School Facilities: America's Schools Report Differing Conditions,* GAO/HEHS-96-103 (Washington, D.C.: GAO, June 1996).

44. Richard W. Stevenson, "Clinton Proposes Spending $25 Billion on Education," *New York Times,* 27 January 1998.

45. *Engle v. Vitale,* 370 U.S. 421 (1962).

46. *Wallace v. Jaffree,* 466 U.S. 924 (1984).

47. *Westside Community Board of Education v. Mergens,* 496 U.S. 226 (1990).

48. *Cochran* v. *Board of Education,* 281 U.S. 370 (1930).

49. *Everson* v. *Board of Education,* 330 U.S. 1 (1947).

50. *Lemon* v. *Kurzman,* 403 U.S. 602 (1971).

51. *Roemer* v. *Maryland,* 426 U.S. 736 (1976).

52. *Board of Education of the Kiryas Joel School District* v. *Grument,* 114 U.S. 2481 (1994).

53. See, for example, Lonnie Harp, "Michigan Bill Penalizes Teachers for Job Actions," *Education Weekly* 13 (27 April 1994): 9.

54. Stephen M. Barro, "Countering Inequity in School Finance," *Federal Policy Options for Improving the Education of Low-Income Students,* vol. 3 (Santa Monica, Calif.: Rand Corporation, 1994).

55. Another equity funding case in Alabama was settled in favor of the poorer district—*Alabama Coalition for Equity, Inc.* v. *Guy Hunt.*

56. *Edgewood* v. *Kirby,* 804, S.W.2D 491 (Tex. 1991).

57. Sam Howe Verhovek, "Texas to Hold Referendum on School-Aid Shift to Poor," *New York Times,* 16 February 1993.

58. Lonnie Harp, "Texas Voters Reject Finance Plan: Consolidation Called Last Resort," *Education Week* 12 (12 May 1993): 1, 16.

59. Lonnie Harp, "Texas Finance Ruling Angers Both Rich, Poor Districts," *Education Week* 13 (12 January 1994): 18.

60. Tamar Lewin, "Patchwork of School Financing Schemes Offers Few Answers and Much Conflict," *New York Times,* 8 April 1998.

61. William Schneider, "Voters Get an Offer They Can't Refuse," *National Journal,* 26 March 1994, 754.

62. Rochelle L. Stanfield, "Equity and Excellence," *National Journal,* 23 November 1991, 3860–64.

63. Reagan Walker, "Blueprint for State's New School System Advances in Kentucky," *Education Week* 9 (7 March 1990): 1, 21.

64. Rochelle L. Stanfield, "Learning Curve," *National Journal,* 3 July 1993, 1688–91.

65. Dirk Johnson, "Study Says Small Schools Are Key to Learning," *New York Times,* 21 September 1994.

66. The Spearman rank-order correlation is -0.26. This finding is to some degree confounded by the different percentages of students taking the SAT in different states. Many of the high scoring states had a small percentage of students taking the SAT.

67. De Witt, "Nation's Schools Learn a 4th R."

68. Rochelle L. Stanfield, "Reform by the Book," *National Journal,* 4 December 1994, 2885–87.

69. "Minority Admissions Dip at U. of California," *New York Times,* 1 April 1998.

Chapter 13. Energy and the Environment

1. Constance Mungall and Digby J. McLaren, eds., *Planet under Stress: The Challenge of Global Change* (New York: Oxford University Press, 1990).

2. Statistical Office of the United Nations, *Yearbook of World Energy Statistics 1996* (New York: United Nations, 1998).

3. Robin C. Landon and Michael W. Klass, *OPEC: Policy Implications for the United States* (New York: Praeger, 1980).

4. Department of Energy, *Annual Energy Review 1997* (Washington, D.C.: DOE, 1998).

5. International Monetary Fund, *Balance of Payments Statistics* (Washington, D.C.: International Monetary Fund, monthly).

6. There may well be more natural gas available, but relatively low prices have deterred exploration. See Mark Fischetti, "There's Gas in Them There Hills," *Technology Review* 96 (1993): 16–18.

7. James M. McElfish and Ann E. Beier, *Environmental Regulation of Coal Mining* (Washington, D.C.: Environmental Law Institute, 1990).

8. Barbara E. Smith, *Digging Our Own Graves: Coal Miners and the Struggle over Black Lung Disease* (Philadelphia: Temple University Press, 1987).

9. Processes of this type have existed for some time; Germany used one like it in World War II. The process is not, however, economically feasible at anything like current energy prices.

10. Felicity Barringer, "Four Years Later, Soviets Reveal Wider Scope to Chernobyl Horror," *New York Times*, 28 April 1990; and David Marples, *The Social Impact of the Chernobyl Disaster* (New York: St. Martin's, 1988).

11. John L. Campbell, *Collapse of an Industry: Nuclear Power and the Contradictions of U.S. Policy* (Ithaca, N.Y.: Cornell University Press, 1988).

12. Richard Balzhiser, "Future Consequences of Nuclear Non-Policy," in *Energy: Production, Consumption, Consequences,* ed. John L. Helm (Washington, D.C.: National Academy Press, 1990).

13. Henry F. Bedford, *Seabrook Station: Citizen Politics and Nuclear Power* (Amherst: University of Massachusetts Press, 1990).

14. Matthew. L. Wald, "License Is Granted to Nuclear Plant in New Hampshire," *New York Times,* 2 March 1990.

15. Rodman D. Griffin, "Nuclear Fusion," *CQ Researcher* 3 (22 January 1993): 51–64.

16. Michael Kenward, "Fusion Becomes a Hot Bet for the Future," *New Scientist* 132 (16 November 1991): 10–11.

17. Todd Wilkinson, "Gone With the Wind" *Backpacker* 20 (September 1992): 11.

18. *New York Times,* 2 March 1980.

19. Michael M. Crow and Gregory Hager, "Political versus Economic Risk Deduction and the Failure of U.S. Synthetic Fuel Development Efforts," *Policy Studies Review* 5 (1985): 145–52.

20. Regina S. Axelrod, "Energy Policy: Changing the Rules of the Game," in *Environmental Policy in the 1980s: Reagan's New Agenda,* ed. Norman J. Vig and Michael E. Kraft (Washington, D.C.: CQ Press, 1984).

21. "Briefing on Energy Policy," *Weekly Compilation of Presidential Documents* 27 (25 February 1991): 188–90.

22. Eugene Feingold, "Finding Trust in Government," *Nation's Health* 24 (May 1994): 2; and "DOE's Growing Fallout," *Environmental Action* 26 (Spring 1994): 6.

23. Amory B. Lovins, *Soft Energy Paths: Toward a Durable Peace* (New York: Harper & Row, 1979); and L. Hunter Lovins, Amory B. Lovins, and Seth

Zuckerman, *Energy Unbound* (San Francisco: Sierra Books, 1986).

24. See National Academy of Sciences, *Our Earth, Our Future, Our Changing Global Environment* (Washington, D.C.: National Academy Press, 1990); and S. George Philander, *Is the Temperature Rising? The Uncertain Science of Global Warming* (Princeton: Princeton University Press, 1998).

25. The journal entitled *Diversity* is a good source of information about the resources existing in these settings.

26. One can, however, identify some twenty-seven other organizations with environmental responsibilities; see Walter A. Rosenbaum, *Environmental Politics and Policy* (Washington, D.C.: CQ Press, 1998).

27. Riley E. Dunlap, "Trends in Public Opinion toward Environmental Issues, 1965–1990," *Society and Natural Resources* 4 (1991): 285–312; and Jerry Spangler, "Survey Shows Environmental Values Deeply Rooted," *Desert News,* 9 October 1997.

28. Margaret E. Kriz, "Jobs vs. Owls," *National Journal,* 30 November 1993, 2913–16.

29. Another manifestation of the issue was the congressional use of a rider on an EPA appropriations act in 1996 to permit more lumbering of old-growth forests.

30. Murray Weidenbaum, "Return of the 'R' Word: The Regulatory Assault on the Economy," *Policy Review* 59 (1992): 40–43.

31. For example, the Safe Drinking Water Act requires monitoring of eighty-three substances, although a number have never been found in any public water supply. See Margaret E. Kriz, "Cleaner Than Clean?" *National Journal,* 23 April 1994, 946–49.

32. Christopher J. Bosso, "After the Movement: Environmental Activism in the 1990s," in Norman J. Vig and Michael E. Kraft, *Environmental Policy in the 1990s,* 3d ed. (Washington, D.C.: CQ Press, 1997).

33. Vice-President Gore's book on environmental politics became a part of the presidential campaign in 1992; see Al Gore, *Earth in the Balance: Ecology and the Human Spirit* (Boston: Houghton Mifflin, 1992).

34. Margaret Kriz, "That Was the Week That Was," *National Journal,* 2 February 1994, 393.

35. General Accounting Office, "Federal Facilities: Issues Involved in Cleaning Up Hazardous Wastes," GAO/T-RCED-92-82 (Washington, D.C.: GAO, 28 July 1992).

36. This has been described as "bureaucratic pluralism," with some even within the EPA itself. See Walter A. Rosenbaum, "Into the 1990s at EPA," in Vig and Kraft, *Environmental Policy in the 1990s.*

37. Margaret Kriz, "Feuding with the Feds," *National Journal,* 9 August 1997, 1598–1601.

38. West Virginia, for example, opposed attempts to impose nitrous oxide standards in 1997.

39. Richard N.L. Andrews, "Risk-Based Decisionmaking," in Vig and Kraft, *Environmental Policy in the 1990s.*

40. Donald T. Hornstein, "Reclaiming Environmental Law: A Normative Critique of Comparative Risk Analysis," *Columbia Law Review* 29 (1992): 562–633.

41. Margaret Kriz, "The Greening of Environmental Regulation," *National Journal*, 18 June 1994, 1464–67.

42. *Lujan v. Defenders of Wildlife*, 112 S. Ct. 2130 (1992).

43. See Michael E. Kraft, "Environmental Policy in Congress: Revolution, Reform or Gridlock?" in Vig and Kraft, *Environmental Policy in the 1990s*.

44. James R. Kahn, *An Economic Approach to the Environment and Natural Resources* (New York: Dryden Press, 1995).

45. For a review of developments, see Debra S. Knopman and Richard A. Smith, "Twenty Years of the Clean Water Act," *Environment* 35 (1993): 17–20, 34–41.

46. "Oil Officials Fear Stricter Water Act Provisions from New Congress," *Oilgram News* 74, no. 218 (1986): 2.

47. James P. Lester, "New Federalism and Environmental Policy," *Publius* 16 (1986): 149–65.

48. Margaret E. Kriz, "Clashing Over Chlorine," *National Journal*, 19 March 1994, 659–61.

49. Margaret E. Kriz, "Clean Machines," *National Journal*, 16 November 1991, 2789–94.

50. James C. McKinley Jr., "10 States Agree on a Program for Air Quality," *New York Times*, 2 October 1994.

51. Mark Crawford, "Hazardous Waste: Where to Put It?" *Science* 235 (9 January 1987): 156.

52. Peter A.A. Berle, "Toxic Tornado," *Audubon* 87 (1985): 4.

53. See Charles E. Davis, *The Politics of Hazardous Waste* (Englewood Cliffs, N.J.: Prentice Hall, 1993).

54. Steven Cohen, "Federal Hazardous Waste Programs," in Vig and Kraft, *Environmental Policy in the 1980s*.

55. Thomas Church and Robert Nakamura, *Cleaning Up the Mess: Implementation Strategies in Superfund* (Washington, D.C.: Brookings Institution, 1993).

56. Environmental Protection Agency, Office of Emergency and Remedial Response, *Superfund Facts* (Washington, D.C.: EPA, annual).

57. Environmental Protection Agency, *A Preliminary Analysis of the Public Costs of Environmental Protection, 1981–2000* (Washington, D.C.: EPA, May, 1990); and Milton E. Russell, William Colglazier, and Bruce E. Tonn, "U.S. Hazardous Waste Legacy," *Environment* 34 (1992): 12–15, 34–39.

58. Zachary A. Smith, *The Environmental Policy Paradox,* (Englewood Cliffs, N.J.: Prentice Hall, 1991), 179–86.

59. Church and Nakamura, *Cleaning Up the Mess*.

60. *Superfund: Backlog of Unevaluated Federal Facilities Slows Cleanup Efforts,* GAO/RCED-93-119 (Washington, D.C.: General Accounting Office, July 1993).

61. Richard A. Epstein, *Takings: Property Rights and the Power of Eminent Domain* (Cambridge, Mass.: Harvard University Press, 1985).

62. Nancie G. Marzulla and Roger J. Marzulla, *Property Rights: Understanding Takings and Environmental Regulation* (Rockville, Md.: Government Institutes, 1997).

63. Charles O. Jones, "Speculative Augmentation in Federal Air Pollution Policymaking," *Journal of Politics* 42 (1975): 438–64.

64. Graeme Browning, "Taking Some Risks," *National Journal,* 1 June 1991, 1279–82.

65. Some analysts have argued that there may be *insufficient* negotiation in the enforcement of environmental legislation, and that better compliance could be achieved through bargaining rather than conventional regulatory enforcement. See Eugene Bardach and Robert Kagan, *Going by the Book* (Philadelphia: Temple University Press, 1983); and David Vogel, *Trading Up: Consumer and Environmental Regulation in a Global Economy* (Cambridge, Mass.: Harvard University Press, 1995).

66. A. Myrick Freeman, "Economics, Incentives, and Environmental Regulation," in Vig and Kraft, *Environmental Policy in the 1990s.*

67. Barnaby J. Feder, "Sold: $21 Million of Air Pollution," *New York Times,* 30 March 1993. For a somewhat skeptical view, see General Accounting Office, *Environmental Protection: Implications for Using Pollution Taxes to Supplement Regulation,* GAO/RCED-93-13 (Washington, D.C.: GAO, February 1993).

68. Margaret E. Kriz, "Emission Control," *National Journal,* 3 July 1993, 1696–1701.

69. See Renee Rico, "The U.S. Allowance Trading System for Sulfur Dioxide: An Update on Market Experience," *Environmental and Resource Economics* 5 (1995): 115–29.

Chapter 14. Protective Policies: Defense and Law Enforcement

1. For some sense of the ups and downs of defense employment (civilian and uniformed), see B. Guy Peters, "Public Employment in the United States," in Richard Rose et al., *Public Employment in Western Democracies* (Cambridge, England: Cambridge University Press, 1985).

2. John D. Steinbruner and William W. Kaufmann, "International Security Reconsidered," in *Setting National Priorities: Budget Choices for the Next Century,* ed. Robert D. Reischauer (Washington, D.C.: Brookings Institution, 1997).

3. See, for example, Robert K. Jervis, *Perception and Misperception in International Politics* (Princeton: Princeton University Press, 1976).

4. Joseph S. Nye, *Bound to Lead: The Changing Nature of American Power* (New York: Basic Books, 1992).

5. Gregory L. Schulte, "Bringing Peace to Bosnia and Change to the Alliance," *NATO Review* 45 (March 1997): 22–25.

6. "Does UN Peacekeeping Serve U.S. Interests?" Hearing before U.S. House of Representatives, Committee on International Relations, 9 April 1997.

7. See, for example, James A. Nathan and James K. Oliver, *United States Foreign Policy and World Order,* 2d ed. (Boston: Little, Brown, 1981).

8. Paul Boyer, *Fallout: A Historian Reflects on America's Half-century Encounter with Nuclear Weapons* (Columbus: Ohio State University Press, 1998).

9. Dunbar Lockwood, "Purchasing Power," *Bulletin of the Atomic Scientists,* 50 (March 1994): 10–12; and "Former Soviet Republics Clear Way for Nunn-Lugar Monies," *Arms Control Today* 24 (1994): 28–29.

10. Even recent evidence points to continuing nuclear weapons development in North Korea, despite its agreements with both South Korea and the

United States. See David E. Sanger, "North Korea Site an A-Bomb Plant, U.S. Agencies Say," *New York Times,* 17 August 1998.

11. Bradley Graham, "Missile Threat to U.S. Greater than Thought," *International Herald Tribune,* 17 July 1998.

12. Patrick E. Tyler, "As Fear of a Big War Fades, Military Plans for Little Ones," *New York Times,* 3 February 1992.

13. David C. Morrison, "Bottoming Out?" *National Journal,* 17 September 1994, 2126–30. See also Donald J. Savoie and B. Guy Peters, "Comparing Programme Review," in *Programme Review in Canada,* ed. E. Lundquist and D.J. Savoie (Ottawa: Canadian Centre for Management Development, 1999).

14. The worst-case scenario appeared to be an outbreak of war on the Korean Peninsula.

15. Julian Critchley, *The North Atlantic Alliance and the Soviet Union in the 1980s* (London: Macmillan, 1982).

16. Robert L. Bernstein and Richard Dicker, "Human Rights First," *Foreign Policy* 94 (1994): 43–47; and William Korey, *The Promises We Keep: Human Rights, the Helsinki Process, and American Foreign Policy* (New York: St. Martin's, 1993).

17. See Christoph Bluth, Emil Kirchner, and James Sperling, *The Future of European Security* (Aldershot, Hants: Dartmouth, 1995).

18. For example, the much-heralded accuracy of "smart bombs" during the Gulf War apparently would be crude in comparison to that of contemporary weapons.

19. For an analysis of the Reagan Strategic Defense Initiative program, see Congressional Budget Office, *Analysis of the Costs of the Administration's Strategic Defense Initiative, 1985–89* (Washington, D.C.: CBO, May 1984); this basic idea has been revived in the 1990s.

20. Lawrence J. Korb, "The 1991 Defense Budget," in *Setting National Priorities: Policy for the Nineties* (Washington, D.C.: Brookings Institution, 1990). See also David C. Morrison, "How Many Carriers Are Enough?" *National Journal,* 4 September 1993, 2162.

21. Gordon Adams, *The Politics of Defense Contracting: The Iron Triangle* (New Brunswick, N.J.: Transaction, 1981); and "Mission Implausible," *U.S. News & World Report,* 14 October 1991, 24–31.

22. Of course, the United States is the only country that has ever used these weapons in war.

23. There were a number of reports of plutonium from Russia being available for sale, potentially to terrorists. The economic crisis in the Soviet Union, especially failures to pay the armed forces adequately, provides even more incentives to sell some of the tons of weapons grade material still available.

24. Owen Cote, "The Trident and the Triad," *International Security Quarterly* 16 (1991): 117–36.

25. Pat Towell, "Pentagon Banking on Plans to Reinvent Procurement," *Congressional Quarterly Weekly Report* 52 (16 April 1994); and Lauren Holland, "Explaining Weapons Procurement: Matching Operational Performance and National Security Needs," *Armed Forces and Society* 19 (1993): 353–76.

26. The program and its sequels have cost approximately $5 billion per year since the mid-1980s.

27. The General Accounting Office has done a number of evaluations of these and other poorly performing weapons systems, e.g., *More Effective Review of Proposed Inventory Buys Could Reduce Unneeded Procurement,* GAO/ NSIAD-94-130 (Washington, D.C.: General Accounting Office, June 1994). See also Scott Shuger, "The Stealth Bomber Story You Haven't Heard," *Washington Monthly* 23 (January 1991): 1–2, 14–22.

28. Korb, "1991 Defense Budget," 136–38.

29. Eric Schmitt, "Military Proposes to End Production of Most New Arms," *New York Times,* 24 January 1992.

30. Eric Schmitt, "Run Silent, Run Deep, Beat Foes (Where?)," *New York Times,* 30 January 1992.

31. Martin Binkin, *America's Volunteer Military* (Washington, D.C.: Brookings Institution, 1984).

32. David McCormick, *The Downsized Warrior: America's Army in Transition* (New York: New York University Press, 1998).

33. *New York Times,* 12 June 1994; C.J. Chivers, "Too Many Officers Trading Fatigues for Business Suits," *USA Today,* 8 October 1998.

34. By this I mean the skills need by hostage rescue and counter-terrorist groups in the military.

35. For example, Molly Pitcher played a partly real, partly mythical part in the Battle of Monmouth during the Revolutionary War.

36. Linda Bird Francke, *Ground Zero: The Gender Wars in the Military* (New York: Simon & Schuster, 1997).

37. See James Kitfield, "Front and Center," *National Journal,* 25 October 1997.

38. Ibid.

39. The Department of Defense argued that the fundamental reason for dismissal of the female pilot was her lying about the existence of a relationship and then continuing once ordered to terminate it.

40. Michael R. Gordon, "Pentagon Spells Out Rules for Ousting Homosexuals; Rights Group Vows a Fight," *New York Times,* 23 December 1993.

41. Tamar Lewin, "At Bases, Debate Rages Over Impact of New Gay Policy," *New York Times,* 24 December 1993.

42. Jane Gross, "Navy Cannot Discharge Gay Officer, Court Rules," *New York Times,* 1 September 1994.

43. Tim Weiner, "Proposal Cuts Back on Some Weapons to Spend More on Personnel," *New York Times,* 8 February 1994. Another version of this is to fight one war while conducting a holding action in another.

44. William W. Kaufman, "'Hollow' Forces," *Brookings Review* 12 (1994): 24–29.

45. Eric Schmitt, "Military Making Less into More, But Some Say Readiness Suffers," *New York Times,* 5 July 1994.

46. Other estimates show substantially greater employment generated by defense purchases. These are rather conservative estimates from the Department of Labor.

47. James Kitfield, "The New Partnership," *National Journal,* 6 August 1994.

48. David C. Morrison, "Painful Separation," *National Journal,* 3 March 1990, 768–73.

49. V. Beiser, "Why the Big Apple Feels Safer," *Macleans* 108 (11 September 1995), 39ff.

50. Generally, young adults are the most prone to commit crimes; this group has been declining rapidly as a percentage of the American population.

51. Hoover himself had a somewhat more complex career. See Anthony Summers, *Official and Confidential* (New York: Putnam, 1993).

52. This organization became very visible during the siege of the Branch Davidian compound in Waco, Texas, in 1993.

53. Actually it does not exhaust the list of federal enforcement activities, e.g., law enforcement by park rangers (Department of the Interior) in national parks.

54. John DiIulio, "Crime," in *Setting Domestic Priorities: What Can Government Do?* ed. Henry J. Aaron and Charles L Schultze (Washington, D.C.: Brookings Institution, 1992).

55. Included here was the (in)famous "midnight basketball," keeping recreation centers in poorer areas open long hours to give young people something more constructive to do than commit crimes.

56. For a discussion of this controversy in the context of the Clinton crime bill, see W. John Moore, "Shooting in the Dark," *National Journal,* 12 February 1994, 358-63.

57. See "Crime in California: Three Strikes, You're Out," *Economist* 330 (15 January 1994): 29-32; and Michael G. Turner, "Three Strikes and You're Out Legislation: A National Assessment," *Federal Probation* 59 (1995): 16-35.

58. Committee on Ways and Means, U.S. House of Representatives, "Children and Families at Risk" (Washington, D.C.: Government Printing Office, January 1994).

59. This appears to be especially true for child and spousal abuse. See David J. Kolko, "Characteristics of Child Victims of Physical Abuse," *Journal of Interpersonal Violence* 7 (1992): 244-76; and Cathy Spatz Widom, "Avoidance of Criminality in Abused and Neglected Children," *Psychiatry* 54 (1991): 162-74.

60. Herman Goldstein, *Problem-Oriented Policing* (New York: McGraw-Hill, 1990).

61. Some students appear to think that the two experiences are equally pleasant.

62. Most correctional officials oppose these changes, arguing that they will only make the prison population more restive and difficult to control.

63. The wording of the amendment is "A well regulated Militia, being necessary to the security of a free State, the right of the people to keep and bear Arms, shall not be infringed."

64. Federal Bureau of Investigation, *Crime in the United States* (Washington, D.C.: Government Printing Office, annual).

65. The legislation was called the Brady bill after James Brady, President Reagan's press secretary, who was wounded severely in the attempted assassination of Reagan in 1981. After that his wife, Sarah Brady, became a vigorous advocate of gun control.

66. Peter H. Stone, "Under the Gun," *National Journal,* 5 June 1993, 1334-38; and Holly Idelson and Paul Nyhan, "Gun Rights and Restrictions: The Territory Reconfigured," *Congressional Quarterly Weekly Report* 51 (24 April 1993):

1021–27.

67. "Gun Owners Don't Fit Stereotypes," *USA Today*/CNN/Gallup poll reported in *USA Today*, 30 December 1993.

68. George Pettinico, "Crime and Punishment: America Changes its Mind," *Public Perspective* 5 (September/October 1994): 29.

69. Welsh S. White, *The Death Penalty in the Nineties: An Examination of the Modern System of Capital Punishment* (Ann Arbor: University of Michigan Press, 1991).

70. *Furman v. Georgia*, 408 U.S. 238 (1972).

71. *Gregg v. Georgia*, 428 U.S. 153 (1976).

72. Gregory D. Russell, *The Death Penalty and Racial Bias: Overturning Supreme Court Assumptions* (Westport, Conn.: Greenwood, 1994).

73. This may not be strictly a constitutional argument, since the Constitution and its amendments do not mention economics as a forbidden category for differentiating among individuals.

74. Stephen Reinhardt, "The Supreme Court, the Death Penalty, and the Harris Case," *Yale Law Journal* 102 (1992): 205–22.

75. Marcia Coyle, "Blackmun's Turnabout on the Death Penalty," *National Law Journal* 16 (7 March 1994): 39.

76. This is called "Mirandizing" an arrestee, after Ernesto Miranda, whose conviction was overturned because he was not told of his right to remain silent (*Miranda v. Arizona*, 384 U.S. 436 [1966]).

77. Kenneth B. Noble, "Ruling Helps Prosecution of Simpson," *New York Times*, 20 September 1994.

78. Prisons are already dangerous enough. See Mark S. Fleisher, *Warehousing Violence* (Newbury Park, Calif.: Sage, 1989); and George M. Anderson, "Prison Violence: Victims behind Bars," *America* 159 (26 November 1988): 430–33.

79. See a discussion of this idea in chapter 3.

80. Moore, "Shooting in the Dark."

81. Senator Alphonse D'Amato (R-N.Y.) went on the Senate floor to complain about the "pork" in the legislation by singing a parody of "Old MacDonald Had a Farm."

82. "Crime Control Issues," *Congressional Digest* 73 (June 1994): 169–70.

83. Morris P. Fiorina, "An Era of Divided Government," *Political Science Quarterly* 107 (1992): 387–410. But see Charles O. Jones, *The President in a Separated System* (Washington, D.C.: Brookings Institution, 1994).

84. Neil A. Lewis, "President Foresees Safer U.S.," *New York Times*, 27 August 1994.

85. Contained in this total is the "midnight basketball" that was so prominent in negative comments about the bill. See Don Terry, "Basketball at Midnight: 'Hope' on a Summer Eve," *New York Times*, 19 August 1994.

86. See Richard Rose, "On the Priorities of Government," *European Journal of Political Research* 4 (1973): 247–89.

Chapter 15. Cost-Benefit Analysis

1. Edward M. Gramlich, *Benefit-Cost Analysis of Government Programs*

(Englewood Cliffs, N.J.: Prentice Hall, 1981).

2. Steven Kelman, "Cost-Benefit Analysis: An Ethical Critique," *Regulation,* 1981, 33–40.

3. Kenneth Arrow, *Social Choice and Individual Values* (New York: Wiley, 1963); and Allan Feldman, *Welfare Economics and Social Choice Theory* (Boston: Martinus Nijhoff, 1986).

4. P. Hennipman, "Pareto Optimality: Value Judgment or Analytical Tool?" in *Relevance and Precision,* ed. J.S. Cramer, A. Heertje, and P. Venekamp (New York: North-Holland, 1976).

5. Nicholas Kaldor, "Welfare Propositions of Economics and Interpersonal Comparisons of Utility," *Economic Journal* 49 (1939): 549–52; and John R. Hicks, "The Valuation of the Social Income," *Economica* 7 (1940): 105–24.

6. Richard Posner, *The Economics of Justice* (Cambridge, Mass.: Harvard University Press, 1983).

7. E.J. Mishan, *Cost-Benefit Analysis,* exp. ed. (New York: Praeger, 1967), 24–54.

8. David Whittington and Duncan MacRae Jr., "The Issue of Standing in Cost-Benefit Analysis," *Journal of Policy Analysis and Management* 5 (1986): 665–82.

9. E.J. Mishan, "The Post-War Literature on Externalities: An Interpretative Essay," *Journal of Economic Literature,* 16 (1978): 1–28; and Neva R. Goodwin, *As If the Future Mattered: Translating Social and Economic Theory into Human Behavior* (Ann Arbor: University of Michigan Press, 1996).

10. John Martin Gilroy, "The Ethical Poverty of Cost-Benefit Methods: Autonomy, Efficiency, and Public Policy Choice," *Policy Sciences* 25 (1992): 83–102.

11. "The TVA—Hardy Survivor," *The Economist* 312 (1 July 1989): 22–23.

12. Edith Stokey and Richard Zeckhauser, *A Primer for Policy Analysis* (New York: Norton, 1978), 149–52.

13. This is referred to as a "hedonic price model," in which the contributions of intangibles to price are assessed. See Paul Portney, "Housing Prices, Health Effects, and Valuing Reductions in the Risk of Death," *Journal of Environmental Economics and Management* 8 (1981): 72–78.

14. Robin Gregory, Donald McGregor, and Sarah Lichtenstein, "Assessing the Quality of Expressed Preference Measures of Value," *Journal of Economic Behavior and Organization* 17 (1992): 277–92.

15. *The Road Back: Endangered Species Recovery* (Washington, D.C.: Department of the Interior, 1998). See chapter 13.

16. Peter Passell, "Polls May Help Government Decide the Worth of Nature," *New York Times,* 6 September 1993. See also J.A. Hausman, *Contingent Valuation: A Critical Assessment* (Amsterdam: North-Holland, 1993).

17. Robert E. Niewijk, "Misleading Quantification: The Contingent Valuation of Environmental Quality," *Regulation* 17, no. 1 (1994): 60–71.

18. Steven E. Rhoads, ed., *Valuing Life: Public Policy Dilemmas* (Boulder, Colo.: Westview, 1980); and W. Kip Viscusi, "Alternative Approaches to Valuing the Health Impact of Accidents: Liability Law and Prospective Evaluations," *Law and Contemporary Problems* 46 (1983): 49–68.

19. Jack Hirschleifer and David L. Shapiro, "The Treatment of Risk and Uncertainty," in *Public Expenditure and Policy Analysis,* 3d ed., ed. Robert H.

Haveman and Julius Margolis (Boston: Houghton Mifflin, 1983), 145–66.

20. For a general discussion of the problems of discounting, see Robert E. Goodin, "Discounting Discounting," *Journal of Public Policy* 2 (1982): 53–71.

21. William J. Baumol, "On the Social Rate of Discount," *American Economic Review*, 10 (1968): 788–802.

22. Marthe R. Gold et al., *Cost-Effectiveness in Health and Medicine* (New York: Oxford University Press, 1996).

23. Ray Robinson, "Cost-Effectiveness Analysis," *British Medical Journal* 307 (25 September 1993): 793–95.

24. David M. Eddy, "Cost-Effectiveness Analysis: Will It Be Accepted?" *Journal of the American Medical Association* 268 (1992): 132–36.

25. Alphonse G. Holtmann, "Beyond Efficiency: Economists and Distributional Analysis," in *Policy Analysis and Economics: Developments, Tensions, Prospects*, ed. David L. Weimer (Boston: Kluwer, 1991); and Elio Londero, *Benefits and Beneficiaries: An Introduction to Estimating Distributional Effects in Cost-Benefit Analysis*, 2d ed. (Washington, D.C.: Inter-American Development Bank, 1996).

26. Peter Self, *Econocrats and the Policy Process: The Politics and Philosophy of Cost-Benefit Analysis* (London: Macmillan, 1975).

27. Peter Self, "Nonsense on Stilts: Cost-Benefit Analysis and the Roskill Commission," *Political Quarterly* 10 (1970): 30–63; and Kelman, "Cost-Benefit Analysis."

Chapter 16. Ethical Analysis of Public Policy

1. Russell Hardin, *Morality within the Limit of Reason* (Chicago: University of Chicago Press, 1988).

2. See Martin E. Marty, *The One and the Many: America's Struggle for the Common Good* (Cambridge, Mass.: Harvard University Press, 1997).

3. Victor Grassian, *Moral Reasoning* (Englewood Cliffs, N.J.: Prentice Hall, 1981).

4. Arnold Meltsner, *Policy Analysts in the Bureaucracy* (Berkeley: University of California Press, 1976), 3–25.

5. Abraham Kaplan, "Social Ethics and the Sanctity of Life," in *Life or Death: Ethics and Options*, ed. D.H. Labby (London: Macmillan, 1968), 58–71.

6. Guido Calabresi and Phillip Bobbitt, *Tragic Choices* (New York: Norton, 1978), 21. See also B. Guy Peters, "Tragic Choices: Administrative Rulemaking and Policy Choice," in *Ethics in Public Service*, ed. Richard A. Chapman (Edinburgh: University of Edinburgh Press, 1993).

7. Sheryl Gay Stolberg, "Live and Let Die Over Transplants," *New York Times*, 5 April 1998.

8. The State of Oregon made this determination as a part of its rationing program (see p. 255). The justification was primarily utilitarian, assuming that the treatments would be less beneficial for people with substance-abuse problems.

9. Dave Davis, Ted Wendling, and Joan Mazzolini, "U.S. Orders Revisions in Rules on Transplants: Current System's Range of Waits is Called Unfair," *Cleveland Plain Dealer*, 27 March 1998.

10. Bonnie Steinbock, *Life before Birth: The Moral and Legal Status of Embryos and Fetuses* (New York: Oxford University Press, 1992).

11. Ronald Dworkin, *Life's Dominion: An Argument About Abortion, Euthanasia and Individual Freedom* (New York: Knopf, 1993).

12. Steven H. Miles, "Doctors and Their Patients' Suicides," *Journal of the American Medical Association* 271 (8 June 1994): 1786–88; and Daniel Avila, "Medical Treatment Rights of Older Persons and Persons with Disabilities," *Issues in Law and Medicine* 9 (1994): 345–60.

13. Jonathan Glover, *Causing Deaths and Saving Lives* (Harmondsworth, Middlesex: Penguin, 1977).

14. Robert Nozick, *Anarchy, The State, and Utopia* (New York: Basic Books, 1974).

15. This individualistic and conservative interpretation of the law was common during the late nineteenth and early twentieth centuries. See, for example, *Lochner v. New York* (1905).

16. Robert E. Goodin, *Reasons for Welfare* (Princeton: Princeton University Press, 1988), 312–31; and Christian Bay, *The Structure of Freedom* (New York: Atheneum, 1965).

17. John Kultgen, *Autonomy and Intervention: Paternalism in the Caring Life* (New York: Oxford University Press, 1994).

18. Desmond King, *Illiberal Policies in Liberal States* (Oxford: Oxford University Press, 1999).

19. See Dennis A. Robbins, *Ethical and Legal Issues in Home Health and Long-term Care: Challenges and Solutions* (Gaithersburg, Md.: Aspen Publishers, 1996); and Bonnie Steinbock and Alastair Norcross, *Killing and Letting Die,* 2d ed. (New York: Fordham University Press, 1994).

20. Some conservatives have argued, for example, that even professional licensure of doctors and lawyers should be abandoned in the name of free choice. In the long run, they assert, the market would take care of the problem.

21. Jerome S. Legge, *Traffic Safety Reform in the United States and Great Britain* (Pittsburgh: University of Pittsburgh Press, 1991); and Kenneth E. Warner, "Bags, Buckles, and Belts: The Debate over Mandatory Passive Restraints in Automobiles," *Journal of Health Politics, Policy, and Law* 8 (1983): 44–75.

22. Howard M. Leichter, *Free to be Foolish* (Princeton: Princeton University Press, 1991).

23. The FDA has to some extent relaxed its usual guidelines for drugs that may help victims of AIDS and a few other extremely deadly diseases, e.g., "Lou Gehrig's Disease." See Harold Edgar and David J. Rothman, "New Rules for New Drugs: The Challenge of AIDS to the Regulatory Process," in *A Disease of Society,* ed. Dorothy Nelkin, David P. Willis, and Scott V. Parris (Cambridge, England: Cambridge University Press, 1991); and Peter Davis, *Contested Ground: Public Purpose and Private Interest in the Regulation of Prescription Drugs* (New York: Oxford University Press, 1996).

24. Sissela Bok, *Lying: Moral Choice in Public and Private Life* (New York: Vintage, 1979).

25. Loch K. Johnson, *Secret Agencies: U.S. Intelligence in a Hostile World* (New Haven: Yale University Press, 1996).

26. See Raymond L. Goldstein and John K. Schoor, *Demanding Democracy*

after Three Mile Island (Gainesville: University of Florida Press, 1991).

27. James C. Petersen, *Whistleblowing: Ethical and Legal Issues in Expressing Dissent* (Dubuque, Iowa: Kendall/Hunt, 1986); Daniel P. Westman, *Whistleblowing: The Law of Retaliatory Discharge* (Washington, D.C.: Bureau of National Affairs, 1991); and Merit Systems Protection Board, *Whistleblowing in the Federal Government* (Washington: MSPB, 1993).

28. See, respectively, Edward Weisband and Thomas M. Franck, *Resignation in Protest* (New York: Penguin, 1975); and David Burnham, "Paper Chase of a Whistleblower," *New York Times,* 16 October 1982.

29. William T. Gormley, *Taming the Bureaucracy: Muscles, Prayers, and Other Strategies* (Princeton: Princeton University Press, 1989). In addition to the academic literature on the freedom of information, the novel *So Now You Know* by Michael Frayn (London: Penguin, 1992) provides interesting insights into the question.

30. See Joseph S. Nye, Philip D. Zelikow, and David C. King, eds., *Why People Don't Trust Government* (Cambridge, Mass.: Harvard University Press, 1997).

31. Michael Walzer, "Political Action: The Problem of Dirty Hands," *Philosophy and Public Affairs* (1973): 160–80; and Thomas Nagel, "Ruthlessness in Public Life," in *Public and Private Life,* ed. Stuart Hampshire (Cambridge, England: Cambridge University Press, 1978).

32. Jan-Erik Lane, *The Public Sector: Concepts, Models, and Approaches* (Newbury Park, Calif.: Sage, 1993).

33. See Robert E. Goodin, *Protecting the Vulnerable: A Re-Analysis of Our Social Responsibilities* (Chicago: University of Chicago Press, 1985). Even such a committed conservative as Charles Murray could argue that "there is no such thing as an undeserving five-year-old"; see his *Losing Ground* (New York: Basic Books, 1984).

34. Richard Allen Epstein, *Takings: Private Property and the Power of Eminent Domain* (Cambridge, Mass.: Harvard University Press, 1985); and William A. Fischel, *Regulatory Takings: Law, Economics, and Politics* (Cambridge, Mass.: Harvard University Press, 1995).

35. Karl Marx, *Criticism of the Gotha Program* (New York: International Universities Press, 1938), v. 29, 14.

36. For an important attempt to provide such a justification, see Goodin, *Reasons for Welfare,* 287–305. See also Bo Rothstein, *Just Institutions Matter: The Moral and Political Logic of the Universal Welfare State* (Cambridge, England: Cambridge University Press, 1998).

37. Edith Brown Weiss, *In Fairness to Future Generations: International Law, Common Patrimony, and Intergenerational Equity* (Tokyo: United Nations University, 1988).

38. Peter S. Burton, "Intertemporal Preferences and Intergenerational Equity Considerations in Optimal Resource Harvesting," *Journal of Environmental Economics and Management* 24 (1993): 119–32; and Laurence J. Kotlikoff, *Generational Accounting* (New York: Free Press, 1992).

39. John Rawls, "Justice as Fairness," *Philosophical Review,* 1958, 164–94, esp. 166.

40. John Rawls, *A Theory of Justice* (Cambridge, Mass.: Harvard Univer-

sity Press, 1971).

41. Ibid., 19.

42. For an earlier literary treatment of this view of fairness, see L.P. Hartley, *Facial Justice* (London: Hamish Hamilton, 1960). On desert, see George Bernard Shaw, *Doctor's Dilemma*.

43. Epstein, *Takings*.

44. This is obviously related to the utilitarian logic that undergirds cost-benefit analysis. See pp. 422–24.

45. Roberto Alejandro, *The Limits of Rawlsian Justice* (Baltimore, Md.: Johns Hopkins University Press, 1998).

46. Richard A. Epstein, *Forbidden Grounds: The Case against Employment Discrimination Laws* (Cambridge, Mass.: Harvard University Press, 1992); and Russell Nieli, ed., *Racial Preference and Racial Justice: The New Affirmative Action Controversy* (Washington, D.C.: Ethics and Public Policy Center, 1991).

47. Douglas E. Ashford, *The Emergence of the Welfare State* (Oxford: Blackwell, 1986). But see T.H. Marshall, *Class, Citizenship, and Social Development* (New York: Doubleday, 1965).

48. See Gareth Davies, *From Opportunity to Entitlement* (Lawrence: University Press of Kansas, 1996).

49. W.E. Leuchtenberg, *Franklin D. Roosevelt and the New Deal, 1932–1940* (New York: Harper & Row, 1963), 133.

50. A few places (e.g., City University of New York) once provided free higher education as well, but budget restraints have forced the imposition of fees in those institutions.

51. See pp. 411–13; and Kimberly J. Cook, *Divided Passions: Public Opinions on Abortion and the Death Penalty* (Boston: Northeastern University Press, 1997).

52. Frances Fox Piven and Richard A. Cloward, *Regulating the Poor*, 2d ed. (New York: Viking, 1993).

53. Amitai Etzioni, ed., *New Communitarian Thinking: Virtues, Institutions, and Communities* (Charlottesville: University Press of Virginia, 1995).

Index

State-centrism, 51–53
Strategic Defense Initiative, 105, 394
"Strategic deterrence," 150
Strategic Petroleum Reserve, 362, 363
Suasion, 11–13
Subgovernments, 29–35
"Sunset laws," 181–82
Supplemental Security Income program, 111, 312–13
"Supply-side economics," 59, 128, 188, 204–8, 230
Supreme Court, 78, 330, 331, 345, 346, 370, 412
Swann v. Charlotte-Mecklenburg Board of Education, 88
Symbols, manipulation of, 56–57
Synthetic Fuels Corporation, 362, 363

"Takings," 379
Tax Equity and Financial Responsibility Act of 1982, 260
Taxes
capital gains, 233–34, 239
corporate, 220, 230, 239
excise, 229–30
flat, 235–36
as governmental instrument, 10–11
income distribution and, 229–30
integrating corporate and personal, 238–39
national consumption, 236–38
politics of, 231–39
property, 230, 327–28, 348
Tax expenditures, 220–21, 239
Tax incentives, 10, 198–99
Tax policy, choices in, 226–31
Tax reform, politics of, 231–39
Tennessee Valley Authority (TVA), 99, 195, 214, 425, 427
Think tanks, 63–64
Thomas, Clarence, 47
Thornburgh, Richard, 272
Time element, in program evaluation, 168
Trade policy, 200, 212
Transportation, Department of, 97
Treasury, Department of the, 97, 129–30, 406
"Troika," 129–30
Truman, Harry S., 271

Twain, Mark, 4

Uncle Tom's Cabin (Stowe), 365
Unemployment insurance, 284
United Nations, 386, 389
Universality, in health care, 275, 277
Urban Development Action Grants, 55
Utilitarianism
alternatives to, 453–54
defined, 437

Value-added tax (VAT), 218, 231, 236, 296
"Veil of ignorance," 450
Veterans Administration, 240
Veterans' Affairs, Department of, 33, 241

Wage and price controls, 189, 210
Walker, Jack, 49
War on Poverty, 104, 116, 171, 309–12, 329, 332, 333, 407
War Powers Act, 74
Warsaw Pact, 389
Water Pollution Control Act of 1956, 370
Water Pollution Control Act of 1972, 119, 135, 373
Water Quality Act, 371
Watt, James, 363
Wealth, 17–18
Welfare reform, 281–82, 302, 304, 309, 313, 315, 317
Welfare state services, 40
Whistleblowers, 446
White House Office, 97
Wildavsky, Aaron, 117, 146
Wilson, Woodrow, 103
Wofford, Harris, 272
Women, in armed forces, 400
Women, Infants, and Children (WIC) program, 120, 312
Workers' compensation, 284
"Workfare," 304, 309
Work Incentive Program, 302
Works Progress Administration, 113–14
World leadership, U.S., 18–19
World Trade Organization, 199

Yeltsin, Boris, 387, 391

Zero-sum society, 191